Meade, Glenn.

Snow wolf.

$24.95

DATE			

SNOW
WOLF

Glenn Meade

ST. MARTIN'S PRESS NEW YORK

A THOMAS DUNNE BOOK.
An imprint of St. Martin's Press.

Design by Scott Levine

Library of Congress Cataloging-in-Publication Data

Meade, Glenn.
Snow wolf / by Glenn Meade.
p. cm.
"A Thomas Dunne book."
ISBN 0-312-14421-0
1. Stalin, Joseph, 1879–1953—Assassination attempts—Fiction. 2. Intelligence service—United States—Fiction. 3. Americans—Travel—Soviet Union—Fiction. I. Title.
PS3563.E16845S66 1996
813'.54—dc20 96-2032
CIP

Originally published by Hodder & Stoughton in Great Britain

First U.S. Edition: May 1996

10 9 8 7 6 5 4 3 2 1

For Geraldine and Alex,
and in memory of Julie-Anne

ACKNOWLEDGMENTS

Some of the events in this book are documented history. Although mention is made of certain well-known figures within the historical context of the period, this book is a work of fiction, and no reference is intended to any living persons. The term KGB is used to denote the Soviet State Security Organization, which went through several name changes before and after the period in which this book is mainly set, until it finally adopted the name KGB in 1954. And although certain events portrayed within these pages are historically recorded fact, they are tempered with a reasonable amount of artistic license in time, place and content.

In the course of my research, there were many people who gave their help and personal insights into these events, and I would like therefore to acknowledge the following:

In the United States: the Association of Former Intelligence Officers (AFIO).

In Finland: the staff of the US Embassy, Helsinki; the SUPO (Finnish Counter-Intelligence) for their invaluable help and courtesy, and allowing me access to certain archival material.

In Estonia: Arzeny Zaharov, Gulag survivor, for his memories of the period and background information; and Ave Hirvelaan for her kindness and support.

In Russia: certain former members of the KGB who, understandably, wish to remain nameless, but who will know the reasons why I thank them. For their expertise on the period and of certain historical episodes in this book: Alexander Vishinsky and Valeri Nekrasov.

Also, I would like to thank Steven Milburn; and the unfailingly helpful staff of the Finnish Embassy, Dublin, especially Hannele Ihonen and Leena Alto.

There were many others, especially former intelligence personnel, who gave of their time and expertise, but as I've discovered, such men and women prefer quiet anonymity in their retirement—to all, my grateful thanks.

"The most difficult thing to predict is not the future, but the past."

Russian proverb

"There is a wolf out there, baying for my blood. We must exterminate wolves."

Remark attributed to Joseph Stalin on 17 February 1953,
over two weeks before his death;
to the Indian Ambassador in Moscow,
the last foreigner to see him alive

THE PRESENT

1

Moscow.

I had come to bury the dead and resurrect ghosts and so it seemed somehow appropriate that the truth and the lies of the past should begin in a graveyard.

It was raining that morning in Novodevichy Cemetery and I was burying my father for the second time.

It isn't often that a man gets to be buried twice, and as I stood alone under the dripping chestnut trees I could see the black Mercedes come in through the cemetery gates and brake gently to a halt near the grave. Two men stepped out, one of them middle-aged and gray-haired, the other a bearded Orthodox priest.

It's a tradition in Russia to uncover the coffin before it's buried, a chance for friends and relatives to kiss their dead and say their last goodbyes. But there would be no such tradition observed this wet day in June for a man who had died over forty years before, just a simple ceremony to finally acknowledge his passing.

Someone had placed a red-flowered wreath beside the grave, I remember that, and then I saw the flashes of forked lightning illuminate the gray horizon, and heard the cracks of thunder.

The Convent of Novodevichy lies south of Moscow, an ancient sixteenth-century Orthodox church surrounded by white-washed stone walls. Five golden cupolas stand on top, and beyond the gates that lead to the cemetery are a maze of narrow roads, overgrown with weeds and crammed with marble headstones and ancient vaults.

Until a few years ago, the cemetery had been closed to the public. Khrushchev's grave was nearby, a massive monument of black and white marble. Stalin's wife and her family off to the right. Chekhov. Shostakovich. Grand marble edifices to heroes of the Soviet Union and writers and actors, men and women who had left their mark on Soviet history. And my father, an American, was strangely among them.

And as I stood there in the pouring rain under the wet trees in the corner of the cemetery I saw the gray-haired man from the Mercedes put up his umbrella and speak quietly with the priest, who nodded and went to stand under one of the trees a short distance away.

The gray-haired man was in his late forties, tall and well-built, and he wore a smart blue business suit under his damp raincoat, and he smiled warmly as he came toward me.

"A wet day for it, wouldn't you say?" He offered his hand. "Brad Taylor, US Embassy. You must be Massey?"

The handshake was firm and as I let go I said, "For a while there I was afraid you wouldn't make it."

"Sorry I'm late, I got held up at the embassy." He took a pack of Marlboro cigarettes from his pocket and offered me one. "Smoke? I hope it doesn't seem disrespectful?"

"No it doesn't, and thanks, I don't mind if I do."

He lit both our cigarettes and looked back over at the priest as he arranged his white vestments under his black raincoat and removed a Bible from his pocket, almost ready to begin.

Taylor said, "Bob tells me you're a journalist with the *Washington Post*? Have you ever been to Moscow before, Mr. Massey?"

"Once, five years ago on a brief assignment. What else did Bob tell you?"

Taylor smiled, showing a row of perfectly white and even teeth. "Just enough so I wouldn't be at a loss when we met. He said you were a friend of his from way back, when you were at boarding school together, and that you served in his unit in Vietnam. And he said to make sure everything went smoothly for you while you're in Moscow. Bob seemed very anxious about that."

Taylor went to say something else then, but hesitated and looked back just as the priest had made himself ready, lighting a small censer of incense before he came over to join us.

Someone had left a fresh marble slab against one of the trees and I could make out the simple chiseled inscription in Cyrillic letters.

JAKOB MASSEY
Born: 3 January 1912
Died: 1 March 1953

Nearby was an old unmarked stone slab that had been uprooted from the grave, green with lichen and weathered by the years. There was another one still lying on the ground, marking a second grave beside my father's, looking just as old, and out of the corner of my eye I saw two gravediggers wearing capes standing a distance away under some trees, waiting to go to work and erect my father's headstone.

And as I stood there I realized how suddenly everything had come together. One of those twists of luck that seem to conspire now and then to make you believe in fate. A week ago and over five thousand miles away in Washington I had received the phone call from Langley, telling me they had arranged the funeral ceremony and that Anna Khorev would meet me in Moscow. It had taken three days to finalize the details and by then I could hardly contain my excitement.

The Orthodox priest stepped forward and shook my hand and said in perfect English, "Shall I begin now?"

"Thank you."

He stepped toward the grave and started to pray as he swung the censer of fragrant incense, chanting the prayers for the dead in Russian.

It was all over in no time at all, and then the priest withdrew and went back to the car. The gravediggers came over and began to place the fresh headstone on my father's tomb. Taylor said, "Well, I guess that's it, except for your ladyfriend, Anna Khorev. She arrived early this morning from Tel Aviv. That's what kept me."

Taylor lit us both another cigarette. "I guess Bob explained the ground rules?"

"Sure. No photographs, no tape recorder. Everything is off the record."

Taylor smiled. "I guess that about covers everything. The place she's at is in the Swallow Hills outside Moscow. Belongs to the Israeli Embassy, one of their staff houses they vacated for the meeting." He handed me a slip of paper. "That's the address. They're expecting you and the appointment is for three this afternoon." He hesitated. "You mind if I ask you a question?"

"Ask away."

He nodded over toward my father's grave. "Bob told me your father died forty years ago. How come you're having this service here today?"

"All I can tell you is my father worked for the American government. He died in Moscow in 1953."

"Did he work for our embassy here?"

"No."

Taylor said, puzzled, "I thought Moscow was out of bounds to Americans during the Cold War, except for those working in the embassy? How did your father die?"

"That's what I'm here to find out."

Taylor looked puzzled and he went to say something else then, but suddenly thunder cracked above us and he glanced up.

"Well, I'd like to stay and talk, but duty beckons." He crushed his cigarette with the heel of his shoe. "I've got to take the padre back. Can I give you a lift someplace?"

I tossed away my cigarette. "No need, I'll find a taxi. I'd like to stay a while. Thanks for your help."

"Whatever you say." Taylor put up his umbrella. "Good luck, Massey. And I sure hope you find whatever it is you're looking for."

* * *

This is what I remember.

A cold, windy evening in early March 1953. I am ten. I am in my dormitory in the boarding school in Richmond, Virginia. I hear the footsteps creak on the stairs outside, hear the door open. I look up and see the headmaster standing there, another man behind him, but this man isn't a teacher or staff. He's wearing an overcoat and leather gloves and he stares at me before he smiles weakly.

The headmaster says, "William, this gentleman is here to see you." He looks meaningfully at the other two boys in the room. "Would you leave William alone for a while?"

The boys leave the room. The headmaster leaves the room. The man comes in and closes the door. He's broad and hard-faced, with deep-set eyes, and looks every inch a soldier with his tight cropped haircut and polished brown shoes.

For a long time he says nothing, as if he finds what he's about to tell me difficult, and then he says, "William, my name is Karl Branigan. I was a colleague of your father's."

There is something in the tone of his voice that puts me on my guard, the way he says *was* a colleague, and I look up at him and say, "What's this about, Mr. Branigan?"

"William, I'm afraid I've got some bad news for you. It's about your father . . . he's dead. I'm sorry . . . truly sorry."

The man just stands there and doesn't speak again. And then I'm crying, but the man doesn't come toward me or touch me or offer any comfort and for the first time in my life I really feel utterly alone. A little later I hear his footsteps go down the creaking stairs again. The wind screams and rushes outside the window. A tree branch brushes against the wall outside, then creaks and snaps. I call for my father. But he doesn't answer.

And then a scream from deep inside me, which echoes still inside my head, a terrible cry of grief, and I can't stop my tears.

I remember running after that. Nowhere in particular. Out through the oak doors of the school and across damp, cold Virginian fields, grief heavy as stone in my heart, until I found the cold river that ran through the grounds. I lay on the wet grass and buried my face in my hands and wished my father back.

It was later that I learned something of my father's death. They never told me where exactly he had died, only that it was somewhere in Europe and it had been suicide. The body had been in water for weeks and it wasn't a pretty sight for a young boy, so they hadn't let me see it. There was a funeral, but no more explanations or answers to my questions, because no one bothers to tell a child such things, but years later those unanswered questions always came back. Why? Where? It was to take a long time to learn the truth.

Ten days ago when my mother died I went back to the rooms where she had lived and embarked on the ritual of going through her things. There were no tears, because I had never really known her. We hadn't seen each other much over the years, a card or two, a brief letter once in a while, because we had never been that close, not the way I had been with my father. My parents had divorced soon after I was born and my mother had gone her own way, leaving my father to bring me up.

She had been a dancer in one of the Broadway shows, and knowing my father even the little I did as a child I always guessed they had never been suited.

She rented a small apartment on New York's Upper East Side. I remember the place was in disarray. An untidy single bed, a single chair, some empty gin bottles and a bottle of blond hair dye. Letters from old boyfriends and some from my father, held together with elastic bands, kept in an old tin box under her bed.

I found the letter from my father. Old and faded with years, its edges curling and the color of papyrus.

It was dated 24 January 1953.

Dear Rose,

Just a line to let you know William is well and doing fine at school. I'm going to be away for a time and if anything should happen to me I want you to know (as usual) there's enough money in my account to see you both through, along with my service insurance. Dangerous times we're living in! I hear they're building air-raid shelters on Broadway because of the threat from the Russians.

I'm keeping well and I hope you are. One more thing should anything happen to me: I'd be obliged if you'd check the house, and if you find any papers lying around in the study or in the usual place in the cellar, do me a favor and pass them on to the office in Washington. Will you do that for me?

Jake.

I read through the other letters out of curiosity. There was nothing much in there. Some were from men, notes sent backstage from someone who had seen her in the chorus line and liked her legs and wanted to buy her dinner. There were a couple more from my father, but none that hinted at how they might have once loved each other. I guess she destroyed those.

But I thought about that line in the letter about the papers. The house that had been my father's was now mine. It was an old clapboard place he had bought when he and my mother first moved to Washington, and when he had died it ran to ruin for a long time until I was old enough to tidy it up. It had taken me years to get it back into shape. There had once been a steel Diebold safe sunk into the floor in my father's study in which he used to keep documents and papers. But I remembered him saying once that he never trusted safes, because they could always be opened by someone determined or clever enough. The safe was long gone, and the room refurbished. But I didn't know of any other place he might have used.

So the day I got back from sorting my mother's affairs I went down to the cellar. It was a place I hardly ever went, filled with long-forgotten bric-à-brac that had belonged to my parents, and boxes of stuff I'd kept over the years and had promised myself I'd get rid of. Remembering the study safe, I shifted the cardboard and wooden boxes around and checked the concrete floors.

I found nothing.

Then I started on the walls.

It took me quite a while before I found the two loose red bricks high in the back wall above the cellar door.

I remember my heart was pounding a little, wondering whether I would find anything, or if my mother had long ago already done as my father had asked, or ignored him as she so often did. I reached up and pulled out the bricks. There was a deep recess inside and I saw the large yellowed legal pad lying there between the covers of a manila file, worn and faded.

There are some things that change your life forever. Like marriage or divorce or someone on the end of a telephone telling you there's been a death of someone close in the family.

But nothing prepared me for what I found behind those bricks in the cellar.

I took the old pad upstairs and read it through. Two pages had been written on in blue ink, in my father's handwriting.

Four names. Some dates. Some details and sketchy notes, like he was trying to work something out, none of it making much sense. And a code name: Operation Snow Wolf.

My father had worked for the CIA. He had been a military man all his life, and had worked in OSS during the war, operating behind German lines. That much I knew, but not much else, until I found that old yellow pad.

For a long time I sat there, trying to figure it all out, my heart and mind racing, until I saw the date on one of the pages, and it finally clicked.

I drove to Arlington Cemetery. For a long time I looked at my father's grave, looked at the inscription.

JAKOB MASSEY
Born: 3 January 1912
Died: 20 February 1953

I looked at those words until my eyes were on fire from looking. Then I went and made photocopies of the written pages I'd found and delivered the originals in a sealed envelope to my lawyer.

I made the call to Bob Vitali an hour later. He worked for the CIA in Langley.

"Bill, it's been a long time," Vitali said cheerfully."Don't tell me. There's a school reunion, right? Why do they always have these things when you're just about getting over those days? The amount of money that place in Richmond cost me in shrink's bills . . ."

I told him what I had found and how I had found it, but not the contents.

"So what? You found some forgotten papers of your old man's. Sure, he worked for the CIA, but that was over forty years ago. Do yourself a favor and burn them."

"I think someone should come and look at them."

"Are you kidding? Is this what this call is about?"

"Bob, I really think someone should come and look at them."

Vitali sighed and I could picture him looking at his watch at the other end.

"OK, what's in there? Give me something I can work with and I'll ask around, see if what you found is important. Remember, it's over forty years. I'm pretty sure whatever you've found has been declassified. I think maybe you're getting excited over nothing."

"Bob, please come and look at them."

Vitali said impatiently, "Bill, I haven't got the time to drive to your place. Give me *something* to go on, for Christ's sakes."

"Operation Snow Wolf."

"What's that?"

"That's what it says on the top of the first page on the pad."

"Never heard of it. What else?"

"There's more."

"Like what more?"

"Come over and look at the pages."

Vitali sighed. "Bill, I'll tell you what I'm going to do. I'll ask some of the old-timers here, or one of the Archives boys, and see what I can come up with. See if this Snow Wolf thing rings a bell." I could hear the impatience in his voice. "Listen, I've got a call coming in, I'll talk to you soon. Be good, man."

The line clicked dead.

I stood up and went into the kitchen and made coffee. It seemed like I sat there for a long time, my heart still pounding, thinking about those pages and what they might mean. I didn't want to tell Vitali *everything* because I wanted to know what Langley knew. My mind was ablaze but I didn't know what to do next.

It must have been an hour later when I heard the screech of car tires outside. I looked out of the window and saw two black limousines pull up, and half a dozen men step out briskly, Bob Vitali among them.

He looked white-faced, and when I went to the door he said urgently, "Can I come in? We need to talk."

The others waited outside on the porch while Vitali came into the room with just one other man. He was tall, maybe sixty, distinguished, with silver hair. He had an arrogant look about him and he didn't smile or speak. Then Vitali said, "Bill, I guess you figured this is about those papers you found . . ."

The other man interrupted sharply. "Mr. Massey, my name is Donahue. I'm a Section Head with the CIA. Bob explained about what you told him. May I see the papers you have, please?"

I handed him the papers.

He looked white. "These are *copies*?"

Donahue's tone demanded an explanation. I looked at him. "The originals are in a safe place."

A muscle twitched in Donahue's face, suddenly stern, then he glanced at Vitali, before reading slowly through the photocopies. Finally he sat down with a worried look.

"Mr. Massey, those papers belong to the CIA."

"They belonged to my father. He *worked* for the CIA."

Donahue's voice was firm. "Mr. Massey, we can argue that point all evening but the papers you hold are still classified top secret. As such, they are government property."

"It's been over forty years."

"It makes no difference—that classification still applies. Anything in those particular papers will *never* be made public. The operation referred to in the file was a highly secret and sensitive one. I can't possibly stress both those words enough. The original papers, please . . ."

"I'll make a deal with you."

"No deals, Massey, the papers, please . . ." Donahue demanded. I was determined not to be bulldozed. "I think you'd better listen to me, Donahue. My father died over forty years ago. I never knew where or when or how he really died. I want answers. And I want to know exactly what this Operation Snow Wolf was he became involved in."

"Out of the question, I'm afraid."

"I'm a journalist. I can have the papers published, write an article, investigate, see if anyone who worked for the CIA back then remembers something. You might be surprised what it turns up."

Donahue paled again. "I can assure you not a paper in the land will publish anything you may care to write on the matter we're discussing. The CIA would not allow it. And your investigation would lead absolutely nowhere."

I stared back at him. "So much for democracy. Then maybe I couldn't publish here," I said. "But there are always newspapers abroad you can't control."

Donahue went silent, his brow furrowed, and I could see his mind was ticking over furiously.

"What do you *want*, Massey?"

"The answer to those questions. I want to know the truth. And I want to meet the people involved with my father on that mission, whoever's still alive."

"That's quite impossible. They're all dead."

"Hardly all of them. There must be someone. One of those four names on the pad. Alex Slanski. Anna Khorev. Henri Lebel. Irena Dezov. Whoever they were. I don't just want a report secondhand. You could tell me anything you want. I want evidence. Flesh and blood evidence. Someone to speak with who knew my father and knew the operation and knows how he really died. And," I said firmly, "I want to know what happened to his body."

This time Donahue really did turn terribly pale. "Your father was buried in Washington."

"That's a damned lie and you know it. Look at the copies, Donahue. There's a date written on the last page, 20 February 1953, in my father's handwriting. You people told me my father died in Europe on that date. That's the date on his tombstone—20 February. Now I may be dumb, but dead men don't write notes. The CIA said my father died abroad but he was *here* in *this* house on that day. You know something? I don't think you even buried my father. I don't think you had a body. That's why you people never let me see it, that's why you gave me all that crap about him being in the water too long. I was a kid, I wouldn't question not being allowed to see the body. But I'm questioning it now. My father didn't commit suicide. He didn't drown himself. He died on this Snow Wolf operation, didn't he?"

Donahue gave a weak smile. "Mr. Massey, I think you're being highly speculative, and really over the top here."

"Then let's not speculate any longer. I went to see my lawyer. I'm having the body exhumed. And when that coffin's opened, I don't think I'll find my father inside. And then I'll have you and your superiors dragged into a public court to explain."

Donahue didn't answer, just went a deep red. He was either totally embarrassed or he wasn't used to being spoken to like that. He looked briefly at Vitali for support, but Bob just sat there, in some kind of shock, like he was dumb-assed or completely in fear of the man or both.

Finally, Donahue stood up, looking like he wanted to hit me. "I want you to understand something, Massey. You do that and you'll find yourself in a whole lot of trouble."

"From whom?"

Donahue didn't reply, just kept staring at me.

I stared back, then adopted a more conciliatory approach. "If you tell me what really happened to my father, what harm can it do? I'll agree to return the papers. And if it's *that* secret I'll agree to sign whatever you want pledging my silence afterwards. And don't talk to me about trouble, Donahue. Not knowing the truth about my father, being told he committed suicide, cost me forty years of trouble and pain." I looked at Donahue determinedly. "But believe me, if someone doesn't tell me the truth, I'll do what I say."

Donahue sighed, then looked at me angrily, and his mouth tightened. "May I use your phone?"

"It's in the hall. You passed it on your way in."

Donahue said, "I think I should tell you at this point that this matter is no longer within my control. I'm going to make a call, Mr. Massey. A very important call. The person I speak to will have to call someone else. Both these people will have to agree before your demands can be met."

I looked at him. "Whom are you going to call?"

"The President of the United States."

It was my turn to react. "And who's *he* going to call?"

Donahue flicked a look at Vitali, then back at me.

"The President of Russia."

The rain had stopped and the sun shone warmly between broken clouds and glinted off the golden onion domes of Novodevichy Convent.

I looked down at the two simple graves lying in the earth, my father's and the worn and weathered slab beside it.

There was no name and no inscription on the slab, just blank stone, the way my father's was.

In all Russian cemeteries there are small chairs facing the graves, a place for relatives to come with a bottle of vodka and sit and talk to their departed. But there were no chairs beside these stones, they were forgotten, the ground around them overgrown with weeds and grass.

I wondered about the grave but knew there was no use wondering, even though my mind was already racing, knowing by some instinct there was something about this , simple unmarked slab that related to my father's death.

There was so little I knew and so much to learn. I hoped Anna Khorev would tell me.

I walked back to the cemetery gates and found a taxi, drove back through the hot, crowded Moscow streets to my hotel room and waited. I lay on my bed and closed my eyes but I did not sleep.

Now the rain was gone the heat lingered like smoke on a windless day.

I had waited over forty years to know my father's secret.

Another few hours was nothing.

The sun was shining on the Swallow Hills, flowers blooming in the gardens of the big wooden houses that overlook the Moscow River. The address was one of the old villas from the Tsar's time. A big, rambling place with a white picket fence and clapboard windows and flower boxes out front.

The taxi dropped me at the gate and when I walked up there were two men in plain clothes, Israeli guards, standing beside a security hut. They checked my passport and one of them examined the bunch of white orchids I had brought, then telephoned the villa, before they opened the gate for me and I walked up to the front.

Unexpectedly it was a young woman who opened the door when I rang the bell. She wore jeans and a sweater and was in her early twenties, tall and dark-haired and deeply tanned.

The smile was warm when she said in English, "Mr. Massey, please come in."

I followed her into a cool marble hall that echoed to our footsteps.

She led me out to the back of the villa. The gardens were dazzling with color but in the bright Moscow sunshine the place looked a little shabby. Creepers grew raggedly on walls and the place looked as if it could do with a coat of fresh paint.

As I followed the girl across the patio I saw the elderly woman waiting at a table. She was tall and elegant, with one of those chiseled, well-proportioned faces that keep their age so well.

She would have been in her late sixties but she didn't look it. She was remarkably handsome. Her face had a Slavic look, high cheekbones, and although her hair was completely gray, she looked like a woman ten years younger. She wore a simple black dress that hugged her slim figure, dark glasses and a white scarf tied around her neck.

She stared up at my face for a long time before she stood and offered her hand.

"Mr. Massey, it's good to meet you."

I shook her hand and offered her the orchids.

"Just to say hello. They tell me all Russians adore flowers."

She smiled and smelled the flowers. "How very kind. Would you like something to drink? A coffee? Some brandy?"

"A drink would be good."

"Russian brandy? Or is that too strong for you Americans?"

"Not at all. That sounds fine."

The girl hovered by her side, poured me a drink from a tray and handed it across.

The woman placed the orchids on the coffee table and said, "Thank you, Rachel. You may leave us now." When the young woman had gone she said, "My granddaughter. She traveled with me to Moscow," as if explaining the girl's presence, and then she smiled again. "And I'm Anna Khorev, but doubtless you know that."

She offered me a cigarette from a pack on the table and I accepted. She took one herself, and when she had lit both, she looked out at the view. She must have been aware of me staring at her but then I guessed she was used to men staring.

She smiled as she looked back at me. "Well, Mr. Massey, I hear you've been very persistent."

"I guess it comes with the territory of being a journalist."

She laughed, an easy laugh, and then she said, "So tell me what you know about me?"

I sipped the brandy. "Almost nothing until a week ago, when I learned you were still alive and living in Israel."

"Is that all?"

"Oh, there's more, I assure you."

She seemed amused. "Go on, please."

"Over forty years ago you escaped from a Soviet prison camp, after being sentenced to life imprisonment. You're the only survivor of a top-secret CIA mission, code-named Snow Wolf."

"I can see your friends in Langley filled you in." She smiled. "Tell me more."

I sat back and looked at her. "They told me hardly anything. I think they wanted to leave that to you. Except they did tell me my father wasn't buried in Washington, but in an unmarked grave in Moscow. He died on active service for his country and you were with him when it happened."

She nodded at me to continue.

"I found some papers. Old papers of his he kept."

"So I'm told."

"Four names were written in the pages, and they cropped up several times. Yours. And another three names. Alex Slanski, Henri Lebel, Irena Dezov. There was also a line written on the bottom of one of the pages, the last line. 'If they're caught, may God help us all.' I was hoping you could help me there."

For a long time she said nothing, just looked at me through her dark glasses. And then she removed them and I saw her eyes. They were big and dark brown and very beautiful.

I said, "That line means something to you?"

She hesitated. "Yes, it means something," she said enigmatically. She was silent for several moments and turned her head to look away. When she looked back she said, "Tell me what else you know."

I sat back in my chair. "The file cover I found, would you care to see it?"

Anna Khorev nodded. I took the photocopied single sheet from my pocket and handed it across.

She read it for several moments, then slowly laid the page on the table.

I glanced down. I had read it so many times I didn't need to read it again.

OPERATION SNOW WOLF.
SECURITY, CENTRAL INTELLIGENCE AGENCY, SOVIET DIVISION.
VITAL: ALL COPY FILES AND NOTE DETAILS RELATING TO THIS OPERATION TO BE DESTROYED AFTER USE. REPEAT DESTROYED.
UTMOST SECRECY. REPEAT, UTMOST SECRECY.

Her face showed no reaction as she looked back at me.

"So when you read this and the other pages and learned your father had not committed suicide or died on the date you were told, you realized there was perhaps more to his death, and went looking for answers?"

"That's when I was offered a deal. If I agreed to hand over the original pages I'd hear some answers, and I'd be present when my father was given a proper burial service. But I was told that the matter was still highly secret, and that I had to sign a declaration promising to uphold that secrecy."

She crushed her cigarette in the ashtray and said, as if quietly amused, "Yes, I know all about your friends in Langley, Mr. Massey."

"Then you'll also know I was told that it was all up to you, whether you'd tell me what I wanted to know."

"Which is?"

"The truth about my father's death. The truth pure and simple about Snow Wolf and how my father ended up in a grave in Moscow at the height of the Cold War."

She didn't answer, but stood and crossed to the veranda.

I sat forward in my chair. "The way I see it, my father was involved in something highly covert, something that people are still reluctant to talk about. I'm not just talking about a secret. I'm talking about something totally extraordinary."

"Why extraordinary?"

"Because the people from Langley I spoke with still wanted to hide the truth after all these years. Because when my father was involved in the operation it was a time when the Russians and the Americans were out to annihilate one another. And you're the only person alive who maybe knows what happened to my father." I looked at her. "Am I right?"

She didn't speak and I continued to look at her.

"Can I tell you something? I lost my father over four decades ago. Four decades of not having a father to talk to, and to be loved by. It was like having a hole in my life for a long time, until finally he just slowly became a wistful memory. I had to live with the lie that he committed suicide. And you—you know how and why he really died. And what's more I think you owe me an explanation."

She didn't reply, just looked at me thoughtfully.

I said, "And I have a question. Why did you want to meet me in Moscow, and not someplace else? I was told you escaped from this country. Why come back?"

Anna Khorev thought for a moment. "I suppose the simple truth of it is I would very much have liked to have gone to your father's ceremony, Mr. Massey, but I considered it your own private affair. But perhaps my just coming here was the next best thing." She hesitated. "Besides, I've never seen his grave. And it was something I wanted to do."

"The second grave, the one beside my father's—it had the same unmarked headstone. Whom does the grave belong to?"

Something passed across her face then, a look like sadness, and she said, "Someone very brave. Someone quite remarkable indeed."

"Who?"

She looked out at the view of the city, toward the red walls of the Kremlin, as if she seemed to be trying to make up her mind, and then she finally turned back to look at me. She seemed to soften suddenly, and she looked down briefly at the flowers on the table.

"You know you look very much like your father? He was a good man, a very good man. And everything you've said is true." She paused. "You're right. All that pain and silence deserves an explanation. And that's why I'm here. Tell me, what do you know about Joseph Stalin, Mr. Massey?"

The unexpectedness of her question threw me and I looked at her for several moments. I shrugged. "No more than most. He was a god to some, I guess. The Devil to others. Depends on which side of the fence you sat on. But certainly one of the great despots of this century. They say he was responsible for as many if not more deaths than Hitler. He died of a cerebral hemorrhage eight years after the war."

Anna Khorev shook her head fiercely. "Twenty-three million deaths. Not including those who died in the last war because of his stupidity. Twenty-three million of his own people whom he murdered. Men, women, children. Slaughtered. Shot or sent to die in camps worse than the Nazis ever imagined, by one of the cruelest men this world has ever known."

I sat back, surprised by the sudden ferocity in her voice. "I don't understand. What has this got to do with what we're discussing?"

"It has everything to do with it. Stalin died, certainly, but not in the way the history books record."

I sat there stunned for several moments. Anna Khorev's face looked deadly serious. Finally she said, "I guess the story I'm going to tell you goes back a long time, to when it first began in Switzerland."

She smiled suddenly. "And do you know something? You're the first person I've spoken to about it in over forty years."

THE PAST

PART ONE

1952

2

Lucerne,
Switzerland.
December 11th

All over Europe that year the news seemed to have consisted of nothing but bad.

In Germany, the past was to resurface at Nuremberg where a tribunal began its hearing into the Katyn Forest massacre of 1940. Four thousand bodies had been unearthed outside a small Polish town, all bound and shot with small-caliber pistols, the grisly remains of what had once been the cream of the Polish Army.

It was the year that also saw the French face an all-out offensive by the Viet Minh, a bloody war was raging in Korea, and in Europe the Iron Curtain was lowered between West Berlin and the surrounding Soviet Zone, the ultimate gesture by the Kremlin that a postwar peace was not to be.

Otherwise, wartime rationing was still in force in Britain, Eva Perón died, Republican Dwight D. Eisenhower beat his Democratic rival, Adlai Stevenson, in the US presidential election, and in Hollywood, one of the few bright moments in a dull year was the debut appearance of a stunning blond starlet named Marilyn Monroe.

To Manfred Kass, stalking through the woods outside the old Swiss city of Lucerne that cold December morning, such things hardly mattered. And although he could not have known it, that day was to mark a beginning, and also an ending.

It was growing light when Kass parked his ancient black Opel on the road in front of the entrance to the woods. He removed the single-barrel shotgun from beneath the blanket on the backseat of the car. It was a Mansten twelve-gauge, getting a little old now, but still reliable. He climbed out and locked the doors before slipping a cartridge into the breech but leaving the gun broken. He shoveled a boxful of cartridges into the pockets of his shooting jacket, then he started to walk into the woods.

At thirty-two, Kass was a tall, awkward man. He walked clumsily and with a slight limp. The clumsiness had been with him since childhood, but the limp had been an unwanted memento from the Battle of Kiev eleven years before. Though he had been born in Germany, being conscripted into Hitler's army had not been one of Kass's ambitions in life. He had intended emigrating to Lucerne before the war, where his wife's uncle ran the bakery business, but he had left it too late, the way he had left many things in his life too late.

"Trust me, Hilda," he had told his wife when the winds of war had started to whisper and she suggested they beat a hasty retreat to Switzerland and her family. "There won't be a war, *liebchen.*"

Two days later Hitler had invaded Poland.

Kass had been proved wrong on many other occasions. Like volunteering for the front at the start of the Russian campaign. He reckoned that because the German army was rolling across the steppes of the Ukraine with such ease, and because the *Russkis* were dirty and stupid peasants, the war against them would be a piece of cake.

He had been right about one thing. The Russians he had met were generally dirty, stupid peasants. But they were also fierce fighters. And the fiercest enemy of all had been the Russian winter. So cold that your own piss froze and you had to snap it off when it turned to solid ice. So razor-sharp were the freezing Baltic and Siberian winds that swept over the steppes that within minutes of defecating, your shit was freeze-blasted as hard as cement.

Kass had laughed the first time he saw his own frozen turd. But it was nothing to laugh at really. Prodding the phenomenon with his bayonet, he had been hit by a sniper's bullet. A clear shot from two hundred meters, into the right flank of his bare ass.

Manfred Kass was used to making mistakes.

But the mistake he was about to make that December morning in the woods outside Lucerne was to be the biggest of his life.

He knew the forest reasonably well. Which paths led where, and the locations of the best rabbit grounds. The rabbits made a good tasty stew to accompany the fresh, floury bread he helped bake six nights a week. And the thought of food made him hungry as he stalked through the forest, snapping the breech of the shotgun closed as he came closer to the clearing in the woods.

The light was reasonably good and getting better. A faint watery mist lingering on the low ground. Not perfect light, but good enough for him to get a clear shot.

As he stepped carefully toward the clearing, he heard the voices. He halted and rubbed his stubbly jaw. He had never met anyone in the woods that early and the sound of voices made him curious. It occurred to him that he might have come across a courting couple, still out after a late Friday-night dance in Lucerne, who had come to make love in the woods. It sometimes happened, he supposed. But he had not seen any car parked on the road, nor any bicycle tracks in the forest.

As Kass moved through the trees to the edge of the clearing, his eyes snapped open, and he halted, riveted to the spot.

A man wearing a dark winter overcoat and hat stood in the center of the forest clearing. He held a revolver in his hand. But what shocked Kass, stunned him, was that it was aimed at a man and a young girl kneeling in the wet grass, their faces deathly white, their hands and feet bound with rope.

As Kass stumbled back, his belly churned and his body broke out into a cold sweat. The kneeling man was crying in pitiful sobs. He was middle-aged, his face painfully thin and sickly gray, and Kass noticed the dark bruises under his eyes and the cuts on his hands indicating he had been savagely beaten.

The child was crying too, but there was a white cloth gagging her mouth and tied behind her long dark hair. She was no more than ten, Kass guessed, and when he saw the frightened, pitiful look on her face, her body trembling with fear, it made him want to vomit.

And then suddenly Kass's anger flared, his veins no longer ice, but boiling now, because there was something pitiful and debauched about the man and the young girl kneeling there as if waiting for death.

He looked at the man. His weapon had a long, slim silencer, but from where Kass stood he couldn't see his face, only his profile. But he noticed a vivid red scar that ran from the man's left eye to his jaw, the blemish so livid that from a distance it looked as if someone had painted it on.

He was talking to the man kneeling in the grass, and in between his sobs the kneeling man was pleading. Kass couldn't hear the words but he could see that the man with the scar was not listening, realized that what he was about to witness was an execution.

And then it happened. So fast Kass hardly had time to react.

The scar-faced man lifted his revolver until it was level with the kneeling man's forehead. The weapon gave a hoarse cough. A bullet slammed into the man's skull and his body jerked and crumpled on the grass.

The child screamed behind her gag, her eyes wild with raw fear.

Kass swallowed, wanted to scream too, felt icy sweat run down his face. He felt his heart was about to explode with terror. He wanted to turn back, to run, not witness what was about to happen, but for the first time he seemed to realize that he held the shotgun in his hands and that unless he did something the child was going to die.

He saw her struggle helplessly as the executioner pressed the tip of the barrel to her head and prepared to squeeze the trigger.

As Kass fumbled to raise his shotgun, he called out hoarsely, "*Halt*!"

A brutal, hard face turned to look at him. The scar-faced man stared coldly at Kass, his thin lips like slits cut in his face with a razor. His eyes seemed to take in everything at a glance, flicking to the forest left and right, then settling on Kass again, assessing his enemy, but no sign of fear in his eyes.

Kass called out shakily, "Stop, do you hear me! Put down your weapon!"

He heard the naked fear in his own voice and barely had time to squeeze the trigger as his adversary swung around and the silenced pistol gave another hoarse cough. The bullet smashed into Kass's right jaw, shattering bone and teeth, slicing through flesh, flinging him back against a tree, the shotgun flying from his grasp.

As Kass screamed in agony he saw the man fire into the child's head. Her body jerked and crumpled.

Kass stumbled back into the trees, but the man was already rushing toward him. As Kass crashed through the woods and fled, oblivious to the pain in his shattered jaw, his only thoughts were of survival and making it back to the car.

Fifty meters to go and he could see the Opel through the trees, could hear the man rushing through the forest after him.

Fifty long meters that seemed like a thousand, and Kass ran like a man possessed, a hand on his bloodied face, his whole body on fire with a powerful will to survive, the savage image of the young girl's execution replaying in his mind like a terrible nightmare, spurring him on.

Please God.

Thirty meters.

Please.

Twenty.

Ten.

God

Please

A bullet zinged through the trees, splintering wood to his left.

Sweet Jesus . . .

And then suddenly he was out of the woods.

As he reached the Opel and yanked open the door the man emerged out of the forest behind him.

Kass did not hear the shot that hit him but he felt the bullet slip between his back ribs like a red-hot dagger. It jerked him forward onto the hood of the Opel.

He was already dead before he hit the ground.

The bodies were found in the woods two days later. Another hunter, like Kass, but this one more fortunate because he hadn't been in the wrong place at the wrong time. He threw up when he saw the child's body.

Her pretty face was frozen and white. The flesh around her head wound and behind her neck had been partly chewed away by forest rodents.

Even the hardened policemen of the Lucerne KriminalAmt thought it one of the most brutal murder scenes they had ever witnessed. There was always something pitiful and particularly brutal about the body of a murdered child.

The subsequent forensic and pathology examinations determined that the girl was aged between ten and twelve. She had not been raped, but there was severe bruising on her legs, arms, chest and genital area, which suggested she had been badly beaten and tortured some hours before being shot. The same with the man's corpse lying next to hers. Both bodies were placed in cold storage in the Lucerne police morgue.

The only corpse that could be identified was that of Manfred Kass. In his wallet was a driver's license and a shotgun permit, and he wore a wristwatch with an inscription, "To Manni, with love, Hilda."

The police learned that the bakery worker had gone hunting after his Friday-night shift and deduced that he had perhaps stumbled onto the slaughter of the man and the child and paid with his life.

But of the murderer or his identity, there was no trace at all.

A month later there was still no evidence that linked the two unknown corpses to missing persons. Both had no personal identification and had been wearing the sort of clothes that could be bought in any large clothing store in Europe. The child's dress and underwear had been purchased in a Paris department store, the man's suit had been bought from a very popular chain of men's outfitters in Germany.

Concerning the bodies, the only clue was a faded, minute tattoo on the man's right arm. It was of a small white dove, centimeters above his wrist.

3

Washington, D.C.
December 12th

It was a little after eight in the evening when the DC-6 carrying President-Elect Dwight D. Eisenhower from Tokyo landed at Andrews Air Force Base in Washington, D.C.

Although he was not to take over the reins of power until January, Eisenhower had flown to Seoul a month after his election to assess personally the war situation in the Far East, wanting to see for himself the state of play on the muddy battlefields of Korea.

His meeting with President Harry Truman the next day was unofficial, and after the brief welcome Truman suggested they take a walk in the White House gardens.

The air was crisp and clear, the ground covered in a moist carpet of brown and gold leaves, as Truman led Eisenhower down the path through the lawns where the Secret Service men stood at strategic intervals.

The two men seemed a strange pair: the small bespectacled President with the bow tie and walking cane who, like a certain predecessor, believed that the way to earn respect was to speak softly and carry a big stick, and the tall, erect military man and former five-star general who had been a professional soldier all his life.

They had reached one of the oak benches and Truman gestured for them to sit.

He lit up a Havana cigar, puffed out smoke and sighed. "You know what I'm going to do the day after I leave office? I'm going to fly down to Florida and bake under a hot sun. Maybe do me some fishing. Seems like I haven't had time for that in years." The President hesitated before he looked at Eisenhower's face and said more seriously, "Tell me, Ike, what's your opinion of Stalin?"

The President called his successor by his nickname, the one that had stuck with him since West Point as a young cadet. Eisenhower ran a hand over his almost bald head. His shoulders tensed as he sat forward and looked out at the White House gardens.

"You mean as a military adversary?"

Truman shook his head. "I meant as a man."

Eisenhower shrugged and laughed bitterly. "I don't think you need to ask *me* that question. I'm on the record in that regard. The man's a despot and a dictator. Shrewd and cunning as they come. You could say he's the cause of all our present problems, or certainly most of them. I wouldn't trust the goddamned son-of-a-bitch an inch."

Truman leaned forward, his voice firm. "Hell, Ike, that's my point. He is the whole damned problem. Forget about the Chinese. We don't have to worry about them for at least another ten years down the road. But the way the Russians are moving so fast with their nuclear research they're going to be way ahead of us militarily. And you know as well as I do they've got some pretty good technical minds working for them. The top ex-Nazi scientists. We've exploded a hydrogen device, but they're working on the actual bomb, for God's sakes. And they'll make it, Ike, you mark my words, and sooner than we think. And when that happens, old Joe Stalin knows he can do pretty much as he likes."

"What do our intelligence people say?"

"About the Russian hydrogen program? Six months. Maybe sooner. But six months at the outside. The word is, Stalin's authorized unlimited funds. And our latest intelligence reports say they've built a test site at a place near Omsk, in Siberia."

Eisenhower frowned. The sun was still warm on his face as he glanced toward the Washington Monument half a mile away. He looked back as Truman put down his cigar and spoke again.

"Ike, this is the first real opportunity we've had to talk in private, and no doubt the CIA will be briefing you in the coming weeks, but there's something else you ought to know. Something pretty disturbing."

Eisenhower studied the small dapper-dressed man. "You mean about the Russian bomb program?"

Truman shook his head and his face appeared suddenly grim.

"No. What I'm talking about is a report. A highly classified report. It was sent to me by the special Soviet Department we have over near the Potomac. I want you to read it. The source is a highly placed contact we have who has links to the Kremlin. And to tell you the truth, the report has me scared. More scared than I've been in a long time. And you're looking at a man who's come through two world wars, like yourself. But this . . ." Truman broke off and shook his head. "Hell, this worries me even more than the Germans or the Japs did."

There was a look of surprise on Eisenhower's face. "You mean the source of the report is a Russian?"

"An émigré Russian, to be precise."

"Who?"

"Ike, even I can't tell you that. That's a matter for the CIA. But you'll know the first day you're sitting in the Oval Office."

"Then why let me read this report now?"

Truman took a deep breath, then stood up slowly. "Because, Ike, I'd like you to be prepared before you come into office. What you're going to be privy to doesn't make for pleasant reading. There are some pretty disturbing things in there, like I said, that scare the pants off me. And whether you like it or not, the contents of the report are going to determine not only your presidency but a hell of a lot else besides. Certainly the future course of this country, maybe even the future course of the whole damned world."

Eisenhower frowned. "It's that serious?"

"Ike, believe me, it's that serious."

The two men sat in the silence of the Oval Office, Eisenhower reading from the manila-colored file, the cover and each page marked in red lettering: "*For President's Eyes Only.*"

Truman sat opposite, not in the President's chair, but on the small floral couch by the window that faced the Washington Monument. His hands were resting on his cane as he looked over at Eisenhower's rubbery face. It was grave and the generous wide lips were pursed.

Finally, Eisenhower placed the report gently on the coffee table. He stood and crossed restlessly to the window, hands behind his back. In another five weeks he would inhabit the President's chair, but suddenly the prospect seemed to hold less appeal for him. He put a hand to his forehead and massaged his temples. Truman's voice brought him back.

"Well, what do you think?"

Eisenhower turned. Truman stared at him, his glasses glinting in the strong light from the window.

For a long time Eisenhower said nothing, his face drawn. Then he shook his head. "Jesus, I don't know what to think." He paused. "You trust the source of the report?"

Truman nodded firmly. "I damned well do. No question. And I've had some independent experts brought in on this. Non-CIA and all top-class people in their field. I wanted them to verify everything you just read. They all agreed with the facts."

Eisenhower took a deep breath. "Then with respect, sir, the day I become President I'm walking into a goddamned minefield."

"I guess you are, Ike," Truman replied, matter-of-factly. "And hell, I'm not being flippant. Just scared. Damned scared."

Truman stood and went over to the window. There were dark rings under his eyes and his soft face looked troubled in the harsh light, as if the strain of eight years in office was finally taking its toll. Suddenly Harry Truman looked very old and very tired.

"To tell the truth, maybe even more scared than I was when I made the decision to drop the bombs on Hiroshima and Nagasaki. This has even wider implications. Greater dangers."

When he saw Eisenhower stare back at him, Truman nodded gravely over toward the desk.

"I really mean it, Ike. I'm glad it's going to be a former five-star general sitting in that President's chair and not me. Florida's going to be hot enough. Who the hell needs Washington?"

France.

While the two men talked in the Oval Office, four thousand miles away in Paris another man lay in the darkened bedroom of a hotel on the boulevard Saint Germain.

Rain drummed against the windows, a downpour falling beyond the drawn curtains.

The telephone rang beside the bed. He picked it up. When he spoke he recognized the voice that answered.

"It's Konstantine. It happens Monday in Berlin. Everything's arranged. I want no mistakes."

"There won't be." There was a pause, and then the man heard the bitterness in the caller's voice.

"Send him to hell, Alex. Send the butcher to hell."

4

Soviet-Finnish border.
October 23rd

Just after midnight the snow had stopped and she lay in the cottony silence of the woods, listening to her heart beating in her ears like the flutter of wild wings.

She was cold.

Her clothes were soaked through and her hair was damp and she was aware of the icy sweat on her face. She was more tired than she had ever been in her life, and suddenly she wanted it to be over.

For the past hour now she had watched the sentry hut beside the narrow metal bridge that ran across the frozen river. Every now and then she rubbed her limbs, trying to get warm, but it was no use, she was chilled to her bones, and she longed for warmth and for a final end to the exhaustion. Her uniform coat was covered in frost and snow, and as she lay in the narrow gully behind the bank of fir trees she tried not to think of the past, only the future that lay beyond the narrow metal bridge.

She could see the two guards on the Russian side, standing by the small wooden sentry hut, their breaths fogging in the freezing air as they paced up and down. One of them had a rifle slung over his shoulder; the other a machine-pistol draped across his chest. The two men were talking but she couldn't hear their words, only a soft babble of voices.

There was a wooden guardhouse off to the left, forty meters away, a bank of fir trees beside it, the branches sugared with snow. A light was on inside, a plume of wood smoke curling into the freezing air. She knew that was where the other guards would be resting off duty, but for over half an hour now no one had moved in or out of the warmth of the guardhouse, only shadows flitting in and out of the yellow light behind the frosted glass. On the metal bridge, electric light blazed from arc lamps in the trees overhead and the red-and-white barrier poles were down at both ends.

She thought she could see the lights of Finland through the trees but she wasn't sure, for there was a flood of light on the Finnish side of the border, and more guards, but this time in gray overcoats and uniforms.

She saw a sudden movement and her eyes went back to the Russian side.

The guard with the rifle stepped into the tiny sentry hut while the other moved into the trees, unbuttoning his fly to relieve himself.

Her body shivered now, knowing what she had to do, knowing that if she didn't move soon she would freeze to death, the icy cold gnawing deep into her bones. She rolled over in the snow and her gloved hand searched in the leather holster and she found the cold butt of the Nagant revolver.

She rolled back slowly and looked over at the guard urinating. She knew this was her moment and she took a deep breath. She stood and her legs trembled with fear. As she came out from behind the cover of the trees, she slipped the weapon into the pocket of her overcoat.

She was down at the sentry hut before she knew it and she saw the guard with the machine-pistol button his trousers and turn abruptly. He stared at her as if she were a ghost.

What he saw was a young woman coming toward him. Her captain's overcoat with green epaulettes and her officer's winter hat looked a size too big, her clothes covered in a rime of frost and snow. Her dark eyes were sunk in their sockets and her lips were cracked from the cold.

For a moment he seemed unsure of himself, as if sensing something was wrong, and then he said, "I'm sorry, Captain, but this is a restricted area. Your papers, comrade."

As the guard unslung his machine-gun, he stared suspiciously at the young woman's face, but he didn't see the Nagant revolver and that was his mistake.

It exploded twice, hitting him in the chest, sending him flying backward. The air came alive with the noise, and birds shrieked as they flew from the forest branches. Moments later the second guard came running out of the sentry hut.

The woman fired, hitting him in the shoulder, spinning him around, and then she started to run toward the bridge.

There was mayhem behind her on the Russian side, sirens going off and voices raised, as the soldiers came rushing out of the guardhouse. She was barely aware of a voice behind her screaming for her to stop as she ran toward the Finnish barrier fifty meters away, dropping the revolver as she ran, her breath rising in panting bursts, her lungs on fire.

Up ahead, Finnish guards in gray uniforms appeared out of nowhere, unslinging their rifles, one of them pointing over her shoulder, screaming something at her.

She didn't see the Russian guard thirty meters behind her take aim, but she heard the crack of a weapon and saw the frosty cloud explode in the snow off to her right, before the bullet ricocheted off the metal bridge.

And then another rifle cracked and she was suddenly punched forward, losing her balance, a terrible pain blossoming in her side, but she kept running, weaving across the bridge.

As she collapsed in front of the Finnish barrier she cried out in agony. Strong hands suddenly grasped her and pulled her aside.

A young officer, his face pale, barked orders at his men, but she didn't understand the words. Other men fumbled at her bloodied clothes and carried her toward the guardhouse.

There were sirens going off now but she was aware only of the flood of pain in her side and a terrible feeling of tiredness, as if a dam had burst inside her head and all the pent-up fear and exhaustion had come spilling out. She was crying now, and then everything seemed to go at once, vision fading, sounds muted.

The young officer was looking down at her face and she heard the urgency in his voice as he screamed at one of his men to fetch a doctor.

She closed her eyes.

All she remembered after that was darkness.

Sweet, surrendering, painless darkness.

5

Helsinki.
October 25th

A man with gray cropped hair sat beside Anna Khorev's bed.

She looked at him.

The rugged face that stared back at her was pitted with fleshy skin and broken veins and his mouth looked set in a grim impression of aggression. It was the face of a man who had seen a lot of unpleasant things in life, cautious and wary and full of secrets, but the light gray eyes were not without feeling and she guessed they missed nothing. One of the Finnish intelligence officers had told her the American was coming and that he wanted to talk with her. The Finns had questioned her, going over and over her story, but she hadn't told them everything. Not because she hadn't wanted to but because the memories seemed too painful just then, and the anesthetic had made her feel sensitive. And besides, she had got the feeling that they were only going through the motions of something that really wasn't their concern. But the man seated beside her bed seemed different. She could tell that simple answers were not going to satisfy him.

He looked in his early forties and as he sat back in the chair his big hands rested on his knees. His Russian was fluent and his voice soft as he smiled over at her.

"My name is Jake Massey. They tell me you're going to make a full recovery."

When she didn't reply the man leaned forward and said, "I'm here to try and fill in some of the gaps in your story. Your name is Anna Khorev, is that right?"

"Yes."

She saw the sincerity in his eyes as he said, "I realize you've been through a difficult time, Anna, but you must understand one thing. Finland gets a considerable number of people escaping over the Russian border." He smiled again, gently. "Not all so dramatically as you did, perhaps. Some of them are genuinely trying to flee Russia. But others, well, let's just say their intentions are not entirely honorable. Your countrymen send people over here to spy.

You understand what I'm saying, Anna? I need to make certain you're not one of those people."

She nodded and the man said, "You feel well enough to talk?"

"Yes."

"The doctors say they hope to have you up and walking by tomorrow." He hesitated, then studied her face again, the gray eyes gentle but probing, his voice suddenly soft.

"Why did you shoot the two guards on the bridge?"

She saw the man was watching her eyes intently.

"To escape."

"Escape what exactly?"

"From the Gulag."

"Where?"

"Near Ukhta."

"Do you know the name of the camp?"

"Nicochka."

"The Soviet Embassy in Helsinki say you murdered an officer at the camp. Is that true?"

She hesitated, then nodded.

"Why did you kill the man, Anna?"

She had answered the question before when the Finns had interrogated her, but she could sense the American was going to be even more thorough. She went to open her mouth to speak but somehow, the words wouldn't come. Massey looked at her.

"Anna, I think I had better be completely honest and tell you the situation. I work for the American Embassy. Your people are making all kinds of diplomatic noises to have you sent back to face a trial. There's no extradition agreement between Finland and Russia, but if your authorities put pressure on the Finns then they may have to agree to return you. The only way they can avoid that is to hand you over to the American Embassy. Once the Finns say you requested political asylum in America, the matter is out of their hands. They want to do that. They want to help you. Russia is not exactly their best friend. That's why I'm here. I was asked to talk with you and help decide if my embassy can be of help. I'm assuming you don't want to go back to Russia and that you would like to request asylum in America. However, I think you ought to know that under the terms of the Soviet-Finnish Treaty, there are grounds sufficient for your return to Russia on a charge of murder."

Massey paused. He must have seen the look of raw fear in her eyes because he shook his head quickly and said, "Anna, that's not something we want to happen, but it partly depends on you."

"How?"

"On how cooperative you are. The people who interrogated you think you haven't told them everything. You see, at least if I know the full story of your background my embassy can best judge if you're a suitable case for political asylum. You understand what I'm saying?"

She nodded. Massey leaned forward in his chair.

"So, you'll help me?"

"What is it you want to know?"

Massey said gently, "Everything you can tell me. About your background. Your parents. Your life. How you ended up at the border crossing. Why you killed the officer at the camp. Anything that you can remember that might be important."

Suddenly it felt like a terrible grief flooded her mind, as if to remember was too painful. She closed her eyes and turned away, unaware that the man noticed the bruises on her neck, the pink patches of skin that showed through her tightly cropped hair. He said softly, "Take your time, Anna. Just start at the beginning."

When the German Army panzers under Field Marshal von Leeb's command swept into the Baltic States in the summer of 1941, there were many inhabitants who were pleased to see them.

On Stalin's orders only a year before the Red Army had swiftly and brutally annexed each of the tiny independent Baltic countries of Estonia, Latvia and Lithuania. Thousands were tortured, executed, or shipped off to labor camps by the invading Russians. And so the German troops arriving in the summer of 1941 were seen as an army of liberation by many of the citizens of the occupied states. People lined the streets to welcome the crack Wehrmacht soldiers. Women threw garlands of flowers at their feet, while every road north and east was clogged with a defeated Soviet army retreating from the mighty German blitzkrieg.

But not all Soviet commanders chose to flee the might of the Third Reich. Some chose to stay behind, fighting a fierce rearguard action that was to give the Germans a bloody foretaste of what was to lie ahead for them on the frozen steppes of Russia.

One of these Russian officers was Brigadier Yegor Grenko.

At forty-two, he was already a divisional commander. A daring officer with a reputation for being headstrong, he had somehow survived the savage purges Stalin had inflicted on his army on the eve of war, when more than half of the senior officer corps were either shot or deported to Siberia, many without trial, simply because Stalin, acutely paranoid, had falsely suspected that they were plotting to overthrow him.

Along the way Grenko had met and married Nina Zinyakin, the daughter of an Armenian schoolteacher. Grenko first met her when she gave an impassioned lecture on Lenin at the Moscow Institute, and he was smitten at once. She was a resolute, fiery young woman of remarkable good looks, and not unlike her husband in temperament. Within ten months of marriage their first and only child was born.

By the time the Germans advanced on Tallinn, Anna Grenko was fifteen years old.

The initial battle orders from Stalin after the Germans had launched Operation Barbarossa had been to engage in the minimum of conflict. Still foolishly believing that Hitler would not push deep inside Russia and that hostilities would soon cease, Stalin had hoped to lessen the conflict by not angering the Germans with a savage counterattack.

Yegor Grenko saw it differently.

Ordered by Moscow to retreat, he had steadfastly refused. In his opinion, Stalin as a strategist left much to be desired. Grenko didn't believe the Germans would hold back at the Russian border. Convinced that within a week the battle orders would change to an offensive, Grenko decided to fight a rearguard action and for days was bombarded with cables from Moscow military command ordering him to retreat. He tore up every signal and even returned one in reply. "*What the hell am I supposed to do? Sit back and allow the Germans to massacre my men?*"

Yegor Grenko was convinced that history would prove Stalin wrong, just as he knew that the first weeks of battle are as crucial as the last. But when he could finally ignore the cables no more, he and his men boarded a troop train near Narva and headed back to Moscow.

When the train pulled into the Riga Station, Yegor Grenko was arrested and marched to a waiting car. When Anna Grenko's mother tried to intervene she was brushed aside and told bluntly that her husband's arrest was none of her business.

The following day came the visit from the secret police.

Nina Grenko was coldly informed that her husband had been tried by a military tribunal and found guilty of disobeying orders. He had been executed that morning at Lefortovo Prison.

A day later, fresh battle orders from Stalin were made public.

Every citizen was to repel the invading Germans with every means, even to death, and no Soviet soldier was to retreat.

For Yegor Grenko, the order had come a day too late.

After the death of her father, Anna Grenko's family home in Moscow was confiscated on the orders of the secret police. Her mother never recovered from the injustice of her husband's execution and in the second month of the siege of Moscow, Anna Grenko came home to find her mother's corpse hanging from a water pipe.

For two days after they had cut down the body Anna lay in her bed, not eating and barely sleeping. There was suddenly a terrible void in her life and no one to turn to. Relatives shunned her, fearing guilt by association and the midnight knock on the door by the secret police.

On the third day she packed what meager belongings she had into one small suitcase and moved out of the apartment into a squalid, tiny room on the eastern side of the Moscow River.

The German army was ten kilometers away, the golden domes of the Kremlin visible through their field glasses. With the city under constant bombardment there was little to buy or eat and almost no fuel; anything that could be burned had long ago been burned. People devoured what meager rations they were allowed. Dogs and cats fetched a month's wages. Bodies were piled high in the suburbs and the German shells and Stuka bombers made life impossible in freezing sub-zero temperatures.

Too young to fight, Anna Grenko was sent to work in an aircraft factory in the Urals. On her seventeenth birthday she was finally called up for military service. Given three weeks' basic training, she was shipped south to the front and General Chuikov's 62nd Army at Stalingrad.

And it was at Stalingrad she was to learn the real meaning of survival.

Fighting from street to street and factory to factory, holding out against the Germans in a siege that was to last for over six months, crossing enemy lines at night in the mud and snow and attacking their positions, the fighting so savage and close she was often near enough to the enemy that she could hear their whispered voices in nearby trenches. The shelling so heavy that every leaf fell from the trees in the city and dogs drowned themselves in the Volga rather than endure the horrendous noise of battle that went on day and night.

Twice she was wounded and twice she was decorated. In the battles that raged in pockets in and around Stalingrad the killing was merciless.

On the fifth incursion behind the German lines she was captured by a detachment of Ukrainian SS. After interrogation, she was brutally raped.

Left for dead in a bomb crater, she had lain there in the freezing cold, a terrible pain between her legs where the five men had torn her flesh in their savage lust.

On the second morning she had woken to the touch of snow on her face.

When she crawled up the gully she saw the Ukrainians on the far side, the same men who had raped her, standing around a lighted brazier, warming themselves and laughing.

Anna Grenko crawled back into the crater and waited until darkness fell. There was a terrible rage in her heart, a need for revenge, a livid urge to kill the men for what they had done to her. It overwhelmed her and went beyond any instinct for survival. When she crawled out again that night she found the Tokarev machine-pistol and the stick grenades on the body of a fallen comrade.

She crawled back up the crater and over toward the soldiers.

One of the men turned and saw her but already it was too late. She saw the horror on the man's face as she unpinned the grenades and lobbed them into the group, firing the Tokarev at the same time, seeing the bodies dance in the light of the exploding flashes and hearing the screams until all was silence again.

When the lines were overrun the next day, she was found by her own troops lying in the crater, a pool of blood between her legs. She spent three weeks in a field hospital in Stalingrad before being called before a military tribunal and questioned, not about the ordeal of her rape, but about her capture by the Ukrainians and how she had allowed it to happen.

For that indignity, and despite her bravery, she received a month's sentence in a military prison.

It was to be the fifth year after the war before Anna Grenko was to find any sort of personal happiness.

Within two years of the war's end Moscow's citizens had found a new zest for life. The city seemed to awaken after a long hibernation and took on an atmosphere of gaiety and abandon. Apartment blocks and cafés, dance halls and beer halls sprang up in every suburb, people wore fashionable clothes and bright colors, and in summer they danced on hotel terraces to the latest popular music.

Anna Grenko found secretarial work in a Moscow factory and with time on her hands she went to night school, and two years later she began to take evening lectures in the Moscow Language Institute. Although often asked out by men, she rarely accepted, and never agreed to their invitations to their homes. Only once did Anna Grenko make an exception.

One of the young lecturers she met was Ivan Khorev.

He was only twenty-four and a slim, pale, sensitive young man, but he was already an admired and popular poet and his work had been published in several respected literary magazines.

One night after class he had asked Anna out for a drink.

They went to a small open-air café on the banks of the Moscow River. They ate *zakuski* and drank strong Georgian wine and Ivan Khorev talked about poetry. When he recited her a poem by Pasternak she thought it the most beautiful thing she had ever heard. He listened quietly and attentively to her opinions and didn't try to dismiss them. He had the ability to poke fun at himself and he certainly didn't take his own literary reputation unduly seriously. And he liked to laugh.

There was a band playing on the terrace, a soft, sad waltz from before the war, and when he asked her to dance he didn't try to touch or kiss her. Afterwards he walked her home, but instead of a goodnight peck he formally shook her hand.

A week later he asked her to his parents' home for dinner. After the meal they all sat up until the early hours, and when she laughed at a joke his father made, Ivan Khorev smiled and said it was the first time he had seen her happy.

She had lain in bed afterwards thinking about him. His quiet assurance and his gentleness and his humor. His ability to speak with authority on almost any topic, his sharp intelligence and his sensitivity. His willingness to listen to her views and take them seriously. He was a loner, too, like her, but a different kind of loner. His independence came from a quiet self-confidence, from a loving family background.

She fell in love and they married a month after she graduated.

For their honeymoon they spent a week together in a big wooden villa on the beach near Odessa, and every morning they went swimming in the warm Black Sea and then ran back to the dacha to make love.

At night he read her the poetry he had written and told her endlessly that he loved her, that he had loved her from the first day he saw her on campus, and when he saw the tears in the corners of her eyes he pulled her close and held her tightly.

When their first child was born a year later, Anna Khorev found her life complete. It was a daughter and they called her Sasha. They were allotted a small apartment off Lenin Prospect where she and Ivan often took their baby for walks in nearby Gorky Park.

She never forgot the first walk they had taken together as a family. She and Ivan and little Sasha. And the look of pride on Ivan's face as he held their daughter in his arms. A man with a camera had taken their photograph by a bandstand for fifty kopecks; the three of them together, she and Ivan smiling, Sasha wrapped in a woolen cap and a white blanket, her face fat and pink and healthy and her tiny lips hungry for milk. She had kept the photograph on the mantelpiece in a silver frame and every day she looked at it, as if to remind herself that her marriage and her happiness were real.

But in that first warm summer of complete joy she could never have imagined the pain that was to come.

The pounding on the apartment door came one Sunday morning at 2 A.M. Three men burst into the room and Ivan was dragged outside to a waiting car. He had been accused of writing and publishing a poem in a dissident magazine. For that crime he was banished to a penal colony in Norylsk in northern Siberia for twenty-five years.

Anna Khorev never saw her husband again.

A week later the men from the secret police came back.

She cried and screamed and kicked and when they took her child she almost killed the men who dragged her to the car waiting to take her to Lefortovo prison, but it did no good.

For her association with Ivan Khorev she was sentenced to twenty years in Nicochka Penal Camp. Her child was to be removed to a state orphanage where she would be brought up like a good communist. She was never to see her daughter again and her right to parenthood was revoked by the state.

She was taken straight to Moscow's Leningrad Station and put on board a cattle truck with dozens of other prisoners. The train wound northward for five hundred miles. When it finally pulled into a siding she and the other prisoners were driven farther west to a prison camp in the middle of nowhere.

There was a blizzard blowing that night and the icy gusts slashed at her face like a thousand razors. She was put in a drafty, squalid wooden hut with five other special-category prisoners. Two were blind and the others were prostitutes with syphilis. The remaining camp prisoners were drunks and political offenders, destined to live out the rest of their lives in the frozen wastes near the Arctic Circle. In the hundreds of penal camps that dotted the Soviet Union, millions of men, women and children labored in mines and rock quarries and makeshift factories. They worked from dawn until dusk for nothing, until malnutrition, the freezing cold, disease or suicide claimed their lives. When they died, a mechanical digger gouged out a pit in the frozen ground and their bodies were bulldozed into a mass grave. No headstone or marker to acknowledge they ever existed.

By the second month of her imprisonment Anna Khorev felt she couldn't go on.

She was allowed no mail, except official state correspondence, and no visitors. She worked from daylight to darkness, and in the first weeks the despair and loneliness almost killed her. If she slackened she was beaten mercilessly by the camp guards. Every day and night her grief seemed overwhelming.

Sasha's face kept coming into her mind and she thought she was going mad. In the sixth month she received a letter from the penal camp information service in Moscow. It informed her that her husband Ivan Khorev had died of natural causes and had been buried in Norylsk. His personal belongings had been confiscated by the state and no further communication on the matter was permitted.

She cried that night until her heart felt it was going to explode with grief. She didn't eat her meager rations of black bread and cabbage soup and within a week she was suffering the effects of severe malnutrition. When she finally collapsed on her work detail she was taken to the drafty wooden hut that served as the camp hospital. The slovenly drunken doctor who visited once a week examined her with little interest and when she still refused to eat she was marched to the camp commandant.

The commandant gave her a stern lecture on his responsibility to his prisoners but she knew by the man's tone that he didn't care if she lived or died.

When the telephone rang in another room and he was called outside, Anna Khorev noticed the map on the wall.

Something took root in her mind because she found herself staring at the map. It was a relief image of the surrounding area, the terrain and border posts, the roads and little red and blue flags marking military bases and civilian prison camps. She moved closer and stared at the image intently for almost five minutes, burning every detail into her mind.

When the commandant finally dismissed her she went back to her barrack hut. She found a piece of charcoal in the metal stove and redrew everything she could remember of the map on the back of the letter she had received informing her of Ivan's death. Every detail she could recall; every road and river and little blue and red flag.

That evening she ate her first meal in eight days.

And that night she made up her mind. She knew she would never see her child again and that her life would never be the same. But she wasn't going to die in the wasteland of the Arctic Circle and she wasn't going to remain a prisoner.

The border toward Finland was a tortuous landscape of thick forest and hills teeming with wolves and bears, glacial ravines and wide frozen rivers. To attempt to escape across such territory in winter would be suicidal. The most accessible crossings were guarded but that was her best chance, even if just as dangerous. She didn't know what might lie beyond the Finnish border but she knew that somehow she was going to escape.

There was a middle-aged camp officer she had noticed, a rough and lustful man who took the risk of bedding the female prisoners, trading extra food for sex. She had noticed the man watching her. She knew by his leering grin that he wanted her body. She let it be known that she was available.

The officer came to her after dark three nights later. They met in a small woodshed at the rear of the camp. She timed the day so the officer was off duty next morning.

She waited until he had undressed her and when he had taken off his coat and tunic and went to suck her breasts she drove the six-inch metal blade deep into his back. It had taken her three weeks to make the weapon in the hours after darkness, but only moments to use it. The man was slow to die and tried to strangle her, but she dug the blade in again and again until the floor was awash with blood.

Ten minutes later she had unlocked the side gate with the man's keys and walked through into the freezing, snowy night, wearing his bloodied uniform and coat and fur hat, carrying his pistol, taking the narrow road through the birch forest. The sentry in the nearest watchtower hadn't even bothered to challenge her.

Within four hours, frozen and exhausted, Anna Khorev had finally reached the border with Finland.

She spoke with Massey for almost an hour.

He sat there listening quietly, nodding his head in understanding when she faltered or the pain of her memories became too much and she had to break off.

Every now and then she saw the shocked reaction on his face as she told him her story, the look in his eyes that was no longer detached, as if he suddenly understood the enormity of her pain and why she had killed as she had.

When she finally finished he sat back and looked at her with compassion, and she knew he believed she was telling him the truth.

There would be other men who would want to speak with her, he said. Other questions to be asked, and maybe she would have to tell her story again, but for now she was to rest and try to build up her strength. The following day they would move her to a private hospital in Helsinki. He would do his best to help her.

She watched him go and then she was left alone in the small white room. Somewhere off in the distance she could hear a radio playing cheerful dance music and it made her think of another time and another place, the first night Ivan Khorev had taken her dancing on the banks of the Moscow River, and in the corridor she heard laughing voices echo beyond the room. She felt the grief suddenly flood in on her like a tidal wave and she tried not to cry.

It was a long way from the icy wastes of Nicochka. A long way from the cold and despair and the pain she had lived with for months, the aching in her breast that felt like someone had stuck a knife in her heart and she was slowly bleeding to death.

And all the time the image in her mind that wouldn't go away.

She and Ivan walking in Gorky Park in summer, Ivan smiling, the look of pride and love on his face as he held Sasha in his arms.

6

Berlin.
December 15th

The Ilyushin transport plane with red stars on the wings bumped to a halt on the icy runway at Schönefeld airport in East Berlin. A thin man with sharp features—a pursed mouth, long face, and small bright eyes—disembarked and walked quickly across the tarmac to a waiting Zis car.

As the car drove out through the gates and headed east away from the city, Colonel Grenady Kraskin took off his cap and rubbed a hand along his thinning hairline. At sixty-two, he was a veteran and senior KGB officer with over thirty years' experience. Answerable only to Beria and Stalin, he was responsible for special interior operations, which came under the control of 2nd Directorate, based in the seven-story KGB Headquarters in Moscow's Dzerzhinsky Square. In this capacity Kraskin had traveled to East Berlin for his monthly inspection tour of top-secret Soviet research facilities, which he carried out with customary thoroughness.

After a thirty-kilometer drive, the black Zis turned off the main Potsdam highway onto a minor road that finally led past the sleepy German hamlet of Luckenwalde. At the end of a road lined with tall fir trees stood a double gate with a metal barrier. Beyond the barrier lay a tarmac track with barbed-wire runs on either side. Two uniformed guards snapped stiffly to attention as the Zis drew up and an officer came out of a concrete guard hut to check the passenger's identity cards. Moments later the barrier was lifted and the car drove through.

A half kilometer down the barbed-wire run Kraskin saw the mouth of an underground tunnel, like giant concrete jaws erupting from the earth. The car drove down and finally came to a halt.

When Kraskin stepped out he was in a vast bunker that looked like an enormous underground car park. There was a sickly smell of diesel fumes and stale air. Intense neon light blazed overhead and a dozen or more military vehicles were parked on the concourse. Off to the right was an elevator, its metal doors open and waiting.

The officer in charge saluted smartly and led Kraskin across. Both men stepped in. The doors closed and the elevator descended.

* * *

The Pan American Airways DC-6, Flight 209 from Paris, was almost empty and the blond-haired man sat in a window seat two rows from the front.

As the aircraft banked to port and came in over Berlin's Wannsee Lake, the man saw the broad ribbon of the Unter Den Linden stretched below him. Here and there the surrounding suburbs were still peppered with old bomb craters, and looking east he saw the still crumbling, gutted buildings in the Russian Zone.

It was ten minutes later when the plane landed in West Berlin's Tempelhof airport. The immigration and customs checks were thorough and there was a military presence everywhere since the Russians had sealed off East Berlin with a ten-yard-wide shoot-to-kill strip. But the uniformed West German official did not spot the false American passport and the man passed through without too much delay.

No one seemed to take any notice of the blond man, and moments later he saw the gray Volkswagen parked opposite the civilian car park. An attractive woman in her early thirties sat behind the wheel smoking a cigarette, and he recognized her dark Russian features. She wore a blue scarf around her neck, and when she noticed him she tossed her cigarette out of the window.

He waited a full minute before he crossed to the car and put his case on the back seat, his eyes carefully scanning the Arrivals area before he moved.

He didn't speak as he climbed in beside the woman, and a moment later she pulled out quickly from the curb and drove toward Berlin.

Colonel Grenady Kraskin looked across at the big, slovenly man seated opposite and smiled. They were in Sergei Enger's office on the first of several floors in an underground complex that had once been built by the Germans.

Kraskin smiled. "Well, Sergei, tell me your troubles."

Sergei Enger was a stout, untidy figure of a man with dark, thinning curly hair and a plump stomach. A physics graduate from Moscow University, he was head of research in the Luckenwalde underground complex. Despite his easy-going manner and untidy personal appearance—Enger frequently wore mismatched socks and carried the remains of breakfast or lunch on his tie—the man had a brain as sharp as a scalpel and a talent for organizing others.

Enger smiled back weakly. Troubles he certainly had, but Grenady Kraskin didn't have the look of a man you shared personal problems with.

The colonel's face was sharp and hard and weather-beaten. There were ruts in his leathery skin, deep wrinkles that almost looked like scars, and combined with a chilling smile, they had a frightening effect. And the man's crisply pressed black uniform and immaculately polished boots always intimidated Enger.

Outwardly a reasonable and intelligent man, Kraskin's external mask hid a dark and savage streak. In one winter campaign near Zadonsk on the River Don in the Caucasus during the Bolshevik Revolution, Kraskin's battalion had engaged a detachment of four hundred Whites, wiping them out in three days of savage hand-to-hand fighting. Promising mercy to the survivors and their families who had surrendered, Kraskin instead had them lined up against a wall and shot, showing no mercy to women and children.

Enger shrugged and toyed with a pencil on the desk. "What makes you think I have troubles, Grenady? The project is going better than I expected."

Kraskin beamed. "Excellent. I'm glad to hear it."

Enger stood up, as if still bothered by something, and crossed to the broad glass window that looked down onto the vast complex below.

The place never ceased to amaze Enger, even after spending two years there. The Nazis had started work on the underground complex ten years before, intending it as a V2 factory, but the Russian advance into eastern Prussia had ended all that. Now it was one of the most secret and advanced research facilities in East Germany, the entire operation sited underground, doing away with the need for camouflage above ground level. Beyond the office, glass lights blazed overhead. The whole area looked as if it were swamped in daylight. Metal boilers and air-conditioning conduits ran along the walls for almost half a kilometer. Here and there men scurried about in white coats.

Enger looked down at the amazing scene for several moments before turning back.

"I left the details you requested in the file on the desk, Grenady. I trust they meet with your approval?"

Kraskin picked up the folder. When he had finished scrutinizing the progress sheets inside he turned back to Enger.

"You've done well, Sergei. The German scientists, they seem to be outperforming themselves." Kraskin grinned. "It's amazing what the threat of being sent to a Gulag will do."

He smiled at Enger. "You look like a man who has the weight of the world on his shoulders. If it's not the project, what is it? Come, Sergei, let's hear whatever's on your mind."

Enger hesitated. "But could I be frank, Grenady? Could I really speak freely?"

Kraskin laughed. "If you're asking me are these rooms bugged, the answer is no. I made a point of deeming you a special case."

"I'm indebted, Grenady."

Kraskin waved a hand dismissively and half smiled. "Nonsense, what are friends for? Say what's on your mind."

Enger removed a soiled handkerchief from his pocket and dabbed his brow. "You've no idea what it's like here. The constant hum of the machines, the conditioned air. I don't know how the Germans stood it. I'm glad my work here is almost at an end."

As he sucked on his cigarette, Kraskin said, "So how much longer before your part of the operation is completed?"

"The way it's going, a lot earlier than we thought. Borosky and the other scientists will be arriving in the next few weeks to link the various projects together."

"So how much longer?" repeated Kraskin.

Enger shrugged. "A month, maybe sooner. Our initial tests have been very promising. And the test site in the Caucasus is nearing completion. I've also read our latest reports of the Americans' progress sent from Moscow. We're going to be ahead of them. Their explosion in the Pacific was small in comparison to the one we intend. Really it was only a triggering device the Americans detonated. I can almost guarantee we'll be the first to explode the actual hydrogen bomb."

"I'm very pleased to hear that, Sergei. I'll make sure to mention your diligence in my report."

Enger paid no heed to Kraskin's statement. His voice suddenly softened and he said, "Do you think there's going to be a war, Grenady?"

Kraskin laughed. Enger looked at him in amazement. "What's so funny?"

"Is that what's been bothering you?"

"It had crossed my mind. You have to admit it's being talked about."

Kraskin grinned. "And what makes you think there's going to be a war, my friend?"

"Damn it, Grenady, it doesn't take a genius to figure it out." Enger nodded back toward the underground bunker. "I've been living down there for the past two years like a mole, not a scientist. Days go by when I don't see sunlight." He hesitated. "The way things are between us and the Americans right now, some kind of conflict looks inevitable. For almost two years now we've been working frantically on our weapons program. And in the past six months since the Americans exploded their first device the funds have suddenly become unlimited. And then there have been the threats. Veiled, but there. To all of us, not just the German scientists. Work harder, much harder, or there will be repercussions. There has to be a reason, Grenady. We're racing against time. Why? Is there something Moscow isn't telling us?"

Kraskin stood up slowly. "There won't be a war if the Americans see sense."

"What does that mean? I'm a scientist, I deal in facts. Give me facts, Grenady."

Kraskin swung around and his words had a savage ring. "The Americans think they own the fucking world. They think they have some God-given right to control this planet, tell everyone how it should be run. Well, we're not going to take that shit from them."

Enger shook his head. "You can't imagine what the next war would be like. These bombs we're working on, they are not like the ones the Americans dropped on Japan. They're much more powerful. Entire cities and their populations can be totally wiped from the map with one explosion. In Nagasaki and Hiroshima people survived some ten kilometers from the epicenter. With a thermonuclear explosion big enough, that isn't even a remote possibility." Enger hesitated. "Besides, I'm not deaf, Grenady. I may be a thousand miles from Moscow but I still hear the rumors."

Kraskin raised his eyes before he drew on his cigarette. "And what rumors are they?"

Enger hesitated. "That we're gearing up for war. That Stalin wants the bomb completed fast, so he can drop it on the Americans before he dies. They say he's taken to walking alone in the Kremlin gardens, talking aloud to himself. That his behavior has become more erratic and unpredictable. They say he trusts no one, not even himself. Doesn't that worry you?"

Kraskin looked sternly at Enger. "And who tells you such things?"

Enger said nervously, "They're simply rumors, Grenady. But everybody here speaks of them."

Kraskin's voice had a hint of menace. "I think you'd be wise to ignore such rumors and not doubt Comrade Stalin's mental health too loudly, my friend. There are people in Moscow who might hear and start to doubt yours. Statements like that could have you locked in a rubber room. Or shovelling salt in a Siberian mine. Or worse."

"Then just answer me this. They say the purges are about to start again. That people are being arrested in huge numbers and shot or sent to the camps. Especially Jews. Is it true?"

Kraskin looked at Enger but left the question unanswered. "You're a Party member and a valuable scientist. You have nothing to fear."

"I'm Jewish, Grenady. It concerns me." Enger's face darkened. "Something's in the air. I can sense it. Please tell me what's happening."

Kraskin said sharply, "I think you're too long down in that bunker of yours talking to rumor-mongers. You'd do better to concentrate on your work. Pay no heed to malicious gossip coming from Moscow."

There was a hard edge of menace in Kraskin's voice, all reasonableness gone. He stubbed out his cigarette and ended the discussion.

"Come, it's getting late, we'd better finish the inspection. I want to be out of this godforsaken place and get back to Berlin."

The blond-haired man stood at the window of the apartment on the Kaiserdamm. It was cold outside, a bitter wind sweeping the street. He heard the rumble of British Army trucks as they passed below the window, but he didn't look down.

He turned as the woman came in. She carried a brown-wrapped parcel tied with string and a doctor's black leather bag. She placed them on the table and went to join him at the window.

She looked at him.

He had an air of stillness and of isolation. Alex Slanski was tall, in his middle thirties, and wore a dark double-breasted suit, shirt and tie. His short blond hair was brushed off his forehead and his face was clean-shaven and handsome.

There was a trace of a smile on his lips, as if fixed there permanently. But it was the eyes which she always noticed. Intense pale blue and infinitely dangerous.

"Kraskin should finish the Luckenwalde inspection by midafternoon. After that he's holding a briefing at KGB Headquarters at Karlshorst. At seven-thirty tomorrow morning he's due to meet with the Soviet Zone Commander, so our guess is he'll go to bed early. He never stays in any of the army barracks, but always uses the private apartment at his disposal. It's by the Tierpark. Number twenty-four, a blue door. Kraskin's apartment is on the second floor, number thirteen." The woman half smiled. "Sometimes not such a lucky number. But for you, Alex, I hope so."

Alex Slanski nodded. The faint smile didn't leave his lips. "Tell me about the crossing."

"You'll use one of our tunnels that exits near Friedrichstrasse. A Red Army jeep will be left parked and waiting there." The woman went over the details for several minutes, and when Slanski was satisfied she handed him an envelope. "Those are your papers. You're a Red Army doctor from the Karlshorst Military Hospital making a call to one of your military patients. Kraskin is a wily old snake, so be careful. Especially if there's someone else in the apartment."

"Should there be?"

"He likes little boys."

"How little?"

"Ten-year-olds seem to be his preference. He also has a boyfriend. A major at Karlshorst named Pitrov. If he's in the apartment, you know what to do."

Slanski heard the hard edge of bitterness in the woman's voice. She nodded at the brown-wrapped parcel. "Everything you need is in there. Make sure you don't fail, Alex. Because if you do, Kraskin will kill you."

He opened the parcel in the bedroom once she had left.

He tried on the uniform and it fitted him well. He felt a shudder go through him as he looked in the mirror. The major's olive-brown waisted uniform with the wide silver shoulder-boards and the polished boots gave him a threatening look. The brown leather holster and belt lay still in the wrapper. He took them out and slid out the pistol. It was a Tokarev automatic, 7.62 millimeter, the standard-issue Russian Army officer's sidearm, but the tip of the barrel had been grooved. He screwed on the Carswell silencer, then removed it again. There were two loaded magazines and he took each in turn and pried out the bullets with his thumb.

He checked the action of the magazines and weapon again and again, until he was satisfied neither might jam, then stripped the gun down and cleaned it with an oily rag left in the parcel. When he had finished, he replaced the bullets in the magazines, slammed home a magazine into the butt of the gun, and slipped it into the holster.

He crossed to the bed and unfastened the buckles on his suitcase and removed the knife from the doctor's black bag he took from inside the case. The silver blade gleamed in the light as he unsheathed it. He stood there running his thumb gently along the razor edge for several moments, feeling the sharpness of the cold steel. He replaced the knife in the sheath, slipped it into the doctor's bag, and snapped the metal catch shut.

Before he removed the uniform he took the photograph from his suitcase and slipped it into the tunic pocket. He wrapped the uniform neatly back in the brown paper. He did not dress again but went to lie naked on the bed.

The alarm clock on the bedside locker said three o'clock.

He would try and sleep until six and then it would be time to go.

It was almost seven when Kraskin's car pulled up outside the apartment block facing the Tierpark. There was a crack of thunder and it started to rain as Kraskin climbed out. The black Zis pulled away and the colonel went up the stairs to the second floor and inserted the key. When he stepped inside and closed the door he took in the smell immediately.

He had been too long a military man not to recognize the stench of cordite after a weapon had been fired, and at once his suspicions were aroused.

The door to the bedroom was open and Kraskin saw the body of Pitrov, dressed in a blue silk dressing gown, sprawled across the bed. Even from a distance his eyes didn't deceive him. He saw the bullet wound to the head and the dark crimson patch spread on the white cotton sheets.

"Oh my God," Kraskin breathed.

"Strange words for a communist, Colonel Kraskin."

There was a faint click behind him. Kraskin turned at once and saw the man. He was seated in the shadows by the curtained window. His face was barely visible. But there was no mistaking the silenced Tokarev in his hand.

Kraskin made a move for his holstered pistol, managed to get the flap undone, but the man stood up smartly and came out of the shadows. He pointed the Tokarev at Kraskin's head.

"I really wouldn't, comrade. Unless you want to lose an eye. Sit down, at the table. Keep your hands on top."

Kraskin did as he was told. The man stepped toward him.

"Who are you?" Kraskin demanded, his face chalk-white.

"My name is Alex Slanski. I'm here to send you to Hell."

Kraskin's face flushed white. "You'll never get away with this." He nodded toward the bedroom door where the body lay. "And for the crime that's just been committed you'll be hunted down like the vermin that you are."

"You're hardly one to talk about crimes, Kraskin. By the laws of any land you ought to be put down like a mad dog. You were responsible for the shooting of at least fifty schoolchildren during the kulak wars. I believe your specialty was to sexually assault them before you dispatched them with a bullet in the head. When they find Pitrov's body and yours they'll put it down to a lovers' tiff that turned tragically violent. The gun I'm holding is Pitrov's. You killed him and then yourself."

"Yes, very convenient," said Kraskin dryly. "So who sent you?" He shifted again in his chair, felt the flap of his holster lift against the tablecloth.

"That really doesn't matter. But this does." Slanski removed a photograph from his tunic pocket and tossed it on the table.

"Pick it up."

Kraskin did as he was told.

"Look at the photograph. Do you recognize the girl?"

Kraskin saw a young dark-haired girl standing on a deserted beach. She was smiling for the camera, and held a child in her arms.

"No, why should I?"

"Her name was Ave Perlov. And this is where it gets personal, Comrade Kraskin. You interrogated her in Riga a year ago. If I'm not mistaken, you had quite a time with her before you sent her to the firing squad. Torture is too mild a word. She had to be taken to the wall on a stretcher."

Kraskin smiled. "I remember now. One of the partisan bitches."

"She was only nineteen, you bastard."

Kraskin saw the flash of uncontrolled anger and knew it was time to make his move. As he tossed the photograph away he saw Slanski's eyes flick to it and Kraskin's right hand reached into his holster and the Tokarev came out smartly.

Kraskin managed to get off a quick shot and it chipped Slanski's left arm below the elbow.

But it wasn't enough.

Slanski leaned in close and shot him between the eyes.

As the gun exploded, Kraskin was flung back in his chair, the close shot cracking open the back of his skull and tearing out half his brain.

Slanski picked up the photograph from the floor and replaced it in his tunic pocket. He looked down at the neat hole drilled in his uniform sleeve, saw the patch of blood spread. There was no pain, not yet, just a dull ache in his arm. He found a towel in the bathroom and wrapped it around the wound before he pulled on the military overcoat.

When he came back into the room, he opened the doctor's black bag and removed the knife. He knew he had very little time before someone reacted to Kraskin's gunshot, but he worked calmly.

He moved back to Kraskin's body and unbuttoned the man's trousers. He removed the flaccid penis. The knife flashed and the organ was severed in a gorge of blood. The man stuffed the severed lump of flesh deep into Kraskin's gaping mouth. He wiped the blade on Kraskin's tunic and replaced the knife in the doctor's bag.

He could hear the noises in the hallway now, fists starting to pound the door, but already he was moving toward the window and the fire escape.

7

Helsinki.
October 26th

That evening two men sat down to a late dinner at Helsinki's Savoy Restaurant, a favorite haunt of embassy staff and foreign diplomats. The tables in the eighth-floor gourmet restaurant overlooking the Esplanadi were spaced generously enough apart for conversations to be conducted in private.

Doug Canning's title at the American Embassy was Political Counselor but his real function was as a CIA senior officer.

Canning had made the initial report on Anna Khorev and the incident at the border crossing to the American Ambassador, and once a joint decision had been made to call in more expert help to interrogate and assess the woman, Jake Massey, a senior Soviet expert and the head of the CIA's Soviet Operations office based in Munich, had been put on a plane for Helsinki that same night. After Massey had delivered his assessment, he got a phone call to join Canning for dinner to discuss the matter.

Doug Canning was a tall, lean Texan with blond thinning hair and tanned good looks. He had Southern charm in abundance and wielded considerable influence with the US Ambassador.

It was the Ambassador who would ultimately decide Anna Khorev's suitability for political asylum. Relations between the Soviets and Americans were at their lowest in years, and those who escaped over the border were often considered more a headache than a help. Massey knew Anna Khorev was a problem the American Embassy would rather not have to deal with and that her worries were far from over.

Canning had ordered a bottle of Bordeaux and the house specialty, *Vorschmack*, for both of them, and when he had sipped his wine appreciatively he smiled across the table.

"It sounds from the report as though the girl had a pretty rough time. But is she telling you anything we could find useful, Jake?"

Massey had hardly touched his food, and now he shook his head.

"There's nothing much she *can* tell us. It's been eight years since she was discharged from the Red Army. So any background information in that regard would be pretty much out of date by now."

Canning looked out toward Helsinki's massive illuminated Dom Cathedral in the distance, then back again. "So I guess she's really no use to us?"

Massey knew it was a crucial question but he replied honestly. "I guess not. But there are other circumstances to consider here, Doug."

"Such as?"

"What the girl's been through. She's taken a hell of a beating in the last six months."

"And you think she's telling you the truth?"

"Yes, I do. I think her story's genuine. Whether or not she can help us with intelligence information, on humane grounds alone I think she has a case."

Canning hesitated, then wiped his mouth with his napkin and sat forward. "Jake, let me give it to you straight. Some pretty strong noises are being made at the highest levels. It seems Moscow has got a bee up their ass on this one. Like it's a matter of principle they get her returned. They say she's a common criminal and in order not to further damage the already delicate relationship between our two countries, we ought to send her back over the border." He smiled. "Now you and I know that's a load of reindeer shit but I want you to be aware of the fact that they don't like the idea of us helping the little lady one little bit."

"What about the Finns?"

"They want us to make a quick decision. But if we don't grant her asylum, they sure as hell won't. As it is, the Russian Ambassador's up their ass with a big stick."

After the Finns had endured a savage and humiliating war with Russia thirteen years before, Massey knew they treated their closest neighbor with caution, like a bear they didn't want to rouse to anger. But Finland also took a delight in frustrating Moscow. They had allowed Anna Khorev to be moved to a private hospital rather than keep her in the special prison on Ratakatu Street, headquarters of Finnish counterintelligence. And they had granted her temporary refugee status while the Americans made up their minds.

"So what do you think's going to happen?"

Canning looked across the table, a concerned look on his face. "We don't need the kind of diplomatic trouble this can bring, Jake. So my guess is that the Ambassador will send her back. And there's something else you ought to know. Helsinki has an agreement with the Russians that allows them to interview any border-crossers convicted of serious crimes. The Soviet Embassy has already made it clear it wants to do that. It gives them a chance to save face and exert a little pressure to try to get the escapee to return with promises of leniency, before they really put on the pressure at embassy level. There's a senior official in town right now who's handling it. Some guy called Romulka, from Moscow."

"*KGB*?"

Canning grinned. "You can bet your ass on it."

"Damn it, the girl's been through hell and back. She shouldn't have to go through all that."

"Maybe, but it's the law, Jake. You know if I had my way anyone who comes over that border who's a genuine political refugee has got my support. But rightly or wrongly she did commit murder. And that makes it pretty difficult for us to grant her asylum."

"Doug, if we send the girl back the Ambassador will be signing her death warrant. He may as well pull the damned trigger himself."

Canning heard the passion in Massey's reply and raised his eyebrows. "Hey, it sounds as if you've got a strong personal interest in the girl, Jake."

"She's been through a hell of a time. She deserves our help. If we send her back, we're only condoning what the Russians do. We're saying go right ahead, punish her. There's nothing wrong with the camps you run. Nothing wrong with killing or imprisoning millions of people, most of them innocent." Massey shook his head firmly. "Me, I'd have a problem going along with that."

Canning hesitated. "Jake, there's something odd about this whole darned thing I haven't told you about but I think you'd better know because it kind of upsets the equation. Despite the fact that the woman's story didn't change during questioning by the Finns, one of their more experienced SUPO officers who questioned her said in his report he didn't believe her."

"Why not?"

"The area where she claims she was in the penal camp, the Finnish officer knows it pretty well. He used to live there when it used to be part of Karelia before the Russians were ceded the territory after the war. This officer says it's impossible for the woman to have made the journey on foot from the camp. The story she told us may make some kind of sense but he says the terrain she's supposed to have crossed is too hostile and even the length of time she said it took her he claims doesn't ring true. He thinks she was left near the border by the KGB. Left there to get over to our side as she did, for whatever reason they have in mind."

"What else does he say?"

"That the whole thing is an elaborate setup by Moscow."

"I don't believe that."

"Moscow could be fooling us, Jake. They've done it before. And whatever they have in mind for the girl, this whole thing about them wanting her back could be another part of the game to make us believe her story."

"I don't believe that either."

Canning shrugged and wiped his mouth with his napkin. "OK, so what do you suggest?"

"Let me talk with the Ambassador before he makes a final decision. And try to hold off letting this Romulka guy talk to her for as long as you can. I'd like to see her again myself. Not for another interrogation, just a friendly chat."

Canning gestured for the waiter to bring the bill, indicating the meeting was at an end, before he looked back at Massey.

"Any particular reason why you want to talk with her again?"

"After what she's been through, I'd guess she needs to talk with someone."

The private hospital was on the outskirts of Helsinki.

It was a big old place on a hill with high stone walls set on several dozen acres. There was a small forest of silver birch trees and a tiny frozen lake, wooden benches set around the perimeter.

Anna Khorev was given her own private room on the third floor. There was a view of the city and the brightly colored timber houses that dotted Helsinki's shore and islands. A guard sat outside her room day and night.

A table stood in a corner, a blue vase on top filled with winter flowers, and there was a radio on a shelf by the window. On the first day she had twiddled with the plastic dial as it spread across the band of short-wave frequencies, listening to music and voices in a dozen different languages from cities she had only read about: London, Vienna, Rome, Cairo.

That afternoon one of the nurses had helped her bathe and changed her dressing and afterwards had brought her fresh clothes. The wound in her side was now just a dull throb, and later she had walked in the hospital grounds. She avoided talking with the other patients on Massey's instructions, though she desperately wanted to see the world beyond the walls and experience freedom. But it was not to be, and she had to content herself with small triumphs, listening to music and reading the newspapers in English.

That first evening a doctor had come to see her.

He was young, in his middle thirties, with the compassionate blue eyes of a good listener. He spoke softly in Russian, explaining that he was a psychiatrist. He asked her about her past and she repeated what she had told Massey. The doctor seemed especially interested in her treatment at the camp, but when he had tried to probe her about Ivan and Sasha she had become withdrawn.

On the following day she turned on the radio and the music that came on was soft and classical and she recognized the strains of Dvořák. It was music Ivan had loved and it made her think of him and Sasha and suddenly a terrible black wave swept in and she felt utterly alone.

As she stood at the window trying to shake off the anguish, she saw a young couple come through the hospital gates.

It was visiting time and a little girl walked between them. She couldn't have been more than two or three and she wore a blue coat and a red scarf. Her woollen cap was pulled down on her head and her hands were wrapped snugly in mittens.

She stared down at the child's face for a long time before the man swept her up in his arms and they all disappeared into the hospital.

As she turned away from the window she switched off the music. She went to lie on the bed and closed her eyes. The sobbing that came then racked her body in convulsions until she felt she could cry no more.

Sooner or later, she told herself, it would have to stop.

She couldn't live with grief forever.

On the third morning Massey came to see her and he suggested they go for a walk down to the lake where they could talk in private.

A tree had been uprooted in a long-ago storm, its rotting tendrils exposed, patches of moss growing on the dead roots. Massey sat beside her on a wooden bench and lit a cigarette.

Anna said, "May I have one too?"

"I didn't know you smoked."

"I don't. Not since the war. But I think I would like one now."

Massey saw the nervousness in her face as he lit her cigarette but he was amazed by the change in her appearance. She had been given new clothes; a thick pale blue woollen sweater that she had tucked into tight black ski pants. One of the staff nurses had loaned her a winter coat that was a size too big for her and it made her look vulnerable, but there was no denying her beauty.

She was different from any of the other Russian women he had met. He had been one of the first Americans to reach Berlin after the Reds had taken the city, and it was the first time he saw female Russian soldiers. There were few beauties among them. Most had been muscled, tough peasant women who looked like they shaved twice a day. He guessed so would he if the Germans had been dropping shells on him for four years.

"Have they been treating you well, Anna?"

"Very well, thank you."

Massey looked out toward the lake and spoke quietly. "I had a talk with Doctor Harlan. He thinks there's something you should be aware of, Anna. It's not going to be easy for you to get over what you've been through. He thinks you'll need time to deal with your pain." He looked at her. "I guess what it comes down to is, no matter what happens you have to try and forget about your husband and your child. Put everything bad that's happened behind you. It sounds easy me saying that, but I know it isn't."

She looked at him without speaking, then said, "I don't think I will ever forget Ivan and Sasha. The other things, maybe, but not Ivan and Sasha."

Massey looked at her. He thought he saw tears in the corners of her eyes. She was struggling hard to fight her emotions, then she bit her lip and looked away. She didn't look back at him when she spoke.

"May I ask you a question, Massey?"

"Sure."

"Where did you learn your Russian?"

He knew her question was a way of deflecting her pain and he looked at her and smiled.

"My parents came from St. Petersburg."

"But Massey isn't a Russian name."

"Polish. It used to be Masensky. My father's people originally came from Warsaw; my mother's were pure Russian."

"But you don't like Russians?"

"What makes you say that?"

"The day you first came to see me at the hospital. The way you looked at me. There was distrust in your eyes, even dislike."

Massey shook his head. "That's not true, Anna. On the contrary. For the most part the Russians are a fine and generous people. It's communism I hate. It kills everything that's noble and good in mankind. Make no mistake, Anna, the men in the Kremlin are only interested in one thing, and that's power. You're looking at the mirror image of Nazism. But instead of a swastika on the flag there's a hammer and sickle and a red star." He paused. "Anna, there's something I have to tell you. Someone from your embassy wants to talk with you."

She looked at him and Massey saw the fear in her eyes. "Talk about what?"

He explained what Canning had told him. "It's only a formality but it's got to be done. Do you think you can go through with it?"

She hesitated. "If you want me to. When?"

"This afternoon. After that, the American Ambassador will make his decision on your case. The Russian official, his name is Romulka. Don't be afraid, I'll be with you all the time. Romulka's not entitled to ask you questions about the crimes you allegedly committed, but he will ask you to return to face trial, and he will promise you leniency. But I guess you know that would hardly be the case."

"The doctor asked me a question this morning. He asked if I regretted killing the men. The camp officer and the guard at the border."

"What did you tell him?"

"I said that I could feel for their wives and children, if they had any. But I didn't regret killing them. I wanted to escape. What was done to me was wrong. I remember Ivan telling me something once. Something he had read. That those to whom evil is done, do evil in return. I only returned the evil that was done to me. It was me or them."

"Then I guess that answers it."

As Massey and Anna sat in the interview room in the city police station, the two Russians in civilian suits stepped in past the policeman who opened the door.

The older of the two was in his early forties, and looked like a powerhouse of energy, tall and broad, his muscled body straining under his suit.

A pair of cold blue eyes were set in a brutal-looking face that was pockmarked with acne scars, and part of the man's left ear was missing. He carried a briefcase and curtly introduced himself as Nikita Romulka, a senior official from Moscow.

The second Russian, a young embassy aide, sat beside him and handed him a file.

Romulka flicked it open and said, "You are Anna Khorev."

The man barely looked at her as he spoke.

Massey nodded to Anna and she answered, "Yes."

When the man looked up he stared at her coldly.

"Under the terms of the Soviet-Finnish Protocol I am here to offer you a chance to redeem yourself by facing the serious crimes you have committed on Soviet soil. I am authorized to inform you that should you return to Moscow your entire case will be reviewed and resubmitted for trial and that you will be accorded the utmost leniency that is due to every Soviet citizen. Do you understand me?"

Anna hesitated, and before she could reply, Massey said in fluent Russian, "Let's cut out all the formal crap, Romulka. What exactly are you saying?"

The cold eyes stared over at Massey, and Romulka's voice was full of scorn. "The question was addressed to the woman, not you."

"Then make it simple so she understands the situation perfectly."

Romulka glared at Massey, then smiled coldly and sat back.

"Basically this—if she agrees to return to Moscow there will be a retrial for her past deeds. If the courts decide she was harshly treated or wrongly accused, then her recent crimes, shooting the border guards and escaping from a prison camp, will be judged in that light. Can I put it any simpler, even for an obviously simple man such as yourself?"

Massey ignored the remark and looked at Anna. "What do you say, Anna?"

"I don't want to go back."

Romulka said firmly, "Diplomatic efforts will be made to ensure you do. But I'm giving you the opportunity to return of your own free will and have your case reviewed. If I were you I would give such a proposal serious thought."

"I told you. I don't want to go back. I was imprisoned for no wrong, I committed no crime before I was sent to the Gulag. And it's not me who ought to be tried, but the people who sent me to a prison camp."

Romulka's face suddenly twisted in anger. "Listen to me, you stupid bitch. Imagine how unpleasant we could make things for your child. Come back and face the courts and you may see her again. Don't, and I swear to you the rest of her life in that orphanage could be made very unpleasant indeed. Do you understand me?"

Massey tried hard to control the urge to hit the man, and then he saw the emotion welling in Anna's eyes, the pain growing on her face until she seemed to snap, all the anguish suddenly flooding out. She lunged across the table and her nails dug into Romulka's face, drawing blood.

"No! You won't hurt my daughter like that . . . You won't!"

As Massey fought to restrain her, Romulka went to grab her hair.

"You bitch!"

Massey and the aide stepped in between them, before the policeman appeared at the door and Massey quickly ushered Anna from the room.

As Romulka removed a handkerchief from his pocket and dabbed blood from his face, he glared at Massey. "You haven't heard the last of this! Your embassy will learn of this outrage!"

Massey stared angrily at the Russian. "Tell who you goddamned like, you piece of shit. But she's made her decision and we'll make ours." Massey jabbed a finger hard in Romulka's chest. "Now get the hell out of here before I hit you myself."

For a moment it seemed as if Romulka would rise to the threat as he glared back at Massey, a fierce rage in his eyes, but suddenly he snapped up his briefcase and stormed out of the room.

Romulka's aide lit a cigarette and looked over at Massey. "Not a very sensible thing the woman just did, considering our embassy will most likely succeed in getting her back. And besides, Romulka is a dangerous man to cross."

"So am I, buddy."

Massey arrived at the hospital that evening and they walked down to the lake. They sat on one of the benches and Anna said, "What I did today didn't help, did it? Has your Ambassador decided what's going to happen to me?"

She looked at Massey uncertainly but he smiled. "After he heard about Romulka's threat he agreed to grant you asylum. We're going to help you start a new life in America, Anna. Give you a new identity and help you settle down and find a job. You won't be given citizenship right away but that's normal in cases like yours. You'll have to be a resident for five years, just like any other legal immigrant. But if you don't break the law or do anything crazy it shouldn't be a problem."

Massey saw her close her eyes, then open them again slowly. There was a look of relief on her face.

"Thank you."

Massey smiled. "Don't thank me, thank the Ambassador. Or maybe you should thank Romulka. Tomorrow you'll be flown to Germany. There you'll be filled in on the arrangements that are being made to help you. After that you'll be flown to the United States. Where to, I don't know. That kind of detail isn't up to me."

For a long time Anna Khorev said nothing. She looked out at the cold lake. Finally she said, "Do you think I'll be happy in America?"

Massey saw the sudden fear in her face, as if it was only now she realized the enormity of what had happened and the uncertainty that lay ahead.

"It's a good country to make a fresh start in. You've been badly hurt and your emotions are in turmoil. You don't know what the future holds for you and your past is a painful memory. Right now you're living in a kind of twilight zone. You'll probably feel confused and lost for a long time. You'll be in a new country with no friends. But you're going to heal with time, I know you will. That's about it. Except for the bad news. And that is we'll probably never meet again. But I wish you happiness, Anna."

"You know something, Massey?"

"What?"

"If things were different, I would have liked to have seen you again. Just to talk. To have been friends. I think you're one of the nicest men I've ever met."

Massey smiled. "Thanks for the compliment. But I guess you haven't known many men, Anna. I'm just an ordinary guy, believe me."

"Will you come to say goodbye at the airport?"

"Sure, if you like." He looked down at her and some instinct made him touch her shoulder gently. "You'll be OK. I know you will. Time will heal your heart."

"I wish I could believe that."

Massey smiled. "Trust me."

There was a patina of snow on the ground as Massey and the two men walked with her to the aircraft. The Finnish Constellation was waiting on the apron and the passengers were already boarding.

Massey hesitated at the foot of the metal steps.

He offered her his hand and she kissed him on the cheek.

"So long, Anna. Take care of yourself."

"I hope I see you again, Massey."

She was looking at his face as she boarded and he thought he saw tears at the corners of her eyes. He knew he had been the first real emotional contact she had had in the last six months and he guessed he had made an impression. He knew it would have been the same with most people who escaped over the Soviet border. Frightened and alone, they grasped the first kind hand offered to them.

He also knew that no matter what his intuition told him he could have been wrong about her and the Finnish SUPO officer who doubted her story could have been right; Massey didn't believe he was wrong but knew only time would tell.

It was five minutes later when he stood in the Departures lounge and watched as the Constellation trundled down the runway before being finally sucked up into the Baltic twilight, its flashing lights sending an eerie glow out into the surrounding cloud.

Massey looked at the empty sky for a few moments before he said softly, "*Do svidaniya.*"

As he pulled up his coat collar and walked back toward the exit, he was too preoccupied to notice the dark-haired young man lounging by the newspaper stand, watching the departing aircraft.

January 13th–27th 1953

8

Bavaria,
Germany.
January 13th,
11 P.M.

It was raining hard all over southern Germany that night, lightning flickering on the horizon, and no weather for flying.

The airfield barracks complex in the heart of the Bavarian lake district was shrouded in low cloud and mist. No more than a runway and a collection of wooden huts that had once belonged to the Luftwaffe's crack Southern Air Command, it now housed the CIA's Soviet Operations Division in Germany.

As Jake Massey came out of the Nissen hut that served as the Operations Room he looked up at the filthy black sky, then pulled up his collar and ran across to a covered army jeep waiting in the pouring rain. A fork of lightning streaked across the darkness and as he slid into the jeep the man sitting in the driver's seat said, "A night for the bed, I'd say. With a good woman beside you and a bottle of Scotch."

Massey smiled as the jeep started along a tarmac road.

"You could do worse, Janne."

"So who have I got tonight?"

"A couple of former Ukrainian SS men bound for Moscow, via Kiev."

"Charming. You always did keep the best of company, Jake."

"It's either work for us or they face a war crimes trial. Nasty types, both of them, part of an SS group who executed a group of women and children in Riga, but beggars like us can't be choosers."

"That's what I like about working for the CIA, you get to meet the most interesting people."

The man beside Massey wore a pilot's leather flying jacket and a white silk scarf. He had a cheerful face and although he was short and stocky his straw-blond hair was unmistakably Nordic.

At thirty-one, Janne Saarinen had already seen more trouble than most men. Like some Finns after the Winter War with Russia in '40 who saw their country's allegiance with Hitler's Germany as a chance to get even with Moscow, Saarinen had thrown in his lot with the Germans but paid a price.

His right leg had been blown off below the knee by a Russian shrapnel burst that tore into the cockpit of his Luftwaffe Messerschmitt at five thousand feet during a Baltic skirmish, and now he had to make do with a wooden contraption that passed for a leg. There was still a piece of the Russian metal somewhere in the ugly mass of scar tissue where the German surgeon had sewn the stump together, but at least Saarinen was still walking, even if with a pronounced limp.

The jeep drove down to a runway situated near a rather large lake, a collection of hangars nearby, the doors of one of them open and arc lights blazing inside.

Massey climbed out of the jeep and ran in out of the rain, followed by Saarinen.

Two men were sitting in a corner by a table, parachutes beside them, smoking cigarettes as they waited near a black-painted DC-3 aircraft with no markings which was parked just inside the hangar, a flight of metal steps leading up into the open cargo door in the side of the fuselage.

One of the men was in his late twenties, tall and thin, a nervous look on his anxious face, which already looked brutal despite his relative youth.

The second was older, a rough-looking specimen and heavily built, with red hair and a hard face that seemed hewn out of rock.

He had a look of insolence about him and he stood up when he saw Massey enter the hangar, and as he walked across the man tossed away his cigarette.

He said to Massey in Russian, "No night for man or beast, let alone flying. Are we still going, *Americanski*?"

"I'm afraid so."

The man shrugged and quickly lit another cigarette, his nerves obviously on edge, then looked back toward his white-faced companion.

"Sergei here has a bad case of the frights. From the look of him he thinks we're doomed. And on a night like this I'm inclined to agree. If the Russian radar doesn't help put us in an early grave, the lousy weather probably will."

Massey smiled. "Oh, I wouldn't say that. You're in good hands. Say hello to your pilot."

Massey introduced Saarinen but because of regulations didn't offer the Finn's name and the two men shook hands briefly.

"Charmed, I'm sure," said the Ukrainian. He looked at Massey more seriously, a small nervous grin flickering on his face. "A small point, but your pilot's got a false leg. I just thought I'd mention it."

Saarinen said, offended, "You could always try taking off without me if it bothers you. And you and your friend over there had better put out those damned cigarettes or none of us will be going anywhere." He nodded over to the aircraft. "There are six thousand pounds of highly inflammable fuel in those tanks. Do it, now!"

The younger man stubbed out his cigarette the moment Saarinen barked the order, but the older Ukrainian stared at Saarinen sullenly, then grudgingly followed suit.

"Who knows? Perhaps it might be a better way to die than taking our chances with a pilot who's a cripple."

Massey saw the anger flare on Saarinen's face and he said quickly to the Ukrainian, "That's enough, Boris. Just remember, your life's in this man's hands so be nice to him. And for your information, you've got the best pilot in the business. No one knows the route as well."

"Let's hope so." The Ukrainian shrugged and said grudgingly to Saarinen as he nodded over to the DC-3, "So you think we'll make it in this American crate?"

Saarinen bit back his temper and said evenly, "I don't see why not. It might be a lousy night for flying but then that means the Reds won't be too anxious to put their own planes up. We should be all right. The danger point is approaching the Soviet-Czech border. After that it's roses all the way."

"Then we're in your hands, it seems."

The second man came over and nodded to Massey and Saarinen. Massey introduced them and the young man said to Massey, "Something tells me I should have taken my chances with a war crimes trial."

"Too late now. OK, let's run through a final check. Papers, belongings, money. On the table."

The Ukrainians emptied out their pockets on the table and Massey sifted through their belongings. "Everything looks in order. Once you get to Moscow and get yourselves organized you know what to do."

Both men nodded.

"That's it, then. Good luck to both of you."

The red-haired Ukrainian grunted and said to Saarinen, "*If* we get to Moscow. Whenever you're ready, my little crippled friend."

Saarinen glared at the man and went to move toward him, but Massey gripped the Finn's shoulder as the Ukrainian turned dismissively and he and his companion walked toward the aircraft, parachutes over their shoulders, both of them laughing.

"Maybe I should drop them in the wrong zone, just for the fun of it, and let the KGB do the work for me."

"Don't worry, the life expectancy of those two isn't long. If they do make it to Moscow, they'll be lucky. You ought to know—most of the agents we send in get caught in the first forty-eight hours, but it's still a chance that's better than a rope or a firing squad."

"And I have to say some of the bastards you use deserve it, Jake. Right, I suppose I'd better get moving."

As Saarinen picked up a parachute and went to move toward the stairs up to the DC-3, a jeep pulled up outside the hangar and a young man in civilian clothes climbed out and went over to Massey.

"Message for you, sir."

He handed across a telegram and Massey tore it open, read the contents, then said to the man, "Carry on, Lieutenant. There's no reply needed."

The man climbed back into the jeep and drove off into heavy rain as Saarinen came over.

"Bad news? Don't tell me, the drop's canceled because of the weather?" He grinned. "Never mind that I've flown in much worse without a co-pilot, like tonight. With a bit of luck I might just make it to a nightclub in Munich, and those two bastards on board can live on their nerves for another night."

Massey said, "Afraid not. And it depends on what you mean by bad news. I've been recalled to Washington as soon as I've finished this week's parachute drops."

"Lucky for you." Saarinen smiled. "Me, I'm taking a rest after this one, Jake. Time to throttle back and rest my wings. Some of these former SS scum you're using are starting to get on my nerves."

Saarinen went up the metal stairs of the aircraft and at the top he hauled in the steps.

"Wish me luck."

"Break a leg."

It was almost nine when Jake Massey drove down to the lake and lit a cigarette as he stared out at the choppy water in the drizzling rain. He wondered about the signal from Washington and why they wanted him home.

As he switched off the engine he heard the faint blast of a foghorn out on the water, glanced up and saw the distant lights of a boat moving in the cold darkness near the far shore.

That sound always reminded him, and for a moment he sat there and closed his eyes.

It was a long ago winter's evening like this when he had first seen the lights of America as a child.

He was only seven years of age but Jakob Masensky still remembered the body smells and the babble of strange voices on Ellis Island.

Ukrainians, Balts, Russians, mixed with Irish and Italians and Spanish and Germans. All hoping to start a new life in the promise of the New World.

He had arrived with his parents from Russia in 1919, two years after the Bolshevik Revolution.

In St. Petersburg, where his father's family had emigrated from Poland two generations before, Stanislas Masensky had been employed by the royal household. Jakob Masensky still had a sharp memory of being taken for winter walks in the grounds of the magnificent gilded palaces of Catherine the Great. Stanislas Masensky was an intelligent man, a reader and chess player who, were it not for the accident of being born into an impoverished family, might have become a lawyer or a doctor and not the humble master carpenter that he was.

And Stanislas Masensky also had a secret which, were it known to his employers, would have caused his instant dismissal.

He was an ardent Menshevik supporter who in his heart despised the nobility and everything it stood for. He believed that Russia's future lay in democracy and freedom and that change was coming whether the Tsar wanted it or not, so when the Reds took St. Petersburg he was not a pleased man.

"Believe me, Jakob," his father was fond of saying. "We will pay the price of this Red folly. We need a new Russia, but not that kind of new Russia."

And no one had been more surprised by the Reds' revolution than Stanislas Masensky. It had come like a whirlwind almost out of nowhere, for the Mensheviks had long been the dominant force for change in Russia. And Lenin's Bolsheviks knew this, and that any threat to their promised revolution would have to be crushed mercilessly.

The Reds had come one day; three men with rifles.

They had marched Stanislas away at the point of their bayonets. His pregnant wife and child didn't see him until his release three days later. He had been beaten almost to a pulp and his arms had been broken. He had been lucky not to get a bullet in the neck but that might come soon, and Stanislas knew it.

So he and his wife had packed their belongings and with a horse and cart donated by a relative had set off with their son for Estonia. What little money Jakob's parents had begged and borrowed went on tickets on a Swedish schooner bound from Tallinn to New York.

It was a difficult winter crossing, made all the harsher because of savage easterly winds. The schooner was buffeted and tossed in twenty-foot swells and in the holds the immigrants suffered the worst. On the fifth day Nadia Masensky went into premature labor.

Stanislas Masensky lost not only a child but a young wife, and when the bodies were buried at sea young Jakob remembered the desolate look on his father's face. The man had loved his young wife deeply, and after her loss he was never the same. A friend of his father's had once told Jakob that the loss of a beautiful young wife was something a man never really got over, and he believed it, watching his father retreat into himself year after year.

Until the Depression came, life had been reasonably good in America for Stanislas and his young son. He had settled in the area of Brooklyn called Brighton Beach, known as Little Russia because of its wave of Russian immigrants who had fled the brutality of the Tsar, Lenin, and Stalin after him, and while Stanislas went out to work on the building sites he found an old *babushka* to take care of his son.

That first day on Ellis Island, like so many thousands of other immigrants from Eastern Europe and Russia, Stanislas Masensky had his name changed to an Anglicized version, Massey. This was partly because of the immigration clerk's impatience and inability to understand or spell the Polish name, and also because it somehow affirmed Stanilas's belief in a fresh start in life and satisfied an unconscious wish to erase his troubled past.

An only child, young Jakob Massey proved to be an ardent pupil at school, but what appealed to him most was to sit at his father's feet and listen to stories of his Russian homeland. About the assassination of the Tsar Alexander and the countless attempts to establish democracy by students and workers put down mercilessly by a succession of Tsars, long before the revolution was even a gleam in the communists' eyes.

And later he was to learn too from the émigré newspapers how the Reds had moved whole villages to Siberia, killed anyone who got in the way of their lust for power; how millions of small peasant farmers called *kulaks* had been savagely annihilated because they dared to speak out against Joseph Stalin's agrarian reforms. Whole families brutally wiped out, villages destroyed or deported, millions shot because of one man's lust for power.

When the Depression deepened and Stanislas couldn't find work, in his despair he never blamed America, but the Reds for forcing him to flee his homeland. When it became harder for him to support his son and their lodgings became squalid tenements, he finally moved to a hostel where he and the boy had to line up for soup from a charity kitchen.

For young Jakob, the nadir came one winter's afternoon at the age of sixteen.

He had walked home from school one day to see his once-proud father standing on a street corner with a placard on which he had scrawled: "I am good honest carpenter. Please give me job."

To Jakob it was heartrending to see the parent he loved reduced to such humiliation. It was the final straw. That day he made up his mind that he was going to be rich and his father was never going to have to beg for work.

But Stanislas was to die on his forty-fifth birthday, a broken and disillusioned man.

Jakob himself never became rich. And it took him longer than he thought to make something of himself. He found a succession of menial jobs just to keep food in his belly. He earned a degree in languages at night school followed by a year at Yale. All paid for with his own sweat. Then in 1939, much to the surprise of his fellow students, he joined the Army as an officer cadet.

After Pearl Harbor there had been rapid promotion for those who sought it but Massey was more interested in action. Within six months of America entering the war he was based in Switzerland with Allen Dulles's OSS, organizing reconnaissance missions deep into German-occupied territory.

After the war, America soon discovered her former Russian ally to be an enemy.

The wartime American Intelligence had little or no knowledge of the KGB and knew still less what went on behind Soviet borders. In a frenzy to gather intelligence information, growing numbers of émigrés—Russians, Balts, Poles, young men with a knowledge of Soviet languages and customs—were recruited from the cities and prisoner-of-war camps all over Europe, and the Americans picked their brightest and best officers to train and oversee them.

It seemed a job Massey was curiously fitted to, and so after the war he had remained in Europe, working out of Munich and dispatching agents onto Soviet soil on long-term reconnaissance missions, hoping they could send back detailed information on the alarming postwar Soviet military buildup—émigrés and patriots, freebooters and renegades, some of them restless men still thirsting for action after a war that had not provided them with enough.

Former SS with Russian-language skills who were destined to face long terms in prison or, worse, death for war crimes, like the two men being dropped tonight, risked nothing by parachuting into KGB-controlled territory. If they performed their tasks and somehow made it back over the border they were free men with a new identity and a clean slate—at best they prolonged their life; at worst, they forfeited it in the gamble.

Jake Massey ran the Munich station with ruthless efficiency, relative success, and nothing short of hatred for the Soviets, and with an intimate knowledge of their wiles. In Washington, it was acknowledged he was among the best.

Massey heard another distant foghorn blast the air somewhere out in the drizzling darkness of the lake and looked up.

There was another thing Jake Massey was unaware of that cold January evening as he looked out at the icy waters.

At that moment, less than two thousand miles away in Moscow, the wheels were already turning in a plot that was to consume the next six weeks of his life and bring the world to the brink of war.

Massey took one last look out at the dark shore, then pulled up his collar against the cold and started the jeep. There was just time to write his monthly report to CIA Headquarters in Washington before bed.

9

Moscow.
January 13th

It was almost 2 A.M. as the Emka sedan and the two Zis trucks trundled out through the massive black gates at the rear of KGB Headquarters on Dzerzhinsky Square.

As the vehicles headed south toward the Moscow River, the plain-clothes officer seated in the front passenger seat of the car removed an old silver case from his pocket, flicked it open and selected a cigarette.

Major Yuri Lukin of the KGB 2nd Directorate knew that his task that morning wasn't going to be a pleasant one, and as he sat back in his seat and lit his cigarette he sighed deeply.

He was thirty-two, of medium build, a handsome man with dark hair and a calm, pleasant face. He wore a heavy black overcoat and a gray civilian suit underneath. His left hand from the forearm down was missing, and in its place was an artificial limb, sheathed in a black leather glove.

As Lukin drew on his cigarette he stared out beyond the windshield.

The snow had come early to Moscow the previous November, and now the streets were piled high with thick banks of slush. It seemed to fall incessantly, giving no letup even to the hardened citizens of one of the coldest capitals on earth.

As the convoy passed through the Arbat and headed east along the banks of the frozen Moscow River, Lukin consulted the list of names and addresses on the metal clipboard on his lap. There were nine, all doctors, to be arrested that freezing morning.

He turned briefly to his driver. "We'll take the next left, Pasha."

"As you wish, Major."

The driver, Lieutenant Pasha Kokunko, was a squat Mongolian in his late thirties. His yellow face and muscular, bow-legged body gave the impression of a man who would have looked more at home sitting on a horse on the Mongolian steppes than driving a four-seater Emka sedan.

As Lukin glanced out at the frozen, deserted streets, the passenger sitting alone in the back leaned forward.

"Comrade Major Lukin, may I see the arrest list?"

Captain Boris Vukashin was somewhat younger than Lukin, and had been assigned to his office only a week before. Lukin handed over the clipboard as the interior light in the back flicked on behind him.

Vukashin said after a few moments, "It says here the doctors are all Kremlin physicians. And to judge by the names, at least five are Jewish. It's about time we got firm with these Jews."

Lukin turned around. There was a smirk on Vukashin's face. He had sharp features and a thin, cruel mouth that suggested a brutal manner, and Lukin had taken an instant dislike to the man.

"Six, actually," he replied. "Not that it matters whether they're Jews or not. And for your information, Vukashin, they haven't been tried and found guilty of anything yet."

"My father says that Comrade Stalin believes the eminent doctors are involved in a plot to poison half the Kremlin, and has suspected them for some time."

Lukin blew smoke out into the freezing cab. Vukashin's father was a senior Party official with friends in the Kremlin. Lukin said dismissively, "Your father ought to keep his opinions to himself, at least until the courts have done their work. One mad physician with a grudge I can understand. But nine? It beggars belief."

Lukin rolled down the window and a blast of freezing air stabbed at his face. As he flicked out the remains of the cigarette and rolled up the window again, Vukashin said frostily, "May I be permitted an observation, Major Lukin?"

"If you must."

"I think your comment was dismissive and insulting to Comrade Stalin. My father was simply repeating what Stalin believes to be true."

Before Lukin could reply, Pasha flicked him an irritated look. "How come we always get the assholes assigned to us?"

Vukashin said to Lukin angrily, "Really, Major. This man makes a mockery of my rank. You ought to report him. And if you don't, I will."

"The man's a Mongol. Allowance must be made for that. Do you know anything about the Mongolian race, Vukashin? Apart from the fact that they were the best fighters the Red Army ever had, they're impossible to discipline."

"I know this one needs to be taught a lesson."

Pasha turned around and glared back at Vukashin. "Why don't you shut the fuck up? You're getting so far up my nose I can feel your fucking boots on my chin."

"That's enough, Lieutenant," Lukin intervened.

The Mongolian was an excellent policeman, a good friend, and totally without fear, but Lukin knew he was wildly undisciplined and quite capable of stopping the car and hauling the captain from the back seat and beating him half to death, despite their difference in rank. Besides, carrying out arrests in the early hours of the morning was always a tense and irritable time, and Vukashin's arrogance didn't help.

Lukin swung around in his seat. "And with respect, Vukashin, I'm in charge here. And my comment was an observation, not a criticism. So why don't you do yourself a favor and just sit back and enjoy the ride."

He turned back and saw Pasha smile faintly.

"Wipe that grin off your face, Lieutenant. Take the next left. We're almost there."

The first address was on the left bank of the Moscow River. It was one of the big old houses from the Tsar's time, converted into apartments, and one of the better areas in Moscow. Street lamps blazed onto the frosty snow and the river was frozen solid.

The cavalcade came to a halt and Lukin climbed out of the Emka. As he lit a cigarette he looked over as Vukashin went to assemble the men. The captain's face looked white with rage.

Lukin had been wrong not to take Vukashin's side but his type irritated him. Arrogant, all polished boots and discipline, and everything done by the book. Lukin saw the men jump down from the backs of the big, sharp-nosed Zis trucks as Pasha came over, rubbing his gloved hands to keep out the cold.

The Mongolian lieutenant snorted. "That bastard's been getting on my nerves all week, Yuri. Can't you get him transferred back to wherever he came from?"

"Impossible for now, I'm afraid. His father arranged his posting. So a word of warning—from now on watch yourself and keep your mouth shut. Are the men ready?"

"Sure."

"OK, let's get this over with."

Lukin crossed to the front door of the apartment block and rang the bell of number eighteen. He saw a light go on behind the frosted glass.

The approach often favored by the KGB was to break down the door of the person being arrested. It immediately put the victim in a state of unease and softened him up for any interrogation. Lukin, however, preferred the civilized approach. See the accused and read him the charge to his face. The first name on the list was Dr. Yakob Rapaport, a pathologist.

A middle-aged woman wearing a dressing gown finally opened the door and peered out. Her hair was covered in a net, curlers underneath. "Yes?"

"My apologies, madam. Is Dr. Rapaport at home?"

Before the woman could reply, Lukin heard a voice in the hallway behind her. "What's wrong, Sarah? Who's calling at this unearthly hour?"

The man who appeared had an overcoat thrown loosely over his shoulders. He wore pajamas and his white beard gave him a distinguished look.

He put on his glasses and peered out at the trucks and men in the street, then at Lukin.

"Who are you? What is this?"

"Dr. Rapaport?"

"Yes."

"My name is Major Lukin. It is my duty to have to inform you that you are under arrest on the orders of KGB 2nd Directorate. I would be grateful if you would kindly get dressed and come with me. And dress warmly, it's cold outside."

The doctor's face turned chalk white. "There must be some mistake. I have committed no crime. I don't understand."

"Neither do I, Doctor. But I have my orders. So please be so kind as to do as I ask."

The doctor hesitated, and suddenly his wife put a hand to her mouth and her face was a mask of fear as she stared back at Lukin.

"Please . . ." the woman pleaded.

"Forgive me, madam," Lukin said as reassuringly as he could. "Hopefully this is all a misunderstanding. But it's best if your husband comes now."

The doctor put his arm around his wife's shoulder and nodded shakily to Lukin.

"Come inside, Major, and I'll get dressed."

It was almost six when the arrests had been completed.

Most of the physicians on the list had come resignedly, but all in shock and some in protest. One had to be dragged forcibly to the back of a truck. None of the doctors seemed to believe that it was happening to them.

At the last address in the Nagatino district there was an incident, and it was recorded in the KGB arrest report for that morning. The doctor in question was a widower in his late fifties, and lived alone on the third floor of the apartment block.

Lukin rang the bell several times but after a minute there had been no reply and he saw a curtain flicker in one of the upstairs windows. In exasperation he rang another apartment, and when the woman tenant appeared and saw the KGB men and vehicles outside she was rooted to the spot and started to shake, but Lukin went in past her, followed by Vukashin.

Lukin reached the third floor and pounded on the door of the doctor's apartment. When Vukashin finally kicked it in, they found the man hiding in the bathroom. The doctor had obviously seen the men come to arrest him and was in a state of shock.

Lukin's orders had been to carry out the arrests discreetly and with no fuss, but before he could get to the doctor, Vukashin had crossed to the cowering man and started to lash out with his fists.

"Get up, you Jewish filth! Get up!"

Lukin came up smartly behind Vukashin and hit him hard across the back of the neck, a blow that sent the captain crashing into the wall.

As Vukashin slid down, blood on his face, Pasha came rushing up the stairs to investigate, his pistol drawn.

Lukin barked, "Get the doctor downstairs. Now!"

Pasha did as he was ordered and Lukin dragged the captain to his feet and stared angrily into his face.

"Understand something, Vukashin. You don't *ever* hit a prisoner while I'm in charge of an arrest. These are people you're dealing with, not animals. Have you got that?"

Vukashin glared at Lukin arrogantly but said nothing. A trickle of blood dribbled from his mouth. Pasha came back up the stairs, and as he came into the room Lukin shoved Vukashin aside.

"Get this idiot out of my sight before I throw up."

Pasha smiled. "A pleasure."

Lukin left KGB Headquarters well after seven that morning.

Lights were coming on all over Moscow as he drove to his home on the eastern end of Kutuzovsky Prospect.

The olive-green BMW 327 Lukin owned had been built in 1940, one of many vehicles confiscated from a defeated Germany at the end of the war, but the powerful six-cylinder engine was still reliable and ran sweetly, and the car was the one worthwhile luxury his KGB officer status allowed.

He parked on the street outside the one-bedroom apartment he and his wife occupied near the Moscow River. It was in a district once favored by Moscow's wealthy merchant class, but now the buildings looked shabby from the outside, the pastel-green paintwork cracked and peeling, but inside the plumbing and the heating always worked, a minor miracle in Moscow. He climbed the stairs to the fourth floor and let himself in quietly.

The apartment was cold and Nadia was still asleep. He filled an enamel kettle in the tiny kitchen and lit the gas stove to make coffee. As he removed his overcoat and unbuttoned his shirt, he crossed to the window and looked down, resting his forehead against the cold pane of glass.

As Lukin stood there he thought about the arrests that morning.

He had lost his temper with the captain but the arrogant fool deserved it, though no doubt Lukin would receive a reprimand.

He knew several of the doctors on the list by reputation. All respected physicians with no hint of crime in their past. The arrests puzzled him, especially since most of them were Jews. No doubt he would find out eventually why they had been taken to the Lubyanka.

The KGB Headquarters on Dzerzhinsky Square which housed the Lubyanka prison was a huge seven-story complex of office blocks that took up the whole northeastern end as far as the top of Karl Marx Prospect. The building was actually a hollow square, with a courtyard in the center, the front and side wings up to the top six floors of which were devoted to the various KGB offices and departments.

And although it contained eight separate directorates, or specialized sections, which dealt with internal and external Soviet security, only four were considered important enough in size and purpose to hold the title Chief Directorate, of which each had a separate and distinct function.

The 1st Chief Directorate was the foreign intelligence branch that operated in Soviet embassies abroad and controlled the networks of agents, foreign informers and sympathizers who provided invaluable intelligence aid.

The 5th Chief Directorate was responsible for internal dissidents, which included Jews and anti-Soviet resistance groups operating from as far apart as the Baltic to the Far East; while the Chief Directorate of Border Guards was responsible for sealing and patrolling all Soviet borders.

The 2nd Chief Directorate, to which Lukin belonged, was perhaps the most important and largest.

A purely domestic security branch of the KGB, its responsibilities were the most wide-ranging, and included the surveillance of all foreigners and foreign businessmen resident or visiting the Soviet Union, foreign embassies and embassy staff; the hunting down and arrest of Soviet nationals who had fled abroad or escaped from prison camps or who had committed murder or serious crimes; the supervision of artists, actors and actresses; recruiting and controlling informers; and curbing the black market. And last, but hardly least, the pursuit and capture of enemy agents from the moment they entered Soviet territory.

There was one other noteworthy section in the bowels of the KGB building: the Lubyanka prison itself, a grim maze of torture chambers and windowless cells where Lukin knew the doctors were destined to be sent.

He poured himself hot coffee and spooned in three spoonfuls of sugar. As he went to sit at the kitchen table, the door opened.

Nadia stood there wearing a pale blue dressing gown. Her head of red hair was down around her shoulders. He saw the slight rise in her belly and smiled.

"Did I wake you?"

She smiled back sleepily. "You always wake me. Are you coming to bed?"

"Soon."

Even that early she looked very pretty. Far too pretty for him, Lukin always thought. She was nineteen and he thirty when they first met at the summer wedding of a friend. As the wedding band played, she had smiled across the table at him and said impishly, "What's the matter? Don't KGB officers dance?"

He smiled back. "Only if somebody shoots at them."

She had laughed, and something in her girlish laugh and the way she had looked at him with her soft green eyes made him know he was going to love her. Within six months they had married. And now, three years later, she was four months pregnant and Lukin felt happier than he ever imagined.

She came over to sit on his knee and began to massage his neck. He could feel her small, girlish breasts brush against his chest.

"How was your night shift?"

"You don't want to know, my love."

"Tell me anyhow."

He told her about his morning's work.

"You think it's true about the doctors?"

"It's probably Beria up to his tricks again. He enjoys killing."

He felt the hands stop massaging his neck and saw the shock on his wife's face.

"Yuri, you shouldn't say such things. You never know who might be listening."

"But it's true. You know how the head of State Security gets his kicks? Marakov, his driver, told me. He's driving along and Beria sees a pretty young girl, maybe fourteen or fifteen years old. He has her arrested on trumped-up charges and rapes her. If she dares to protest, he has her shot. Sometimes he has her shot anyway. And nothing is done to stop him."

"Yuri, please. Skokov might be listening."

Every apartment block, every house, had its KGB informer. Skokov, the block janitor who lived on the ground floor, was theirs. It wasn't beyond the man to crease his ear against someone's door. Lukin saw the fear in his wife's eyes and stood and cupped her face in his hands and kissed her forehead.

"Let me get us some coffee."

Nadia shook her head. "Look at you. You're tense. You need something better than coffee."

"And what would you suggest?"

Nadia smiled. "Me, of course."

Lukin saw her pull back her dressing gown to reveal her flimsy pink underwear. Even though she was petite, she had perfect legs and full hips, and there was something faintly erotic about the gentle rise of her stomach which embarrassed him.

She smiled. "A surprise for you, Yuri Andreovitch. I bought them on the black market."

"Are you out of your mind?"

"Where else in Moscow can a woman buy underwear like this? You don't think Comrade Stalin would have me sent to Siberia for a pair of panties?"

As she laughed she brushed herself against his body.

Lukin smiled despite himself.

"Do you know what the French say?"

"No, but I think you're going to tell me."

"When a woman opens her legs for a man, her secrets fly away like butterflies."

He looked into her face. "But with you, somehow the secrets multiply." He kissed her forehead and her arms went around him. "I love you, Nadia."

"Then come to bed."

He gently caressed her belly. "You don't think making love would be bad for the baby?"

"No, silly, it would be good for the baby." She giggled. "Make the most of it while you can. In another few months you'll have to keep your fly closed."

She took his hand and led him into the bedroom. The bed was still warm as Lukin and his wife made love, and beyond the glass the early morning traffic hummed as Moscow came awake.

10

Washington, D.C.
January 22nd

The collection of wooden buildings on the bank of the Potomac River looked to the passerby like a dismal, run-down barracks.

The walls inside were pockmarked with holes, the plaster ceilings were smudged with damp stains, and the rain leaked through the fragile roof. The view from the two-story building was equally dismal: a decayed red-brick brewery and a distant roller-skating rink. Only a handful of the shabby buildings had the distinction of overlooking the famous reflecting pool further along the river.

Originally a First World War army barracks, the ramshackle collection of wooden huts had later housed the offices of the OSS, the Office of Strategic Services, the organization responsible for America's wartime foreign intelligence. Transformed only in name and function four years after the Second World War, the buildings now housed America's Central Intelligence Agency.

Fresh CIA recruits, expecting their role in intelligence work to be glamorous, soon found their expectations rapidly diminished when they got their first glimpse of their dingy offices. It was difficult to believe that these same buildings had been home to one of the most intrepid wartime agencies, one that had taken on the collective intelligence might of Germany and Japan.

The CIA barracks complex was divided into sections with alphabetic titles. The "Q" building, overlooking the river, housed the section known simply as the Soviet Operations Division. Living up to its title, it was here that highly sensitive and secret operations were planned and executed against the Soviet Union, clandestine work known only to a handful of highly trusted and trained senior intelligence and government personnel.

The office at the end of a long corridor on the second floor of the building had no title on the door, just a four-digit number.

It was pretty much like all the other offices, with the same green desk and filing cabinet and standard-issue calendar, but on the desk alongside the photograph of his wife and two grown children, Karl Branigan had placed a Japanese officer's ceremonial dagger on a brass mounting.

At fifty-six, Branigan was a blubbery but muscular man with a tightly cropped GI haircut and a fleshy ruddy face. Despite his name he was neither Irish nor German in background but third-generation Polish, the surname arrived at by having a Brooklyn-Irish cop for a stepfather. And despite the close-cropped army haircut and the ceremonial dagger, Branigan had never seen front-line action but had been a desk-bound intelligence officer most of his working life. But the presence of the keepsake gave some indication of Branigan's character. He was certainly a tough man, a man who made decisions quickly and decisively, who was almost savage in his dedication to duty, and as a senior CIA officer those virtues were valued by his superiors.

It was almost two o'clock that cold January afternoon when his secretary rang to say that Jake Massey had arrived.

Branigan told her to organize a car to take them to the morgue.

A small elevator led down to the morgue. There was just enough room for the three passengers—Massey, Branigan, and the attendant.

When the elevator halted and the attendant opened the door, they were in a cold, large, white-tiled room with four metal tables at the far end. Two of the tables had forms under the white sheets. The attendant pulled back the sheet on the first table.

Shock and a terrible anger registered on Massey's face when he looked at the body underneath.

The man's face was frozen and white as marble, distorted in death, but he at once recognized the features. There was a hole drilled through Max Simon's forehead, a purple swelling surrounding the wounded flesh. Massey noticed the traces of a powder burn around the skull wound, then the tattoo of a white dove above his wrist. He grimaced and nodded and the attendant drew back the sheet and moved to the second table.

When the sheet was pulled back this time, Massey wanted to be sick.

He saw the perfect white face of the child, the eyelids closed, the same neat hole in the flesh of the forehead. Nina lay on the metal table as though asleep. Her long dark hair had been combed and for a moment Massey thought that if he touched her she might come awake. Then he noticed the dark purple bruises on the body, around the arms and neck, and the marks where the forest rodents had gnawed at her flesh.

The attendant pulled the white sheet over the girl's body and the two men turned and left the room.

Jake Massey and Karl Branigan had known each other for almost twelve years and their relationship had not improved with time.

There was often an air like crackling electricity between the two men which some claimed was the result of professional rivalry. Both were capable and hardened men and both were dangerous to cross. Today, however, Branigan seemed civilized and courteous.

"Tell me how it happened."

Branigan hesitated. "I guess you and Max Simon were friends a long time?"

"Thirty years. I was Nina's godfather. Max was one of the best people we had." Massey's face suddenly flushed angrily. "Goddamn it, Branigan, why were they killed? Who did it?"

"We'll come to that later." Branigan's hand stretched to a cigarette box on the table, popped a cigarette in his mouth and lit it. He didn't offer Massey one.

"But I'm sure you realize that what happened to Max and his daughter was an execution pure and simple. They were both shot in the head at close range. I assume the girl was killed because she saw whoever shot her father, or they meant her death as a further warning."

"They?"

"Moscow, of course."

"What do you mean, a warning?"

"Max was gathering some pretty sensitive information for us before he was killed. We didn't know about the deaths until a routine Interpol report reached our office in Paris. We had the bodies identified and shipped back." Branigan hesitated. "Max arrived in Lucerne from Paris on the eighth of last month, after traveling from Washington. He took his daughter with him for the trip. She'd been ill recently, and he wanted her to see a Swiss doctor."

"Is that the reason he was in Switzerland?"

"No, it wasn't. He was there to arrange a meeting with a highly placed contact from the Soviet Embassy in Berne. They were to meet in Lucerne, but Max never made the meeting, nor did his contact. We think Max and his girl were abducted from their hotel, or maybe outside in the street. The police checked but no one saw anything. You know the Swiss, they're upright citizens. They see you parking a car on the wrong fucking side of the street and they scream for the cops. It would have been reported if anyone had seen an abduction. But one thing the Swiss police do know is that the hunter, Kass, stumbled on the executions, tried to stop them, and was killed for his trouble."

A flood of anger registered again on Massey's face and he stood and crossed to the window. "Why did they have to murder the girl, Karl? She was only ten years old."

"Because we both know the people who did it are ruthless bastards. Simple as that."

"Have you any idea who murdered them?"

"Why? You got revenge on your mind?"

"A year ago Max Simon moved out of my operation in Munich to work for Washington. Now he's dead and I'd like to know why."

"Who did it I can tell you pretty much with certainty. A man named Borovik. Gregori Borovik. We think he followed Max from this country and was ordered to kill him in Switzerland. Borovik's not his real name. He uses a whole lot of aliases. Kurt Braun is one. Kurt Linhoff is another. I could go on but you get the picture."

"Who is he?"

"A hired killer the Soviets use. He belongs to one of their hit squads. The guys Moscow take from prisons and put on the payroll to do their dirty work in return for their freedom. East German national, speaks English and Russian fluently. Operates all over the goddamned place. Europe and Stateside, and a mean son-of-a-bitch if ever there was one. We've got at least three murders put down to him. But I'd get revenge out of your mind. Besides, we've got other plans for you."

"What plans?"

Branigan smiled. "All in good time. And it's revenge of a kind if you care to look at it that way."

Massey sat down. "Then tell me what it was Max was doing for you that cost the lives of him and his daughter."

Branigan shrugged. "I guess I can tell you that. He'd been buying information from the Soviet embassy official I told you about, information important to Washington. Only someone in Moscow got to hear about it and didn't like it one little bit. The official was called back home. What happened to him you can guess."

"What sort of information?"

"Pretty high-grade stuff out of the Kremlin. Some of it pretty hot."

"How hot?"

Branigan smiled thinly. "On a scale of red hot to boiling, it would probably bust the fucking thermometer."

"Has this got something to do with why I was recalled?"

Branigan shifted his heavy bulk in the chair. "We knew you'd want to see the bodies. You and Max went way back. I heard you knew each other as kids in the streets of Little Russia. I remember Max told me once you were kind of like brothers. But you're right, that's not the real reason you're here. There's something I want you to see. I guess it'll explain everything."

Branigan unlocked a drawer with a key he kept on a ring in his pocket. He slid out a buff-colored file and placed it on the table. Stamped along the top in red letters was "*For President's Eyes Only.*" He looked at Massey.

"Needless to say, the classification says it all. But it seems you're a special case."

He slipped his jacket from the back of the chair and pulled it on, smiling thinly as a hint of aggression crept into his voice.

"Only get this straight. You tell nobody about the contents of that file unless you're cleared to do so. Which I guarantee you won't be—ever, not in a million years. I'm going to leave you alone for say fifteen minutes. That ought to be enough time to read what's inside and prime you for what you're going to hear later. When I come back I'm taking you to see Wallace. He's expecting us at his place. Another thing. If you need to use the john, use it now."

"Why?"

Branigan found another key on the ring. "Because I'm going to lock the door after me while I go get a coffee and let you read that in peace. No one else in this building gets to see what's in the file except you and me. And I've given orders no one's to knock so you won't be disturbed. You need to use the john?"

"I guess not."

Branigan stood. "OK, just two more instructions you ought to know. One, this meeting never happened. Two, as of today you're officially on indefinite leave on health grounds and you're about to take it on full pay. For the records, you're depressed, and you need a break from intelligence work."

Massey frowned. "Do you mind telling me what the hell's going on?"

There was an edge of irritation in Branigan's voice. "It's all in the file. And between those pages you'll find the reason why Max Simon and his kid were murdered, and it doesn't make pleasant reading."

When he saw Massey stare at him, Branigan shrugged his shoulders. "The instructions ain't mine." He pointed a finger to the ceiling. "They come from high above."

"How high?"

"The President."

11

Washington, D.C.
January 22nd,
4 P.M.

The white-painted house in Georgetown looked as imposing as any in the select neighborhood that housed Washington's elite.

Built of wood, the clapboard three-story colonial property sat secure in a vast walled private garden of cherry and pear trees, and although it was winter the three men sat out on the back patio in wrought-iron garden seats.

The Assistant Director, William G. Wallace, was a Yale man, silver-haired and in his late fifties, and his tanned face bore the vestiges of a recent winter vacation in Miami.

When the small talk was over the Assistant Director looked over at Massey, smiled faintly and said, "You read the file, Jake?"

"I read it." Massey nodded.

"Have you any questions?"

"One, who knows about this?"

"Besides you, Branigan and me? Only the President and the Director." The Assistant Director smiled."There is one other I should mention, who's aware, shall we say, of our intentions, and not what you've read, but we'll come to that later."

Branigan interrupted. "Maybe I better fill in the gaps, sir?"

The Assistant Director nodded. "I guess you better, Karl. I want Jake to be crystal clear about what he's read."

Branigan ran a hand through his cropped hair and looked at Massey.

"Jake, what you saw back in the office was a confidential report written by Joseph Stalin's private physicians. It was the last report we received from Max Simon a month before he was murdered. You know the contents but I'll go over them again to clear up any points. Number one, Stalin has had two strokes in the last six months and as a result his speech and movement are impaired.

"Number two, his medical people all agree that either as a result of the strokes or another medical condition, he's become mentally unstable. He's displaying signs of paranoid schizophrenia. Put simply, the man's going crazy."

Branigan smiled. "Now we and the world know he's already a certifiable nut, but this report confirms it and puts it in perspective. Something else you ought to know. The doctors in the Kremlin who wrote the medical report were arrested on a charge of trying to poison Stalin. Whether it's true or not we don't know, but we do know they were taken to the Lubyanka prison. We've got no information on their fate, but I'd guess it ain't exactly rosy. Most of the doctors were Jews. Stalin's made no secret of the fact he hates the Jews. Pogroms have already started in Russia and we think it's a sign that he's going to start his purges again. And something worrying you should know about—our intelligence people have confirmed Stalin's already building concentration camps in Siberia and the Urals. He intends to finish what the Nazis started. Sounds kind of familiar, doesn't it? A buildup to another situation like the one we had with Adolf Hitler."

Massey stared at Branigan. "What exactly are you saying?"

The Assistant Director interrupted. "Jake, we know Max Simon was receiving those reports from a highly placed and reliable Russian contact in the Berne Embassy. He was a Jew. I say *was* because I doubt he's still alive. But he was worried, like some of his Kremlin friends, not all of them Jews, about the direction Moscow's going in. Jake, let me put it simply. Stalin is a danger. And I don't mean only to America but the whole damned world, including his own people. Everybody from Congress to the man in the street believes there's another war on the horizon. And this one won't be like the last—but it may well *be* the last. The potential for worldwide destruction is enormous. Stalin has set his sights on completing his hydrogen bomb program before we do and we know for sure that's going to happen. And that's a mighty dangerous scenario.

"Hell, we're building fallout shelters all over this country as fast as we can but that's pretty much all we can do—we're not prepared for war. But Uncle Joe has made it pretty plain in the past what his intentions are. He sees a war with us as inevitable. I guess it's an obsession with him. A death wish. And a crazy old man with an obsession is pretty likely to want that wish satisfied."

Massey looked impatiently from Branigan to the Assistant Director. "Will someone kindly tell me just what in the hell all this is leading to?"

"Jake, the President believes Stalin's going to use that bomb just as soon as it's ready. We're talking months, not years. Now we can either sit on the fence and wait for the worst to happen or we can come up with a solution to remove the problem. A solution that's much better for everyone in the circumstances. It calls for a pretty special operation. And I want you to head it."

Massey said, "And what solution is that?"

It was Branigan who answered. "We kill Stalin."

The silence went on for several long moments. The Assistant Director looked out at the bare winter trees, then back at Massey.

"You don't look happy, Jake. I thought you'd be impressed."

"Whose idea was it?"

"It was a decision made at the highest level."

"Meaning?"

The Assistant Director smiled. "Meaning the answer to that question is classified."

Massey frowned and pushed himself up from the chair. "With respect, sir, what you're suggesting is impossible. It would be suicide for whoever goes in."

"And that's exactly why it would work. Moscow would never expect it. Stalin is seventy-three. He's an old man in poor health. You could say why don't we simply wait until he dies?" The Assistant Director shook his head. "Jake, he could live another five, ten years. We can't take that risk. We've got to fight dirty on this one. And in a barroom brawl you can't fight by the Marquess of Queensberry rules. Short of a pre-emptive war, which we're not prepared for on that scale, it's the only sensible solution we've got. We're not prepared to sit back and let another Pearl Harbor happen. Not ever. Naturally, it's a solution not without its risks. That's why the mission will be limited to a small number of personnel operating externally, one we would disassociate ourselves from if it went wrong. The operation would be yours and yours alone. This is not an order to accept, Jake. But I guess if it comes to it, I could make it one."

"Why me?"

The Assistant Director smiled. "Easy. I can't think of anyone more qualified or experienced. Damn it, Jake, you've sent more men across the curtain than anyone I can think of."

Massey crossed to the end of the patio and looked back at the Assistant Director and shook his head. "It's a crazy idea."

"Crazier ideas have worked for us before. And if we'd done something like this some time back, someone like Hitler would never have started a war."

Massey shook his head. "You don't understand. Getting someone close enough to Stalin to kill him is impossible. People have tried before and failed. Émigré groups. The Nazis. Remember the NTS report?"

Massey saw the Assistant Director nod, a look like distaste on his face."Sure I remember."

The NTS, or *Narodny Trudovoy Soyuz*, was a group of ethnic Russians and Ukrainians in Europe and America, controlled by the CIA, who were devoted to the destruction of the Soviet regime. Many of its members had volunteered to be parachuted onto Soviet soil on CIA reconnaissance missions after the war. Many had also paid with their lives, both inside Russia and without, victims of Stalin's murder squads, dispatched to Europe and America to kill any prominent Soviet émigrés who actively opposed Moscow. Two years after the war, determined to step up their campaign, NTS had set about evaluating an assassination attempt to kill Stalin in Moscow.

Massey looked back at the Assistant Director. "Their report speaks for itself. For one, Stalin's quarters in the Kremlin are impregnable. Walls twenty-four feet high and five feet thick. Even thicker and higher in places. Then there's the security measures Stalin employs. Over five hundred guards are stationed in the Kremlin Armory, all hand-picked, all fanatically loyal to Stalin. Less than a half-kilometer away there's a reserve of three thousand Kremlin troops in case they're needed. And those are only the visible deterrents.

"You both know that inside the Kremlin there are secret entrances and exits that go back to the time of the Tsars, ready to be used if needed. And at his villa at Kuntsevo his personal security is impossible to breach. A twelve-foot-high fence. Guards with dogs stationed all around the perimeter. You enter that area of forest and come within a mile of the place without a special pass and you're dead, shot or chewed to death.

"And it doesn't end there. Every morsel of food Stalin takes, every sip of liquid that passes his lips, is first tasted to prevent someone trying to poison him. He even has a woman assigned solely to serve him tea. Each sachet is kept in a locked safe before it's served. Once, a sachet was found not fully sealed. You know what happened? The woman got sent to the cellars of the Lubyanka to be shot."

Branigan interrupted. "Jake, every suit of armor has its chink. It's a matter of finding the right chink. You know that."

Massey shook his head firmly. "In Stalin's case, there are no chinks. His security is airtight. Some people thought there were chinks and tried to kill him, but they all failed. Even the Germans failed. And if crack Nazi troops could fail, what hope have we?"

The Assistant Director sat forward. "Jake, what if I told you we have a plan? Ways to get close enough to Stalin to kill him. Right now, it's only a rough blueprint, if you like, but with your experience you could fill in the details of getting our man into Moscow and make it work."

"Then I'd like to hear it. But who's going to carry out the plan?"

"You are."

"That wasn't what I meant. Who had you in mind to send to Moscow?"

Branigan smiled. "We all know there's only one man capable of pulling this off. Alex Slanski. He can play a Russian to the hilt and he'd have no hesitation in putting a bullet in Stalin's head."

Massey thought a moment. "You're right about Slanski. But what makes you think he'll agree to do it?"

The Assistant stood up. "He already has, in principle. He's the one other person I told you about who knows of our plan, but not the details, and he hasn't seen the file you read. But we can rectify that."

Massey sat back and shook his head. "Sir, sending Slanski into Moscow alone would be suicide. He's an American, born in Russia, but he hasn't been in Moscow since he was a kid."

The Assistant Director smiled. "We've been thinking about that. He'll need help. Someone to act as his wife on the journey until he reaches Moscow and help him get his bearings. There's a woman named Anna Khorev. Border-crosser. I believe you met her in Helsinki. She's been in America almost three months."

Massey frowned. "She's a Russian."

The Assistant Director smiled again. "I would have thought that was perfect for what we had in mind. She seems just the type we need and besides, she's about the only suitable candidate we have. She knows Moscow. For the purpose of the mission she won't even know what Slanski is after. And once she helps him get to Moscow we take her back. But I have to ask you a question, Jake. Are you still certain about her? I read in her file that even though we accepted her story, one of the senior Finnish officers who interrogated her claimed we'd been sold down the river. He didn't trust the lady one bit."

"I trusted her then, and I'd still trust her now." Massey hesitated, doubt clouding his face. "But you're assuming she'll help you in the first place. Why should she? She's already been to hell and back."

"So I read. But I guess we'll have to take your word about her being trustworthy—I trust your judgment, Jake. In regard to why she'd do it, she'll have a motive. Or at least we'll give her one."

"What motive?"

The Assistant Director smiled broadly and turned to Branigan. "Karl, why don't you go get us all a drink while I explain to Jake. I think we're going to need one after this."

It was two hours later when Massey reached his house east of Georgetown.

He called the boarding school in Richmond and made arrangements to see his son the next day. He was looking forward to seeing the boy and he knew he had been less of a father than he should but he felt that somehow the boy understood.

Then he went into the bathroom and ran the cold-water tap and splashed the icy liquid on his face.

He seldom looked at himself in the mirror but that evening he was aware that he looked older than his forty-one years. He had seen a lot of unpleasant things in his life, but the image of the frozen bodies that came into his mind, white, lying in the morgue, the holes drilled in their heads, their flesh chewed away by rats, disturbed him.

He had known and respected Max Simon for many years. They had grown up together, joined OSS together, been friends all their lives. A Jewish kid who lost his father to the Reds and had made it to America on a tough winter crossing like Massey and his father.

Massey looked down as he rolled up his sleeve.

There was a small tattoo on his wrist, of a white dove. Two urchin kids up in Coney Island for a day's fun and chasing girls, and Max had wanted the tattoos to cement their friendship. He had been a gentle soul, Max, who only wanted to do his best for his adopted country, and the little girl had been the only family he had. Massey shook his head and felt the anger rise inside him again, then toweled his face dry and went into his study.

He made the phone calls he needed to make and then he poured himself a large Scotch and took a pad and pen and went over the plan again, looking for flaws.

The Assistant Director was right about one thing; the plan was something Massey could work with. But there were innumerable dangers. For starters, Stalin's Moscow was an alien place and few Westerners were allowed to enter the city.

He thought of Anna Khorev as he sat there sipping the Scotch and making notes. The details of the plan would be up to him, and even though her background was ideal for the mission he disliked having to use her. According to Branigan, the latest report by her case officer had been favorable and she had settled into her new life and was making good progress. But Massey really wondered if she would be up to such a mission mentally and physically after barely three months since her escape. He also knew he was sending her to certain death if it failed.

And something worried him about sending her in with Slanski.

He had the file Branigan had given him and although Massey knew Alex Slanski's background it still made interesting reading.

He was a naturalized American citizen, but Russian-born, aged thirty-five. They had worked together during the war when Slanski was one of a small group of highly trained assassins OSS ran into occupied France and Yugoslavia to help the resistance groups operating against the Germans. Slanski had worked under the code name Wolf. If a German commander or Nazi official in the occupied countries became particularly unpleasant to the resistance, OSS sometimes sent in an assassin to kill him. But it had to appear like an accident so the Germans wouldn't suspect partisan involvement and exact reprisals against the civilian population. Slanski was one of their top agents and expert at making the deaths look a mishap.

Concerning his past, Massey knew there would be very little in the file, except to indicate a determined but lone character.

As a boy, Alex Slanski had escaped from a state orphanage in Moscow. He had managed to get aboard a train for Riga and eventually stowed away on a Norwegian frigate bound for Boston.

When the American authorities were landed with him they didn't quite know what to do with an obviously disturbed twelve-year-old. They guessed something distressing had happened to the child because of his psychological state—he was withdrawn and rebellious and behaved like a wildcat—and he told them virtually nothing about his past, despite the best efforts of the psychologists.

Eventually, someone had the idea to send him to stay with a Russian-speaking émigré living in New Hampshire, a trapper and hunter, who agreed to take the boy for a time. The forests up near the Canadian border had once teemed with Russian immigrants. It was remote, wild territory where the long cold winters and the snow made their exile seem less alien.

Somehow the boy settled in and everyone gladly washed their hands of the matter. There he remained until he joined OSS in 1941.

No one ever learned what happened to his family and parents but everyone who worked with Slanski in OSS guessed it was something pretty bad. One look at those cold blue eyes of his told you that something disturbing had once happened to him.

Long ago Massey thought he had guessed the truth. There was a sick joke Stalin had devised. If anyone opposed him, he as often as not had them killed. If the victim was a man with a family, his wife and any children above the age of twelve were also put to death. But if the children were younger than twelve they were sent to a state orphanage and brought up like good communists, turned into the one thing their parents probably despised.

He guessed that had been Alex Slanski's fate.

Another thing—the KGB had the pick of the orphanage crop. They ran every state orphanage in Russia, and many of their recruits came from those same institutions. Massey always reckoned they probably lost the best killer they ever could have had in Slanski.

He spoke fluent German and Russian and could kill ruthlessly and in cold blood. The most recent assassination had been of a senior KGB officer visiting East Berlin, which Slanski had carried out for the CIA at the request of the émigré group, NTS.

Massey removed an envelope from the file and slid out a photograph of the colonel named Grenady Kraskin. It showed a hard-faced man with thin lips and small, evil eyes.

Assassinated was too nice a word. Kraskin had his penis cut off and stuffed in his mouth. It wasn't a calling card Slanski inflicted on his prey, but according to the file Kraskin had liked to perform that particular kind of brutal mutilation on his male victims. Slanski liked to make the punishment fit the crime, ignoring orders to desist from such behavior. But Branigan and Wallace had been right; there was no one more suitable Massey could think of to carry out the mission.

He slid the photograph back into the envelope. He had a 7 A.M. start and it was a long drive to Kingdom Lake in New Hampshire.

The grim sight of the bodies of Max and Nina lying in the morgue kept coming into his mind, and Massey knew that no matter what Branigan had said, he personally couldn't let the matter rest there. Whoever was responsible for what had happened to Max Simon was going to pay the price, even if it meant stepping outside the bounds, something Massey rarely if ever did.

But this was personal.

It was almost an hour later when he looked up and heard distant bells chime in the church of the Holy Trinity. He stood and went down to the basement and selected the key from the ring in his pocket and unlocked the door.

The two loose firebricks were above the cellar door, a safe hiding place he used whenever he was working at home, rather than leave any notes or files lying around or in locked drawers or a safe that could be broken into. He placed the yellow pad with his notes and the manila folder inside the recess and replaced the bricks. Slanski's file he would return to Branigan.

It was just after 5 P.M. on the afternoon of Thursday, 22 January, two days after the inauguration of Dwight D. Eisenhower as President of the United States.

12

New Hampshire.
January 23rd

The New England towns and villages with their brightly painted clapboard houses looked pretty in the light dusting of snow.

Jake Massey crossed the Massachusetts state line into New Hampshire in the late afternoon and took the road northwest to Concord. There was hardly any traffic on the road and half an hour later he drove the Buick down through a thickly forested track that led to Kingdom Lake. He saw the snow-capped mountains in the distance and a signboard at the track entrance proclaimed, "Trespassers Keep Out!"

Massey switched off the engine and climbed out of the Buick. There was a narrow wooden veranda at the front of the cabin and he went up the steps. The front door was unlocked and the room he stepped into was empty.

Massey called out "Anybody home?" but there was no reply.

The room looked neat and tidy but he thought the place could have done with a woman's touch. It was barely furnished with a scratched pinewood table and two chairs set in the center, and several pairs of deer antlers hung on the walls. There was a tiny kitchen in the back, the utensils and plates neatly stored on the spotless wooden shelves. Massey noticed a rifle storage rack in a corner. Two of the weapons were missing.

There were some books on a shelf and a photograph in a wooden frame on the wall over the fireplace. A very old family photograph, the image cracked and worn, of a man and a woman and three small children; two boys and a blond little girl.

Massey guessed Slanski and the old man had probably gone hunting. He decided to walk down to the lake.

The water was choppy and rain clouds were gathering overhead. A razor-sharp icy wind suddenly whipped across the lake, and as Massey stood beside the boat he said aloud, "Jesus, that's cold . . ."

He heard the barely audible click of a weapon behind him and the voice a split second later.

"You'll be a damned sight colder, mister, if you don't take those hands out of your pockets. Keep them in the air and turn around very slowly. Otherwise you're going to be crawling around on stumps."

Massey turned and saw the man. There was a thin crazy smile on his unshaven face and he looked thoroughly dangerous and unpredictable. He was of medium height, blond, and carried a canvas bag slung over his shoulder. He wore a heavily padded windbreaker over his sweater, and his corduroy trousers were tucked into knee-length Russian boots. He held the butt of a Browning shotgun lightly against his waist, the barrel pointed at Massey.

The man's face creased in a grin. "Jake Massey. For a second there I thought you were a trespasser up to no good. You almost got yourself peppered."

"I guess I got here earlier than expected." Massey smiled and nodded to the shotgun. "You planning on using that thing, Alex?"

The man grinned and lowered the shotgun as he stepped forward and shook Massey's hand. "Good to see you, Jake. No problem finding us, then?"

"I saw the sign at the entrance road. Talk about wanting privacy. Who in the hell's going to bother coming up to this godforsaken place?"

Slanski smiled. "Poachers, for one. The land and water all around here belong to Vassily and he doesn't take warmly to strangers stealing from his traps."

"Then one man's meat must be another man's poison. Me, I'd go crazy up here."

"If you've got time later I'll give you the guided tour. We've even got bears in the woods."

There was a brief look of alarm on Massey's face.

Slanski laughed. "Relax, Jake. It's still a lot safer than New York."

Massey suddenly noticed the old man standing in the woods fifty yards away, a deer carcass slung over his shoulders.

He carried a Winchester rifle and his long black hair was tied back from a weathered face that looked as brown and deeply wrinkled as a walnut. He looked like an Indian from a distance, but Massey recognized something familiar in the features. It was a face that had the same look as the Russians who live north of the Arctic Circle; dark hair and features not unlike the Laplanders.

Slanski waved over at him, the merest of gestures, and when Massey glanced back the old man had disappeared into the woods.

Suddenly it started to rain, a heavy, drenching downpour, and a squall of wind threw freezing water in their faces.

Slanski smiled. "How about we go up to the house? I've got a bottle of bourbon put by that'll warm that old Russian heart of yours."

They sat at the pinewood table and Slanski opened the bottle and poured bourbon into two shot glasses.

He was lean but well built, and he moved stealthily. A strange combination of restless energy and measured control, as if he was in command of every muscle in his body. As Slanski sat, Massey noticed the man's eyes. Deep, slate blue. There was more than a hint of torment in them, but the strange smile hardly left his face.

Slanski raised his glass. "*Za zdorovye.*"

"*Za tvoyo zdorovye.*" Massey sipped his drink, stood and crossed to the bookshelf in the corner and picked up a book.

"Dostoevsky. Last time it was Tolstoy. Whatever are we going to do with you, Alex? An assassin as well as a scholar. Quite a dangerous combination."

Slanski smiled. "He appeals to the darker side of my Russian nature."

"Where's Vassily disappeared to?"

"He's in the woods someplace. Don't worry about him."

Massey swallowed the bourbon and pushed forward the glass. As Slanski refilled it he said, "You want to talk?"

Massey said, "What did Branigan tell you exactly?"

"Enough to get me interested. But seeing as you're going to be running the show, I want to hear it from the horse's mouth."

Massey undid the security lock on the briefcase he had taken from the car, removed the file marked "*For Presidents Eyes Only*" and handed it across.

"Inside you'll see two reports. One is the result of almost two years' work. Highly secret intelligence work carried out for the CIA by the Moscow contacts of some of the anti-Stalinist émigré groups. It gives details of the old Tsarist escape tunnels in the Kremlin that date back hundreds of years. One tunnel in particular is interesting. It leads from the basement of the Bolshoi Theater to the third floor of the Kremlin and comes out in a room next to Stalin's quarters. We also learned there's a secret underground train line that runs from the Kremlin to Stalin's villa at Kuntsevo, just outside Moscow. Stalin's got several villas; however, that's the one he uses most often. But the underground line is only ever used when he needs to travel in haste or in an emergency. We discovered it can be easily breached two blocks from the Kremlin, and leads right under the Kuntsevo villa. Both tunnels, like all the others, are checked at weekly intervals by the Guards Directorate, visual checks and using mine detection equipment and dogs, but normally they're not guarded, except at the entrances and exits, as you'd expect. But you wouldn't be going in through a regular entrance. And a man of your abilities would find a way of getting past the guards. The Kremlin and the Kuntsevo villa are the most likely places Stalin is going to be. Those are your ways in and out of both, whichever should be necessary to use."

It took Massey several minutes more to outline the exact details of the operation, and when he had finished Slanski looked through several pages of the file and said, "I'm impressed, Jake."

He picked up the bourbon bottle, poured a measure into the glass and downed it in one swallow, then fixed Massey with a stare. "But I've got some questions."

"Ask away. You're the one this depends on."

"Why wait until now to kill Stalin? It should have been done a long time ago."

"Look at the file again. There's a second report I told you about, at the back. It ought to explain."

Slanski took the file and read. When he finished he looked up and smiled. "Interesting. But I don't need a report to tell me Stalin is crazy. He should have been put in a rubber room long ago."

"Maybe, but this time we're in deep enough trouble to have to put the man down for the dangerous beast that he is. Do you remember Max Simon?"

"Sure. He was a friend of yours, as I recall."

Massey explained about the deaths of Max and his daughter, and why they had been killed. A look of utter distaste crossed Slanski's face. He lit a cigarette and stood.

"There's something I don't like."

"What?"

"Bloody the waters in a pool full of sharks and it's difficult to get out with all those teeth chopping. Assuming I do the job, the KGB and militia are going to be swarming all over Moscow afterwards, if there is an afterwards. There are five hundred Kremlin Guards behind those red walls, another three thousand a stone's throw away. That's a lot of angry comrades."

"I was coming to that."

Slanski grinned. "I kind of hoped you were."

"You leave the Kremlin or the *dacha* the same way you enter. But there'll also be alternative exits just in case you need them. As soon as I have everything organized, I'll tell you the details. But assuming it all goes according to plan, after that you lie low in a safe house I'll set up in Moscow. A week later, if things work out the way I intend, I take you out."

"How?"

Massey smiled. "I'm working on it. But either way you don't go in without the safe house and exit being in place. Otherwise it's a suicide mission."

"I figured it was that already. Who else knows about the plan?"

"Only Branigan and the brass who approved it, but the exact details are up to me. And that's the way it stays. The fewer people who know the better."

"Branigan said there's going to be a woman?"

"She'll be with you as far as Moscow, then we take her out of the picture."

Slanski shook his head. "You know I always operate alone, Jake. Taking a woman along will only slow things up."

"Not this time. It's for your own good. Traveling alone to Moscow might make you a target for suspicion. Besides, she's part of the plan. She'll accompany you acting as your wife but for the obvious security reasons she won't know the target."

Slanski crushed his cigarette in an ashtray on the table. "You'd better tell me about her."

"You know the rules, Alex. Whenever we drop two or more people onto Soviet territory we don't reveal their backgrounds to one another. No real names, no real identities. That way there's less trouble for either of you if one gets caught."

Slanski shook his head firmly. "The rules don't apply. If I'm going into the lion's den I want to know who I'm going in with. Especially if it's with a woman I know nothing about."

Massey spread his hands on the table and sighed. "OK. I'll give you the basics. Her name's Anna Khorev. Age twenty-six. She escaped from a Soviet Gulag near the Finnish border three months ago and we gave her asylum."

Massey saw the look on Slanski's face as he put down his glass.

"Jake, you must be crazy picking someone with that background. How can you trust her?"

"She wasn't my choice. And if I had my way I'd leave her out of it. But not for the reasons you might think. She can definitely be trusted, Alex, take it from me. And she's the best we're going to get at short notice. It would take months to train another woman, even just so that she wouldn't stand out like a sore thumb on a Moscow street or turn white with fear every time she was asked for her papers by a militiaman."

"Can she handle herself?"

"She can use a gun, if that's what you mean. But all she's really got to do is play the part of being your wife and make your cover seem plausible until you reach Moscow. We can use Popov for a week or so to put you both through your paces. But I'll be relying on you to look after her. The girl's already had some basic military training with the Red Army."

There was a flash of anger or doubt on Slanski's face, Massey couldn't tell which.

"Branigan never said she was Red Army."

"She was a conscript during the war. She didn't volunteer out of ideology. And I would have thought her military background, however brief, was an advantage."

"What about the rest of her background?"

Massey explained briefly about her parents but said nothing about Anna Khorev's personal experience before her imprisonment in the Gulag.

Slanski shook his head in disbelief. "This gets crazier by the minute."

"What does?"

"Her father a Red Army officer."

"Past tense, and hardly in the Red Army mold. And it doesn't taint the girl. I told you, you can trust her."

"Then why was she in a Gulag?"

"You know the way the system works. There doesn't have to be a reason. She was an innocent victim. She did nothing wrong."

Slanski frowned. "So why has she agreed to go back into Russia?"

"She hasn't agreed to anything yet, because I haven't told her. But her reasons will be personal and nothing to do with you."

Slanski crossed to the window and looked out. "Another question. Why did your people come to me?"

Massey glanced over toward the photograph on the wall before looking back. "You know the reasons. I don't have to tell you."

"Tell me anyhow."

Massey pushed away his empty glass. "You were the best man OSS ever trained. You speak fluent Russian. You've been behind the curtain before. And the best two reasons of all. I figure you want to kill the son-of-a-bitch and you're bold enough to try."

Slanski smiled. "Thanks for the vote of confidence. You really have it all worked out, don't you, Jake?"

"You're just about perfect for the part. You've got no family ties, no wife and children. No emotional baggage to tie you down."

"Getting into Moscow is going to be difficult enough despite the plan. It's probably going to be a close hit, not one done with a rifle from a safe distance. And going in with a woman I don't know from Judas doesn't help."

"I never said it would be easy. That's a risk you take. But you stick to the plan and you both stand some chance of getting out of this alive. But trust the girl, Alex. Me, I'd stake my life on her."

"This is going to be no ordinary walk in the woods, Jake. You think it's fair that she doesn't know how deep and dangerous she's getting in?"

"I don't have any choice. That's the way Branigan wants it. And maybe it's best. If she knew she probably wouldn't go."

Slanski thought for a moment. "Where have you got in mind for training?"

Massey shook his head. "Not the regular base we use in Maryland. It's too much of a security risk." He smiled and nodded over toward the window. "I kind of thought maybe here. The terrain is pretty similar to what you'll be crossing. If that's OK with you?"

"I guess Vassily won't object. I'll tell him we need to do some training. He won't ask why and he'll keep out of the way."

"There's another reason why I'd like to use her maybe you ought to know about. After Anna Khorev escaped, the Russians wanted her sent back. They claimed she was a common criminal. I figure that's a load of crap, but she did kill a camp guard and a border guard during her escape. Maybe I'm wrong, but I figure the KGB just might try to find her and take her back illegally. God knows, they've done it before with other escapees and defectors. Up here I'm pretty sure she'll be safely out of harm's way. And if and when she makes it back after the mission, I'll make sure she'll have deep enough cover so that she'll never be found."

"Interesting. You never told me about her killing the guards."

"If you're still unsure about her, I'll let you have the relevant details about her escape from her file."

"Do that."

"Any more questions?"

"Just tell me the odds on the plan working."

Massey shook his head. "I can't answer that. Nobody can. At best you succeed, at worst you die. There's going to be no radio contact once you go in and you'll both be on your own, apart from the safe houses I'll set up. Your chances depend on yourselves and lady luck. And let's just hope she smiles on you both, my friend."

He saw a sudden look of doubt on Slanski's face and said, "You're still in?"

Slanski was silent for several moments. He looked out of the window. Without turning back he said, "On one condition. I have the final say on whether the woman's in. You let me meet her as soon as she's made up her mind."

Massey thought for a moment. "Let's cross that bridge when we come to it." He picked up the file he had shown Slanski. "We've got a code name for the operation—Snow Wolf. But I keep the file, I'm afraid. It's eyes only. No one but you, me, and the folks at the top get to see it. We'll both go through all the details again later, so there won't be any mistakes, but the file stays with me."

He replaced the file in his briefcase, then removed another, placed it on the table and slid it across. "Joseph Stalin" was written on the folder cover in blue ink.

"In the meantime, you'd better read this."

Slanski picked up the folder. "What is it?"

"Everything we know about Joseph Stalin. His background, his personality, his weaknesses, his strengths. Even medical data. His present security arrangements, as far as we can ascertain. The layout of the Kremlin and the dachas he uses. I want you to study it carefully. This isn't an ordinary mission, Alex. You're going to try and kill the devil incarnate. You know the rule—know your enemy like you know yourself. Needless to say, you don't show the file to anyone. Destroy it when you've memorized everything you need to."

Slanski half smiled. "Then all things being equal I guess there's really only one more question."

"What's that?"

"When do I go in?"

"A month from now."

13

New York.
January 26th

The apartment was on the top floor and she came to the door as soon as Massey knocked.

"Hello, Anna."

For a moment she hesitated, then a smile lit up her face. "Massey . . . !"

"You look surprised."

"I thought I'd never see you again."

She took him by the hand, led him inside and closed the door. The apartment was a studio with a single bed, a table and two rickety chairs. There were some winter roses in a vase by the window and the view looked down to a liquor store below, Brooklyn and Queens in the distance.

The place didn't look like much but then Massey guessed she would have been happy with anything after her experience in the Gulag. She had done her best to make it pretty, but there were no family photographs on the walls and it made him feel sad, knowing how lonely she must have felt.

He handed her the brown wrapped parcel. "For you."

She smiled and the surprise lit up her face. "I don't understand. What is it?"

"Open it and see."

She opened the brown paper. It was a box of Kuntz's chocolates. The big brown eyes looked almost childlike as they met his face.

Massey said in Russian, "My way of saying hello again. One Russian to another. How have you been, Anna?"

"Good. And even better now I've seen you again. Thank you for the present, Jake."

"It's nothing." He looked at her figure. "Don't get angry when I say this, but you've put on weight since Helsinki and it suits you."

She laughed. "Then I'll take it as a compliment." She held up the box of chocolates. "And these are not going to help, but thank you again." She stood up as she said, "I found an émigré store that sells really good Russian tea. Would you like some?"

"You read my mind. I'll have it Russian-style." He smiled. "Seven sugars but don't stir."

She laughed and went into the tiny kitchen.

They sat at the table. Massey sipped the tea and spoke in Russian.

"It's good to see you smile, Anna. I guess last time we met you didn't have much to smile about. I hear you have a job?"

"In a garment factory owned by a Polish-American. It's a crazy place, but I like it. And the girls I work with are not how I thought American girls would be."

"In what way?"

"They talk a lot more than Russian girls. And they laugh more. And eat more." She smiled. "A lot more. That's why I put on weight."

"I guess you must make big dresses, huh?"

She laughed. "Not that big."

"Have you made many friends?"

"Some."

Massey looked around the room. "Don't you get lonely here all on your own?"

"Sometimes." She shrugged. "It's not so bad. But I'm so glad you came to see me, Jake."

"Actually, it's unofficial business, not pleasure. But it's good to see you too."

She put down her cup and looked across at him. "I don't understand. I was told someone wanted to talk to me about my work permit. Is that why you're here?"

For several moments Massey sat there, not saying anything. When he finally spoke his voice was quiet and serious.

"Anna, I didn't come here to talk about that. I came to talk about something else."

When he saw the confusion on her face he said, "Will you do something for me, Anna? Will you just listen to what I have to say? Then we can talk some more. But for now, just listen."

Anna hesitated, then nodded.

Massey stood up. He ran a hand through his hair and looked down at her face.

"First, I want you to understand one thing. What I have to tell you is strictly confidential. If you speak about it to anyone I can promise that your right to remain in this country will be revoked. You may even face court charges." He saw the sudden look of fear on her face and said, "I'm sorry for being so blunt, Anna, but you'll understand why when I've finished. I want to put a proposition to you. If you say no to what I'm going to propose then I walk away from here and you never see me again and this conversation never took place. If you say yes, then we talk some more. Is that much clear, Anna?"

She was still looking at him, confusion on her face, and Massey said gently, "Don't be afraid. Whatever your answer is, it in no way affects your right to remain in America. But I want to make it clear that you speak to no one about this conversation."

She nodded slowly. "I understand."

"Good. Now we've got that part out of the way." He sat down and took his time before he began. "Anna . . . The people I work for, they need a woman to be part of a mission. A very sensitive mission."

She stared back at him. "What sort of mission? You mean something to do with the military?"

Massey shook his head and half smiled. "Not the military, Anna. And I can't tell you who right now. But let's just say these people plan to send a man, an American, into Russia. Moscow to be precise. They need a woman to accompany him, someone who's recently been in the Soviet Union. Someone who knows her way around and wouldn't feel or look out of place. This woman would have to act at being the man's wife. It would be dangerous and difficult and there's no guarantee she'd come back."

"I don't understand. What has this got to do with me?"

"The people I spoke about want you to be that woman."

Massey studied her face. She looked totally confused. For several long moments she stared back at him.

"I don't understand? You're asking *me* to go to Moscow?"

"I know it sounds crazy. What you escaped from doesn't bear thinking about. To ask you to go back again is like asking you to return to hell. But not for nothing, Anna. Like I said, there's something these people can do for you in return."

She looked at Massey, totally dumbstruck, then she said, "What?"

"Get you your daughter back."

Massey studied her reaction. It was as if a painful, terrible wound had opened. Her face drained of color and she didn't speak for several moments, the dark eyes probing Massey's face.

"Anna, I told you before this conversation began all I needed to know after I put the proposition to you was do we keep talking, or do I walk away from here and we never see each other again."

She stared at him and Massey saw the wet eyes. "You didn't lie when you said you can get Sasha out of Russia? You can really do that? You can bring her to America?"

"It can be done, Anna. You'll just have to trust me." He stood up slowly. "Do you want a little time to think about what I've said? If you like I can take a walk and come back in an hour."

She stared back at him. For several moments she stood there, tears at the edges of her dark eyes.

"No, I want to hear what you have to say."

Massey put a hand gently on her shoulder and said, "How about I fix us some more tea? Then we can talk this over."

She sat there listening intently. When Massey had finished she asked, "How long would I be in Russia?"

"At the outside, ten days. But that's not something I can guarantee. We'll do our best to keep it as brief as possible. But it will be dangerous, Anna. Make no mistake. I'd be lying if I told you otherwise."

"What is this man going to do in Moscow?"

"Kill someone."

Massey said the words so matter-of-factly he thought she would be shocked, but she didn't react, her face blank.

"Who?"

"That's not something you need to know."

"Then am I allowed to ask why?"

"You don't need to know the answer to that question either. But you'll be long gone from Moscow before it happens." He paused. "Anna, I'll be honest with you. It's a very difficult and dangerous operation. And like I said, you may not come back. But that's a risk you're going to have to take to get your daughter back."

She hesitated a moment."Why did you come to me?"

Massey smiled. "I guess the people I speak for think you have all the right qualifications for the job. You speak Russian and you know the country."

"You didn't tell me how you'd get my daughter out. You didn't tell me how you'd find her."

He shook his head. "And I can't. Not until I know you agree to go along with what I've proposed. But what we do know will help. She's in an orphanage, probably in Moscow. We have contacts in Moscow through the émigré organizations. Underground groups and dissidents. People who could help us find your daughter. It's not going to be easy—in fact, it's going to be downright difficult—but if you go along with this then you'll have my word the deal will be kept. Not only that, but I'll arrange new identities for you and Sasha, and whatever you'll need materially to start a new life together afresh."

The tears had stopped but Massey saw a look like grief on her face. He guessed she had tried hard to put her daughter from her mind but had found it impossible.

He stood up slowly. "Maybe things are moving a little too fast for you right now. And I guess my vagueness hasn't helped, but like I said I can't tell you any more until I know where I stand."

He wrote down a phone number on a slip of paper. "You need to be alone to think this through. I'm staying at the Carlton off Lexington Avenue. Room 107. You can contact me there when you make up your mind. There's someone at the hotel I want you to meet. He'll have the final decision whether you go to Moscow or not. But call me tonight one way or the other."

As Massey left the note on the table Anna shook her head. "That's not necessary. I've already thought about it. The answer is yes."

Slanski sat in the room on the eighth floor of the hotel off Lexington Avenue, sipping a Scotch. He heard the footsteps outside, then the door opened and he saw Massey standing in the doorway.

A woman stood beside him. She was very beautiful. She had high cheekbones and dark hair. She wore a simple, inexpensive black dress that emphasized her figure, and he couldn't help but admire the splendid curves of her body.

But it was her face that held him; a face he instantly reacted to. Something in those dark Slavic eyes that suggested a curious mixture of strength and remorse. It seemed like a long time before his eyes left her face, as Massey said, "Alex, meet Anna Khorev." Anna stood there staring at the man. There were a few moments of hesitation, and then she saw his eyes take her in.

It was as if they bored into her very soul, terribly frightening and terribly reassuring both at once, and it seemed he was trying to make up his mind about something.

Then he glanced at Massey, and as he looked back at Anna he suddenly smiled broadly, raised his glass in a toast, and said in Russian, "I guess it's welcome to the club."

The two men sitting in the black Packard across the street from the hotel had followed the yellow cab from Manhattan's East Side.

As Massey and Anna had climbed out, the man in the passenger seat had rolled down the window and steadied the Leica.

The light was bad but there was a wash from the blaze of lights at the front of the building and the man got two shots of the couple as they got out of the cab, another three as they went up the steps into the hotel.

14

New York.
January 27th,
8 P.M.

The man who called himself Kurt Braun had his eyes on the girl's breasts as she leaned over to place his double Scotch on the table. They were magnificent in the low-cut top, even in the dim lighting of the dingy bar on Manhattan's Lower East Side docks.

"That'll be a dollar, sir."

Braun smiled at the girl as he peeled off two singles from the wad he took from his pocket.

"Keep the change. You look like you're new here."

"Thanks, mister. I started Friday."

"Where do you come from?"

The girl smiled back. "Danville, Illinois. You ever hear of it?"

"No, I can't say that I have."

"Maybe that ain't such a bad thing."

Braun grinned back and glanced around the bar. The private club Lombardi ran as a sideline was doing good business. It was only eight but the place was buzzing already. Friday night and every young tough from the docks and visiting sailors were coming in for drinks and a look at the girls. A record was on in the background, Kay Kyser and his orchestra playing "On a Slow Boat to China."

He looked back at the girl. "Do me a favor and tell Vince that Kurt Braun is here."

"Sure."

She walked away and Braun watched her retreating buttocks wobbling beneath the tight skirt before he looked around the bar. There were a couple of dozen men in the place, and a handful of the girls were working the tables. They looked like the hookers they were, all lipstick and too much makeup and cheap flashy clothes that showed off their bedroom assets.

It was five minutes later when Vince, Lombardi's bodyguard, came to the table. Broad and well built, he had a nose that looked like it had been flattened into his face with a sledgehammer. The man hadn't a hint of grace in his body and there was a bulge under his left arm where Braun knew the holstered pistol would be.

Despite the man's appearance, Braun knew he could kill him with little effort. The two men looked at each other a moment, like prizefighters sizing each other up, before Vince spoke.

"Carlo is waiting upstairs. He said to go right on up."

Braun finished his Scotch and stood.

The sign in scratched gold lettering on the door of the second floor above the club said "Longshoreman's Union. C. Lombardi—District Chief."

Carlo Lombardi was a small fat Sicilian in his middle forties with a pencil-thin mustache. As his title suggested, he ran the Manhattan Lower East Side dockland as if it was his private territory, and besides the club downstairs he had numerous business interests, including a share in the profits from three local brothels that serviced visiting merchant sailors. Despite his harmless appearance, Lombardi had a reputation for violence, especially with a knife. The only vanity he allowed himself was occasionally combing his hair to cover the pink scalp that erupted like an angry rash through the hair.

A smart hick in the bar had once joked that Lombardi combed his hair with a wet sponge, and Lombardi had taken pleasure in waiting for him in an alleyway a block away and sticking a knife in his eyeball and twisting till the shit-kicking hick screamed like a stuck pig. No one slighted Carlo Lombardi and walked away unhurt.

He heard the knock as Vince opened the door to admit Braun.

The visitor looked small beside Lombardi's muscular bodyguard, but had a livid red scar on his left cheek and an air of menace about him that suggested he was equally as dangerous.

"Mr. Braun to see you, Mr. Lombardi."

"Leave us, Vince."

The door closed and Lombardi came around slowly from behind his cluttered desk to greet his visitor. The office blinds were drawn, cutting out the view of the East River and docks beyond the window, but the light was on overhead, and when Lombardi had shaken the man's hand, he said gruffly, "You wanna drink?"

"Scotch."

Lombardi poured two Scotches from a chrome cabinet by the window and threw in some ice cubes. He came back and handed Braun his drink before he sat down.

"You want the story on the broad?"

"That's why I'm here."

"You mind if I ask a personal question? The fuck is up? You got me watching her for months now. She does nothin'."

Braun sipped his Scotch, sat back in his chair and said sharply, "Just give me the story, Lombardi. That's why you get paid."

Lombardi sighed and reached toward a drawer and pulled out a large brown envelope, clusters of gold rings on his fat fingers. As he looked back up he smiled and said, "The new girl downstairs, you see her?"

"I saw her."

Lombardi smiled and gripped his crotch. "She's as green as cow shit but she's a fucking rodeo in the hay. She also likes it rough, know what I mean?"

Braun didn't smile. "Tell me what you have for me."

"That's what I like about you, Mr. Braun. Everything is click-click. Direct and to the point. Busy man. Places to go, things to do." Lombardi handed across the envelope. "It's all written up the way you wanted it. Nothing much new, except the girl had a visitor."

"Who?"

"A guy. Stayed one night at the Carlton, off Lexington Avenue. Name of Massey. Took the girl there too. She left after a couple of hours. That's all I know from shit." Lombardi nodded to the envelope. "It's all in there, anyway. Including the pics."

Braun opened the envelope and examined the contents briefly, looking at the photographs, then closed it again and put his hand in his inside pocket, took out another envelope and handed it across.

"For you."

"Amigo, I thank you from the bottom of my black heart."

Lombardi took the envelope in his fat hand and looked at Braun. "So what's with the Russian broad?"

"Who says she's Russian?"

"Mister, I've had my guys watching her for over two months. You think I don't learn nothing?"

Braun smiled, a cold smile, but didn't reply. Lombardi's fat hand stuffed the envelope into a drawer and banged it shut.

"OK, you pay the tab so we play it your way. As long as I don't get no Feds crawling up my ass with a hot poker."

"You won't. Just keep watching her." Braun finished his drink and stood. "It's been a pleasure doing business, Lombardi."

"Sure."

Lombardi looked up at his visitor's scarred face. "Seeing as I got to keep you happy, you want a girl before you go? No charge for the hick from Illinois if she's what you want."

This time Braun smiled back. "Why not?"

It was almost ten when Braun arrived back at the one-bedroom apartment in Brooklyn. He climbed the stairs to the fourth floor and let himself in, leaving the lights off as he closed the door. The curtains were open and he went into the kitchen to the refrigerator and picked a bottle of beer off the shelf.

As he came back into the front room he saw the man sitting in the shadows by the window. He wore an overcoat and hat and smoked a cigarette, a full glass in his hand. In the faint wash of light from the windows, Braun saw the grin on the man's face.

The man said, "Working late, Gregor?"

Braun let his breath out and said, "Christ . . . I wish you wouldn't do that, Arkashin."

The man named Arkashin laughed and stood up. "I helped myself to some of your excellent Scotch. I hope you don't mind."

Feliks Arkashin was short and stocky. His fleshy cheeks were limp and sagging, small eyes hard in a weathered face. It wasn't a handsome face; there was a large dark mole on his left jaw, tufts of hair sprouting from the blemish, and his skin had the texture of leather. At forty-eight he was an attaché with the Soviet Mission to the United Nations in New York. In reality he held the rank of major in the KGB. Braun looked at him.

"You're taking a risk coming here. You could have been followed."

Arkashin smiled. "They tried as usual. And as usual I lost them in the subway. A wily old fox will always lose the hunter, my dear Gregor. Besides, I quite like the thrill of the chase."

Braun crossed to the window. The lights of New York dazzled him beyond the glass and as he stood there he drank from the bottle and smoked his cigarette.

"So why the visit?"

"You have the report on the woman?"

Braun raised his eyebrows, a trace of anger in his voice. "Is that all? You could have waited until you picked it up from the drop tomorrow."

"There's been a directive from Moscow on the woman in today's diplomatic bag. I need to make a decision tonight."

Braun looked back, surprise on his face. "What directive?"

"Let's hear your report first, Gregor."

Braun told him and Arkashin scratched the mole on his jaw and raised his eyebrows.

"Interesting. You trust Lombardi?"

"I'd sooner trust the devil himself. Moscow may secretly contribute to his union, but he has his fat fingers in a lot of pies, most of them illegal. And that's dangerous."

Arkashin shrugged. "We have no choice but to use him. If the Americans discovered us mounting our own surveillance operation, there would be hell to pay. This way, we keep everything at arm's length. Besides, Lombardi owes us. Without our help he'd still be a union steward."

"So who do you think this man Massey might be?"

Arkashin put down his glass. For a long time he seemed to have difficulty making up his mind about something, then he said, "Who knows? The photographs Lombardi's men took are not the best quality, amateurish really, but they may help. I'll have our people check and see if any of our station officers recognize him."

"And in the meantime?"

"In the meantime you tell Lombardi you want the woman watched more closely. A twenty-four-hour operation. And tell him you may have a job for him soon that will pay well." Arkashin grinned. "I'm sure Lombardi will appreciate that."

"What sort of job?"

Arkashin looked across and smiled. "You know Moscow doesn't like it when the Americans slight us, Gregor. We need to let them know they can't make fools of us."

"Is she that important?"

"No, but it's a question of principle."

"So what does Lombardi have to do?"

Arkashin said, "When the time is right we're going to take the girl back to Moscow. We'll need Lombardi to kidnap her. You think he'll do it?"

"He'll do anything you tell him for money. But taking her back to Moscow is going to be difficult."

Arkashin put down his glass and stubbed out his cigarette. "I agree. But Lombardi controls the docks. Getting her on board a Soviet vessel shouldn't be difficult. But we have another option should it prove impossible."

"And what's that?"

"A repeat performance of the one you carried out so well in Switzerland." Arkashin smiled. "You kill her."

PART THREE

February 1st–22nd 1953

15

New Hampshire.
February 1st

She saw the lake and the wooden house as they came around the bend in the narrow private road. There was snow on the mountains in the distance and the forested scenery below looked remarkably wild and beautiful, like a Russian landscape.

When Slanski halted the car, Massey opened the door for her and took her suitcase. "Let's get you settled in, then I'll fill you in on what happens next."

Anna looked out at the water and the forest landscape and said to Slanski, "Jake said it was beautiful here, but I never expected it would look like a part of Russia."

Slanski smiled. "There used to be parts around here where Russian was spoken. Small communities of fur trappers and hunters mostly, who came over in the last century. I guess the scenery made them feel at home."

He took them inside and showed Anna to a small bedroom upstairs.

"This is your room. It's a bit basic, I'm afraid, but it's warm and reasonably comfortable. When you've finished unpacking I'll be downstairs."

She noticed Slanski look at her, his eyes faintly lingering on her face a moment, and then he left. There was a single bed and a chair and the window overlooked the lake. Someone had left some flowers in a vase by the window and fresh towels beside an enamel water jug and basin on a stand in the corner. When she had unpacked and washed she went back downstairs and found Massey and Slanski sitting at the pinewood table drinking coffee.

Slanski said, "Sit down, Anna."

She sat and Slanski poured her coffee. She studied his face when he wasn't looking. It was neither handsome nor unattractive, but there was a look in his eyes she had noticed when she first met him, a look like something wasn't right about the man, and there was a faint smile at the corners of his mouth that suggested he found life oddly amusing.

Now he looked across at her and sat. The smile was gone from his face as he said, "First things first. You're completely sure you know what you're doing?"

"I wouldn't have come here if I wasn't."

"Jake told you that you might have to face dangers. But are you certain you're prepared to face them?"

She looked at Slanski steadily. "Yes."

"Then there are some ground rules I want you to understand that apply as long as you're here. About the mission, you don't talk to anyone you meet apart from us here. Did Jake explain about Vassily?"

"Yes, briefly."

"Although he's completely trustworthy, for the sake of security you don't discuss the mission with him. But don't worry about that, he won't ask. We'll be doing some preparation together for the journey but in ten days' time a man will arrive. His name's Popov. He's going to put us through some pretty rigorous training, both in Soviet weapons and self-defense. It's a precaution really, for your sake, so you'll know how to handle yourself if you get in a difficult situation. But on no account do you talk to Popov about our intentions or discuss anything about our plans. Is that understood?"

She looked briefly at Massey. He was staring at her. "Anna, while you're here Alex is in charge. You do as he says."

She looked back at Slanski. "Very well. I agree."

"Good. Another rule. You work hard and do your utmost to absorb everything you're going to learn. I want to be sure of who I'm going in with. I want to be sure I can depend on you."

"You can."

Slanski stood up slowly. "OK. Concerning the mission itself, and just to let you know, when the time comes we'll be going into Russia through one of the Baltic states, landing by parachute. Estonia to be precise. You've been to Estonia?"

Anna nodded. "My father served there as a commander with the Red Army."

Slanski said shortly, "Then let's just hope when we get there the Estonian resistance we're depending on to help us don't get to know about it. At all times during the mission, while it's necessary, we'll behave as man and wife. If things go according to plan, we'll make our way to Moscow using regular transport, trains and buses, via Leningrad. We'll have a predetermined route and enough contacts to help us as we need. If things go against us for whatever reasons, then we'll just have to change our plans to suit the situation. Once we reach Moscow—*if* we reach Moscow—you'll be passed on to another contact to be taken back to America."

"How?"

"Jake will tell you all that before we go. As well as everything else you need to know." Anna looked from Massey to Slanski. "You make it sound easy. What about the routine checks on travelers in the Soviet Union? What about the paperwork needed for the journey? What happens if we're separated or one or both of us are caught?"

"It *won't* be easy. In fact, it's going to be damned difficult. Especially just after we parachute. Estonia is crawling with Soviet troops. It's a garrison country and some of the Baltic Fleet are based there. In many ways traveling in Estonia will be more difficult than Russia itself. As to your other questions, you'll get the answers all in good time."

Anna said, "I've never parachuted before."

Slanski shook his head. "Don't worry, we'll sort that out too."

He checked his watch before saying to Massey, "I've got to pick up some supplies in town. You want to show Anna around? Vassily should be back soon. He's taken the boat out on the lake to do some fishing."

Massey nodded. Slanski picked up some keys from the table and crossed to the door and went out. Anna heard the jeep start up moments later and drive off.

Massey looked at Anna's face. "What's wrong?"

"Something I saw in his eyes. Either he doesn't like me or he doesn't trust me."

Massey smiled. "I wouldn't say that. If Alex is blunt, it's because he has your safety in mind. But he's always blunt when it comes to tactical business. Granted, he's also a difficult man to get to know. But don't worry, you'll be fine."

"I'm not worried, Jake."

"Good." Massey smiled. "Come on, let's see if we can find Vassily. I think you're going to like him."

As they reached the lake minutes later a small boat was coming in, its outboard motor rupturing the silence, sounding like a metal wasp as it came into the shore.

The old man sat in the bow, and when he saw Massey he waved. He wore a deerskin jacket and an old woollen deerstalker cap with the ear flaps pulled down. There was a big sheathed knife on a leather belt around his waist, and Anna recognized something familiar in the man's features as he climbed out of the boat and tied up. He studied her face briefly before he shook Massey's hand.

He spoke in English, his accent heavily broken. "Massey. Welcome. Alexei told me you'd be coming."

"Vassily, I'd like you to meet Anna. Anna, this is Vassily."

Anna looked at the man again. Though far from handsome, there was something warm about his face, a kindness in his brown eyes she found instantly endearing, and when she offered her hand and the old man shook it, she said instinctively, "*Zdrastvuti.*"

He smiled and replied in Russian. "Welcome, Anna. Welcome to my house. Alexei never said you were Russian."

"From Moscow. And you?"

"Kuzomen."

Now she recognized the old man's features, the dark Laplander looks of those who inhabited Russia's northern tundra.

"You're a long way from home."

A big smile creased the man's brown face. "A very long way and too far to go back. But this place is just like home. And we Russians are like good wine. We travel well." He looked at Massey. "Where's Alexei?"

"Gone to town to pick up supplies."

"Did he offer our guest bread and salt?"

It was an old Russian tradition with visitors, and Massey smiled and said, "Just coffee, I'm afraid."

The old man removed his hat and shook his head. "Typical. Like all the young he forgets tradition. Come, let me do the honors, Anna. Give me your arm."

Vassily held out his arm to her and Anna slipped her hand through his.

She winked at Massey as he stood there amused, and let the old man lead them up to the house.

Anna looked up as Massey smiled over at her.

"You know, I think he likes you."

Massey was standing at the window smoking a cigarette twenty minutes later when he saw the jeep pull up outside.

Slanski climbed out and carried two cardboard boxes of supplies up to the house. Massey opened the door for him and when Slanski had put the boxes away he looked at the two long wooden crates Massey had placed on the floor and kicked one of them with his boot.

"What's in the boxes?"

Massey said, "Everything you'll need for when Popov arrives. Better stash it in a safe place; there's enough weapons and munitions in there to start a war."

"There's a cold storage room under the kitchen. We can leave them there."

"Where's the girl?"

"Vassily's taken her for a tour of the place. He's taken quite a shine to her."

"It's just been a long time since he's smelled perfume. But suddenly I'm not so sure about her, Jake."

"You've got doubts already? What happened to your instinct?"

Slanski shook his head."One look at her was enough to tell me she's got what it takes. But it's her life you're risking. I don't think she fully realizes what she's getting herself into here. Once she's with me, I think she'll be OK. But if we have to part company because of trouble I'm not sure she's capable of making it on her own."

"You ought to give her more credit, Alex. I told you. Trust me. And remember, she's spent almost a year in the Gulag. Anyone who can survive that and do what she did to escape isn't going to give in easily. And she'll be fine once Popov puts her through her paces."

"Another thing. She's far too pretty. She'll attract attention."

"Then why did you agree to having her along?"

Slanski smiled. "Maybe for that very reason. You know me, I'm a sucker for a pretty face."

Massey smiled back and shook his head. "You're anything but, my friend. But we can have that problem sorted out when the time comes. It's amazing what clever make-up and a bad hairstyle can do to alter someone's appearance."

"You ought to know, Jake."

"Funny."

Massey removed an envelope from his inside pocket and handed it across.

"What's this?"

"Your list of contacts in Russia and the Baltic. You need to memorize the details between now and the day of departure, then destroy the list."

Slanski glanced at the envelope. "How did you get in touch with them?"

"I haven't, not yet, but leave that to me. If there's any change in the names I'll let you know. I've arranged to make contact with our partisan friends in Tallinn who'll pick you up after you drop, if everything goes according to plan."

Slanski put the envelope in his pocket. "So what do you want me to do with the girl in the meantime?"

"Give her a couple of days to let her get used to the place, then start to get her into shape. And yourself. Daily runs and exercises. Be tough with her. It's for her own good. It's a long way from Tallinn to Moscow and you don't know what to expect, so you both want to be fit. Another thing, seeing as you'll both be parachuting in and we can't use any of our training camps, you'll have to do the best you can in that department. Seeing as Anna hasn't dropped before you'll have to cover the basics to make sure she doesn't do damage to herself when she falls."

"And what will you be doing while we're sweating it out here?"

"Me?" Massey smiled. "I'll be in Paris enjoying myself."

16

When the Red Army rolled over the plains of Poland on its way to crush Berlin and the German Reich, Henri Lebel had been liberated from Auschwitz concentration camp.

The Russian officer who had gone through the camp huts with his men searching for the still living among the dead had taken one look at the Frenchman's emaciated body lying on the lice-ridden bunk, at the spindly legs and arms and soulless eyes, and said, "Leave him. The poor bastard's dead."

It was only when they carried Lebel's body to the mass grave along with the other wasted corpses and heard the faint gasp of breath and saw the flicker of life in Lebel's eyes that they decided the man was definitely still alive.

There had been two long months spent in a Russian field hospital to build up his strength before he was handed over to the British and allowed to return to his native Paris.

Lebel had survived the war but it was a war that had cost him his wife, gassed, then burned in the ovens of Auschwitz, not only because she was Jewish, but because Lebel had been a member of the French Communist Resistance.

For the last eight years he had resumed the furrier trade his father, an émigré Russian Jew, had begun in Paris. Henri Lebel had gradually built it up into a flourishing business, outfitting the Parisian rich with the best of Russian sable and fur, and in the process turning himself into a wealthy man, with a resident suite at the Ritz Hotel and a luxury villa in Cannes.

There were frequent trips to Moscow, where his resistance connections had gone down well with the Soviet authorities, and as a result Lebel had managed to turn his company into a virtual monopoly, with sole rights in Europe to sell the finest Russian sable and fur. And with America beginning to boom in the postwar years, he had even opened a thriving branch on New York's Fifth Avenue.

Life, it seemed, despite its horrors, had turned out reasonably well for

Henri Lebel. But unknown to his business contacts in Moscow, he had a dark secret he kept hidden from them.

There were milestones in his troubled life which Henri Lebel remembered with great clarity. The day he and Klara were arrested by the Gestapo. The day he had met Irena Dezov. And the day he had begun to live again after the horror of Auschwitz.

The first, the arrest in Paris two years after the Germans invaded, he could never forget.

It was his wife's birthday, and after several months of hiding he had decided to risk taking her out to celebrate. As he sat in the Paris café with Klara that Saturday morning, barely enjoying the wartime ersatz coffee and the stodgy cakes, the door had burst in and three men in plain clothes entered. Lebel saw the black leather coats and gloves and the slouch hats and an icy chill ran through his veins. As it stood, he was already a wanted man for his resistance activities.

The three men stood in the center of the café, hands on their hips, the sharp voice of the man in charge still perfectly clear in Lebel's memory.

"*Papieren*! Everybody get their papers ready!"

And then the grim joke that rang around the café as the Gestapo man grinned. "And if there are any Jews among you, start saying your prayers."

The laughter that followed from the Gestapo men still echoed in Henri Lebel's ears. He had looked at his wife, her beautiful face draining of color. Lebel could still remember the feeling that spring morning. Icy fear. Sweat breaking out all over his body, his heart pumping in his ears, ready to burst. He was a *résistant*, and worse, a Jewish *résistant.*

The three men went through the café checking papers. The one in charge came to Lebel's table. He smiled down at Klara, then looked at Lebel.

"Papieren, bitte."

Lebel promptly handed over his papers. The Gestapo man was tall, thin-faced, with piercing blue eyes. It was a face that was to live vividly in Lebel's head day and night. The eyes flicked slowly from the photograph in the papers to Lebel's face, as if the Gestapo man were trying to make up his mind about something.

The eyes narrowed. Lebel's hands were shaking and he guessed the man noticed.

The Gestapo man smiled coldly and said, "Where were these papers issued?"

Lebel could hear the silence in the café as the man spoke. He saw his wife glance at him nervously.

"Marseilles, sir," Lebel answered respectfully, trying to keep his composure. The place of issue was already stamped on the papers. Lebel had got rid of his own papers and had been given forged ones by the Resistance. His new family name was Claudel. It had worked for six months. But now Lebel thought the Gestapo man sensed something wasn't right.

He continued to scrutinize the papers, then looked up. "Your occupation, Herr Claudel?"

Lebel swallowed. His occupation was typed on the document. "I am a salesman." He paused, decided to be bold and risk everything. "Is there a problem with our papers? There really shouldn't be, you know."

"That's for me to decide," the Gestapo man snapped back, then looked down at Lebel's wife. There were tiny beads of perspiration on Klara's upper lip, her hands trembling in her lap as she clutched her napkin.

The Gestapo man had sensed her fear. He looked back at Lebel and said, "Your wife, Herr Claudel, she seems afraid of something. I wonder what?"

The question hung in the air like an accusation. Lebel felt his heart sink. He answered as calmly as he could.

"She hasn't been well, I'm afraid."

The man looked at Klara. "Really? And what has been the matter, Frau Claudel?"

Lebel decided to brazen it out.

"Really, officer," he interrupted. "My wife's health is no concern of yours. We are both upright French citizens. And if you must know, my wife suffers with her nerves. And really, this intrusion of yours is not helping matters. So please be so kind as to return our papers if you have finished examining them." He held out his hand boldly as he tried to keep it from shaking.

The Gestapo man sneered before he slowly handed back the papers.

"My apologies, Herr Claudel," he said politely. "I hope your wife's condition improves. Enjoy your coffee and cake."

The Gestapo men left. Lebel could not help the feeling of relief and triumph that surged through his body.

It did not last long.

They came later that night.

Lebel heard the screech of tires in the street below their safe apartment, heard the pounding fists on the door. As he flicked on the light and went to grab the pistol he kept hidden under the pillow, the door burst in on its hinges.

Half a dozen men in plain clothes crowded into the room, the thin-faced man from the café leading them, a sneer on his face.

He smashed Lebel in the mouth with a leather-gloved fist. Then Lebel was on the floor and the man was kicking him senseless. "Get up, Jew! Get up!"

When they dragged him to his feet two of his ribs were broken and his shoulder dislocated. The other men were already moving through the apartment, ransacking the rooms. His wife was dragged screaming from her bed and bundled downstairs.

Everything after that was a troubling, painful memory. Lebel could never forget the nightmare that followed. The separation from Klara. The brutal interrogation in the Gestapo cellars on the avenue Foch. And when they told him his wife had been sent to Poland for resettlement, Henri Lebel knew it was a lie and feared the worst.

For a week the Gestapo tortured him, trying to pry information from him about his resistance connections. Despite the beatings, the torture, the sleepless nights, he held out and told them nothing. Two days later he was put on a cattle train to Auschwitz extermination camp. There he endured almost two long years of painful humiliation, surviving only because of his will to survive.

And there he first met Irena Dezov.

A young Red Army driver in her late twenties, she had been captured and sent to Auschwitz along with a ragged convoy of Russian prisoners. She was eventually put to work in the warehouse where Lebel had to sift through the clothes from the cattle-train transports of prisoners sent to the camp. Irena Dezov was a handsome woman, and despite the appalling camp conditions she was full of humor and vitality, and with a fondness for the illegal vodka the prisoners distilled. But although Lebel spoke fluent Russian he had hardly exchanged a word with her in the two months they had worked together, until, that was, the day he found out with certainty the fate of his wife.

Since arriving at Auschwitz he had been driven half mad wondering what had happened to Klara, hoping that somehow she might still be alive. When he learned that a trainload of French Jews had reached the camp two days before his own arrival, he gave Klara's name and a description to a kapo in the women's section he had become friendly with and asked her to help.

The woman came to him a week later and confirmed his fears. "Your wife was gassed the day she arrived. Then burned in the crematorium. I'm sorry, Henri."

Lebel had looked at the woman in horror, expecting the worst, but not wanting to believe it. He went to his filthy bunk and lay there, curled up in a ball, weeping.

Images and memories raged like a fire through his mind. The day he had first met Klara, and how innocent she looked, and how much he had wanted to protect her. The first time he told her he loved her, and the first time they made love. The grief and anguish that flooded his body was unbearable. When he finally dragged himself from his bed he removed his camp tunic and tied it to the top bunk. He put his neck in the noose. Then he let his body go with the fall.

As he slowly strangled, he heard the scream.

"Henri!"

Irena burst into the hut and struggled to free him, Lebel protesting, wanting to die. But Irena would have none of it, the two of them struggling on the floor, Lebel gasping and punching the young Russian woman.

"Get away! Leave me to die!"

"No, Henri, no . . ."

It took Irena all her might to calm Lebel, to help him to the bed. And then he was curled up in a ball again on the bunk, crying his eyes out. Irena put a hand firmly on his shoulder. "The kapo told me. I came here to see if I could help comfort you."

Tears streamed down Lebel's cheeks. "You should have let me kill myself. Why did you stop me? Why? You have no right . . ."

"I do have a right, Henri Lebel. We Jews must stick together. You and I, we're going to survive. Do you hear?"

Lebel looked into Irena's face. "You . . . a Jew?"

"Yes. Me, a Jew."

"But the Germans don't know?"

"And why should I tell them? They have enough Jews to kill."

Lebel stared back at her, his pain deflected. "Why didn't you tell me?"

Irena smiled and shrugged. "What does it matter what a man or woman is? Does it change your opinion of me?"

"No."

"Good. Take some of this."

She handed him a small bottle of illegal spirit. He refused, but she made him drink.

She looked into his face, this cheerful Russian woman, and he saw compassion in her eyes.

"And now, Henri Lebel, I want us to say *kaddish* together. And then you're going to go back to work and you're going to try to forget your pain. But remember one thing. The death of your wife does not have to go unpunished. Some day, the world will want to know about this camp. But for that to happen some of us must survive. Do you understand me, Henri Lebel?"

Lebel nodded. He wiped his eyes.

Irena took his hand and smiled. "Come, let us kneel and say *kaddish* for your family."

It was so unreal. In the midst of all the pain and death around him, Lebel had knelt with the young Russian woman and said the ancient prayer for the dead. Afterwards he had cried again, and Irena had put a hand on his shoulder and hugged him. And then she had made the supreme gesture any woman could make to comfort a man. She offered him her body.

Not for sex, but for solace. Despite the filthy barrack surroundings and their unwashed bodies, there was a beauty and a touching kindness to the lovemaking which somehow reaffirmed Henri Lebel's belief in humanity, and as Irena held him close afterwards, she had whispered in his ear, "Remember, my little Frenchman. Only in surviving will there be justice."

After that day, Henri Lebel and Irena Dezov had become friends as well as lovers. They endured the endless humiliations of camp life, laughed together when they could, shared what scraps of food they managed to scavenge to supplement their meager rations of watery turnip soup and stale black bread, and got drunk on illegal spirits whenever possible, anything to relieve the agony and pain around them.

The last time Lebel saw Irena was three days after the Russians finally liberated the camp. She was being helped to climb onto the back of a truck to take her behind Russian lines, her long frail legs barely able to stand. They kissed and embraced and promised they would write, and as the truck drove out through the gates Irena managed a smile and a wave. Lebel cried that day as much as he had when he had learned the fate of his wife.

In the five years after the war, Lebel tried to forget his past. A succession of nubile young models eager to parade in his furs on the Paris catwalks and also to give him solace had temporarily dulled the pain, but somehow Irena Dezov never left his mind.

A year later he had to visit Moscow on business, an opportunity he was to be allowed with greater frequency because of his expanding business.

On one such trip, as he came out of the Moscow Hotel, he saw a woman across the street and he froze, rooted to the spot with shock. She *looked* like Irena, only somehow different, and then Lebel realized she was no longer the emaciated skeleton in his memory but a full-figured, handsome woman, much like the one he had seen the first day she had arrived in Auschwitz. But it was *definitely* Irena. She climbed on board a tram and in panic Lebel did something he had never done before.

He evaded the KGB man delegated to chaperone him and hopped on board the tram at the last moment. His heart pounding, he sat behind the woman. When she got off he followed her to an apartment off Lenin Prospect, took note of the address, then reluctantly returned to his hotel.

The KGB chaperone was furious; Lebel was sent for by his contact in the Ministry of Foreign Trade, who demanded an explanation for the evasion.

Lebel pretended angry indignation: as a trusted friend of Russia he ought to be allowed to travel in Moscow more freely. He considered it a matter of mutual trust and he gave his word as a gentleman that he would not break that trust. Besides, he had strong business interests in Moscow and he would hardly destroy those interests by doing something he shouldn't, now would he?

The man from the Ministry merely smiled and said to him, "Impossible, Henri. You know the way it works here. Foreigners are suspect. Even if you do nothing we have to watch you."

Lebel said indignantly, "Then *you* realize this. I can buy excellent fur from the Canadians and the Americans and without the irritation of being followed everywhere I go in New York or Quebec."

The man's face paled just a little, but then he smiled. "Is that a threat, Henri?"

"No, simply a fact. And another thing. I fought for the Communist Resistance in France. I lost my wife and was sent to Auschwitz for my ideals. You people know I'm not a spy."

The man laughed. "Of course we know you're not a spy, Henri, but you're a businessman, not a communist."

"That doesn't stop me from having certain . . . sympathies." Lebel's sympathies had long since vanished but business was business. "Besides, some of the wealthiest businessmen in France supported the Communist Resistance during the war."

"True. But I still can't grant you your request."

Lebel tossed aside the refusal and said very angrily, "Then I suggest you seriously consider this. I'm tired with these petty games you people play. Tired of being followed like some mistrusted schoolboy. Tired of being scrutinized like some unwelcome guest and feeling half a dozen pairs of eyes on me every time I go to the bathroom. I'm considering no longer representing your interests in Europe. Quite frankly, it's not worth the bother. I can buy my furs elsewhere."

The man permitted himself a knowing grin. "But not sable, Henri. You have to come to us for that. Besides, we could simply have someone else represent us."

It was true—and Russian sable fur was the finest and the most sought-after—but Lebel had an ace up his sleeve.

"Not *Russian* sable. But a firm in Canada have bred a marten species not unlike yours and believe me the sable pelts are the finest I've come across. So either we stop this petty pantomime and you trust me, or I go to them."

Lebel stood up to leave.

"No—wait, Henri. I'm certain we can resolve this."

That settled it. A couple of phone calls to the upper echelons of the Ministry and a fine sable coat for the official's wife finally clinched the deal. Lebel would be bestowed with honorary Soviet citizenship, which would do away with the need for him to be under surveillance as a foreigner.

The next day he went back to the apartment off Lenin Prospect, checking to make sure he wasn't followed. He wasn't. It was still a terrible risk but he considered it worth it. He knocked on the door and Irena appeared.

When she saw him she went white, and when the shock subsided her eyes were wet as she led him inside the two-room apartment.

For a long time they embraced and kissed and cried. There were two things Lebel learned that day. One, that he still loved Irena Dezov, and much more than he even realized, and two, rather more disturbing, that she was married. Or rather had been when they had their affair in the camp. The husband, a much older, stern-faced army colonel, had later died in the final battle for Berlin.

Somehow Lebel wasn't unduly bothered by conscience about their affair in the camp. With death so close you took what human comfort you could. Besides, there was no such thing as a truly honest businessman, and in business he had sometimes committed sins considerably worse than adultery. And Irena wasn't sad about it, quite the opposite. She confessed that the day she learned of her husband's death she opened a bottle of vodka and got quietly drunk with joy. The man was a brute and the only good he had done was leave her an army widow's pension and a country dacha on the outskirts of Moscow.

They made love that day with an intensity Lebel had never known, and did so every time afterwards that they could get to Irena's dacha, which offered them privacy.

That first day together in years, as they lay in bed, she had prodded his generous stomach and laughed.

"You're no longer a skeleton, Henri. You've grown fat, my little Frenchman. But I still love you."

He *had* grown plump, but he saw the look on her face when she said it and knew she still loved him too.

Irena Dezov was certainly no longer a skeleton. Her body had filled out, her bust rather larger and even more comforting than he remembered, her lust for life and lovemaking still unquenched.

But Lebel knew Irena would *never* be allowed out of Russia, despite his connections. *Nobody* was allowed out of Stalin's Russia. Dissidents were shot, committed to asylums, or imprisoned for life, not given exit visas. Even applying for an emigrant visa condemned the applicant as a traitor, which meant the firing squad or the Gulag. And each time he and Irena met, four, six times a year, more if possible, he had to take particular care he wasn't followed, developing an elaborate sense of subterfuge and timing to travel to the dacha.

It wasn't perfect, and it wasn't safe, and every time he saw her he feared their relationship would be exposed and, worse, stopped.

But they would still take the risk and meet every time he was in Moscow.

And it would be their secret.

17

Paris.
February 3rd

The clouds hung gray and sullen over Paris that afternoon in early February, threatening rain all day, but in the luxury penthouse suite on the fifth floor of the Ritz Hotel, Henri Lebel's mind was on anything but the weather.

The sight of the two voluptuous young models who stood before him almost naked as he sat in the couch by the window sent a rippling, erotic shiver down his spine. They were tempting, too tempting almost. The curtains were drawn and the lights were on, three powerful Xenon bulbs flooding the suite, and as the fashion photographer effected some last-minute adjustments, Lebel lit a cigar and smiled at the youngest of the two girls.

"Very, very nice, Marie. Turn around now if you please."

The girl was twenty, with short dark hair and a dusky-skinned body any full-blooded Frenchman would gladly kill for. She wore only a pair of stiletto high heels and black silk stockings and a suspender belt. The girl turned, displaying a rear view of her long, elegant legs and perfectly rounded buttocks. She cocked her head as she giggled back at a smiling Lebel.

"What about the coat, Henri?"

Lebel pursed his lips and grinned. "In a moment, my sweet. Let me drink this moment in like good wine."

Marie laughed as she stood there with her hands on her hips, not a shred of embarrassment in evidence as Lebel's eyes wandered over her body.

Lebel thought: The girl is stunning, no question about it, and really ideal.

"*Très bien*, Marie. And now Claire. Your turn. Nice and slowly."

The second girl was fair-haired and nineteen. She gave Lebel a cheeky smile and turned her buttocks to him. She had splendid breasts, and as she turned Lebel was given the full benefit of their firm, pert mounds. Her ass wasn't as tantalizing as Marie's, or her legs as long, but she was a beautiful creature nonetheless, and her breasts more than made up for the deficit.

Lebel felt a warm electricity in his loins and had to suppress a sigh of pleasure.

"*Très bien*, Claire."

He stood and stubbed out his cigar in the crystal ashtray on the coffee table.

He turned to the photographer, an effete middle-aged man in a sweater and slacks, with a cravat tied around his neck, and slapped him on the shoulder. "You did well, Patric. The girls have just the look I want for the New York catalog."

"As always, a pleasure to work with you, Henri."

Despite his busy schedule, Lebel always found time to supervise personally the catalog photo-shoot for the coming winter collection, and the sumptuously decorated suite in the Ritz provided an ideal backdrop.

The photographer clapped his hands. "The sables first, girls. Let's start with the best."

The photographer had shot off a quick dozen frames with the girls in various poses, Lebel offering suggestions as he felt necessary, when there was a knock on the door. A tall sharp-featured man with the dour face of an undertaker and dressed in a black suit entered the room. He barely glanced at the two beautiful models. Charles Torrance was English and as Lebel's butler and chauffeur was discreet and had just the right air of gravitas. His honeyed voice spoke softly across the room in perfect French.

"A visitor, sir."

"Tell whoever it is to go away," Lebel snorted. "Can't you see I'm busy, Charles?"

"It's Mr. Ridgeway, sir. He says he has an appointment."

Lebel sighed. He had almost forgotten his secretary had phoned him about the appointment three days before. "Very well, tell Mr. Ridgeway I'll see him in the study." Lebel glanced back at the girls and photographer and smiled. "Champagne for everyone when they're finished, Charles. And a little caviar would be nice. The Crimean red the Soviet Ambassador sent."

The penthouse suite Henri Lebel lived in on the fifth floor of the Ritz had one of the most pleasant views in Paris, overlooking the magnificent cobbled Place Vendôme.

The suite had been occupied during the war by a senior Gestapo officer who had the luxury quarters expanded to a five-room apartment to impress his Parisian mistress. It was elegantly fitted out with period furniture and silk tapestries, and had the distinct advantage of having three separate entrances and exits. Lebel's registered offices and warehouses were in the suburb of Clichy, but he seldom if ever used them to conduct business. The suite in the Ritz was far more private.

As he stepped into the study that afternoon he saw Massey standing by the window, staring out at the pigeons swirling above the sodden Place Vendôme. The record player in the corner was on, Maria Callas in *La Bohème* playing softly in the background.

Lebel smiled as he crossed to the window, offering his hand. "Jake, good to see you." He pronounced the name like the French *Jacques*, and shook Massey's hand before glancing back at the source of the music. "I see you took the liberty. She's quite superb, Callas. Remind me if ever you want tickets when she's playing in Paris. I have a friend at the Opéra."

"Hello, Henri. I hope I didn't disrupt your afternoon? Charles said you had company."

Lebel took a cigar from a humidor on the lacquered table, lit it and blew out a cloud of smoke. "So what brings you to Paris, Jake?"

Massey looked at the chubby Frenchman. His pencil-thin mustache was neatly clipped, and close up his face was covered in fine wrinkles, masked from a distance by a deep Riviera tan, the gold Rolex watch and diamond cufflinks giving him an air of affluence.

"Just a brief visit to have a chat, Henri."

Lebel nodded toward the record player. "Is that why you put the record on, just to be certain we can't be overheard?" The Frenchman grinned. "Jake, you wouldn't trust God himself."

"That's how I've lived so long."

Lebel's eyes took in the room. "The suite is completely safe, believe me. No listening devices. I checked the rooms myself." The record playing softly in the background was unnecessary, but Lebel understood. He poured two Cognacs and handed one to Massey.

"So to what do I owe the pleasure of this visit? It's years since we last met. You never rang or wrote like you promised. You break my heart, Jake. If you were a woman I'd have given up on you long ago."

Massey smiled. "So tell me, how is business?"

"One can't complain. In fact, it's very good. Since the war ended your rich Americans have no shortage of cash. They like the best money has to offer. And they particularly like my sables and ermine. I grossed five million francs from America alone last year. A quarter of my business."

Massey's eyebrows rose. "That's good, Henri."

"Wait until next year when they see my new catalog. It's going to be even better."

Lebel smiled confidently and leaned forward and touched Massey's knee. "But enough of business. Why are you in Paris?"

"You still see any of the boys from the resistance?"

"Once a year we meet and crack open a couple of bottles and remember the dead. You should come next time. They still remember you fondly. Killing Germans was the highlight of their lives. Now they raise chickens or kids and live boring lives. How could life ever be the same?"

Massey looked around the elegant room. "You don't seem to be doing too badly. This place must be costing you plenty."

Lebel smiled. "True. But it's all down to luck and a twist of fate, *mon ami*. You know that."

"Being in the resistance has been good to you, Henri."

Lebel shrugged. "It had its price, but of course, I don't deny it. They helped with my Moscow business contacts after the war."

"That's partly why I'm here. I need a favor, Henri."

Lebel smiled. "Is it something highly dangerous or simply illegal?"

"Both. And it has to do with Moscow."

A nervous look flickered on Lebel's face, emphasizing his wrinkles. He became serious.

"Explain."

Massey put down his glass. "A man named Max Simon and his daughter were murdered in Switzerland two months ago. Both of them were shot through the head. Moscow sanctioned the killings."

Lebel put up a pudgy hand. "Jake, if it's politics, you know I don't get involved."

"Hear me out. The man responsible is an East German killer named Borovik. Gregori Borovik. That's not his real name. He uses a whole lot of aliases. He's scum, Henri, and I want to find him."

Lebel sighed and shook his head. "Jake, the contacts I have don't talk about such things."

"All I'm asking is that you make a few discreet inquiries. You know everyone in the Soviet Embassy in Paris. You're personal friends with the Ambassador."

"It's not a friendship that extends to discussing the nastier side of intelligence life."

"Max Simon was a personal friend of mine. His daughter was only ten years old."

Lebel's face paled slightly with distaste before he shook his head firmly. "Jake, I'm sorry to hear that, but you're wasting your time."

Massey sighed and stood up. "OK, let's put that aside. Right now you're the biggest dealer in Russian fur in Europe. Apart from diplomatic staff and a handful of Western businessmen in oil, tobacco and diamonds, you're one of the few people allowed to visit Moscow almost at will. And seeing as Moscow's pretty much a closed city right now, I guess that makes you kind of special."

Lebel nodded thoughtfully before sipping his cognac. "That's true. But to use an American expression, cut the crap, Jake. Get to the point."

Massey smiled back and his face didn't flinch when he said, "I need you to take some people out of Moscow for me on one of your private goods trains."

Lebel's mouth opened and before the cigar could fall from his mouth he pinched it hard between his thumb and forefinger and frowned in disbelief.

"Let me get this right, Jake. You want *me* to smuggle people out of Russia?"

Massey nodded. "Three people, to be exact."

Lebel laughed, a derisory snort. "Jake, have you lost your mind?"

"I'm not asking you to do it for nothing. It's a business arrangement, pure and simple. You'll be well rewarded."

"Correction, *mon ami*. It would be suicide, pure and simple. Besides, money I don't need."

Lebel looked down at the square below. The rain had finally come, lashing down on the shiny cobbles, pigeons scattering to the rooftops. He looked back at Massey.

"Jake, please understand, I'm a fur dealer, not a travel agent. I make a good life out of my trade with the Russians. You know what would happen if they found out I was smuggling people out? I'd be making snowballs in some godforsaken camp in Siberia for the rest of my life."

"Hear me out first, Henri."

Lebel shook his head. "Jake, it's pointless. God himself wouldn't convince me to take such a risk."

Massey stood. "I said hear me out. How many trainloads of furs do you take out of Russia each year?"

Lebel shrugged his shoulders and sighed. "Four, maybe six in a good year. It depends on demand."

"In sealed carriages?"

"Yes, in sealed carriages. Six carriages a train."

"And you're always there to accompany the goods?"

Lebel nodded. "Of course. With such a valuable cargo, I can't take a risk. Even with Stalin in command there are bandits near the border with Finland. I lease a train privately from the Russians that travels from Moscow to Helsinki."

"Do the Russians check you both sides of the border, going in and coming out?"

Lebel smiled. "The border guards check all the carriages with sniffer dogs, Jake. Believe me, nothing goes in or out of that country without Moscow knowing about it."

"You mean *almost* nothing."

Massey took an envelope from his inside jacket. He handed it across to Lebel.

"If that's money, Jake, I told you, forget it."

"It's not money. It's a confidential report. I want you to read it, Henri."

Lebel took the unsealed envelope and opened it. Inside was a single page. He read the page and his face dropped. As he looked back at Massey the Frenchman had the startled look of a fox caught with a chicken in his mouth.

"What's the meaning of this?" Lebel said almost angrily.

"As you can see, it's a report on the last three consignments you exported from Russia. You've been a naughty boy, haven't you, Henri? You had a hundred and twenty more sable pelts than you claimed in the customs declaration, all hidden in a secret compartment under the train."

Massey held out his hand and Lebel returned the report, white-faced. He slumped into his chair and stared up at Massey. "How did you know?"

"The Finnish customs found the compartment under the carriage's floorboards. They had a discreet look at your train in Helsinki Station after it came back from Moscow two trips ago. Naturally, they reported it to us, just in case our friends in Moscow were up to something. But now I know they're not. It's your operation, isn't it, Henri? Who else knows about this? Anyone in Russia?"

"The train driver," admitted Lebel. "In fact, the method was his idea. He saw it done during the war by certain criminals in Moscow, when food was being smuggled in from the country for the black market."

"Can he be trusted?"

Lebel shrugged. "As much as any crook can be trusted. He has a weakness for a certain ravishing young Finnish lady who lives near the border in Russian-occupied Karelia. A big girl whose tastes run to expensive French champagne and naughty silk underwear which I provide him with. I guess he'll do anything for sex and money, but then won't most men?"

"But it is your operation, isn't it, Henri?"

An anxious smile flickered on Lebel's pale face. "Jake, you've no idea what the Finns charge me in import taxes. Their inland revenue would put a highwayman to shame."

"So naturally, when your friend found a way around it, you jumped in."

Lebel gestured with his cigar at the report in Massey's hand. "Until you showed me that I thought I'd done the clever thing, but now I know I was foolish. OK, Jake, what's the story? You get the gendarmes to slap the bracelets on me and haul me away?"

"The American Embassy in Helsinki advised the Finns to hold their fire for the moment." Massey smiled briefly. "But I've a feeling things might get pretty difficult for your company if the Finns prosecute. And after that I think you'd find America was a closed door for your business. You'd be ruined, Henri."

"Don't tell me, but you can save me from all that?"

Massey smiled. "If you were willing to cooperate."

Lebel sat back with a sigh. "I was waiting for this."

"First tell me how you got around the Russians. Don't they check your train?"

"Of course, but only coming in over the Finnish border, not coming out. The carriages are examined by the Finns after we cross the Russian border into their territory."

"Who else is in on this?"

Lebel hesitated. "Certain greedy associates I deal with in Russia. Bureaucrats and railway officials. In fact, it was they who put the train driver up to it. For a small consideration they make sure the Russian guards turn a blind eye when the train passes through the border checkpoint."

"Did you ever take out *people* for Moscow?"

Lebel shook his head fiercely. "Jake, I don't work for the KGB. Nor do the people I deal with, I swear it. Their sole motivation is money. But to take people instead of furs would be impossible, believe me, and the train driver would never agree. Furs are one thing, people quite another. He'd be shot for such a thing, not to mention me if I was caught."

"What if the plan was foolproof?"

"Jake, no plan is foolproof, especially where the Russians are concerned."

"Foolproof and worth half a million francs. Swiss francs, that is. Paid into your own Swiss account once you agree to help. And if you do what I ask about Max Simon, there's a cherry on the cake."

"A formidable sum, but I'm still not interested." Lebel frowned with curiosity. "What's the cherry?"

"The Finns throw away their file on you so long as you promise not to be a bad boy again. Otherwise, Henri, I can assure you, your hide's going to be nailed to the wall and you'll never move another trainload of fur out of Russia."

Lebel's face showed his displeasure. "Jake, you're a hard man."

"Believe me, I'm a pussycat compared to the people who'll come after you."

There was a distracted look on Lebel's face as he lit another cigar. For a long time he was silent, his brow creased deep in thought, then he looked at Massey.

"What if I said I would consider helping you, but not for money?"

"It depends on what you have in mind instead."

"An extra passenger."

Massey's eyebrows rose. "You'd better explain."

Lebel told him about Irena.

Massey said, "She's Jewish?"

Lebel nodded. "Another reason why I'd feel safer if she got out of Moscow. And I can't pretend some of my contacts there haven't become noticeably icy toward me of late. I thought we had left all that behind us with Hitler, but it seems not. Many times I thought of trying to get Irena out, but the risks were too great. If the Finnish authorities were to find her on board the train they might send her back to Russia and me to prison. But you could make sure that wouldn't happen, couldn't you, Jake? And get her a legal passport and citizenship?"

"You're a dark horse, Henri. This dacha Irena owns outside Moscow. Is it safe?"

"Of course, that's why we use it. Why?"

"I'll explain later. Do you love this woman?"

"What do *you* think?"

"I think we can do a deal."

18

***New Hampshire.
February 3rd***

It was almost seven when Anna awoke. It was cold in the small bedroom, and when she opened the curtains it was dark outside and she saw the thin fall of snow. The view down to the lake was really quite special, she thought. She threw on her dressing gown and went downstairs.

Slanski was sitting at the table drinking coffee. He wore a military parka and sturdy boots, a small rucksack on the floor beside him, and he looked up at her silently as she sat down.

Not for the first time she noticed the photograph over the fireplace. A couple and three small children. A pretty blond girl and two boys, one dark, one fair. She thought one of them resembled Slanski, but she looked away when she noticed him watching her.

Vassily placed a breakfast of eggs, cheese and corn bread in front of her and said, "Eat, little one."

When the old man had poured her more tea and left the room, she looked at Slanski. "Perhaps you'd better tell me what we'll be doing today."

"Nothing too strenuous to begin with, just enough to start getting you in shape." He smiled. "Not that there's much wrong with your shape as it is."

"Is that meant to be a compliment?"

"No, an observation. But it's really a question of building up your stamina. The training is purely a precaution. It's over six hundred miles from Tallinn to Moscow, a relatively short route, and that's why it was chosen. But if something goes wrong and you have to look after yourself, then you had better be fit and prepared."

"I'm quite capable of looking after myself."

He smiled again. "Let's make certain of it. We'll take a gentle walk in the woods. Ten miles to start with. When Popov arrives in a couple of days the real training begins. Then, I assure you, it gets a lot tougher." He stood. "One more thing."

She looked up and saw the blue eyes stare down at her and for a moment she felt an odd flutter in her chest.

"What?"

"Something Massey will explain, but I think you'd better know now. You'll be given a pill when we go in. Cyanide. It kills instantly. You'll have to use it in a situation where it's likely you're going to get caught and there's no way out. But let's hope that doesn't happen."

Anna hesitated. "Are you trying to frighten me?"

"No, just making sure you know this is not some elaborate game we're playing here. And that there's still time for you to change your mind."

"I'm quite aware it's not a game. And I won't change my mind."

She dressed in the warm clothes Massey had bought her, fur-lined walking boots and heavy trousers and a thick sweater and navy oilskin. It was still dark as they set off through the forest. The snow had stopped when they came to a clearing after half a mile, and Anna saw the first rays of sunshine on the far horizon, streaking the sky orange and red.

She noticed the way Slanski moved through the woods. It was almost as if he was familiar with every inch of the forest, every branch and twig, but she knew that was impossible. He halted in the clearing and pointed toward a sloping mountain that rose up in the distance through a thin bank of pine trees.

"See that plateau on the mountain? It's called Kingdom Ridge. That's where we're headed. Ten miles there and back. Think you'll be able to manage it?"

There was a smile on his face and she thought he was goading her but she didn't reply, simply marched on ahead.

She was exhausted after the first two miles. The rising ground made it hard on her legs, but Slanski walked as if he were on flat ground and the tilt of the land seemed to make no difference to his stamina. Once or twice he looked around to check on her, but by the fifth mile, as they reached the top, he was way ahead.

She came out of the forest onto the ridge, exhausted, fighting for breath, and by then the sun was up, the view of the lake and forest below quite stunning. In the distance was an enormous ridge of snow-capped mountains. In the morning light the rock looked as if it were tinted blue.

Slanski was sitting on a rocky outcrop overhanging the ridge, smoking a cigarette. When he saw her he smiled. "Glad you could make it."

"Give me a cigarette," she almost gasped.

He handed her one and lit it for her.

When she had caught her breath she said, "The view is incredible."

"The mountains you see are called the Appalachians. They stretch over a thousand miles."

She looked out at the view again, then back at him. "Can I ask you a question, Slanski?"

"What?"

"You didn't want me to be part of this, did you?"

He grinned. "Now what makes you think that?"

"From what you said back in the cabin. And besides, you strike me as the kind of man who likes to do things alone. Tell me about yourself."

"Why?"

"I don't want to know your life history. Just enough to know you better. We're going to have to pretend to be man and wife and I presume that means sleeping in the same bed if necessary. I'd like to know something about the man I'll be sharing a bed with."

"What did Massey tell you?"

"Hardly anything. Were you ever married?"

"It crossed my mind once or twice. But what woman in their right mind would want to live up here?"

She smiled. "Oh, I don't know. It's really quite beautiful."

"To a visitor, maybe. But most of the local girls can't wait to get the hell out and head for New York."

"There weren't any women you ever met that you liked?"

"Some, but not many I'd care to lead up an aisle."

"The photograph back in the house. Tell me about it."

There was a sudden look of pain on his face and he stood as if to stop the conversation going any further.

"A long time ago, as they say. And a tale not for the telling. We'd better be getting back."

"You still haven't told me about this Popov. Who is he?"

He looked down at her. "Dimitri Popov is a weapons and self-defense instructor. With a knife and gun and fists he's probably one of the best there is."

"He's Russian?"

"No, Ukrainian. And that means he hates the Russians. He fought against them during the war with a Ukrainian SS regiment before he finally joined the émigré movement. He's a nasty piece of work but in a matter like this he's worth his weight in gold. That's why Massey's people use him. Right, let's get back. Unless, that is, you want to sit here all day and admire the view."

She looked at him with irritation on her face. "I don't have to like you, Slanski, and you don't have to like me. But if I'm supposed to be your wife then I have some rules of my own. In my company you'll be more polite. You'll treat me like you would a wife or at least like a human being. Or do you think that would be too difficult?"

His eyes blazed back at her a moment, and then he tossed away his cigarette and said dismissively, "If you don't like the arrangement, you don't have to put up with it. Now let's get going."

As Anna went to stand she slipped off the rock. He caught her wrist and pulled her in and at that moment she looked up into his face.

The blue eyes stared at her and suddenly for no reason at all he went to kiss her, his mouth moving on hers. For a few moments she was caught up in it all but then she pushed herself free.

"Don't . . . !"

He smiled. "Like you said, I ought to treat you as a wife. That *is* what you wanted, isn't it?"

She knew he was simply provoking her and said angrily, "Understand one thing—if we have to sleep together for the sake of appearances on this mission I don't want you ever to touch me, is that clear?" He turned and started to walk back down the ridge.

Helsinki.
February 8th

The southwest coast of Finland, seen from the air in winter, looks like a shattered jigsaw puzzle of frozen green and white shapes, as if some giant hammer had smashed land and frozen sea into a million particles.

Islands and ice meet whenever a harsh winter freezes the Baltic, and that winter it was no different. To the west lay Hango and Turku, ancient seafaring towns that had both seen invaders come and go—Russians, Swedes and Germans. For almost all her history Finland had had to endure invasion by her Baltic neighbors. To the east lay Helsinki, and to the south, fifty miles across the narrow frozen Gulf of Finland, lay the Baltic states occupied by Stalin's army.

It was almost noon when Massey arrived in Helsinki on the morning flight from Paris, and Janne Saarinen met him in the Arrivals area. As they drove west along the coast in Saarinen's little gray Volvo, the Finn looked across at Massey.

"I thought I was going to have a rest from covert mission flying until I got your phone call. Who is it this time, Jake? Not more types like those two SS creeps I dropped last month from Munich?"

"Not this time, Janne."

Saarinen smiled. "Thank God for small mercies. How many passengers do you want to drop?"

"Two. A man and a woman."

"What is this, Jake? Something special? Your people don't normally drop from up here in winter. The weather's usually too bad."

"Between you and me, Janne, it's an unrecorded drop. You'll be well paid, but that goes without saying."

Saarinen grinned. An unrecorded drop meant it was highly secret and unofficial, and usually highly dangerous.

"Smells like danger, and I could do with a bit of that right now. Say no more. We can discuss money when it's done."

The roads were icy, but the sturdy little Volvo was equipped with snow chains and they came to a small fishing village twenty minutes later. It was no more than a clutch of brightly painted wooden houses set around a frozen harbor.

There was an inn at one end and Saarinen pulled up outside it and said to Massey, "This will do nicely. Belongs to a cousin of mine. There's a room at the back where we can talk and won't be bothered. Let's go inside where it's warmer, Jake."

The Finn eased his false leg out of the car and they went into the inn. It was surprisingly large inside and all done in pine, a blazing fire roaring and a ceramic stove going at the same time, and the view looked out onto the frozen harbor locked in solid ice. There was a man behind the bar, tall and blond, wearing a spotless white bar smock and reading a newspaper.

Saarinen said to him in Finnish, "Give us both a drink quick, Niilo, before we freeze to death. We'll use the room at the back, if you don't mind. I've got a bit of business to discuss."

The man behind the bar placed a bottle of vodka and two glasses on the table and handed Saarinen a set of keys.

Saarinen led the way to a room at the side of the inn and unlocked the door. Inside, it was icy cold. He grinned as he closed the door.

"Don't know why Niilo bothers to open half the winter. Most of the locals stay at home. I think he must be missing a couple of slates off his roof. In summer the place is crawling with kids from Helsinki out on a bender, but in winter it's as quiet as the morgue. So tell me what you have in mind."

"The two people I spoke about, I want them dropped near Tallinn."

Saarinen raised his eyes. "Why Tallinn? It's a garrison town. Crawling with Soviet troops."

"There are two reasons for the drop in that area," Massey explained. "Number one, it's only a short hop across the Gulf of Finland to Estonia and the Soviets would never expect a drop in that area in winter. And number two, there'll be a welcome committee from the Estonian resistance waiting to help my people on their way."

"I see. Where to?"

"Sorry, Janne. That I can't tell you."

"Fair enough. As long as you know the dangers. Where do you plan to take off from?"

"I had thought the place you've got farther up the coast, if it's not too close to the base at Porkkula?"

"Bylandet Island? Why not, it's where I keep my plane hangared in winter and it's pretty much ideal. And don't worry about the Soviet base on Porkkula."

The Porkkula peninsula, over thirty kilometers from Helsinki, was occupied by a small Soviet military and naval force. Such an occupation was a touchy subject for Finns. But having sided with Germany in the war, Finland had been forced to allow a small part of its country to be used as a Russian base until Helsinki had paid Moscow its war reparations in full.

"By air, the peninsula is over ten kilometers from Bylandet Island," Saarinen explained. "But the Soviet base has never caused me any problems—it's strictly out of bounds to Finns and the Russians keep to themselves. And if we go from Bylandet the crossing shouldn't take more than thirty minutes. Maybe forty at most if there's a headwind."

"You think the weather will be a problem?"

Saarinen smiled, a rakish smile. "It's always a problem up here. But if it's bad it can work to our advantage in a situation like this. We can use cloud cover most of the way in. Stick right in it almost until the drop."

"Isn't that taking a big risk?"

Saarinen laughed. "Not as big a risk as getting blown out of the sky by the latest Mig fighter. There's a squadron of the latest all-weather model stationed south of Leningrad that covers Baltic coastal patrols. Those machines are pretty damned good—the fastest thing around right now, even faster than your latest American fighters. And the Russians have got radar on board."

"What if they pick you up on their radar?"

"The news is the Soviet pilots are not that familiar with the new equipment, so they won't stay in the cloud too long at the kind of speeds they cruise at. They prefer to be able to see where they're going. And if it's really bad, like heavy snow, they'll stay safely on land getting drunk in the mess."

"Can your plane stand the kind of buffeting you'll get if the weather's bad?"

Saarinen grinned. "The little Norseman I've got could come through a blizzard of shit in one piece."

It was almost eight that evening when Saarinen dropped Massey off at the Palace Hotel in Helsinki.

They had one drink in the bar together before the Finn bade him goodbye. When Massey went up to his room there was a message waiting. Henri Lebel had called from Paris. Massey made the return call after waiting twenty minutes for the Helsinki operator to patch him through to Paris on a crackling line.

"Jake? I'm going to be in Helsinki the day after tomorrow and I thought we could meet to discuss our business arrangement further."

Massey knew Lebel meant to show him the hidden compartment in the private goods train the Frenchman leased from the Finns, before Lebel traveled on for a brief visit to Moscow.

"What about the other information I require?"

"I'm working on it, but it hasn't been easy, *mon ami*. A matter of greasing the right greedy palm. But I hope to have something for you soon."

"Good, Henri. Give me a call when you get here."

When Massey replaced the receiver he crossed to the window that overlooked the harbor. If Lebel got the information he wanted he knew what he had to do next, despite what Branigan had warned.

In the moonlit winter's darkness the entire Baltic seemed frozen white as far as the eye could see. As he stood there looking out at the scene, Massey couldn't help thinking of Anna Khorev. Two weeks from now she'd be flying out over that frozen gulf with Slanski, taking the biggest risk she had ever taken in her life.

New Hampshire.
February 11th

Anna was standing at the window when she saw the old black Ford pull up outside the house.

The man who climbed out was big and powerfully built. His dark bushy beard and greasy black hair gave him the appearance of a wild-looking mountain man. When he and Slanski came up the veranda and stepped inside the cabin, the big man saw her and grinned, broken teeth showing behind his beard.

"So this is the woman," the man said to Slanski.

Slanski said, "Popov, this is Anna."

The man held out a huge bearlike paw. Anna didn't offer to shake it but said to Slanski, "When you want me I'll be outside," then walked past the Ukrainian and down the steps of the veranda.

Popov watched her retreating figure appreciatively as she walked toward the woods.

He grinned and stroked his beard. "A good one to have beside you in a bed on a cold night, I'll say that much. But did I say something wrong?"

"I don't think former Ukrainian SS are among her favorite types, Dimitri."

Popov grunted. "Massey said she was Russian. Russians and Ukrainians have always fought like cat and dog. The *Russkis* have tried to grind us to dust for centuries." A brief smile flashed on his face. "Still, I'd call a truce as far as that one's concerned. Nice ass on her, I'll say that."

"You're here to do a job, Dimitri. Get fresh with her and I'll take it personally."

Popov frowned as Slanski glared at him. There was a flash of anger in Popov's bearded face as he went to say something, but then he seemed to think better of it and broke into a wide grin.

"You know me, Alex, always willing to keep the peace for the sake of harmony."

"Let's go down to the lake. I want to talk."

Popov left his things in the car, and as they walked down to the water Slanski said, "You think you can cover everything in ten days?"

"You I know about. The girl I don't. It depends on her."

"Massey thinks she should be OK."

"And what do you think?"

Slanski smiled. "Much as I hate to admit it, she's good. The last week she's put her heart into getting fit."

"Better let me be the judge of that. But if anyone can do it, Popov can."

When Popov had settled in he met them downstairs in the dining room. Slanski had poured coffee and the three of them sat at the table.

The Ukrainian looked across at Anna and Slanski. "First things first. The program. You wake every morning at four-thirty. We take a five-mile run, even if there's snow, then back here for more exercises. After breakfast we do some self-defense training, how to defend yourself, and also how to kill." He looked at Slanski. "You too, Alex. The day you think you know it all, you're dead. The woman here, I know nothing about her background, so I'll have to assume she knows nothing and go on from there." He looked directly at Anna. "What kind of experience have you had of this kind of thing?"

Slanski interrupted, "She's had some, Dimitri."

Popov raised his eyebrows and grunted. "I asked the girl, Alex. So let her answer." He looked at Anna. "Show me your hands."

"What?"

"Your hands. Give them to me."

Anna held out her hands and Popov studied them. Then he reached over and gripped them painfully hard. He seemed to take pleasure as his big strong fingers pressed cruelly into her flesh, as if he was trying to hurt her, but Anna only winced and didn't cry out.

Popov grinned, then released his grip. "Good. You've known pain before. So what's your background?"

Slanski said, "Massey said no questions, Dimitri."

Popov turned to stare at him and spoke gruffly. "I'm not asking her life history. But I need to know how much training she's had. How much pain she can take."

"I've had military training, if that's what you mean," Anna answered sharply.

Popov's bushy eyebrows rose. "Which army?"

"Dimitri . . ." Slanski went to interrupt.

Popov stared back at him. "You realize as well as I do it's important I know something of her background, considering what she might have to face when the time comes. I need to know what I'm working with." He looked back at Anna. "Which army?"

"The Red Army."

Popov frowned, an unpleasant look crossing his face before he grinned again and stroked his beard. "I guessed as much. So, we were once enemies.

This should make for an interesting time. But I can tell you that such military experience will hardly help you. The Red Army are a rabble. Undisciplined. Unruly."

Anger flared on Anna's face. "Even at Stalingrad?"

Popov grinned. "First blood to you. Stalingrad is the exception."

"And no doubt the SS were better?"

Popov heard the bitterness in Anna's voice and glanced at Slanski before looking back at her.

"So, you know something of me? As fighting men, the SS were infinitely better, believe me."

"Except the Ukrainian SS. They were rapists and scum."

Slanski looked at Popov, whose face turned red with fury. Slanski stood up to break the tension.

"Let's get this under way. Whenever you're ready, Dimitri."

Popov stood and pushed back his chair. "There's still light outside. Let's start with ways to kill." He looked at Anna. "We'll see who was scum. Go change." He grinned at Slanski. "You know, I think I'm going to enjoy this."

They were out behind the house, their breaths fogging in the freezing air, but the cold didn't seem to bother Popov, who had removed his parka and sweater, and stood there in his dirty vest. The smell from the man's body was unpleasant, a mixture of stale sweat and wood smoke.

He faced them, his feet spread apart as he hitched up his trousers.

"OK. Basics first. To kill properly you need two things. Determination and skill. Forget anger. It makes for mistakes and distracts you. You must be clear-headed about your purpose. OK, without weapons first. Let's start with you, Alex. Step forward."

Slanski stepped forward.

"Give me your hands. Palms up," commanded Popov.

Slanski offered his hands. Popov grasped one, held it up and splayed the fingers.

He looked at Anna. "Five fingers. Five simple but deadly weapons on each hand. You use them to gouge and poke out eyes. To strangle and choke. Then there's your feet. And your head, but using that for anything other than thinking can be both painful and dangerous. Better to stick with the other parts—legs, hands and feet. OK, Alex, tell me how you can kill with your hands."

Slanski's hand touched a point behind Popov's left ear and pressed.

"Pressure points left and right sides of the neck where the veins carry blood to the brain. Depending on the amount of pressure applied, you can knock a man unconscious or kill him in five to ten seconds."

"That's assuming, of course," said Popov, "you've got time. What if you haven't? What if it must be done instantly? A sentry, perhaps? Someone you wish to silence without a sound and at once?"

Slanski showed his hand, gestured with the edge like a blade. "Side cut to the throat shatters the Adam's apple."

"And if you're coming from behind?"

"The quick way is the side cut or punch to the pressure points."

"But if it doesn't kill him?"

"Stamp on his throat."

"But if he's still standing?"

"You get him down on the ground as quickly as possible. Crush his throat with your hand or foot."

"Which part of the foot?"

"The heel is the strongest."

"OK, do it to me."

Popov turned, offering his back. Slanski came up behind him and went to attack. As his hand came cutting through the air, Popov turned quick as lightning and grasped Slanski's arm and twisted. Slanski didn't scream even though the bone almost cracked. Popov released his grip and grinned. "First mistake. I'm surprised at you, Alex. You've grown rusty. Always anticipate. Always be ready for the unexpected. Anticipate that the guard is going to turn and look or have a piss." He looked at Anna. "If the guard sees you, it can cost you your life, and worse, the lives of the others with you. Never expect things to happen as you plan them. In short, expect fucking anything to happen. And when you're making that kill, every sense must be alert. Not only the ones you're using right now."

He stepped back a little. "Now try it again." He turned, offering his back again. Slanski came at him. As he was about to strike, Popov turned once again, but this time Slanski was ready. As Popov's hand came around, Slanski grabbed it and twisted, at the same time bringing his knee up and halting it an inch from smashing Popov's face, then his hand cut through the air and struck Popov a glancing blow on the neck.

It stunned the man but he was powerfully built, and as Slanski's hand came down sharply to strike again Popov grunted and wrenched free, his hand grabbing Slanski's hair, wrenching it back painfully from the scalp.

"Better. But not quite good enough. You would have killed me, but not silently. We'll improve on it. Remember, always anticipate. The SS trained their men to expect everything." He looked at Anna and grinned. "And now you. Step forward please, madam."

There was something in the way Popov said madam that was almost goading. Anna took two steps forward. The grin behind the Ukrainian's beard widened.

"With women," Popov said dismissively, "it's even more difficult. They haven't got the natural strength a man has. But even nature's weaklings can be taught technique. Remember, always anticipate and react. And it must be quickly, or your life gets snuffed out. Got it?"

"I think so."

"We'll see. OK, the same again. Try and remember what you saw Alex do. Come at me from behind."

Popov turned again, showing Anna his back.

There was a swishing sound and Popov felt the force of the kick as a foot slammed hard between his legs. He vomited as he went down, his face turning purple as his hands went to cover his genitals.

At the same time Anna came around in front of him. Her hand sliced through the air and hit Popov a glancing blow to the side of the neck as he pitched forward.

As Popov writhed in pain, Slanski saw the barely concealed smile on Anna's face, and then it was gone, her face deathly serious as she looked back at him.

"His first mistake. He didn't heed his own advice to anticipate. That's the sign of a poor instructor."

Slanski grinned. "I'd have to agree. What's the idea, are you trying to kill him?"

"There are many ways to stop a bear. The Mongolian troops I served with at Stalingrad taught me that. That's how they've silenced a sentry since the time of Genghis Khan. A hard, sharp kick between the legs to a man's most vulnerable spot. The pain is so intense he can't scream or cry out even if he wants to. He goes dumb with shock. Then you kill him."

Slanski smiled over at Popov squirming on the ground. "I think you've made your point."

"Then tell him for me I hope the rest of the training is better. And remind him a good instructor should always practice what he preaches. Tell him that. I'll be inside when your friend has recovered."

Slanski watched as she turned and went back up to the house. He saw Popov try to struggle to his feet, cross-eyed with pain as he tenderly massaged his genitals and moaned.

Slanski laughed and lit a cigarette. "I guess she's better than you thought, Dimitri."

Moscow.
February 12th

It was almost noon when the Finnish DC-3 carrying Henri Lebel landed at Vnukovo airport. Situated ten kilometers southwest of Moscow, Vnukovo served as the city's main civilian airport, but it was also a military airbase, ringed by a high-security fence and guarded by a battalion of crack paratroops.

Lebel remained quietly in his seat long after the aircraft had taxied to a halt. There were only a dozen passengers on board that Thursday morning, and among them Lebel recognized several faces he had seen before on Moscow flights—two prominent Dutch diamond merchants, a German oil magnate, and a minor Finnish embassy official. They all waited patiently in their seats, frequent visitors to Moscow who knew the drill that was to follow.

Lebel glanced out of the window and saw an Emka car drive the short distance across the snowy tarmac to the plane. He noticed that, as always, there were few Western aircraft on the aprons.

The Emka halted below on the apron and the two passengers climbed out and came up the metal stairway. The procedure was always the same. The two men were KGB, and they came on board but remained at the door. Before the passengers were allowed to disembark, the Finnish stewardesses went through the cabin removing any Western newspapers and magazines and storing them away in a locked cabinet in case anyone was tempted to take one.

Lebel and the passengers were finally led across the snowy tarmac to the terminal by one of the KGB men. Inside, two more men were waiting, standing beside a long metal table, where the passengers' bags would be examined.

Lebel identified his bag from a trolley and the man opened it and thoroughly examined the contents. When he had finished, he indicated for Lebel to move to another official sitting nearby, waiting to check passports. The man, whom Lebel knew from previous visits, was KGB. He examined the passport along with the official document declaring Lebel an honorary Soviet citizen, then stamped the passport and handed it back without a flicker of recognition.

There was a Zis and a driver waiting, as usual, for since his outburst years before the Ministry of Foreign Trade had treated Lebel royally. When he stepped inside it drew away from the curb.

Lebel liked the cosmopolitan, noisy atmosphere of Moscow—there were Russians, Slavs, Mongolians, lots of Chinese, and a hundred other ethnic faces. It reminded him a little of New York, except that it was slower, colder, there were no really excellent restaurants, and it was much more drab.

But nothing could have been drabber than Moscow's hotels. There were only four in the capital which were used for foreign visitors, and the best by far was the Moskva on Marx Prospect, with a grand frontage and a summer café terrace that overlooked the Kremlin. The Moskva was the chief hotel assigned to important visiting foreigners and dignitaries. Lebel used it as his office, although he already had an official bureau assigned to him with a staff of three Ministry of Foreign Trade employees, situated near the Arbat. It was a drab two-room place he avoided as much as possible.

As the Zis pulled up outside the hotel, there was a uniformed militiaman on duty at the entrance, wearing a long blue overcoat with red and white tabs. Lebel told the man from the Ministry he wouldn't need him or the car until the next morning at nine—he had a meeting to discuss his next shipment—and the Zis drove off.

Whenever Lebel stepped into the Moskva it reminded him of a magnificent, if somewhat dismal, palace. Vast, with miles of deserted polished marble halls and glittering chandeliers, it still gave a bleak impression—there was no flower shop or newspaper stand, no concierge, and not a uniformed bellboy in sight. Guests were expected to carry their own bags.

Lebel went to check in. The clerk was busy talking with two men in civilian clothes at the far end of the desk, who were riffling through some index cards. One of them had a gloved false hand, and the other was a squat Mongol with slit eyes. The two men glanced briefly at Lebel, then went back to their discussion with the clerk. When the clerk finally came to attend to him after a long delay, he handed over his room key—always for the same suite on the fourth floor—but did not ask to see a passport. That was up to the office known as the Service Bureau, across the hall, which was in reality the KGB's office in the hotel.

When he had finished checking in, Lebel carried his bag across to a glass-fronted door.

He saw a woman seated behind a desk smile and gesture for him to enter.

"Back for more sable or just the sinful delights of Moscow, Henri?"

Lebel knew the woman well. She had once worked at the Trade Ministry and spoke six languages, all fluently. Lebel smiled. "Wild horses can't keep me away."

The woman took out a batch of forms and began filling them in. "How long's your stay?"

"Two nights."

"Tickets for the opera, the ballet?"

"Not this time, Larissa. I've a busy schedule." Lebel handed over his passport and document of citizenship, and the woman placed them in a metal tray that would go in the office safe. Both passport and document would be kept until his departure.

"Any foreign currency? Valuables?" the woman inquired.

"No valuables, but I've got five hundred US dollars in cash. The same in Finnish marks."

Like all visitors and citizens, Lebel was not allowed to carry foreign currency, only rubles. He removed the money from his wallet, handed it across, and said playfully, "All for you, my sweet Larissa, if you'd let me take you out to dinner."

The woman frowned and Lebel said, "It's only a joke, Larissa."

"Don't joke, Henri. The duty officer's around, doing his usual check on arriving visitors. He might come back and overhear and get the wrong impression."

Lebel had come to know most of the Service Bureau personnel but had never got used to Russian paranoia and their fear of authority. "Who's on duty this time?"

"A Major Lukin. You haven't met him before and he's only filling in. But he shouldn't keep you long. He and a comrade just left the office to check the register."

Every foreign visitor had to have his passport checked and registered by the KGB 2nd Directorate officer on duty in the Service Bureau. Performing such duties, the KGB men always wore civilian clothes. All guests from abroad, important or not, were their responsibility. Lebel knew he had nothing to fear. His document of honorary citizenship meant it would be merely a perfunctory check. But this time, knowing what he had to discuss with Irena, he felt a little nervous. He watched as the woman counted out the dollars and marks, filled in a form, then put the bills in the tray alongside the passport and had Lebel sign for both.

The door opened and the two men Lebel had seen chatting with the desk clerk came in.

"M. Lebel? My name is Lukin, and this is Comrade Kokunko." The man with the leather glove extended his good hand and shook Lebel's. The Mongol said nothing, just stared at him through slit eyes, which made Lebel feel distinctly uncomfortable.

"How do you do," Lebel answered.

"Just a short visit this time, I believe?" Lukin said.

"I have a meeting with the Ministry of Foreign Trade tomorrow morning. I think you'll find everything is in order."

"I'm sure it is." Lukin held out his hand to the woman. "May I see M. Lebel's passport, Larissa?"

The woman handed it across, along with the document of citizenship. The major studied both, then held up Lebel's document. "You have honorary citizenship, I see. We don't come across too many of these."

"I do a lot of important business in Moscow. I'm a fur dealer and have an office here. I'm here to arrange a shipment of sable."

For some odd reason, even though the major seemed polite enough, the man made Lebel feel uneasy. He put it down to his own conscience, knowing what he was *really* in Moscow to do, and he tried hard to appear calm. In another two hours he would hopefully be out on the streets of Moscow, going through his well-rehearsed routine of checking to make sure he had not been followed, before he carefully made his way to Irena's dacha. He was desperately looking forward to seeing her again, and excited by the prospect of their future freedom together. But out of nervousness, he seemed to be explaining too much to Lukin.

The major was watching his face. He seemed an intelligent sort, with eyes that looked at you intently, as if pressing you to fill the void and talk. His Mongol colleague also just stood there, staring silently across. Lebel had the feeling that the major was suspicious of something, but he tried to put it down to his own heightened sense of anxiety on this trip. He checked himself, stared back at Lukin, and said nothing more.

Finally, the major handed back the passport and document to the woman, and said politely, "Enjoy your stay in Moscow, M. Lebel. I hope your business goes well."

"I'm certain it will."

20

New York.
February 19th,
5 P.M.

In the tenth-floor office of the Soviet Mission in the United Nations building in Manhattan that late afternoon, Feliks Arkashin stood hunched over the half-dozen black-and-white photographs and frowned as he scratched the mole on his jaw.

He turned to the man standing beside him and said, "You're certain about this, Yegeni?"

Yegeni Oramov was small and thin and wore thick black spectacles. He had the look of a distracted professor about him, wild tufts of wiry black hair sprouting from his head, but despite his appearance he held the rank of KGB captain in the New York Soviet Mission.

"Certain as we can be. I had the photo prints checked out with our people here and in Europe. It definitely looks like the man named Massey."

"Tell me about him."

"He runs the Munich CIA operations office. Apparently, he's been a thorn in our side for a long time. The question is, what do we do about it?"

Arkashin shook his head. "The question is, surely, what's he doing with the woman, Anna Khorev?"

Oramov smiled. "That's where our station in Helsinki comes in. I checked through the file you gave me, the one on the woman. Then I had some copies of these photographs sent to Helsinki in one of our diplomatic bags. We think Massey was present when our people interviewed her, although as you'd expect he used a different name. Colonel Romulka's aide remembers him, and the description would seem to fit. Also, our man who watched her at Helsinki airport saw the photographs and thinks Massey was with the Americans who escorted her to the plane."

"What about the second man?"

Oramov smiled."Now that's where it gets even more interesting. We're not a hundred percent sure, but we're pretty certain it's a man named Alex Slanski."

Arkashin said, "*The* Alex Slanski? The one they call the Wolf?"

Oramov nodded. "The same. Moscow has a price on his head, as you know. We've wanted him a long time. Remember Grenady Kraskin who got hit in East Berlin over two months ago? We think Slanski did it."

Feliks Arkashin stepped toward the window and rubbed his fleshy face. Beyond the glass lay East 67th Street with its cluttered chaos of traffic, and to the west, Central Park. He always considered the situation in America's commercial capital to be ridiculous, and the Americans tolerant fools. Under cover of the Soviet trade mission, consulate, or Soviet news agencies, and sealed off from the other parts of the UN mission and with their own independent communications to Moscow, their files immune from search and with reasonable ability to move freely about New York, KGB branch chiefs and their officers went about their daily business as if they were working in Moscow Headquarters itself. Crazy, but it worked to their advantage.

For several moments Arkashin was deep in thought, then turned to his visitor and said, "You can go now, Yegeni. Leave the photographs. Well done."

The man left and Arkashin lit a cigarette. Yegeni Oramov had supplied him with the confirmation he needed of Braun's latest report. He stood there a moment before he crossed back to his desk. He picked up the internal telephone and dialed a three-digit number to his superior's office. As he waited for the other end to answer he glanced over at the portrait of Joseph Stalin on the wall above his desk. The face stared down at him, a wry smile on the lips. Arkashin shivered. The line clicked.

"Leonid? Arkashin here. Can I come up? This won't take a minute. Something's come up I think is important and I'd like your opinion."

Leonid Kislov was a stout man in his late fifties who chain-smoked four packs of American cigarettes a day.

As senior KGB station officer in the New York Mission, with the rank of colonel, he had a lot of worries, not least of which were a duodenal ulcer and a fiery Georgian wife who harried him constantly. That morning he was in a foul mood, his ulcer playing up, and as he gestured for Arkashin to sit he said, "Make it quick, Feliks, I've got a meeting with the Ambassador in half an hour."

"Problems?" Arkashin asked sympathetically.

Kislov burped and rubbed his chest before he slipped a couple of tablets from a glass bottle and reached for a glass of water on his desk.

"There are always fucking problems." He swallowed the ulcer tablets and sipped the water. "Washington is up the Ambassador's ass again over the matter of the Jewish doctors. They want to know what's going on."

"What will he tell them?"

"That it's none of their fucking business." Kislov grinned. "But politely of course. That's what diplomacy is all about. Just as well they don't know what else is going on. They'd have a fucking fit. But fuck them, I say. Their day's going to come, and sooner than we all think."

"Anything you'd care to tell me?"

Kislov looked across sternly. "It's none of your business, comrade. But I'll slip you a little hint. If things go according to plan we won't be here in another six months. This hydrogen project of ours is almost complete. There's a plan to evacuate us before the trouble starts. And start it will, you can be sure of that."

Arkashin went slightly pale. "You mean Stalin's almost ready to start a war?"

Kislov grinned. "Like I said, it's not your business." He tapped a cigarette from the pack on his desk and lit it, glanced at his watch and said gruffly, "What did you want to see me about?"

Arkashin explained about the photographs and the woman as he lay the shots on the table and Kislov examined them.

The photographs were taken from a distance and rather clumsily too. The images were grainy and of poor quality.

"These photographs are crap," commented Kislov.

Arkashin half smiled. "True. But Lombardi's men are not trained photographers and they couldn't risk getting too close in case they were spotted. Still, we're as sure as we can be that the two men in the shots are Massey and Slanski."

Kislov knew about the woman, but up to now hadn't been interested in the details and preferred to let Arkashin get on with it. But now he leaned forward and drew on his cigarette.

"Interesting."

"That's what I thought."

"But it hardly matters in the overall scheme of things, does it? Why Moscow wastes its time on piffling matters such as this is beyond me."

"As you know, Colonel Romulka has taken a personal interest in the woman's case." Arkashin smiled faintly. "Apparently, she made quite an impression when she met him in Helsinki. There's more to it than that, of course, but no doubt Romulka wants his pound of flesh. And with respect, Leonid, I'd hardly call the Wolf a piffling matter. He's been a scourge for quite some time."

Kislov sighed. "I suppose you'd better fill me in on what's been happening."

"We're using Lombardi to watch the woman, of course, but Braun's acting as the link."

"Braun? That animal?"

"Even an animal has its uses. That's why we brought him here as an illegal. He's so adept at killing troublesome émigrés."

"I'm aware of that. So what do you propose?"

"Something tells me Massey is up to something. And with this Slanski in the picture it might suggest Massey perhaps has an agent drop in mind. Maybe even using the girl. She'd be an ideal choice, considering she knows our country."

Kislov shrugged his bulky shoulders. "Possible, but speculative. So why come to me?"

"We have three choices. One, take out the woman, as we intended. Two, take her out and kill Massey and Slanski in the process as a bonus. Or three, we keep tailing them and see what they're up to. If it's a drop Massey intends, we could try to find out where and when and take them when they land on Soviet soil."

Kislov sat farther back in his chair and thought for a moment, then drew on his cigarette.

Finally he shook his head. "The second option is not the best way to go and the third is risky and speculative. We may not be able to discover when or where they're going to drop, if that's what's happening. The first seems the best choice, and besides, it's what Moscow ordered." He frowned. "You never told me how you know where these people are? Massey, Slanski, the woman?"

Arkashin smiled. "Simple really. Lombardi had a couple of his men follow Massey and the woman when they took a train to Boston. They were met there by this man—Slanski." Arkashin pointed to a grainy photograph taken at Boston railway station of Massey shaking hands with Slanski, Anna Khorev beside them.

"The woman had a suitcase with her," Arkashin went on, "so it's likely she was going to stay somewhere. Lombardi's men followed the three of them out of the station but lost them after they drove off in a vehicle driven by the man we think is Slanski. But they got the license number—a New Hampshire registration—and had it checked out. It's definitely registered to an Alex Slanski, with an address at a place called Kingdom Lake in New Hampshire, which confirms his identity."

"Go on," prompted Kislov.

"Curious, but the terrain around there is not unlike Russia. It would seem an ideal place for mission training if Massey is planning a drop."

Kislov nodded. "Anything else?"

Arkashin half smiled. "There's a Soviet cargo ship due in New York docks in five days, which rather suits us if things go the way I plan. I'll need you to authorize a dollar payment for Lombardi if we're to go ahead with the woman's abduction."

"Can Lombardi be trusted with such a delicate matter as this?"

Arkashin grinned. "He's as shifty as a sewer rat, but a true capitalist who'll do anything for money. Besides, he's not averse to killing."

"Surely Lombardi won't get involved in this personally? He'll want to leave it to his men."

"I'll insist that he does, considering what we'll pay him. I don't want this business botched."

Kislov thought a moment. "Could Braun and Lombardi make the deaths of Massey and Slanski look like accidents? So that the Americans can't come back at us?"

"It could be arranged, I'm certain."

Kislov grinned slightly. "Then perhaps your second option was best after all. There could be promotion in this for both of us."

Arkashin smiled back. "That's what I thought."

"But just remember, the woman is the priority. It's her we want. It's fine if Massey and Slanski are there when we take her, we can deal with them, but if not, just make sure you get that bitch. And tell your people to be careful. By all accounts this Wolf is a dangerous proposition."

New Hampshire.

Popov had recovered, and the following days had been spent on weapons training. He didn't reproach Anna but Slanski saw the blaze of anger in the Ukrainian's eyes every time he looked at her. The man was earning his money the hard way.

It had started to snow that early afternoon, a light fall that covered the forest and land in a sprinkling of white. They spent an hour examining Soviet weapons which Popov had laid out on the table in the front room.

"Some of these you may meet on your travels, so it's important you know what you're up against and how to use them if you have to." He picked up the first weapon. "Kalashnikov assault rifle," he said. "Not really a rifle at all, but a machine-pistol and rifle combined. It can fire single shots, semi-automatic or automatic bursts. Designed by an NCO in the Red Army by the same name in 1947. That's how it got its model number—AK47. It fires 7.62 ammunition. An excellent weapon, I have to admit. Hardly ever jams and you can throw it in the mud and dance on it and it will still fire.

He put it down and picked up another weapon with a drum magazine. "PPsH machine-gun. Standard issue to Soviet NCOs during the war. It's noisy and inaccurate, and it fires too fast. Steel pressed parts. It's still in use in all countries behind the Iron Curtain. Fine if you're up close to a kill or need to spray a room at speed but otherwise a waste of fucking time."

He replaced it and selected another. "And now for the *crème de la crème*. German MP40 machine-pistol, sometimes inaccurately called the Schmeisser. The Soviets captured thousands of them from the Germans. The Reds even preferred this weapon to their own models during the war. They've armed some of the militia with the MP40 in Soviet Bloc countries until they're replaced with the latest Soviet arms. A lethal weapon, way ahead of its time. Nine-millimeter parabellum shells, thirty-two rounds in a clip. Better than any of the others you've seen, in my opinion."

Popov put down the German machine-pistol and turned to a couple of handguns.

"Only two that should really concern you. The Tokarev TT-33 automatic pistol and the Nagant revolver. Both reasonably accurate and reliable. The shortcomings of the Tokarev are it's an awkward design and badly finished. The Nagant is really a Belgian weapon, but the Soviets manufacture a direct copy. It's a good, solid, dependable revolver."

He looked up at Anna. "Pick them up. Handle them. Feel the weight and get used to the mechanical action. You too, Alex. You can never have enough practice. Then outside in the woods in ten minutes."

Anna had begun to feel fit again. The running through the woods and the excruciating exercises had toned her body and she felt more alive than she had in a long time. Slanski had covered the rudiments of parachuting and he and Popov had rigged up a basic training drop to teach her how to land properly. The entire regime had given her little time to be alone and think, her days preoccupied by what she was doing and her nights a haze of sleepy exhaustion.

It was snowing on the second to last day of training, and when they had finished supper and Slanski and Vassily had cleared away the plates she threw her coat over her shoulders, left the cabin and walked down to the lake.

She heard the voice behind her minutes later and turned. Popov came down to stand beside the water. He looked over at her.

"So, we only have another day together. No doubt you're happy to see me go. But I hope you've learned enough to save your life in an awkward situation?"

She looked at him coldly. "Are you worried about me, Popov?" He grinned in the darkness. "I always worry about my pupils. But it's up to them to take as they will of what I teach them. Either they learn enough to survive or they don't and they're dead." He hesitated. "When did you escape?"

"I don't think that's any of your business. And who says I escaped?"

Popov grinned. "How else could you have got out of Russia? Still, I wouldn't like to see a woman as pretty as yourself caught by the Reds, if that's the case. You know what they would do to you?"

"I can imagine. Now why don't you leave me alone."

"Believe me, if they caught you, rape would be the mildest thing. Then torture. Excruciating torture. After that, death would be a welcome companion. And with the KGB, that usually happens slowly."

"Are you trying to frighten me, Popov?"

The grin behind the beard widened. "I doubt if that's possible. I'm just making sure you know what to expect. You have better nerves than most men I've trained." He crushed the cigarette under his boot. "But whatever you're going to do I hope it hurts the bastards. Good night."

He stared over at her before he turned and walked back up to the cabin. As she stood there looking out at the darkened lake she heard the voice.

"Nice conversation."

Anna turned. Slanski stood there in the shadows, smoking a cigarette—

she saw the glow from the tip of his cigarette before she saw him. He strolled down to stand beside her.

"He's not as bad as he looks or sounds."

"If you say so."

"You don't like Popov much, do you?"

"No."

"What you learned from him could save your life, remember that."

"That doesn't mean I have to like him."

Slanski smiled. "I guess not." He flicked away his cigarette and it cartwheeled into the lake. "Tomorrow I'll take you into Concord. There's a hotel, it's not up to much, but the cooking's better than Vassily's. And there's a dance during dinner."

She looked at him, surprised. "Why should you take me there?"

"No reason, except maybe you deserve it after all your hard work. And besides, like you said, maybe it's time we started to act like man and wife. Massey's going to be back tomorrow night to go over some final things, so we haven't much more time to get to know one another." He went to turn, but hesitated. "Wear a dress tomorrow night if you have one."

She hesitated. "Why are you doing this?"

"Doing what?"

"Going into Russia. What's your motive?"

"Why do you want to know?"

"I think maybe you volunteered. And happy men don't volunteer."

Slanski looked up at the night sky, then back at her. "None of your business, I'm afraid. Just as yours is none of mine. You'd better get back up to the house soon. You'll catch your death out here."

He turned without another word and walked back up to the cabin.

As he sat in his bedroom Slanski heard Anna come in ten minutes later and climb the stairs. He heard her wash and undress and then the creak of springs as she climbed into bed. The house went silent again, except for Popov's snoring down the hall.

He crossed to the corner of the bedroom. Hunching down near the window, he took out his penknife and flicked open the blade. He slipped the blade between the two short wooden floorboards and pried. The wood gave easily, and he removed the two foot-long sections. He put his hand into the recess and removed the old rusting biscuit tin, and beneath it, the single manila file Massey had given him to study.

This had been his childhood hiding place when he first came to the cabin. He had trusted no one then, not even Vassily. It had once hidden the only possessions he had brought with him to America as a boy.

Now he opened the file on Joseph Stalin and read through it again. It contained only the information Massey had said, and no details of the mission.

Stalin's habits, information on his health, his personal security arrangements, and particulars of his elite bodyguard. The entire bodyguard system comprised almost fifty thousand people, dedicated to his protection and divided into departments according to their expertise: Stalin's transport, his food, his health, his physical protection, his entertainment.

Every morsel he ate was produced on special farms, rigidly controlled by the Guards Directorate, which supervised the growing of foodstuffs and the slaughtering of animals, and then transported these supplies along guarded routes to its own storehouses. And even then the food was laboratory-tested and fed to test animals, as well as Stalin's personal staff, before being consumed by Stalin himself.

The file also contained two detailed maps, one of the Kremlin and Stalin's personal quarters, and another of his Kuntsevo villa with information on its security system.

Before the drop Slanski would commit every word and detail to memory. When he had finished studying the file he replaced it in the recess in the floor.

He picked up the rusted biscuit tin, opened it and removed the contents. Two locks of hair tied neatly with red binding thread and a small photograph album, its black lacquered cover cracked and worn.

He remembered how he had clutched them both for months after his escape, clutched them hard to his chest, especially during the long cold journey across the tossing Atlantic swells, hidden in the hold of the stinking boat, hunger in his stomach like a pain but not as bad as the terrible pain in his heart, what was in that little box the only tangible reminder of his family. It offered a small lost boy the only sanity in the whole wide, confused world.

He looked down at the locks of hair. He had loved them both, Petya and Katya, had always wanted to protect them. He vaguely remembered the night a storm came, and little Petya had been so afraid. Lying in his bedroom in the darkness, Slanski heard him crying, fearful of the noise and light, of the terrible and frightening sounds outside.

"Are you afraid?"

Lightning flashed and thunder rolled beyond the bedroom window. Petya wouldn't stop sobbing.

"Don't be afraid. Come, sleep beside me."

Petya had snuggled in beside him, a mass of dark curls and puppy fat, still sobbing as Slanski's arms went around him and hugged him close.

"Don't cry, Petya. I'll always keep you safe. And if anyone or anything ever tries to hurt you I'll kill them. You understand, Petya? And when Mama has her baby, I'll keep baby safe too."

He had held Petya close all night, warm and safe.

But he hadn't kept him safe afterwards. Nor Katya.

Slanski put the locks of hair aside, one dark, one faded blond, all that remained of Petya and Katya, then opened the old album and stared down at the images.

* * *

The two men had parked the car five miles away off the forest road and trekked through the snowy woods in darkness up to the clearing. It stood on a ridge across the lake, sheltered by pine trees, and it was the best location they had found the previous day, with a reasonable view of the cabin.

It took them twenty minutes to set up the equipment, the white camouflage canvas tent and the tripods for the powerful military binoculars. By then it was after two and bitterly cold, a light dusting of snow on the ground, and they climbed wearily into their sleeping bags and tried to sleep.

21

Manhattan,
New York.
February 21st

Carlo Lombardi sat opposite Kurt Braun in the private office above the club on the Lower East Side docks. Lombardi said, "Your friends are still here at the lake house. I have my people watching it, but nice and discreet. Another guy arrived last week, big guy with a beard, looks like a fucking hick. He's still staying at the cabin. It was in the last report."

Braun frowned and leaned forward. "I read that. You got photographs of him?"

"Not this time, and it's too risky for my men to get close." Lombardi made a face as he looked at the map. "Who the fuck in their right mind would want to live up there? Real shit-kicking country."

Braun said, "This man who arrived at the cabin, I'll need to know who he is and what he's doing there."

Lombardi shrugged. "Tell your friend Arkashin, he'll figure something out. Me, I don't want to blow this thing just to have my boys get a closer look." He looked at Braun. "So what's the deal?"

Braun spoke for almost a minute. When he finished explaining, Lombardi whistled. "Serious business." He whistled again. "Serious fucking business."

Braun removed an envelope from his pocket and threw it on the table. Lombardi picked it up and riffled through the thick wad of bills inside. He suppressed the urge to whistle again.

He had a broad grin on his face as he stood. "Vince can come along."

"I presume he's capable?"

Lombardi smiled. "Capable? Mister, let me fucking tell you something, Vince cut his teeth on guns in the fucking cradle. So when do you want it done?"

"Considering the Soviet vessel will be arriving in New York in twenty-four hours, I think the sooner the better, don't you?"

New Hampshire.

Slanski parked the pickup in the town's main street. The windows of the pretty New England town were lit up in the evening darkness as they walked to the hotel on Concord Street. There was a dance band playing on the rostrum and the waiter showed them to a window table set with fresh flowers and a red candle. He came back with two bottles of beer and poured it into their glasses before taking their order and leaving. Anna looked around the hotel restaurant. It was Friday night and the people there were mostly middle-aged, but some young couples were on the dance floor.

When their meal came Slanski said, "It's not exactly New York, but this is where the locals come for their night out."

"It's the first time I've been to a place like this in America."

He smiled at her. "You know, you look very pretty tonight."

She looked across at him. He was staring at her. Her hair was down and she had put on lipstick and makeup and she wore the black dress she had worn the first night she had met him in New York.

"Is this where you come to find girlfriends?"

He smiled and shook his head. "Hardly, it's only my second time." He looked across and said, "Tell me about yourself, Anna."

"What do you want to know?"

He sipped his beer and put down the glass. "Anything you want to tell me."

"No," she said. "First you tell me about *your*self."

He raised his eyes, faintly startled, a little amused, and suddenly he seemed more at ease. "There isn't much to tell. Maybe it's better if you ask me what you want to know."

"How did you come to live in America?"

He toyed with his glass as if he seemed to be wondering how much to tell her. He didn't look at her directly when he spoke.

"My family lived in a village near Smolensk. When my parents died my younger brother and sister and myself were sent to an orphanage in Moscow. I was twelve. I hated the place. It was cold and heartless. So I made up my mind for us to escape. A relative of my father's lived in Leningrad and I thought he'd take us in. The night we planned to escape we were caught. But I managed to get away alone and climbed aboard a train at the Leningrad Station. When I reached Leningrad the relative wasn't very pleased and wanted to hand me back. I wandered the streets until I found myself at the docks looking at a ship. I didn't know where it was going and I don't think I much cared. But I knew that ship was destiny waiting for me." He smiled briefly. "You know what the Russians say. The seeds of what we'll do are sown in all of us. So I stowed away on board."

"What happened afterwards?"

"Two weeks later I was on the docks in Boston, cold and very hungry."

"For a boy of twelve what you did was remarkable."

He shook his head. "Not so remarkable. I didn't know it until I landed in Boston but there were four other stowaways on the same ship. In those days it was a lot easier to escape."

"How did you end up with Vassily?"

Slanski smiled. "I proved a little troublesome after I arrived in Boston. They sent me to an orphanage just like in Moscow, only the food was better and the people were kinder. But it didn't help. And then someone had the bright idea to send me up here."

"He's a good man, Vassily."

"The very best type of Russian. Good and kind."

"And your brother and sister, what happened to them?"

He didn't reply and as Anna looked at him she realized it was the first time she had seen any real sign of emotion in his face. There was a flash of pain but he seemed to want to suppress it as he leaned forward and the smile came back again.

"Now it's your turn."

"What do you want to know?"

"Do you like Massey?"

The question surprised her. She hesitated and looked away a moment. When she looked back she said, "He was the first good man I met when I escaped to Finland. The first honest and caring human being I'd known in a long time. He trusted me and helped me. They would have sent me back to Russia had it not been for him. For that I'll always be grateful."

"Were you ever married, Anna?"

Suddenly she wanted to tell him the truth, but she said, "Do we have to talk about it now?"

"Not if you don't want to."

"Then I don't want to." She changed the subject."Do you trust Popov?"

He laughed. "Of course."

"The Ukrainians were the worst beasts in the SS. They killed women and children without regard, without so much as a second thought. How can you trust him?"

"Is that why you kicked him between the legs?"

"He got what he deserved. He should have taken heed of his own advice."

"You really don't like him, do you, Anna?"

"Men like him were traitors. They betrayed their own people by fighting for the Germans. They raped, they murdered."

He heard the anger in her voice and said, "You're wrong about Popov, Anna. And you're neglecting an essential truth. In Russian schools they teach you a very biased history. The Ukraine was not always a part of the Soviet Union. Lenin subdued the country with his Bolsheviks. Then Stalin. He had almost five million Ukrainians killed or sent to Siberia. Men, women, children. Whole families uprooted and massacred. You have no idea of the scale of it and Soviet history books never tell the truth."

"And Popov is different?"

"He wasn't a war criminal. He was a camp instructor, and a good one. Besides, he hates the Reds."

"Why?"

"During the *kulak* wars when Stalin stole all the grain from the Ukraine his people perished in the famine. What the Germans did was terrible, but what the Russians did to the Ukraine was worse."

He looked at her but she didn't speak. He put down his napkin as if to change the subject and stood and held out his hand.

"Come on. Let's dance. This is getting too serious."

"But it's a long time since I danced."

"It's never too late to start again."

He led her onto the floor just as the band changed to a slow dance. He held her close and as they danced he said, "What happened at the ridge . . . I owe you an apology."

She looked up at his face for a moment. "You don't have to apologize."

"But I do. You were right, I didn't want you along, but not for the reasons you thought. I just didn't want you to be hurt getting involved in this."

"And do you still think it would be better if I didn't come along?"

He smiled. "Now I'm not so sure."

They danced two sets, and she was aware of Slanski holding her tight and how comforting it felt. There was some lively music at the end which had people kicking their legs in the air as a man played a fiddle. The dancing made her laugh, and when they came back to the table some more people came over to say hello and she saw several women nearby give her envious glances.

Slanski smiled. "You know you're going to ruin my bachelor reputation in this town?"

"Does it bother you?"

"Not one little bit."

It had been a long time since she had danced with a man. She remembered the night Ivan had danced with her on the banks of the Moscow River and suddenly it seemed a long time ago and she felt a little sad.

When they finished the meal they walked back to the car, and Slanski draped his coat around her shoulders to keep out the cold.

As they climbed into the pickup neither of them noticed the dark blue Ford sedan parked across the street, the two men inside watching them.

Massey's car was parked outside the house when they got back. He was sitting at the table drinking coffee with Vassily when they went in and when he saw Anna he smiled.

"It looks like you two have been enjoying yourselves."

Slanski said, "All part of the training, Jake. Where's Popov?"

"Gone to bed. He's starting early back to Boston tomorrow. Pull up a chair."

They sat and talked for ten minutes over coffee, and then Vassily went to bed. Anna said good night shortly thereafter. Massey waited until she had gone upstairs and said, "Something's different about her tonight."

"Like what?"

"A look in her eyes. What have you two been up to?"

Slanski found the bottle of bourbon and poured them one each. "A dance and a meal and a few drinks. It did her good."

"So how's she shaping up?"

"Better than I thought." He told Massey about Popov's experience and Massey smiled.

"He ought to have known better. Maybe he's getting old."

"How was Paris?"

Massey told him about the arrangements in Paris and Helsinki. "We'll use Lebel's girlfriend's dacha when you two get to Moscow. It's ideal—remote and safe."

"You think it's right getting Lebel's friend involved?"

"She won't be. If things go according to plan, as soon as Anna and you arrive in Moscow, Irena and she will leave on Lebel's train. Then you'll have the place to yourself."

Massey went over the details and then Slanski looked across at him. "You look like you've got something on your mind, Jake."

Massey drank his bourbon and put down the glass and stood. "Remember what I told you about Max Simon and his little girl? I think I've found who did it. A man who uses the name Kurt Braun. One of Moscow's hired killers. And he's in New York as an illegal."

"What's he doing in New York?"

"God only knows, but he can't be up to much good."

Slanski half smiled. "Why do I sense something coming?"

"From what I've heard of Braun, he's the worst scum you could meet. He's a psycho, Alex. He was serving time for manslaughter and rape in a German prison before the Germans got desperate for men and put him in an SS penal battalion. The Russians captured him in forty-five. They gave him a choice. Work for them or freeze to death in a Siberian camp. Not surprisingly, he chose the first option."

"So what are you going to do?"

Massey crossed to the window and looked back, a look of anger on his face. "Branigan wants me to forget about him."

"But you have other plans, right?"

"I checked with immigration. Braun arrived using a West German passport in the name of Huber three months ago. I've got his address. An apartment in Brooklyn. I want to pay it a visit. If it's him, I'm going to settle the score."

"What about the Russians?"

"There's nothing they could do about it. Braun's an illegal and they can't even acknowledge he exists. And hopefully he won't after we're finished."

"And Branigan?"

"He needn't ever know if we do it properly."

"We?"

Massey said hopefully, "I was kind of expecting you'd come along for the ride. Just the two of us. I'll need someone watching my back. Anna can stay here with Vassily."

"You're sure you know what you're doing, Jake?"

Massey nodded and Slanski said, "When?"

"Tomorrow."

It was almost seven when Massey and Slanski left for New York the next morning, but Dimitri Popov had risen early and left at six to drive back to Boston.

It was ten minutes later when Popov saw the Packard with New York license plates overtake him at speed. Five minutes later he saw the same Packard parked off the road, the driver kicking the front nearside wheel in anger.

The man waved him down and Popov pulled in and rolled down the window. "What's the problem?"

"I hit a fucking pothole in the snow. I ask you, mister, is this what we pay our taxes for?" The man held up a wheel jack. "The tire's warped as a bent nickel and my jack's broken. You got one I could borrow?"

Popov grunted and stepped out of the car. The little fat man with the thin mustache looked useless, all blubber with a New York accent and gold rings on his pudgy fingers. Popov found the jack in the boot and brought it over to the man, then pushed him aside and said, "Here, let me."

"Hey, thanks, mister, you're an angel."

The tire looked undamaged but as Popov bent down to examine it he felt the crushing blow of something metallic on the back of his skull and then another before he keeled over.

Then a foot slammed hard into his crotch and before he could yell in agony he heard the rush of feet from out of nowhere and the fat man's voice saying, "Get the fucking hick into the car."

Then something sharp jabbed into his arm and he went under.

22

***New York.
February 22nd***

It was just after one and raining hard as Massey pulled up outside the apartment block in Brooklyn. It was an old red-brick tenement building with a fire escape at the back, and the place looked seriously in need of attention.

"How do you want to handle it?"

"The simplest way is always the best." Massey smiled and held up a piece of headed paper with the seal of the US government. "Internal Revenue come to have a friendly chat. Braun's apartment is on the top floor at the back. You go up the fire escape and cover me, while I go in the front. Once I'm inside, we take him."

Slanski tossed his cigarette out of the window and took out a Tokarev pistol with a silencer, then slipped it into his waistband under his coat. "You're sure you know what you're doing, Jake?"

Massey removed a snub-nosed Smith and Wesson .38 from the glove compartment and checked the chamber before slipping it into his pocket.

"Trust me."

Feliks Arkashin was tired. There were dark rings under his eyes from lack of sleep and as he turned from the bedroom window of Braun's apartment he looked at Popov's body slumped in the chair.

Two of Lombardi's men had delivered him, and the ropes around the big man were tied securely, but Arkashin knew there was no need. The man was barely conscious from the drug and hardly capable of moving.

Arkashin lit a cigarette and came back from the window. He stared down at Popov's bruised face, at the trickle of blood running from his mouth down his beard, then his hand reached over and lifted the man's chin.

"You're really making this very difficult. Don't you think it would be a lot easier if you told me what Massey is up to at the lake?"

Popov grunted and his eyes flickered, then his head rolled in Arkashin's hand and slumped to one side. Arkashin sighed. He and Braun had spent an hour trying to make the man talk and he had barely uttered a word.

His wallet lay on the table. His name was Dimitri Popov, which told him nothing except he was Russian or Ukrainian. No doubt one of the émigrés the Americans used. There was a hypodermic syringe on the table and a phial of scopolamine, the truth drug, Arkashin's last resort. As he reached for them he heard the knock on the door and turned, slightly alarmed.

He was about to reach for the Walther pistol on the coffee table when he heard the voice.

"I really wouldn't, not unless you want to lose your fingers."

The blond man who stood behind him held a silenced Tokarev pistol in his hand and the window that led to the fire escape was open, the curtain blowing in the breeze. Arkashin paled when he recognized Slanski.

"Just drop the gun on the table, then be a good boy and open the front door, nice and easy."

Arkashin did as he was told, placing the Walther on the table, breaking out in a cold sweat as he crossed to the door. His face dropped when he saw who stood there.

As Massey came in, Slanski said quietly, "Jake, I think you'd better take a look at who our friend's got in the bedroom."

Massey sat in the chair opposite Arkashin and said in a hard voice, "You'd better tell me what the hell is going on here, and fast."

Arkashin smiled nervously. "I could very well ask the same. It would be interesting to know what you're up to. But I ought to tell you I'm an accredited diplomat with the UN Soviet Mission and as such immune from law."

"Wrong. It makes your situation all the more difficult, so cut the crap." Massey held up the gun in his hand and clicked back the hammer. "Five seconds and I'm counting."

Just then Slanski came back into the room supporting a dazed-looking Popov. When the big Ukrainian saw Arkashin his eyes blazed.

"If you don't pull the trigger, Jake, I will."

Massey said to him, "Tell me what happened."

Popov wiped a trickle of blood from his mouth and pointed to Arkashin. "Our friend here's after the woman. They've been tailing her. After I left the cabin some of his men fooled me into stopping my car and knocked me unconscious. Then they took me here and tried to get me to talk. His name's Arkashin."

Slanski tossed a handful of maps and photographs on the table. "These were in the bedroom. It looks like Arkashin's got a keen interest in photography. And in us."

Massey looked at the photographs. Some of them were of Anna alone, others of him and Anna and Slanski together coming out of a hotel and at the Boston railway station. The maps were of New Hampshire and he noticed the markings that circled the lake.

Massey turned pale and looked over at Arkashin. "Where's your friend Braun?"

Arkashin said gruffly, "I don't have to answer any of your questions."

Massey crossed to him and put the gun against his forehead and said, "That might be true or not, but if you don't so help me I'm going to punch a hole in you so big you could run a train through it."

"I really don't think that would be wise or necessary."

"I don't give two shits for your immunity, Arkashin. And it doesn't apply. What you're involved in here is kidnapping. That's a serious federal offense. So talk before I lose my patience and this thing goes off."

Arkashin sighed and spread his hands in a gesture of helplessness. "You understand, we couldn't let the woman get away just like that."

"Who's we?"

"The embassy had orders from Moscow."

Suddenly everything was clear to Massey and he stepped closer. "How did you know where to find her?"

"We tailed her from Helsinki. We've been following her since she arrived in this country."

Massey was silent, then he said, "Why? She's a nobody."

Arkashin smiled faintly. "Where people like you and me are concerned, ours is not to reason why, Massey. We simply do what our masters tell us."

"How do you know my name?"

"Your activities are well known to us. Finding out your identity from the photographs wasn't difficult."

Massey's face flushed angrily. "Where's Braun?"

When Arkashin hesitated, Slanski pushed the silenced Tokarev hard into his temple until the man's eyes opened wide in terror.

"Gone to get the woman."

"Alone?"

Arkashin shrugged. "Does it matter now? You won't be able to stop him."

"What's he going to do with her?"

"Put her on a Soviet boat in New York Harbor."

"How long has Braun been gone?"

When Arkashin didn't reply, Slanski struck him hard across the face with the pistol, drawing blood.

Arkashin staggered back. When he had recovered he wiped blood from his nose. "That wasn't necessary."

Slanski's face was white with rage and he gestured to Popov and said, "It'll get a lot worse if I let my friend here repay you for what you did to him. When did Braun leave?"

Arkashin glanced nervously over at Popov, then said, "He left for Boston two hours ago by train."

Slanski said to Popov, "Take him inside and tie him up. Good and tight. So he can't move or talk."

"With pleasure. And then I'm going to beat him to pulp."

Massey glared at the Russian. "After this you won't see daylight for a long time, Arkashin. Assisting an illegal resident, intent to murder, kidnapping, carrying an illegal weapon. And I'm sure there's more your immunity won't cover. You're finished."

Arkashin turned noticeably pale.

As Popov went toward him, Arkashin grabbed for the Walther on the table. When Popov reached to wrench it from him he was too slow and the gun went off, hitting the Ukrainian in the face. As Popov was flung back, Slanski fired once, hitting Arkashin in the heart.

Massey had turned white as he went to feel Popov's pulse. "Christ . . . he's dead . . ."

Slanski came back from Arkashin's body sprawled on the floor, the Russian's clothes bloodied from the wound in his chest.

"Arkashin too. Jake, this is getting muddier by the minute. What now?"

"We get out of here fast. Leave everything as it is. I'll figure out what to do later."

Slanski said softly, "We're never going to get to the lake in time. It's six hours away by car and Arkashin's people have a head start."

"Then let's get going."

Massey was already moving toward the fire escape when Slanski gripped his arm and said, "Wait . . . !"

He crossed to the table and picked up one of the maps. There was sweat on his face as he looked back at Massey and said, "There may be a quicker way. But it's just a chance."

New Hampshire.

Carlo Lombardi hated the countryside. He was used to the smell of gas fumes and smog—chirping birds and trees weren't really his thing. He wrinkled his nose as Vince rolled down the Packard's window and the blast of cold fresh air swept in.

"Put the fucking thing up. What you trying to do? Kill me?"

Vince did as he was told as Braun sat silently in the back. They had come off the highway ten minutes ago, Lombardi doing the driving after picking up Braun from Boston station. The quaint New England wooden houses flashed past, but Lombardi wasn't impressed.

"What's the story with the hick with the beard?"

Braun flicked him a look. "He's Arkashin's problem now. How much farther?"

"Another hour."

Lombardi turned to Vince. "You know the plan. Anybody gets in the way you blast them. You got the pieces?"

Vince reached down and hefted up a canvas bag. He reached in and removed three handguns, two sawn-off shotguns and an MI carbine.

Lombardi said, "Jesus . . . what the fuck you expecting? Bears?"

Vince shrugged. "You said there could be trouble. You never know."

Lombardi turned to Braun seated in the backseat and smiled. "I'll say this for the kid. He comes prepared."

Vassily stepped out of the boat and helped Anna onto the wooden walkway.

They had spent an hour fishing on the lake and caught three large trout, and as they walked back up to the cabin together Anna said, "Tell me about the photograph in the cabin. Is it of Alex's family?"

"His father and mother, brother and sister. He told you about them?"

"Enough to make a guess about the photograph."

"Then he must like you, Anna."

"Why do you say that?"

He looked at her knowingly for a moment, then said, "Alex never talks about them. I think you must have found a chink in his armor."

She smiled. "When I came up here the first day I have to admit I found him difficult."

Vassily laughed. "That's nothing compared to the first day *he* came here."

"What was he like?"

"Like a wild little wolf cub. Impossible to tame. He'd refuse to eat or talk. Just wanted to be on his own, like he had a pain so deep in his heart no one could reach."

"But you reached it."

Vassily shook his head. "I don't think anyone's ever reached it. And I don't think anyone ever will."

"So why did you let him stay?"

They had reached the cabin and Vassily put down the fishing things and the trout and sat on the veranda.

"I knew he'd been through a bad time and didn't trust anyone but himself. He needed distraction and he needed a father. I did what I could and taught him about the woods and about hunting. I don't know of anyone who could survive better in those woods than Alex, even me. It took his mind off things and he gradually settled in. And after everything that had happened to him he needed space, not people around him."

"What happened to his parents?"

"He didn't tell you?"

"No."

Vassily thought for a moment, then shook his head slowly. "Anna, some things a man is allowed to keep private. If Alex wanted to tell you, he would have. You'll have to let him tell you that story himself. Now, why don't you fetch some kindling for the stove and I'll cook these fish."

Anna stepped off the veranda. She looked back at him as she brushed a strand of hair from her face.

"Vassily . . ."

"What?"

"I like you. I like you very much."

Vassily smiled before she turned away. Then he stood up and went inside. At the window he hesitated and saw her disappear into the woods. Then he went into the kitchen to gut the fish.

An hour later Lombardi saw the sign on the road, TRESPASSERS KEEP OUT!, and turned the Packard onto the snowed-under dirt track.

Fifty yards further along they saw the lake in the distance. Lombardi pulled in and Vince and Braun were already climbing out as he switched off the engine.

Braun nodded down toward the cabin and looked at Lombardi. "That's it?"

"That's it. Uncle fucking Tom's cabin. Ready when you are."

Vince handed out the weapons, and Lombardi checked that he had the knife in his waistband, then said, "OK, let's get this fucking thing over with. And Vince, try not to sound like a fucking bear coming through the woods, understand?"

Braun said, "I'll take the back way, you two take the front. And be careful."

Vassily saw the two men come out of the woods as he stood at the kitchen window.

They were fifty yards away and one carried a shotgun and the other a carbine as they moved toward the front of the cabin. He put down the gutting knife and wiped his hands before picking up the Winchester rifle.

He stepped out onto the veranda and said to the men, "Didn't you see the sign? You're on private property. Turn around and go back the way you came."

The fatter of the two strangers appeared to be in charge, the one with the thin mustache. The younger man beside him was nervously fingering his carbine.

The fat man smiled and went to move closer. "Hey, take it easy. We got lost. Maybe you can help us."

Vassily raised the Winchester and said, "No closer, or I'll help you to the cemetery. I said you're on private property."

The fat man said boldly, "Put down the rifle, old man. That way you won't get hurt."

Vassily hesitated. "Who are you and what do you want?"

"Just a friendly talk with the woman. Where is she?"

Vassily turned pale and cocked the Winchester's hammer with his thumb. "You step any closer, fat man, and I kill you."

"This is none of your business. Just bring out the woman and no one gets hurt. We just want to talk with her."

"Is that why you come here with guns?"

The fat man stepped closer.

Vassily aimed the Winchester. "Drop your weapons—now. Or I kill you."

"Fuck you," said Lombardi.

The shotgun in his hands came up and exploded and the shot hit Vassily in the right shoulder and he was flung back against the wall. As he fell back onto the veranda the men were already moving toward him, and when he grabbed for the Winchester one of them kicked it away and he saw the flash of the blade as the fat man knelt over him. "Too slow, old man. Where's the woman? Don't fuck with me. Where is she, or I cut your fucking heart out, you red-faced hick."

Halfway through the woods Anna heard the gunshot and her heart skipped.

As she turned she saw the man off to her right and froze. He held a shotgun in his hands and at first she thought he was a hunter, but the shot had come from the direction of the cabin and when she saw the look on the man's face she knew something wasn't right.

The man raised the weapon at her and grinned. He had a livid red scar on his face.

"Stay where you are."

Anna halted, and as she looked at the man, confused, he came toward her and she saw the grin widen.

"Nice and easy now. We're going to move back the way you came."

Her first instinct was to turn and run, but when she went to move the man came after her and grabbed her savagely by the hair. As she was spun around she lashed out with her foot. She kicked the man in the knee and he crumpled, dropping the shotgun, but when she tried to grab the weapon the man yanked her hair painfully hard and pulled her up.

"You little bitch!"

He struck her hard across the face, again and again, so hard she thought her jaw had broken, and then his fist struck her in the back of the neck and all she remembered after that was darkness.

23

The small harbor in the broad inlet sixty miles south of Boston known as Buzzards Bay was deserted. The man who walked across to the waterside hangar with Massey and Slanski was tall and thin, with sad eyes and a permanent six o'clock shadow. He had a dour face that suggested he found life an unpleasant experience, and his movements were heavy and unhurried.

"You know, it's really quite irregular, Mr. Slanski, especially in this weather. There ain't no cloud but that damned wind's pretty near sharp enough to skin a dog."

"I appreciate that, Abe."

"What's the big rush that you got to get up to the lake?"

"An emergency."

Abe Barton looked out doubtfully at the sea and scratched his jaw.

"Well, I ain't too keen about taking off in those waves and coming back in darkness, but I guess on account of it's an emergency I can oblige. I wouldn't do it normally, mind."

It had taken Slanski and Massey almost three hours to drive north to the bay and the tension on both their faces showed.

The harbor town had no more than a dozen wooden houses built around it and the hangar was at the far end of the sea wall. There was a skid ramp for launching the flying boat into the water. The hangar doors were closed.

The flying boat worked out of the bay taking hunting and fishing parties up to northern New England in season, and Abe Barton was the pilot, mechanic and caretaker. He unlocked the padlock to the hangar and rolled back the doors, to reveal a bulbous-nosed Seebee single-engine flying boat inside. A tarpaulin covered the nose and Barton pulled it away.

He rubbed his stubby jaw. "She'll need to be refueled. There's just enough in the tanks to warm her up."

"How long will that take?"

"Ten minutes should do it. There's fuel in the storeroom back up at the house."

Slanski said impatiently, "Then I suggest we get moving. We'll leave the car here."

Barton sighed and crossed to the door. There were a couple of small two-wheel upright trolleys by the hangar door for carrying the fuel barrels and he dragged one out morosely.

When he had gone Slanski said to Massey, "It's going to be dark in an hour. Landing on the lake in daylight is difficult enough if the water swell's bad. In near-darkness it's pretty near impossible."

Massey looked over at the flying boat. "You're sure Barton can fly this damned thing?"

"Judge for yourself. He knows the lake area pretty well." Slanski nodded to another trolley in the corner. "We'd better give him a hand with the fuel or we'll be here all day."

Five minutes later they all came back, Barton dragging his trolley like a condemned man. Massey and Slanski quickly helped him load the fuel with the mechanical pump.

When they had finally winched the Seebee into the water, Barton climbed into the cockpit and started the Franklin engine. It throbbed into life first time.

Anna came awake with a throbbing headache.

She was in the cabin, lying on her back on the floor. Vassily was beside her, tied in a chair.

She looked at him in horror. His skin was white and his eyes half closed, an ugly wound in his right shoulder, blood oozing from it, his face badly cut where he had been beaten. His head was slumped to one side and a strange gurgling sound came from his lips.

Anna screamed.

"Shut the fuck up, lady."

When she looked over she saw two men. One was the man with the scarred face from the woods. He sat in a chair by the window, smoking a cigarette, a shotgun across his knees as he stared over at her silently.

The second man, the one who had spoken, was short and fat and had a thin black mustache. He sat on the table, a slim knife in his hand as he picked at his nails with it and grinned. "So, you're back in the land of the living?"

She ignored them both and struggled to her feet. There were tears in her eyes as she moved beside Vassily. His eyes flickered as he recognized her.

"Anna . . ."

"No, don't speak, Vassily."

He was still losing blood and she felt his pulse. It was weak. She looked back at the men.

"He'll die if he doesn't get help. You have to do something . . . Please!"

The fat man said, "I'll fucking kill him if you don't get away from there."

He slid off the table and came over and grabbed Anna by the hair and threw her into a chair.

"Now you sit there and keep that mouth shut."

"He's dying . . . !"

The scar-faced man stood and came over and slapped her hard across the face, then his hand gripped her jaw painfully and he stared into her face as he spoke in Russian.

"Massey and Slanski, where did they go?"

Anna felt the blood drain from her, a sudden overwhelming fear in her heart, and she opened her mouth to speak but no words came, a terrible truth dawning on her.

The man slapped her hard again. "I asked you a question. Where are your friends?"

"I . . . I don't know."

The man lifted his shotgun and aimed it at Vassily. "The truth, or I kill him."

"I . . . I don't know . . . they left . . . this morning . . ."

"To go where?"

"I don't know."

"When will they be back?"

"I don't . . ."

The man eased back the hammers of the shotgun and aimed at Vassily's head.

Anna said, "Tonight. They said they would be back tonight. I don't know when. I'm telling you the truth . . . please."

For several seconds the man just stood there, aiming the weapon at Vassily, then he grinned and lifted Anna's face.

The grin vanished as he gripped her face hard, grinding his teeth as he said, "Don't lie to me. Lie to me again and I kill you, understand?"

There was a noise from behind and another man came into the room from the kitchen, young, heavily built, carrying a long wooden box.

"Guess what I found?"

He put the box down on the table and flipped open the lid. Anna saw it was the weapons they had used in training with Popov.

The young man grinned. "They were in the back. There's a trapdoor under the kitchen floor, kind of like a storage room, full of food and stuff."

The fat man with the mustache came over and looked through the box of weapons, then whistled as he picked up a Tokarev machine-pistol.

"Heavy stuff. Looks like our friends here are going to start a war." He looked at the man with the scar. "What the fuck's going on here, Braun?"

Braun thought for a moment, then flicked a look at Vassily. He said to the younger man, "Take the woman outside. I'll deal with her later."

When they had gone, Lombardi said to Braun, "What's the story here?"

Braun ignored the question, stepped over to Vassily and gripped his face hard. He was still conscious, but his eyes were barely focused. Braun said, "What else are Massey and Slanski hiding, old man?"

Vassily's eyes flicked up weakly at Braun, but he didn't speak. Braun slapped him savagely across the jaw. "I won't ask again. Next time I tell my friend outside to hurt the woman. Hurt her bad. This is your property. The weapons were here. Why?"

"Massey . . . brought them. I . . . don't know why," Vassily gurgled.

"What else did he bring?"

"I . . . don't know."

Braun said sharply to Lombardi, "Bring the woman back."

"No," Vassily pleaded hoarsely. "I told the truth."

"What other hiding places have you got in the cabin?"

Vassily's head slumped onto his chest and Braun grabbed his hair and stared into his face. "You want to watch while the woman's raped? Because that's what's going to happen to the bitch if you don't talk. Then I kill her. Slowly."

Vassily's eyes came open drowsily. He seemed to be having difficulty breathing. "Don't . . . don't hurt her."

Braun grinned. "You help me, and I won't."

But before Vassily could speak again his eyes rolled and his head slumped to one side. Braun hit him across the face, again and again, in frustration, but Vassily didn't return to consciousness.

Lombardi said, "You're wasting your time, the hick's out of it, he's lost too much blood."

Braun picked up the shotgun and moved toward the stairs. He said to Lombardi, "Search the storage room again. And search downstairs thoroughly."

"Where you going?"

"To see what else I can find."

Fifteen minutes out from Buzzards Bay the clear air was turbulent and Barton had to increase altitude to five thousand feet to avoid the worst of it.

The takeoff had been bumpy to say the least, but Barton seemed to know exactly what he was doing. The Seebee had finally lifted off gracefully and climbed to two thousand feet before banking northwest.

It was growing dark in the cabin and they could see the vast speckle of lights that was Boston coming on in the stretch of dusk off to the right. Barton turned back and said above the engine noise, "Another ten minutes and we'll be over the state line into New Hampshire. I'll try to get as close to the cabin as I can, but I can't promise, mind. Depends on what the water's like."

Slanski said, "Forget the cabin. I want you to land further away up the lake, a mile up the shore. And leave off the landing lights on the way in."

Barton looked puzzled and glanced from Slanski to Massey. "Hey, I thought you folks said this was an emergency?"

"It is."

"Well, I need those lights to see what the water's like," Barton protested.

"If I hit whitecaps too damned hard they can crack the prow or make me dip a wing into the water."

Slanski put a hand on Barton's shoulder. "Just do as I ask, Abe. And as soon as you touch down and we get away, do me a favor and wait half an hour in case we need you to take us back. No longer than that, or you'll have trouble landing back in Buzzards Bay."

"I got trouble enough as it is doing what you ask. I need those damned lights."

"Please, Abe, just do as I say."

Barton frowned in puzzlement, then he shrugged and turned back to the Seebee's controls.

Braun went through the rooms upstairs one by one. Even though he knew the house was empty he moved cautiously, stepping into each bedroom with care, the shotgun ready in his hands.

He found the woman's room first and searched through her clothes and a small suitcase under the bed. There was nothing of interest, but when he found her underwear he fondled it and smiled.

The other rooms were bare and functional. The old man's had nothing much besides tatty clothes, some tobacco and a couple of old books in Russian.

When he found Slanski's bedroom he went through it with much more care. He searched through the clothes in the wardrobe, emptying the pockets, and two leather suitcases full of old clothes, lying at the bottom. He turned over the mattress and looked underneath, but found nothing.

In frustration, Braun kicked over the bedside locker and it toppled onto the floor. He went to the window and idly lit a cigarette, and as he stood there something made him look down. The locker had rattled the roughly hewn wooden floorboards under the window and one of them felt loose as he stepped on it. He knelt and pried it with his nail. He saw the rusting biscuit tin in the recess and opened it. After several moments examining the contents he flung them away. Then he saw the file lying below. There were four pages inside the folder headed "Joseph Stalin," and he read them quickly.

For several moments he stood there, guessing the value of his discovery, then he smiled to himself. Moscow would pay for what he had just found, no question.

He folded the file and tucked it carefully down his trousers, then searched through the rest of the contents of the box before discarding them without interest. When he had finished checking the other rooms thoroughly he went back downstairs.

It was growing dark outside and Lombardi was trying to light an oil lamp. He burned his fingers in the process and said to the old man slumped unconscious in the chair, "Ain't you hicks ever heard of fucking electricity?"

Lombardi looked over at Braun. "There were only provisions downstairs. The rest of the place is clean. What did you find?"

"Nothing," Braun lied.

Lombardi said, "So what next?"

"We leave and take the woman with us."

"I thought we were going to wait for the broad's friends?"

"There isn't time."

Lombardi frowned. "Whatever you say. What about the old man?"

"He's seen our faces. Kill him."

The Seebee circled the lake in a perfect arc, then Barton nosed her down to three hundred feet above the water.

Dusk was falling rapidly and the lake was in almost complete darkness, just a faint shimmering of silver light on the water. Barton insisted on flicking on the landing lights briefly to see what the water surface looked like below. It seemed calm enough but toward the shore there were choppy waves, and as Barton turned back he said to Slanski, "Better make sure you're strapped in and holding on, this could be a mite bumpy."

There was sweat on Barton's brow as he dropped down to a hundred feet and started gently to ease the flying boat down. They were headed toward a stretch of shore about a mile north from the cabin, coming in alongside the land, about a hundred feet from the bank.

At sixty feet the Seebee started to bump with the updraft over the water, a sudden gust hitting them and throwing them off to the left, closer to the land.

Barton said, "*Jeez . . .*," and corrected, then continued to ease forward the control stick. At twenty feet he pulled back on the throttle and the Seebee hit the water hard, bumped, then settled, and it was down, skimming and bumping over the lake as the propeller idled and Barton let out a sigh, easing the boat closer to the shore before looking back over his shoulder.

"This is as close as it gets. You folks are going to have to get wet."

They were twenty feet from the shore, and Slanski was already tearing open the cabin door and climbing out, Massey behind him. Slanski jumped out into the waist-high water and started to wade toward the bank.

Barton said to Massey, "I'm waiting no longer than half an hour, understand? What the hell kind of emergency is this, anyhow?"

Massey didn't even reply but plunged into the water after Slanski, who was already at the shore.

"You hear something?"

Lombardi had crossed to the open door, then he stepped toward the veranda and stood there, his head cocked to one side. He looked back in at Braun. "I heard a fucking engine."

Braun came and stood beside him, listening. Finally he said, "I hear nothing."

"It sounded like a plane." Lombardi cocked his ear again. "But it's gone."

Braun shook his head. "Forget it."

He crossed to the table and picked up the oil lamp and said to Lombardi, "Untie the ropes on the old man."

"Why? What you got in mind?"

Braun removed the glass cowl on the oil lamp. The flame guttered for a moment, then burned brightly again.

Lombardi frowned. "You going to set the place on fire?"

"As a lesson to our absent friends. The nearest town is five miles away. With this terrain no one will see the flames. First, go outside and shoot out the tires on the jeep and pickup."

Lombardi took the .38 from his pocket. "You're not going to plug the old man?"

Braun smiled coldly. "I thought that pleasure would be yours."

A mile into the woods and Massey was out of breath.

He saw Slanski racing ahead of him in the dusk, running like a man possessed as he scrambled through the forest. He was running fast and silently, but Massey had trouble keeping up, tripping over deadwood and fallen branches.

Five minutes on and he saw Slanski slow and look back, pointing to tell him he was going on ahead, and Massey waved back. He saw Slanski give a burst of speed and then he disappeared.

A hundred yards on Massey had to slow down to catch his breath, then suddenly, somewhere off in the distance back toward the lake, he heard the roar of an engine and recognized the sound of the flying boat.

Massey swore. Barton hadn't waited long.

Suddenly Massey heard another sound, a gunshot, then another, half a dozen shots one after another and then moments later a couple more.

When Lombardi came back he undid the ropes around Vassily. Braun lit a cigarette from the naked flame of the oil lamp, then said calmly, "Move back."

Lombardi stepped back and Braun tossed the lamp into a corner of the room and the fuel spread on the wooden floor and ignited.

As the flames started to lick the corner walls, Braun said to Lombardi, "I'll take the woman to the car. Finish the old man."

"A pleasure."

Braun stepped out. Vince came back in moments later and stood at the door. "Mind if I watch?"

Lombardi handed him his shotgun and took out the pistol again and held it by his side as the knife flashed in his other hand.

"You might learn something, kid. I'll show you how to gut a shitkicker. Watch closely, this is going to be quick."

As Lombardi went toward Vassily, he sensed a presence behind him.

Lombardi looked around as an angry voice said, "Touch him and I kill you."

A blond man stood there in the kitchen door, his face covered in sweat. He had a pistol in his hand.

Lombardi said, "What the fuck . . . ?"

The pistol in Lombardi's other hand came up and Slanski shot him in the eye. Lombardi screamed, then Slanski shot him again in the head, and as Lombardi was punched back out of the door, the second man fired both barrels of his shotgun in panic.

It went wide and the blast hit Vassily in the chest and flung him back into the flames.

Slanski screamed, "No!"

As the second man wrenched out a pistol and went to shoot again, Slanski fired, hitting him in the head, then the chest, then the head again, a terrible rage in him as he kept firing.

The flames rose and spread in the cabin and smoke filled the room, choking the air, and as Slanski tried to move frantically toward Vassily's limp and bloodied body engulfed in flames, he already knew there was nothing he could do.

Braun was hardly fifty yards from the cabin when he heard the shots and the scream, instinct telling him something was terribly wrong.

He looked back and saw the flames lick inside the cabin but no sign of Lombardi and his bodyguard. The woman suddenly tried to struggle free and Braun grabbed her and dragged her at a run toward the car, impulse telling him to get away.

"Move, you bitch! Move!"

He had gone another twenty yards when he looked back and saw the blond man come down the veranda dragging a body out of the burning cabin, then the man looked up and saw Braun and broke into a run toward him. Braun fired off two quick shots in his direction, then pulled the woman against him as a shield and shouted to the man, "Come any closer and I kill her!"

The man slowed but kept coming, and then Braun saw the gun in his hand. He recognized him from the photographs. Slanski. The Wolf.

He flicked an anxious look back at the Packard. It was thirty meters away along the narrow track through the woods.

Close enough to get away.

He moved backward smartly, still holding the woman in front of him.

He looked back. Slanski had started to move toward him again.

Braun pressed the gun hard into the woman's head and roared, "Another step and I kill the bitch!"

Slanski halted thirty meters away. There was sweat on Braun's face as he reached the car, but he knew now Slanski was too far away to stop him. He smiled as he yanked open the driver's door and shoved Anna inside. He fumbled for the keys in the ignition. They were gone.

"Kurt Braun?"

Braun spun around in his seat, a look of panic on his face as he heard the voice.

Another man sat behind him in the back, rage in his eyes and a .38 in his hand, the weapon aimed at Braun's face.

"I asked are you Kurt Braun?"

Before Braun could reply Massey squeezed the trigger.

The cabin was still in flames as Slanski held a storm lamp over the bodies laid out a distance away.

There was a terrible look of grief on Slanski's face as Massey looked down at Vassily's body. They had searched the others for forms of identity but Braun's was the only one Massey was interested in.

Vassily's body was badly burned and there was a gunshot wound in his chest, another in his shoulder. Massey looked at Slanski for a long time. It was the first time he had ever seen such a look of anguish on his face, and he touched his arm.

"This is my fault. I'm sorry, Alex."

Slanski was suddenly white with anger. "It's no one's fault but the people who did it. He didn't have to die and they didn't have to kill him." He looked at Massey, a frightening rage in his eyes. "Someone's going to pay for this, Jake. Someone's going to pay dearly, so help me . . ."

"Leave that to me, Alex. But right this minute, all bets are off. We're canceling the operation."

Slanski shook his head fiercely. "You do that and I go in alone, with or without your help. I told you someone's going to pay and I know who it is . . ."

Massey said grimly to Slanski, "Not now, we talk later."

"I mean it, Jake. I go in with or without your help."

"We can't do it, Alex. Branigan would never go along, not when he hears what's happened to Arkashin. And what's happened here only makes it worse. It's a security risk."

"When they find Arkashin's body no one's going to know who did it. And Arkashin couldn't have known what we intend. Besides, he's dead."

Massey shook his head. "Maybe, but Branigan will hear. Popov's body is in Braun's apartment. And Branigan will put two and two together."

Slanski looked over at Anna and said to Massey, "Either way it's going to take time before Branigan finds out. Anna can stay if you're worried. But me, I'm still going in."

Anna looked at him and said quietly, "If you go, I go too."

Massey looked at them both. For a long time he seemed to hesitate, then he said to Slanski, "You're angry, but are you really sure about this?"

"Me, I'm on this ride to the end of the tracks. You'd better ask Anna that question."

"Anna . . . ?"

She hesitated, then looked over at Slanski's face and said, "Yes, I'm sure."

For a long time Massey seemed unable to make up his mind, then he sighed and said, "OK, Alex, we do it your way. We'll have to bury the bodies in the woods in case anyone comes by. I'll worry about Branigan later." Suddenly Massey seemed at a loss for words. "I'll help you bury Vassily."

Slanski shook his head and said fiercely, "Not in the woods with those vermin who killed him. Down by the lake."

Massey said quietly, "There's a shovel in the jeep. I'll get it."

Grief flooded Slanski's face again as he looked over at the burning cabin, flames searing up through the rafters and raging in the darkness. There was a crash and an explosion of sparks as part of the roof caved in.

He stared at the flames, his mouth tight in anger, and as Massey went to move toward the jeep he grabbed his arm and said in a hard voice, "Just tell me, when do we go in?"

"There's a flight to London from Boston tonight, with a connection to Stockholm and Helsinki. We can make it if we hurry. We'll use Braun's car. I've got passports for both of you."

"You didn't answer the question. How long before we go in?"

"Forty-eight hours."

PART FOUR

February 23rd–24th 1953

24

New Hampshire.
February 23rd

It was almost 9:00 A.M. the following day when Collins drove up to Boston airport from New York.

He met the group off the Canadian Airlines flight from Ottawa, two women and a man, younger than himself, and by the time they had hired the camper and equipment in Boston and applied for the hunting permits in New Hampshire, it was almost noon.

The man named Collins was thin but well muscled, in his early forties, and his eyes had the steely, detached look of someone who had seen death and even dispensed it. The younger man wore glasses and his dark hair was cropped short. There was a faint hint of the Slav in his high cheekbones but his demeanor and manner were pure North American.

The two women were in their late twenties, both pretty and vivacious, but Collins knew they would be as capable as he was with any kind of weapon, even their hands. For the purpose of the mission they were friends who had met on a camping holiday the previous summer at Lake Ontario, renewing their acquaintance. The briefing they had received had been specific about using extreme caution.

The hired camping trailer had been Collins's idea. Under cover of a hunting party they wouldn't arouse suspicion. All of them were illegals with no police or criminal record, unknown to the CIA or the Royal Canadian Mounted Police. The rifles and pistols were legally bought and licensed in their own names.

They turned onto the road that led down to Kingdom Lake just after one that afternoon. Snow chains had been fitted on the tires so they wouldn't leave identifiable tracks. The landscape seemed totally deserted. It reminded him of the Caucasus of his homeland, and who he really was, despite almost eight years as an illegal American citizen—Major Grigori Galushko, KGB 1st Directorate.

They parked the trailer a mile from the cabin on the lakeside and decided to cook lunch before venturing closer. That way they were covered if anyone who had seen them came to investigate. But no one came and it was almost four when they changed into their hunting clothes, all of them wearing gloves, and started to stroll toward the cabin, the men carrying the rifles. They walked in couples and they made as much noise as they could, joking and laughing as they strolled, acting like a quartet of married friends out for a winter shooting holiday, but their eyes were everywhere, watching any movement, hearing every sound.

A hundred yards from the lakeside cabin they stopped for a cigarette and to drink from hip flasks. Galushko's eyes flicked nervously about the landscape. There was almost no snow in the forest itself, the ground protected by the trees. He still saw no movement, heard no sounds, only those of the wind and lake water lapping gently, some pigeons in the pine trees above cooing their arrival.

They saw the boat tied up at the promontory and the burned-out cabin, smoke still curling from its embers, the jeep and the pickup parked nearby, the tires shot through, but no sign of life.

Galushko's face had a worried look. Instead of walking directly toward the cabin, they skirted it and walked back into the woods. It took them another half-hour to determine that the area was deserted, circling it carefully, until they finally came back to the charred remains of the cabin. Each of them moved more like practiced hunters now, careful and watchful, as if they were stalking some animal hiding inside.

It was Galushko and the younger man who went toward the cabin first, moving cautiously onto the remains of the veranda. The women remained a distance away, watching in case anyone appeared.

"Anybody here?"

Galushko called out twice, but no one appeared. He could hear the two women doing the same outside, their voices carrying on the breeze and out onto the cold lake like ghostly cries for help. But still no one came and no voice answered.

Then Galushko and his companion took their time, sifting through the remains.

When they checked the area around the cabin they saw no sign of a disturbance at first, but then Galushko's practiced eyes saw the dark stains on the ground, the patchy snow all around melted from the heat. When he bent to examine the stains he knew it was blood.

He stood and glanced anxiously at his companion.

After that they moved more quickly.

It took them almost half an hour, searching the area as thoroughly as they could, then checking the vehicles and the boat and the perimeter of the lake, before they moved out into the woods again.

Another hour later they had found nothing and Galushko was frustrated. They were about to go back to the trailer, had walked back along the lake shore, when one of the women went off to relieve herself in the woods, the cold biting at them all. Galushko saw her undo the buttons of her jeans as she walked away, watching her figure as she retreated farther into the forest for privacy. When he looked back at one moment, he saw her white buttocks appearing in the forest gloam like some strange and bloated ghostly apparition as the woman squatted and relieved herself. Galushko smiled faintly before he turned back toward the others.

They had almost reached the camper when she came running after them breathlessly. Galushko saw the look on her face, not fear, these women didn't show fear, but something else, and then she was beside Galushko, but looking at the others too, saying, "I think you'd better come back and have a look."

Moscow.

Hours later in New York, on that same late February evening, Leonid Kislov, the KGB station head in New York's Soviet UN mission, boarded a Pan Am flight to London, with onward connections to Vienna and Moscow.

He carried with him a diplomatic briefcase handcuffed to his right wrist, and he hardly slept throughout the entire twenty-two-hour journey.

As he climbed tiredly into a cold Zis, Kislov found a blanket on the back seat and pulled it over his freezing legs. The driver climbed in front and looked around cheerfully. "You had a pleasant flight, comrade?"

Kislov didn't feel like small talk, his head aching after the long flights, especially with the knowledge of what he carried in the briefcase gnawing at his brain.

He said gruffly, "The Kremlin, quick as you can."

The driver turned back at the rebuff and eased the Zis across the snowy tarmac toward the airfield exit.

25

Finland.
February 23rd

The scheduled SAS Constellation from Stockholm landed in darkness at Helsinki's Malmi airport a little after five that February afternoon.

Three of the passengers on board were Massey, Slanski and Anna Khorev.

As the plane taxied in, there was little to see in the almost Arctic darkness beyond the cabin windows. Ten minutes after the aircraft touched down they came through Arrivals.

A blond-haired man wearing a worn leather flying jacket and a white woollen scarf came out of the waiting crowd and shook Massey's hand cheerfully.

"Good to see you, Jake. So this must be the cargo?"

Massey turned to Anna and Slanski. "I'd like you to meet Janne Saarinen, your pilot. One of Finland's best."

Saarinen smiled as he shook their hands. He looked small for a Finn and his face was a mass of angry scars, but despite the disfigurement he seemed a cheerful sort.

"Don't pay any attention to Jake," Saarinen said in perfect English. "He's an old flatterer. You must be exhausted after the flight. I've got a car outside, so let's get you to our base."

It was very cold and eerily dark outside, just a faint trace of watery light on the Arctic horizon.

As Saarinen took Anna's case and led them to the parking lot, Massey saw the look on their faces as the Finn limped his way ahead of them, swinging his leg out in front with each step.

When he was out of hearing, Massey said to Slanski, "What's wrong?"

"In case you hadn't noticed I'd say your friend's missing a leg."

"Don't let it bother you. It hasn't bothered Janne. Believe me, he's the best there is."

Saarinen climbed in the front of a small muddied green Volvo, and Massey slid in beside him, Slanski in the back with Anna. As they drove out of the airport minutes later she was already asleep, exhausted after the long journey, her head resting on Slanski's shoulder.

* * *

"Welcome to Bylandet Island," said Saarinen.

They rattled over the bridge and came to a small cove that consisted of a couple of bright-painted wooden buildings, a stretch of curved frozen beach in front and a thick forest behind. Saarinen drove toward a big, solitary two-story green-painted wooden house, its shutters firmly closed, and halted in front. Wood fuel was piled high against one of the walls, and the remains of a fishing boat languished nearby, a clump of ancient frozen netting hanging from a rusty hook on the side of the house.

"The place used to belong to a local fisherman, until he drank himself to death," Saarinen told them. "Not surprising really. This is the only house on this part of the island and it's off the beaten track. Hardly anyone comes here in winter apart from wildlife, unless like us they're completely mad, so we won't be bothered."

The house was all bright-colored pine inside and freezing cold. Saarinen lit a couple of oil lamps and showed them around. A large room downstairs served as the kitchen and living room area, sparsely furnished with a pine table and four chairs and an ancient settee and dresser, but the place was kept neat and tidy. A small wooden table in a corner of the room was covered with a heavy canvas sheet that hid something bulky underneath. There was a wood-burning stove in the corner and when Saarinen had lit it, pouring some kerosene on the logs to get the blaze going, he showed them their rooms upstairs.

They were comfortably furnished with simple pine beds, an oil lamp and locker beside each; but the rooms smelled unpleasantly of must and salty sea air. When they went downstairs ten minutes later, Saarinen had got the electric generator going and made coffee.

In the kitchen a single light was on overhead, and a couple of maps were spread out on the table, showing the southern coast of Finland and the western coasts of Russia and the Baltic countries in detail. On one Saarinen had marked the intended flight route with a red pen.

He smiled. "The house isn't exactly the Helsinki Palace, I'm afraid, and the salt smell can't be helped, but it's just for one night. Right, now to business. The crossing shouldn't take more than thirty-five minutes, forty at the outside, depending on any head winds we might meet after we take off from here."

He pointed to the map and the red curved line he had drawn which ran from Bylandet Island to a point across the Baltic Sea, just outside Tallinn, Estonia. "From the island here to the drop point near Tallinn it's exactly seventy-five miles. A snap, really, if things go according to plan."

Anna looked at him. "Where's the runway on the island?"

Saarinen shook his head and grinned. "There isn't one. The aircraft is fitted with skis so we can take off from the ice. Don't worry, it may be a tiny bit bumpy to start with but you'll hardly notice the difference."

Massey said, "What about the latest weather reports?"

Saarinen smiled, a rakish smile. "According to the Helsinki office, it couldn't be better for a covert drop. Strong winds tonight, followed by a heavy cold front with a threat of some cumulonimbus cloud across parts of the Gulf of Finland, possibly down to a thousand feet from five, expected by tomorrow evening. That kind of cloud can give snow and hail and even thunderstorms, and we'll have to try and avoid the worst of it, if that's possible."

He shrugged. "Flying through heavy snow cloud isn't a pleasant way to travel for the passengers because it can get pretty rough up there, only it's less likely the Soviets will have their Migs patrolling the airspace in such extreme conditions, but of course I can't guarantee that. Let's just say I'd be optimistic." He smiled again, looking as if he were actually about to enjoy the bad-weather flying and the danger involved.

Slanski lit a cigarette. "Isn't that taking a risk, flying in such bad conditions in a light aircraft?"

Saarinen laughed. "Sure, but not as big a risk as the certainty of getting blown out of the sky by the latest Mig jet fighter in clear weather. Those machines are the fastest thing in the skies, even faster than anything the Americans have got right now."

"What about radar?" asked Slanski. "Surely the Soviets scan the area?"

"You can bet your backside on it." Saarinen tapped a finger at a point on the map near Tallinn. "There's a Soviet airbase right here, equipped with the Mig 15P all-weather interceptors with on-board radar that's only just been introduced. It operates a Baltic air patrol jointly with another base outside Leningrad for a full twenty-four-hour shift. If any aircraft comes into Soviet airspace, they blast it out of the skies, without asking questions.

"But the way I understand it, in really bad snow, the Mig pilots keep above the cloud because they're not yet fully used to operating the new on-board radar. However, there's a radar unit at the airbase itself, another in the main Soviet Army headquarters in Tondy barracks, just outside Tallinn, and yet another positioned in the old town in a church tower, Saint Olaus, next to the local KGB headquarters, probably the tallest point in the town. Between the three of them they keep the patrolling Migs informed."

He smiled. "On a clear day I believe the post in the church can pick up the buzz of a wasp. But on a bad one, with snow and hail, the Soviet radar units often can't discriminate between a target and the clutter produced on their screens by the weather. That's where really bad conditions help us. But anyway I'm going to stay as low as I can within the cloud to avoid being picked up on their screens. The real risk, however, is once we come out of the cloud briefly for the drop zone. There's a chance we'll be noticed by their radar and Ivan will get interested. That's why I've got to find the target quickly and drop you. But at that stage, it would really be my problem, and nothing for you to worry about. Even if Ivan did respond, you'd have parachuted by then and with luck I'd be on the homeward leg."

Massey crossed to the window and looked out at the frozen bay. Up here in the north he knew a man was lucky if he saw a couple of hours of weak sunshine in winter. The twilight had a curiously depressing effect. He looked back at Saarinen. The man was a very capable pilot, but he was also plainly crazy to be so enthusiastic, considering the dangers. Massey wondered if some of the shrapnel in his leg had lodged in his brain as well.

"OK, Janne, so what's the schedule? When can we get under way?"

Saarinen sat on the edge of the table. "The cloud is expected due southeast of here by eight tomorrow night. If the weather boys are right, it should give us cover as far as the coast of Estonia. If we leave at twenty-thirty, then according to my predictions we should meet the cloud about twenty miles out on our course. The route we take is this." He pointed to the red line on the map. "Almost straight across the Baltic to the drop area. I know the frequencies of the Russian beacons and I can use them for more exact navigational reference when we get near Tallinn so I can pick up the drop reference."

Massey frowned. "And what happens if the weather really is bad, like you say?"

"Don't worry. I'll pick it up. I can go in low, to within five hundred feet of the ground if necessary. I should be able to make out the lights of Tallinn once we're out of the cloud. And the terrain profile is pretty flat around there so hopefully we're not going to bump into any mountains when we're flying blind in cloud. Right, any more questions?" No one spoke and Saarinen smiled broadly. "Good, that must mean you trust me." He swung his leg off the table and said to Massey, "Come on, I'll show your friends the little beauty that's going to take them into the jaws of hell."

Saarinen led them out across the wooden promenade to the hangar.

It was a converted boat shed, and there were two sets of double wooden doors, one each at the front and rear of the building. Saarinen swung them both open to reveal a short, sturdy-looking single-engine aircraft with high wings, painted all white. It had no markings and its landing wheels had been replaced with combination skis and wheels, so that it could take off and land on ice or a runway. The engine cowling and propeller had a thick woollen blanket thrown over them. Saarinen ran a hand lovingly over the edge of the starboard wing.

"A beauty, isn't she? The Norseman C-64 light transporter, Canadian design, as used by the American Air Force during the war. I picked her up for next to nothing at a military surplus auction in Hamburg. She's ideal for cold-weather countries and can fly at a hundred and forty knots with up to eight passengers. But in these temperatures she needs to be looked after like a baby. You've got to keep the engine turning over several times a day, otherwise the oil freezes and the engine metal cracks from severe cold." He looked at his watch. "Almost time now. Better stand well back."

They stood well beyond the open rear doors of the hangar and Saarinen pulled off the heavy blanket over the engine and propeller. He hefted himself with relative ease into the cockpit, swinging his false leg in last. He started the engine, opening the throttle and revving for ten minutes, the noise almost deafening, letting the oil run hot. Then he pulled back on the throttle to idle for another five minutes before closing down the engine and climbing out.

"Well, that's it for another four hours. Now it's time to keep myself warm. Like most sensible Finns at this or any other hour during this godforsaken winter, I'm going to have a couple of stiff drinks to keep myself from cracking up and my blood from freezing. Care to join me inside?"

Massey said, "Sounds like a good idea."

He looked over at Slanski and Anna. There was tension around the corners of Slanski's mouth, his eyes full of nervous energy. He looked like a caged animal anxious to be let loose and Massey thought that the strain of everything was beginning to show. Anna appeared calm, but he could sense her restlessness.

Slanski said, "Thanks for the offer, Janne, but another time." He looked at Massey.

"What's next on the agenda?"

"We'll go over the weapons, clothes and papers tonight. Everything you need for the drop and afterwards. But in the meantime, there's nothing to do but wait."

"Then how about I take Anna for a little diversion?"

"What kind of diversion had you got in mind?"

"A drive into Helsinki and back, if we could borrow Janne's car."

He looked over at Saarinen. "How about it, Janne?"

The Finn shrugged. "It's OK by me." He found the keys to the Volvo and tossed them to Slanski. "Just watch the roads, they're pretty icy this time of year. And don't hit the bottle before you drive back. It's about the only thing the police are strict about in these parts."

Massey said to Slanski, "OK, but I want you both back here by nine, no later."

"A last taste of freedom before we go. Jake, I think you owe us the price of a good dinner."

Massey took out his wallet and handed Slanski some Finnish marks. "I reckon you're right. Compliments of Washington. Don't get lost on me, either of you. And be careful, for God's sake."

26

Washington, D.C.
February 24th

It was just before 2 A.M. and raining hard as the unmarked black Ford sedan drew up outside the rear entrance to the White House.

As the three passengers climbed out, Secret Service men led them briskly through to the Oval Office.

President Eisenhower was already seated behind his desk, wearing a dressing gown, his face looking tired and drawn, and he stood briefly as the three men were ushered into the room. "Take a seat. Coffee's on the table if anyone's interested."

There was a pot of steaming coffee and a tray of cups on a side table but no one bothered to touch the refreshment. Lights from the security arc lamps outside blazed beyond the tinted windows onto the expansive lawns. There was an air of anxious restlessness as the men sat.

Allen Welsh Dulles, the Acting Director of the CIA, took the chair next to Eisenhower. Appointed Director only six weeks previously, and not to be sworn into office for another four days, the sixty-year-old Dulles was to be the CIA's first professional director, but neither looked nor behaved like one.

A big, wide-shouldered New Yorker with rumpled white hair and a mustache, he had an easy manner and a taste for party-going. That early morning, however, his face appeared tense and there was no sign of the charming seductiveness for which he was noted. A distinguished intelligence chief, he had led America's OSS in Europe from his wartime base in Switzerland, being responsible for secret missions into Nazi Germany and, more notably, Operation Sunrise, the surrender of all German troops by SS General Karl Wolff in the last and bloody stages of the war in Italy.

Normally a calm and relaxed man, that February morning Dulles seemed a bundle of nerves.

The other two men in the room were the Assistant Director of the Soviet Division, William G. Wallace, and Karl Branigan, the Special Operations Chief. Both men sat facing Eisenhower's desk, and both, like Dulles, looked tense and restless.

It was exactly two when Eisenhower opened the meeting, in a voice raw from sleep and a lifetime of too many cigarettes.

"You had better begin, Allen. It's bad enough being woken at one-thirty A.M., so let's not waste any more time."

Dulles leaned forward and formally introduced the other two men present. "Mr. President . . . the Assistant Director of the Soviet Division you know already."

The Assistant Director nodded to Eisenhower. "Mr. President . . ."

"Good to see you, Bill." Eisenhower frowned and smiled slightly. "Or maybe not, as the case may be."

"Sir, this is Karl Branigan," Dulles went on quickly, "Soviet Division's Special Operations Chief."

Branigan raised himself briefly from his chair, but Eisenhower indicated with a wave that he should remain seated. "Relax, Mr. Branigan, we don't stand on formality at two A.M. in the White House. Right, Allen, let's get to it. I presume this isn't going to be good news?"

Branigan sat down again as Dulles cleared his throat. "Sir, I believe we have a major problem."

"I already gathered that from your call," Eisenhower said sharply.

Dulles placed a red folder in front of Eisenhower. It was stamped "*For President's Eyes Only*."

"Mr. President, sir, as of this morning we believe Moscow may be aware of our intention in regard to Operation Snow Wolf."

At once Eisenhower reacted. There was a look of alarm on his face and he instantly paled. "You're certain about this?"

"As certain as we can be."

Eisenhower sighed deeply and ran a hand across the back of his neck as if to ease a growing tension in himself. He said softly, "Jesus Christ."

The anger showed instantly on his face as he stared over at the other two men in the room, then back at Dulles. "You mind telling me how in God's name one of the most sensitive, top-secret operations your department's ever handled has been blown? What in goddamned hell's gone wrong?"

Dulles opened the file and shakily handed it to Eisenhower. "Inside you'll find all the details, Mr. President. But I'll run through them to save time. At exactly ten-thirty last night a diplomatic attaché named Kislov from the Soviet UN Mission in New York boarded a plane for London, with onward connections to Moscow. As you might expect, Kislov is no attaché—he's the KGB station head in New York. He had with him a diplomatic bag. We believe it contained information from a copy of a secret file we had given Massey on Stalin's personal security and habits."

Eisenhower frowned. "And what makes you assume that?"

"It's rather complex, Mr. President."

"Then tell me as simply as you can."

Dulles explained about the bodies found by the police in the Brooklyn apartment after a shooting had been reported, and that one had been identified as Dimitri Popov, who worked for the CIA. The body of the second man was Feliks Arkashin, a Soviet attaché and KGB major. It took Dulles several minutes more to outline the complete details of how the CIA had been alerted by the FBI. Branigan had learned of the alert and knew Popov had been seconded to Massey for agent training, so Branigan had decided to have the house in New Hampshire visited for the sake of security.

Dulles went on worriedly, "The cabin had been burned to the ground and Massey and his people had vanished. Branigan called in one of our teams to check the property. As of an hour ago four bodies have been found, three in the woods, another near the lake by the cabin. One of the bodies is of a killer named Braun who worked for the Soviets, and the body had a single file hidden on it—the file I referred to. Massey had been supplied with a copy for Slanski to study. It contained details on Stalin's background, his personality, his weaknesses, his strengths. Even his medical data. His present security arrangements, as far as we can ascertain. The layout of the Kremlin and the Kuntsevo dacha he uses. It was top secret."

"Did the file contain any details about Snow Wolf?"

"No, sir, it did not."

Eisenhower said impatiently, "Then just how do you suppose the Soviets could have deduced what we intend? This man Braun is dead and the file didn't contain any suggestion of our intentions."

Dulles hesitated. "I think maybe the Assistant Director can better answer that question, sir." Dulles nodded to William Wallace, who sat forward.

"Mr. President, as you know, for the sake of security and the extremely sensitive nature of the mission, Snow Wolf was ultra-covert. No one knew about it but us four here in the room and the people directly involved. By that I mean Massey, and the man we're sending in, Slanski. Not even the woman accompanying him knew the target."

Eisenhower said abruptly, "Get to the point."

The Assistant Director looked uncomfortable. He glanced at Dulles for support, but when none came, he said, "Our forensic people believe Braun's body had already been disturbed before we found it. We also now suspect Moscow had been watching the woman and sent Braun to kill or abduct her. It seems the likely scenario. Braun must have found the file in the cabin, sir, before he was killed, most obviously by Massey or one of his people. We concluded that when Braun and the others didn't return, the KGB sent someone, possibly another team, to check. We don't think Kislov flew to Moscow just to report Arkashin's death and the deaths of the others—that would hardly warrant such a trip. We think he flew there because the team sent to find out what had happened to Braun also found the file. They examined it but left it on the body. Kislov was informed and realized what the information might suggest. A man like Kislov is no fool—with the kind of details in the file and with Massey being involved, it's more than likely he'll have reasoned we intend an operation against Stalin, and soon, considering most mission training is done shortly before a drop takes place." Eisenhower waited silently until Wallace had finished. There was a frustrated look on the President's face, then he read quickly through the file himself. When he had finished he closed it with a heavy sigh.

"It seems like we've landed ourselves one big mess, haven't we?"

"It's pretty bad, sir," Dulles agreed.

Eisenhower sat down and said quickly, "OK, first things first. Has the team gone yet?"

"No, sir."

Eisenhower sighed. "Thank God for that. If there's one thing I've learned, it's when you're in a hole you stop digging. At this stage, we can't be absolutely certain Moscow will know exactly what's going on, but if there's a risk of that, then the obvious answer is for us to abort the whole operation. It's a damned pity. The way things are going with us and Moscow I had hoped your people stood a chance, however slim." Dulles went to speak again but Eisenhower put up a hand. "Let me worry about the Soviets if they do start making noises, diplomatically, about this man Arkashin. For now, we'll just have to wait and see what develops." He shook his head resignedly. "But God only knows where it's going to lead if you're right. So where's Massey?"

The Assistant Director looked uncomfortable. "Sir, despite what's developed, we know he's flown to Finland for the final stage of the mission, but we don't know exactly where in Finland he is."

Eisenhower stared over at Dulles. "I thought you said the operation hasn't started yet?"

"We can really only assume that, Mr. President, because we haven't received the 'Go' code. As you know, the operation was entirely run on Massey's discretion. We provided a rough plan, a template if you like, and Massey filled in the details. One of our instructions to Massey was that we receive a signal from him when the operation proceeded to the final and imminent stage, by that I mean just before he was ready to drop his people. It was to give us a chance to cancel the operation if we so wished. So far, that hasn't happened. And considering the fact that Massey hasn't informed us of his problems at the base, we can't be certain he will signal the code."

"Jesus . . . this gets worse by the minute."

"There are also several other factors at play that would suggest the operation hasn't yet become active."

"Such as?"

"We believe Massey left Boston the night before last with the two people on a scheduled flight to London, and from there onto Stockholm and Helsinki. Going by the schedule he used, that means he'd have arrived in Helsinki within the last fourteen hours, Washington time. We've had the immigration departments of those countries contacted as a matter of urgency and we've verified that the false passports supplied by our Soviet Division were used. The Finnish authorities also confirm Massey and his team landed in Helsinki yesterday evening. But because of the weather, our belief is that Massey won't carry out the drop until tonight."

Eisenhower said quietly, "Then how in hell do we contact him?"

"Like I said, contact was left at his discretion. That's what we agreed. It would distance us from the operation if it went wrong. Massey was simply instructed to get in touch if there were problems, and to call a Washington number with the 'Go' code." The Assistant Director swallowed. "Sir, we can only assume he's still intent on going ahead with the plan, for whatever personal reasons he might have."

"Is the man dumb or crazy? I thought you said he was one of the best we had?"

"He is the best, sir. Mr. Dulles worked with him in Europe during the war and can attest to that. And I can't imagine what's made him behave so unprofessionally."

The Assistant Director shifted uncomfortably in his chair and Eisenhower stood up. He was angry, his face whiter than ever, the eyes dark and narrow.

"The only chance of success this thing stood was if it remained covert. That's plainly no longer the case. From what you've told me, Moscow may already have a hint something's in the air. If these two people make it onto Soviet soil and they're captured, there's only one outcome for us. And that's a possible disaster. I think we all know how the Russians would respond once they have the evidence."

Eisenhower looked around. "We're not just talking about a cause for a war, gentlemen. We're talking about *the* war. We're talking about a Soviet response that could put us back twenty years. They can march into West Berlin and anywhere else in goddamned Europe on the pretense that it's now a question of security or retaliation. We're talking about the greatest potential disaster that could ever hit this country and our Allies."

Dulles looked back at Eisenhower uncertainly. "Mr. President, needless to say, we're doing everything we can to locate Massey. But as you'll appreciate, because of the sensitive nature of this situation, we'll need our own people on the ground in Finland. Branigan here has already assembled a team and they're on their way. There's a jet aircraft waiting at Andrews. As soon as he's through here, he'll be on it to connect with his team in Finland. But we'll need your intervention with the US Embassy in Helsinki to ask their complete cooperation as well as that of the Finns, if necessary."

Eisenhower took a deep breath and let it out in a long, worried sigh. "That's valuable time, gentlemen. What happens if you're too late? Where in hell does that leave us?"

"With respect, Mr. President, we can still locate and stop them," said Branigan.

"Then for God's sake tell me how?"

"It's a question of timing," Branigan explained. "Most operations into Russia and the Baltic are weather-dependent. If the weather's good, the CIA never drop by air because the Russian radar can easily track our aircraft. The report Massey was shown recommends an air drop for the penetration into the Baltic area and I'm certain that's the way he'll do it. He'll most likely need a local pilot, someone with experience of flying in Russian airspace. We've checked the weather report for the region. It suggests a bad snowstorm moving in from the northeast Baltic area tonight, that's eight P.M. Helsinki time. That's around the most likely time Massey's people would go, which gives us some leeway. With enough manpower we could find them before that happens. And with the cooperation of the Finns and their air force we could make it impossible for Massey's team to make the crossing. With enough of their aircraft patrolling the area, they could make sure the plane doesn't get anywhere near its destination."

"You mean blow it out of the sky?"

"If necessary."

Eisenhower looked around at each of the three men in turn. The steel that was always just beneath the surface of the friendly blue eyes showed itself immediately.

"Then I don't care how, but I want it done. I want Massey and the others found. Found or stopped any which way you can. Even if it means their deaths. An unpleasant thought, gentlemen, considering they're brave people, but the consequences are far too threatening otherwise. You all understand that?"

The three visitors nodded in turn.

Eisenhower's face was still pale as he looked at his wristwatch to end the meeting. His gaze shifted back to Dulles.

"Make whatever arrangements you have to. Needless to say I want the clamps on this. And I want hourly reports until this thing is through. Just make sure you stop them, understood?"

"Yes, sir, Mr. President."

Finland.
February 23rd

Slanski parked the Volvo along the Helsinki sea front and they took a tram the rest of the way into the city.

Lights were still on everywhere and they strolled around the old harbor market and the cathedral square for half an hour before finding a small restaurant on the Esplanadi main boulevard.

The restaurant was warm and bustling and they found an empty table beside the window. Slanski ordered schnapps and *Vorschmack* for both of them. They ate silently, and when they had finished they walked back out along the coast road toward Kaivopuisto. A wind had come up, and it blew in off the frozen sea, bitterly cold.

Slanski stopped and pointed to a bench, his face serious. He lit a cigarette and offered her one as she sat beside him. "How do you feel?"

She brushed a strand of hair from her face. "How should I feel?"

"Scared." He saw the tension around the corners of her mouth.

"A little, I guess."

"It's not too late to change your mind."

Slanski looked back toward the city. "The Swedish Embassy is ten minutes' walk from here. You could ask for asylum and I won't stop you. To hell with Massey. I think he'd even understand. I could still go through with this alone."

"Why are you telling me this? Why the sudden concern?"

There was a look like pain on Slanski's face. "You saw what happened to Vassily. And Popov was right about what the KGB do to women agents they arrest. I've seen it myself."

"Tell me."

He glanced away again. "Two years back I was sent to the Baltic to organize a resistance group. One of the partisans I helped train was a girl of nineteen. The KGB caught her when they stormed one of the forest camps the partisans used. What they did to her doesn't bear telling."

"Did you love her?"

"That hardly matters, does it? Let's just say I repaid the bastard who tortured her. He's lying six feet under."

Anna looked away. Out in the bay she could make out the solid mustard-colored walls of an island fortress, and the small islands nearby looked like frosted moles on the sea.

"I'm afraid. But not so afraid that I won't go through with it." She looked back at Slanski's face. "What happened at the cabin, the way you reacted, it wasn't just to avenge Vassily, though that was part of it. There was a look in your eyes, it was like you came alive when you faced danger. Don't you ever feel afraid?"

"What's there to be afraid of? Death comes to us all sooner or later. Maybe when we're faced with it that's the moment we truly define ourselves." He smiled. "It's not the heroes who stay to look trouble in the eye—there's no such thing—only fatalists with nothing to lose."

"Don't you have anything to lose?"

"Not much."

"Didn't you ever love anyone besides Vassily? A woman?"

"Typical of a woman to ask that question. But what's it got to do with it?"

She looked at him intently. "Maybe nothing, maybe everything."

"What do you want to know?"

"Tell me what you liked to do most when you lived in Russia as a boy. Tell me about your family."

Slanski looked away uncomfortably. Anna said, "Something bad once happened to your family, didn't it? Is that why you left Russia?"

He said dismissively, "Hardly any of your business. Besides, it's all water under the bridge. A long time ago. Forget it."

"But that's the point. I don't think you can forget it. I think it's what makes you the way you are. Angry and vengeful. And always living close to death, as if you wish it."

He looked at her defensively. "What is this, amateur psychoanalysis? Is that something you picked up in New York?"

She realized he was more sensitive than angry, and some instinct made her reach across and briefly touch his hand. "You're right, it's none of my business. But what happened to Vassily, I'm truly sorry. He was a good man."

For a long time he didn't speak, and then he said quietly, "He was one of the finest men I knew. But he's gone now, and nothing can bring him back."

She saw the look of grief flood his face, and he stood up as if to kill the emotion.

Anna said, "Why do you always do that?"

Slanski frowned. "Do what?"

"Hide your feelings like a typical Russian man. Never let emotions in. But yet you always repay pain with pain. Like Vassily and that partisan girl. Why?"

He said flippantly, "A long story. Remind me to tell you some time."

The wind in the harbor grew harsher. Street lamps flickered along the promenade and behind them a tram trundled past on its metal tracks, electric blue flashes sparking in the darkness overhead.

Anna said, "I don't think you've ever trusted anyone enough to let them get really close, have you, Alex Slanski? Inside you're still that same little boy who had to escape halfway across the world on his own, with no one to rely on but himself."

He didn't reply and Anna looked toward the sea and suddenly shivered.

Slanski said, "What's wrong?"

She put her hands in her coat pockets, a deadness in her voice when she spoke.

"I'm not sure. It's odd, but I have a feeling we're both doomed across that sea. What happened at the cabin is like an omen. And people like you and me, maybe we have too much bad fortune in our pasts to be lucky."

"Then why not forget about it and do as I said?"

"Like you say, maybe like you I've nothing to lose."

They spent the rest of the evening going over the weapons, equipment and the forged papers with Massey in the kitchen.

He gave them each a Tokarev 7.62 pistol and a spare magazine. He also produced a Nagant 7.62 revolver which had most of the barrel sawn away and a silencer attached. He handed it to Slanski, who checked the weapon before slipping it into his pocket and half smiling at Anna.

"A little something extra just in case the Tokarev jams."

Slanski had three sets of papers; one for an Estonian worker named Bodkin, home on leave from a collective farm in Kalinin, another for a Red Army captain named Oleg Petrovsky, on leave from the 17th Armored Division barracks at Leningrad, the third in the name of Georgi Mazurov, a KGB major attached to the 2nd Directorate, Moscow. Anna had another three sets in the same family names, posing as his wife in each case, and there were photos of them together and separately, along with personal letters to support their relationship and past.

The other papers included various regional passes and work cards, all in drab official paper and aged deliberately, the photographs in black and white and officially stamped. When Massey had gone over their aliases and backgrounds again he said, "The papers are the best I've seen and they should pass close scrutiny, but of course there's no guarantee. All I can say, if it's any comfort, is that the forgers are the best in the business and worked damned hard to get them right."

Anna picked up her worn-looking set and examined them. "I don't understand. How can they look so used?"

Massey smiled. "An old trick from the war. The forgers fray them with very fine sandpaper and then tape them under their armpits for a couple of hours. Human sweat has an aging effect on paper. As you can see, it works wonders."

Anna made a face and Massey smiled. "An unpleasant thought, but a simple thing like that may save your life. The KGB might become suspicious of passes printed on fresh paper and if they look closely enough they can sometimes tell if chemicals have been used to age them artificially. Whereas the sweat process is undetectable."

He opened a leather pouch containing several wads of rubles, and gave the largest wad to Slanski. The money was creased and aged and there was a handful of coins each.

"If you need any more rubles you can pick them up at the safe houses between Tallinn and Moscow," he explained to Anna. "Otherwise, if you're searched and found with a large amount of cash, it might arouse suspicion. The weapons and some of the clothes and extra papers, of course, are going to be a problem for the first set of false identities if you're stopped and searched soon after you land. That's the danger time. I'm afraid there's no way of safely hiding everything incriminating on your person, but it's a temporary risk, so you'll just have to play the game as it happens. Bury them somewhere near where you land and retrieve them later if you think it's going to be a problem. OK, let's look at the other equipment."

The jumpsuits were made of heavy green canvas and contained generous pockets to hold items they would need immediately after landing. A flashlight each and a knife to cut the parachute free if it caught on a tree, and short folding spades to bury their equipment. There were helmets, goggles, gloves, and thermal suits for each of them.

"It's going to be pretty cold up there when you jump, so you'll need the thermals to stop you from freezing to death before you land. Now let's see how well the tailors have done."

He produced two frayed suitcases with their personal belongings and clothes inside, and after he had handed them out Anna went upstairs to try her clothes on.

When she came down ten minutes later her hair was tied back severely with a ribbon. She wore a heavy woollen skirt and a thick white blouse, a woollen scarf and an overcoat that was just the right size.

Slanski had changed and stood there dressed as an Estonian peasant, wearing a tweed cap, an ill-fitting jacket and a baggy corduroy suit that was a little too short in the legs. Anna couldn't help laughing and Slanski said, "What's so funny?"

"You look like the village idiot."

"A fine way to talk to your husband."

Massey said, "The clothes and uniforms are all the genuine article, taken from Soviet army defectors or refugees who came over after the war. You should wear the clothes tomorrow to get used to them. You're happy, Alex?"

"Happy as I can be apart from these trousers."

Massey smiled. "Can't be helped, I'm afraid. Besides, an Estonian laborer is hardly going to be dressed to perfection. Anna, is there anything you want to ask?"

She shook her head and Massey said, "Then I guess that's it, except for one last thing."

He took two miniature tin boxes from his pocket, opened their lids and emptied the contents on the table. One box contained only two black capsules. The second contained several dozen blue ones, and both types of capsules were different sizes.

"Pills. Two types. One good, one bad, but both invaluable. As you can see they're different sizes and colors so hopefully you can't get them mixed up."

"What are they for?" Anna asked.

"The blue pill is an amphetamine. It gives you an energy boost to overcome fatigue. Commonly used by special forces and pilots during the war to stave off tiredness." Massey picked up one of the black pills. "And this little baby here is the one you've got to be careful about. It's only to be used in a dire emergency."

"What is it?" Anna asked.

"Cyanide. It kills you in seconds."

* * *

It was almost midnight and Slanski lay in the dark, smoking a cigarette, listening to the wind rage outside. He heard the door open and Anna stood there in a cotton nightgown, holding an oil lamp.

She said softly, "Can I come in?"

"What's the matter?"

"I can't sleep."

"Come in, close the door."

Her hair was tousled and there was something childlike about her face in the light of the lamp as she came to sit at the end of the bed. He noticed she was trembling and he said, "Are you cold?"

She shook her head. "Just frightened. Maybe I've suddenly realized everything about this is deadly serious. Especially when Massey gave us that pill. Now it's not a game any more. In the air raid shelters in Moscow during the war, when people were afraid of the bombing, complete strangers used to hold and kiss each other. I once even saw a couple make love."

"It makes sense. A natural instinct to preserve the species when it's under threat. Soldiers got married for the same reason before they went to war."

She bit her lip. "Will you do something for me?"

"What?"

"Just hold me. Hold me tightly. It seems like it's been such a long time since someone did that."

He saw it in her face then, a real and terrible fear, and it made her look very young and vulnerable. He realized she was more afraid than he had ever imagined, and his hand touched her cheek as he looked into her eyes and said, "My poor Anna."

Her arms went around his neck and she held him tightly. She moved under the covers beside him, snuggling close for warmth and comfort, and then suddenly for no reason at all she was crying and kissing him fiercely.

"Make love to me."

When he hesitated, she kissed him again, her tongue finding his, and he felt himself reacting, growing hard. Her body trembled as he pulled up her nightgown and slid off her underwear. His hand traced the firm outline of her breasts, his fingers gently squeezing the nipples until they were hard and he took one in his mouth. She was panting as his hand slid over her belly and moved down to the warmth between her legs, his fingers caressing her until she was wet.

Without a word her hand came up and gripped his hardness and when he moved on top she moaned as she guided him inside.

It seemed after that as if they were in a frenzy, their bodies in the grip of some kind of urgent desperation, until finally they both shuddered and spent themselves. And then Anna started to cry again, a deep sobbing that racked her whole body.

"What's wrong, Anna?"

She didn't reply, her eyes full of tears, and then she said, "Do you want to know why I'm going back to Russia with you?"

"Only if you want to tell me."

She told him, told him everything, and she was still crying when she finished.

Slanski held her close and whispered, "Anna. It's all right, Anna."

He stroked her face but it was a long time before her tears stopped. Then he blew out the lamp and held her gently, wordless in the dark, until she finally fell asleep.

27

Finland.
February 24th

It was just after nine the next morning when Janne Saarinen came in the front door, a gust of icy wind raging into the room before he kicked the door shut with his boot. His face looked blue with cold and he carried two parachutes over his shoulders.

"You slept well?"

"Well enough, considering."

The Finn grinned as he flung the packs on the table. "Your 'chutes. I've repacked them twice just to be certain."

"Nice to know someone cares. Thanks, Janne."

Slanski looked out of the window and saw Anna and Massey out walking on the wooden boardwalk together, their collars up to keep out the biting cold. Saarinen came to stand behind Slanski and offered him a cigarette.

When he lit their cigarettes, Saarinen nodded out at the boardwalk. "She's quite a looker, your ladyfriend. I'd almost risk it just to go in with her myself."

Slanski examined the parachutes. "She's a good woman. It's just a pity she has to be a part of this. Going over is never easy and always dangerous."

"Tell me about it."

"Which reminds me. That was a nice show you put on for yesterday's briefing."

The Finn blew out smoke and grinned. "You didn't believe the bravado, did you? Didn't think you would."

"There's a couple of important things you left out. Like the fact that half of the agents parachuted onto Russian soil are caught within forty-eight hours because they injure themselves when they drop, or else the radar picks up the flight. And that most of the boys in the air who bought it during the war weren't shot down by the enemy, but died because of engine failure or bad weather."

Saarinen eased himself into a chair. "I've done this particular route maybe half a dozen times and each time it gets more difficult. The Russians are making their air defenses tighter and tighter and the new Mig fighters don't help the likes of me. I only made it sound easy for her sake. As for our chances, cloud cover is our one real hope, despite the obvious dangers if the weather turns really nasty, but I can vouch for that little aircraft out there, mechanically and structurally. If the cloud stays in our favor, I'd almost guarantee you'll at least make the drop. If not . . ." Saarinen grinned and shrugged. "We may get blown out of the sky."

"Did anyone ever mention you've got a total disregard for life and death?"

Saarinen laughed. "All the time. It comes from having looked the grim reaper in the eye too many times and found out it's not such a big deal. Before '39 I was studying English at Helsinki University, then the war came and the first time I flew into battle I was bitten by the bug. After that I couldn't get enough jeopardy and excitement. You realize everything else lacks a certain dangerous edge. But after the shooting died down and it was all over, you know you're just living on borrowed time anyway, so you keep sailing close to the wind just for the hell of it. If I'm not mistaken, you have the same look about you yourself. What was it Kant said? 'That steely unmistaken look in a man's eyes that tells its tale of war, and death the grim reaper too often faced.' "

Slanski smiled. "So what about the radar on the other side?"

"Like I said, if the weather's on our side it shouldn't bother us." Saarinen shook his head. "It's not all black, just shades of gray. But I told you, I'm lucky. I also speak fluent Russian. So even if their air traffic control calls us up, I can try and bluff my way out."

"A man of many parts."

Saarinen grinned and tapped his wooden leg. "Not all of them good, I'm afraid."

Helsinki.

The wheels of the US Air Force B-47 Stratojet bit the icy runway with a squeal as they touched down at Helsinki's Malmi airport in a flurry of light hail at exactly 6 P.M. Karl Branigan was exhausted after the long and turbulent flight from Washington, a journey of almost ten hours and over four thousand miles, an experience he had never before endured and never wished to repeat again.

Twenty minutes later his car drove up into Kaivopuisto Park, the city's diplomatic belt, and came to a halt outside the American Embassy compound. Two immaculately uniformed Marines on the gate checked the passengers before raising the barrier and allowing the car through.

As the Ford drew up at the front entrance to the embassy, a tired-looking Branigan stepped out, turning up his coat collar against the cold. A tall, lean man with tanned skin came out of the double oak doors, an anxious younger official at his side.

"Mr. Branigan? I'm Douglas Canning," the man said in a Texan drawl as he offered his hand. "My secretary here is already looking after your men, but if you'll come this way, the Ambassador is waiting to meet you."

Branigan grunted a reply and followed Canning as he led the way inside.

The small garden at the front of the embassy compound was deserted in the Baltic darkness. The grim-faced Ambassador stood at the window looking down at the scene, frowning.

He had finished reading the one page letter Branigan had presented him, signed by Allen Dulles, studying it silently before handing it to Canning, his face blank.

Canning finally looked over at the Ambassador. "Sir, would you care to respond?"

The Ambassador looked around. His thinning gray hair was groomed neatly, but the distinguished look on his face was momentarily lost to astonishment as he stared back at his visitor.

"First, let me get this right, Mr. Branigan. You want to locate a certain three people in Finland who are engaged in a covert operation, and apprehend them as a matter of urgency. If apprehension is not possible you want to stop their mission, even if it means their deaths. And you want my help in this."

Branigan's face was drawn and had an unmistakable five o'clock shadow, his limbs still aching and tense after the cramped flight, and he didn't feel like playing the diplomat.

"That's correct," he said briskly, almost forgetting who he was talking to, and added, "Mr. Ambassador, sir."

"And I'm not permitted to ask what the exact nature of this operation is that these people are intent on carrying out?"

Branigan shook his head and said bluntly, "You read the letter from Mr. Dulles. That's the exact position and all you need to know. And I'd appreciate it if you didn't ask me any further questions in that regard."

The Ambassador's face registered his annoyance at the disrespect, but he carried on.

"But you're requesting I put my entire embassy staff at your disposal, if necessary, in the pursuance of this matter. You also want my personal intervention at the highest level in Finland, to request that their air force prevent these people leaving Finnish airspace. Shoot them down if they're airborne."

"Correct."

"Mr. Branigan, I would suggest this is all somewhat without precedent." There was a look of frustration on the Ambassador's face. "So what in damnation is going on here?"

Branigan looked pointedly at his watch. "You'll have to address that question to Mr. Dulles, not me. I've simply got a job to do and quickly. Time's ticking away. So, can I rely on your help?"

The Ambassador came back behind his desk and sat down. "Mr. Branigan, quite frankly, I find this matter not only lacking in protocol, but rather disturbing. What do you think, Canning?"

Canning hesitated. "Everything we've been asked is really rather impractical. Perhaps we ought to contact Mr. Dulles ourselves to discuss this further?"

Branigan shook his head impatiently. "Not possible. My orders say no telephone contact with CIA Headquarters from Helsinki right now. As you've gathered, the nature of this mission is extremely, and I repeat *extremely*, sensitive and covert."

The Ambassador looked over smugly and made a steeple of his fingers. "Then I'm afraid I'll have to remind you, sir, that your Mr. Dulles is only *Acting* CIA Director. His official appointment doesn't take place in Washington until later today, and he won't be sworn into office for several more days. For such formidable requests as these, I'll need higher authority, I'm afraid."

Branigan stood up angrily and grabbed the letter from Canning, replaced it in his pocket and glared across at both men.

"Now how about we cut out the shit right here and now. If either of you pair of assholes don't want your balls in the Washington grinder I suggest you do as the letter says. And another thing, I need a senior liaison man here from the Finnish SUPO. Someone who can be relied on to be completely discreet. And I need every goddamned trustworthy and available man you can spare. And I want to tell you something else for nothing. Either you or they breathe a word about this operation to anyone, and I'll personally see to it the offender gets a bullet in the head."

The Ambassador's face suddenly flushed angry red at the blatant, unseemly threat and disrespect being shown his high office, but Branigan ignored it as the telephone on the desk jangled.

The Ambassador glared over in shock before he grabbed the phone.

"What the hell is it!"

There was a long pause, then the Ambassador went pale as he flicked a switch to activate the scrambler, and the first words Branigan heard the Ambassador say were, "Mr. President, we're doing everything we can."

The dimly lit temporary operations room in the back office of the east wing of the embassy was thick with sweaty men, cigarette smoke and the babble of voices. Branigan had a dozen telephones rigged up and they stood on six trestle tables in the center, a half-dozen personnel from the embassy huddled around them.

The Finn who stood beside Branigan was tall but chubby-faced, his dark hair graying slightly at the sides, and he spoke perfect English.

Henry Stenlund, the Deputy Director of SUPO, Finnish Counter-Intelligence, and a lawyer by profession, stared over at the bustle of men and equipment with nothing short of amazement.

Finland's security police had its entire operation housed in a grim and drafty three-story granite office building on Ratakatu Street, and was comprised of ten men, three worn-out Volkswagen cars, and a half-dozen rusting Raleigh bicycles for his best agents. The offices had nothing like the bustle of this, and it generated a certain excitement in Stenlund that he hadn't experienced since the Germans had left Helsinki.

He had received the call just as he was leaving the office and had brought the files to the embassy as Branigan requested. Stenlund knew better than to ask too many questions, except the bare facts, for he knew from the grim look on the face of the CIA man that the matter was serious indeed and sensitive enough for him to be summoned by the Director himself. Now he stood beside Branigan as they went through a list of names.

All were mercenary pilots who risked their lives flying into Soviet airspace from the Baltic on covert Finnish military and CIA reconnaissance and agent-dropping missions, an activity Finland officially denied. Apart from one daring, highly decorated but demented German ex-Luftwaffe mercenary pilot, with more Russian shrapnel in his head than brains, all were Finns. Not surprising really, as Stenlund's country had long been an enemy of Russia, and old hatreds and grievances ran as deep as his country's fear of its powerful neighbor.

Branigan looked on as Stenlund consulted the list. "What have we got?"

"According to my files, fifteen men who operate freelance with their own aircraft for either our people or yours. They're all very capable pilots. Unfortunately, we're talking about places as far apart as the east coast of Helsinki, near the Soviet border, to Arland island in the west. A distance of several hundred kilometers."

Branigan ran a hand across the back of his neck. "Jesus Christ."

Stenlund puffed on his pipe and shrugged. "However, we can eliminate most by assuming the people you're looking for will want to cross the Baltic in the quickest possible time, and that means the pilot would possibly have a base within close proximity to Soviet soil. Also, weather is an important consideration. And right now, the imminent bad weather we're expecting would favor a drop."

Branigan nodded. "So who are the likely suspects?"

"Two strong possibilities, seeing as both have worked for the CIA at one time or another. A man named Hakala who lives in a small fishing village near Spjutsund. He's got an aircraft hangared there, a German Fiesler Storch. The second is a man named Saarinen."

"How far is the first?"

"Spjutsund? About twenty kilometers east of Helsinki. An hour there and back by car."

"And the other guy?"

"Janne Saarinen." Stenlund consulted a file. "An excellent pilot. Ex-Luftwaffe. According to our intelligence reports, he sometimes uses a place at Bylandet Island, thirty kilometers west of here. Both men would be based pretty much the same distance from Tallinn as the crow flies."

"Which would you pick?"

Stenlund shrugged. "Like I said, they're both likely candidates. They're excellent pilots and, as I understand it, reckless enough to try a crossing in the type of weather we're expecting."

Branigan hesitated, the tension in the small room stifling. "OK, we try the nearest. Hak . . . ?"

"Hakala."

"Him first, then this guy Saarinen. I'll get us a car."

"As you wish."

Branigan reached for a shoulder-holster with a Smith and Wesson .38 pistol and buckled it on, then checked the chambers before slipping the gun back in its holster and turning to beckon several burly-looking men waiting in the room, who began to check their firearms. Stenlund looked on, alarmed, and when Branigan turned back, said nervously, "You think there'll be shooting?"

Branigan put on his jacket and overcoat. "If there is, leave it to me and my men."

Small beads of sweat had already appeared on Stenlund's forehead. "My pleasure. Personally, I never carry a weapon since the war. Having the Gestapo forever up my nose was quite excitement enough."

Stenlund stood and tapped out his pipe, then pulled on his overcoat and glanced over at the clock on the wall.

The hands read exactly 7 P.M.

28

Bylandet Island.

Slanski sat down at the table and Massey pulled up a chair. His face was serious as he looked across. "There are a couple of things I want to make clear, Alex, and they've got to do with Anna."

Slanski lit a cigarette. "Fire away."

"No matter what happens I don't want to see her hurt. Either by the KGB, or anyone else."

"What's that supposed to mean?"

"She likes you, Alex. I can tell. A man and woman going on a dangerous mission together are bound to be drawn close, for comfort if nothing else. But I don't want her put in any unnecessary danger on the mission, or hurt by getting too close to you. There's a good chance she'll make it back. You may not be as lucky."

Slanski said defensively, "You sound like you have a personal interest in Anna."

Massey thought for a moment, choosing his words carefully. "She's been through more pain than most. Let's just say I feel protective toward her."

Slanski stood. "It's not my intention to hurt Anna. But I can't help whatever happens between us, Jake. If you feel more for Anna than you're saying, and I think maybe you do, then you should have considered that before this thing began."

Massey was silent for several moments, and his face looked grim. "Then just promise me one thing. If your backs are ever to the wall and there's a chance you're going to be caught, and she can't swallow her pill in time, just make certain those KGB bastards don't get her alive."

For a moment Slanski didn't reply. He saw the genuine concern in Massey's face, then said, "Let's hope it never comes to that."

Anna came down the stairs five minutes later, dressed in her peasant clothes, the thermal suit underneath making her look bloated, and carrying her suitcase. There was a bottle of vodka and some glasses on the table and Slanski went to pour one for each of them. He handed one to Massey, then Anna.

"Nervous?"

She looked at him, something passing between them, and said, "I'm shaking."

Slanski smiled and raised his glass. "Don't worry, it'll be all over before you know it."

Massey nodded to the corner of the room to where the parachutes, canvas jumpsuits, helmets, goggles and gloves waited. There was an extra 'chute for Saarinen.

"You can leave those until Janne's almost ready to go. One more thing. If you somehow separate from each other after you jump, or your contact who's to meet you at the drop doesn't make it, the rendezvous will be the main railway station in Tallinn, the waiting room on the main platform, nine A.M. tomorrow morning. If either one of you or the contact don't show, go the next day an hour later, taking the precautions I told you about. If there's no show on the third day, you're each on your own, I'm afraid. Anything you need to ask?"

Anna said, "You never told me who the contact meeting us is."

"It'll be a member of the Estonian resistance. Any more than that I'm afraid I can't tell you, Anna, just in case you're caught."

Anna looked back at Massey doubtfully, but said nothing, and he put a hand gently on her arm. "Just stick close to Slanski and you'll be fine."

The door opened with a blast of freezing air and Saarinen appeared carrying a heavy-duty electric flashlight. He wore a yellow oilskin and scarf over his flying suit, and a pair of thick woollen gloves.

"Christ, what a night," he said, closing the door. He shook his clothes and nodded to the vodka bottle. "One of those would go down nicely."

Massey said, "You think that's wise?"

Saarinen grinned and pulled off his gloves. "Relax, Jake. I never drink and fly. One limb is penalty enough without being completely legless." He checked his watch and looked at Anna and Slanski. "Ten more minutes, I reckon. You'd better get into those jumpsuits."

As Anna and Slanski went to put on their suits, Massey crossed to the Finn. "How's the weather turning out?"

"It seems a bit rougher than expected, but don't worry, I've seen worse."

Massey nodded. Saarinen came back to the table, picked up the vodka bottle and filled each of their glasses generously, then poured himself a tiny drop of spirit.

Slanski and Anna had dressed in the green canvas suits and helmets and goggles, but left the gloves until last.

Saarinen smiled and raised his glass. "It looks like I'm breaking the habit of a lifetime. Just enough to wet my lips in a final toast for luck. *Kipiss.*"

He knocked back the vodka, and the others did the same.

Massey could feel the growing tension in the room. It was almost physical. He put down his glass and looked over at Anna and Slanski, then Saarinen.

"Are we ready?"

Saarinen nodded and smiled. "Onward and upward."

He picked up the flashlight and his parachute, and they followed him out of the door.

The tiny office that served as the operations room of the Finnish Air Force Liaison Unit at Helsinki's Malmi airport was bitterly cold, despite a tiled stove going full blast in the corner. The wing commander had been summoned from a dinner party at the Palace Hotel and his pinched face showed his irritation as he looked up at the warrant officer standing in front of the desk.

"They can't be serious, Matti?"

The warrant officer was in his late twenties, tall and lean. He wore an air force greatcoat and scarf and gloves.

"I'm afraid so, sir. It's Priority One. If the aircraft manages to get airborne it's to be stopped at all costs before it reaches Russian airspace."

"They must be out of their tiny minds at the Defense Ministry wanting us up in this weather. What the hell's going on? Where's the authorized signal, the paperwork?"

The warrant officer shrugged. "I wish I knew, sir. But you know the Ministry brass."

The wing commander shook his head doubtfully. "Well, it's damned irregular. And I want the orders verified."

"I already did, sir. I contacted the C-in-C by telephone. The order stands."

"Does he realize we'll be risking the boys' lives? I wouldn't send up a balloon in weather like this."

The warrant officer shrugged. "The orders were quite specific, I'm afraid, sir. The aircraft is to be stopped at all costs."

"What type is it?"

"Possibly a Norseman C-64, though we can't be absolutely certain. One thing will be, though. It'll be the only light aircraft flying up there tonight. I have the likely flight projection here."

The wing commander studied the paper the warrant officer handed him, then stood and crossed to the window. He sighed. "Well, I suppose we had better do as we're told. But I'll check with the Ministry myself, just to be absolutely sure. You're quite certain we're to blast this thing out of the sky?"

"Those were the orders, sir. No question."

The commander scratched his chin and sighed. "I suppose it could be some Russian spy trying to beat a hasty retreat? It's about all that makes sense on a dog's night like this. If that's the case, I hope it's worth the risk to get the bastard, that's all I can say."

He nodded to the warrant officer and reached for the telephone. "Very well, Matti, give the order to crank up. We'd better warn the boys to be extra careful. It's going to be pretty damned rough up there."

* * *

The two Fords came off the Espoo main road and turned left, taking the narrow track that led down to Bylandet Island.

Branigan gritted his teeth in frustration. His watch said 8:10. The visit to the pilot near Spjutsund had been a waste of time. The man was laid up with a broken leg and hadn't flown in weeks. The roads had been bad, hard-packed snow and ice all the way. An hour wasted.

He looked at the SUPO officer impatiently. "What about the local police near the island? Couldn't we have got in touch with them?"

Stenlund smiled indulgently. "That *was* something I considered, Mr. Branigan. But you did say you wanted this done discreetly and that the people you're looking for will be armed and possibly dangerous. The nearest police station to Bylandet Island is over half an hour away by car, but all the local policemen have are bicycles. In this weather, we'd probably have passed them on the way."

Branigan leaned over and tapped the driver on the shoulder. "Can't you go any faster?"

The man was embassy staff and glanced back nervously. "If I do that we end up in a ditch or worse. These roads are treacherous."

"Just put your goddamned foot down!"

Darkness had swallowed up the sea and the sky was pitch black.

The wind slashed at their skin and the four of them shivered as they walked down to the hangar, Saarinen ahead of them, playing the flashlight beam in front.

A long stretch of electric cable ran from the generator out onto the ice, and when Massey and Slanski helped open the hangar doors Saarinen flicked a switch on the wall. A single string of yellow lights glowed brilliantly out on the ice, and stretched into the gloom for a hundred meters.

"Our runway lights. Simple but effective." Saarinen said to Massey. "You can leave the lights on, I'll be back in no time." He removed the blanket from the engine and took away the chocks from the skis.

"OK, let's move this baby out," he said.

They all helped to slide the Norseman out and down the ramp onto the ice. It kept on sliding for a couple of meters, then came to a halt. Saarinen told them to move back before he started the engine, then opened the door and hauled himself into the cockpit.

Moments later the Norseman's engine erupted into life, exploding the silence as the propeller turned, sounding like the buzz of a giant angry wasp. As Saarinen checked the instruments and moved the control surfaces, going through his pre-flight check, Massey looked up at the sky.

The storm was obviously getting worse. Flakes of snow began to fly around them in gusts. Anna and Slanski started to haul on their parachutes, looking a little absurd in their jumpsuits, helmets and goggles with the worn suitcases beside them.

Massey looked back as Saarinen shouted above the engine noise, "Whenever you're ready." At that moment he looked up at the sky and pursed his lips.

There was a tangible tension everyone could feel. Massey said to Slanski and Anna, "Well, I guess this is it."

He shook Slanski's hand, then Anna's. "Good luck."

It seemed as if there was nothing else to say. For a moment Anna hesitated, then she leaned forward and kissed Massey full on the lips.

"*Do svidaniya*, Jake."

For a long time Massey looked at her frozen face, but before he could reply she climbed into the Norseman, Slanski after her, closing the cockpit door as Massey stood back.

Immediately Saarinen revved up the engine and the snow gusted around Massey like a blizzard. In the surge of power as the aircraft strained to move, he looked at the three faces in the cabin, Saarinen working at the controls, Anna and Slanski in the back. He gave a thumb's-up sign and Slanski did the same.

There was a crunching sound as the skis started to move out slowly onto the ice to the right of the string of yellow lights. Moments later came a sudden harsh growl of power as Saarinen eased forward the throttle. There was a momentary lag before the propeller bit the air hard and then the Norseman started to move more rapidly.

It took only a couple of seconds for the speed to build up and then the little aircraft was skimming fast over the uneven surface of the frozen sea, the skis bumping every now and then when she hit a rough patch of ice.

The sound of the engine faded in the wind and the plane was sucked up and disappeared into the swirl of snow and blackness.

At fifteen thousand feet, skimming above the clouds in darkness, Lieutenant Arcady Barsenko, aged twenty-one, watched the rush of black and winking stars against the cockpit glass of the Soviet Air Force Mig 15P and the scene almost put him to sleep. He yawned. The noise of the Klimov turbojet engine roared in his ears and he rubbed his nose tiredly with his fur-lined leather glove.

Shit.

He could have done with being back in the mess in Tallinn toasting his feet at the stove. A crazy night to be out with the storm below, but the commander of Leningrad Air Base had insisted the patrols go ahead, and warned the crews to be extra vigilant.

Crazy.

Barsenko ran his gloved fingertips lightly over the panel instruments and grinned.

She was a beautiful machine, the latest-model Mig. A thousand kilometers an hour with an engine that sounded like a pack of wild jaguars were fighting in the back of the aircraft.

Barsenko loved the Mig.

His one regret was that he had been too young for the war. Machine and man in perfect harmony in a battle through icy Baltic skies. And with a machine like this he would have blasted those fucking Germans out of the blue, no question. His leather thumb playfully rubbed the smooth red cap at the tip of the control stick. Underneath the hinged cap were the red plastic buttons that fired the twin 23mm and single 37mm cannon.

As for the Finns . . . Bah!

Those reindeer-eating slobs hardly ever crossed into Soviet airspace. Still, they had fiercely held the might of the Red Army at bay in Karelia in 1940, he'd give them that. His own father had been among the dead. That's why he had particularly wanted this posting. If the opportunity ever arose and a Finn came into his airspace, Barsenko was going to make the most of it and scorch the bastard.

The Mig bumped fast in sudden clear turbulence, then settled. Barsenko checked his instruments. Everything was fine, all the white pointers on the dials perfectly and correctly aligned.

Six more minutes to go and he would be ready to set a course home for Tallinn and base. A couple of large vodkas in the mess and then meet Magda. His busty Estonian girlfriend could drop her pants even faster than a Mig. Barsenko grinned at the thought of the evening's pleasure ahead.

He had the new on-board radar switched on and he idly twiddled the knobs until the indicator that showed the position of the antenna inside the Mig's nose cowl pointed down into the gray mass of cloud below. He glanced at the green illuminated glass. Nothing but clutter.

Suddenly he saw a bright white blip, twenty miles ahead and below. Then another. And another. Three blips.

They vanished.

Fuck!

Barsenko came wide awake and rubbed his eyes. Had he really seen something? Snow sometimes gave you ghost images in bad weather. Or else the radar was acting up.

But three strong blips . . . ?

Three fast aircraft out there in the blinding swirl of the storm at eleven o'clock, still in Finnish airspace but coming his way.

What the fuck was going on . . . ?

His radar had to be playing tricks on him.

It was probably clutter. He could call up Tallinn radar, but those lazy shits hardly ever answered in lousy weather, or the reception was too bad to decipher what they were saying.

Still, no harm in having a look below. The cloud was broken in places and maybe he'd see something. He eased back on the throttle and the roar of the jet engine softened to a hush, then the nose of the Mig dipped into a gentle dive.

Barsenko kept his eye on the radar and anxiously fingered the red cap on the control stick.

Anyone tried to move into his territory and they were going to get blasted out of the fucking skies . . .

Massey stood over the stove and nervously lit a cigarette.

His hands shook as he tried to warm them. They were numb from the chill outside and he went to pour a glass of vodka to stop himself shaking before he checked that the radio was still working. The red light glowed on the panel. Good. A heavy gust of wind raged outside and he looked up as he heard snow dash against the window clapboards. He thought, "Jesus, what a night."

He swallowed the vodka in one gulp and refilled the glass, then pulled up a chair beside the stove. Suddenly figures stormed into the room out of the darkness and crashed into him. He was winded and fell back onto the floor, knocking over a chair.

"What the . . . ?"

As Massey struggled to his feet something as hard as steel hit his skull.

29

Janne Saarinen had smelled trouble for some time now. He was sweating, perspiration running down his face.

Twenty minutes after takeoff and the Norseman was rocking violently. It plowed through the thick swirl of cloud in blinding whiteness at fifteen hundred feet, the little aircraft tossing about like a balloon in a hurricane. He was fighting hard to keep her under control and some instinct told him it was going to get worse.

He turned to glance at his passengers. The girl's face was a mask of white, and she looked as if she was going to throw up. The American seemed calm enough, but he was gripping the seat hard to stop himself being thrown about. Luckily the two of them were strapped into their seats.

As the Norseman bucked wildly again Saarinen looked back. A flash of light appeared on the window and the cockpit glass glowed brightly. Thick veins of electricity coursed rapidly all over the panes like creeping vines in a glowing, blue-green color, until they covered the front windows. It was an eerie sight, and Saarinen shouted over to his passengers.

"St. Elmo's fire. A strange phenomenon. You often get it in weather like this. Don't worry, it's relatively harmless."

Slanski said, "How long before we drop?"

"About fifteen more minutes should do it. We can't stay in this cloud for much longer."

He turned back to scan his instruments, fiddling with a knob on the panel while Slanski and the girl checked their parachute harnesses.

Slanski looked at her. "OK?"

Anna's face was green. "You didn't tell me it was going to be like this."

He smiled. "Some things you're better off not knowing. Don't worry, we'll be out of it soon enough."

There was a sudden violent crack and the Norseman lurched wildly, then another crack, and Saarinen had to work the stick feverishly to maintain control as the aircraft slewed to the left. Anna gripped Slanski's arm painfully hard.

"What's the matter?" Slanski shouted at the Finn.

"Lightning strikes. Christ, this buffeting is too severe. If it keeps up, it could do damage."

Suddenly a sound like machine-gun fire hit them in a fierce wave, juddering the aircraft, shaking it hard. The sensation ebbed away, then slowly built up again, only this time more intensely, until the whole structure of the plane seemed to be trembling violently.

Saarinen shouted above the noise, "Jesus Christ."

"What the hell's that sound?"

Sweat dripped from Saarinen's brow. "There's hail the size of tennis balls hitting us. We've got to get out of here fast. We'll just have to take our chances out of the cloud."

He pushed the stick forward and eased off on the throttles and the Norseman began to nose down. The hail and buffeting became even worse for several moments, then they broke into misty clear air at twelve hundred feet and it subsided, wisps of thin cloud and flakes of snow bursting past them, the frozen Baltic below. Saarinen pointed to a faint haze of lights far over on the left.

"That's Tallinn. The drop's another eight minutes east of here."

There was a sudden swish of violent air and Saarinen looked up as the Norseman rocked fiercely in a wash of turbulence and a flash of gray rocketed past on their port side.

"Holy Jesus!"

"What was that?" shouted Anna.

Before Saarinen could reply they saw a burst of tracer fire off to the right, and another flash of gray roared past out of nowhere.

"Fuck . . . this isn't our night. We've got company. Let's see what we can do about it."

He quickly applied power and pulled back on the stick, dropped the flaps, and the Norseman rose back into the turbulent cloud again, shuddering as it was sucked up into the air and the buffeting resumed as before.

"What the hell's up?" Slanski asked.

"You tell me," said Saarinen frantically. "Those were Focke-Wulfs from the Finnish Air Force. I don't understand it. Those guys shouldn't be up in weather like this. And they're in Soviet airspace. We must have been picked up on Helsinki military radar and the Air Force decided to investigate. They probably think we're a Russian reconnaissance plane making the most of a bad night, that's why they're firing, but it doesn't make sense."

"What do we do?"

"The only thing we can. Stay in cloud and carry on. Uncomfortable, but safer than having one of my own countrymen shoot us out of the sky."

Saarinen quickly retracted the flaps and checked his instruments. There was sweat glistening on his face and the instrument panel was shaking fiercely with the turbulence. It felt as if the little Norseman were driving over cobblestones, then the sensation slowly reduced as the flaps came in, but it didn't go away completely.

"Another thirty seconds and we'll be over Estonian soil. If those Focke-Wulf pilots have any sense they won't follow us in. Seven minutes to the drop zone by my reckoning. When I give the word, open the door and be ready to jump. And don't hang around."

He turned back to his instruments. The waiting seemed to go on forever as the Norseman was rocked fiercely from side to side. Finally he roared back, "I'm coming out of the cloud. Get ready with the door. I'm going to try and find your drop!" Slanski and Anna readied themselves and then Saarinen eased back on the throttle and pushed the stick forward. Seconds later they broke cloud at twelve hundred feet into almost completely still air. The night was still misty with light flakes of snow, but they could see faintly the glow of Tallinn's lights again off in the distance. Saarinen had his earphones on and he was fiddling with a knob on the radio receiver, at the same time watching his instruments and compass.

"Shit!"

"What's up now?"

He glanced over at Slanski. "I'm just getting crackle where the Russian beacon ought to be. It's the damned weather."

He looked out of the side window into the misty darkness, perspiration dripping from his temples as he tried to make out the contour of the land below. It seemed impossible to Slanski and Anna that he could discern anything out there, the land below all starched white in the blackness, here and there tiny pinpricks of light, but suddenly he tensed as he concentrated on the earphones. He fiddled with an instrument knob on the panel, then turned back and shouted, "Got the beacon! Drop's coming up in twenty seconds. Open the door!"

Slanski pushed open the door. A blast of freezing air raged into the cabin. It was almost impossible to get the door fully open, the force of the air against it like a ton weight, and then finally it gave and Slanski locked it in place. He gripped Anna's arm, pulled her closer and indicated that she go first.

She moved across him to the door and then Saarinen roared, "Go! Go! Go!"

For a second she seemed to hesitate, then Slanski pushed her out, counted to three, lunged after her and was swallowed up by the rush of freezing air and darkness.

In the cockpit, Saarinen held on to the stick with one hand, reached back and released the arm catch and the door slammed shut with a thunderclap. He locked it, then turned back as the Norseman lurched violently again, then settled.

He let out a sigh of relief, wiped the lather of sweat from his face, then banked the plane around in a perfect arc. He just hoped those Focke-Wulfs were not still lurking out there somewhere, because if they were he might be in trouble. It meant he would have to stick in the cloud, despite the risks.

He gritted his teeth and sighed again. "Right, my sweet, let's see if we can get you home in one piece."

The blood was pumping through Arcady Barsenko's veins like fire as the Mig tore through the cloud at five thousand feet, with four hundred knots on the airspeed indicator.

A minute ago he had seen another blip on the radar. Slower and smaller. A light plane, he guessed. Seconds later it had vanished in the clutter on the screen. Barsenko frowned. He had definitely seen the blip off to his right, maybe five miles away and moving slowly. No question about it.

The other three blips he had detected earlier had come and gone on the screen at intervals and he couldn't get a good fix on them. It was the damned weather making the radar act up, but they were definitely there. Three fast aircraft and a little light plane out there in the blinding swirl of cloud.

It didn't make sense in these conditions. Like playing Russian roulette. The light aircraft could be a reconnaissance maybe, but even that didn't figure in this weather, and if he wasn't mistaken it appeared like the three faster planes were hunting the light one.

Unless the light aircraft was Soviet?

A reconnaissance from the Leningrad air base that had strayed into enemy airspace and the Finns were looking for him. It was the only explanation. Barsenko scratched his chin and glanced at the radar.

Seconds later the three fast blips showed up again. Five miles away, and coming at him fast. This time they stayed on the screen. But no sign of the light aircraft. Maybe the Finns had already shot him down?

Barsenko grimaced angrily at that thought and said to the three blips, "Just stay right where I can see you, you bastards."

He decided to come out of the cloud and see if he could make visual contact. If he could, then he was sure as hell going to blast the Finns right out of the sky. He could argue about it afterwards. The aircraft were damned close to Soviet airspace and by their maneuvering and speed they could only be military. Barsenko grinned as he disengaged the autopilot, eased forward on the stick, and pulled back on the throttle.

The Mig reduced speed and dipped into the cloud with a terrible buffeting that seemed to go on forever, but ten seconds later, as he broke cloud at fourteen hundred feet into a sudden clear pocket of air and started to pull back on the stick, Barsenko's jaw dropped and his eyes opened wide in horror.

He saw the little light aircraft dead ahead, approaching on a direct collision course. He banked frantically to starboard.

If there was a hell, then this was it, Janne Saarinen decided.

Static arced across the cockpit window, veins of electricity dancing before his eyes, and the little Norseman bucked like a wild horse, shuddering as big lumps of hail smashed into the fuselage again.

He had been in bad weather many times before, but nothing as bad as this. Besides, if you saw storm cloud you avoided it if at all possible.

This time it wasn't possible. A second later, as he scanned his instruments, a sudden downdraft dropped him out of the cloud, and as the aircraft was spat out into a patch of clear dark sky, instinct made him look up sharply as he heard a faint howling in his ears.

"Jesus!"

He saw the lights of the Mig as it roared toward him.

"Jesus . . . NO!"

He frantically pushed the stick to the right and the Norseman banked sharply with such a force that his skull cracked into the cockpit door.

The Mig crashed into Saarinen's left wing, tore it off with a terrible, juddering bang, and then came a grating sound of shearing metal, exploding in his ears, the Norseman yawing violently to the left.

Saarinen suddenly felt an odd sensation, as if he were suspended in midair, and then came a second bang somewhere behind him as the Mig exploded in a burst of violent, intense light.

The third explosion came a split second later, but this one tore through Saarinen's cockpit like a roll of thunder as his own fuel tank ignited.

There was a brief, intense feeling of searing hot pain, and then he was consumed by a ball of orange flame.

Slanski sank through the freezing air, a vicious cold cutting into his bones, icy wind rushing in his ears.

A sparkle of lights that was Tallinn glowed in the distance off to his left. He had counted to ten and now he tugged hard on the ripcord. There was a deafening crack as he was sucked upwards, his breath snatched away as the parachute blossomed.

As he floated down he saw fields of white and patches of dark forest below. He tried quickly to find his bearings and saw a ribbon of road far off to the right, pools of light and shadow from street lamps on either side. What appeared to be the lights of a convoy of military vehicles snaked along the road, and he guessed it was a highway. He craned his neck and swung in the harness, trying to see Anna's parachute.

Nothing.

When he looked down again the snowy fields were coming up rapidly to meet him. As he braced himself to hit the ground a sudden gust of wind blew him to the right. He saw the dark outline of a bank of trees looming up and tried frantically to steer himself away, kicking his legs and avoiding the trees just in time, holding firm on the harness straps until the last moment, and then he let his body tension go, hitting the snow hard and rolling right.

He tore off his harness and gathered up his 'chute as he stumbled to his feet and looked around him. Behind lay a tall, thick line of birch trees on top of a raised bank of earth. In front of him he could make out the frosty Baltic in the distance, a dim expanse of gray ice. He figured he was a couple of hundred meters away from the drop zone.

But where was Anna?

It took him several minutes to remove the jumpsuit and bury the parachute and equipment. He decided to remove the uniform from the suitcase and buried it fifty meters away, digging a hole near some undergrowth, and then he tugged on his cloth cap and started to move up toward the bank of trees, carrying his case.

As he came down the other side of the bank, he saw a narrow road below, then froze when he saw a Zis army truck with red stars pulled in by the side.

As he reached for the Tokarev he heard the click of a weapon and spun around.

A beam of light suddenly flashed in his face from somewhere in the trees, blinding him instantly, and a voice said in Russian, "Don't move or I shoot!"

Slanski blinked. The beam of light moved slowly off his face and traced down his body. Then the light moved out from the trees and he could make out two men in uniform, another figure between them. One of the men was armed with a pistol and the other held a flashlight.

"Come forward. Slowly."

Slanski moved closer. He saw that one of the men was a young KGB captain in his twenties, the other a burly army sergeant, and then his heart sank.

Anna stood between them. Her helmet and goggles were gone, her hair tousled and her jumpsuit torn, and there was a look of pain on her face as the sergeant held her firmly by the arm.

The captain with the Tokarev looked over at him and grinned.

"Welcome to Estonia, comrade."

PART FIVE

February 25th–27th 1953

30

Moscow.
February 25th

The black Zis glided silently to a halt outside the Kremlin Armory courtyard at exactly three minutes to midnight.

Major Yuri Lukin stepped out of the car into thickly falling snow. A young captain waiting at the bottom of the courtyard steps was dressed immaculately in a Kremlin Guard's uniform, and as he stepped forward he said, "This way, Major. Please follow me."

The captain climbed a flight of stone steps up to an archway and Lukin followed, two uniformed guards standing either side snapping smartly to attention. There was a large battery of trucks drawn up at one end of the square, crack Kremlin Guards with blue bands on their caps sitting in the back, armed with machine-pistols.

Lukin felt the sweat on the back of his neck and wondered what was going on.

The call to his apartment had come half an hour ago. He was to be ready within ten minutes for an urgent appointment at the Kremlin. The sleek black Zis pulled up on the street outside even as he spoke on the telephone, and three minutes later he had dressed in his best uniform and kissed an anxious Nadia goodbye before he went down the stairs to the waiting car.

Now, as he walked beside the Kremlin Guards officer, the feeling of apprehension and confusion still had not left him. He guessed his summons to the Kremlin at so late an hour could only spell trouble of some sort.

At the top of the steps two massive oak doors were set in the archway. Another two uniformed guards snapped off salutes before the captain opened one of the doors. "Inside, Major. Watch your step."

Lukin entered a long, ornate hallway. The captain followed him inside and shut the door. A draft of warm air hit Lukin's face, mixed with the smell of wax polish and damp must. The walls were pastel blue, and plush red carpets covered the floor. A glittering chandelier hung overhead; there was a pair of shining floor-to-ceiling doors at the end of the hallway, more guards either side. Security at the Kremlin was always tight, but tonight it seemed extraordinary to Lukin, and again he wondered what was happening. The captain's face was set in a blank stare and Lukin said quietly as they walked, "I presume you know why I'm here?"

The young man shook his head and smiled briefly. "I haven't a clue, Comrade Major. My orders are simply to deliver you."

"Security seems rather tight here tonight?"

"Not my business, Major. I'm just to make sure you get to your destination."

Before Lukin could speak again they reached the end of the corridor and one of the guards examined the captain's signed pass carefully before admitting both men. They entered a large, plush outer office of red carpet and magnificent Tsarist tapestries and Bokhara rugs. A faint sound of music came from behind a pair of double oak doors directly opposite.

A fat, pasty-faced colonel sat at a mahogany desk flicking idly through some papers, his double chins spilling over his collar. On either side of him stood a couple of armed Kremlin officers, hands resting on their holstered pistols, and at a desk opposite was a stern middle-aged woman in uniform.

The captain showed him the signed pass, saluted and left.

The colonel smiled at Lukin. "Comrade Major, please, take a seat."

He led Lukin to a chair opposite and said politely, "Some tea or coffee? Or perhaps you'd prefer mineral water?"

Lukin shook his head. He flicked a look at the officers nearby. Their watchful eyes studied him before he looked back at the colonel.

"Am I permitted to know why I've been brought here, comrade?"

The colonel shot a meaningful look at the woman, then looked back at Lukin and grinned.

"Relax. You'll know soon enough."

Lukin sat and tried to relax, but it was impossible, and his stomach churned with apprehension. The stump of his hand hurt, the cold metal prosthesis like a block of ice. It had been freezing in the back of the Zis, the cold outside fifteen below. Off in the distance he heard the Kremlin clock tower chime midnight, and at that precise moment one of the oak doors burst open.

A colonel in KGB uniform stood half in, half out of the room, blue light flickering in the darkness behind him.

Lukin didn't recognize him, but he looked like a man of powerful energy, tall and broad, his muscled body straining under his immaculate uniform.

Cold blue eyes were set in a brutal-looking face, pockmarked with acne scars. Lukin noticed part of the man's left ear was missing. A pair of black leather gloves was tucked into his tunic belt and he carried a manila file under his arm. He looked at the fat colonel, who jerked a thumb at Lukin.

The rugged colonel stared over at Lukin. Then he wagged a finger and said curtly, "This way."

Lukin stood and stepped toward the door.

* * *

There was a blaze of colored light and music and a strong smell of tobacco smoke. As the door closed behind him, Lukin saw he was in a large private cinema. Several rows of plush red leather seats faced the front, heads jutting from the darkness in the front row. A color film flickered on a screen as Lukin looked up.

He had never seen the actors or actresses before but he guessed it was an American film. Girls in frilled dresses danced on a bar while a man wearing a cowboy hat sang in English and strummed a guitar. The scene looked ridiculous.

The colonel prodded Lukin with a finger like an iron rod.

"In there, Lukin. And keep quiet." He pointed to one of the chairs in a row at the very back. "The show isn't over yet and the Kremlin doesn't like its entertainment interrupted."

Lukin sank into a deep red leather seat and the big colonel slipped into the seat beside him.

It took several moments for Lukin to accustom his eyes to the semi-darkness. There were perhaps half a dozen men in the front row. A blur of cigarette smoke curled to the ceiling and a table was set against the far right wall, a shaded lamp on top, its pool of yellow light spilling about the floor.

Two uniformed orderlies stood on either side and Lukin saw the silver trays of vodka, brandy and mineral water laid out neatly. A large box of chocolates lay open beside one of the trays, an enormous basket of fruit next to it. Plump grapes, oranges and pears and bright red apples. Such fruit was rarely seen in Moscow in winter, but obviously the Kremlin had no problem with luxury supplies.

Every now and then a hand rose and waved from the blackness to be silhouetted against the screen, and moments later an orderly crossed to the table to pour some refreshment and place some chocolates or fruit on a small tray and return.

Ten minutes later the film reeled to a close and a fit of coughing erupted, but no one moved and the lights stayed off. Lukin sat there in confusion. He saw the projectionist, a young man in a captain's uniform, flick on a torch and feverishly load a fresh can of film. The screen flickered to life again.

This time the images were silent and in black and white. White words on a black background announced GUILTY OF CRIMES AGAINST THE SOVIET PEOPLE AND STATE.

The banner faded out.

A cobbled courtyard covered in snow appeared on the screen. A half-dozen frightened men and women were led out in single file and made to stand against a wall. Lukin realized that one of the men was a scrawny boy of no more than fourteen, his face drawn and pinched from cold and fear, and he appeared to be crying.

A firing squad was lining up, a line of uniformed KGB men readying their rifles.

Lukin saw the officer in charge raise his hand and silently bark a command. Puffs of smoke erupted from the rifles and the men, women and boy were punched back against the wall and slumped to the ground.

As they lay there, the boy's body twitched. The officer stepped forward and unholstered his pistol and aimed at the boy's head. It jolted obscenely and the body fell still. Then the officer walked along the row of corpses and fired a single shot into each. Lukin turned away in revulsion.

The colonel beside him seemed to be enjoying himself, his mouth set in a cruel grin.

For another ten minutes the brutal film rolled on, the executions repeated as more groups were led out to the courtyard. At least fifty men, women and children were brought out into the snow and shot. In the middle of it all, a hand rose in the darkness of the front row and an orderly placed some fruit and chocolates on a silver platter and brought them over.

Just when Lukin thought he could stand no more, the film reeled to a close and the lights came on overhead.

Lukin blinked. There was an outburst of coughing as fat, weary bodies pushed themselves slowly out of their plush seats.

Lukin froze in shock.

The figure of Joseph Stalin rose from one of the seats in the front row, the withered left hand, the bushy gray eyebrows and hair, the heavy mustache unmistakable.

He wore a simple gray tunic and looked frailer than Lukin imagined, his skin pale and waxen, but he was smiling as he lit his pipe and went to stand among a group of well-fed men. They were laughing, as if someone had made a joke.

Lukin recognized the other faces instantly.

Nikolai Bulganin, the sober-faced former Defense Minister, and beside him a grinning Georgi Malenkov, the fat, baggy-trousered senior member of the Communist Party Presidium.

One other figure stood out from the group. A bald, stunted, heavy-set man in a black baggy suit. His pumpkin head seemed to have no neck, and behind his wire-rimmed glasses, dark, watchful eyes looked full of menace. His portrait adorned every wall inside Dzerzhinsky Square.

Lavrenty Beria, head of State Security.

Lukin sat rigid in his seat in a cold sweat. What was going on? Why had he been summoned here?

The colonel next to him stood, his big frame towering above Lukin.

"Wait here."

And then he was gone toward the front row.

The room started to empty.

Lukin saw an officer open a door to the right and Molotov and Malenkov stepped out. Moments later Joseph Stalin shuffled toward the door, but at the last moment he hesitated, then looked back, his eyes narrowing. He stared over at Lukin.

Lukin felt his pulse race. He was unsure if Stalin was smiling or glaring at him, but the man was definitely looking his way, and with a look that suggested distaste. Uncomfortably, Lukin went to rise from his seat, but just then Stalin turned abruptly and went out of the door.

Lukin let out a breath, not knowing what to make of it all. He glanced anxiously around the room. Only the big colonel who had led him in, the projectionist and Beria remained.

Suddenly the colonel beckoned for Lukin to join them. Lukin stood and moved down to the front row.

The colonel said bluntly, "Major Lukin, Comrade Beria."

Beria was standing, his stunted body lost next to the towering figure beside him.

Reptilian, olive-black eyes bored into Lukin from behind his glasses, the pasty face grinned crookedly and a silky voice said, "So this is Major Lukin. The pleasure is all mine, I'm sure."

"Comrade Beria."

Beria didn't offer a hand, but slumped into a leather chair. The man had a frightening, grotesque appearance. In the red leather chair he looked not much taller than a circus dwarf, his feet dangling over the edge of the seat. The feet, large and flat and awkward, seemed out of proportion with the rest of his body. A diamond pin glinted on a gray silk tie.

Plump fingers gestured to a seat. "Sit, Lukin."

As Lukin sat, Beria turned to the projectionist. "Leave the last reel loaded and go."

The man did as he was told and saluted, then scurried out, closing the door after him. Beria said, "Well, Lukin, did you find our last film entertaining? Speak up, Major."

"It wasn't pleasant, Comrade Beria."

Beria smiled thinly. "Nevertheless, such punishment is often necessary. Those you saw executed were guilty of serious crimes. Vagabonds and thieves and common criminals. As such they deserved execution, wouldn't you say?"

"I'm sure the comrade knows better than I."

"You're being a diplomat, Lukin. You disappoint me. I prefer directness."

Beria snapped his fingers at the colonel opposite. "The file, Romulka."

The colonel stepped forward and handed over the file. Beria flicked it open idly.

"I've been reading your background, Lukin. An interesting story. Of a once renowned officer who fell from grace." He grinned crookedly and glanced at Lukin's hand. "Were it not for your little error in '44, doubtless you'd be a full colonel by now and still have your hand."

Lukin said uncomfortably, "I presume there is a reason for my visit here, Comrade Beria?"

"I haven't finished. By all accounts you were one of the best counter-intelligence officers we had during the war. You had a particular talent for hunting down enemy agents the Germans slipped into our territory."

"That was a long time ago, Comrade Beria."

"Not that long ago, I think. Besides, some talents we are born with. Tell me, I heard all the best people in your department, the ones who tracked down German enemy agents, were orphans. Is that true, Lukin?"

"I couldn't say, comrade."

"But an odd fact, I'm sure? No doubt the psychologists might make something of it. A passion for seeking and finding, as if such people had a thirst to discover their own truth. But you, Lukin, stood head and shoulders above them."

"Those days are behind me, Comrade Beria. The war's over and now I'm just a simple policeman. Such matters don't concern me."

"Don't demean your position, Lukin. You're far from simple and the KGB doesn't recruit fools."

"I meant . . ."

"Forget what you meant," Beria said abruptly, and sat back. "What if I told you there was a threat to our glorious Comrade Stalin's life? Would that concern you?"

Lukin stared at Beria, then at the colonel opposite. When Lukin looked back he said, "I'm not sure I understand."

Beria gestured to the KGB colonel. "This is Colonel Romulka, one of my personal staff. Tell Lukin the present situation."

Romulka stood with his hands behind his back, his chest pouting.

"Two hours ago one of our Mig fighters on patrol in the Gulf of Finland disappeared from radar control in Tallinn. We believe the pilot had detected an intruder in Soviet airspace. We sent three other Migs to the vectors where the aircraft disappeared. An hour ago the wreckage of the missing Mig was spotted in the ice in the Baltic Sea. There also appears to be the wreckage of a light aircraft it collided with. A special foot patrol is on its way across the ice to examine the crash site."

Beria looked back at Lukin. "Not terribly interesting, you might say. However, according to our intelligence sources, the Americans intended infiltrating two agents, a man and a woman, into Moscow with the purpose of killing Comrade Stalin. We believe a parachute drop of these people may already have taken place near Tallinn and the light aircraft was their transport. Despite the errors in your past, certain senior officers still speak highly of your talents, Lukin. I want you to find the man and woman and bring them to me, preferably alive."

Lukin looked stunned. "I don't understand."

"It's simple, Lukin. I'm going to give you a chance to redeem yourself. As of this moment you're in charge of this case, on my direct orders."

Beria handed a file across. "Take that and study it. Inside you'll find everything we have on the woman and man we believe the Americans have sent. The man in particular should prove a particularly interesting quarry. Besides, I think you and he have certain, let us say, characteristics in common. Age, for one. And intelligence and ability, I imagine. You may both be suitably matched. Wasn't that a device your people sometimes used during the war? Pick a man with similar attributes to his enemy to hunt him down and kill him? Some quack psychologist's suggestion, no doubt, but surprisingly I believe it sometimes worked."

"This man and woman, who are they?"

"It's all in the file, as much as we know, including how we surmised the Americans' intentions. There are photographs, which should be of some help. The man will prove a capable adversary, I believe, so be careful, Lukin. And another thing. You will have absolute authority to do as you see fit to apprehend these criminals."

Beria produced a letter from his pocket and handed it across with a flourish.

Lukin read the letter and Beria said, "Should anyone doubt your authority, that states you are working directly for me and all assistance demanded by you will be given without question. You report to me personally. Choose any personnel you need from among your own staff. Colonel Romulka here will act as my personal representative in the case. He's of superior rank but you will be in command. Needless to say, Romulka will give you any assistance you require. You look shocked, Lukin."

"I don't know what to say, comrade."

"Then say nothing. A Mig is standing by at Vnukovo to fly you to Tallinn as soon as the weather clears. The local KGB and military have already mounted patrols to find the couple and will be expecting you. Local commanders have been informed of the hunt for these people, but obviously not their mission's intention, for now that remains classified. Colonel Romulka will join you later. If there are any further developments, the duty officer will contact your office."

Beria snapped his fingers and Romulka crossed to the projector and switched it on. Then Beria looked back, his eyes flashing dark and dangerous, as a threatening look clouded his features.

"These are high stakes, Lukin. So don't fail me. I'd hate to think of you up on this screen some day in front of a firing squad. Find the man and woman. Find them and bring them to me. The moment you do, Stalin himself has promised to make you a full colonel. Fail me and I will be unforgiving. You have your orders. You are excused."

Beria waved a hand dismissively and poured himself more champagne. Moments later Romulka pressed a switch and the room plunged into darkness, before the screen flickered to life seconds later.

Romulka came back and led Lukin out.

At the door, something made Lukin glance back. The film on the screen was in black and white, with no sound, just the clicking of the projector reel as a series of disturbing, vivid images appeared. What Lukin saw made his blood run cold.

A naked girl was tied down on a long metal table. She was dark-haired and very young. Her arms and legs were splayed wide apart with leather straps and her eyes were wide open in horror. Froth spewed from her mouth, as if she were having a fit. She squirmed wildly, helplessly, her mouth open in a silent scream. Her head bounced off the metal table as she tried in vain to free herself.

A man came into the picture. He wore a thick rubber apron over his KGB uniform. His fingers probed roughly between the girl's legs and then he began inserting a thick electric probe into her vagina, a long wire flex attached to the probe.

Lukin saw the look of pained horror on the child's face and turned away in disbelief, in disgust, unable to bear watching the film a second more, as Beria sat there, sipping his champagne, looking at the screen.

Romulka grinned as he pulled on a black leather glove. "What's the matter, Lukin? Can't stand seeing a woman tortured?" He flicked a look at Lukin's hand. "No wonder that German bitch disfigured you. I would have shot her between the eyes."

Romulka slapped the other leather glove into his hand and went out grinning. Lukin waited a moment, then followed, wanting to be sick.

Half an hour later Lukin was smoking a cigarette and reading through the file Beria had given him when Pasha entered.

The Mongolian lieutenant brushed snow from his overcoat. "It's really coming down out there. So what the fuck's up that you get me out of bed at one A.M.?" He stared over at Lukin. "Hey, you look like you've seen a ghost."

"Not exactly, but something just as shocking. First things first. Have you any of that Siberian vodka of yours?"

Pasha grinned. "I always keep an emergency supply, just in case I start to sober up. But be warned, it's like sticking a lighted candle down your throat."

"Pour me one."

"On duty? It's not like you. I'm surprised, Major."

"Not half as surprised as you're going to be."

Pasha locked the office door and took a bottle and two glasses from his desk. He handed one to Lukin and poured.

"Chase the devil away and put a little sunshine in your stomach. *Za zdorovye.* So what's up?"

Lukin swallowed. "Keep the toast for another time. You're on a case with me."

"Who says so?"

"I do. I've just had the dubious pleasure of being summoned to the Kremlin."

Pasha frowned, his eyes thin slits in his yellow face. "Are you serious?"

"A visit to the Kremlin is not something I'd joke about, Pasha."

"What was the occasion?"

Lukin told him everything, then gave him the file. Pasha read it, whistled softly and crossed to his desk. He threw off his overcoat and put his feet up, taking a sip of the vodka.

"There's not much in there, but what little there is makes for interesting reading."

"There was even less on this American, Slanski, the one they call the Wolf. And as you probably noticed, there were a couple of pages missing from his file, if the page numbers were properly sequenced."

"I wonder why?"

"Probably classified."

"But it's usual that an investigator be given access to *all* information for the case he's working on. Why leave out just two pages?"

"When has Beria ever been known to tell everything? He'd only tell us what we need to know. Still, I agree, it's odd."

Pasha said, "It's a pity about the woman. She's obviously had a difficult time. She must have been pretty desperate to escape the Gulag. The photographs won't be much help. The woman's must have been taken after she was arrested. She looks scrawny and her hair's cropped short. And this one of Slanski was taken from a distance. The shot's too fuzzy to be of real use. Besides, a man like that will know how to alter his appearance, and they'll both probably have enough false documents to paper the walls."

Lukin nodded. "The First Directorate kept the file on him. His background seems to be something of a mystery. But they know he speaks fluent Russian and suspect he had a military background. They seem to think he was responsible for the deaths of at least half a dozen senior KGB and military officers, including Colonel Grenady Kraskin in Berlin a couple of months back."

Pasha almost smiled. "He sounds formidable. But Kraskin was one evil bastard I wasn't sorry to see go."

"I'd watch your tongue, Pasha. Especially where Beria is involved."

"You think Beria's right about these two trying to kill our lord and master? That the Americans would really send this Wolf to try to kill Stalin?"

"It's possible." Lukin paused. "Did you ever hear of a Colonel Romulka on Beria's staff?"

Pasha raised his eyebrows and said, "Colonel Nikita Romulka?"

"I didn't hear his first name."

"Then I'll give you a description. A big ugly bastard with half his left ear missing. A face that looks like it caught fire and they tried to beat out the flames with a shovel."

Lukin smiled faintly. "Sounds like him."

"From what I heard, he's one of Beria's henchmen, with special responsibility for security affairs in the Gulags. Why?"

"He's working with us. It seems he has a special interest in the case. Beria wants him to liaise with us."

Pasha stood and said worriedly, "That kind of help you can do without. Romulka's just a vicious thug. I heard Beria sometimes uses him for the really dirty work, like torture and rape, to extract confessions from special-category prisoners. A word of advice, Yuri. Don't cross swords with Romulka. He's dangerous, and he never forgives or forgets. And he'll suck your eyeballs out like grapes if the mood takes him."

"I'll try and keep that in mind." Lukin scratched his head absently. "You know what really bothers me?"

"What?"

"Why did Beria pick me? It's been a long time since I did this kind of work."

Pasha grinned. "He picked you because you were the best tracker the directorate had. You ran down every top Abwehr agent the Nazis sent at us. There were three names everyone in the department knew in those days. Guzovsky, Makorov and Lukin."

Lukin shook his head dismissively. "A long time ago, Pasha, or maybe it just seems like it. I'm just a policeman now. And frankly, I'd rather stay that way."

"It seems you don't have much choice. Besides, you're being modest and you know it."

Lukin looked down at his false hand. "Maybe I've earned the right to be."

"Because some German girl shoots your hand off with a machine-pistol?"

"I stood there and let it happen."

"A temporary lapse of judgment. You should have shot her first but you couldn't. Personally, I've never killed a woman in my life, even during the war, and I don't think I ever could, but it was you or her. You hesitated because it was a woman and it cost you half a limb. It could have cost you your life if someone else hadn't shot her."

"Perhaps, but why didn't Beria pick Guzovsky or Makorov?"

Pasha poured another drink for himself and topped up Lukin's glass.

"Guzovsky's too old. Sixty-four next birthday and his eyes are almost gone. And he drinks so much he couldn't track a fucking elephant in snow. As for Makorov, he's got so lazy and careless I wouldn't send him out for my shopping."

Lukin smiled. "Still, there are others more capable. And besides, working directly for Beria has its dangers. He could have me up against a wall and shot if I fail. And I don't trust him."

"Who does? Not even Stalin himself, I hear. The little beady-eyed bastard would scare a ghost. Only you can't refuse. But if you ask me, he knew what he was doing and picked the best. So what happens now?"

Lukin thought for a moment. "I'll need you to stay in Moscow for now and organize an operations room. I'll need telephones. Lots of telephones. And a telex. Tables, chairs, a couple of beds. Large- and small-scale maps. A couple of Emkas for transport. Anything you think we might need. Beria's orders are clear. This Wolf has to be found. And the woman. With luck, the patrols already in the area may find them, but if not, it's up to us."

Pasha said, "Then God help the poor bastards if Beria and Romulka get their hands on them, that's all I can say." He looked over at Lukin and smiled. "And what will the major be doing while I'm up to my ears in the shitty work?"

"There's a Mig standing by. The duty officer's going to phone just as soon as the weather improves or anything turns up I should know about."

As Lukin drained his glass the telephone rang.

31

Bylandet Island.

Massey came awake on his back with a splitting headache.

Jesus.

Slowly, the pain and fog washed away. He opened his eyes and looked about the room. He was in one of the bedrooms of the island house, the blankets tossed carelessly around him on the bed. He heard the wind gusting wildly outside and the brightly lit room was bitterly cold. He remembered the darkened figures bursting in through the front door and the blow across the back of the neck, but after that, nothing.

Who the hell was it who had struck him? He got to his feet in a panic and stumbled to the window, ignoring the dizzying spasms of pain. He pulled back the curtain.

Flakes of snow dashed against the glass and he saw a blaze of light below. Two black American Fords were parked outside the house and half a dozen men stood around, rubbing their hands to keep out the cold. Massey recognized none of them.

Suddenly he heard footsteps climb the stairs and looked around.

The footsteps halted outside the door. Massey felt his heart race as the door opened.

Branigan stood there, grim-faced. He wore an overcoat and scarf and leather gloves.

He stepped into the room.

"So, you're back in the land of the living."

Massey said hoarsely, "What the hell's going on, you son-of-a-bitch? You almost killed me."

"I could ask you the same question."

Massey went to brush past him but Branigan moved to block his way. "And where do you think you're going?"

"Downstairs—there's a radio beacon—landing lights on the ice—"

"If you're thinking about your friend Saarinen, forget it."

"What do you mean?"

"He's dead."

Massey turned white.

Branigan looked at him coldly. "We need to talk."

Tallinn,
Estonia.

The Zis army truck jerked to a halt and Slanski raised himself from the floor and peered out beyond the canvas flap.

They had halted in a narrow alleyway beside what looked like an ancient inn. Beyond lay a deserted cobbled square. Shabby, brightly painted medieval houses ringed the square. He guessed they were in the old town of Tallinn.

Anna sat beside him, and as she dragged herself up they heard the doors of the front cab open and the sound of feet hitting the ground and crunching on snow. A moment later the sergeant tore back the canvas flap. The KGB officer grinned up at them.

"Right, bring your things and follow me."

Slanski jumped down and he and the sergeant helped Anna from the truck. They followed the officer down a foul-smelling alleyway to a door at the side of the inn. The place stank of stale beer.

The officer brushed snow from his face and knocked on the door. They heard the sound of metal bolts and then a big, stoutly built man with a bushy red beard appeared in the open doorway. He wore a filthy white smock and a cigarette dangled from his bearded lips.

The officer smiled and said in Russian, "Your guests arrived on time, Toomas. Got a bit of a shock when they saw the uniforms. Good job we found them before the army did. Those bastards are swarming all over the place." The officer jerked his thumb at Slanski. "For a moment there I thought our friend here was one of them."

The innkeeper wiped his hands on his smock and grinned. His teeth were stained yellow and his red beard hid half his face.

"You'd better not hang around, Erik. Get that truck back to the barracks immediately."

The officer nodded and was gone, and they heard the Zis start up and move out from the alleyway.

The innkeeper ushered them into a hallway. When he had closed and locked the door he shook their hands.

"My name is Toomas Gorev. Welcome to Estonia, my friends. I take it everything went well with the drop despite the lousy weather?"

Slanski said, "Apart from the shock of having the KGB waiting for us, reasonably good."

The innkeeper grinned. "A necessary change of plan, I'm afraid. Some shit of a Russian general decided to put the army on maneuvers at the last minute. Two divisions are moving south toward the coast for the next couple of nights. The area you landed in was smack right in the middle of their route. Using the army truck was the only way our resistance could pick you up. But don't worry, you're safe now."

Slanski said, "There's a problem. I buried some belongings back in the woods."

Gorev shook his head. "Then I'm afraid you'll have to leave them there. For the next few days there's going to be too much military activity in those parts. It would be more trouble than it's worth."

He gestured toward an open door at the end of the hall, a shabby kitchen beyond. Dried fish and moldy-looking slabs of meat hung from hooks.

"In Estonia, we have a saying. Never welcome a guest without offering liquid refreshment. Come, I have a bottle of vodka opened. I'm sure you both need warming after dropping through that filthy storm."

The staff car turned into the main square of Tondy barracks just after 3 A.M. and ground to a halt.

As Lukin climbed out tiredly he looked around him and shivered. The snow had lightened but the early morning air was ice cold. The old barracks had once belonged to the Tsar's cavalry, its red brickwork faded and crumbling, but now it served as Red Army Headquarters in Tallinn. There was a captain waiting at a barrack door.

He saluted. "Captain Oleg Kaman. I was ordered to be at your service, sir."

"Carry on."

The captain led Lukin up a stone stairwell to an office on the third floor. The room overlooked a broad square and was barely furnished; just a desk and a couple of hardwood chairs and a rusting filing cabinet set against one wall. A map of the Baltic states and Estonia hung on another. A red-colored folder lay on the desk, and when the captain had taken Lukin's overcoat he said, "Some tea or coffee, Major?"

Lukin shook his head. "Perhaps later. You're familiar with Tallinn, Captain?"

"My father comes from these parts and I've been stationed here for five years. My commander was called away to supervise winter maneuvers and sends his regrets."

"Good. You have a progress report ready for me?"

"Yes, sir."

"Then proceed."

Lukin sat back tiredly in the chair. In Moscow there had just been time for a quick phone call to his wife before a Zis had sped him away to the airport. The Mig had lifted off during a lull in the snow but the flight had taken half an hour longer than expected as the pilot tried to avoid the worst of the weather, Lukin cramped in the rear cockpit seat. The visibility at Tallinn airport was dangerously bad and the landing had been frightening, the lights of the runway only visible for the last one hundred meters.

Now Lukin looked up and saw Kaman stare at him.

Lukin said, "Well?"

"I'm sorry, Major. You seemed distracted."

Lukin's stump itched in the cold and he scratched his arm. "It's been a tiring night. Give me your report."

The captain picked up the folder from the desk and opened it. He cleared his throat. "So far, what we know is that at approximately nine P.M. local time a Mig 15P all-weather fighter on coastal patrol disappeared. The aircraft was being tracked here in Tallinn, from the radio tower in St. Olaus's Church near Pikk Street, but because of bad weather only intermittent contact was made."

The captain pointed to an area of sea on the map. "We think the Mig vanished somewhere here. When the alarm went up three other Migs on patrol north of Leningrad were sent to scour the area. They flew low and spotted two areas of wreckage in their lights, crashed onto the ice. One was the Mig. The other appeared to be what remained of a light plane."

When the captain hesitated, Lukin said, "You're certain about the second aircraft?"

"Absolutely. That's what the pilots reported. They suggest a midair collision occurred. The weather's now cleared a little over the Gulf of Finland, but it's still pretty bad. We've sent a foot patrol out onto the ice but it may be dangerous to go too close to the wreckage. After the crash the ice nearby will be weakened. But the patrol ought to be able to get a better look as soon as they get there. We've already alerted the local militia that enemy agents may have been dropped and the commander ordered a dozen patrols out to scour inland and along the coast, but we've turned up nothing so far." The captain paused. "That's it, basically."

"How long before the foot patrol reach the crash site?"

The captain glanced at his watch. "A couple of hours. But it depends on the weather conditions, obviously. They're in radio contact."

Lukin rubbed his eyes. "You think the light aircraft managed to drop these people before it crashed?"

"Difficult to know, sir, but it's likely."

"Why?"

Kaman pointed at the map. "The local radar picked up several spurious blips west of Tallinn, along this route here. Three fast, one slow. Assuming the slow one was the light aircraft, its altered heading would suggest the drop had already been made and it was turning back. The radar people suggest that Finland was the likely destination. So we must assume the drop has been made and the man and woman you're seeking are on Russian soil."

Lukin stood. The file Beria had given him had contained a photograph of the woman, Anna Khorev. Despite her scrawny appearance she looked rather beautiful, which helped him. It was always easier for the militia to spot a good-looking woman. Plain ones tended to blend into the crowd.

There were details in the file as to why she had been arrested and sent to the Gulag, and information on her escape. The woman's past made unpleasant reading. She was the daughter of a disgraced army officer, her husband had died in a camp, and her child was in the care of a Moscow orphanage.

The man's file didn't go into much detail. Alexander Slanski, a Russian-born, naturalized American citizen. Lukin had read the brief character sketch compiled by the 1st Directorate with interest, but there was no information concerning Slanski's childhood in Russia, and Lukin had wondered about that. Such information might help him.

"A question, Captain. If you were an enemy agent parachuted onto Russian soil, with your destination being Moscow, how would you proceed?"

"I don't understand."

"What route would you take? What disguises would you use? How would you try to avoid the enemy?"

The captain thought a moment. "It would depend."

"On what?"

"On whether I knew the enemy was aware of my arrival."

"Go on."

"If the enemy was unaware, I'd probably take the direct route, with precautions. A train, main line, or some such public transport, bus or plane. I'd probably not travel in uniform because there are periodic checks on military personnel at such stations."

"And if your enemy did know of your arrival?"

The captain thought a moment. "Lie low for a couple of days. Then take a less direct route using public transport. But in disguise. And I would try to behave like a local, so as not to arouse suspicion. Assume a local's dress, his demeanor, his habits. Walk the way he walks, speak the way he speaks."

Lukin nodded. "Good. Though these people would hardly know the aircraft has crashed. But allowing for both scenarios I want checkpoints placed on every major and minor road, every railway and bus station, and the airport. Identity checks at all those points. Use every available man. You'll be looking for a woman aged twenty-seven. But cover the ages between eighteen and forty.

"As for the man, his description is less helpful. We know he's in his mid-thirties. Again, check all males between twenty-five and sixty. Take particular note of identity papers. And remember that makeup or disguise can change appearances. Put any backup men in plain clothes, not uniforms. That only attracts attention. And I want hourly reports. Inform the local militia that if anyone is spotted acting questionably, or if parachutes or any suspicious equipment are found, I want to know about it. If all that dredges up nothing we start sector searches. Area by area, house by house." Lukin handed over the photographs. "Have copies of these made and distributed to the officers involved. The images are not the best, I'm afraid, but they're all I have."

"Very good, sir."

The captain gestured to a door leading off from the room. "I've taken the liberty of having a bed made up for you in the next room."

"Thank you, Captain. Carry on."

Kaman saluted and left.

The meeting with Beria and the implicit threat had disturbed Lukin. Of one thing he was certain. He couldn't fail. He could imagine the outcome if he did. The way Beria played the game, Lukin would forfeit his own life, and perhaps even Nadia's. The man was that merciless.

The executions and the image of the girl being brutally tortured replayed in his mind like a bad dream. To men like Beria and Romulka, torture and death were pleasures and all part of the game.

But not to him.

He remembered a spring day in a forest near Kursk. The young German girl he had cornered, no more than eighteen, parachuted in on a reconnaissance mission behind Russian lines by the Abwehr in a last-ditch German offensive.

He and two of his men had tracked her down to an abandoned house in some woods. She was wounded, helpless, and frightened. Lukin had gone in by the back door with his gun drawn, but when he saw her young face, frozen white with fear, huddled in a corner with a coat thrown over her, something had made him drop his guard. The girl had reminded him of a long-ago innocent face. His young sister, aged four, crying as she clutched a rag doll on their father's doorstep, with the same frightened, helpless look. The resemblance was uncanny. But the indecision had proved almost fatal. The ragged burst from the girl's machine-pistol hidden under her coat had nearly torn off Lukin's arm.

One of the other men had to shoot the girl. Two months after he recovered, Lukin was transferred back to Moscow.

His heart wasn't in it any more.

But now was different. Now it was find this man and woman or die. With the descriptions and information he had and the swiftness of Moscow's response, he imagined it would be over quickly. By dawn, hopefully. Estonia was a small country, Tallinn a small town, the places the couple could run to or hide in limited.

And this time there could be no mistakes.

32

Tallinn.
February 25th

The kitchen at the back of the inn was warm and cosy and a table was set. Plates of cold fatty meat and oily salted fish, goat's cheese and dark bread. Despite Gorev's effort at hospitality, the food looked unappetizing. Gorev poured three measures of vodka into large tumblers before he lit a cigarette.

"Eat. The fish are called salty manyards. They go well with the vodka. In fact, it's about all they go with. The alcohol kills the taste. Since the Russians took over the food's been lousy."

He dug a hand into the plate of tiny salted fish and scooped out half a dozen, swallowed them heads and all, then washed them down with a gulp of vodka.

Slanski drank the vodka but he and Anna ignored the food. "Where did your friends get the truck and uniforms?"

Gorev laughed. "The truck came from the Red Army supply depot in Tallinn. The Estonian resistance, the Forest Brothers, supplied the KGB uniform. The officer and sergeant who took you here are Red Army conscripts."

He saw the look on their faces and his grin widened. "Don't worry, they're also in the resistance and completely trustworthy. And Erik happens to be well in with the quartermaster. He told him he wanted a truck to travel to Parnu to meet his girlfriend. For a crate of good Estonian beer, the quartermaster obliged."

"You trust him?"

"The quartermaster?"

"I meant Erik."

The innkeeper looked offended. "Don't worry about the natives in these parts, my friend. We hate the Russians. Half the country has had family shot or shipped off to Siberia by the bastards."

"And you?"

Gorev nodded up at a family photograph on the wall. "My wife, she died during the war. The young man on the left was our only son, a priest. Erik and he were like brothers. After the war the Reds came to Tallinn and took my son away. I haven't seen him since." He spat on the floor in contempt, then looked over at them. "You'd better tell me who you're supposed to be while you're here."

"I'm your niece from Leningrad," Anna said, "on my honeymoon with my new husband."

Gorev smiled, sucked on his cigarette and blew out smoke. "It's believable enough, I suppose. We get quite a lot of Russian visitors to the old town. Tomorrow night, I plan to put you both on the train to Leningrad. After that you'll be out of my hands. You'd better show me your papers so I'll get the names right if I'm asked."

Slanski and Anna handed Gorev their papers and as he examined them there was a rumbling noise of vehicles beyond the windows and they all stood. Gorev went to peer through a chink in the curtain. After a few moments he came back.

"Russian army trucks heading toward the coast. Those damned maneuvers will keep half the town awake."

He saw the look of alarm on Anna's face. "Don't worry, girl, they're not going to bother us. Not even Beria's KGB friends will touch you here."

"What makes you so certain?" Anna asked.

"Because I've got two KGB officers staying at the inn."

Slanski and Anna stared at him in alarm and Gorev grinned. "They're both harmless. Here for a few days of drinking and carousing. And having the KGB as guests is always an advantage. That way the militia don't harass me."

"Who are the officers?" Slanski asked.

"A colonel and a young captain. Old customers paying a return visit to a couple of local tarts they met while stationed here a while back. They prefer to stay at the inn rather than Tondy barracks. It's more discreet and a lot safer and believe it or not the food's better. Besides, every once in a while our boys come out of the forests and shoot up the barracks. It keeps Ivan on his toes and let's him know we're still in business."

He handed back their papers, then drained his glass and slapped it on the table. "Right, let's get you settled in. You'll sleep upstairs. My two guests are still out on the town with their girlfriends and no doubt they'll be drunk out of their minds when they get back, so they won't bother us."

Gorev led them along the hallway past the inn's bar and dining room, up a flight of creaking stairs to the second floor. He took a key from a metal ring hanging on his greasy belt and opened a door and flicked on a light.

Inside was a small, shabby, oak-beamed bedroom.

"It isn't the height of luxury, but it's warm and comfortable and you have your own bathroom." He grinned. "And seeing as though you're on your honeymoon I trust you won't have any objection to sharing a bed? I've left clean sheets and blankets. Breakfast is at eight in the dining room beside the bar. I expect to see you there, playing the newlyweds."

"Thanks, Toomas."

"My pleasure. Like they say, my enemy's enemy is my friend. Sleep well."

He bid them good night and closed the door. Slanski turned the key and looked at Anna as she made the bed. He sat on a chair and studied her face as he lit a cigarette.

"What are you looking at?"

"You. Has anyone ever told you how beautiful you are, Anna Khorev?"

She couldn't resist a smile. "You sound like a very bad actor reading an even worse script. And remember my name for now is Anna Bodkin. Aren't you going to sleep?"

"I'd rather sit and watch you."

She looked at him, her voice suddenly more firm. "Understand something. What happened last night is not going to happen again. I was vulnerable, that's all. And if you're waiting for me to undress you're wasting your time. I'm going to do it in the dark."

"Can I ask you something?"

"What?"

"Do you love Jake?"

She thought for a moment, surprised by the question. "What I feel toward Jake is none of your business. But if you must know, he's one of the finest men I've ever known."

"I think he's in love with you, more than just a little. And you know what's really odd? I'm not sure that makes me feel entirely happy."

Anna didn't speak, just sat there, considering what he had said.

Slanski put his cigarette in the ashtray, then stood up and pulled her toward him. She could feel his strength but she resisted, and then his mouth was on hers, kissing her fiercely.

She pulled back and said, "No! Please, Alex, don't. And put out that cigarette or we might both be burned to death and save the Russians the bother of killing us."

"Interesting."

"What is?"

"You said 'the Russians.' As if you were no longer one of them."

"Put out the cigarette and get some sleep."

He stubbed out the cigarette and as Anna went to switch off the light he reached again for her hand.

"I said no . . . !"

But he held her while his other hand began to undo the buttons of her blouse. She went to stop him but he gently pushed her hand away and put a finger to her lips.

"Don't speak."

There was a determined look in his eyes. Part of her wanted to protest, but another part of her wanted to feel close to him, to be held and protected again.

He undid her bra, untied her ribbon, and her hair spilled about her shoulders. He looked into her eyes. "Anna, what happened between us, I want you to know it was good. Maybe the closest I've ever felt to a woman."

"No doubt you tell that to every woman you sleep with?"

"Not true. Maybe you were right. Maybe I've never really trusted anyone enough to let them get close."

She looked up at his face and she knew in all honesty he meant it. A feeling of guilt came over her, but it passed, and then something stirred inside her. She felt a surge of passion overcome her and she kissed him fiercely on the mouth in the darkness.

Helsinki.

A log fire blazed in a corner of the room on the second floor of the American Embassy, and as Branigan came in his face was grim as he stared across at Massey seated nearby.

"The doc says you've got a mild concussion but you'll live."

Massey rubbed his neck and said, "How do you know for certain Saarinen's dead?"

"The Finnish Air Force tried to stop him at our request. They picked up the crash on their radar when Saarinen was on the homeward leg, and the signals went dead. By all accounts it looks like he bumped into a patrolling Mig."

A look like pain appeared on Massey's face. "Why did you try to stop him, for God's sake?"

Branigan looked him in the eye. "I should have thought that was obvious. You really fucked up, didn't you, Jake? You're going to get the book thrown at you for this." Branigan slammed his fist on the desk. "And don't look so dumb and innocent, buddy. I didn't come all this way just to have a fireside chat. I'm talking about the bodies in the woods. I'm talking about Braun—and Arkashin."

Massey had turned quite pale, then he said quietly, "How did you know?"

"After we learned about Arkashin and Popov we decided to pay the cabin a visit." Branigan paused, and said angrily, "You should have contacted me as soon as you had problems. Why didn't you?"

"The men at the cabin came looking for trouble. But I figured they only wanted Anna. After it was over we buried the bodies. Slanski still wanted to go through with the mission. Nothing was going to stop him after Vassily was killed. I went along with him. Maybe I was wrong, but too much planning had gone into it and I wanted it to succeed. I knew once you learned what happened you'd want to reconsider the mission or cancel. But I thought that would be a mistake. I figured how could it really matter if we went ahead? Arkashin or the men who came to kill Anna couldn't have known about the operation and they were all dead. I figured maybe we had enough time to go ahead with the plan before you figured out what had happened."

Branigan leaned in closer. "You broke the rules, Massey. And it mattered all right. You want to know how much?" Branigan explained about the Stalin file found on Braun's body, and the suspicion that a Soviet team had visited the cabin.

Massey was deathly silent, then he said, "Slanski thought the file was destroyed in the fire."

"Well, it wasn't. And if your two friends landed safely my guess is they've walked into big trouble. Kislov and his pals in Moscow are going to put two and two together. And they're going to hope that we go ahead with our plans, because that way they just might catch your friend Slanski and the woman when they land. That's why they didn't remove the file. That Mig we think bumped into Saarinen's plane, it wasn't a coincidence. Within two hours of Kislov landing in Moscow every damned Soviet border post, naval and air base were put on alert—including the one outside Helsinki, at Porkkula. Kislov's people in Moscow may not know when or which way Slanski is coming, but they'll figure out the likely bets, the ways we've used before, and they'll hedge them."

Branigan saw the shock on Massey's face and sat down.

"And you know what's going to happen if Moscow captures them alive? Shit, there's enough meat in this pie to start World War Three. First, you'd have a show trial, and when the evidence came out in court, every country in the world is going to point an accusing finger at Uncle Sam. After that, Moscow can do pretty much as it wants, and do it self-righteously, because we're knee-deep in our own dirty washing—we sent in an assassin to kill a world leader and that's a naughty thing to do by any standards."

"Slanski would never let himself be taken alive."

"You can't guarantee that, Massey. No one can. It's aces wild right now, and anything could happen. And the fact is, Moscow's probably already on his tail, and that ain't good. That's why we've got to stop this thing before it gets out of hand. That's why I want to know exactly how this plan of yours works and how you planned to get them into Moscow. I want names and safe houses and routes. Every last detail. I want answers and I want them fast. Because sure as hell, old buddy, we're going to abort this mission, no matter what it takes."

Branigan stared into Massey's troubled face.

"I think you'd better talk, Jake, and talk fast. Before it's too late for all of us."

Tallinn.

The two KGB officers were already seated in the dining room when Slanski and Anna came down to breakfast the next morning. Both stood up politely when they saw Anna enter the room, their eyes red from a late night and too much alcohol.

The older of the two was middle-aged with a ruddy face, a large stomach and bushy mustache. He had a cheerful gleam in his eye and he introduced himself as Colonel Zinov.

The second man was a boyish-looking captain. His eyes took in Anna's body as he offered his hand.

"Captain Bukarin at your service, madam." He smiled amiably. "Your uncle just told us about your arrival. This must be your husband." He shook Slanski's hand and then it was the colonel's turn.

"Pleasure to meet you both. You chose a bad time coming to Tallinn in winter, but I do hope your honeymoon will be pleasant. Will you be staying long?"

"A couple of days, just enough time to visit relatives and see the old town," Slanski replied.

The captain smiled over at Anna. "Perhaps you'd both care to join us for drinks tonight?"

"I'm afraid we already made plans, but thank you for the offer."

Bukarin smiled charmingly and clicked his heels. "Of course. Another time, perhaps. Enjoy your breakfast."

Breakfast was more thick slices of fatty meat and chunks of goat's cheese and another plateful of oily fish, but there was fresh white bread and butter. When Slanski led Anna to a table by the window he noticed she was pale.

As they sat, he whispered, "What's the matter?"

"The way those two looked at me made me shiver."

Slanski touched her arm and smiled. "I'd say they both have an eye for the ladies. Relax. And remember, they think we're on our honeymoon. So cheer up."

Beyond the window the sky was clear and blue. On the cobbled square outside there seemed to be some kind of market going on, groups of countrymen in cloth caps standing around examining horses.

Gorev came in moments later carrying two jugs of steaming tea and coffee. He chatted with the two officers a moment before they finished their breakfast and left the room.

He came over. "Looks like you both passed with flying colors." He winked at Anna. "And the young one, Bukarin, has definitely taken a fancy to you, I can see that."

"I'm supposed to be a married woman."

"That hasn't stopped either of them before."

Slanski stood up and went to the window. Horses' hooves clattered on cobblestone and the square was crowding with people. "What's happening outside?"

"Horse market day," said Gorev. "The horseflesh dealers meet here every month."

An Emka was parked outside and moments later they heard heavy footsteps in the hallway and the sound of a door opening; then the two officers stepped into the car before it rattled off noisily over the cobbles, leaving upset horses and dealers in their wake.

Slanski said, "Where have your two guests gone?"

Gorev poured coffee and said scornfully, "Off to pick up their girlfriends for more drinking and carousing. The bastards even had me make them up a picnic. I hope it kills them."

When Gorev fell silent, Slanski said, "What's the matter?"

Gorev wiped his hands anxiously on his apron. "It may be nothing important, but one of the delivery men who came this morning, he said there were plain-clothes militia at the railway station, checking papers. They seemed quite thorough. But what struck him as odd was that they were checking both men and women."

"What's odd about that?"

Gorev tugged at his beard. "More usually the militia are in uniform when they're at the station, and trying to catch army deserters. Only this time they seemed to be paying as much attention to the women. I'll have to contact Erik and ask him to find out what's happening, but it may take a couple of hours. In the meantime, I suggest you remain here at the inn."

Slanski came back from the window and finished his coffee. He looked at Anna. "I don't know about you, but I need some air."

Anna looked at Gorev, who shrugged. "Personally, I would prefer it if you both waited until I hear from Erik. Who knows? There may be trouble."

"What sort of trouble?"

"That's God's guess. But if there's a lot of militia about, you can be sure something's up and it may be unwise to tempt your luck."

Slanski produced his wallet and examined his papers and food coupons.

"Maybe now is our chance to see if our papers stand up to the test. I'd say it's as good a time as any." He smiled over at Anna. "What do you say?"

"Maybe Toomas is right. Perhaps it would be safer to stay here. But if you think we should . . . ?"

Slanski grinned. "You're playing the compliant wife. Leaving the decisions to your husband."

"Then let's just hope, my darling husband, that it's the right one."

Slanski put away his wallet and saw the worried look on Gorev's face. "Don't fret, we'll be back before you know it. You have a map of the town?"

Gorev wiped his hands nervously on his apron. "In the back room. But I hope you're doing the right thing. And if you must go out, an hour, no more. Otherwise I'll start to worry."

Lukin came awake a little after eight, his head aching and his mouth dry. He had slept for only three hours and there were dark shadows under his eyes.

When he had shaved, an orderly brought him a tray with a samovar of tea. It tasted vile but he drank it thirstily and ignored the single slice of burned toast on the plate.

Five minutes later as he dressed there was a knock on the door and Kaman entered.

"Sorry to disturb you, Major. Some news just came in."

Lukin picked up his false hand lying beside him on the bed and began to strap it on. He saw the captain wince at the sight of the mangled stump.

"What's the matter? Haven't you seen a war wound before?"

Kaman blushed. "It just occurred to me, how do you manage to shave?"

"With great difficulty. Your report, Kaman."

"The foot patrol managed to get within twenty meters of the wreckage sites. One's definitely the missing Mig."

"And the other aircraft?"

"A light plane, make unknown, but definitely not one of ours."

"Any bodies?"

"Two. The Mig pilot and the other pilot in the light aircraft. The patrol couldn't get close enough to remove the corpses, and apparently there wasn't much left of either of them. Both appeared burned beyond recognition."

Lukin crossed to the wall map. "They're not going to be much help to us anyway. Have the checkpoints turned up anything yet?"

"Nothing except a half-dozen deserters and a black marketeer. One of the deserters was shot and wounded trying to escape."

"Excellent. At least we've done some good for the state. Tell me, do you think the Estonian resistance might be helping our quarry?"

"It's possible, but they usually confine themselves to the forests, and the nearest group we know of is a hundred kilometers east of here."

Lukin crossed to the window and looked down at the barrack square. A couple of dozen soldiers marched by smartly in double file, and it was still dark outside.

He said without turning back, "Have you ever read Turgenev, Captain?"

Kaman shrugged. "I come from a simple farming background, Comrade Major. Reading books wasn't half as important as milking cows."

Lukin smiled. "Nevertheless, Turgenev made an interesting observation. He used to say that when you're searching for something, don't forget to look behind your ears as well."

"I don't understand."

"If you wanted to hide a couple of enemy agents in Tallinn, where would you put them?"

Kaman scratched his chin. "Lots of places. Parts of the old town go back to the fourteenth century and the place is like a rabbit warren. Underground vaults and passageways from the days of pirate smuggling. I'm sure there are cellars and tunnels there we don't even know about."

"My point exactly." Lukin thought a moment. "And the outskirts of the town?"

Kaman hesitated, then shook his head. "Too few people. And country folk would spot a stranger a mile off." He smiled. "In that part of the world, people would talk if you part your hair on the wrong side. Besides, half the population of Estonia are Russian plants. They'd be quick to inform the militia of suspicious strangers."

Lukin nodded. "Very well, forget about the rural areas for now." He pointed to the city map. "Concentrate on the city and the old town. For now I want checkpoints and roadblocks here, on all the main roads and the old entrance gates of the citadel. Maintain radio links to the barracks and inform KGB Headquarters on Pikk Street of our intention. These agents could have landed anywhere within a twenty-mile radius, but my guess is they'll try to hide where a new face doesn't look amiss. Anyone fitting the ages or descriptions is to be stopped and their papers checked thoroughly. And I mean thoroughly."

"Yes, Comrade Major."

Lukin dragged on his tunic. "Arrange an Emka and driver. And a mobile radio and maps. I'll be inspecting the checkpoints personally at intervals."

"As you wish, sir." Kaman snapped to attention.

As the captain turned to leave, Lukin looked down at the tea and burnt toast.

"And Kaman, a decent breakfast might be in order. You can't expect a grown man to get through the morning on this."

Kaman blushed. "I'll have the cook see to it at once."

The ancient citadel of Tallinn had once been part of the old Hanseatic League, an ancient port and trading fortress and home to prosperous merchants and craftsmen, until the Russian Tsar had invited himself in and turned it into a colony. Then Stalin, then the Germans, then Stalin again.

Despite a long history of invaders, it looked as if time had not touched the narrow medieval cobbled streets. Sunlight splashed on yellow and blue pastel walls, and all around were oak-beamed inns and houses, and gilded onion-domed churches.

As they walked along Pikk Street, the main avenue that cut through the length of the town, Slanski looked in the drab shop windows.

In a butcher's premises a single scrawny carcass of beef hung from a solitary hook. In another shop window, a bored woman arranged a couple of pairs of cheap rubber shoes. Slanski decided to try his coupons, and when he bought a bottle of vodka in a shop off Pikk Street the girl behind the counter took his coupon and money without batting an eye.

As they came onto Lossi Square, dozens of attractive girls sat around on the park benches, their legs crossed, smiling at passing uniformed sailors from the Soviet Baltic Fleet. Slanski noticed there were numbers chalked on the soles of the girls' shoes.

"The girls are prostitutes from Moscow, here for the sailors," Anna explained, smiling. "Prostitution is against the law and a Gulag offense, but the militia can't arrest the girls until they catch them soliciting by asking a price. So the girls write their fee on their shoes and they're not breaking the law."

"All very civilized and clever. You think they'd take coupons?"

Anna laughed. "Slanski, you're crazy."

"The name's Bodkin, remember."

"And it suits you in those trousers."

They came to a park on a hill at the top of the town, with a view down to the sea. Despite the clear blue skies it was freezing cold. Behind the park was some kind of large official residence, two soldiers in uniform on guard duty outside. The park was empty except for a couple of elderly ladies walking their dogs and a strolling soldier and his girlfriend.

They found a bench and Slanski uncorked the vodka and took a sip, then handed the bottle to Anna. "Here, put a little sunshine in your heart."

She took a sip. Slanski was watching her face and said, "Stalingrad. Tell me about it."

"Why do you want to know?"

"No reason. Just curious."

She looked out at the park. "It was terrible. The savagery. The house-to-house fighting. The endless days and nights without sleep. The intense cold. And always wondering if you were going to have enough to eat that day, or if you were going to die. The shelling was the worst. The noise went on for months, day and night. It got so bad even the dogs would drown themselves in the Volga—they couldn't take any more." She hesitated. "But it taught me how to survive. After Stalingrad, nothing could really frighten you."

Slanski said quietly, "What do you believe in, Anna?"

She shook her head. "I think I stopped believing in everything the day they took my daughter away."

"You never told me how Massey intends getting her out."

"The same way he intends getting me out, whatever way that is. Just as soon as he finds out what orphanage she's in. Stalin's made so many orphans, and there are so many orphanages in Moscow, Jake said it's going to take time to find Sasha. Some of the children are often given new names, to make them forget their backgrounds and their parents. But he promised me he won't fail." She paused. "And you, what do you believe in?"

He took in her figure and smiled faintly, and Anna said straight-faced, "Besides that? If you don't believe in anything, then what would please you?"

He thought for a long time. His face looked more serious. "What would please me? To be able to walk in my father's garden again. To smell the scent of apple trees and cherry blossoms. To be with my parents and brother and sister once more."

"You're such a strange man, Alex."

"In what way?"

"You're a killer. And yet you talk of the scent of apple trees and gardens. Or maybe you're just a typical Russian. Sentimental when you drink vodka for a memory that can never be recaptured."

He laughed and said, "Or maybe I'm just trusting you enough to let you get close."

She saw something vulnerable in his eyes then, and as he offered her the bottle she shook her head.

"I think I've had enough. Any more and you'll have to carry me back."

When he looked away over the town she studied his face. The words he had spoken had obviously affected him. There were no tears, but there was a tightening around his mouth and a distant look in his eyes, as if what he had said of his past had been painful to remember.

She wrapped her scarf tightly around her neck and stood. "I think it's time we were getting back. Gorev will be worried."

Slanski looked up. "Anna . . ."

"What?"

"Do you have any regrets after what happened last night?"

She thought for a moment, then shook her head. "No regrets." Her hand reached out and a finger gently brushed his lips. "It's been a long time since someone had their arms around me. A long time since I felt so secure and safe and wanted."

"And did you want me?"

"Maybe I've wanted you since the first day I saw you. Only I didn't want to admit it." She smiled. "Women can be like that, you know. It's a kind of foolish pride."

He stood and kissed her. "So, do you really think I'm crazy?"

There was a kind of childish innocence to the question that suddenly made her feel very tender toward him. She smiled faintly.

"Perhaps just a little. But then all of us Russians are."

34

Gorev, his face pale, looked from Slanski to Anna as they sat in their bedroom. The innkeeper had ushered them upstairs as soon as they returned.

"Bad news. I had a visit from the local militia sergeant."

Slanski said worriedly,"What did he want?"

"To see the inn's guest register. Luckily I hadn't written in your names. When he saw the ranks of the two KGB officers in the register he left. We're in the clear for now but it doesn't look good."

Gorev wiped his hands anxiously on his grimy smock. "According to Erik, the army and militia are setting up roadblocks everywhere. They're watching the bus and railway stations and the airport with great interest. It seems almost everyone's papers are being checked. Apparently, some KGB major arrived here from Moscow last night to take charge of the operation. His name's Lukin, and barrack rumor has it he's working directly for Beria. Erik says he's got everyone on their toes. The militia shot one man already at the railway station. A deserter, poor bastard."

"Did Erik know exactly why this Major Lukin was in Tallinn?"

"That's the really rich part. Erik heard he's looking for two agents who parachuted in last night. Apparently, a Mig disappeared and crashed off the coast. A foot patrol was sent out onto the Baltic ice last night. This morning they found the wreckage, and another of a light aircraft that had crashed mid-air into the Mig. No doubt it was the aircraft that dropped you. That explains why the army and militia are swarming all over Tallinn like flies on shit."

Slanski went noticeably white. He looked at Anna. There was a shocked look on her face. He turned back to Gorev.

"But how could this Lukin have known about us?"

"Search me. Maybe some yokel found your buried parachutes. But he does and that spells trouble for all of us."

Slanski saw Anna's face pale.

Gorev said quickly, "My intention was to put you on the train for Leningrad, but that's out of the question now with the station being watched.

Even the buses are being stopped and checked, and the airport is definitely out, security will be too tight."

Anna said anxiously, "What can we do?"

Gorev stroked his beard nervously. "God only knows. Normally our resistance people in the forests would hide you. But getting you through the roadblocks would be too difficult and their nearest camp is too far. I doubt Erik could try to borrow the truck again, that would be tempting luck too far. Besides, this Lukin seems to have commandeered every available vehicle and man at the barracks. And even if I got you to our resistance there are risks involved. The boys may not welcome your company right now; they get enough flak from the Reds as it is."

Slanski slammed a fist on the table in frustration.

"Damn it to hell!"

Gorev said, "Erik tells me they'll start house-to-house searches if they haven't found you both by tomorrow."

Anna glanced at Slanski, a look of indecision on her face, and then she said, "What do we do?"

"Either way, I'm on this ride to the end of the tracks. But if you want to take your chances alone trying to hide out with the partisans, I'm sure Gorev will oblige and I won't stop you."

She thought for a moment, then shook her head. "No, I stay with you."

"Then there's no choice at all, really. We have to move. We haven't a chance in hell staying here."

"But that doesn't seem possible. How can we get out of Tallinn?"

"You could try the sewers under the old town, but you'd be asphyxiated by the fumes before you got ten meters."

"Where do the sewers lead?"

"To the edge of the old town. But after that where do you go? And Erik says the Reds are everywhere."

"It could be worth a try."

Gorev shook his head firmly. "Forget it. We used the sewers once to hide weapons from the Germans. The gases killed two of our men and another died from blood poisoning. A couple of sniffs of that foul air and you'd be on your backs in the mortuary. And even if you did manage to stay conscious, most of the tunnels lead to under the KGB headquarters. You take the wrong turn and you'd save this Major Lukin the effort of finding you."

"Still, it looks like we'll just have to take our chances. Could Erik find us some gas masks at the barracks?"

Gorev shrugged. "I can ask, but there's still the risk of drowning or poisoning yourselves in the effluent. But it's your heads on the chopping block, I suppose."

They all heard a screech of tires on the cobbled street below and they looked out of the window anxiously.

The Emka had drawn up and the two KGB officers, Zinov and Bukarin, stepped out, two young women accompanying them. They all looked the worse for drink and the women laughed as the young captain staggered drunkenly toward the inn.

Gorev's face screwed up in disapproval. "Drunken bastards. Back for more drink at the bar and a roll in the hay with those tarts from the town."

Slanski thought for a moment, then said, "Did you tell your guests who we were?"

"Only that you were my niece and her husband on honeymoon. Why?"

"Nothing more? No names?"

Gorev shrugged. "It didn't seem important to elaborate. Besides, they didn't seem that interested."

"When do your two friends leave?"

"Zinov drives back to Leningrad tomorrow morning, presuming he's sober enough to drive. Bukarin, the younger one, tells me his girlfriend wants him to stay behind another couple of days. Why?"

"Maybe there's another way out of this rattrap." Slanski smiled. "You think you could find me an army officer's uniform?"

Zinov was sitting at the bar when Slanski went in. One of the women, a blond, busty girl, sat next to the colonel, nibbling his ear. A bottle of champagne was in front of them, two glasses poured. The young captain and his girlfriend were nowhere to be seen.

Zinov said, "Ah, my friend, you're just in time for some champagne. We helped ourselves, I'm afraid. No sign of Gorev."

The colonel's eyes were glazed from alcohol, and as Slanski sat down he said, "Your wife isn't joining you?"

"Tired, I'm afraid. She decided to have a nap."

Zinov grinned crookedly. "My captain friend and his lady had the same problem. Shame. This Crimean champagne is really excellent. It has Maria here as tight as a rusty nut."

The young woman giggled and almost fell off her stool. Zinov grabbed her. "Hey, steady, old girl. We've still got another night to go."

The girl was pretty, her blond hair cut short, but she wore too much make-up. Her blouse was open a couple of buttons to reveal an ample bosom and her skirt rode halfway up her thighs. She tried to focus on Slanski as she patted the bar stool next to her, a cigarette dangling from her fingers.

"Here, you sit beside me."

Zinov sipped champagne and grinned. "You're talking to a newly married man, old girl. Right now he's beyond temptation. Give him a couple of years of married life and try again."

"Well, I still think he's nice," the woman gushed drunkenly.

"We're all nice until you marry us." Zinov patted the girl's thigh and winked at Slanski. "Perhaps it's just as well that good wife of yours isn't here, my boy. She probably wouldn't approve. I know mine wouldn't." The colonel chuckled at his own joke.

"Each to his own, Colonel."

"That's what I always say. Well, don't just stand there with a dry mouth. Have a drink."

Zinov poured a glass of champagne for Slanski and another for himself and the girl. Slanski said quickly, "Actually, I came to ask you a favor."

"Oh, and what's that?"

"I received an urgent call to report back to Leningrad. My unit is setting out for winter training maneuvers tomorrow night."

"Funny, I thought you had a slight look of the army about you. But why didn't Gorev say you were a military man? What's your rank and division?"

"Captain. The 17th Armored. I brought my uniform with me, half expecting a call, but not so soon."

"What a damned shame. Rather upset your honeymoon plans, hasn't it? I know one or two of the boys up the military ladder in Leningrad. You want me to try and twist a few ears so you can stay on?"

"Thanks for the offer, sir, but I'm anxious to get back. I've already promised my wife to make up for the honeymoon with a trip to Odessa."

"Good for you. Duty first, eh?"

"I was really hoping you might be able to oblige us with a lift. The last train for Leningrad left half an hour ago and the first one tomorrow morning leaves too late. Toomas mentioned you were traveling to Leningrad and I wondered if you had a couple of empty seats in the Emka. But forgive me if I'm speaking out of turn."

Zinov smiled drunkenly. "Nonsense. A pleasure, and I'd be glad of the company. I have an early start, mind. Seven A.M. Does that suit you?"

"Perfectly." Slanski finished his champagne and put down the glass. "My thanks for the drink, Comrade Colonel."

"You're going so soon?"

"I've got some packing to do, I'm afraid. And I'd better tell my wife."

"Right, see you at seven, then."

The girl began rubbing Zinov's chest and the colonel slapped her thigh. "That's assuming, of course, this little tigress here doesn't kill me with passion before the night's out."

It was almost midnight and Slanski sat at the bedroom window smoking a cigarette. Anna came over and looked at him.

"You think it will work?"

He shrugged. "I can't think of anything else besides the sewers, and we can't stay here. There's a chance the checkpoints won't be as suspicious of a car with two officers in uniform. And an officer's wife traveling with her husband shouldn't arouse too much curiosity."

"What if we're stopped?"

"Try not to seem like you're frightened. The KGB can smell fear."

"You think it was Janne's plane that alerted them?"

"Probably."

There was a knock on the door. Slanski opened it and Gorev came in carrying an army captain's uniform, brown leather belt and holster, overcoat, cap and boots.

"It's the best I could do at short notice. Erik got everything from the army stores. The size should be all right, but the divisional flashes are a problem, I'm afraid. All they had was the 14th Armored."

"I'll just have to manage and hope Zinov was too drunk to remember I told him otherwise. Where is he?"

"In his bedroom with his girlfriend, drinking and wrecking my bed."

Slanski smiled. "Thanks, Toomas."

Gorev nodded and said anxiously, "Well, good luck, both of you. See you in the morning."

When he had left Slanski tried on the uniform. He buckled on the holstered Tokarev pistol and leather belt over the tight-waisted officer's smock tunic, then adjusted his cap in the mirror.

Anna came in from the bathroom where she too had been dressing and Slanski said, "What do you think? Do I pass?"

She looked at him. The blue eyes stared out arrogantly from under the broad-peaked officer's cap, and in his polished boots and captain's stiff shoulderboards and waisted tunic he looked the part.

"I have to admit it suits you. Only try not to look so menacing."

"I'm a Russian officer. It comes with the territory. Right, let me see what you'll be wearing."

Anna had changed into her clothes for the morning, a dark pleated skirt and a blouse opened at the neck. Her hair was down and her make-up emphasized her good looks. Slanski shook his head. "An officer's wife ought to look suitably attractive, but not that attractive. Your blouse would be better buttoned up to the neck and your hair's got to come up. Try to look a little dowdy."

"Thanks."

He reached over and pulled up her hair and tied it severely with a bow.

"That's better. Any militiaman will be drawn to look at a pretty face. Use your make-up more cleverly to avoid looking too good and keep your scarf up around your neck. Are you wearing underwear?"

"*What?*"

He half smiled. "You heard me. Are you wearing underwear? The flimsy variety or something sturdier and warmer? The kind my old *babushka* used to swear by."

"It's been ten below freezing outside. What do you think?"

Slanski smiled. "Good. Tuck those into your underwear tomorrow." He handed her his sets of false papers. "I suggest you do the same with your own, just in case they try a body search at the checkpoints. A militiaman usually won't feel between a woman's legs, unless he's a complete animal. But if he does, play the cards as they fall."

Anna took the papers.

Slanski said, "And you'd better leave your pistol with Toomas before we go. If we are stopped and searched and they find it on you, it would only complicate matters."

"What about you?"

"I'm in uniform."

"How would you explain the silenced Nagant revolver?"

He smiled. "Let me worry about that." He looked at her face seriously. "It's not going to be easy from now on, Anna. You understand that?"

"Yes, I know."

"And you know what to do if we get separated and there's a risk of being caught?"

She nodded solemnly.

Helsinki.

Branigan was standing at the window on the second floor of the American Embassy, drinking his third cup of coffee. Massey sat in a nearby leather easy chair, looking grim as he stared out at the lights of the islands out in Helsinki bay.

There was a knock on the door and Douglas Canning came in holding a slip of flimsy paper in his hand. Massey stood anxiously.

"Bad news, I'm afraid. I did as you asked and according to our radio monitoring boys here in the embassy there's a hell of a lot of transmission activity going on in Tallinn. Some kind of search, by the sound of it. Our boys gather from the gist of it that they're looking for two people, a man and a woman. Looks like your two friends are definitely in for trouble."

Branigan put down his coffee and snatched the paper from Canning's hand and stared at it, then crumpled the paper and flung it angrily against the wall.

"*Damn . . .*"

Canning said to Massey, "Doesn't anyone get to tell me what's going on here?"

Massey didn't reply, and Branigan looked across at him sternly. "I told you already, no questions. This is a top-secret matter. You keep your mouth shut or I'll shut it for you."

The diplomat flushed and looked offended. "Look, like you say, it's none of my business, and I don't know what the hell is going on, but what's the story here? Are you and your people planning on staying around here?"

Branigan sighed and shook his head. "We're into a whole different ball game." He looked over at Massey. "I was right. You really fucked up, Jake. Big time."

Massey said worriedly, "What happens now?"

Branigan ignored the question and said to Canning, "I need to make an urgent call. Have you got a secure line I can use?"

Canning smiled. "Sure. But I wouldn't suggest you phone the Ambassador this late. The old man gets mighty sore about late-night calls to his home."

Branigan stared back at the man with angry contempt. "You moron. I don't want to talk with the goddamned Ambassador. I want to talk with the President."

35

Tallinn.
February 27th

Zinov looked red-eyed from a blinding hangover when Anna and Slanski entered the dining room before seven. His jowls were like rubber and his brow furrowed as he sat alone at a table.

He waved to them silently across the room, and returned to his breakfast. When Gorev came in to serve them coffee, Slanski noticed that the innkeeper's hands shook.

"What's the matter?" he said quietly.

Gorev leaned over to pour coffee and whispered, "I took a walk down to the market square at six. The town is crawling with militia and KGB and there are checkpoints everywhere. Without sounding like a defeatist, the moment you're gone I'm going to go and stay with my friends in the forest until I think it's safe to reappear. If you're caught, that could be never."

Across the room, Zinov suddenly stood, wiped his mouth with his table napkin, and came over. He managed a weak smile at Gorev. "That champagne of yours could kill a man. My head feels like someone's been pounding it all night with a rubber club."

"Every indulgence has its price, Colonel."

"Indeed," replied Zinov dryly. He looked at Anna and smiled again weakly. "May I say you look very fetching this morning, my dear."

Anna wore heavy make-up that was far from pleasing and guessed Zinov was being polite. "Thank you, Colonel. My husband told me you're driving us to Leningrad. I'm very grateful."

"Nonsense. We have to look after our men in uniform. I'm just sorry this business of his has upset your honeymoon plans." Zinov looked at his watch and said briskly,"I'll be leaving in ten minutes, so try not to dally. They're expecting me in Leningrad for a staff lunch at one."

He turned to go, then hesitated and said to Slanski, "We'll leave by the old East Tower, by the way. It takes us directly out onto the coast highway. And just so you know, I heard last evening the authorities are looking for a couple of enemy agents who parachuted in the other night, so there are probably going to be checkpoints, but hopefully they shouldn't bother us."

Slanski pretended surprise. "Really? Enemy agents from where?"

"You know, I didn't even ask. A man and a woman. That's all I know."

Lukin had woken at six, still exhausted after sleeping badly. He shaved and dressed before sitting at the table and reading through the night's reports which Kaman had brought in.

Kaman had also left a samovar of tea and some fresh rolls and foul-tasting plum jam on a breakfast tray. Lukin had dismissed the captain, saying he would call if he needed him.

Now he spread the reports in front of him and sifted through the pages. The words danced on the paper, his eyeballs raw and sore from lack of sleep.

There was nothing much of interest. Every hotel and inn in the city and old town had been visited and all the guests had been accounted for, their backgrounds checked and verified by KGB Headquarters on Pikk Street.

The deserter tally had risen to twenty-one arrested.

There was a joke in the army that if you were going to desert, you headed west to the Baltic. The women were beautiful and the drink stronger and at least a man might have some fleeting enjoyment before being sent to a Siberian penal colony for desertion.

Lukin looked up briefly to stare out at the darkness. Winter in this part of the Baltic was dark and brooding, only three hours of sunshine at most, and he always found winter depressing. He longed for some warm Crimean sun; the scent of orange blossoms and wild jasmine and a hot wind on his face. He had promised to take Nadia to the Crimea this summer. He wondered if he would still be alive by then to keep his promise.

He thought of her now, and dreaded to consider what might become of her if he failed. He couldn't fail. Lukin sighed in despair and concentrated again on the reports, tension and frustration coiled up inside him like a spring.

Twenty-one deserters, a black marketeer, and a youth of fifteen with a rusting unlicensed German Luger but no ammunition. The boy had been arrested during the night, and questioned about the parachute drop, but it was obvious he knew nothing. Reading between the lines of the report by the local KGB, the boy had been tortured during interrogation. It was unlikely he was even a partisan. They hid in the forests, brave but futile Estonian men and women armed with decrepit German weapons, but they still harried the army even eight years after the war.

Lukin shivered as he put the report aside. The poor boy would most likely be shot. Having an unlicensed weapon in the occupied territories meant certain execution, regardless of age.

He pushed back the chair and lit a cigarette, felt the strong makkorka tobacco reach the pit of his lungs. There was a knock on the door and Kaman entered and saluted.

"The car's ready for your checkpoint inspection, sir. The East Tower is first, I believe."

Lukin stubbed out his cigarette. "Very well, Kaman, the East Tower it is."

It was pitch dark and freezing as the Emka rattled down the narrow cobbled roads of the old town.

Like most small Russian cars, the Emka was pretty basic and had no heater, so Zinov wore a heavy sheepskin jacket to keep warm. He had suggested that Anna and Slanski sit together in the back seat, and use the heavy woollen blanket he kept for passengers to cover their legs. When he turned left into a narrow road that led toward one of the ancient granite towers, they all saw the checkpoint ahead.

A group of plain-clothes men and uniformed militia manned a temporary red barrier placed across the road between two oil barrels, just in front of the tower. There was a line of three vehicles in front, two delivery trucks and a private car, halted and waiting to be allowed to pass. The militiamen appeared to have finished searching the first truck and it drove through when the barrier was removed.

Zinov eased on the brakes and pulled in behind the car in front. He tapped the steering wheel impatiently with his fingers.

"Damn it. I suppose there's not much we can do but wait our turn." He looked back at Slanski and Anna as he pulled out a pack of cigarettes. "Smoke, anyone? Crimean black. Guaranteed to leave you gasping."

Slanski took one, but Anna declined. Slanski touched the flame of his match to Zinov's cigarette, then looked back at Anna. Her mouth was tense with strain and she stared back at him.

They all heard a vehicle rattle on cobbles. Slanski looked ahead and saw a green army Zis drive up to the checkpoint from the opposite direction. The car braked to a halt and a man stepped out.

He wore a black KGB uniform and officer's cap and a heavy black overcoat and galoshes. Slanski noticed he wore only one leather glove on his left hand. The hand looked stiff and he guessed it was false.

The KGB man crossed to a uniformed officer at the checkpoint and spoke heatedly with him. Moments later the officer turned and barked an order and the militiamen manning the checkpoint started to work more smartly.

Klieg lamps and arc lamps sprang to life, flooding the cobbled street. More militia appeared, as if some of them had been sleeping in the back of their cars and had been shaken awake. The KGB officer had obviously made an impression because the second truck was being searched more thoroughly. There was a bustle of activity and the darkness came alive with stern orders and answering voices.

Slanski felt Anna's hand grip his tightly as they watched the scene. He counted twelve militia and army personnel, plus the KGB man with the leather glove and his driver. Five agonizing minutes passed and the truck showed no sign of being allowed through. Behind them, more vehicles had joined the queue.

Zinov finally slammed his fist on the steering wheel. "Damn it to hell! At this rate we'll be lucky to make Leningrad by midnight."

Suddenly the truck was allowed through and the car in front of them started to move up. It was searched just as thoroughly, the driver's papers scrutinized, and the KGB man watched it all with interest as he leaned against a wall smoking a cigarette. Slanski swore to himself and felt a cold sweat break out all over his body.

He quietly unbuttoned the flap of his Tokarev pistol and made sure the safety catch was off. He leaned across to Anna, sensing her growing fear.

"Get ready to move if we have to run for it," he whispered. "Try to make it back to the inn."

Zinov glanced around suddenly. "You said something?"

Slanski smiled and said quickly, "Perhaps we should have taken the train, Colonel."

"My apologies, this is damned ridiculous."

"Not your fault."

"True, but I think it's damn well time I had a word with the officer in charge. We can't hang around all day, for heaven's sake, or we'll both be late."

But suddenly it was their turn as the car in front was waved through. The barrier came down again as Zinov advanced the Emka, halted and rolled down his window. The flood from the arc lamps washed the car in a blinding pool of light and a militiaman ran forward.

"Right, get out of the car and have your papers ready."

Zinov flushed red at the militiaman's bluntness. He flashed his ID. "You're talking to a colonel in the KGB. Watch your damned manners." He waved toward the barrier. "Allow us to pass and be quick about it."

The militiaman looked at Zinov's ID and shook his head. "Everyone's got to be checked and their vehicles searched. So just do as you're told and we'll get this over with as quickly as possible."

Zinov could hardly contain his anger at the man's impertinence. "We'll damn well see about that! Who's in charge here?"

"It won't make any difference, comrade. His name's Major Lukin, KGB Moscow. So in the meantime, step out of the car."

Slanski and Anna tensed at the mention of the name, but Zinov seemed completely to lose his head.

"Shut up, you insolent fool, and tell the officer in charge I want to see him. Now!"

The roar from Zinov made the militiaman jump. The man turned and raised a hand and signaled the KGB man, the one named Lukin, who had been watching the proceedings.

He strode over. "Is there a problem?"

"Look here, Lukin, or whatever your name is," said Zinov. "You're talking to a colonel in the KGB, and my friends and I are in a hurry. We've got important business in Leningrad."

"I'm afraid no one passes without being checked and searched."

"On whose damned authority?"

Lukin produced his ID and held it out for Zinov to inspect. "On mine. There is a search for enemy agents in progress."

Zinov examined Lukin's ID and said, "That's all very well, but as you can appreciate, you're delaying us."

"I'm delaying everyone, Colonel, but I'm sure you realize I have a job to do. Now, would you all please step out of the car and have your papers ready."

Zinov flushed a deep red, then stepped out and slammed the door after him. The militiaman examined his papers first while two men moved to search the car. Slanski and Anna slid out from the rear as Lukin's eyes showed a sudden interest.

He stepped forward. "Papers, please, Captain."

Slanski handed them across. For a long time the major looked at Slanski's face, then examined the papers, before he looked up and said, "And who is this lady?"

"My wife, Comrade Major. We've been staying in Tallinn on a short visit."

"And the purpose of your visit to Tallinn, Captain Petrovsky?"

Slanski smiled and nodded at Anna. "Our honeymoon, comrade."

"Where were you staying?"

"With a relative of my wife's in the old town. Is there a problem, Comrade Major?"

Lukin studied Slanski's face. "Indeed there is. We're looking for a man and a woman, enemy agents who parachuted into Estonia the night before last. As it happens, our information suggests they're about the ages of you and your wife here." He looked at Anna. "So you say this lady is your wife?"

Slanski said proudly, "Indeed she is, comrade. We were married three days ago." He smiled. "And I can assure you, Major, she's not an enemy agent."

There was a laugh from one of the militiamen standing nearby, but Lukin's expression didn't change.

He said evenly, "My congratulations to both of you. May I see your papers also, madam?"

"Of course."

Anna fumbled in her handbag and handed them over. Lukin examined the documents thoroughly, flashing his light on the paper, feeling it, rubbing his thumb against the page. He didn't hand them back to Anna but looked at Slanski, then examined his papers again, doing the same.

"Your destination, Captain Petrovsky?"

"Leningrad."

"For what purpose?"

"To rejoin my division."

"And which division is that?"

"The 14th Armored. There are winter maneuvers imminent at Novgorod and I'm afraid I have to rejoin."

The major glanced at Slanski's 14th Armored uniform flashes. "Would you mind if we searched your luggage?"

Slanski shrugged. "Of course not, Major."

Lukin snapped his fingers and a militiaman appeared. "Remove the captain's luggage and search it thoroughly. His wife's also." He looked at Slanski again as suddenly two militiamen came forward with their Tokarev machine-pistols at the ready, as if sensing trouble.

Zinov came over and interrupted. "Look, Major, is that really necessary? We're in a damned hurry. This officer is known personally to me. And also the young lady. I happen to stay frequently with her uncle here in Tallinn."

"Quite. And I'm sure you are in a hurry. But so are we all. This won't take long."

Zinov flushed angrily. The militiaman removed all the bags and Lukin said to Slanski, "Please indicate your luggage."

Slanski pointed out their two suitcases. Lukin examined both suitcases externally first, very carefully, running his fingers along the joins. Slanski stood there, feeling the sweat on the back of his neck, trying to judge how many shots he could get off rapidly, deciding there and then to shoot Lukin first.

The major looked up. "Open the cases please, Captain."

Slanski did as he was ordered. Lukin knelt and flashed a light through the belongings. He examined the clothes' labels and felt the material of each garment. Finally he stood up and studied Slanski again. There was a look of indecision on the major's face, indicating something was bothering him.

"You look familiar, Captain. Have we met before?"

"I can't say we have, Major."

"Did you serve during the war?"

"With the Fifth Kursk."

"Infantry?"

"Yes, sir."

"Really? You knew Colonel Kinyatin?"

Slanski pretended to think for a moment, then shook his head. "I was only with the Kursk for three months before I was transferred. I'm afraid I never heard of the man."

Zinov shivered from the cold and interrupted again. "Really, Major, the poor fellow and his wife have had their honeymoon plans upset as it is. You can see he's a genuine officer. Are you going to make a fool of yourself and arrest him or are we all to just stand here and freeze to death?"

The major gave Zinov a withering stare, then looked at Anna and Slanski again, as if still unable to make up his mind.

"A question, Captain. What's your wife's month of birth?"

"Sir?"

"Her month of birth. A simple question."

Slanski smiled faintly. "July. A man could hardly forget that, especially being just married, sir."

"You seem a little old to be just getting married, Captain."

"Sir?"

"Is this your first marriage?"

Slanski shook his head and looked as if he was suitably hurt. "No, sir. My first wife died in the war. Really, sir, is this all necessary?"

Lukin hesitated for a long time, then slowly handed back the two sets of papers. "My apologies for the delay. You may proceed. Have a pleasant trip, Captain. You too, madam. And you, Colonel."

"About damned time too," said Zinov, puffing a breath of steaming air.

They all climbed back into the car. As Slanski slid in beside Anna in the back and threw the woollen blanket over their legs, he felt her hand reach for his and grip it very tightly, her fingers digging painfully into his flesh. He felt her shaking and there was sweat dripping inside his own shirt despite the cold, his heartbeat hammering in his ears.

As the Emka moved off and rattled over the cobbles, Zinov was muttering angrily to himself in the front. "Those Moscow types think they run the damned show." He growled venomously, "And don't you worry, Major Lukin, you jumped-up little shit. I'll see to you when I get to Leningrad. You've no fucking respect for senior rank."

As he kept on cursing, Slanski glanced back through the rear window.

The KGB major stood staring after the car, a faint look of uncertainty clouding his face.

Slanski turned back. The major had been clever, asking harmless questions, but questions that could have told him a lot. Somehow, by the look on his face, he was still not completely convinced. Slanski tensed and shivered as the Emka rounded the next corner.

Anna whispered in the darkness of the cab, "What's wrong?"

"I think someone just walked over my grave."

It was just before nine when Lukin returned to the Tondy barracks.

Kaman was waiting with a sheaf of papers. He looked exhausted.

"Some more reports for you, Major. Still definitely no sign of the man and woman, I'm afraid." He placed the papers on the table. "You think at this stage we're wasting our time?"

Lukin fixed him with a stare. "On the contrary. I want the operation continued and expanded."

Kaman sighed. "Has the major considered that these people could have been killed when they parachuted into Estonia? Parachutes sometimes fail. Perhaps we should be searching the countryside for bodies?"

"One death from an unopened parachute I can accept, but not two. The order stands. Widen the net to include up to fifteen kilometers beyond the town center. Every house, inn and shop in the town is to be thoroughly searched."

"But that will take days!"

"You have twelve hours."

"Major, what you're proposing will include a quarter of the population of Estonia!"

Lukin rounded angrily. "I don't give a damn. Just do it. And quickly, man!"

"Yes, Major." Kaman saluted and left, closing the door.

Lukin ran his hand through his hair in exasperation. He had been harsh on the captain—the man looked as tired as himself—but too much was at stake. The roadblocks and checkpoints and the checking of the hotel registers should have yielded something.

But nothing. Not even a suggestion that the man and woman were in Tallinn.

The man and the woman ought to be somewhere out there. It was ridiculous. With so many checkpoints something should have turned up by now.

He thought of the captain and his young wife at the East Tower. Something odd about him he couldn't quite figure. He was sure he had seen the man's face somewhere before. The remark had been no ploy, like some of the other questions. But where had he seen him?

The captain's wife was attractive but hardly beautiful. Her makeup had spoiled her face. A little too heavy. Maybe it was deliberate? The man had said they were on their honeymoon. She should have been happy. She didn't look too happy, just anxious. Or was it his imagination?

But the man had shown no sign of fear, just bemusement. Lukin had found it hard to decide about him.

The question he had asked him about his wife's birthday had influenced his decision, but only just. He had once caught a couple of German agents in Kiev who had been traveling as man and wife. A husband always remembered his real wife's birthday and the German had faltered too long, then finally made a run for it before he was caught. But the captain that morning had known.

Still, the couple were borderline, and he should have checked their story. The colonel's statement that he had known his passengers personally had swung it in their favor.

But what really bothered Lukin still was the man's face. He was certain he remembered him from somewhere. Something about him that seemed oddly familiar. But he was too troubled, too stressed, and memory worked best when the mind was at peace, not tired and in turmoil. It would come to him, eventually, but right now, even though he racked his brain, it was a total blank.

He picked up the photographs of the woman and the man known as the Wolf. He looked down at them for a long time. The Wolf's picture was really too blurred to be useful and had been taken from too great a distance. Another thing kept bothering Lukin—the fact that there were two pages missing from the man's file. Perhaps Beria had his reasons for withholding the pages, but Lukin felt somehow less than trusted. It was as if his path were being made deliberately more difficult.

Pasha was right. It was usual that an investigator be given access to all information concerning a case.

The photograph of the woman showed her with no make-up, her hair cropped short and her face gaunt. There were obvious dark circles under her eyes from stress or lack of sleep, or both.

Lukin tried to imagine what she would look like with more flesh on her cheekbones and her hair longer and wearing make-up. Impossible, really. A woman could completely change her appearance with cleverly applied make-up. Still, instinct told him something wasn't right. And the checkpoints had turned up no other likely suspects.

He picked up the phone and quickly dialed Kaman's extension.

"Lukin here. I want a Captain Oleg Petrovsky checked out immediately. See if he's with the 14th Armored at Leningrad. Get onto his commanding officer, or whoever's next in line. I want details from his personal file. Background, marriage, and so on. And verify if the division is planning winter maneuvers at Novgorod. Have them call me."

Kaman said, "Who is he?"

"Never mind that for now, just do it. And phone the local air force commander and have a helicopter stand by in case I need it. If he quibbles, put him onto me. And find out where a KGB colonel named Zinov was staying in Tallinn."

Lukin replaced the phone. There was still plenty of time to stop the Emka before it reached Leningrad. The drive took five hours, so that left Lukin the best part of three.

He checked his watch. Nine A.M.

With luck, the information should be back from the Leningrad Divisional Headquarters within ten minutes.

PART SIX

February 27th 1953
9:15 A.M.–6:30 P.M.

Estonia.
February 27th

They took the main highway to Kivioli, then once past the town followed the coast road for Leningrad.

Brightly painted fishing boats lay rotting on the shoreline, abandoned nets like giant spider's webs. The skies were clear but off to the west a mass of threatening snow clouds hovered above the frozen Baltic.

It was over three hundred kilometers to Leningrad, five hours on the highway, but once they left Kivioli the roads were clogged with military traffic. A long column of tanks and trucks trailed jets of muddy slush in their wake as they moved westwards, and Zinov had to drive slowly until they reached the coast.

"Good to see Stalin still likes to let the Balts know that we're in business," commented Zinov. "Smoke, anyone?"

Slanski accepted a cigarette. As Zinov handed back his lighter, he said casually, "I must say, that major back in Tallinn seemed very uncertain about you."

Slanski smiled. "I must have a suspicious face, Colonel."

Zinov laughed. "Well, if you had been enemy agents you certainly would have picked the wrong traveling companion in a KGB colonel."

After another hour there was almost no traffic apart from occasional peasants on horses and donkeys and carts and Zinov made up for lost time.

They passed squalid Estonian towns and villages, and here and there the ruins of houses dotted the countryside, still deserted since the war, charred buildings and derelict cottages with their roofs caved in. Rusted, scavenged hulks of German Panzers and artillery pieces were still decaying, lying abandoned in open fields.

As they passed through a deserted village Slanski and Anna saw that the timber houses had been recently razed to the ground and the local church gutted. Two black paint strokes on a sign had obliterated the village name.

"A couple of months ago that was a thriving village," Zinov remarked. "Until some partisans decided to blow up an ammunition dump in a nearby barracks. The local commander shot all the men and had the women and children sent to Siberia. Drastic, but then drastic measures are sometimes called for, I think you'll agree, Captain?"

"Of course."

Zinov turned back and smiled. "These crazy partisans think we can be defeated. But they're wrong. Like that madman Hitler and that fool Napoleon. Do you know the famous monument in Riga? On one side it reads: 'In 1812 Napoleon passed this way to Moscow with two hundred thousand men.' On the other side it reads: 'In 1813 Napoleon passed this way from Moscow with twenty thousand men.' Zinov laughed.

They passed Narva half an hour later and Zinov suggested they stop and stretch their legs before they pressed on to Leningrad.

"We'll have some food and vodka. Nothing like a little refreshment and fresh air to clear the head."

Slanski glanced at Anna. Something about the major at the checkpoint in Tallinn had made them both uneasy and unwilling to delay getting to Leningrad.

He said to Zinov, "Perhaps we ought to press on?"

"Nonsense, we've plenty of time. We'll be in Leningrad in under two hours. There's a perfect spot up ahead. I sometimes stop there for a break."

It was still dark, a gray twilight and the moon out, as Zinov turned off the highway minutes later and drove along a forest road. Either side narrow lanes led off into the woods and after a hundred meters they dipped over a rise and came out in a clearing beside a small frozen lake.

The view over the lake was really rather beautiful, the towering birch trees along the shoreline sugared prettily with snow, and there was a sense of peaceful isolation after the highway.

Zinov climbed out and said to Slanski, "Splendid, isn't it? Get the vodka and food, man, it's in the trunk. There's some smoked eel and bread I bought in Tallinn. I'm sure your wife's hungry."

Slanski went around to the trunk and removed a picnic basket. As he turned back he heard a small cry from Anna and saw Zinov grab her savagely by the hair, his pistol pointed at her head.

"Put your hands in the air," he ordered Slanski. Zinov's face looked stern and he was suddenly all business. "Undo your pistol belt very slowly. And I mean slowly. Then throw it over here. You do as I say or the woman gets a bullet in the head."

"What's going on? Is this some kind of joke?"

Zinov's eyes narrowed suspiciously. "Something's not right with you two. That major back in Tallinn, he was right. You're both enemy agents."

"Colonel, this is nonsense," Slanski said reasonably. "Our papers were in order at the checkpoint. Put the gun away. You're making my wife nervous."

Zinov said sharply, "Shut up. I've listened to your accents. Neither of you are from Leningrad. I've lived there all my life. The woman here, she's from Moscow, but you, I can't figure you out. A little while back something else occurred to me. Last night you told me you were with the 17th Armored. But you told the major at the checkpoint you were with the 14th. Perhaps you'd care to explain?"

"A mistake. I don't know what I was thinking of. And I never said my wife was from Leningrad."

"Mistake, my ass."

Slanski shifted his stance, ready to move, but he was standing well back, too far to get closer to the colonel.

Zinov fingered his pistol. "I really wouldn't try anything. I'm an excellent shot." He aimed the pistol at Slanski. "Now, you're going to tell me just who you really are or I pull this trigger."

Lukin sat in the freezing dome of the MIL as his eyes swept the ribbon of highway that snaked below the helicopter.

They had taken off in darkness from the Tondy barracks an hour before, flying at barely fifty meters above the main Leningrad road. Acres of endless birch forest ran either side, coated white, the lights of villages and street lamps burning in the winter grayness that stretched ahead.

The helicopter pilot turned to Lukin and shouted above the cabin noise. "We can't go much farther, Major. There's a bank of snow cloud moving in from the west. Flying in both darkness and bad weather is not permitted by regulations."

Lukin had had difficulty convincing the pilot's commander to allow the helicopter to fly in darkness, until he produced the letter from Beria, and the man had given in grudgingly, warning Lukin of the dangers of flying in poor light. The MIL wasn't equipped for it and the pilot would have to stay close to the ground.

Now Lukin shook his head. "Forget regulations. You turn back when I tell you. You have enough fuel?"

"For another two hundred kilometers, but—"

"Then keep flying. Shout if you spot anything."

The pilot started to protest, but then he saw the grim look on Lukin's face and returned to his controls.

Lukin looked down at the map on his knee. He had a small reading light in his hand and he flicked it over the map while he continued to glance down at the highway. There was a column of tanks moving south, their lumbering gray shapes like giant metal snails in the twilight.

The news had come back from Leningrad ten minutes after Kaman had made the call. There was no Captain Oleg Petrovsky with the 14th and definitely no winter maneuvers in Novgorod. Lukin's instinct had been right. But *damn*, he should have followed it at the checkpoint.

The inn where Zinov had stayed had been visited by the KGB, but the place was locked and the owner nowhere to be found. The men had broken in but a quick search of the premises had produced nothing. There was only one other name on the inn's register, a captain named Bukarin. Lukin would just have to wait and see if either the captain or the innkeeper showed up.

By his own calculations, the Emka had to be somewhere close up ahead. Even traveling at eighty kilometers an hour, the maximum distance the car could have traveled was two hundred kilometers. Allowing for traffic, more likely a hundred and fifty.

That put them about five minutes ahead.

Lukin considered that the colonel driving the Emka could have taken a minor road, but that was unlikely. No roadworks blocked the main highway, and the minor roads were clogged with military traffic. The pilot had already swooped low on several Emkas, come alongside them in the darkness, disbelief on the faces of the passengers as the helicopter hovered alongside to get a closer look at the occupants. But so far, no sign of the colonel's car. Lukin still couldn't figure if the KGB man had been an innocent dupe, or whether he was part of it.

He looked down at the highway again. Empty. They had passed the last column of tanks minutes ago. He shouted to the pilot. "You have a searchlight under the fuselage?"

The man looked back and nodded.

Lukin said, "If there's nothing in the next ten minutes, we go back and check the minor roads, those that lead into the forest. The car could have pulled in somewhere."

The pilot looked worried, pointed up ahead at a bruised-looking sky, and shook his head. "There's going to be snow soon. Besides, there are high-voltage cables off the main highway. In this poor light we could clip one. It's too dangerous."

"Do as I tell you," Lukin commanded.

The pilot shook his head firmly. "No, Major, I'm in charge of this aircraft. I must insist, it's too dangerous. And if we get snow it could be treacherous. We turn back—"

The pilot turned away and tilted the control stick, and the MIL started to bank right, heading back the way they had come.

Lukin removed the pistol from his holster, cocked it, and put it to the man's head.

The pilot glanced over at him, open-mouthed.

"Are you fucking crazy?"

"Maybe, but you'll be dead if you don't do as I say. Switch on that search beam, Lieutenant, or I'll take your damned ear off!"

"Colonel, you're making a mistake."

Zinov stood there, his weapon pointed at Slanski. "Talk. Before I'm tempted to shoot."

"I have nothing to say. Except I'm going to report this. Your behavior is uncalled for."

There was a brief look of uncertainty on Zinov's face and then he said, "You're trying my patience."

"Might I make a suggestion? We drive down to the nearest militia barracks. You phone my commanding officer. He'll verify my identity."

Zinov smiled. "And meantime, you both try and make a run for it. I'm not an idiot. And it's me who's going to get the credit for capturing you, not that jumped-up fool of a major back in Tallinn. So tell me who you are."

"Captain Oleg Petrovsky, 14th Armored Division."

Zinov stepped closer and angrily leveled the gun at Slanski. "Don't fuck with me."

Anna said, "Colonel, I think you ought to know the truth."

Slanski went to speak, but Anna interrupted. "No. I have to tell him." She looked at Zinov steadily. "We're not married to each other. My husband is an army officer in Leningrad. This man is who he says he is. But we went to Tallinn to be alone together."

Zinov grinned. "Lovers? Nice try, but you'll have to do better than that."

"In my bag you'll find a photograph of my husband and me."

Zinov hesitated, suddenly unsure. "Get it for me. Just remember not to try anything or your friend here loses his head."

Anna moved to the car and found the handbag on the back seat.

Zinov stepped closer to her and said, "Toss it here."

Anna threw over the bag and as it landed Zinov bent to pick it up.

She crossed the distance quickly and as Zinov reacted and raised the gun in panic her hand chopped down hard on his neck. He screamed in pain and Slanski was already moving, racing across the ground between them, but he wasn't fast enough.

Zinov fired off a shot and it clipped Slanski's tunic, just as his foot came up and kicked the gun from the colonel's hand and his fist smashed into his jaw. Zinov fell back into the snow, blood streaming from his mouth.

As Slanski grabbed the weapon, Zinov looked up pleadingly, real fear in his eyes. "Please don't kill me. Please, I'll tell no one. Please—"

Slanski shot him between the eyes.

Anna put a hand over her mouth in horror and Slanski said, "Get back to the car."

She didn't move as she stared down at the colonel's body. There was blood pumping from his wound. For several seconds she stood there, stricken, until Slanski touched her arm.

"Anna . . . !"

"Get away from me!"

As she pushed him away, Slanski grabbed her arm angrily and pulled her face up to his. "Listen to me. You're in shock. You think I like this? This is war, Anna. This is life or death. He would have killed us both. And just remember he was KGB, the same people who put you in the Gulag. The same people who took your child. Remember that."

His words suddenly jolted her back.

"You'd better help me bury the body. See if there's anything in the car we can dig with. Quickly. I don't want to be here all day."

She watched as he turned over the body and began searching through the pockets. Suddenly she looked up at the sky as she heard a faint chopping sound, but then it faded and was gone.

"What's wrong?" There were beads of sweat on Slanski's face and he was staring at her urgently.

"Nothing. I thought I heard something . . ." and then she started toward the car.

It took them five minutes to bury the body in a shallow grave in the snow, digging with their hands and using a tire iron from the car. When they finished they were soaking wet and their clothes were covered in blood.

Slanski said, "You'd better change. I'll get the suitcases."

She started to strip and Slanski fetched the suitcases from the trunk and undressed himself. He put on the corduroy suit and cap and when Anna had finished dressing he took one last look around the area and said, "Give me your clothes."

She handed them over and Slanski crossed to some bushes and scrabbled in the snow with his bare hands until he had dug a hole deep enough to bury their clothes. He then covered the hole with soil and snow again until the earth looked as if it had not been disturbed.

"Let's go."

When they reached the car, Slanski looked at her face. It was pale and drawn and he could see real fear in her eyes.

"Anna, what I did was necessary, you know that."

"Yes, I know." She shivered.

"What's the matter? Cold?"

"And frightened."

"We can be in Leningrad in less than two hours. With luck, no one's going to know Zinov's missing for some time."

His hand touched her face, then he removed his jacket and placed it gently around her shoulders.

Anna protested. "You'll freeze."

"Take it."

She looked up at him. "Alex . . ."

"What?"

She started to say something, then seemed to change her mind and shook her head.

"Nothing."

She turned to look back at their footprints in the snow. "What about those?"

"There's more snow on the way, by the look of it. They'll be covered up quickly enough. Come on, let's go. The quicker we're away from here the better."

He stowed the suitcases in the trunk and they climbed into the car. He turned on the headlights and lit up the track through the woods that led back to the highway.

There was a sudden dull chopping noise that filled the air, high above them, and they saw a powerful beam of light sweep through the forest behind, the sound growing louder until it became a deafening thunder.

Suddenly a helicopter reared above the trees, the light from under its fuselage dazzling as it caught them in its beam.

Two shadowy figures became visible in the cockpit, one of them taking aim with a pistol through the open side window of the machine.

A shot rang out and the Emka's passenger window shattered.

Anna let out a cry as the bullet zinged past her.

"Hold on!"

Slanski frantically started the Emka. It gave a roar and the wheels spun wildly before they gripped in the snow, then it shot forward down the forest track.

37

Lukin rubbed his eyes and peered down.

They were over forest now, skimming acres of dense birch trees. The searchlight was on, its silver finger probing the foliage below them, swinging left and right as the pilot controlled the yaw of the aircraft. Every now and then the man looked over at Lukin nervously. Lukin still held the gun in his hand. If they dropped too low they might clip the trees or the electric power lines running close to the highway.

They had been sweeping along the road for almost ten minutes, criss-crossing to the woods on either side, but had seen nothing. Lukin swore in frustration.

There was sweat on the pilot's brow as he looked over and said nervously, "Major, if we don't turn around now, we're going to be in big trouble. We won't have enough fuel to get back to Tallinn and the weather's going to be against us . . ."

Lukin peered out through the dome. The man was right. There was a dirty-looking bank of snow clouds moving toward them from the west.

"Keep flying."

"Major . . . I must protest!"

"I'll take responsibility for the aircraft. Do as I say!"

The pilot gritted his teeth and turned back to the controls. There was a growing edge of desperation in the man's voice.

It happened then.

The searchlight passed over a narrow road in the forest and Lukin suddenly picked out the tire tracks of a car.

"Over there!" He pointed and the pilot saw the marks. Up ahead Lukin glimpsed a small rise in the forest and beyond it what looked like the outline of a frozen lake.

"Go lower!"

"Major, if we get too close to those tree tops . . . !"

"Do it, man!"

The pilot shook his head in exasperation but obeyed the order, the searchlight picking out the twin snail-like tracks cutting along the woodland road. They led up through a rise to the frozen lake. As they came sweeping over the lake shore, suddenly Lukin saw the black Emka and his heart skipped. He saw the two figures fleetingly as they climbed into the car.

He screamed at the pilot, "Hold it here! Hold it!"

The noise in the cockpit was almost overwhelming as the MIL suddenly halted in midair, shuddering as it hovered above the Emka, tossing the trees furiously and kicking up flurries of snow.

Lukin saw the couple's surprised faces through the windshield, frozen in the searchlight for an instant, the same couple from the checkpoint.

There was a moment of frantic indecision, then he tore open the small window at the side of the helicopter, aimed his pistol at the car and fired.

He saw glass shatter on the passenger side and then suddenly the car lurched forward and sped through the forest.

"After them!" Lukin roared.

The pilot turned the MIL in an arc and began to clatter over the trees after the car.

Slanski sweated as he gripped the steering wheel hard, the car bumping down the narrow road. Freezing air blasted into the cab from the shattered window but he was hardly aware of the icy chill as he drove, all his senses concentrating on the way ahead. Every now and then the car bumped violently as it hit a rut and Anna held onto the door for her life.

Seconds later the noise of the helicopter roared above as it suddenly overtook them, spun around and hovered in midair, the searchlight cutting into their eyes. Slanski swore as the light blinded him and for an instant he lost control of the car as it lurched and he fought for control.

The Emka skidded. He put on a burst of speed and then they were ahead of the beam again. There was a narrow track off to the right and he yanked the wheel around and turned into it, the helicopter following until it was ahead of them once more. Then they heard a metallic thump as a bullet ripped through the roof of the car and Anna screamed as the lead embedded itself in the rear seat.

"Hold on tight!"

Slanski gripped the steering wheel with one hand, rolled down the side window and wrenched out his Tokarev. He eased on the brakes and slowed. Seconds later the helicopter came tearing over the trees and floated directly ahead of them, the machine swinging left and right as it tried to settle itself. Slanski suddenly saw the major's face in the cockpit.

He aimed, fired three quick shots, and saw holes blossom on the glass dome as the pistol cracked.

The helicopter lurched but continued to hover and then Slanski saw the major aim out through the side window. Puffs of white exploded in the snow to the left of the Emka.

Seconds later Slanski saw the main road fifty meters in front. Off to the left, ahead of them, was a towering electric pylon, thick metal cables running high either side.

He yelled at Anna, "Keep your head down!"

He gave a sudden burst of speed and the Emka roared toward it.

The throaty clatter of the blades was deafening as the MIL tore through the air. There was an atmosphere of desperation in the cockpit as the pilot fought to control the machine, turning in sharp banks, following the Emka as it twisted and turned and snaked through the woods.

Lukin's eyes were on the car. He had the Tokarev stuck out through the side window, trying to get a clear shot at the driver, but it was almost impossible. Every time the MIL got ahead of the car it veered off onto another track and the helicopter yawed violently to keep up.

He roared at the pilot, "Try to keep this damned thing steady, can't you!"

"I'm doing my fucking best!"

The Emka suddenly slowed and they overtook it again. As the MIL swung around and the pilot tried to settle the searchlight on the car there was the sound of rapid gunfire and three holes cracked in the glass above their heads. The MIL lifted as Lukin ducked his head instinctively, aimed through the window and got off two quick shots, but both went wide. The Emka started to move again, turning right, then back onto the forest road that led down to the highway.

"Keep after them! Don't lose them!"

They were fifty meters from the highway when Lukin suddenly felt a frightening shuddering.

The pilot screamed, "Oh my God . . . !"

In horror Lukin saw the towering electricity pylon almost dead ahead. The pilot tried frantically to veer away at the last moment, but a second later the blades clipped the electric cables and there was a powerful blinding flash of blue corona, sparks bursting like fireworks in front of their faces.

There was an almighty harsh metallic crash as the MIL yawed into the massive pylon and then the noise of the blades died abruptly and the helicopter sank in a burst of flame.

Leningrad.
February 27th

The tram halted on the Nevsky Prospect and Anna and Slanski climbed down.

It was early afternoon and traffic clogged Leningrad's broad main street. He took Anna's hand as they walked along the lengthy crowded avenue. It had started to snow and the entire stretch was a chaos of noise and pedestrians.

The Alexander column in the Winter Palace and the magnificent dome of St. Isaac's Cathedral rose behind them in the distance. The lime-colored Tsarist buildings lining the canals that ran either side of the Nevsky Prospect looked dazzling in the snow, easing the general impression of grayness. But on almost every side street there were still ruins standing from the war, blackened shells of buildings half demolished or supported precariously with struts of heavy timber, testament to a siege that had lasted almost a year, destroyed nearly half the city, and cost the lives of over half a million of its inhabitants.

Strung across Nevsky Prospect was a giant banner of a beaming Joseph Stalin, smiling down at the traffic trundling past: trucks and cars, buses and trolley cars and trams; German BMWs and Volkswagens and Opels, surrendered or abandoned by a defeated Nazi enemy and gratefully confiscated by the city's wrathful population.

Slanski stared up at the banner of Stalin, then turned to Anna as they walked through the crowd. She was tired and pale and there was a look of tension in her eyes.

They had abandoned the Emka on a side street in the suburb of Udelnay, ten kilometers away, taken a bus to the edge of the city and then one of the yellow city trams the rest of the way. Within half an hour they were in the center of Leningrad.

When they reached the corner opposite the main railway station for Moscow, Slanski found a telephone coin box and dialed the number.

The thin-faced man placed three tumblers of vodka on the shabby table.

He drank one quickly and looked at the man and woman before wiping his mouth with the back of his sleeve and smiling over.

"Drink up. You're going to need it."

The man was middle-aged, and his dark, lean face showed no sign of nervousness.

He was a Ukrainian nationalist, and after the war he had lived in Paris as a refugee, working as a photographer, until the Americans had helped send him into Russia with the identity of a Soviet prisoner-of-war caught up in the advancing Allied lines at Göttingen. Once he had been handed over with hundreds of other Russian soldiers there had been weeks of brutal interrogation at the hands of the KGB, and even then he had to endure two years in the Gulag for his supposed mistake of being caught by the Germans.

After that it was easy.

He got a job in the photography studio near the Petrograd Embankment and took flattering photographs of senior officers from the Leningrad Naval Academy. They were so pleased they came back to him with their friends and families and now and then he took shots of them and their comrades at naval functions.

Every month he delivered copies and biographies of interest to an émigré agent in Leningrad, to be passed on down the line to the émigré office in Paris, and eventually to the Americans.

A dangerous job. But he was getting his own back at the Reds for what they had inflicted on his country.

He had met the couple in the park near the Winter Palace an hour after the phone call to his studio. He took them on several roundabout tram rides back to his home, not resting until they sat in the filthy two-roomed tenement off an alleyway along the Moika Canal near Nevsky Prospect.

"What's the problem?" asked Slanski.

"Everything you've told me suggests a problem. You're both fucked, or my name isn't Vladimir Rykov." He looked at Anna and shrugged as he blew out smoke and offered the pack to his guests. "There's really no other way of putting it, I'm afraid, my dear."

As Slanski accepted a cigarette, suddenly across the landing a couple could be heard arguing at the tops of their voices, swearing at each other, doors banging and voices raised. A scream curdled the air; there was the sound of someone being slapped and a voice boomed, "Get your hands off me, you filthy pig!"

Vladimir raised his eyes toward the door and half smiled. "Love. Where would we be without it? Russians like to argue and throw things. What they can't do to authority they do at home." He nodded toward the door. "Don't worry about those two, they're at it night and day. Any moment you'll hear the door banging, the husband will call his wife a bitch, and then he'll be off to get drunk."

At that moment a door slammed, an angry voice shouted, "Bitch!" and footsteps clattered down the stairs.

Vladimir laughed. "See? If only everything in life was as reliable as my neighbors."

Slanski said, "You were about to tell us why we're in trouble."

The man looked back and sucked on his cigarette. "For two reasons. Number one, from what you told me the KGB and militia are doubtless going to be looking for you. Number two, whatever route you take is going to be difficult."

"We could leave if you're worried," Slanski offered. "But we've nowhere else to go."

Vladimir shook his head resignedly. "Don't worry about me. My worry went out the door with the war. I lost my wife and family. There's only me left. What is there to worry about?" He stood and reached for the vodka. "Let the bastards shoot me if they want."

He refilled his glass as Slanski stood and crossed to the window and looked down. There was a small courtyard below that led in from an archway on the street. At one end of the courtyard wall was a line of padlocked wooden doors belonging to what looked like outside storage rooms for the tiny flats. The yard was littered with refuse and patrolled by scrawny, scavenging cats.

Slanski had explained about the incident with Lukin, the KGB major. Not because he wanted to but because whatever happened from now on would affect their journey and perhaps put Vladimir in danger. But he had been surprisingly unruffled by the information.

Slanski looked back at him. "We have to get to Moscow somehow."

Vladimir stubbed out his cigarette, tore a hunk of bread off the loaf and chewed. Then he washed it down with a mouthful of vodka and wiped his mouth.

"Easier said than done. By rail, there's the Red Star express. It runs overnight between Leningrad and Moscow and takes twelve hours. But given what you've told me the railway station will probably be watched. Flying's the quickest way. Aeroflot flies to Moscow every two hours. But tickets are hard to come by and you'd probably have to wait a couple of days to get them, and that's if you're lucky. And no doubt the KGB and militia will be watching the airport too, just like the railway stations. Of course, you could always steal a car and drive, but that takes a day and a half allowing for rest stops and you'd be only asking for trouble if you were stopped at a checkpoint in a stolen car."

"What about traveling by bus?"

Vladimir shook his head. "There's bus service, of course, but no direct one to Moscow. You'd have to change every so often and the journey could take days. It's damned awkward if you don't know your way."

Slanski looked over at Anna and sighed in exasperation. She stared back at him, then she said to Vladimir, "There must be some other way?"

Vladimir grinned and spat a fleck of tobacco on the floor. "Maybe." He thought a moment, then looked at them. "I've got an idea. It may work. Come, I'll show you."

He headed toward the door and Slanski and Anna followed.

Estonia.

It was a nightmare.

Lukin woke, shivering, in freezing darkness. His limbs were painfully stiff and it felt as if ice flowed through his veins.

He was numb, soaked in sweat, feverish.

There was frost on his clothes and face and he felt like someone had sealed him in a block of ice. Cold bit into his flesh and bones like fire.

As he lay there in the snow, half in, half out of consciousness, he became aware of a strong smell of kerosene fuel, mixed with an acrid, sugary stench.

He remembered the stench. Anyone who had been near battle never forgot it. Like an animal carcass, but sweeter.

Burning human flesh.

He craned his neck to look around and felt a pain shoot down his left arm which made him scream in agony.

He closed his eyes slowly, then opened them again, and looked down at his body, as much as he could in the poor light.

He was lying in the snow and the back of his head was touching something hard. From the way he lay he saw he was propped against a fallen tree trunk. There was a dull ache at the back of his skull and he felt a throbbing pain flow through his body. His clothes had been shredded by the explosion, the material scorched, and he smelled of burned material and fuel.

And something else.

To his horror he saw his false hand had been sheared off, exposing his stump, and the end of the flesh had burned to black.

Lukin stared at the wound in agony and alarm. He tried to move his arm but the stump refused to budge, his whole body frozen stiff, from cold or shock, he couldn't tell which.

Perhaps he was paralyzed and the explosion had shattered his spine?

He couldn't recall, but he must have been doused in fuel when the helicopter's tanks ignited. All he remembered with certainty was the awesome crash as the MIL hit the ground and an eruption of flames moments before. He vaguely recollected the passenger door bursting open from the force of the fall. He had been flung out and his skull had hit something hard.

After that was blank.

He had landed in the snow. It must have damped the flames on his clothes and arm and prevented them from spreading. Still, the pain in his stump was excruciating.

A thought occurred to him; if his back was broken would he still feel pain in his limb?

Somewhere near he could sense light and heat.

There was a tangle of hissing metal, steam rising from the wreckage of the

MIL. The forest had not caught fire but there was a small blaze in what remained of the cockpit, lying at the base of a huge electricity pylon. Severed metal cables swung in the wind, a shower of sparks erupting every time they brushed against the pylon.

Flames licked in the center of a tangled heap of metal. He saw the body of the pilot lying half in and half out of the shattered wreckage. His body had been half burned, the man's left arm dangling over a chunk of jagged metal. The bone had cracked cleanly and was only held on by the exposed tendons.

Lukin winced. The man was certainly dead and it was his fault. He had been too intent on capturing Slanski and the woman. Too intent on stopping them from escaping. But they had escaped and he had lost them.

So close . . . he had been so close.

He was unaware of how much time had passed but he guessed it hadn't been long because the wreckage was still burning. Flakes of snow began to fall and hiss on the flames.

He was barely conscious but he knew he couldn't remain in this temperature for long. He tried to move but still his body felt numb.

Suddenly he was aware of a flash of light through the trees and heard the rumble of an engine. He remembered the highway. Perhaps someone had come to investigate the explosion or the damaged pylon.

He cried, hoarsely, "Help!"

It was a weak cry, a cry of desperation, and no one answered.

Seconds later the noise and the light vanished beyond the trees.

It was useless. Waves of pain rolled up from his scorched arm. His eyelids fluttered.

He wanted to close his eyes and sleep, forget about his suffering.

Not sleep, he thought: *I'm dying.*

For a moment, in his feverish mind, he saw Nadia's face, smiling at him.

Leningrad.

The storage room at the end of the courtyard was in pitch darkness when Vladimir unlocked the two heavy padlocks and flicked on the switch. The room flooded with light and he beckoned them inside and closed the door. The large room had obviously once been one of several individual stables belonging to the house during the Tsar's time, entered through the courtyard. Vladimir's storeroom was packed with ancient rotting furniture and on a narrow workshop table were bits of engine parts. There was a dusty sheet in a corner, covered with paint stains.

Vladimir pulled it off to reveal a German Army BMW dispatch rider's motorcycle with twin leather saddle pouches hanging at the back. The bike's gray paintwork had been repainted dark green and the tires were broad, deeply grooved thick rubber made for rough terrain. Vladimir smiled and ran a hand lovingly over the leather saddle.

"I could say a lot against the Germans but the bastards still made the best motorcycles. There are lots of these models still around and they're much better than the Soviet variety. Even the army uses them. I took her for a spin last week. The engine still runs sweetly." He wheeled the BMW out into the center of the room and said to Slanski, "You've ridden a motorcycle before?"

"Never."

"Christ! Now you are fucked, little brother."

"I could learn, quickly."

"On Russian roads? You may as well put a gun to your head and squeeze the trigger. Here, you'd better start it and try it for size. Don't worry about the neighbors, they're used to me riding this thing."

Slanski took the handlebars and climbed onto the machine. It felt rugged and heavy.

"Of course, it'll be damned cold riding it," Vladimir remarked. "You have to be well wrapped up or your balls will freeze hard as rocks."

"I'll try to remember that."

Vladimir smiled at Anna. "Sit on the back, dear. Get a feel for it."

Anna slid onto the machine behind Slanski and put her arms around his waist.

Vladimir said, "Right, start her up. The kick starter's on your right. That's the metal arm that swivels out."

Slanski found the kick starter, flicked it out, gave it a blow with his foot and the machine started first time. A steady, reassuring throbbing filled the storeroom.

Vladimir smiled. "See? She still starts first time. Well, what do you think?"

"Considering we don't have many options, it's worth a try."

Vladimir poured them each another vodka as they sat in the kitchen again and spread out the map.

"Not bad for a first-timer. You did well."

Slanski had ridden around the yard for half an hour to get the feel of the machine. Difficult at first, but with Vladimir's instructions he managed to keep the BMW reasonably well controlled, learning how to change gears, operate the various switches on the handlebars, and what to do if the engine flooded. A group of curious, scrawny children had come down from the tenement flats to beg Vladimir for a ride until he had shooed them away and wheeled the BMW back into the storeroom.

Now Slanski looked at the man and said, "Tell us what you have in mind."

"The KGB and militia are probably going to be checking the railway and bus stations, the airport, and maybe even doing spot checks on the Metro." He pointed to the map, a web of roads leading out of Leningrad to all points on the compass. "They may even set up roadblocks on all the main roads out of the city if they haven't already found that car you abandoned. And when they do find it they'll definitely get to work trying to find you. It's over six hundred kilometers to Moscow. Using the motorcycle you should be able to avoid the main roads out of Leningrad. But the one road they probably won't be checking is the road *back* to Tallinn."

Anna said, "I don't understand."

Vladimir grinned. "Simple. You double back on the Baltic road, past Pushkin, to here." He pointed to a place on the map. "It's a town called Gatchina, approximately eighty kilometers from the city. At this point you take any of the minor roads that fork southeast to Novgorod. That leaves you with just over five hundred kilometers to cover to get to Moscow. But once you get to Gatchina and beyond, there are so many minor roads through hilly, uninhabited forest that it would take half the Red army to find you, and you could make it to Moscow without much difficulty.

"That motorbike out there was designed for rough terrain and can easily travel over dirt tracks, no trouble. The route I'm suggesting is an indirect one, and longer, but probably the safest, considering the circumstances. Don't worry about getting lost; you can keep the map and I'll give you a compass. With luck you could be in Moscow in just over twelve hours. There are also several trains that run there by an indirect route from smaller towns along the way if you have to abandon the motorcycle. It means changing trains many times, of course, but that can't be helped and this is the best route I can suggest. Don't worry about removing the license plates on the bike if you ditch it. Like most of the German motorcycles still around, mine isn't registered." He grinned as he looked at them. "How does all that sound?"

Slanski smiled. "When do we leave?"

"Who knows how long before the city is ringed with checkpoints? For your own sake, the sooner you leave the better."

Slanski checked his watch. "Let's say this evening. As soon as the traffic starts to fill the main roads it'll help give us a better chance of not being noticed."

"That would be perfect."

Estonia.

Lukin heard a sound like an animal cry and came awake with a start. The pain in his stump hadn't gone away and his body shivered with agony. How long had he been lying here?

He moved the fingers of his left hand, slowly. An effort. But there was no pain *there* and at least he could move *something*. He tried his wrist next. It budged slightly. Enough so he could read his watch.

A quarter past one.

He had been lying in the frozen woods for over three hours.

Blasts of freezing air raged through the trees in gusts. His limbs still felt like ice and his bones ached through with the intense cold. His teeth chattered. He licked his lips. They felt like slivers of ice. He inhaled and the chilled air bit into his lungs and made him cough.

He heard the cry again.

He had heard that sound before, in childhood. He and his brother as small boys, playing in a field near their father's house one winter's evening. His father off in the distance by the house, chopping wood, looking up, waving at them.

And then the noise that startled them. When they looked around they saw the two pairs of piercing yellow eyes staring at them from the trees, until the eyes moved out of the woods and became bodies.

Two white wolves.

Snow wolves.

Their white coats so bright they were almost luminous. Lukin had screamed in fright and run back to his father as the man raced toward him. He swept him up in his arms and Lukin still remembered his comforting smells, an odd mixture of disinfectant, soap and sweat.

"Wolves, Papa!" Lukin had screamed.

"Bah! He's afraid of everything," his brother Mischa protested, laughing.

He looked at his brother accusingly. "Then why did *you* run too?"

Mischa smiled. "Because *you* ran, little brother. And I couldn't stop you."

His father said, "Wolves don't kill humans. Not unless they're threatened. Remember that. Now, come, Mama has supper ready."

His father carried them into the warm, happy house and there was bread on the table and hot soup their mama had made. A log fire crackled in the hearth and cast shadows about the big old room. His mother was hugging them, fussing over them, her belly swollen with a child, warning them not to go to the woods again alone.

And afterwards? What had happened afterwards? He tried to think, but a fog rolled in. It was a long, long time ago. Faces and memories a blur the years had eroded. He remembered so little of that time, before Mischa had died. Proud and brave Mischa.

Maybe he was remembering now because he was close to death; the way they said recollections flashed before dying eyes. He blinked and pushed the fleeting memories from his mind. Now was important, not the past.

He focused on the wreckage and the half-burned corpse of the pilot. Maybe the wolves had smelled the cooked human flesh.

He tried to push that prospect from his mind. The fire was still dying, the hot embers smoldering. If he could get closer to the fire for heat, maybe he could thaw out his bones. Slowly, he dragged himself over to the fire. It took a long time, an age, trying to block out the pain in his stump, but he finally made it.

The heat from the embers was like a balm as it started to soak through his body.

God, it feels good.

There were two sparking cables dangling beside the smoldering debris. Lukin couldn't understand why someone hadn't come to investigate the damaged pylon. Until he noticed that there were still half a dozen or more cables intact at the top. The repairmen would come, eventually. But when? And by then he could be frozen to death. The helicopter's radio would have been useful if it was still working, but the wreckage told him that thought was a waste of time.

After five minutes, he tried to stand, but his legs felt like rubber.

He swore. He needed more heat. The fire was definitely helping. He shifted around until his legs were closer to the embers.

The shock had gone now, replaced by anger. Somehow he had to get down to the highway. If he could alert the militia in the nearest town—though he knew that by now the man and woman could be in Leningrad, or at any other point on the compass—there was still a slight chance he could catch them. He could alert every barracks along the route and have roadblocks set up on the highway.

He felt his legs start to warm. He tried to haul himself up.

As he did so he heard the rustle in the undergrowth and a low growl.

He instinctively reached for his pistol. The belt and holster were gone. The rustling came closer.

A magnificent white wolf appeared out of the woods.

Lukin's heart almost stopped and he froze.

The animal stood staring at the wreckage, eyes pinpricks of yellow in the shadows. He lay still as the wolf moved cautiously out from the trees and nosed toward the wreckage. It hardly seemed to notice Lukin. When the animal came to the dead pilot it sniffed the half-severed limb, then started to lick the flesh. Finally, it sank its fangs into the arm, tore it from its socket, and tossed it to the ground with a shake of its head.

The wolf chewed hungrily at the flesh.

Lukin's heart hammered in his chest.

Wolves were not supposed to attack live humans, unless provoked, but he guessed any animal would if hungry. And this wolf looked sleek and hungry.

There was another rustling in the bushes and a second wolf appeared. This time Lukin saw the animal stare at him.

He tried not to move his head as he looked around frantically for something to defend himself with. He saw his empty belt and holster lying among the scattered wreckage. It must have come loose when he was tossed through the door of the MIL. In horror, he saw that the pistol wasn't in the holster.

It had been in his hand, he remembered, he had been firing out through the helicopter's window. Then he saw something metallic lying off to his right. The butt of a pistol.

The wolf padded out of the forest and toward him.

Lukin screamed, then twisted his body and rolled over, grabbing at the gun.

The wolf bared its fangs in a snarl, then the other wolf started, stopped chewing and growled at him.

Lukin fumbled with frozen fingers, aimed at the animal nearest him and squeezed the trigger.

Click.

The gun was empty.

Frantically, he grabbed the holster. There was a slim pouch in the leather for a spare magazine and he wrenched it open, found the magazine, and with fingers shaking desperately tried to load the pistol again with his one hand.

The wolves were less than two meters away. He could smell them. They bared their fangs again, growling as they crouched, ready to pounce.

Lukin cocked the pistol and fired in the air.

The explosion echoed around the forest. The wolves yelped.

He fired another shot, then another.

The animals bolted back into the forest.

He wiped cold sweat from his face. The wolves wouldn't stay away for long. They had been threatened, were obviously hungry, and it was only a matter of time before they risked coming out again for food.

He staggered to his feet, ignoring the waves of pain burning through his arm. He looked toward the highway. Flashes of headlights flickered through the trees as a convoy of vehicles trundled past.

The road was his only hope.

He stumbled through the forest, his legs weak, his lungs on fire with the effort. It took him over ten minutes to cover the fifty meters to the edge of the highway.

It was deserted, only tire marks slashing the white surface.

Lukin swore, breathless.

Suddenly a pair of headlights appeared up ahead as a truck came around a bend and loomed at him out of the falling snow.

Lukin stumbled into the middle of the road and waved his gun.

Leningrad.

It was after four and already dark outside as Vladimir came in from the kitchen and handed Anna a brown-wrapped parcel.

"Some food for the journey. It's not much, only bread and cheese and some vodka, but it should fill your bellies for a while and help keep out the chill."

"Thank you." Anna took the parcel as Slanski came back from the window.

Vladimir gave him a rolled-up leather pouch, a pair of thick woollen gloves, an ancient helmet, and a tattered black overcoat that smelled as if a dog had recently slept on it.

"The coat ought to keep you warm on the bike if you can stand the stink, but it's all I've got that's heavy enough to keep out the chill. There are some tools in the pouch for any minor repairs. But try not to get a flat, because you'll have no spare tire."

"Is there enough fuel in the tank?"

"It's full." Vladimir handed Slanski some official coupons. "If you have to refill you'll need those. But finding a fuel station isn't so easy after dark, and especially on remote country roads you won't have a hope. There's enough fuel in the tank for over four hundred kilometers if you don't drive like hell, and I've left a full container in one of the saddle pouches that should give you a further two hundred. It'll just about get you all the way. But there's only one helmet and pair of goggles, I'm afraid, best worn by the driver, otherwise that icy cold out there will cut your eyes out when you get up to speed."

Slanski checked his papers and Anna's, then looked restlessly at his watch and said to Vladimir, "How much longer before we can go?"

Vladimir looked out at the darkness below and scratched his stubble.

"Another hour ought to do it. By then the traffic should have thickened." He spread the map on the table again. "Meanwhile, let's go over the route one more time. The last thing you want is to get lost."

"You want *what*?"

Lukin looked at the red-faced colonel across the desk and said, "Every available man you have put at my disposal. All railway, bus and Metro stations and the airport patrolled and every passenger checked. Every hotel register in the city scrutinized and the identity of guests verified. That's just to start with. There'll be more, I assure you."

"You're out of your tiny fucking mind, comrade."

"Perhaps I ought to telephone the Ministry of State Security and you can tell that to Beria personally?"

The colonel's face turned an even angrier red, then suddenly paled.

"I'm sure that won't be necessary."

"I'm sure it won't," Lukin answered. "You've seen my authorization. Please be so good as to comply with the order."

He replaced the letter in his breast pocket as the colonel stood up and sighed in frustration. He looked as if he wanted to hit Lukin for his impertinence.

He was a big, stocky man, with cropped red hair the color of rust. They were in his large office on the sixth floor of the red-brick building on Liteiny Prospect which housed the KGB Headquarters in Leningrad. Lights blazed in the city beyond the broad panoramic window, flurries of snow brushing against the glass.

There were photographs on the walls, one of a smiling Beria. Others, more personal, taken in Berlin, Warsaw, Vienna. Groups of soldiers smiling in the after-ruins of battles. Lukin recognized the colonel in all of them, hands on hips, his chin and chest stuck out self-importantly.

Next to the colonel's desk stood his adjutant, a young captain in uniform.

The adjutant looked across at Lukin.

"You're asking a lot of us, Major," he remarked. "We've already alerted militia patrols about the car. Have you any appreciation of the scale of such an operation as you're demanding?"

"Just as I'm quite certain Comrade Beria would demand your lives if you failed to give every assistance." Lukin stood and stared at the men. "And I'm sure you'd much rather deal with me than him." He looked pointedly at his watch. "So, can I count on your help?"

The adjutant shot a nervous glance at his colonel, who stood up, nodded at Lukin and gave a heavy sigh.

"Very well, Major," he said reluctantly. "Let me explain the situation and we'll take it from there."

The colonel crossed to a map on the wall near the window and Lukin followed. His arm hurt, the stump throbbing. He still reeked of fuel and smoke. A shower or bath would have been welcome. Down in the street he saw an elderly woman wearing several thick skirts, sturdy boots and a headscarf sweeping snow away from the front of the building. The broad frozen Neva River lay beyond the rooftops of the city that had once been the Tsar's capital. The battleship *Aurora*, whose cannon-shot had signaled the storming of the Winter Palace and the start of the Revolution, lay anchored in the ice, the magnificent island fortress of Peter and Paul behind it, illuminated in a blaze of arc lights.

Lukin turned back as the colonel picked up a slim wooden baton and tapped it on the colored map of Leningrad, red flags pinpointing military installations and barracks.

"You're familiar with Leningrad, Major?"

"Unfortunately not."

"We're talking about a city of almost two million inhabitants. There are ten railway stations. One civilian and three military airfields. A public transport system that includes trams, buses and a Metro. Perhaps eighty transport stations in all. Major highways here . . ." The colonel pointed to several blue veins leading from the heart of the city. ". . . here, and here." He gave a thin, flickering smile. "And this one is the Baltic highway where you stopped the army truck after your unfortunate crash. We have a patrol on the way there now to recover the pilot's body and search for the missing colonel."

Lukin ignored the jibe. "What about hotels?"

The colonel shrugged. "Maybe forty, large and small, in the city. More on the outskirts. I can have my men do a check on new arrivals in the last six hours over the phone. That's the easy part. The difficult bit comes when we go to seal off the minor roads. There are hundreds leading in and out of the city. Have you any idea of the kind of traffic volume we're talking about? Over a quarter of a million people in transit at any one time, and much more during the peak rush-hour periods. You try to cover everything, you're going to stretch resources."

"How many men can you assemble?"

"At short notice? Perhaps a thousand, including militia. Any more and you'll have to wait."

Lukin said, "Very well. If these people have already found refuge with a contact in the city, as I suspect, it's going to make our task difficult, therefore you should instruct your informers and block janitors to keep their eyes and ears open for the arrival of any strangers similar to the man and woman you have descriptions of—indeed, *any* strangers. And alert all militia and traffic police to be on the lookout. Also, as well as civilian, I want any military traffic stopped and checked."

The colonel snapped. "Military traffic? But that's ridiculous . . . !"

"Hardly. The man has already impersonated an army officer. He may still be in that disguise, and both of them using their assumed names, though I doubt it. But I can't afford to take that chance."

The colonel sighed. "Is there *any* category we can eliminate to save time?"

"Animals and children. Everyone else, I want their papers checked. Disguise is a distinct possibility. And remember, I suspect the man and woman have already murdered a senior officer. They'll be armed and highly dangerous. If there's the slightest doubt about anyone's identity or their papers, they're to be detained or arrested with caution."

"I can see us filling every damned jail and barracks in the city," the colonel said irritably. "We *are* probably talking about checking the papers of half the population of Leningrad, you realize that, Major?"

"I don't care if I'm talking about the *entire* population. These people must be found. Is that understood?"

Spittle appeared on the colonel's lips and he looked as if he was going to have a fit. He didn't like being ordered about by a lower rank, but to hell with him, Lukin thought.

The colonel bit back his anger with a grim, tight-mouthed expression. "Understood."

Lukin crossed to the door. "Please arrange everything immediately. As soon as you can assemble more men, cover the minor roads in and out of the city. I'm giving you an hour to do it. And I'll need an office, manned with as many telephones as you can provide. Radio links to all the checkpoints we spoke about. And make sure any mobile patrols have field radios. I also want a fast car and a driver at my disposal who knows the city, with a couple of militia motorcycle outriders as guides. If there's any news, I'm to be contacted at once."

The colonel flung down his baton in obvious anger. "Anything *else* while we're here, Major?"

Lukin ignored the sarcasm and said, "Yes, there is. Do you have a doctor in the building?"

The man looked at Lukin's stump, at the charred and ragged sleeve of his uniform, and wrinkled his nose at the smell of burned flesh. The major was obviously in pain but had refused a doctor earlier, first demanding to see whoever was in charge.

"No. But I can have one brought here."

"Then do so. And I'll need fresh clothes."

The colonel picked up his baton again and glared. "By the way, Lukin, for your information we alerted Moscow as to your accident as a matter of courtesy. A Colonel Romulka phoned back. He said to tell you he's on his way here by air force jet. He should be arriving within an hour." The colonel half smiled. "If it's the same Colonel Romulka I think it is, he seemed rather interested in your progress. Naturally, I could tell him nothing since we hadn't spoken."

Lukin said grimly, "Thank you."

The door closed.

The colonel waited until Lukin's footsteps had receded down the hallway, then he flung his baton against the wall in a rage. It bounced off the picture of Beria and clattered to the floor.

"The fucking jumped-up shit! Who the hell does he think he is, talking to me like that?"

The adjutant looked suitably sympathetic. "Who's this Romulka, sir?"

The telephone rang. The colonel picked it up and snapped, "What the fuck is it?"

He listened for several moments, then said, "Have it brought to headquarters immediately," and slammed down the phone.

The adjutant said, "More problems?"

"The militia found a car matching the Emka abandoned in Udelnay. They're bringing the vehicle here."

The adjutant smiled. "So, we've made a little progress?"

The colonel glared. "Hardly, you idiot! The passengers could be anywhere by now. If they're not still traveling in the car it only makes our work more difficult trying to find them. Go after Lukin and tell him. And arrange everything he wants and fucking fast. The last thing I need is that little shit Beria nosing up my ass."

Slanski wheeled the BMW into the middle of the storeroom and climbed on. He pulled on the helmet and goggles and wore the stinking heavy winter coat Vladimir had given him. Anna wore two sets of clothes under her coat to keep out the cold and their small suitcases were strapped to the carrier at the rear.

She climbed on and put her arms around Slanski's waist.

"You have the map?" Slanski asked.

"In my bra."

He laughed. "Whatever you do don't lose it or we're in trouble."

He nodded to Vladimir who stood by the door. "Ready when you are."

"Don't forget to take the route through the city I told you about. And take it easy until you reach the main Baltic highway. Breaking the speed limit won't help matters. The last thing you want is to be chased by a militia patrol car with a wailing siren."

Slanski nodded. "Wish us luck." He kicked the starter arm and the BMW came to life, the engine purring solidly under them.

Vladimir opened the door and then Slanski throttled the engine and kicked the machine into gear, but didn't release the clutch.

Vladimir went out into the street, looking left and right to check that there were no militia about before signaling for them to move out. Slanski drove out through the mouth of the archway.

Vladimir slapped Anna on the shoulder. "Go. And may the devil ride with you both."

The BMW roared off into the night. There was a crunch of gears as Slanski slowed and changed down, and then they drove at a leisurely speed along the Moika Canal.

Vladimir watched anxiously as the red taillight disappeared toward the Nevsky Prospect, then he went back and turned off the storeroom light and padlocked the door, before going up to his flat.

As soon as he was inside he opened the bottle of vodka and poured a large glass.

He wondered what the man and woman were up to in Moscow?

Still, it didn't really matter.

After what they had told him and the man's lack of skill on the BMW he doubted they'd ever make it. Just so long as they didn't incriminate him.

He shivered slightly at the prospect.

As he thought of the couple he lifted the glass in a toast and said, "Good luck, you poor bastards," and swallowed the vodka in one gulp.

A female doctor dressed Lukin's arm.

They were in a large room on the second floor which the adjutant had organized, and already uniformed personnel were setting up telephones and a powerful radio transmitter.

The doctor gave him a mild shot of morphine, Lukin insisting that the injection not be so strong as to make him drowsy and unable to concentrate. Then the woman basted a foul-smelling green ointment onto his stump to ease the pain, and after dressing the wound she pinned back the sleeve of the fresh tunic an orderly had brought.

The doctor was young and pretty with gentle hands.

She smiled. "You're as good as new, Major. The wound isn't too bad, but you'll need to have a surgeon examine your stump. The morphine and bandage are only a temporary fix. Some of the burned flesh may have to be cut away. You were lucky. You have no other injuries apart from bruising and a large bump on the back of your head. Your skull seems to have suffered no really serious damage but I'd like to take an X-ray, just to be certain."

Lukin winced as the woman examined the back of his skull again.

"Another time, but thank you, Doctor."

The woman sighed and looked up as a man carrying several telephones and a roll of cable brushed past.

"As you wish. I can see you're a busy man. Do you mind telling me what's going on here?"

Lukin didn't reply as he looked at his arm and the folded-back sleeve. The false hand was bad enough but now he really did look like a cripple. He had a spare he kept in his desk, a crude affair with a metal hook on the end which he had first worn some months after he had been wounded, until his stump had healed enough for a proper prosthesis. It would have to wait until he got to Moscow.

Suddenly the door burst open and Romulka appeared, wearing an overcoat slung loosely over his shoulders, a swagger-cane in his leather-gloved hand.

"There you are, Lukin. The adjutant told me I'd find you here. Still alive after your mishap, I see." He jerked his thumb ignorantly at the lady doctor and said, "You—get out."

The woman took one look at Romulka's frightening presence in the black uniform, packed up her black bag and scurried out. The other men setting up the equipment in the room took the hint and followed her.

Romulka pulled up a chair and sat. He lit a cigarette and looked around the room.

"They seem to be looking after you, I see. I've spoken with the colonel in charge. A car has been found, I believe." He glanced at Lukin's arm. "Tell me what happened."

Lukin told him. When he had finished, Romulka grinned maliciously. "Not a very promising start, was it, Lukin? You let the couple slip from your grasp. Comrade Beria won't like that."

Lukin said shortly, "Why are you here?"

"This case is my responsibility too, or had you forgotten? I'm here to assist you and ensure your health is sufficient to continue."

"It is. And if you've come to gloat over what happened, I can do without that kind of help."

Romulka stood, towering above Lukin. "Let's cut out the fencing, Lukin. I may be here on Beria's orders but I want you to know I also have a personal interest in this case. The woman especially." He tapped Lukin's chest with his stick. "As soon as she's caught I want to interrogate her, you understand that?"

"And in case you've forgotten, I'm in charge. If she's caught alive, I decide who interrogates her."

Romulka's eyes narrowed in an icy stare. "I suggest you don't cross me, Lukin. Life wouldn't be worth living."

Lukin looked at the mess of equipment in the room and nodded toward the door. "I'm busy, Romulka. There's work to be done. Is there anything else you wish to say before you leave?"

Romulka grinned. "Actually there is. Another aspect to the investigation I thought you ought to know about. Unfortunately I won't be remaining in Leningrad. I'm leaving the pursuit in your hands. It is after all your apparent specialty, though I'm hardly inspired by the evidence so far. I have other pressing matters to attend to."

"What matters?"

"In case you failed to realize it, Lukin, it struck me the Americans would need someone in Moscow to help them. Possibly some person or persons to aid their escape once the deed is done, which it won't be if you do your job."

"I didn't fail to realize it. But what of it?"

Romulka removed a sheet of paper from his pocket and handed it across.

"What's this?"

"A list of names. Foreigners who, because of important business interests vital to the state, are allowed to come and go in Moscow virtually unchecked."

Lukin examined the list. Almost all were European businessmen, with the exception of two Turkish gold dealers and a Japanese oil buyer.

He looked up. "What are you suggesting?"

"One name on the list particularly interests me. A man named Henri Lebel. A French fur dealer."

"I know of him."

"Then perhaps you'll know that during the war he was a member of the Communist Resistance branch in Paris."

"I didn't, but go on."

"The man has considerable liberties in Moscow because of his trading status and monetary contributions to the French Communist Party. But that's about to change."

"What do you intend?"

Romulka smirked. "I've a feeling about Lebel. He isn't due in Moscow for another three days, but we can get around that considering the urgency of this matter."

"How?"

"Our friends in Paris can arrange it. We question him, discreetly. If he knows nothing, we let him go on his way."

"Presumably unharmed? The man is a suspect, not a culprit."

Romulka grinned. "That depends on how cooperative he is. If he's innocent, he has nothing to fear. But there's something to consider that implicates him."

"What?"

"We know he had connections through the resistance to the man named Massey who was involved in organizing the American mission."

Lukin thought for a moment, and nodded. "Very well. But I suggest you proceed with this cautiously. No doubt Lebel has important connections in Moscow and we don't want any embarrassment."

Romulka took the list and slipped it back into his pocket. "Whether you agree or not, Lukin, the matter of this Frenchman is my responsibility. It's already been agreed to by Beria. Besides, I have a feeling about Lebel. I assure you I won't be proved wrong."

Romulka turned toward the door and glared. "One more thing, Lukin. I meant what I said about the woman. Remember that. Do keep up the good work."

He laughed as he went through the door just as the adjutant came in, almost knocking the man over.

The startled adjutant said to Lukin, "A friend of yours, sir?"

"Hardly. Well, have you any news?"

"Nothing positive from any of the checkpoints. We're scouring the neighborhood where the car was found and alerting block janitors. We've also questioned people living in the area as to whether they saw a couple resembling the one we're looking for, but so far no one saw anything. As for the car, it was brought here ten minutes ago, but there was nothing in it of interest or that could have belonged to the couple. No blood on the seats to suggest you wounded anyone either. Our patrol recovered the body of the pilot in the woods, also the missing colonel. He was buried in a shallow grave nearby. He'd been shot through the head, I'm afraid."

Lukin sighed. "What about the hotels?"

"Most have been checked, and we're working on the others. So far any persons remotely resembling the ones we're looking for have had their identities and backgrounds thoroughly investigated."

"And?"

A smile flickered on the adjutant's face. "All we got was a divisional major sleeping with an adjutant's wife in the Kremski Hotel and a couple of homosexual army officers caught in a compromising position in a flea-ridden hotel near the Finland Station. I could go on, but I won't bore you with such unimportant details."

Lukin ignored the flippant remark and crossed to a map on the wall. The adjutant followed.

"We've also drafted another two thousand men, including army personnel, and done everything you've asked, Major. Field radios were issued and linked to the transmitter we've installed here and another in the exchange in the basement. I've got people standing by the radio and telephones there also. The pins on the map indicate where we've set up checkpoints. Now all we have to do is wait until something turns up."

Lukin stared at the wall map for a few moments.

"Something wrong, Major?"

Lukin looked back absentmindedly. "Something just occurred to me. The roads you've placed checkpoints on, they're all leading north, south or east of the city."

"That's so, Major."

"But not west toward the Baltic? You're supposing these people won't turn back."

The adjutant half smiled. "If they turn back then maybe you've nothing to worry about."

"The object is to catch them," Lukin said sharply. "We haven't manned the roads to the Baltic. Traffic either way. In or out." Lukin stared at the man, waiting for a reply.

"Of course, but the question of manpower—"

"Arrange it."

The traffic was heavy when they reached the Neva River, and Slanski veered left and took the road out toward Pushkin. He drove slowly, still getting the feel of the powerful BMW, flicking switches on the handlebars to familiarize himself with the machine. When they stopped at traffic lights on Turgenev Square, he spoke over his shoulder to Anna.

"All right back there?"

"Apart from the fact that I'm freezing to death."

Slanski smiled. "Push your body closer to mine. It may help."

"Help you or me? That coat you're wearing smells like it belongs in a pig sty."

Slanski laughed and she held him tighter as the lights turned green. He was about to change into gear when they both heard a whistle blow. A young policeman standing outside a traffic kiosk in the center of the square was staring at them and waving them over.

"Oh my God," said Anna.

"Relax. Let me do the talking."

"Can't we just drive on?"

"Do that and we're asking for trouble."

The traffic policeman blew his whistle again and Slanski nudged through the traffic and drove over. The man scrutinized the BMW as he slapped a black truncheon into the palm of his open hand.

"Just what the hell do you think you're on, comrade?"

"Sorry?"

"A motorbike or a suicide mission?" The man looked at Slanski with narrowed eyes, then tapped his truncheon on the headlamp. "You're driving with no lights on."

Slanski leaned forward to look at the headlight. He must have switched it off when he had been trying to familiarize himself with the machine and forgot to switch it on again. He smiled innocently at the policeman and began to fumble at the handlebars, looking for the switch. When he couldn't find it, the policeman said, "This your machine, comrade?"

"Yes."

"And you don't know where the light switch is?"

Slanski continued feeling for the switch, but the policeman reached over, flicked a knob on the handlebars, and the lights sprang on.

"Well, comrade? What's the matter? Are you dumb as well as blind?"

Slanski tried to look suitably fearful of the man's authority. "Thank you, comrade. I'm sorry. I only bought the machine today. I'm not familiar with the switches."

"If you're not familiar with it, why are you driving the beast? Let me see your papers."

Slanski told Anna to climb down and he propped up the heavy bike and found his papers. A second policeman, a sergeant, came over from the kiosk, curious.

"A problem?"

"This *durak* here thinks it's OK to drive with no lights."

The sergeant smiled thinly. "A serious offense. But if you want to commit suicide you should do it in your own apartment where you won't hurt anyone. Use gas like everyone else." The man began to examine the BMW. "Good machine. How did you acquire it, comrade?"

"A friend sold it to me."

"His name?"

"Does it matter, Sergeant?"

"It matters if I ask." The face looked up at Slanski's. "Your friend's name?"

"Grenady Stavinka. From Pushkin."

"And this is . . . ?" He looked at Anna.

"My wife."

The sergeant looked at Anna. "Your husband, is he always so reckless?"

"It's why I married him. Now I'm beginning to think it was a mistake."

The sergeant laughed. He turned to his colleague. "At least the girl's got a brain. Let her man go with a warning this time, Boris. The woman has more sense than he has."

He looked back at Slanski. "Take heed of your wife, comrade. You'll live longer."

"She's a treasure indeed, little brother."

"She is that. And if you want to keep her alive too, learn to use that light switch."

"I will, comrade, thank you."

"Be off, now."

Slanski climbed onto the machine and Anna followed him. He kicked into gear and the BMW drove away shakily.

The two policemen strolled back to the traffic kiosk in the center of the square and climbed inside.

"Fine ass on that woman, Sergeant."

"He ought to stick with saddling her and forget about the bike."

The policeman sniggered. The telephone rang in the kiosk. The sergeant picked it up and spoke.

"Traffic Kiosk 14, Turgenev Square."

The sergeant listened to the sharp voice at the other end, then said finally, "Don't worry, we'll keep our eyes open."

He slowly put down the receiver and stared out at the ring of lights as traffic flowed around the kiosk. The other man looked at him.

"A problem, Sergeant?"

The sergeant's face looked a little pale as he scratched his chin. "I'm not sure. That was the central exchange. KGB Headquarters want us to keep a lookout for a man and a woman. The description could have been those two on the BMW."

"Did they say why they wanted them?"

"The man is armed and dangerous. An enemy agent. The woman's Russian, probably traveling as his wife. It's imperative they be stopped and arrested. They've already killed an army officer."

The other man gave a low whistle. "You think it was that idiot on the bike?"

"Unlikely. That fucker wouldn't know his ass from his elbow. I've seen the type before. Fourteen years in this game and you get to read faces, Boris. That *durak* wasn't a killer. Even my missus looks a lot more dangerous after she's had her quart of vodka."

"Still, they could have been the couple. Maybe I should report it?"

The sergeant looked over at his colleague as if he were a complete idiot.

"And have those guys from Central crawling up our asses asking all sorts of questions?" The sergeant shook his head. "Besides, according to the exchange, half the fucking army, the KGB and the militia are out looking for them. Every road around the city has been sealed off. Rest assured, they won't get far, wherever they are."

Baltic Highway,
Leningrad.

As they came around a bend on the Baltic Highway, Slanski saw the string of red taillights up ahead. He pulled to the side of the road and doused the headlight.

Alarmed, Anna said, "What's wrong?"

"Take a look."

As cars swished past, Anna peered over Slanski's shoulder. She could see several army and militia vehicles blocking the highway a hundred meters ahead, a traffic tailback of rear lights glowing in the darkness. Men in uniforms milled around, checking drivers' papers and climbing into trucks and cars. Traffic coming from the opposite direction looked like it was receiving the same scrutiny.

Slanski said, "Whenever I get suspicious, I get a headache. And right now I've got a blinder. I'll bet you a ruble it's us they're after."

"What can we do?"

"There was a minor road a couple of kilometers back. Let's try our chances there."

He kicked the machine into gear and swung around. He left the lights off until they had gone a couple of hundred meters, and when they reached the minor road on the right he turned into it. The country road was covered in patches of slush and Anna held on to him tightly as the freezing rush of air slashed at their faces.

They had driven another five kilometers when Slanski came around a sharp bend and they suddenly saw the blaze of lights up ahead. It was too late.

Two covered jeeps stood in their path. An army sergeant with a Kalashnikov and a militiaman wielding a rifle stood next to one of the jeeps, another young militiaman sitting in the front seat, manning a portable radio, his rifle resting across his knees.

The officer in charge stood nearby, casually smoking a cigarette.

Slanski felt Anna's arms tighten around his waist. He slowed the machine as the officer, a lieutenant, raised his hand for them to stop.

Slanski brought the BMW to a halt but kept the engine running.

The lieutenant came forward and said loudly, "Douse that light and switch off the engine."

Slanski did as he was told. The lieutenant flashed a light in their faces.

"Well, what have we got here? Two lovers out for a ride in the country?"

The men and the sergeant laughed. Slanski tried to assess the situation. Of the four men, the sergeant and the lieutenant looked capable enough, big and strong, their necks wider than their foreheads. But the two militiamen were barely out of their teens and they fingered their rifles nervously.

The officer tossed his cigarette away and stared at them suspiciously.

Slanski said calmly, "What's the problem, comrade? You frightened the hell out of us. I could have plowed into those jeeps of yours."

The lieutenant looked at the motorcycle, then Anna.

He said to Slanski, "Papers, both of you."

Slanski handed over his papers and Anna did the same. The lieutenant flashed the light from the papers to their faces. He didn't hand them back but said, "Your destination?"

"Novgorod," replied Slanski.

"That's a long drive on a cold night like this. Your purpose?"

Slanski jerked a thumb back at Anna. "My wife's mother is unwell. They don't think the old woman is going to make it through the night. You know how it is, Lieutenant. My wife needs to see her before it's too late."

"Where have you come from?"

"Leningrad. What the hell's going on tonight? This is the second time we've been stopped on this road."

The lieutenant hesitated. Slanski's reply seemed to ease his tension, then he slowly handed back the papers. "We're looking for two enemy agents. A man and a woman. They killed a KGB officer."

Slanski whistled and looked suitably worried. "Will the road be all right from here on? I mean, I hope we're not in any danger, comrade? My wife is distressed enough."

The officer smiled. "I doubt you'll be bothered. But if you do see anyone acting suspiciously, inform the nearest militia. You may proceed."

"We'll do that, comrade." He glanced back at Anna. "Come, let's do as the lieutenant says."

They mounted the BMW, but then the lieutenant said softly, "One moment."

He stepped closer and shone the flashlight again in Slanski's face. Then Anna's. The light lingered on her.

He said suspiciously, "Where was the last checkpoint where you and your husband were stopped?"

The question seemed to hang in the air like a threat. When Anna hesitated, she felt Slanski's body stiffen under her arms. She noticed the two militiamen finger their rifles, taking up the cue from the sergeant, who was readying his Kalashnikov.

The lieutenant continued to stare at Anna. "I asked you a question."

"Three kilometers back. There was a car and two militiamen."

The officer's eyebrows rose. "We drove that way not half an hour ago. There wasn't a checkpoint." He turned smartly to the young militiaman manning the radio in the jeep and called out, "Kashinsky, call up central exchange. Ask them if they have a checkpoint where the woman says."

The militiaman picked up the radio hand-mike and began to talk into it.

Slanski said to the lieutenant, "Look, comrade, my wife is upset enough . . ."

"Relax, it won't take long. If there's a checkpoint back on the road then we're wasting our time hanging around here."

The militiaman in the jeep was talking away on the radio but Slanski couldn't hear the words, just a babble of static and crackle.

Finally the militiaman in the jeep climbed out with his rifle, a look of alarm on his face, beginning to speak before he reached the lieutenant.

"The bitch is lying! There's no checkpoint on that part of the road!"

It happened quickly. As the officer went for his pistol and the other men raised their weapons, Slanski flicked the switch on the handlebar and the headlight blazed into the darkness, blinding the men for an instant.

He wrenched the Tokarev from his coat and shot the officer in the chest, then fired twice at the sergeant, hitting him in the throat and face and punching him back.

He fired two quick shots at the two young militiamen as they scurried for cover behind the jeep, then he screamed back at Anna, "Hold on tight!"

He kicked the starter and the BMW revved wildly and roared forward, the front wheel lifting with the sudden burst of power, before he tore between a narrow gap in the jeeps.

Lukin was sitting at a table in the staff canteen eating a plateful of cabbage and pickled beef and potatoes, but despite his hunger he was barely tasting the food. A dozen or so officers and men sat around, eating and smoking during their break.

He had hardly taken a couple of mouthfuls when the adjutant burst in through the swinging doors. Lukin put down his fork and wiped his mouth as the adjutant strode over, carrying a map.

"Some news just in. A militia mobile patrol stopped a man and woman on a BMW motorcycle who resembled the ones we're looking for. It happened on a minor road west of Pushkin, near the Baltic Highway, about three minutes ago. When the couple were challenged, the man produced a gun and killed a lieutenant and a sergeant. The other two militiamen managed to raise the alarm. Right now they're pursuing the culprits in a jeep."

Lukin jumped to his feet and grabbed the map and spread it on the table. "Show me where."

The adjutant pointed to a spot on the map. "Here. About thirty kilometers away. By fast car, maybe half an hour if the roads are not bad. But it's going to be difficult to catch up with a motorbike, and they've got a head start. I've told the exchange the details and ordered six other patrols in the area be alerted. Several are moving to surround the region right now. Maybe if we can fence them in we've got a chance. Make them go around in decreasing circles until we've cornered them like rats."

Lukin grabbed the map and his pistol and holster and said, "Get my car. You have two motorcycle outriders ready?"

"Ready and waiting in the basement garage, along with your driver . . ."

Lukin was already moving toward the door like a man possessed, shouting back over his shoulder at the adjutant. "You man the radios here. I want to be kept in touch at all times!"

Slanski was sweating as Anna clung to him and the BMW roared along the dark, narrow country road.

He was doing sixty kilometers an hour, taking corners as fast as he dared, skidding dangerously each time he tore around bends.

Anna shouted, "Slow down or you'll kill us both!"

"Those two militia are going to radio in what happened," Slanski roared back. "We have to get away from here fast."

At the next bend he didn't heed her warning, and as the motorbike rounded the sharp curve he felt the wheels start to go from under him and suddenly the bike skidded on a patch of slush. There was a screech of rubber and they careened across the road into a ditch, Slanski ending up on top of the revving motorbike, Anna flung off and landing in some bushes.

Slanski swore and struggled free, the engine still running. "Damn!" He switched off the engine and went to help her.

"Are you all right?"

She took his outstretched hand and he pulled her out of the ditch. "I . . . I think so . . . I don't know."

The BMW's headlight was still working and Slanski saw that there was a deep cut on her forehead. Her clothes were covered in slush and bramble, and her hands were scratched. He wiped her face with her headscarf and then tied it around her bloodied forehead.

"It'll have to do for now, I'm afraid."

"What about the motorbike?"

"I'll have a look."

As he went to retrieve the bike he looked back and saw a blaze of headlights approaching at speed behind them on the road.

"The militia must have followed us or alerted another patrol."

He quickly righted the BMW and checked it as best he could. There didn't appear to be any real damage but the front wheel was tangled with grass and bramble.

He went to work frantically, tearing it away, and then he mounted the machine and kicked the starter arm.

The engine made a sputtering sound and died.

"Christ . . . !"

"Try it again!"

He did. It sounded the same.

They both looked back. The headlights were coming closer, moving rapidly. Slanski took out his pistol and handed it to Anna.

"If they get close enough, try to shoot out their headlights."

He tried to start the BMW once more but the engine died again.

"Damn it to hell!"

Suddenly Anna pointed and cried, "Look!"

Coming in the other direction along the road Slanski saw a convoy of lights, perhaps three vehicles in all, maybe a kilometer away or less. He turned back frantically, sweat on his face.

Across the road up ahead, twenty meters away, was a gate leading into a field covered in snow. It led down a long slope into darkness.

He pointed to the gate and shouted to Anna, "Open it!"

"What?"

"The gate—open it—quickly!"

Anna ran across the road and went to push the gate open. It refused to budge. She tried again. It was stuck hard.

Slanski ran over to her and kicked at the gate, hammering at it madly until it burst open. He said to her, "Stay there!"

He ran back to the BMW, climbed on, and with all his weight kicked the starter arm with terrific force and the engine thundered at last.

The convoy was almost on top of them but at that moment they heard the roar of an engine from the other direction, as a covered jeep came around the corner at speed, skidding to a halt.

Slanski drove toward Anna at the gate as they were both caught in the sudden glare of the jeep's headlights.

Suddenly from both directions there were blasts of gunfire, bullets kicking up snow and stitching across the road, as voices barked orders and vehicles screeched to a halt, men jumping out of cars and trucks.

Slanski grabbed Anna's arm and pulled her onto the bike, revved the engine, and they tore through the open gate into the field and down the slope, as bursts of rifle and machine-gun fire crackled behind them.

Lukin's heart was pounding.

The wail of the siren screamed into the night as the Zis ate up the road, the driver working hard to keep the big car from skidding.

They had already covered thirty kilometers in twenty minutes, the two militia motorbike riders in helmets and goggles on either side of the car racing ahead every now and then to clear traffic in the way. As they sped through a country village the radio crackled and Lukin picked up the hand mike.

"Lukin."

The adjutant's voice came back. "Base here, sir. We ran into them again. The same country road six kilometers east."

"What happened?" Lukin said urgently.

"They're still on the motorbike. When the patrols caught up with them they drove into a field and disappeared."

"Don't lose them!" Lukin roared into the mike. "Cut them off! Cut them off!"

"We're doing that, sir. The patrols have gone after them on foot. According to one of the militia, the field runs down to a valley and a stretch of forest. Four minor dirt roads leading in and out. I'm having them all covered as we speak."

"Whatever you do, don't let them escape! I'm on my way." Lukin dropped the mike and said to the driver, "You heard him. The same road. And keep your foot down. We haven't got all day!"

The BMW roared down the slope and when they came to the bottom Slanski braked. There was a narrow frozen stream, a dark forest beyond it.

Anna looked back over her shoulder and saw lights. Figures were running down the incline after them, bullets cracking into the trees on either side.

Slanski shouted back, "Hold on as tight as you can. This is where it's going to get rough."

Once across the frozen stream the headlight illuminated a rugged track through cavernous woods.

The tires crunched and bumped over the track, the smell of pine in the forest almost overwhelming. Minutes later they cut out onto a broader, heavily rutted road that had obviously been used by forestry vehicles. There were banks of freshly felled trees stacked nearby and Slanski said to Anna, "Have we been followed?"

"I haven't seen anyone. Not since we left the field."

He stopped the bike and pulled up his goggles, his face covered in dirt.

"Give me the map."

Anna removed it from her blouse and Slanski lit a match and tried to read it in the spluttering light.

"Where are we?"

"A place called Bear Valley Forest, by the looks of it. But how we get out of it, God only knows. There are no roads marked on the map."

Slanski looked around at her face. It was pale and frozen and he could see the terrible strain and fear. "Anna, if we get into trouble, keep your pill ready, you understand?"

"I thought we were in trouble already."

He smiled grimly. "Then let's hope it doesn't get any worse. OK, let's see if we can find a way out of here."

He revved the throttle and turned right onto the forest road.

Lukin's car halted and he saw the headlights and activity up ahead, half a dozen vehicles cramming the narrow road, uniformed men milling about.

He climbed out of the car and ran up to a captain who looked in charge.

He flashed his ID. "Major Lukin, KGB Moscow. I authorized this pursuit. What's going on here?"

The captain saluted. "They got away, sir. The crazy bastards drove into a forest down below. I've sent a dozen men down after them but we haven't got suitable transport to pursue."

Lukin noticed that a gate into a field was open, a single tire mark cutting down the starched white field. He saw figures at the bottom of the slope with flashlights. Loud voices reached him from the darkness below.

He turned back to the captain urgently. "Get on your radio and make sure all roads leading out of there are blocked off. I want every available man ringing those woods. Do it, man!"

"It's already been done, sir . . ."

"Then get on the radio again and make sure it is. I'm holding you personally responsible. And inform any patrols going into the area I'm on my way down." Lukin looked around frantically, already knowing what he had to do. He saw a sergeant with a Kalashnikov and said to the captain, "I want that man's weapon."

"Sir?"

"The Kalashnikov, bring it here."

As the captain scurried over to the sergeant, Lukin ran back to the two motorcycle riders who had dismounted. He grabbed one of the machines, climbed on and kicked it into life.

As the startled rider began to protest, Lukin roared, "Out of my way!"

He drove over to the captain, grabbed the Kalashnikov from him and slung it around his neck.

The captain looked at Lukin doubtfully as he sat on the machine with only one good hand, and stepped in front of the motorbike. "Sir, it might be better if you waited. Going after those two alone is only begging for trouble. Besides—"

"Besides what? I'm a cripple? The advantage of one good arm, Captain, is that it soon gains the strength of two. Out of my way!"

The machine roared and the captain jumped back just as Lukin drove across the road, through the gate and down the slope.

Slanski was lost.

The forest was a maze of narrow paths and in the darkness it was impossible to guess which led where. There were no signposts and more than once he had to stop to check the map and the compass.

Sweat dripped down his face and every time he glanced back at Anna he saw the raw fear in her eyes.

Suddenly the road widened and a wooden sign before a bend up ahead said "Caution—Exit to Kolimka Road. Traffic ahead."

As he came around the bend he squeezed hard on the brakes and skidded to a halt.

Half a dozen jeeps and trucks and a line of soldiers and militiamen stood across the road, waiting silently in the darkness, readying their weapons.

A voice called out, "Halt! Dismount and throw down your weapons!"

Slanski revved and frantically spun the BMW around.

There was a terrible volley of fire which exploded through the forest, lead zinging through the air and cracking all around them, as Slanski tore back the way they had come.

It was almost impossible.

Lukin had to use his feet for balance, finding it hard to control the machine with one hand.

He halted on the bumpy lane that led through the woods, his good arm aching from the effort of gripping the handlebar, sweat pumping from every pore.

He had followed the tire marks through the forest but now he switched off the engine, listening for noises in the woods or the sound of an engine, but all he heard was his own heart thumping in his ears.

And then—

A thunderous volley of gunfire erupted somewhere close and his heart skipped.

He started the motorbike again and drove toward the noise. He had gone only another fifty meters when he cut out onto a broader road.

He saw the single headlight flashing through the trees off to the right, coming toward him, and his heart almost stopped.

He pulled back in off the road and cocked the Kalashnikov slung around his neck.

The BMW roared past and he saw the man and woman.

He shifted into gear and drove after them.

He was twenty meters behind the BMW when the woman looked back. Lukin saw her face in the beam from his headlight, her mouth open in a terrible look of fear and surprise.

And then she was turning, thumping the man's shoulder and screaming to warn him.

The man glanced around briefly, his face masked by his helmet and goggles.

The BMW suddenly picked up speed, racing dangerously fast over the forest path.

Lukin found it almost impossible to keep control of the motorbike, his feet skimming over the ground for balance. If he could only aim the Kalashnikov at the rear tire he stood a chance of slowing them, but it was impossible with one hand and he could barely manage to keep up speed as it was.

The man and woman were racing ahead of him now.

As the BMW rounded a corner in the forest, suddenly Lukin saw a bank of headlights, army trucks and jeeps straddling the road a hundred meters ahead, as another roadblock obstructed the way.

The BMW slowed and swung a hard right to avoid it, roaring up a bank leading into trees. Lukin realized that Slanski was trying to cut around the patrol.

The BMW shot up the bank and Lukin went after it.

He had gone hardly a couple of meters up when the machine wobbled beneath him, snaked violently, and he came off and landed hard.

He saw the BMW put on a burst of power and growl up the rise, but just before it reached the top it suddenly seemed to stall, bucking like a horse unwilling to jump the final fence.

The woman was thrown off, hit the earth hard, and rolled back down.

Lukin stumbled to his feet and raced toward her.

Up on the top of the rise he saw the driver fighting hard to control the machine, until it nosed down and the tires gripped and then it was safely at the top. Lukin saw the driver look back down in horror as the woman's body rolled to a halt at the bottom of the bank.

There was a moment of indecision, then a scream of despair. "Anna . . . !"

Lukin gripped the Kalashnikov and fired wildly, the volley showering the woods with splinters, but the man turned and sped away into darkness.

Soldiers from the trucks ran forward, firing into the woods and climbing the rise after the BMW.

Lukin tossed away the Kalashnikov and lunged at the woman, just as she was trying to put something into her mouth, and as he landed on her hard she cried out in pain.

He shoved his fingers into her throat.

February 27th–March 2nd 1953

41

Paris.

It was just before ten that same evening when the sleek black Citroën pulled up on the boulevard Montmartre and Henri Lebel climbed out.

It was pouring rain, and as the chauffeur handed him an umbrella Lebel said, "You can go, Charles. Pick me up from Maxim's at midnight."

"Very good, sir."

Lebel stood watching as the Citroën disappeared into the sheeting rain before he crossed the boulevard and turned down a narrow street and came to a littered alleyway. A cat scurried past him out of the shadows, and when Lebel reached the end of the filthy lane he came to a blue-painted door on the right. A floodlit sign above it said "Club Malakoff. Members only."

Lebel knocked on the door. A grille opened and a man's unshaven face appeared.

"*Oui?*"

"M. Clichy. I'm expected."

There was a rattle of bolts and the man opened the door and peered out into the rain-soaked alleyway before admitting his visitor.

Lebel went down a winding metal staircase to a packed, smoky room, the tables occupied by tough-looking working men drinking glasses of beer and cheap wine. An elderly man wearing an apron and polishing glasses behind a zinc bar smiled when he saw Lebel, then came over and said, "This way, monsieur, follow me."

Lebel followed him through some curtains behind the bar up a narrow flight of stairs to a door at the end of a shabby hallway.

The old man knocked and a voice said, "Come in if you're good-looking."

"It's Claude. Your visitor has arrived," the man said, and opened the door.

Lebel stepped into a tiny smoky room with a single lightbulb dangling low in the center, the rest of the room in shadows, an ancient scratched mirror covering one wall. A man in his middle thirties sat at a table in the center of the room, a bottle of pastis and two glasses in front of him. He was small, wiry, and had a hunched back. His two front teeth were missing, and the shabby black suit he wore was flecked with cigarette ash.

As he lit a Gauloise he winked to the barman. "Leave us, Claude."

When the door closed the man at the table gestured to a chair in front. "Henri, my old flower, always good to see you."

Lebel sat opposite and removed a pair of exquisite hide gloves. "Unfortunately, Bastien, I wish I could say the same."

"As always, the diplomat. Take a seat. Drink?"

"You know I only drink champagne. Anything less upsets my stomach."

Bastien grinned. "Tough. All I've got is cheap pastis. Not even the Chairman of the Party can afford the finer things in life, Henri."

"Then I'll decline."

Bastien shrugged and poured a drink for himself. He looked over at Lebel, who wore an expensive suit and silk tie with diamond pin, the collar of his beautifully tailored camel-haired overcoat trimmed with sable.

Bastien smiled, his missing incisors leaving a black gaping hole in his mouth. "You're looking well as usual, Henri. Business good?"

"I presume you didn't ask me here to discuss such a repulsive subject as my money-making? So perhaps you'd get to the point. What is it this time? Another contribution to the Party?"

Pierre Bastien stood up. Lebel always considered that the man wouldn't have looked out of place swinging in the bell tower of Nôtre-Dame. Unkind, perhaps, but the man before him was a particularly nasty piece of work behind the simulated bonhomie.

"Actually, just a friendly talk, Lebel, and there's no need to get snotty, comrade."

"I'm not your comrade."

"Fighting the Germans together for two years counts for nothing, I take it?"

"Let's get the facts right as to who did the fighting. You like to tell people the Gestapo knocked out your teeth and injured your back when we both know it was really your former wife who did it. She pushed you down a flight of stairs as repayment for leaving her and your children alone to face the Gestapo who raided your home. Naughty, Bastien, especially since some of us had to endure real hardship and torture, while you sneaked from one safe house to another and never fired a shot at the Germans until the Allies had safely secured Paris. Still, it got you the Croix de Guerre from De Gaulle. And you really ought to get something done about those missing teeth of yours. For too long you've been wearing that gap in your mouth like a badge of honor."

A look of contempt twisted Bastien's face. "Don't belittle me, Lebel. I did as much as any man. Besides, it was important I wasn't captured, for the sake of the Party, to continue the struggle after the war."

"Indeed. And remember this is the same scum who contributes so generously to your cause. Get to the point. I've a dinner appointment at Maxim's."

"No doubt with some tarty model?" Bastien said with a sneer.

Lebel sighed. "Envy will get you nowhere. Existing in the hell of a concentration camp with death hanging over me taught me two things. One, you can rely only on yourself, and two, enjoy life when you can. I do both every day and my private life is none of your concern. So, what do you want to talk about?"

Bastien grinned maliciously. "A sensitive matter. That's why I asked you here in person. You took the usual precautions?"

"Naturally. From the look on your face I can only conclude you have some unpleasant news to impart?"

Bastien finished his drink and slapped his glass on the table. "A man named Jake Massey. Do you know him?"

Lebel looked up a little unsteadily, thrown by the question, and tried hard not to show his alarm.

"What's this got to do with?"

"I asked a simple question. Do you know him?"

Lebel sighed and idly glanced at his watch so as not to betray his unease. "Look, Bastien, can we get to the point."

"That is the point. Do you know this Massey?"

"The name sounds familiar. He was an American OSS officer working with the resistance during the war. Why?"

"Have you seen him recently?"

Lebel saw that Bastien had a slight grin on his face, which was always dangerous. He decided to tell the truth.

"Actually, yes. He was in Paris recently and called at my suite to say hello. But what's this got to do with? Are you checking up on my social calendar, Bastien?"

"So, just a friendly visit, was it, Henri?"

"Of course. Look, what's the point of all this? I told you, I've got an appointment."

"What did Massey want to see you about?"

"Nothing in particular. I told you, he called to say hello and talk about old times. I asked him to join me for dinner, but he said he had another engagement."

"That's it?"

"That's it. Now, Bastien, unless there's anything else . . ."

As Lebel went to rise, Bastien's hand fell on his shoulder. "Sit down. I'm not finished yet. Some important people have been asking questions about you."

"Who?"

"None of your business. But because we're old resistance comrades I asked you here to pass on a warning. The last thing I'd like to see happen is for you to get hurt. Then where would we be? Your contributions to us are quite generous, Henri."

Lebel shrugged. "I do what I can. But hurt how, by whom? What kind of warning?"

"To be careful about the people you meet. And you can cut out the shit. You contribute because you have to. Because it ensures Moscow looks favorably on you and your business."

"You haven't answered my questions. How might I be hurt? And by whom? For what reason?"

"It's best not to ask. But do yourself a favor. Next time Massey contacts you, tell me. He was OSS. Now he's CIA. Your private life may be no concern of mine but it is to Moscow. You get mixed up with someone like that, people may get the wrong impression."

Lebel pretended alarm. "Massey CIA? I had no idea . . ."

"Well you do now. OK?"

Lebel nodded. "If you say so."

"I do."

Lebel said, "Is that it?"

Bastien nodded. "That's it. Just remember what I said."

As Lebel stood, Bastien grinned slyly and said, "By the way, there's someone I'd like you to meet." He turned toward the mirror. "You can come in now, Colonel."

A door opened somewhere in the shadows and a man appeared. He was big and brutish, his face a mass of pockmarks and scars, and part of his left ear was missing. Bastien said, "Colonel Romulka, KGB Moscow, meet Henri Lebel. Colonel Romulka here tells me you were due to travel to Moscow in two days' time. He wants to rearrange your travel plans and get you there a little earlier."

Lebel said palely, "What's going on here?"

Romulka snapped his fingers and two men appeared from behind the door. They grabbed Lebel and rolled up one of his sleeves and Romulka came forward and jabbed a hypodermic in his arm.

Washington, D.C.
February 27th,
8:30 P.M.

Rain streaked against the Oval Office French windows and a flash of lightning lit up the black evening sky beyond the Washington Memorial.

Eisenhower sighed as he sat down heavily at his desk and looked at the three other men in the room.

"Let me get this straight. You're telling me now it's impossible to stop this thing?"

Allen Dulles, the head of the CIA, sat near the President, Karl Branigan and Jake Massey in front of the walnut desk.

There were dark shadows under the President's eyes, the famous grin nowhere to be seen. The weather outside seemed to match his black mood.

Branigan sat forward in his chair. "I'm afraid it looks bad, Mr. President. As Massey explained, the only way we could get word to Slanski in Moscow was through Lebel. But now Lebel has vanished."

Eisenhower said bleakly, "Tell me what happened."

"As you know, sir, Lebel was due to fly to Moscow in two days' time. We had our Paris desk try to contact him but Lebel couldn't be found. His chauffeur claims he was to pick him up from Maxim's club at midnight, Paris time, where Lebel had a business appointment. Our men were waiting for him at the club but Lebel never turned up. But something else did."

"What?"

"Our Paris desk monitored an unscheduled Soviet diplomatic flight leaving from Le Bourget airport with a flight plan for Moscow, not long after Lebel was dropped off on the boulevard Montmartre by his chauffeur. There's a club near the boulevard, the Club Malakoff, used by known French Communist Party members. We also know from our contacts in French counterintelligence that Lebel has been observed occasionally visiting the club. Lebel's chauffeur says his boss took a phone call earlier in the evening and claimed he had a private meeting to attend but didn't say where, only that he wanted to be driven to the boulevard Montmartre.

"But there's something much more worrying to consider. There were several passengers bundled on board the Soviet flight just before takeoff, one of them on a stretcher and accompanied by a doctor. According to the French, the Soviets claimed he was a member of their Paris embassy staff being taken to Moscow for urgent medical treatment. However, from talking with the French authorities who checked the Soviet passenger manifest and getting their descriptions of the people who went on board, we suspect now the man on the stretcher may have been Lebel."

"*Jesus.*"

"Which leads me to believe Moscow has figured out Lebel's connection to Massey and they want to interrogate him."

Eisenhower put a hand to his face and rubbed his eyes. "It gets worse by the hour."

"Mr. President, taking Lebel to Moscow would suggest he hasn't already cooperated. But in my opinion, no matter what we had ordered Slanski to do at this stage, I'm convinced he'd ignore our command."

Eisenhower looked up. "Even a direct command from me?"

"Even a direct command from you, sir, if it were possible to relay one to him."

Eisenhower sighed again and turned in his chair. "Mr. Massey, do you want to say anything?"

Massey looked up. There were dark rings under his eyes and his face looked troubled. He had hardly slept for the last forty-eight hours, the long flight from Helsinki to Washington swiftly followed by a grueling four-hour debriefing by Branigan, the Assistant Director, and Allen Dulles, every detail of the operation gone over. There was a gnawing feeling of doom and a sickness in the pit of his stomach that hadn't left him in all that time. The news about Lebel only added to it, and there was an atmosphere of hopelessness in the room.

He looked over at Eisenhower, who was staring at him. "I don't know what to say, Mr. President."

Eisenhower flushed angrily. "Considering you're partly responsible I think you had better contribute something to this conversation. You've been sitting there for the past ten minutes like a man who's lost his way home. Don't you have any suggestions?"

"If Lebel's been abducted and taken to Moscow, then we've no way of stopping Slanski, short of sending someone in there to reason with him. As for Lebel's abduction there's no answer, unless you consider shooting down the aircraft he's on."

"Impossible, even if I considered it," Eisenhower answered sharply. "By now it'll be inside Soviet territory. And in answer to your first suggestion you heard what Branigan said. Slanski would never listen. What's your opinion about this Lebel? Do you think he'll break easily under interrogation?"

"Lebel was in a concentration camp after being caught and tortured by the Gestapo, so he's been through the ordeal before. He may refuse to talk and deny his involvement, depending on what evidence Moscow has to implicate him. But they must have some, and they must be in a hurry, otherwise why abduct him, especially when he was to arrive there in two days' time? Or Lebel may just as easily tell Moscow everything. I've no way of knowing."

"But you know the man, right? Give me your honest opinion. Will he talk?"

Massey thought for a moment. "I'd say Lebel will hold out as long as he can. He's no fool, and he'll probably try to deny everything at first. But considering the way the KGB have refined the art of torture, I wouldn't expect that to be for more than a couple of days, maybe a little more."

Allen Dulles was wiping his glasses when he looked up slowly. "It strikes me that if Lebel can be counted on to hold out, that gives us time, and maybe a way out of this mess."

"How?" asked Eisenhower.

"We kill Slanski and Khorev. Callous as it sounds, it's about the only solution I can think of."

There was silence in the room. Massey looked over at Dulles and said with feeling, "We're talking about two people risking their lives for us. Two people who had the guts to carry out this operation, and you want to kill them?"

Dulles fixed Massey with a stare. "This isn't a perfect world, Massey. But it's the only solution I can think of, and maybe the only shot we've got left." He looked back at the President. "Branigan and I have been doing a little homework, trying to figure this thing out."

He plucked a file from the briefcase beside him. "Right now we've got four agents in Moscow. To each we send a brief encoded message usually every four weeks to keep in touch and let them know we haven't forgotten about them. The transmissions are made on regular radio programs on The Voice of America at prearranged times. To any ordinary listener the transmission sounds harmless, but our agents, once they decode a certain passage transmitted at a certain time, have got a message from us."

He leaned over and handed the file to Eisenhower. "These are two agents of ours in Moscow we think could help."

As the President picked it up, Dulles added, "They're freebooters. Former Ukrainian SS. In fact, Massey himself had them parachuted into the Ukraine six weeks ago. They arrived in Moscow a week later."

Eisenhower quickly read the file and replaced it on the desk.

"So what are you proposing?"

"We're due to send a routine message to these men on schedule tomorrow night. But instead we tell them about the man and woman we want located. Massey here has told us about Lebel's ladyfriend whom Slanski is to meet in Moscow. She's got a dacha he's going to use as a safe house. If we can confirm that Slanski and the woman will show up there, well then, I think you can guess the rest. But I figure we'll need someone in place in Moscow to make sure the plan is carried out. There's no room for error. And it's got to be done fast. Like Massey says, our friend Lebel is eventually going to be made to talk and then the KGB will know about the dacha."

"Is there any chance Moscow could decode your radio message?"

Dulles shook his head. "Highly unlikely, Mr. President. The message is decoded on one-time pads, and impossible to break."

"There's something vital you're leaving out. How in the hell do we get someone to Moscow?"

Dulles said, "We're working on it, Mr. President. Mossad seems the most likely bet. They've got contacts through their Jewish League in Russia and Eastern Europe, and we know they have a number of agents and highly placed informers in Moscow, in the KGB and the Soviet military. If you give us the clearance, we ask Mossad's assistance without divulging our reasons. I think they'll agree. As you know, we've got a formal agreement with them on mutual security matters."

"You really think it could work?"

Dulles said, "It's going to be risky and difficult, sir. And it needs to be done with great speed but also with great care. There's no room for error. Me, I think it's a chance we've got to take. But I believe Massey's the one to answer that question. He sent each of these people in."

All faces turned to Massey, and finally Eisenhower said, "Well, Mr. Massey, tell me if it's possible? Can it work?"

Massey thought for a moment, then said flatly, "I don't know."

Eisenhower's face turned red. "Answer the goddamned question."

Massey looked over at him, and the President heard the anger in his voice. "Me, I don't want any part of this."

Eisenhower flared. "The question I asked was can it work? And let's not forget why we're here, Massey. You're partly responsible for what's happened. Answer the question."

Massey went to get up angrily and Eisenhower said, "Stay right where you are!"

He looked at Dulles and Branigan. "Take a walk, gentlemen. Leave us."

Dulles and Branigan stood and both of them left the Oval Office.

As Massey sat there, Eisenhower lit a cigarette with shaking hands, still angry, as he stood and walked over to the French windows. He opened them and stepped out onto a porch. There was a rush of cool air and the sound of pelting rain beyond the patio and Eisenhower said over his shoulder, "Step out here, Jake."

Massey went out to the patio. Rain came down in sheets beyond the porch, and as Eisenhower stared out he said, "Have you got family?"

"A son."

"What about your wife?"

"We're divorced."

Eisenhower looked back. "Would you consider yourself a patriot, Jake?"

"Mr. President, I love my country. I wouldn't be doing this job if I didn't. But I can't go along with this. Alex Slanski's a brave man, a man who's doing what no one else would dare do. As for Anna Khorev, she only agreed to go along to get her child back. But she's still a courageous woman, nonetheless. And maybe we've used her. But we can't kill her. It isn't moral and it isn't right."

Eisenhower sighed and flicked his cigarette away. "I want to tell you a story I haven't told to anyone in a long time. When I was a young officer I served in Panama. There was a boy I knew from my home town served with me. A nice red-haired kid, a good pal to get drunk with and always quick with a song. Had a sweetheart back home he was crazy about.

"One night our company got sent into the jungle where some guerrillas had artillery that was giving our battalion hell. Our objective was to silence those guns. Halfway through we got pinned down in the darkness by machine-gun fire. The kid I knew went ahead to silence one of the guns and took a hit in the belly. He crawled back through the jungle toward us with his guts hanging out, screaming his head off for someone to help him. The trouble was, he was giving our position away.

"I was maybe the best rifle shot in the company. My commander ordered me to shoot the kid. I couldn't bring myself to do it, so I fired wide. Someone else tried and failed. Five minutes later the guerrillas stormed our position and killed ten of our men."

There was a look like remorse on Eisenhower's face. "If I had had the guts to shoot that kid, maybe those men wouldn't have died. And there was worse. After we retreated the guns went on firing and decimated our battalion. I let my commander and my fellow men down. I let my country down."

He looked out grimly at the rain. "This ain't no jungle in Panama with the lives of ten men in the balance, or even the lives of a battalion. This is a war we're talking about. Not twenty lives or more at stake, but maybe twenty million. If I learned one thing that night in the jungle it's that you cut your losses when you have to and you take your pain. Hard decisions, sure, but we're talking about hard facts—two lives for a whole lot of others. Including maybe your son's. Because, make no mistake, if we fail to stop this thing there *will* be a war. If Slanski and the woman are caught alive, Moscow will have evidence and reason enough to start one. A war America's not ready for. A war we can't win. They're six months ahead of us with the hydrogen bomb and Stalin's just itching to use it if he has an excuse to. And with that kind of power he can blow us off the face of the earth."

Massey studied the President's face. There was a hard, determined look in the man's blue eyes and a grimness around his mouth he had never seen before in any of his photographs.

Eisenhower stared back."The question I asked you was can the plan Dulles suggested work? I'd like your answer to that."

Massey sighed. "Maybe. But it's only an outside chance. Slanski's no fool and he's the best man we ever trained. Killing him won't be easy."

"Then even if there's just a slim chance we've got to take it. There's only one man I can think of who can identify Slanski and the woman and stop them. And that's you. I know you don't want to kill them, but you and I both know why you have to. Don't make the mistake I did all those years ago. Don't save two lives when you may lose millions."

Eisenhower looked into Massey's eyes. "I'm asking you, Jake, don't let your country or me down on this one."

42

Dzerzhinsky Square,
Moscow.

A scream echoed somewhere in the distance and Anna came awake, her body drenched in sweat.

A single lightbulb shone overhead and it almost blinded her.

She was lying on a hard wooden bed in a tiny windowless cell. Water seeped down the shiny granite walls and the place smelled of damp and urine. There was a metal door in the far wall and beyond it she could hear the faint clanking of doors being opened and closed.

She guessed she was in a prison somewhere, but she had no idea where, or if it was day or night, or how she had got there.

One moment it seemed she was being choked by the KGB man and the next she was here. But everything in between was a blur. Where was Slanski? Was he dead? Alive? In another cell?

The anxiety consumed her. She remembered the scream beyond the cell door. Had she been dreaming or had the scream been real? Perhaps it was Slanski? She felt totally confused and helpless, a terrible fear gnawing in her stomach which made her feel ill.

Her left shoulder was stiff and her mouth felt dry and her body weak. She looked at her shoulder.

A dressing had been applied, the bandage so tightly wrapped that it cut painfully into her flesh. She tried to move her arm and felt a sharp pain stab through her shoulder to the base of her back.

She cried out in agony.

She guessed her shoulder had been dislocated when the KGB major threw himself on top of her in the forest. She remembered the sharp pain when he landed, as if a bone had broken. Then she noticed a small red welt in the soft flesh of her arm where a hypodermic had punctured skin. They had put her to sleep.

As she went to drag her legs over the edge of the bed and sit up she heard the scream again, followed by a tortured cry that rang through the corridor outside.

She shuddered, and the pain stabbed through her again.

Where was she? What was happening? Who was screaming?

She heard the clatter of boots outside, a key being inserted in the lock, then the metal door creaked open on its hinges.

Two men in black KGB uniforms stood there. They crossed to the bed and gripped her roughly by the arms, jerked her up. The pain shot through her shoulder in agonizing waves.

As they dragged her from the cell she blacked out.

When she opened her eyes she was sitting on a chair in a room with black steel bars on the windows.

The room was bare and functional. Green walls and a wooden table and two chairs facing each other. The table was fastened to the floor with steel brackets. The metal door in the far wall had a small grille and a tiny peephole.

She felt sick with fear and she could still feel the waves of pain in her shoulder.

Watery sunlight flooded in through the window. Beyond the glass she heard the sound of engines starting up and moving off, gears crunching, and far off the faint hum of traffic.

She pushed herself painfully from the chair and went to the window.

There was a large cobbled courtyard below. She counted seven floors on the opposite side of the building, and there were bars on all the windows. A dozen or more trucks and cars were parked in one corner of the courtyard, and a half-dozen motorcycles were sheltered in a corrugated shed. Men crossed the courtyard busily, some in civilian clothes and carrying sheaves of papers, others in black KGB uniforms.

Her heart sank. As she turned away from the window the door opened suddenly.

The KGB man stood there. He wore his black uniform with major's shoulder boards and carried a manila file under his arm, but there was something different about his false hand this time. In place of the leather glove was a metal hook. He locked the door with a key from a chain in his pocket and put the folder on the table.

"How are you feeling?"

The voice was soft, inquiring, and when she didn't reply Lukin removed a packet of cigarettes and a lighter from his tunic pocket and placed them on the table. He pulled up the chair opposite and sat.

"Please, sit down. Cigarette?"

Again Anna didn't reply and Lukin lit a cigarette and glanced at her shoulder. "My fault, I'm afraid. You've got a nasty dislocation a physician had to reset. Nothing's broken but it's going to take a couple of days before the pain goes away." He smiled faintly and tapped his own arm. "Quite a pair of walking wounded, aren't we, Anna?"

Now that she saw him close up the man looked exhausted. There were swollen dark rings under his eyes, the strain and tiredness making him look older.

"Sit down, please."

She sat facing him.

"Even though we've met before perhaps I should introduce myself formally. My name is Major Yuri Lukin. I'm sorry you were hurt. I had hoped it wouldn't come to that. Can I get you something? Tea? Coffee? Water? Some food?"

"I'm not hungry, or thirsty."

"That's impossible. You haven't eaten or drunk anything in almost twelve hours. If you think by accepting my offer it would seem like a sign of weakness, you're being foolish, I assure you."

When she didn't reply, Lukin said, "As you wish."

There was another scream from somewhere far away, the sound of a dull crack, as if a human skull was being struck against a wall. Lukin's eyes flicked to the door, a look of distaste on his face. He sighed and stood up. "I know what you're feeling, Anna. Fear. Anxiety. Confusion." He glanced at her shoulder, then back at her face. "Pain is the smallest and least part of it. Do you know where you are? Dzerzhinsky Square, Moscow. You passed out when I made you cough up this." Lukin took the cyanide pill from his breast pocket and held it up. "I managed to stop you crushing it just in time."

She looked at the pill, then turned her face away. "How long have I been here?"

"You were brought in late last night, by military transporter. I'm afraid it's not the most pleasant of places, with a deservedly bad reputation." He paused, and said without humor, "Some call it the First Circle of Hell, and perhaps they're right."

He dropped his cigarette on the floor and crushed it with his shoe, then opened the file on the table and flicked through the pages.

"I've been studying your file. You've had quite a life, Anna Khorev. A lot of pain. A lot of grief. So many tragedies. Your parents' deaths. Your husband's trial." He paused. "Not to mention everything that happened afterwards. And now this."

Anna looked at Lukin in amazement and said suddenly, "How . . . how do you know who I am?"

"We've known you were involved in this for a long time. Even before you landed on Soviet soil. You and Slanski both."

Anna started to speak, but she felt so shocked the words wouldn't come.

Lukin said, "Anna, if you help me by telling me everything you know, it will be easier on both of us."

She looked at him steadily. "I have nothing to tell you."

"Anna, there are people here who could make you talk. People who would take pleasure in hurting you. Take pleasure in hearing your screams. Raping you. Torturing you. I am not one of those people. But I've seen their work and it's not pleasant. And if you don't talk to me, they will make you talk, please believe that."

Anna didn't reply.

Lukin said, "I know Slanski came to kill Stalin."

She looked up at Lukin suddenly, her face deathly white.

Lukin continued to look at her. "I believe you were simply used by the Americans to help him get to Moscow, to pretend to be his wife and hence avoid arousing suspicion. But Slanski's mission has already failed. Last night he escaped, but he can't have gone far. And most certainly one of our patrols will hunt him down and find him. In the meantime, you may as well help me by telling me all you know. Who your contacts were when you landed in Estonia. Who were meant to be your contacts in Moscow and en route. I want to know how you were trained and by whom. And everything you can tell me of Slanski's plan to kill Stalin. Help me answer those questions and I will do my best to help you in return."

For a long time she stared at Lukin, the enormity of what he had said still ringing in her ears. "*I know Slanski came to kill Stalin.*"

Lukin said, "I can help you by pleading for mercy when your case comes to trial."

There was a look of resignation on her face and she didn't reply.

He said quietly, "Anna, you're either being very brave or very obstinate, but I have a job to do. To find Alex Slanski dead or alive and arrest whoever else is involved in this mission."

He picked up the folder and put it under his arm. "I'm going to give you a little time to reconsider. For your sake I hope you will talk to me, rather than the others. I really don't want to see you hurt any more than you have been."

He picked up the cigarettes and lighter from the table. As he stood there a moment Anna looked up at him. There was something in the soft brown eyes which seemed to suggest compassion, the way he looked at her and called her by her first name, but she dismissed the thought from her mind.

He crossed the room and unlocked the door. As she went to step out, he looked back at her.

"I'll have some food and water sent to you. We've a lot to talk about and you'll need to keep up your strength." He paused. "May I ask you a personal question, Anna?"

"What?"

"Are you in love with Slanski?"

She didn't answer.

Lukin stared at her for a moment, then the door clanged shut.

Only when she heard his footsteps fade beyond the door did she bury her face in her hands.

* * *

There was a message on the desk to call Beria's Kremlin office urgently. Lukin ignored the message and pushed it aside.

He had sent a report that morning. No doubt Beria would have some sharp comments on how he had allowed the Wolf to escape, but right now he felt too exhausted to worry about it.

The pain in his stump came and went in short, savage bursts. He looked at his hand; the primitive metal hook would have to do for now. He picked up the telephone and dialed the operations room. Pasha Kokunko answered.

"How did the interrogation go?" The Mongolian sounded tired. He had been up all night manning the telephones and communications equipment in the operations room.

"Not too good. Can you come over here, Pasha?"

"I'm on my way."

Lukin put the receiver down. He rubbed his eyes and felt the tiredness take hold, flooding his body. The woman had been unconscious in the military transporter to Moscow, despite the Ilyushin aircraft's buffeting in bad weather, out cold from the sedative she had been given. But he had slept for less than ten hours in almost three days. He felt exhausted, the words in the file a blur now. There was a cup of steaming coffee on the desk and he picked it up, sipped and swallowed.

The woman's capture had been a small victory, but really the whole business had been a defeat. The Wolf had escaped. And Lukin didn't like the look he had seen on her face when he questioned her. He knew from experience the kind who talked under interrogation and she wasn't one of them. There was a grim resignation in her face that was almost a death wish.

She was afraid, of course, but everyone imprisoned in the Lubyanka was afraid. He sensed that if he tried to cajole her into talking it wouldn't work. He decided the best approach with a woman like her was honesty. There was another way that might make her talk and he shuddered thinking about it.

But he had to find the Wolf.

Where was he? Out there somewhere. But where? An order had gone out to army, militia, and KGB commanders within a two-hundred-kilometer radius of the forest to mount patrols and checkpoints in case he had evaded the dragnet. But so far nothing had turned up, despite a search lasting through the night. If the Wolf had escaped and was headed toward Moscow, it made Lukin's job more difficult. There were so many places a man could hide in a densely populated city.

As he sat there, he again thought about the two missing pages in the Wolf's file. Why had Beria not allowed him to see them? What was in there that could be so secret? Something occurred to him. It was well known in Dzerzhinsky Square that Beria secretly despised Stalin, and ultimately wanted to succeed him. If the Wolf achieved his goal, that might play into Beria's hands. Perhaps he really wanted to impede Lukin's efforts? If there was some clue in the missing pages which might help Lukin, then it was a dangerous game he was caught up in. The simplest way was to ask Beria for the pages and see what happened, but even that might be courting trouble.

The door opened and Pasha entered. His uniform was crumpled and his eyes bloodshot.

Lukin said, "You look like you've been sleeping in a ditch."

Pasha rubbed his neck and grinned. "No, just one of those bunks divisional stores stuck us with—a ditch would probably be more comfortable."

"Any more word from the patrols and checkpoints?"

"They still haven't found him. But something has to turn up soon—he can't have vanished off the face of the earth. So the woman didn't talk?"

"Not yet. I want you to arrange something for me." He wrote a phone number on a slip of paper, handed it across, and explained to Pasha what he wanted him to do.

Pasha looked unhappy. "You're sure about this, Yuri?"

"I'm afraid so. Beria wants to see me, and he's going to want results fast."

Pasha shrugged and left. The telephone rang and Lukin picked it up.

"Lukin."

"Yuri?" Nadia's voice. "Is everything all right?"

Right now Lukin felt he wanted to lie in his wife's arms and sleep, drain the exhaustion from his body. He had been away three days. Three days that seemed like hours to him, but must have seemed like weeks to Nadia because he hadn't contacted her.

"Yes, everything's fine, my love."

"I called yesterday. They wouldn't tell me anything. Where you were or when you'd be coming home."

"The case I'm working on, it's taking longer than I thought. How are you?"

"Missing you. Come home tonight for dinner. I know you when you're like this. You get so involved. Please, Yuri. It'll help you relax."

"I can't say, Nadia. You'd better not expect me."

The line was silent for a long time. "I love you, Yuri."

"I love you too."

Then it clicked dead.

It was almost two o'clock when Lukin drove through the main gates of the Kremlin and parked in the Armory courtyard.

Five minutes later he was ushered into Beria's sumptuous office on the third floor by a Guards captain. There were silk tapestries on the walls and Bokhara rugs scattered on the floor and the furniture was expensive Finnish oak. Beria sat behind his desk and he looked up from some papers as Lukin entered.

"Major, sit down."

Lukin pulled back a chair.

Beria looked over. "I believe congratulations of a sort are in order."

"Thank you, comrade."

Beria reached over to a cigar box on the desk and selected one. He frowned. "But you let the man slip from your grasp. Not good at all. You disappoint me, Lukin. Has the woman talked?"

"Not yet, comrade."

Beria's eyebrows rose as he lit the cigar. "But you interrogated her?"

"This morning."

"Considering the seriousness of the matter I thought even some slight progress would have been made by now. In the old days we used to be able to break women within hours. They're much more susceptible to torture, especially the threat of rape."

Lukin suppressed an urge to look away in disgust. "It will take a little time. She was injured, as my report explains—"

"I read the report," Beria interrupted sharply. "You failed to capture the American not once, not twice, but three times. I expected more from you, Lukin."

"I can assure you I'll find him, Comrade Beria."

"To do that you must have some idea where he is. Do you?"

Lukin hesitated. "I believe he's still in the forest area, hiding out. In that kind of weather and terrain he can't have gone far. There are over a thousand men searching the area as we speak. I've also alerted regional KGB commanders and requested roadblocks be set up on all major and minor roads in the area. All public and private transport will be searched. It's only a matter of time before the Wolf turns up, dead or alive."

"I hope that's so, Lukin. For your sake." Beria fingered a pen on his desk, the slim fingers playing with it a moment, then he said, "But so far you haven't exactly inspired confidence. Perhaps I should interrogate the woman myself? I think it's time to take off the gloves, don't you? A little violence to soften her. I know you think it's easier to catch flies with honey than vinegar, but you see, we old hands do have a way in these matters."

Lukin looked at him. He could see the gleam in Beria's eye as a grin played on his face. The images Lukin had seen on the screen flashed before his mind and he felt sick.

"With respect, I don't believe simple torture is going to work in her case. I don't believe she'll respond to it. I need just a little time to gain her trust and confidence. The best way to do that is to deal with her alone. Just me and her."

"But will she talk then?"

"I believe so."

Beria toyed with his pen, as if trying to decide. He sighed. "Very well. We play it your way for now. I'll give you forty-eight hours. Forty-eight hours to make her talk and to find the man. After that, if you haven't succeeded, you hand her over to me and Romulka will deal with her and take over the case. You're dismissed. That is all."

When Lukin hesitated, Beria stared at him. "What's the matter, Lukin? Is there something on your mind?"

"I have a request to make."

"And what request is that?"

"I couldn't fail to notice there were two pages missing from the Wolf's file. I'm certain Comrade Beria had good reason not to include those pages in my copy. However, it strikes me that all information concerning the Wolf should be made available to me. It may help me apprehend him."

Beria half smiled. "You're quite right about the pages, Lukin. But you already had the chance to catch the Wolf and failed, three times, *without* the supposed benefit of the pages you speak of. But believe me, you have all the information relevant to your mission. Your request is denied. You may leave."

Lukin stood and walked to the door.

"Lukin . . ."

He turned back. The black piggish eyes stared at him.

"I believe you and Romulka had a slight disagreement yesterday. Try to remember, you're working together, not as adversaries. See that it doesn't happen again. And something else you should know about. Romulka is bringing the Frenchman, Lebel, to Moscow, arriving this afternoon. I think it best that Romulka deal with him alone. He's much more experienced in these matters." He paused and puffed on his cigar. "Forty-eight hours. Not a second more. Don't fail me, Lukin."

Moscow.
February 28th,
8:30 A.M.

The underground train thundered into the Kiev Station with the sound of a thousand pounding hammers and squealed to a halt. As the doors rolled open, Slanski stepped out onto the platform.

Like most of Moscow's Metro stations, the Kiev was an absurdly ornate construction; an underground palace of glittering chandeliers and marble walls, decorated with bronze reliefs and red flags hanging from the ceiling.

The station was packed with early morning commuters and the air reeked of stale food and tobacco and sweating bodies. As Slanski stood there trying to get his bearings, he felt a tap on his shoulder and spun around.

A young Tartar wearing a blue militia overcoat over his uniform stood there. He held a cigarette in his hand as his slanted eyes stared at Slanski.

"You have a light, comrade?"

Slanski hesitated, then shook his head. "*Niet.*"

The Tartar grumbled and moved away into the crowd.

The militiaman had startled him. He stood there for several moments, sweating, trying to regain his composure as people swarmed past. He was on unfamiliar territory and the noise and the crowds made him feel uneasy. He saw the steep escalators at either end of the platform and took one to the top.

There was no letup in the crowds when he reached ground level. The station entrance hall teemed with milling bodies. He saw a number of military uniforms in the crowd, mostly army officers carrying briefcases as they hurried briskly to and fro, but they paid him no attention.

There was a public toilet across the hall and he went inside. The place was filthy and stank to heaven but there was a wash basin and a cracked mirror on the wall. He looked at his face.

It was a mess.

His eyes were red and swollen from lack of sleep. Disheveled and unshaven and covered in grime, he still wore the coat Vladimir had given him. But he had abandoned the motorbike in a remote wood outside the suburb of Tatarovo, buried Anna's and his own suitcase and the helmet and goggles a distance away, using his hands to dig in the hard-packed snow. He had worn the extra clothes to keep out the cold on the motorbike and now the garments stuck to him with sweat. He had walked a kilometer to the nearest train station at Tatarovo before transferring to the Metro. He ached for sleep. He had been driving for almost fifteen solid hours through forest and on minor roads, having to avoid at least half a dozen checkpoints in the first two hours alone.

As he ran the water he thought: *I look terrible.*

The fear of what might have happened to Anna had left him depressed and he tried desperately to keep the black mood from crowding in on him. But it refused to go away. Was she still alive? Had Lukin caught her? He hoped for her sake she had bitten the pill, even though that thought made him more despondent, but he remembered looking back at the last moment, recognizing Lukin, and seeing him lunge at her. Somehow the major had survived the helicopter crash. How, it didn't matter. All that mattered was that the man was alive and determined to catch them.

If Anna was alive, he dreaded to think what Lukin might do to her, and suddenly a terrible surge of hate flooded him. He wanted to kill Major Lukin. Kill him with a vengeance.

The door to the toilet opened. A sergeant in army uniform came in and began to use the urinal. After a few moments the man glanced over idly.

Slanski finished washing himself and stepped out into the station hall again. He glanced back but the sergeant hadn't followed him. He noticed a number of militia and army personnel moving through the crowd, but none of them seemed remotely interested.

He left the station quickly and walked two blocks to Kutuovsky Prospect, the charge of people and traffic in the morning rush hour almost overwhelming.

It took him almost ten minutes to find the right bus stop on the Prospect and he looked behind him before he climbed on board, but saw no one watching or following him.

The sign above the wrought-iron gates said "State Orphanage Number 57. District of Saburovo."

Lukin showed his pass to the attendant in the lodge and drove the BMW in through the gates. Pasha sat beside him in the car. He looked uncomfortable.

"You mind going in alone, Yuri? These places always give me the creeps."

"Me too. But as you wish."

When Lukin halted outside the grim four-story red-brick building and climbed out, he saw the massive front doors open. A middle-aged woman wearing a white doctor's coat came slowly down the steps. Her face was a picture of stern authority and her cold eyes studied him before she held out a limp hand.

"Major Lukin, I presume? I'm the orphanage matron."

Lukin ignored the woman's hand and showed her his ID. Her hard stare registered the affront and she inspected his ID card closely before she looked back at him.

"I must say the request your comrade lieutenant made was most unusual. No doubt you have the written authority I require?"

"I think that ought to cover everything."

Lukin handed her the signed letter from Beria. The woman's tone changed immediately.

"Why . . . of course, Comrade Major."

"My time is rather limited. The child, if you please."

"Follow me."

The matron went back up the steps, opened one of the massive doors and stepped inside. A smell of carbolic soap and stale food wafted out of the building.

As Lukin went to follow the matron up the steps, some instinct made him look up.

At a window on the second floor, two scrawny-faced young boys stared down wide-eyed at the green BMW with Pasha sitting inside. Their faces had the look of caged and frightened animals. When they saw Lukin notice them they vanished from the window.

Lukin felt a shiver down his spine as he followed the matron inside.

The dacha was in the Ramenki district, eight kilometers from Moscow.

Slanski got off the bus two stops early and walked the last five minutes down a secluded birch-lined road until he found the address.

The wooden house was big, two-story and painted green. It was set in its own large grounds surrounded by tall birch trees. There were several other dachas nearby, lining either side of the road, but judging by the shuttered windows they were deserted.

A narrow pathway led up to the dacha and there was a large woodshed off to the right toward the back.

He watched the place for five minutes, walking up and down the empty street. Because of everything that had happened he was two days early, and he wondered if the woman was home. The shutters were open but he saw no movement behind the curtained windows. He decided to risk knocking on the front door.

He walked up the pathway and knocked hard. Moments later the door opened and a woman appeared. He recognized her from Massey's description.

She looked at him cautiously. "Yes?"

"Madame Dezov?"

"Yes?"

"I'm a friend of Henri's. You were expecting me."

The woman went visibly pale. She studied Slanski for several moments, then looked out nervously into the street.

"Come inside."

She led him into a large kitchen at the back. There was a stove lit in one corner, and beyond the kitchen window Slanski saw a long broad garden dotted with withered fruit trees and bare vegetable plots.

The woman said anxiously, "You're here two days early. And there were supposed to be two of you? I was expecting a man and a woman."

Slanski looked at her. She was undeniably handsome. She had a full figure, generous hips and breasts. She wore nail varnish, and the long nails were perfectly manicured, her eyebrows plucked and darkened. He noticed she wore no wedding ring.

"I'm afraid there was a problem. My friend didn't make it."

The woman said hesitantly, "What happened?"

Slanski told her but didn't go into detail or mention Lukin. He saw the look of fear on the woman's face and said, "Don't worry, she knew nothing about you."

"Are you certain?"

"You have my word you're safe."

He looked at the woman. He realized he was more nervous than he thought and that made him suspicious. He noticed the concentration camp numbers tattooed in blue ink on her wrist, then he saw a framed photograph on the wall. It showed a man in a colonel's uniform. A hard and ugly face that looked like it had been beaten with rifle butts.

"Who's that?"

"My husband, Viktor. He was killed during the war."

"I'm sorry."

The woman laughed, then looked at the photograph with contempt.

"Don't be. The man was a pig. I wouldn't have cut him down if he was hanging. All I ever got from him was a widow's war pension and this place after he died. I only keep his picture there to remind myself how lucky I am without him. Every anniversary I get drunk and spit at it. Are you hungry?"

"Starving."

"Sit down. I'll make you something."

The woman busied herself cutting several thick slices of bread and sweaty goat's cheese. As Slanski ate ravenously she heated a pot of soup on the stove, then poured them each a glass of vodka and joined him at the table.

"You look like you've been to hell and back."

"I guess that's close enough."

"Eat and drink some more. Then I'll heat some water for you to wash and shave." The woman wrinkled her nose. "You smell worse than a cattle train. Give me your jacket and shirt for a start. There's some old things of Viktor's somewhere that should fit you."

"If the KGB took my friend to Moscow, where would they have taken her?"

The woman shrugged at the question. "The Lubyanka prison. Or Lefortovo. But most likely the Lubyanka, because it's part of KGB Headquarters. Why?"

Slanski didn't reply as he removed his jacket and shirt and stood there bare-chested as he handed them over.

"You're certain I'm safe here? What about the neighbors?"

"Perfectly safe. Most of the dachas around here are never used in winter. They're owned by army officers and Party officials." The woman smiled. "And if anyone asks, you're my cousin come to visit. Whether they believe it or not is another matter, but they won't bother us."

"I'll need transport."

The woman crossed to the stove and poured thick *soliyanka* soup into a bowl and placed it in front of Slanski, cut more bread and poured another vodka for him.

"There's an old Skoda under a tarpaulin in the woodshed. Viktor brought it back from Poland in '41, along with a mistress and a bad case of syphilis. The car still works perfectly well and the tank's full."

"Can you drive?"

The woman nodded. "I was a driver in the army during the war. I sometimes take the Skoda into the city."

"Can you show me around Moscow?"

"Will it be dangerous?"

"I doubt it. Just a nice leisurely drive to help me get my bearings. You have a map of the city?"

"An old one, from before the war."

"That'll do fine."

The woman stood. "I'll get the map. Have your soup before it gets cold."

"One more thing."

The woman looked at his face and Slanski said, "What do I call you? Madame Dezov?"

Her eyes took in his bare chest as she laughed.

"You? Anything you want. But Irena will do for now."

Moscow.
February 28th,
2 P.M.

The small park off Marx Prospect was empty that afternoon.

With its ponds and landscaped gardens and wooden pavilions, the park had once been a favorite haunt of Tsar Nicholas until the KGB had decided to acquire it for their own private use. Tall birch trees protected it from the prying eyes of passers-by and the wrought-iron gate was constantly guarded by an armed militiaman.

Lukin was sitting in the BMW outside when he saw the Emka pull up in front of the gate.

Two plain-clothes KGB men climbed out of the back. Anna Khorev was handcuffed to one of them. Someone had given her a man's overcoat and it hung loosely over her shoulders.

Lukin climbed out of the BMW and crossed to the men. "You can take off the handcuffs. That'll be all, I don't need you any more."

When the handcuffs had been removed the two men left.

Lukin saw the confusion on Anna's face. In the oversized coat she looked vulnerable. He nodded to the militiaman to open the gate, then looked back at her. "Come, let's walk."

Silver birch trees lined the narrow walks and the place was peaceful apart from the faint hum of traffic. As they strolled toward a pond, Lukin pointed to one of the wooden benches.

"Let's sit, shall we?"

He brushed away a dusting of snow and when they had sat down he looked at her. "How are you feeling?"

"Why have I been brought here?"

"Anna, I told you my job is to find Slanski dead or alive. I'm going to be honest with you and tell you so far our searches have turned up nothing. He could be dead, of course, but I believe he's still alive. He's a very resourceful fellow. By now he could even be in Moscow. You're the only one who can help me find him. I told you I'd give you time to consider your situation. But I have to be frank and tell you my superiors are becoming impatient. They want answers and they want them fast. If I can't get you to talk, then they'll use someone who will. The kind of brute I told you about."

"You're wasting your time. I told you already. I can't help you."

"Can't or won't? You know the people who helped you on your journey to Moscow. And there may be other things you know that could offer me some clue that could help me find Slanski."

"I have nothing to say."

"Anna, I'm asking you to think again. Even if Slanski is alive and in Moscow, it's impossible for him to succeed. The Kremlin or Stalin's villa can't be breached. And make no mistake, sooner or later Slanski will be caught. It would be better for your sake if you played a part in that by helping me. I know you won't break easily under pressure. Anyone who has suffered as you did has to have nerves of steel. But in the Lubyanka cellars even a strong woman would talk eventually. These people have drugs, implements of torture. They've made braver and more stubborn people than you confess to crimes they didn't even commit." He hesitated, then shook his head. "I don't want you to have to suffer that. It's not worth it, Anna. Not for someone who's going to be caught eventually."

Something in the tone of Lukin's voice made Anna look at him. That same look of compassion was discernible in his soft brown eyes.

"Do you mean it when you say you don't want me to be hurt?"

"Of course. I'm not a beast, Anna. But if I don't succeed, you'll be tortured and hurt. Much more terribly than you can imagine."

"Then if I asked you to kill me to save me from that pain, would you do that?"

"You know I couldn't do that."

"You know what I think? I think you just want me to believe that you're half human. And that way you think I'll confide in you and talk."

Lukin sighed and stood. He took a deep breath before he looked down at her. "My father, you know what he used to say? Begin with the truth. He was a principled man. Perhaps far too principled for this life. I've tried to begin with the truth. I've tried to tell you what will happen if you refuse to talk. You know that your position is impossible. But there may be a future for you if you help me."

"You know I won't be set free."

"True, but any alternative to death is a welcome one."

"What alternative?"

"If you help me, I'd ask the prosecutor to consider penal servitude in the Gulag instead of a death sentence when your case comes to court."

For a long time Anna said nothing. She looked out at the trees and the snow on the ground, then she looked back.

"Have you ever been in the Gulag, Major Lukin?"

"No."

"Then you've never seen what goes on there. I think if you did you'd know that death is a better alternative. There's nothing but brutality and hunger and slow death. You're treated worse than an animal. I can't tell you what you want to know because I really don't know where Slanski might be if he's alive. Whether you believe me or not is up to you but it's the truth. And even if I did know, I wouldn't tell you. Your friends in the cellars can do what they want, but the answer will be the same. As for those who helped us they knew nothing of Slanski's plans. To tell you their names wouldn't help you find Slanski, but simply expose them to suffering and death."

"But you can still reveal what you planned to do when you reached Moscow. You can still tell me their names."

"I'll only tell you one thing. Go to hell."

Lukin saw the angry defiance on her face as she turned away.

"I'm sorry it's come to this. I admire your bravery but I think you're being a foolish woman. Foolish because your bravery is unnecessary and foolish because you have a choice. Help me and I will try to help you. It may mean having to face a life sentence in a camp, and that's not pleasant, I agree, but it's surely better than the alternative." He paused. "But whatever your decision, I want you to have this moment."

She looked up at him and frowned. "What do you mean?"

Lukin nodded to the militiaman at the gate. A moment later Pasha appeared. A little girl clutched his hand. She was very pretty. She wore a red winter coat and a woollen hat and gloves and tiny brown boots. She looked about her uncertainly.

When Lukin turned back he saw the shock reaction on Anna Khorev's face. Disbelief and confusion, a look of both joy and pain. Her cry shattered the silence of the park.

"Sasha!"

The little girl started at the sound of her name and her face looked a mask of confusion. She stared over at her mother uncertainly, then her lips trembled and she began to cry.

Pasha let go of her. Anna ran to her daughter and swept her up. She smothered her in kisses, touched her face and stroked her hair, washed away all the confusion the child felt, until finally the little girl had stopped crying and her mother held her tightly.

For a long time Lukin stood there watching, until he could bear it no longer.

He looked at Anna. Her wet eyes met his.

He said, "You have an hour. Then we talk again."

Slanski unfolded the street map and stared out beyond the Skoda's windshield as Irena drove.

The broad boulevards of Moscow were jammed with yellow trolley buses and covered trucks spurting black clouds of exhaust. Droves of small Emka taxis whizzed by, and a few shiny black limousines, Soviet officials sitting stern-faced beside their drivers.

Irena drove the little gray Skoda erratically, paying no heed to the icy slush that covered the streets as she wove in and out of the chaos of traffic. It was anything but a leisurely drive, but Slanski noticed that most of the other vehicles seemed to be driving just as carelessly.

Irena explained that because most cars had no heaters, drivers often drank vodka to keep out the cold.

The pavements seemed crowded with a million different faces: Russians and Slavs, dark-eyed Georgians and yellow, flat-faced Tartars and Mongolians. When they reached the Arbat, the old merchant district of the city, Slanski saw the golden domes and cupolas of the Kremlin in the distance. Waves of raw plastered apartment blocks lay beyond in the suburbs on either side of the Moscow River.

They drove around the city for another half-hour, Slanski referencing the streets to the map, until Irena said, "Now what do you want me to do?"

"Drive to KGB Headquarters on Dzerzhinsky Square and drop me off."

Irena looked at him in disbelief. "Are you crazy?"

"Pick me up outside the Bolshoi Theater in an hour."

Irena shook her head in horror. "Definitely, your brain has to be missing. The KGB are looking for you and you want me to leave you outside their front door?"

"That's the last place they'll look for me."

A car honked as Irena cut recklessly across its path. She honked back and raised her arm in an angry gesture.

"Idiot!"

"What did you drive in the war, Irena? A tank?"

She looked over and smiled. "A Zis truck. Don't laugh, I was a good driver. I told you, most of the madmen on the roads are drunk. At least I'm sober."

"The war's over, so take it easy on the accelerator. The last thing we need is a militiaman troubling us for speeding."

"Bah! You can talk about trouble! You're the one who wants to be left at Dzerzhinsky Square."

The Skoda had suddenly left the Arbat and then Slanski saw the red walls and the mustard-yellow buildings of the Kremlin. On a broad cobbled street in front stood St. Basil's, its candy-colored towers soaring into the skyline. Minutes later Irena had turned into a series of narrow cobbled streets near the Bolshoi Theater and finally came out onto a massive square.

A giant metal fountain stood in the center, the water turned off in the icy temperature in case it froze and cracked the metal, and traffic and trolley buses hurtled around it. Directly across the square stood a huge seven-story yellow sandstone building.

Irena pointed to it. "Dzerzhinsky Square. KGB Headquarters. The place once belonged to an insurance company before Felix Dzerzhinsky, the head of the secret police, took it over."

Slanski saw a pair of massive brown oak doors set in the front entrance. Searchlights ringed the top and uniformed militiamen patrolled the pavement around the building.

Irena said, "The entrance to the Lubyanka prison is around the back. There's a pair of big black metal gates and security is tight—no one's ever escaped, anyone in Moscow will tell you that." She looked at Slanski's face as he studied the building. "Even if your friend's in there, you're wasting your time if you think you can rescue her. You'd be committing suicide to even try."

"Let me out over there."

He pointed to a huge wrought-iron archway on the left side of the square opposite the KGB building. A sign above the archway said "Lubyansky Arcade." The pavement was crowded with people entering and leaving the arched entrance, and beyond it Slanski saw lines of drab-looking shops down either side of the arcade.

Irena drove over and pulled in but kept the engine running. "Only the KGB could think of having a public shopping arcade next to a house of torture."

Slanski opened the passenger door. "An hour from now, at the Bolshoi."

Irena touched his arm. "Be careful."

He smiled at her as he climbed out and then he slammed the car door and moved onto the crowded pavement.

Lukin looked at Anna Khorev's face as they sat on the park bench.

She looked miserable and her eyes were red from crying. The park was empty again. Pasha had taken the little girl away. Lukin had seen the grief on Anna's face when she refused to let go of her daughter. She had clung to the child as if her life depended on her. The little girl was confused and upset and had started crying again, and the militiamen on the gate had to help Lukin hold her mother down while Pasha took the child to the car.

Tears had racked Anna Khorev's body as she saw the car drive away. Then she slumped onto the bench, inconsolable, in despair.

Lukin felt overcome by a terrible feeling of guilt. He had put her through a terrible trauma; she had not seen her daughter in well over a year. He had given her the child, and taken her away again. He imagined Nadia in such a situation, having to endure the same trauma, and he felt sick.

He understood her pain, wanted to tell her so, but knew she wouldn't believe him. It was pointless. Besides, he was becoming emotionally affected, not a good thing. He took a handkerchief from his pocket and dabbed her wet face.

She pushed him away.

He touched her arm.

"Anna, before I take you back to the Lubyanka we have to talk."

She pushed him away again.

"Don't touch me!"

Her tears had stopped but she seemed in shock, her eyes glazed, and he wondered if she had gone over the edge. There was something deeply disturbing about the look on her face and he wondered if he should take her to a doctor.

"Anna, look at me."

She didn't look back at him as she spoke, the red eyes staring into space, pain in her voice. "Why have you done this to me? Why have you put me through this?"

"No matter what happens I thought you would want to see Sasha again."

"Because I'm going to die?"

"I told you the alternative. And if you help me, I'll do all I can to make sure that you be allowed to take your daughter with you."

She looked at him, grief in her face. "And what sort of life would that be for my daughter? Living in the hell of a camp in some frozen wasteland. You think she'd survive that?"

"At least you'd be together."

"She'd survive in the orphanage. In a camp she'd be dead within a year."

Lukin sighed, not knowing whether to say it, seeing the desolation in her face. "Anna, if you don't talk, it's not only you who'll die. Sasha may die with you."

He saw her face turn white as she stared at him. "No . . . you couldn't do that. She's . . . she's only a child . . ."

Lukin stood and looked down at her.

"It's not up to me, Anna. But I know Beria. And I know Romulka, the man who will interrogate you if I fail. They'd do it if they can't make you talk. I'm going to be honest with you. Beria's given me until tomorrow night. If I fail, I hand you over to him. He'll break you, Anna, be certain of it. And once you're out of my hands I'll have no say in the matter."

He looked down at her wet eyes. "Help me, Anna. For Sasha's sake, help me find Slanski."

As Slanski walked through the crowded Lubyansky Arcade, bodies pressed in on him, people bustling past and jostling to squeeze into the tiny, drab shops that lined the arcade.

When he came out of the arcade at the far end he was in a narrow cobbled street. He turned right and came around onto the street opposite the side entrance of the west wing of KGB Headquarters. He saw another pair of tall double oak doors like those at the front, but here there was no guard. Twenty meters beyond the doors he noticed a cobbled street at the back of the KGB building. It was crowded with parked military trucks and a couple of civilian cars.

He saw a pair of massive black gates set between the stone walls and guessed it was the entrance to the Lubyanka prison. Two uniformed guards stood beside a sentry hut, rifles slung over their shoulders. Powerful search-lights ran the entire length of the top of the building and every window had steel bars.

The place looked impenetrable.

Suddenly the guards stood back and the gates swung in and a covered Zis truck thundered out and turned left into the traffic.

Slanski glimpsed a courtyard inside and ranks of parked trucks and cars and then the gates swung shut again.

As he stood there one of the guards on the gate noticed him. He turned around and walked back along the square.

One whole side of the square seemed to consist of dingy cafés and restaurants. As he passed the window of a café he saw a number of men in dark blue uniforms sitting inside. He guessed from their appearance and uniform markings that they were guards from the prison on their break.

He went inside the café and got in line to pay for a glass of tea, then took his receipt to a stoutly built woman serving behind the counter. She handed him the glass in a metal cup and he took it to a table near the prison guards.

He made a mental note of the guards' rank and uniform markings. They were a hardened-looking bunch of men, talking in whispers among themselves. He wondered if any of them were guarding Anna. If she was alive.

There was a burst of coarse laughter from behind.

When Slanski glanced around he saw a flash of color. Half a dozen small, wiry men, their Uzbek faces brown and wrinkled, were leaving their table and heading toward the door. Wisps of beards dangled from their chins and their short-cropped heads were covered in brightly colored skull caps. Some wore brightly dyed silk or cotton gowns over their shoulders and they chatted in a dialect Slanski couldn't understand. They looked like a flock of exotic birds in the drab surroundings.

He looked back at the KGB building across the street. Suddenly he heard a jabber of excited voices and saw two of the Uzbeks push their way to the window and stare out into the street. A distinctive olive-green BMW had halted at a set of traffic lights in front of the café. The Uzbeks pointed excitedly at the car and jabbered among themselves.

Slanski looked at the man and woman seated in the BMW and his blood froze.

Lukin sat in the driver's seat, Anna beside him.

Slanski could hardly believe his eyes. It was definitely Lukin. The false hand was unmistakable, but this time it was a metal hook. And Anna's face he saw clearly through the windshield.

Suddenly the traffic lights turned green and the BMW started to move. Slanski stood up frantically and pushed past the Uzbeks, knocking one of them over in his race toward the door.

As he stepped out, the BMW was already moving away toward the back of Dzerzhinsky Square and the entrance to the Lubyanka.

Slanski broke into a run. He was hardly aware of passers-by staring at him; he was like a man possessed as he chased after the BMW, wanting to wrench Lukin from the car, shoot him, grab Anna and run.

Up ahead now the BMW halted in the middle of the road, the right indicator on as it waited for a break in the oncoming traffic to turn into the cobbled street that led to the Lubyanka.

Slanski kept running along the pavement, pushing through the crowds, his eyes on the car.

Fifty meters.

Forty.

He saw Lukin's fingers tapping the steering wheel impatiently.

Tapping.

Tapping.

Thirty meters.

Twenty.

He moved out onto the road and as he ran he kept his eyes on Lukin, watched the fingers still tapping on the steering wheel, waiting for the traffic to let him pass.

Ten meters.

Close enough to get a shot.

He wrenched the Tokarev from his inside pocket.

At the angle he approached the BMW he could see only the back of Anna's head, but he saw Lukin's face clearly, and hate raged inside him like an inferno.

Five meters.

Lukin still hadn't turned to see him.

Slanski cocked and aimed the Tokarev.

Suddenly a truck coming in the opposite direction screeched to a halt. Slanski saw the truck driver stare in disbelief at the gun.

Just as he reached the BMW, Lukin applied a burst of power, thinking the truck driver was stopping for him. The BMW screeched forward and accelerated as it swung right toward the massive black gates of the prison.

One of the guards hammered on the gates and they swung open and the car disappeared inside.

Slanski caught a glimpse of Anna's face before the guards swung the gates shut again.

He swore as he quickly put the gun away.

Too late.

The Gates of Hell had opened and closed and swallowed her up.

45

Henri Lebel opened his eyes.

Not that it mattered much because it was dark. For a while he lay there, his body so stiff he couldn't even feel that the hard wooden bed under him had no mattress. Whatever was in the syringe had knocked him out cold for a long time. And then something clicked in his head and he was filled with a terrible unease.

He got to his feet shakily, took a cautious step forward and bumped into a stone wall. He stepped back and turned, took three paces, his hand outstretched, and felt another wall. Four hesitant paces to the left took him to a metal door.

He was in a cell, no question.

He stumbled his way back to the wooden bed and sat down, overcome by a dreadful feeling of doom. The same black feelings he had endured in Auschwitz returned.

He remembered what had happened at the club. What did the colonel named Romulka want? But Lebel knew, and that thought filled him with an even greater dread. He should never have got involved in this. Never. He had signed his own death warrant. Or something worse than death—harsh imprisonment in a labor camp.

As his body shook with fear he suddenly heard voices outside, feet scraping on concrete, and a light burst on overhead, blinding him, as the cell door opened.

He blinked and saw Romulka step into the cell.

"So, our sleeping beauty is awake."

"Where am I? What's the meaning of this outrage?" Lebel demanded.

"To answer your first question, you're in the Lubyanka prison."

Lebel looked at Romulka in disbelief.

"As to the second, I think the reason for your presence ought to be obvious."

Lebel shook his head. "I . . . I don't know what you're talking about."

"Really, Lebel, you're wasting my time. I know all about your connection to Massey. So let's put the pretense aside and get down to business, shall we? My time is limited." He stepped closer. He held a riding crop in his left hand and he put the tip of it under Lebel's chin.

"Your intention in Moscow was to help a certain couple. I want to know how, when and where you were to meet them and who your accomplices are."

"You're out of your mind."

"Something else disturbs me that's turned up in my investigation. A man named Braun who used to work for us, who's now unfortunately dead. You made certain inquiries about him from an employee at the Soviet Embassy in Paris in return for a considerable sum of francs. Do you deny it?"

Despite his best effort, Lebel went noticeably pale. "I really don't know what you're talking about. This is some sort of conspiracy—"

The riding crop flicked back and struck Lebel a stinging blow on the face. He cried out and put his hand to his cheek. He felt a gash and saw blood on his fingers.

"How dare you. You have no right to treat me like this. I have important connections in Moscow. I demand to see the French Ambassador."

Romulka's crop prodded his chest. "Shut up, you filthy little Jew, and listen to me. You can demand all you like but I want answers and I want them quick. Talk, and I have you back in Paris on a plane before you can say good-bye. Refuse, and I'll grind you to dust. Understand? Now, are you going to talk?"

"I told you . . . I don't know what you're talking about . . . You're making a dreadful mistake."

"Very well, play it your way." Romulka turned and snapped his fingers. "In here."

Two brutal-faced men in black KGB uniforms came through the door and crowded into the cell. They each grabbed Lebel by the arms.

Romulka said, "Take him down to the cellars. A little Lubyanka hospitality ought to soften him up."

"I tell you, this is a mistake!"

As Lebel protested, Romulka smashed a fist hard into his face, and the men dragged him from the cell.

Lukin stood at his apartment window.

Across the river he saw the lights of the late evening traffic moving across Kalinin Bridge, headlights probing the thin icy fog that had descended on Moscow.

Nine P.M.

He had arrived home an hour ago, needing to get away from headquarters and from the powerful grip of hopelessness he felt crushing him.

And he needed to see Nadia.

She had made supper for them both, soup and cold sausage and a half-liter of Georgian wine. The wine had lifted his spirits just a little but now its effect had worn off and he felt wretched again.

To make matters worse he had hardly spoken to Nadia during the meal.

He saw her reflection in the window as she cleared away the supper plates. She looked over at him for a moment, then went into the kitchen. When she came out again he was still standing at the window.

"Yuri."

He looked around absentmindedly. She stood watching him. She wore a cardigan over her shoulders, and as she brushed a strand of hair from her face, she said, "You hardly touched your food."

Lukin smiled weakly. "The soup was good. I just wasn't hungry. I'm sorry, my love."

"Come. Sit with me."

She went to sit on the couch. Her brow was creased in a worried frown and the corners of her mouth were turned down with tension. He hadn't helped to improve her mood. His own was worse. He felt desperate, totally lost.

Anna Khorev still hadn't talked. And now there was nothing he could do to save her. That prospect troubled him.

The roadblocks and the searches to find the Wolf had turned up nothing. If the man was still alive, Lukin felt certain he was in Moscow. But where? And how did you scour a city of five million souls?

Nadia's voice brought him back. "Sit beside me, Yuri."

Lukin went to sit next to her on the couch. She touched his arm. "This is the first time I've seen you in four days. But you're not really here in spirit, are you, Yuri? Is there anything you need to talk about?"

Lukin reached for her hand and kissed it. He never talked to his wife about his work. It was a rule he had made with himself. But right now he had a powerful urge to tell her everything and lighten the terrible weight that crushed him.

"I'm sorry, my love. It's not something I can talk about."

"I understand. But you worry me, Yuri."

"Why?"

"Because whatever's troubling you is tearing you apart. I've never seen you like this before. Distracted. Lost. Dejected. You're like a different man."

He let out a deep sigh of frustration and stood. His body ached all over. He had gone almost three nights without sleep. He looked down at his wife and shook his head.

"Please. Not now, Nadia."

"What time do you have to leave?"

"Six A.M."

She stood. Her hand gently touched his face, then fell away. "You're exhausted. You need to sleep. Let's go to bed."

* * *

Lukin went into the bedroom, undressed and got into bed.

When Nadia came in she removed her clothes and lay down beside him. He felt the heat of her body as she snuggled up close, her small, hard nipples brushing against his bare chest.

"The baby is kicking. Can you feel it, Yuri?"

He laid his hand on his wife's belly and felt the rise, and then suddenly a feeling like a sharp jolt. He put his head on Nadia's stomach and kissed her bump.

For a long time, as he lay there silently, Nadia's hand stroking his hair, he thought of Anna Khorev in the park that afternoon. Her screams when they took her daughter away. The memory playing over and over in his mind until it almost crushed him and he felt smothered by a wave of remorse. He sighed, a long, troubled sigh.

Nadia whispered, "Tell me, Yuri. For God's sake, tell me what's troubling you before it breaks your heart."

For several long moments he didn't speak, then he said, "I can't. Please, don't ask me."

He heard the anguish in his own voice and then her arms went around his neck and she held him close.

Something seemed to break then, like a dam bursting inside his head. His whole body shook and his shoulders trembled.

In the darkness he heard himself crying, for Anna Khorev, for Nadia, for his unborn child, for himself.

Slanski sat in the kitchen at the back of the dacha. Irena sat facing him. She had returned from Moscow in the Skoda minutes before, carrying a large shopping bag and looking exhausted.

Slanski said, "OK, tell me what you got."

She searched in her pocket and placed a slip of paper on the table. "The most important thing first. Have a look at that."

He picked up the slip of paper, read what was written on it, and smiled. "Did you have any problems?"

"There were over a dozen Yuri Lukins listed in the city telephone directory in the post office in Gorky Street. I called them all just to be certain, but when I got to the last I was pretty sure I might have got the right one."

"How?"

"A woman answered. I asked for Major Yuri Lukin. She said he wasn't there and asked who was calling. I said I was with the army pensions office. Some of our files had got mislaid and I was trying to trace a Major Yuri Lukin who had served with the Third Guards Division of cavalry during the war. She said it couldn't have been her husband; he was certainly a major but he hadn't served with the army. I apologized for calling the wrong number and put down the phone. Only one other Major Yuri Lukin turned up in all the calls I made. But he was attached to an artillery battalion in Moscow."

"What happened then?"

"I went to the address given in the phone book. It's an apartment off the Kutuzovsky Prospect. I spoke to one of the neighbors' children. It must be the same Lukin. He drives a green German BMW. And the long and the short of it is, he's married with a wife and no kids. The apartment is on the second floor."

"Good. Did you get to see his wife?"

"Are you joking? I wasn't going to knock on the door and let her see my face. That might've been tempting fate too far." She hesitated. "You're a very brave man but something tells me this could get us both killed."

Slanski shook his head. "Relax, Irena. You're not going to be in any real danger."

"What you're going to do is still crazy and you're playing with fire. You said your friend in the Lubyanka knew nothing. Why try and rescue her?"

"Because the plan's simple and with a little luck it can work. Just open the bag, Irena. You got everything I asked?"

She opened the bag and spread the contents on the table. "It wasn't easy. But you can get anything you want on the black market once you have the money."

"Let me have a look."

He examined everything carefully. There was a heavy-duty army flashlight with two sets of batteries, several thin ropes and an army penknife. There was a hypodermic syringe and two small glass bottles, one of clear glass and the other opaque brown. He picked up both. They each contained clear liquid. He examined them, then put them down again.

"You did better than I hoped. Had you any trouble getting these?"

"The Adrenalin and the hypodermic were easy enough." She picked up the brown bottle of liquid. "But this was difficult. Ether isn't easy to come by. It cost two hundred rubles. I could live for a month on that."

Slanski smiled. "I'll remember you in my will. Did anyone ask why you needed this stuff?"

She laughed. "Are you joking? The gangsters in the Moscow black market would deal with the devil himself if he had a wallet full of rubles. And they keep their mouths shut. A loose tongue means a trip to the Gulag or the firing squad."

"What about the rest of the things?"

"Viktor's old uniform I've taken in so it should fit. The divisional markings are probably out of date but you'll have to live with that. Considering what you're going to do, Viktor is probably turning in his grave right now and it serves the bastard right."

"The man didn't deserve you. Thanks, Irena."

"I must be mad to go along with this."

He had explained everything to Irena that afternoon because he needed her help. He had lost his chance to rescue Anna but now he had a plan. A simple plan. When he told Irena she had turned pale.

"*What*? Now I know you're really insane." She had shaken her head resolutely. "I'm not getting involved. If you want to risk your life, you go ahead. Me, I'm taking enough risks as it is. I don't want more trouble."

"There won't be any trouble if you do as I tell you."

When she still refused, Slanski said, "The woman's your passport out of here. You think Lebel is going to like it when you turn up without her?"

Irena had hesitated then, doubt on her face. It had taken Slanski another half an hour to convince her and to go over the details of the plan, but even though she still didn't like it, in the end she reluctantly agreed.

"On one condition," she demanded. "If it fails, you forget about her and I leave Moscow alone."

"Agreed."

The plan had come to him as he walked back to the Bolshoi. The image that kept coming into his mind was of Lukin sitting there in the car, tapping the steering wheel impatiently with his fingers. And then Slanski remembered the ring. A gold wedding ring on his hand. Major Yuri Lukin was married. He had a weak point that could be exploited. If the plan worked Anna would be free and Lukin dead.

If it worked.

He glanced at his watch and looked back at Irena.

"You'd better get some sleep. We've got a busy day tomorrow." He saw the fear and strain on her face. "Thanks for helping."

"You know what I think?"

"What?"

"I think maybe you love this woman."

Moscow.
March 1st

Lukin arrived at Dzerzhinsky Square the next morning at six.

While he drank his first coffee of the morning, he spread out the map of Moscow and laid several sheets of paper on his desk. He looked at the map. If the Wolf was in Moscow, as he suspected, people had to be helping him. Perhaps Romulka was right about the Frenchman, Lebel. He had phoned Romulka's office the previous evening but so far he had not returned the call. He would deal with that later. Right now there were other avenues to explore.

He spread the sheets of paper in front of him. They were lists of names of dissidents, mostly Jews, known supporters of the émigré groups. If any group were suspect and likely to be involved, it was this one. Eight pages that contained 312 names and addresses. It was a mammoth task to check them all, search their homes and pull them in for questioning, but it had to be done. Some of the people on the lists had already endured harsh prison sentences. Others were allowed to remain free but were secretly watched by the KGB and informers.

There was the chance, of course, that whoever was helping Slanski wasn't even on the list at all, and at this thought Lukin sighed. The hotels in the city still had to be checked, but he doubted that Slanski would be so foolish as to stay in a hotel. It was too public, a guest had to register, and besides, there weren't that many hotels in Moscow in which to hide. But they would have to be eliminated. He considered visiting the woman's cell again, but felt it was pointless. In the meantime, he had to do *something*.

He would need at least fifty men to check the hotels and pick up all those on the list.

As he reached for the telephone to call the rostering office, the door opened and a tired-looking Pasha came in. He had stayed through the night in case any news came in from Leningrad. Lukin put down the phone as Pasha went to sit in the chair opposite, put his feet on the desk, flung off his cap and yawned.

Lukin said, "Any news?"

Pasha shook his head and ran a hand over his face. "Not a whisper. It's been as quiet as the grave. Apart from a visit from Romulka, that is."

Lukin sat up. "What happened?"

"He turned up last night. Said to tell you he had a Frenchman named Lebel. Who the hell's he?"

Lukin explained and Pasha said, "Who knows? Romulka might be right. He also said he wanted to see the woman."

"And?"

"And I wouldn't let him. I told him he'd have to see you first. He said he's going to put me on report. But I say fuck it, the mood he was in he would have probably done her damage. Let Romulka crawl to Beria and moan all he likes. What can they do, send me to a labor camp? Where I come from, it gets much colder and the food's no worse."

"Thanks, Pasha." Lukin guessed that Romulka had ignored his phone call because of Pasha's refusal. "How is she?"

"Awake, last time I looked."

"How does she seem?"

"Like someone switched the lights off inside her heart."

"You tried to talk with her?"

Pasha nodded. "Sure, like you asked. I brought her some food and coffee last night and this morning. But she just sits there, saying nothing and staring at the walls." He sighed. "You really think she'll talk?"

"God only knows, but somehow I doubt it. And I don't have much time left. The question is, can she really help us? I doubt it somehow. I get the feeling she may not know where Slanski is, as she claims. The problem is, that means we're going to have to hand her over to Beria soon. It wouldn't be beyond him to harm the child to make her talk. We have to find Slanski, if only for the child's sake."

Pasha stood. "Whatever happens, either way the woman's dead. You know that, Yuri. Beria won't send her to a camp. He'll kill her."

Lukin said solemnly, "I know."

"What happens now?" asked Pasha.

Lukin told him what he intended. "It may turn up something, but I wouldn't count on it."

Pasha said, "I've been thinking about the missing pages in the Wolf's file. If we could see the original, maybe there's something in there that could help us. Relatives he had in Moscow, friends of his family he might be tempted to approach if he's desperate."

"I already asked Beria. He said no. If Beria doesn't want you to see everything in a file, you don't see it."

Pasha grinned. "True, but there are other ways to crack a nut."

"How? The Archives office is out of bounds without a permit. There are sensitive files kept there, top-secret files. A man could lose his head if he's caught."

"The Chief of Archives is a Mongol. He drinks like a camel after a month without water. I could get him drunk and borrow his keys and have a look for the original."

"Forget it, Pasha, it's too risky, and it's unlikely the Wolf would use such people in Moscow. He's been away too long."

"How about I simply ask the Chief?"

Lukin shook his head. "I told you what Beria said. His word is law. And there's probably nothing much in there relevant to the case. Besides, it isn't worth it if you're caught riffling through files without permission. Forget it."

Pasha shrugged. "If you say so."

It was dark as the Skoda pulled up on Kutuzovsky Prospect just before seven that morning.

Slanski climbed out dressed in the major's uniform and said to Irena, "You know what to do. I'll be as quick as I can."

"Good luck."

He watched as Irena drove off and then he walked back along the street. There was hardly any traffic but the trolley buses were running, blue sparks illuminating the morning darkness as they whirred along the Prospect. He could make out the numbers of the big old apartment houses under the porch lights and he counted them off as he walked.

Number 27 looked much like its neighbors. It was a big old granite four-story residence from the Tsar's time, which had obviously once been the home of a wealthy family but was now converted into apartments. There was no sign of the olive-green BMW outside in the street.

Slanski saw that the blue-painted entrance door was open and walked up the front garden path. He saw the names and numbers of the occupants written on small white cards above recessed letter-boxes inside on the porch.

Apartment 14 sported the name Lukin. He pushed open the front door and stepped into a long dark hallway.

A stairway led up from the hall and there was a faint wash of light from one of the upstairs landings. The hallway smelled of lavender polish. Two bicycles were stood against a wall, and he heard muffled voices somewhere off in the building.

He climbed the stairs up to the second floor. The landing light was on and he saw the door, number 14 stenciled on the wood. No name, just the number. He examined the locks. Two. One top, one bottom. He put his ear to the door but heard no sound from inside. He guessed Lukin's wife was still sleeping.

He went down the stairs again and walked around to the rear of the apartment block. The side path had been freshly swept of snow. There was a long communal garden at the back, covered in a blanket of white. A lamp was on, illuminating a paved walkway. There were a couple of wrought-iron summer benches set under bare cherry trees and some overgrown melon patches under a small glasshouse partly covered by snow.

He looked at the back of the block. There were some lights on but the curtains were still closed. At the end of the garden he saw a wooden door set in a crumbling granite wall. He guessed it led to an alleyway at the back. He went down the path and saw that the door was almost rotted through. He pushed. It barely moved and he had to kick away the snow piled at the bottom before the wood budged. The door opened onto an alleyway behind the house, as he had expected. It was dark and appeared deserted, but to the left and right at the end of the alleyway he saw street lights. He guessed the alleyway led to side streets off Kutuzovsky Prospect.

He stepped back into the garden and went halfway up the path.

He looked up at the second floor, counting off the windows until he guessed that number 14 was situated to the right of the middle. There were no lights on behind the curtain and he walked back around to the front of the building.

As he walked back down the front path suddenly a voice behind him said, "Can I help you, comrade?"

Slanski turned and froze. An old man stood just inside the porch. He wore a greasy black peasant's cap and a patched overcoat with string tied around the waist, a thick woollen scarf around his neck. He looked like he wasn't long up, his eyes red raw, and he had a garden broom and some twigs and dead leaves in his hands.

Slanski smiled. "I'm looking for an old friend of mine."

"Really. And who would that be?"

He guessed the man was the block janitor. A pair of cautious eyes stared at him suspiciously.

"Major Lukin. I believe he's in apartment fourteen."

"He's a friend of yours, is he?" The old man took in the uniform shoulder boards.

"From the war, comrade. I haven't seen him in years. I'm on leave in Moscow. Just got in from Kiev this morning on the overnight train. Is the major at home?"

"He left early, I'd say. His car's not here. You ought to find him at Dzerzhinsky Square. But his wife ought to be back soon. She usually goes shopping early on Saturday mornings to the vegetable market. She gets back before eight."

"Of course, Yuri's wife. I'm afraid I can't remember her name?"

The old man gave a cackled laugh as he leaned on his broom handle. "Nadia. A redhead. Good-looker."

Slanski smiled back. "That's her. Lukin did all right for himself." He looked at his watch. "I'll call back later. But do me a favor. If you see Nadia, don't tell her I called. I'd like to surprise her. You know how it is."

The old man winked as he touched his cap. "As the major wishes."

Slanski tapped him on the shoulder and looked down at the swept path. "You're doing a fine job here, comrade. Keep up the good work."

Slanski walked back and crossed over to the other side of the street. A café stood fifty meters beyond. The lights were on and he went inside.

It was a dismal-looking place but full of early morning workers. Taxi and tram drivers and sleepy-looking shop girls from the stores along Kutuzovsky Prospect having coffee or breakfast. It smelled of rancid food and stale cigarette smoke and everyone in it looked bored to death or half asleep.

It took him almost ten minutes to get a glass of tea. He found a free table by the window.

He sat smoking a cigarette. The street lamps were on and the light was reasonable, so he had a good view of the apartment block across the street. The old janitor was still clearing away debris from the front garden, but ten minutes later he disappeared into the building.

Meeting the old man had been a help—now he had the name of Lukin's wife and a brief description—but he could also be a problem. If he didn't stay out of the way, Slanski would have to deal with him, and he hoped to avoid complicating things.

It was fifteen minutes later when he saw the woman across the street. He didn't notice her red hair at first because she wore a fur hat, but when she turned into the pathway he spotted the flame-red color at the nape of her neck. She carried a heavy shopping basket and was dressed in a fur-collared coat and knee boots. From the brief glimpse he had of her face she looked pretty. He watched her go in the front door.

He sat in the café for another five minutes, waiting to see if the janitor reappeared. He didn't, and Slanski crushed out his cigarette and stood up.

He crossed the street briskly, and when he rounded the corner nearest the apartment block he saw Irena sitting in the parked Skoda, a woollen scarf partly covering her face. The Skoda's license plates were muddied and unreadable.

He tapped on the passenger window and he saw her start as she looked around, then she opened the door for him and he climbed inside.

Irena looked frozen. "What kept you? I was beginning to get worried you weren't coming back."

"Lukin's wife was out. I think she's just come back. She's alone, so far as I can tell."

"What if she isn't?"

"Let me worry about that. I'll just have to play the cards as they fall. There's an alleyway around the next corner that leads to the back of the apartment block."

Irena nodded. "I saw it."

"A door leads out from the garden. It's about midway along. Wait for me at this end of the alleyway."

"What if someone asks me what I'm doing there?"

"Just tell them the car's broken down and you're waiting for a friend. Keep the scarf covering your face."

He saw the doubtful look on her face and smiled. "Trust me."

"You're a crazy man, and I don't know why but I do."

"See you soon."

He stepped out of the Skoda and walked back around to the front of number 27.

He went up the path and still saw no sign of the janitor. He climbed the stairs to the second-floor landing.

He took the bottle of ether out of his pocket and uncorked the top. He doused a handkerchief with a splash of the liquid. The pungent vapor was sickly and overpowering and he quickly stuffed the bottle and the handkerchief back in his pockets. He checked that his holster flap was undone and left the safety off. He knocked on the door.

The woman appeared almost at once. It was the same woman he had seen go up the path. Red-haired, pretty. She had removed her coat and wore a dress and cardigan and a kitchen apron. When she opened the door she frowned slightly at the sight of the uniform, but when Slanski smiled she smiled back and wiped her hands on her apron.

"Yes?"

Slanski glanced over her shoulder. The narrow hallway behind her looked empty.

"Madame Lukin? Nadia Lukin?"

"Yes."

At that moment Slanski pushed in the door and lunged at the woman.

As she started to scream his hand went over her mouth and he kicked the door shut behind him.

Lukin was standing at the office window shortly before noon, smoking a cigarette, when he saw the gates in the courtyard below swing open and two Zis trucks drive in and brake to a halt on the cobbles. Plain-clothes KGB men and uniformed militia jumped down and began to force a crowd of civilian prisoners from the trucks, beating them with rifle butts.

As he stood watching there was a knock on the door. "Enter."

Pasha came in, his eyes bloodshot from lack of sleep. "I thought I'd see how the men were making out with the city hotels."

"Any luck?"

"They've covered half on the list but nothing so far."

Lukin nodded down into the courtyard as the trucks disgorged their cargo. "What's going on down there?"

Pasha came to the window and looked down. "More work for the bully boys in the cellars, by the look of it. They're the people on the dissident lists being brought in for questioning. The rest are still being rounded up. The interrogation teams will let us know if anything turns up. We should have everyone on the lists covered by tonight. The men are working flat out."

Lukin sighed and nodded. "Hardly quick enough. OK, keep checking the hotels. When you're finished, I want you to have the men check all the co-operative guest houses to within a twenty-kilometer radius of Moscow."

"Yuri, there must be hundreds . . ."

"And I want them checked, Pasha. All of them. And another thing . . ." Lukin nodded down at the courtyard. "Tell whoever's in charge below to go easy on the prisoners. They're citizens, not cattle for the slaughter."

"As you say." Pasha nodded and left.

Lukin looked at his watch. Another twelve hours and Anna Khorev's time was up. If she didn't talk soon, he'd have to deliver her to Beria and face him himself. He'd have to try to interrogate her again.

The door burst open without a knock.

Romulka stood there grinning."I thought I'd find you here. Well, Lukin, any progress?"

"Not as yet. What do you want?"

"Just a friendly chat."

"The prisoner, Lebel, where is he?"

"Odd, but that's what I came to see you about. Right now he's in one of the cellars being softened up."

"I told you to be careful, Romulka. The man has connections. I want to see him."

Romulka shook his head. "I'm afraid not, Lukin. The Frenchman is mine. And Beria will tell you that if you care to ask."

"As officer in charge I demand it."

Romulka stepped closer and tapped the riding crop in his palm. "Demand all you like. Of course, we could always come to an agreement. Let me interrogate the woman and you get access to Lebel in return."

"Go to hell."

Romulka grinned. "A pity. I would have enjoyed a little fun with her. Still, another twelve hours and she'll be mine."

"You're the lowest form of life, Romulka."

"A matter of opinion, surely? Think about the offer, Lukin. And remember, it's not my life at stake, it's yours."

With that he went out of the door. Lukin returned to the window and bit back his anger.

He heard more vehicles entering the courtyard. Another two Zis trucks pulled up and this time a couple of militiamen tied back the canvas flaps and jumped down. As they unslung their rifles, a group of frightened-looking men and women prisoners began to climb out of the trucks. One of the women fell to her knees and a militiaman struck her across the face with his rifle.

As Lukin went to turn away in frustration, he saw Pasha cross the courtyard and have words with the sergeant in charge.

So many people were going to suffer unnecessarily because of the Wolf. Many would end up in prison or the Gulags. Some would die.

He shook his head and rubbed his eyes. He had slept badly last night, tossed and turned for four hours, and his mood had upset Nadia. He wanted to forget he had ever become part of this nightmare. But he *had* to get the woman to talk.

As he reached for his cap, the telephone jangled. He picked it up.

A man's voice said, "Major Lukin?"

"Yes, this is Lukin."

There was a pause, then the voice said, "Major, we need to talk."

47

Lukin saw the white plaster walls of Novodevichy Convent in the wash of the BMW's headlights. As he swung around onto the entrance road and braked to a halt, his heart was pounding in his chest.

He switched off the engine, doused the lights, and stepped out.

The gilded onion domes of the deserted convent rose up into the twilight. A frozen river lay at the rear and he walked down toward it. Blood hammered in his temples and his body was drenched in perspiration.

When he reached the river he found the bench near the edge of the bank and sat. There was a small birch wood behind him and he peered anxiously over his shoulder but saw nothing except the dark outline of trees and bushes.

His mind was on fire.

"Novodevichy Convent," the note said. "Be at the east wall, the second bench by the river at three o'clock. Come alone and unarmed or you don't see your wife alive again."

No signature on the note but he had no doubt it was Slanski.

It was almost three o'clock now and darkness was falling.

Two minutes after the call to his office, Lukin had driven frantically to his apartment.

The man's voice on the telephone had said, "*We need to talk.*"

"Who is this?"

"An acquaintance of yours from Tallinn, Major Lukin. I've left a message for you at your home."

And then the line clicked dead.

At first Lukin had been confused, and then a terrible realization dawned and he felt an icy chill go through him—it was Slanski, it had to be. He felt a surge of fear and cold rage.

No. It wasn't possible!

Nadia.

If Slanski had harmed Nadia . . .

He had left the office in a daze. Ten minutes later he was bounding up the steps to his apartment. When he unlocked the door there was a pungent smell in the hallway. A handkerchief lay tossed on the floor, a small brown bottle beside it.

He called out Nadia's name and when he got no answer he felt his stomach sink.

He picked up the handkerchief and moved into the rooms. A flowerpot and stand had been knocked over. There had been a struggle here, Lukin was in no doubt. He was shaking with rage and fear, consumed with worry for Nadia. *God, don't let her be harmed.*

He put the handkerchief to his nose and sniffed the pungent smell.

Ether.

He checked the bedroom—empty—then moved into the kitchen. He saw the note on the table. He read it and turned even paler, and his body shook. He raced back down the stairs to look for the block janitor. He found him in the boiler room, drinking vodka.

Yes, a man had called, early that morning. Tall, blond, smiled a lot. Said he knew you. Friend from the war, he said. When your wife wasn't here he said he wanted to call back and surprise her. Why? Is everything all right, Major Lukin? You look pale, Major Lukin.

Lukin had looked at the old man distractedly and lied. "Yes . . . yes, fine. Thank you. I imagine they've gone somewhere together."

He went back upstairs and sat at the kitchen table for almost an hour, wondering what to do next.

Nothing.

He could do nothing until he met Slanski.

He felt a livid urge to kill the man. If he harmed a hair on Nadia's head he'd tear him apart.

What if she had been hurt? What if Slanski had injured her?

God . . . let her be safe. She's all I have.

And then another thought: how had Slanski known where he lived? Had he been watching him? Had he simply found his address from the city telephone directory? Lukin was too confused to think straight. He left the question aside. All that mattered was Nadia's safety.

He imagined Nadia hurt, Nadia ill, Nadia frightened and locked up somewhere, and he almost drove himself insane with worry.

He had to stop it. He went into the bathroom, splashed icy water on his face. The mood wouldn't go away. God, he wanted to destroy Slanski.

Why had Nadia been taken?

Why?

And then he understood.

Slanski wanted to trade. Nadia for Anna Khorev.

It was so obvious that in his turmoil he hadn't seen it.

But that would be impossible.

It was two hours later when Lukin left the apartment. Slanski had chosen his meeting place well. Novodevichy Convent was deserted, the nuns long ago shot or deported to the penal camps.

And as Lukin sat by the frozen river, he tried hard to control himself. Would the Wolf come himself or send someone?

He heard the rustle behind him and turned.

A man stepped out of the shadows. He wore a long dark overcoat and his face was visible in the twilight. Slanski. He held a Tokarev pistol in his right hand.

Rage erupted inside Lukin. He felt an overpowering urge to rush Slanski and wrench the gun from his hand.

"Where's my wife?"

"Stay where you are. Don't move and don't talk."

Slanski reached over and his free hand searched Lukin's body.

Lukin said, "I'm unarmed."

"Shut up."

When Slanski finished he stepped back. Lukin said again, "My wife, where is she?"

"She's safe. For now. But her safety really depends on you."

"What do you want?"

"I want Anna Khorev. And I want her tonight."

Lukin felt sweat drip down his back. He shook his head. "That's impossible. I can't release her, I don't have the authority. You must know that."

"Don't lie to me, Lukin. You can do anything you want."

"I couldn't release her without permission. It's impossible."

"Impossible or not, you bring her here tonight. Eight o'clock. Just you and her. You tell no one what you're doing. My people will be watching you every step of the way. Just like we watched you taking her into the Lubyanka this afternoon. And these are the rules—you fail me, or try anything foolish, you won't see your wife again. Is that understood?"

Lukin was numb with shock. Slanski had him watched. In the middle of Moscow this American had *him* watched. He felt the anger flare inside him and clenched his teeth.

"I have a condition."

"No conditions."

"You bring my wife here tonight. I get her back when I hand over the prisoner. You agree or I don't bring the girl."

"I'll think about it."

Lukin shook his head. "No, no thinking. You agree or you don't. I don't trust you."

"Very well. But remember the rules. You do anything foolish, you get no second chances."

"And you understand. When this is over, I'm going to find you and I'm going to kill you."

Slanski grinned."But you'll have to catch me first." He pointed the Tokarev in Lukin's face. "Close your eyes, tightly. Count to twenty. Nice and slow."

Lukin shut his eyes. Silence. Cold. But not feeling the icy air; his anger boiling, like a furnace inside his head. A wind whistled through branches.

He counted to twenty.

When he snapped open his eyes the Wolf was gone.

The Lenin Hills were covered in a patina of white as Lukin parked the BMW on the rise of a hill and climbed out. He ran the rest of the way to the top of the hill.

In the valley below, Moscow was a million winking lights. When he reached the top he knelt, panting, in the snow. His body shook. So close to Slanski. So close and he couldn't kill him. He felt he was losing his grip, his mind throbbing with confusion as the image of Nadia raged through it.

He felt hopelessly lost.

The Wolf was clever. Very, very clever.

He smashed his fist into the snow. He wanted to scream but closed his eyes instead, opened them again, blinked several times.

Whichever way he looked at it, he was dead.

By releasing Anna Khorev he was signing his own death warrant. Perhaps Nadia's also.

How could he explain to Beria? *How?*

The man would never listen.

There had to be a way out of this—had to be. He just couldn't see it.

How had Slanski known where he lived? How had he known about him taking the woman out of the Lubyanka that morning?

Slanski had to have help in Moscow. And the man was far more capable than he ever imagined.

Lukin drew a deep breath, let it out sharply. He tried to think furiously but his head felt like a block of ice. Not responding.

Think.

Think.

He forced himself to think hard, until the action was like an ache in the top of his skull. A wind raged across the hill. The icy chill gouged at his eyes, but his mind was racing now, as a plan started to form in his head.

It was dangerous, very dangerous, but it was his only hope. If it went wrong, he and Nadia were dead. They were dead anyway if he released the woman.

This way they stood some chance. He had to risk it.

He checked his watch. Four P.M. He had enough time to do what he needed to do before taking Anna Khorev from the Lubyanka to the convent.

He turned and started to race back down the hill.

Austria.

The hilly streets of the old wine town of Grinzing in the Vienna woods were busy that Sunday afternoon, the cosy restaurants and taverns crammed with off-duty Allied occupation troops and Viennese couples enjoying their first spring weekend.

Gratchev stepped off the number 38 tram and crossed the street. The snow lay thin on the ground but the air was crisp and dry and he walked for several minutes until he reached the tavern near the end of the town. When he was satisfied he hadn't been followed, he stepped inside.

The place was crowded and there was a three-man ensemble with accordions and zither playing lively Austrian folk music as they moved through the noisy tavern. Gratchev made a face. He hated that sort of fucking music and the sound did nothing to improve his mood.

He recognized the handsome, dark-haired woman seated alone in a wooden booth. It had been a year since they had last met and her slim, firm body still brought out an urge in him. She smiled when she saw him but Gratchev didn't smile back.

He crossed over and eased his bulk into the seat opposite. He was short and stockily built with bushy eyebrows and, like most men used to a lifetime of wearing a military uniform, he wore his civilian clothes uncomfortably.

The woman said, "It's good to see you, Volya."

Gratchev looked at her and grunted. "I wish I could say the same."

"What's it to be? Vodka?"

"These days I prefer American bourbon. Ice and water."

The woman called the waiter and ordered their drinks. When the waiter had gone she lit a cigarette and offered her companion one.

Gratchev accepted the cigarette. "What made you pick this place?"

The woman smiled. "Everybody's too busy getting drunk to pay any attention to two old friends talking. Besides, your people watch the city."

"True enough. So what's this about?"

The waiter returned with their drinks and as the woman lit his cigarette she looked at her companion's face. It was a lived-in face. Deep lines like scars on his jaws and forehead and the narrow Slavic eyes that were dark and unpredictable. A Russian face, no question. Deep and brooding, but with a touch of humor, wrinkles at the corners of the man's mouth from smiling. But he wasn't smiling now.

She said, "You got my message?"

"Would I be here if I hadn't?" He looked at his watch dismissively. "I presume you didn't come to talk pleasantries, Eva. I'm supposed to be at an opera matinée. It finishes at five and I've got to be back at the base by six. I had to tell my driver I was seeing a certain lady acquaintance. It cost me a bottle of vodka to keep his mouth shut. And even that's compromising. So tell me why you're here."

The woman leaned forward. "I have a favor to ask, Volya."

"I guessed as much." The Russian put down his bourbon almost angrily. "When will you Jews ever leave me in peace?"

"Mossad has asked very little of you, Volya. But if you do this one thing we wipe the slate clean and we never contact you again. Ever."

Gratchev's eyebrows rose. "That's a promise?"

"You have my word."

Gratchev sighed. "Then it must be important. Tell me what it is you want. More of your friends flown to Vienna?"

The woman glanced around the room. The tavern buzzed with conversation and music as the three musicians wandered from table to table. No one was paying her and her companion the slightest attention. She looked back at the Russian.

"Not this time. We need to get a man into Moscow secretly, and back if necessary. We need you to do it and provide him with the necessary travel papers."

Gratchev's eyes opened wide. "Moscow? Impossible."

"Hardly. You're a colonel in the Soviet Air Force. Such a thing would not be beyond possibility."

"I may be a colonel, but what you're asking is dangerous and impractical. Who is this man?"

"One of our people."

"Mossad?"

"Yes. And we need it done tonight."

The Russian blinked, then sat back and laughed. "My darling Eva, you need to cool that pretty head of yours. It's been frying too long in the Middle East sun."

"I'm not joking, Volya."

The Russian nervously fingered his glass. "Then you're crazy."

The woman hesitated. "If you don't agree to help, your file will be handed over to the Soviet Embassy in Tel Aviv tonight."

Gratchev's face turned red and he clutched his glass so hard the woman thought it would shatter.

"You little bitch! To think I once loved you."

"Temper, Volya. I'm only a messenger."

The three men with the accordions and zither wandered over to the table, playing with beaming smiles on their faces.

Gratchev looked at them icily and said, "Why don't you fuck off and bother someone else?"

The grins changed into a shared look of affront, and the musicians moved on.

The woman laughed. "I see you haven't lost your charm and diplomacy."

Gratchev snorted. "Remember how those Kraut bastards used to play the same music near the front lines? It still drives me crazy."

The look of anger disappeared from Gratchev's face. His mind flashed back almost ten years. A captain, he had been shot down over southern Poland in '43 and captured by the Germans. For four days and nights he had been frightened and in solitary confinement, while the Gestapo had interrogated him in the local police barracks and in the process almost beaten him to death. On the fifth day a group of partisans attacked the barracks to rescue one of their comrades.

Jews, mostly, who had escaped the Warsaw uprising, they showed no mercy to the captured Gestapo, executing them on the spot. Eva Bronski was in command. She had asked Gratchev if he wanted to join them, and he, grateful for the reprieve, had no difficulty saying yes. They battled the Germans together for over a year, and he had loved her for her courage and beauty like he had loved no other woman, not even his wife.

When the Russians had eventually pushed south and overrun the German lines, she took Gratchev to the district Red Army commissar and explained that he had been shot down over partisan territory. She told the commissar that Gratchev had helped lead and organize the partisans, and the way she told it he had been a hero, the bravest man she had ever known. She made no mention of his capture and interrogation by the Gestapo, for that could have cost him a prison sentence, his rank, and maybe even his life.

They said their emotional good-byes that same day, and by the end of the war he was a wing commander, decorated by Stalin, two years later a full colonel.

The first month he was posted to the Soviet air base in Vienna. Three years later he was sitting in a coffee house minding his own business when a woman sat opposite him. Gratchev's face dropped.

Eva said, "Hello, Volya."

Before he could reply she slid an envelope across the table and told him to open it. When he did he saw copies of his Gestapo arrest documents, a transcript of his interrogation, with replies by him that would have been enough to destroy him utterly.

It was simple blackmail after that. The woman had saved him to use him. He was forced to help smuggle Jews on Soviet Air Force flights to Vienna, bound for the new state of Israel. Not often, but often enough to give him sleepless nights.

Now, sitting in the tavern, Gratchev sighed and stood up. "Walk with me."

"Where?"

"Outside, in the street."

Gratchev tossed some notes on the table and they went outside and walked until they found a spot that overlooked the lights of Vienna. Gratchev stopped.

"You were serious? About leaving me in peace?"

"If you do this, definitely."

"Your man speaks Russian, obviously."

"Obviously."

Gratchev sighed and thought for a moment. "There's a military transporter leaving for Moscow from Vienna at six this evening. There's a house on Mahler Strasse. Number four. I have a mistress there. Have your man at the address at five o'clock. No later."

He looked at the woman. "So this is the last time we meet?"

"You have my word."

He continued looking at her face almost wistfully. He went to kiss her, then seemed to change his mind and let his hand trace the outline of her face. "*Shalom*, Eva. Think of me sometimes."

"*Shalom*, Volya."

He turned and walked back toward the town and the tram stop.

Moments later a black Opel pulled up at the curb and the woman climbed in. The man in the driver's seat turned around.

Branigan said, "Well? How did it go?"

The woman nodded at Massey, sitting beside her. "Your friend leaves tonight."

There was an expression of relief on Branigan's face as he looked at Massey.

"I guess you're in luck, Jake."

Massey didn't reply. Branigan tapped the driver's shoulder and the car pulled out from the curb.

Moscow.

The guard unlocked the cell door and Lukin stepped inside.

Anna Khorev barely acknowledged him as she sat on the edge of the wooden bed. As the door clanged shut behind him, Lukin said, "Anna?"

She looked up at him slowly but didn't speak. Her eyes were red from crying, her face drawn and pale. Lukin thought she looked as if she were in a trance. What had happened in the park appeared to have left her deeply traumatized.

He said, "Anna, I want you to listen to what I have to say. I'm releasing you."

She looked up, a puzzled frown on her face.

He said, "It's no trick. Something's happened you need to know about."

He told her what had happened to his wife and when he had finished he saw the shocked reaction but she didn't reply.

"I'm exchanging your life for hers. That's what Slanski wants. If I don't agree he says he'll kill my wife."

When she still looked unconvinced, he said, "Anna, this is no elaborate trick, you must believe me. You have to come with me now, there isn't much time. Please."

"Where are you taking me?"

"A rendezvous near Moscow. The convent of Novodevichy. As far as the chief warden is concerned you're being transferred to Lefortovo prison. But I need your cooperation. Please don't do anything rash when we leave the building and don't speak to anyone but me. And when we meet Slanski I want you to do something for me."

"What?"

"Persuade him not to harm my wife. She's pregnant. Slanski can do what he wants to me, but if he harms my wife, I'll kill him. Whatever's between Slanski and me doesn't concern her. Will you do as I ask?"

Anna Khorev continued to look at him as if she didn't believe what was happening. She seemed to be studying his face.

His voice had sounded dead with despair. She must have seen the dark rings under his eyes and the tension in his body, and he was aware how absurd the situation was; he was no longer the interrogator, but pleading with her. He didn't know whether she hated him or not, or if she was getting some grim satisfaction from his dilemma, but then she nodded.

"Yes."

"Thank you." Lukin moved toward the door. "We'd better go."

"What will happen to you?"

"Because of this? Does it matter? Ultimately we're all dead. You and Slanski because I doubt you'll get out of Moscow alive after Beria learns about this. And my wife and I for what I've allowed to happen."

"What will happen to my daughter?"

"Anna . . ."

"Tell me."

Lukin saw the utter misery in her eyes. She was on the edge of tears but she didn't cry. He shook his head. "I can't answer that, Anna. I honestly can't."

He saw the grief flood her face and despite his own despair it almost broke his heart.

He touched her shoulder gently, "We'd better leave now. There isn't much time."

Anna sat in the front passenger seat as Lukin drove. She stared out beyond the windshield at the lights of Moscow.

He had signed the release and transfer papers in front of a warden before he put the handcuffs on her. Five minutes later they drove out of the Lubyanka courtyard and he had pulled up to the curb and removed the handcuffs.

After that he had been silent. She didn't care whether he spoke or not. All she could think of was Sasha. It had almost broken her heart to see her again. Holding the child in her arms had brought back a flood of memories and she thought she was going mad with anguish. She felt as if someone had stuck a dagger in her heart.

So much about her daughter had changed and yet she was still Sasha. She remembered the smell of her, the feel of her skin. And then came a flood of grief when she realized all the moments they had missed together in their lives.

And then Lukin had taken her away and she would never see her again.

She had wanted to die at that moment in the park, because only death would put an end to her suffering. And now she was consumed with worry; what would happen to her daughter?

Despite what Slanski had done, somehow she didn't seem to care. She looked at Lukin as he drove. She hated him. Hated him for what he was and what he had done to her.

She wanted to kill him.

Looking at his face, she realized he was close to the breaking point. For a brief moment in the cell she had felt compassion for him, but now she thought of Sasha again and her anger came back.

Finally, she couldn't bear the silence any longer.

"Give me a cigarette."

Lukin looked across at her. "Are you all right?"

"Just give me a cigarette."

He pulled in and searched in his pocket. He gave her his cigarettes and lighter and pulled out from the curb again. Anna lit a cigarette and saw that her hands were trembling.

"May I have one too?"

She lit another and handed it across. Lukin glanced at her. "Slanski must love you."

"Why?"

"To do what he's done. He's either very courageous or else he loves you so much he's being reckless."

When Anna didn't reply, Lukin said, "Does he love you?"

"He's not doing this for love."

"Then why is he doing it?"

"Because he doesn't want to see me harmed or killed by bastards like you."

Lukin looked across at her steadily. "Anna, let me tell you something. I've never killed or hurt a woman in my life. And I didn't ask for the job of finding Slanski, I was ordered to. But one thing I will tell you. If he harms Nadia, I'll kill him."

Lukin switched off the engine and doused the headlights. As he stepped out of the car he said to Anna, "Please wait, and don't leave the car."

He started to walk toward the deserted convent. Halfway there he looked back at the BMW. Anna Khorev was still sitting in the passenger seat. He heard an owl hoot.

There was an arched entrance in front which led into the convent. When he reached the archway he halted. A rusted trellis gate stood at the end. He stepped up to the gate. It was padlocked with a heavy chain. Beyond stood a collection of dilapidated whitewashed buildings set around a small courtyard with a fountain in the center.

He heard a voice behind him.

"Turn around slowly."

Lukin turned, his pulse racing, as Slanski stepped toward him out of the shadows, the Tokarev pistol in his hand.

"Up against the wall and spread your feet."

Lukin bit back his rage and did as he was told. When he had finished searching him, Slanski said, "Where's Anna?"

"In the car."

"You came alone?"

"Only with the woman. Where's my wife . . . ?"

"Later."

Lukin was spun around to the right and Slanski pushed him forward. "Walk toward the car."

"My wife . . . we agreed, Slanski."

Lukin glanced back and felt the barrel of the gun in his neck.

"How do you know my name?"

"We knew all about you and the woman before you parachuted onto Soviet soil."

"What else do you know?"

"You're here to kill Stalin."

There was a silence, then Lukin felt the gun press hard into his neck. "Keep looking straight ahead and walk. You try anything and I drop you."

"You're either a very brave man or a complete fool. After tonight you won't stand a chance of getting near Stalin. The entire army will be searching Moscow for you. Take my advice and forget what you came to Moscow to do. You're throwing your life away. And Anna's."

He felt the sudden sharp blow on the back of his skull and a bolt of pain jolted him.

"Now why don't you shut the hell up and keep walking."

They reached the BMW and Slanski flashed an electric flashlight in Anna's face. "Are you alone?"

"Yes."

"Were you followed?"

"I . . . I didn't see anyone."

Slanski shone the light around the inside of the car. "OK, step out slowly."

When Anna stepped out, Slanski said, "At the back of the convent there's a road by the river. You'll see a car parked. Someone's waiting in the driver's seat. Get going, fast."

Suddenly Slanski fired a shot into the BMW's right front tire. It hissed and deflated. He did the same with the driver's side.

He came back and aimed the Tokarev at Lukin's head, then said to Anna, "What the hell are you waiting for. Go!"

Anna didn't move as she looked at Slanski. "What about Lukin's wife?"

"Get going. Leave this to me."

"Don't kill him."

"Just do as I say. Get going. Now!"

"No. Not until you release his wife and promise me you won't harm them. Not until you do that."

Slanski stared at her in disbelief. "Just whose side are you on, for God's sake! Move!"

Anna didn't flinch. "I mean it. I'm not going until I know his wife's safe and you won't harm him."

Slanski had a wild look on his face and for a moment Anna thought he would kill both her and Lukin.

"Please, Alex."

He said angrily, "Go to the car. The woman's inside. Bring her here. Quickly. I haven't got all night."

"You won't kill him?"

"No. Now *move*. Get his wife."

She moved away toward the convent at a run.

Slanski gestured to Lukin with the gun. "Get down on your knees. Then lie flat on your stomach."

Lukin turned pale. "Are you going to kill me?"

"Do it or I take your head off now."

Lukin knelt, then lay in the snow on his stomach. "If you're going to kill me do it now. Do it before my wife comes. I don't want her to see this."

Slanski put the tip of the barrel against the back of Lukin's skull. He cocked the hammer.

For a long time he hesitated, then he said, "It's tempting, but not this time, Lukin. I think your life's just been saved. I can't think why. But let me tell you this. If I see you again after tonight you're dead."

Slanski heard a noise and turned. Anna raced out of the shadows of the convent wall, clutching Lukin's wife by the arm.

They had come halfway when Slanski shouted, "That's far enough! She comes the rest of the way alone."

Anna let go of the woman's arm. Slanski was already moving back toward the convent, the Tokarev still aimed at Lukin. He passed Lukin's wife and then shouted at Anna, "Get back to the car."

For a second she hesitated, as if to be certain that Lukin and his wife were safe, then she turned and ran. Slanski started to follow her, moving backward, the gun still trained on Lukin, until finally he turned and trotted toward the convent walls.

When Slanski was twenty meters away, Lukin pushed himself up from the snow and grabbed Nadia.

"Get in the car!"

He saw the naked fear on his wife's face as he pushed her into the BMW.

"Yuri—please—what's going on—?"

"Start the car. Drive to the end of the street and wait there. Drive carefully, the front tires are punctured. But get the hell out of here fast. Do it, Nadia, no questions!"

He slammed the car door and already he was reaching under the left front fender.

He worked feverishly, fumbling until he found the knotted cord and tugged. He felt the Tokarev revolver slip free as the knot released. He placed the weapon on the hood and felt under the fender again, tugged at the second cord, and the big-barreled Negev flare gun plopped into the snow.

He worked like a man possessed, sweat dripping down his face. He put the Tokarev under his arm and grabbed the flare gun. When he looked back through the windshield he saw Nadia's face stare at him in horror as she saw the weapons.

"Go! Nadia, get the hell out of here!"

For a moment she seemed to hesitate, then he banged on the hood with the butt of the Negev and roared at her.

"Quickly, woman! Go!"

The BMW exploded into life.

The car started to move, slowly at first until the punctured tires gripped the snow, then it shot forward.

As the BMW roared away, Lukin looked back at the convent. He could still see Slanski's figure moving toward the river in the shadows of the wall, sixty meters away.

For a moment Slanski appeared to turn, hearing the roar of the BMW as it raced away. Lukin dropped the Tokarev in the snow, cocked the Negev flare gun, raised it above his head and squeezed the trigger.

A deafening crack erupted as a burst of brilliant orange light exploded above in the darkness and the flare turned night into day.

In the glare of light Lukin saw Slanski halt, his figure illuminated. Already he was turning, reacting.

At the same moment a black Emka came roaring out of nowhere, its engine screaming like some wild animal. As the car skidded to a halt in front of Lukin, Pasha burst out of the driver's door clutching a machine-pistol.

Lukin dropped the flare gun and grabbed the Tokarev. In one swift movement he knelt, rested his elbow on his knee and cocked and aimed the revolver. He caught Slanski clearly in his sights and squeezed the trigger.

The shot missed and ricocheted off the convent wall. As he aimed again, suddenly Pasha opened up with the machine-pistol, flame leaping from the barrel as lead exploded in puffs of snow in front of Slanski, shots ringing around the convent walls. What happened next Lukin could hardly believe.

Slanski calmly knelt, aimed and fired twice.

The first shot kicked up snow but the second hit Pasha and he screamed and rolled over.

Before Lukin could aim again, the orange light started to flicker and a tendril of smoke plummeted to the ground. The flare extinguished and light plunged into gloom. Lukin heard an engine splutter to life.

He clambered to his feet, running forward like a man possessed, ignoring Pasha's body lying in the snow, firing the Tokarev blindly into the darkness after Slanski.

When he reached the road by the river he was just in time to hear a car roar away.

49

Ramenki District,
Moscow.

The Skoda pulled up outside the dacha and Slanski, Anna and Irena climbed out.

Irena led them inside, and when she had lit the wood stove and oil lamps she went into the kitchen and came back with a bottle of vodka and three glasses. She poured them each a drink with trembling hands and swallowed her own quickly.

Her face was white with anger as she stared over at Slanski.

"We all could have been killed tonight. I thought you said there wouldn't be any trouble?"

Slanski put a hand on her shoulder. "Take it easy, Irena. It's all over and you're safe."

"Safe? When I saw the sky light up and heard the shooting I thought I was dead for sure. We're lucky we didn't have half the army on our backs after what happened. And it's hardly over. Look at me, I'm still trembling."

Slanski picked up his glass. "But you're still alive, Anna's free, and no one followed us. All in all, not a bad end to the evening, I'd say."

Irena saw the slight smile on Slanski's face and shook her head in exasperation. "If you're trying to be funny, your humor's wasted—my nerves are too frayed."

She poured another vodka and swallowed it before she said to Anna, "I don't know whom I'd rather face. This lunatic friend of yours or the KGB. The man's as crazy as Rasputin." She put her glass down and touched Anna's arm. "What about you, are you all right?"

"Yes."

"You don't look it. You look like death. Take a drink, it'll calm your nerves. Me, I'm that shook I'm going to drink until I'm legless. You're going to need a bath and a change of clothes. I've got some in the room at the back. I'll get them and heat some water."

When Irena went out, Slanski said to Anna, "Drink. Irena's right, you look as if you need it."

Anna ignored the vodka. "Where are we? Where is this place?"

Slanski told her. He had already explained about Irena, but the atmosphere in the car as they drove to the dacha had been charged and anxious, as if they each expected a roadblock or a police siren at any moment, and they had hardly spoken.

Now Slanski said, "There's something wrong, isn't there?"

"I told you, I'm fine."

"Then why is it I get the feeling something about you is different? I would have thought getting you out of the Lubyanka was cause for a celebration. Instead, you look like someone's just spoiled your evening."

As she stood there, Slanski saw a lifeless look in her eyes and said, "Tell me what's wrong."

"Lukin told me you came to Moscow to kill Stalin. Is that true?"

Slanski didn't reply.

For several moments she stood there, looking at him, and then she said, "If that's true, you're insane."

"Wrong man. It's Stalin who's insane. And yes, I came here to kill him."

"You could never do it. It's impossible. You'd simply be wasting your own life."

"Best let me be the judge of that."

Anna was going to continue, then hesitated. Slanski said, "There's something else, isn't there? Did Lukin hurt you? Is that it?"

"He didn't lay a finger on me."

"You know you almost got us killed tonight? You can't trust Lukin. How could you be such a fool? You should have let me shoot him when I had the chance."

"He didn't deserve to die like that."

He looked at her and laughed harshly. "I can't believe you're saying that. The man tries to kill us and you're defending him."

"Lukin took me to see Sasha."

He saw the pain in her face and suddenly put down his glass. "Tell me."

She told him everything that had happened since he had lost her in the woods.

When she had finished, Slanski said, "So that's why you were with him in the car? Listen to me, Anna, there's only one reason Lukin would have allowed you to see your daughter, and that's to make you talk."

"There was nothing I could tell him to help him find you. I think Lukin knew that all along, even when he took me to meet Sasha. What he did tonight any man in his position who loved his wife would have done. Lukin thinks she'll be punished too for what you did. He had to try and stop you."

"Listen to me, Anna. Lukin's no different from any of those other KGB bastards. He tried it on with you with a sob story and hoped you'd fall for it and you did. You should have let me put a bullet in him when I had the chance." He shook his head. "He was playing games with you, Anna. Playing games to get you to trust him. And even if he meant what he said about saving you from a firing squad, what sort of a life would it have been for your daughter, imprisoned in a camp?"

He saw her struggle to hold back her tears. His hand reached out and touched her face.

"Anna, I'm sorry. If there was something I could do to get Sasha back I would, but it's too late for that and too dangerous, and even if I knew where she was you can be sure after tonight Lukin will have her closely guarded. I can't take the risk of trying to rescue her, it would only jeopardize what I came here to do. And it's come too far to let that happen."

She turned away, a flood of grief on her face. Slanski went to touch her again but she pushed him away, and he saw the tears at the edges of her eyes.

"I can't give up now, Anna, not when I'm so close. And if Lukin thinks I'm finished he's got a surprise in store."

Anna looked back at him. "You're being reckless. You know what you intend is impossible. Stop before it's too late."

He smiled, but the smile never reached his eyes. "Definitely too late for that, Anna. Irena will drive you to a railway station outside Moscow before it gets light. There's a goods train leaving for the Finnish border and you'll both be on it. A man named Lebel will look after you. Irena will tell you everything when the time comes. I'm truly sorry about Sasha."

He looked at her face and she knew he meant it. He turned toward the kitchen door. "Where are you going?"

"To get some air. Maybe you need to be alone."

As he opened the door, Anna said, "You know you're dead if you stay in Moscow?"

Slanski pulled up his collar. "Like they say, the seeds of what we'll do are in all of us. Maybe that's my fate. I mean to finish what I started. And no one's going to stop me now. No one. Least of all Lukin."

And then he turned and was gone out of the door.

The man had driven halfway down the unlit street in the van and pulled in under a tree. It was deserted and the dachas on either side were in shadow. He removed the binoculars from under the passenger seat and stepped out into the snow.

It took him almost ten minutes to find the address in the darkness. Five minutes later he had found his way around to the back of the property and came out in a clump of trees at the rear of the dacha. He saw the yellow glow of an oil lamp burning behind the downstairs curtained window and he smiled to himself.

He settled down in the freezing woods. The binoculars were pretty useless without any light, and he trained his eyes on the dacha, scanning the curtained windows for any sign of movement.

As he sat there he suddenly saw the back door open. In the flood of light that filled the doorway a man stepped out onto the patio and closed the door after him.

He lifted the binoculars. It was too dark to see the man's face clearly and he swore to himself. Then a light flared in the blackness near a woodshed as the man lit a cigarette, and he locked onto the figure and saw the face clearly for an instant and froze.

The man put down his binoculars and picked his way back through the woods to the van. It was five minutes later when he drove into the nearest town and found a public telephone.

He went to stand under the rusting metal canopy and inserted a coin and dialed the number. It took a long time before the phone was lifted at the other end.

"Boris?"

"Da."

"It's Sergei. I think I've found them."

50

Moscow.

Nadia came out of the kitchen with a bottle of vodka and two glasses. Her hands were trembling.

Lukin said, "You really think you ought to drink?"

"I need it. So do you."

"Perhaps I should call you a doctor?"

She shook her head. "One patient is enough for tonight. Sit down, Yuri."

There was a firmness in her voice Lukin hadn't heard before. He sat on the couch and she poured two glasses and came to join him.

As Lukin sat there, he felt numb inside. What had happened was a nightmare. They had left Pasha at the office of a Mongol doctor he knew. A bullet had chipped his shoulder bone but the wound wasn't life-threatening. The doctor had given him a shot of morphine and cleaned the wound, then Pasha had called Lukin aside.

"Go home, Yuri. I'll call you when I get out of here. Look after Nadia. She looks pretty upset."

"You're sure you'll be all right?"

Pasha lifted his arm and grimaced in pain. "I'll just have to learn to drink with my left." Lukin knew the humor was forced. He consulted the doctor.

"He's lost some blood," the doctor said, "but I know this lunatic. He'd live through anything. What about you and your wife? You both look shaken."

Lukin didn't want to complicate things further. The less the doctor knew the better. But he had him examine Nadia in the next room.

When the doctor came back he said, "Your wife's pretty distressed. Because she's pregnant, I've given her some mild sedatives to help her relax. Make sure she takes them. Do you want to tell me what happened?"

Lukin shook his head. "She wasn't hurt?"

"There's no sign of any physical injury. She just needs to rest. What about you?"

"Just make sure Pasha's taken care of. And if anyone asks, you were told his wound was an accident."

Now Lukin put his head in his hand as he sat on the couch. He felt drained, exhaustion and stress fogging his brain.

"Drink this."

He looked up. Nadia handed him the glass of vodka.

When he had swallowed a mouthful, she sat beside him. "Tell me what's going on. Tell me why that man kidnapped me." She looked at him. "What happened to your hand?"

Lukin heard the anger in her voice as she stared at him.

"You'd better tell me everything, Yuri. Because if you don't I'm packing my things and leaving. My life's been put in danger. And the life of our child."

"Nadia . . ." He went to touch her but she pushed him away.

He understood. At first, her reaction was fear and shock, now anger, because he had put their lives in danger.

He shook his head helplessly. "Nadia . . . regulations don't permit me . . ."

"I mean it, Yuri. After tonight you owe it to me to tell me everything. And to hell with your regulations. What if that madman hadn't released me when he did?"

"Pasha would have tried to follow him."

"That was still putting my life in danger."

"Nadia, there was no other way . . ."

"Tell me the whole truth, or so help me, Yuri, as much as I love you, I'm leaving you. Who was the man?"

Lukin saw the look on her face and knew she meant it. He put his glass down very slowly, took a deep breath and let it out.

"An American assassin. His name's Alex Slanski. He's also known as the Wolf. He's in Moscow to kill Joseph Stalin."

Nadia turned white. She put down her glass, disbelief on her face.

Lukin told her everything. When he had finished, Nadia stood up and said, "Oh my God."

"After tonight the situation looks hopeless. When Beria learns I've released the woman he'll have me arrested and shot. It won't matter that I did it because your life was in danger. To Beria that's no excuse. Duty comes first. And he'll see you as an accomplice who should be punished."

He saw the look of anguish on his wife's face and said, "Nadia, you wanted the truth and I've told you."

"I . . . I don't believe this is happening."

He felt the perspiration run down his shirt. "Listen to me, Nadia. No matter what way you look at it I'm dead and you're in danger. It's not going to take long before Beria learns the truth. Tomorrow at the latest. I want you to leave Moscow. Go somewhere you stand a chance of not being found. Somewhere far away. The Urals. The Caucasus. I'll arrange false papers. You take every ruble we have. It's your only hope. If you stay, you'll be shot or sent to a camp. This way at least you stand a chance."

"I'm not leaving you here alone."

"You have to, if only for our child's sake."

"And what will you do?"

"I stay in Moscow. If we leave together there wouldn't be any mercy shown. But if I stay there's a chance Beria won't trouble himself about you."

Nadia seemed to crack then, and Lukin saw the flood of tears before her arms went around his neck and he pulled her close.

"No tears, Nadia. Please . . ."

"I won't go without you."

"Then think of our child."

She pulled away from him, sobbing. Lukin stood. Seeing her like this was killing him.

"Tell me what happened this morning. What did Slanski do to you?"

Nadia wiped her eyes. "He came to the door and forced himself in. He put something over my mouth and I blacked out. When I came to he had a gun to my head. He said he'd kill us both if I didn't do as he said. I thought he was some escaped madman."

"Did he hurt you?"

"No."

"Tell me what happened after he took you outside."

She told him and Lukin said, "When Slanski took you to the car, was he alone?"

"No, there was someone waiting in the driver's seat."

"Who?"

"I couldn't see. I was still drowsy. As soon as I got in the backseat he blindfolded me. The next thing I knew I was in a room somewhere. That's all I remember."

"Do you remember what type of car?"

"I . . . I'm not sure."

"Think, Nadia. What type? What color?"

"Everything happened so fast. I don't remember what type."

"Do you remember the color?"

"Gray, maybe. Or green. I can't be certain."

"What about the license plates? You didn't see the license plates?"

"No."

Lukin sighed. "Do you remember anything about the driver?"

"He had his back to me."

"Think, Nadia. *Please.*"

"When the smell of the drug went away I could smell something else . . ."

"What?"

"A clean smell. Like perfume . . . but I'm not sure."

"Could the driver have been a woman?"

Nadia shook her head. "I don't know. I suppose, but I really don't know. Can we stop this, please, Yuri . . ."

Lukin saw the strain and tension on her face. She was close to breaking point but he needed *some* clue. *Something* that might help him.

"Tell me about the room you were kept in."

"I told you, I was blindfolded."

He put his hand to his wife's face and covered her eyes. She started to move away but he held her still. "Nadia, this is important. Imagine you're in that room again. Imagine you're blindfolded. What smells were there? What sounds?"

"There was no . . . no sound of traffic. I heard birds outside but it was very quiet and still. It seemed like somewhere in the country, but it was Moscow, I'm sure of it."

"Why are you sure?"

"When I was taken to the convent I was still blindfolded but I couldn't have been in the car for more than half an hour. But where we drove from . . . I don't know . . . it could have been anywhere."

"*Think*. What else do you remember?"

Nadia went to push his hand away but he kept it there.

"Yuri, please . . . I can't take any more, please . . ."

Lukin removed his hand. Nadia was crying, tears streaming down her face. He pulled her close and held her tightly.

"It's all right, my love. It's all right. Come into the bedroom. Try and sleep."

She wiped her face and pushed away from him. "How can I sleep after what you've told me?"

"Because you need to. Take one of the pills the doctor gave you." He stood up and saw the alarm on her face.

"Where are you going?"

"Nadia, I have to try to find Slanski. He won't come back here, he wouldn't risk it. But if it makes you feel better I'll have one of the men come over and stay. But tell him nothing and lock the doors while I'm away."

He picked up the brown bottle. "This is what Slanski used to put you asleep—ether. It's a controlled substance, an anesthetic and solvent. And that means it can only be bought through legal channels. I need to check if any of the names on the lists of dissidents are chemists or doctors, or work in hospitals where they could have access to such supplies, or even if any has been reported stolen. It's not much to go on, but it's all I can think of. If Pasha calls, tell him where I've gone. I'll have one of the men stop by as soon as I get to my office."

"Yuri, please be careful."

He kissed her forehead. "Of course. Now try and rest."

Lukin watched as she crossed to the bedroom door. She looked back at him, a frightened look that almost broke his heart, and then she went into the bedroom.

He put his hand to his forehead and sat there, in turmoil. Everything had gone wrong. The ether was a thin strand, but he had to give Nadia some hope. He *had* to find Slanski and find him fast before Beria discovered that the woman was missing. He found it difficult to concentrate as he tried to rack his brain for clues.

Nadia's information hadn't been much. Maybe a house on the outskirts of Moscow. A quiet place in the country with no traffic. A dacha, perhaps. Maybe a woman involved. It was nothing much to go on. Nothing.

He needed *solid* clues. He looked down at the ether bottle. Right now it was all he had.

It was almost ten that evening when the Tupolev 4 military transporter arriving from Vienna touched down on the snowy runway at Moscow's Vnukovo airfield.

Among the military-only passengers that evening was a bulky man in his early forties with cropped gray hair. He wore an air force major's uniform and had hardly spoken throughout the bumpy four-hour flight, pretending to sleep in his seat at the rear of the aircraft, while the other military passengers drank and played cards or wandered up and down the aisles to ease the boredom.

Now, as he carried his duffel bag down the metal steps, an imposing black Zis drew up alongside the Tupolev and a young lieutenant in air force uniform introduced himself and led the major to the waiting car.

It took almost ten minutes to exit the airport, the papers the lieutenant produced being checked thoroughly at the special gate reserved for military traffic. But the documents were all in order and the Zis was waved through.

Half an hour later the car pulled up on a dark country road on the outskirts of Moscow. The young officer looked around and smiled.

"This is where I was told to drop you, sir."

The major looked out of the window at the falling snow and said, "You're certain this is the place?"

"Certain, Comrade Major."

Massey climbed out silently, dragging his bag after him. The lieutenant watched him disappear into the darkness as the snow fell lightly beyond the windshield.

51

Lukin pulled up opposite the entrance to the small park near the Kiev Metro station. As he stepped out of the car, he noticed that the lights were on in the park. He saw a dozen or more tough-looking men huddled beyond the bare trees twenty meters away. Most of them had the dark look of the south: Uzbekistans, Turkestans, Georgians, gypsies from the Crimea with ugly, elaborate tattoos on their hands and arms. Hardened petty criminals who ran the Moscow black markets and risked five years in Siberia for illegal trading.

He saw the rusting green Emka parked across the street, but there was no sign of Rizov.

He noticed that some of the men under the trees were closing suitcases and canvas bags, stashing them onto the backs of bicycles or carrying them to the trunks of rusted cars and vans outside the park. Another ten minutes and the place would be deserted.

Through the bare trees Lukin saw a trader with a heavy black mustache. A barrel-chested fat man with one leg shorter than the other, wearing loose, baggy clothes and a bushy black beard. Oleg Rizov. Rizov the Bear.

He was arguing with a woman carrying a shopping bag. The woman held up a dented can of tinned peaches, trying to bargain. Rizov kept smiling a gold-toothed smile and shaking his head from side to side. Finally the exasperated woman flung the can into the bushes in disgust and uttered a mouthful of expletives before turning on her heel. The other men standing under the trees laughed and Rizov growled at them, then limped over and retrieved the can of peaches and swore after the woman.

Lukin watched as moments later Rizov picked up two worn suitcases and came out through the park gates to the rusted Emka, waddling like a man with legs of rubber. Rizov locked the cases in the trunk, then went around to the front. He removed two windshield wipers from inside his coat and fitted them to the wiper arms, then climbed into the Emka.

It started in a puff of blue exhaust smoke and moved out from the curb. Lukin pulled out after it.

*   *   *

The apartment block off the southern end of the Lenin Prospect had been built just after the war, but despite its newness it looked shabby. Raw unplastered cinder block and lines of frozen washing hanging on balconies.

The Emka halted and Lukin saw Rizov climb out, retrieve his two suitcases and remove the wipers again before he locked the car. He stepped on a line of wooden planks that covered the slushy patches in front of the building before he limped into the apartment block.

Lukin locked the BMW and followed.

He went up to the third floor and knocked on Rizov's door. There was a rattle of bolts and locks and Rizov appeared. His face dropped when he saw Lukin.

"Major . . . what a surprise . . ."

Lukin brushed past him.

The room was squalid, untidy and in disarray, but it was a storehouse of luxury. The two suitcases from the car were open, their contents scattered. Jars of Dutch jams and some cans of peaches and red caviar. From hooks in the ceiling hung sides of smoked salmon and bunches of dried salted herrings. On the table Lukin saw half a dozen bottles of Ukrainian champagne and a couple of kilo jars of pickled sturgeon's roe.

"About to give a party, Oleg? Or did I disturb your supper?"

Rizov closed the door and nervously licked his lips. "What can I say, Major?"

"Caught red-handed would do nicely. For this little lot alone you could get five years." Lukin rummaged through one of the suitcases and plucked out two bright red camisoles.

"Yours?"

"I'm holding on to them for a friend."

"The French Ambassador's wife, no doubt?"

Rizov smiled nervously. "Consider them a gift."

Lukin let the garments fall. "Sit down, Rizov."

Rizov pushed some dirty clothes off the bed and sat. "Perhaps if the major told me to what I owe the pleasure of his visit? Can I get the major a drink?"

"You know, it never ceases to amaze me, Rizov."

"What does?"

"We must have the tightest borders and ports in the world and yet people like you still manage to smuggle in just about anything."

Rizov shrugged amiably. "The major knows if I can provide a service for the good citizens of Moscow, it makes me feel good. I consider it social work, not crime."

"I'm sure a judge would see it differently. You'd sell your own grandmother for a profit, Rizov. You're a rogue beyond redemption." He removed the brown bottle from his pocket and placed it on the table.

"What's that?"

"Ether. You've heard of ether, Rizov. A chemical liquid used as an anesthetic."

"I know what ether is." Rizov pointed to the bottle. "But what's this got to do with me?"

"Do you know how to get ether in Moscow?"

"No, but I've got a feeling the major will tell me."

"Unless you're a doctor or a hospital administrator or work in certain industries, it's impossible to buy. Its purchase is strictly controlled and monitored."

Rizov shrugged. "You learn something every day. What's it got to do with me?"

"If somebody wanted a small quantity of ether and fast, no doubt your friends on the black market would find a way to oblige for a price?"

Rizov pursed his lips and nodded at the bottle. "Was it bought on the black market?"

"Perhaps. Or stolen from a hospital or surgery."

Rizov shrugged. "I heard some of the illegal abortion clinics buy it on the black market."

"Among your friends, who'd be daring enough to steal it?"

Rizov shook his head. "Major, really, I know nothing about such things. Food and drink, sure. But stuff for hospitals, forget it. Five years in a camp is one thing. A bullet in the neck for stealing proscribed chemical substances is another."

"Answer the question, Rizov. I'm not in the mood for playing around. This is important. Who'd be daring enough to steal ether?"

Rizov sighed and put a hand to his forehead and thought for a moment, then looked up. "Perhaps the Crimean gypsies. Or the Turkmenistans. They're a bunch of reckless bastards who deal in drugs and stuff. They'd steal the food off a policeman's plate if they thought there was a profit in it."

"Give me names."

Rizov shook his head and laughed. "Major, as Stalin is my judge, I keep away from that lot. They're not only mad, they're dangerous. Even sending them to the camps doesn't frighten them. Like weeds, they'd thrive in fucking shit."

Lukin's hand slapped hard on the table. "*Names*, Rizov. I want *names.* They're acquaintances of yours. You work the black market together."

"On the grave of my dead mother I know none of them. And even if I did and ratted they'd have my balls for worry beads."

Lukin grabbed the little man by his shirt collar. "You're a lying rogue, Rizov. And your mother's alive and living in Kiev."

"I don't associate with these people, Major. Drugs, stuff like that, it's too risky. Me, I stick to food and clothes."

Lukin looked about the room. "You like living here?"

Rizov threw an eye quickly over the filthy, tiny flat and said flippantly, "Sure. I love it." He saw the look on Lukin's face and his tone became more respectful. "It could be worse."

"Worse than a log hut in some icy corner of Siberia?"

"It's just as cold here, believe me. The plumbing hardly ever works. Not that I'm complaining, mind, just that in winter your balls feel like lumps of ice."

"Rizov, get it into your thick skull, I'm not playing games here."

"You wouldn't have me sent to Siberia, Major Lukin. You're too kind a man. Besides, what have I done?"

Lukin nodded at the suitcases on the bed."That stuff's worth five years if I report you. Ten if the prosecutor's in a bad mood. Even longer if I recommend it. And believe me, I'll recommend it if you don't cooperate."

Rizov's face drained. "Major—"

"Think about it. An old dog like you doesn't need the hard road. Talk with your black-market friends. Use all your charm and cunning. If anyone bought ether in the last few days I want to know about it."

He saw the puzzled frown on Rizov's face and said, "Someone used it to carry out a serious crime. Don't fail me on this one or I swear I'll have you on a prison train to Archangel by morning."

He let go of the little man and put the empty bottle on the table. "Take this. It may help your Turkmenistan friends remember. Tell them from me that if they don't come up with answers, they'll be keeping you company on the train."

He took a slip of paper from his pocket and slapped it on the table. "You have an hour, no more. Call me at this number."

He crossed to the door and skewered Rizov with a steely look.

"I mean it, don't fail me. One hour. It's a matter of life and death."

The room stank like a sewer and so did Lebel.

A blinding light blazed in the ceiling and his body was drenched in sweat.

As he came awake in the filthy cell and struggled to sit up he found he couldn't. He was lying on a metal table and tied down with leather straps.

He had come awake to the sound of distant screams and it didn't take much imagination to know where he was.

The cellars of the Lubyanka.

His body ached with pain and his mouth felt twisted. He tasted blood on his lips. The two men had beaten him senseless, punching and kicking him in the kidneys and stomach until the pain was unbearable and he threw up.

Then they started on his face. Punches and blows that made his head swim and finally left him unconscious. When he came to they started all over again, this time with rubber hoses, until he passed out once more.

Now he moaned and looked down at his body. His shirt and vest were gone. And his shoes and socks, although he still had his trousers. He had wet his pants after the painful blows to his kidneys.

He slumped back on the table.

He had been through it all before with the Gestapo. And what worried him was that he knew the real torture hadn't even started yet. The men had only softened him up. The worst was yet to come.

As he lay there in agony, he tried to consider his options. He had none really, except to tell Romulka everything. And then what? The man would probably kill him. He wondered what Romulka already knew. Very little. Otherwise, why bring him here? He was probing, trying to find answers.

He could hang in there playing dumb and hope that Romulka would tire of the interrogation and let him go. But he guessed that Romulka wasn't the type to tire. Besides, the bastard seemed to enjoy inflicting pain.

Lebel had connections in Moscow. Someone would intervene. But when? And by then it might be too late. Confessing wouldn't help Massey. And it wouldn't help Massey's friends. Above all, it wouldn't help Irena.

That thought worried him. Imprisoned, he had no way of warning her.

But he wasn't going to talk. He wasn't going to give her away. Besides, Romulka couldn't *kill* him. No, he just had to hold out and deny everything.

A door clanged open. Romulka came into the room flanked by the two men who had given him the beating.

"Have you reconsidered, Lebel?"

Sweat ran down Lebel's face. He said hoarsely, "I told you, you're making a dreadful mistake . . . I'm an innocent man . . . your superiors will hear of this . . ."

Romulka stepped closer and gripped Lebel's face hard. "Listen to me, you little Jew. I haven't the patience or the time for games. You either talk or, I swear, what the Gestapo did to you is nothing compared to the little treat you have in store. In fact, Lebel, I can promise you that you'll never see daylight again."

"On my life . . . I don't know what you're talking about."

"Then let's try and change that."

Romulka stepped over to a table in the corner. Lebel craned his neck and saw to his horror a selection of instruments and tools of torture which made his blood run cold.

"I always find concentrating on a man's weaknesses is the best approach."

Romulka selected an odd-looking implement with two small cup-shaped metal scoops with leather pads inside and a screw handle on the end.

"A little something we borrowed from the Tsar's secret police. They considered it most effective. It's a genital clamp. Know what it does? Enough turns of this handle here and it crushes a man's testicles. Splits them wide open. But slowly, very slowly, and very painfully. Let's give it a try, shall we?"

Romulka turned to the men and nodded. One tied a gag around Lebel's mouth, while the other pulled down his sodden trousers and underpants.

Romulka came forward and Lebel watched in horror as the implement was slipped under his scrotum and secured.

He gritted his teeth as he struggled behind the gag.

Romulka turned the screw handle and the implement tightened around Lebel's right testicle.

There was an excruciating, sickening pain, and Lebel felt as if a bolt of electricity had shot through his spine. His brain exploded with agony and he saw stars and felt the nausea to the pit of his stomach.

He screamed behind the gag and passed out.

The large house in the Degunino district north of Moscow was built of wood and brick and had once been the home of a wealthy Tsarist officer, but now it was badly dilapidated and the roof leaked.

Massey sat in the front room of a shabby second-floor apartment. It was sparsely furnished with a table and two chairs. An iron bed and a wardrobe in the small bedroom next door were the only other items of furniture, but there was a new valve radio sitting on a box near the bed. The place smelled of rot and damp and it was biting cold, despite the wood stove lit in the corner.

Massey had changed out of the uniform and now he wore a cloth cap and a coarse, frayed suit under his overcoat. On the table in front of him was a bowl of cabbage soup and some fresh bread, but he ignored the food and concentrated on the map of Moscow lying next to it.

The man seated opposite poured vodka into two glasses and said gruffly in Russian, "You want to tell me what the fuck's going on, *Americanski*?"

Massey looked up. The man was big and red-haired and powerfully built. He wore a filthy woollen scarf around his neck and his black suit was worn and shiny.

He was the former Ukrainian SS captain Massey had dispatched from Munich six weeks before. It seemed so long ago Massey had difficulty remembering the face when the man had ushered him into the apartment. He looked older; his jaws were unshaven and his narrow eyes had the nervous look of a man under stress.

Massey said flatly, "You got the signal with your instructions."

"On The Voice of America. It said to give you total assistance, that it was top priority . . ."

"Then that's all you need to know. Tell me about the dacha."

A war spent in SS uniform had taught the Ukrainian not to argue with an order. He nodded and pointed to a place on the map.

"Sergei's there now, covering the place. So far it seems the occupants haven't moved."

"How many people?"

"Sergei saw two, he thinks the man and woman you're after, but the signal said there was another woman. He hasn't seen her, but she could be inside."

"Can we contact Sergei by phone?"

The Ukrainian laughed. "Listen, this is Moscow, not Munich. I was lucky to get this dump of a place a month ago after I found work. It hasn't even got a fucking bath and I have to piss in the sink rather than walk to the downstairs toilet. The only way Sergei and I can keep in touch is a communal pay phone in the hallway below. Sergei has to drive to a kiosk in a village five minutes from the dacha if he wants to contact me." The man shrugged. "An unhelpful situation, and hardly conducive to surveillance, but there you have it."

Massey saw the tension on the man's face. He was living on his nerves, constantly in fear of being caught.

"How have you both been?"

The Ukrainian grimaced. "Munich seems like a lifetime ago, but we were lucky to get here. That crippled Finnish pilot of yours dropped us two miles from our target, in a fucking swamp that it took us half the night to wade out of. I think the bastard did it deliberately." He shrugged. "But we're still alive, and that counts for something. We've both found jobs. Lucky for you, Sergei as a delivery driver, that's how he borrowed the van. So far, the papers your people supplied have worked and no one's bothered us."

Massey turned back to the map. "Tell me about the dacha."

The man took several minutes to describe the location and the layout of the property, then Massey said, "How far is it from here?"

"By taxi, over half an hour. But I suggest we take public transport. It's more reliable and less conspicuous. An hour ought to do it. Sergei can take us back."

"What if he telephones while we're gone?"

The man shrugged. "Can't be helped, I'm afraid. We'll have to take the risk and hope your friends stay put. But if they move I gave Sergei orders to follow them." He hesitated. "You still haven't told me why we're watching these people."

Massey stood and crossed to where he had left his duffel bag. He removed a large, heavy cotton cloth and laid it on the table. He unrolled the cloth. Inside were two Tokarev pistols with silencers and spare magazines. There was also a disassembled Kalashnikov AK47 automatic assault rifle with a folding stock.

The Ukrainian looked at the weapons, then over at Massey, and grinned. "We're going to kill them?"

"You've both had weapons training so I don't have to show you how to use these."

The Ukrainian picked up the Kalashnikov and expertly assembled the parts. He checked the magazine and clicked it home.

"My type of weapon—lethal. You didn't answer my question, *Americanski*. We're going to kill the people at the dacha?"

"Yes."

"You don't look too happy about it."

Massey ignored the remark and picked up a Tokarev and silencer. As he slipped the weapon and a spare magazine into his pocket, the Ukrainian looked at him.

"I don't have to know why they're going to die, but this *is* Moscow. What happens if we run into trouble and get caught?"

Massey held the man's stare. "The dacha's remote so it's unlikely the militia will turn up. We ought to have this over and done with and be back here in a couple of hours. Any problems with the militia showing up and we still finish the job, no matter what it takes. Then we get out of there fast. I've got air transport out and I take you and your friend with me. After this, you both have your freedom."

The Ukrainian grinned. "That sounds better. This could turn out to be interesting. A little action won't be bad after a month flattening my ass sitting in this dump. I've got a feeling it's going to be just like old times for Sergei and me, killing *Russkis.*"

Massey didn't reply, just stood there grimly, then picked up the other Tokarev, silencer and magazine and handed them across.

"For your friend. Let's not waste any more time."

The telephone rang on Lukin's desk.

He picked it up. Rizov's voice.

"Major Lukin?"

"This is Lukin."

"I've done as you asked. One of the Turkmenistans claims he sold a bottle of ether to a woman two days ago at the Kazan market."

Lukin grabbed a pencil and reached for the pad on his desk. "Did he get a description of the woman?"

"Late thirties. Matronly build. Good-looking. Dark hair. Reasonably well dressed. The man I spoke to sometimes sells anesthetics and drugs to the illegal abortion clinics, but this woman wasn't one of his usual customers. And she seemed to have no shortage of rubles."

"What about the woman's name?"

"Are you joking?"

Lukin sighed. "Come on, Rizov, there has to be more. That description could fit a quarter of the women in Moscow."

"The man never saw her before, that's what made him remember. He remembers seeing her getting into a Czech Skoda parked across the street. Also, the woman bought another drug. Adrenalin. And a single hypodermic syringe. He thought that was odd. That's all I've got."

Lukin thought for a moment. He knew a shot of Adrenalin could be used to give a person an energy boost to overcome exhaustion. He had seen it used during the war. Someone in Slanski's position might need such a drug, to ward off tiredness. His pulse quickened.

"Was there anyone else in the Skoda?"

"The man didn't notice."

"The color of the car?"

"Gray."

"License number?"

Rizov snorted. "Major, these Turkmenistans in the black market can buy and sell like nobody's business, but they can hardly read and write. License numbers they don't notice."

"There's nothing else your friend remembers?"

"Nothing, I swear it."

Lukin tore the sheet from the pad. He knew Rizov was telling the truth, but it was still little to go on. It might not even be the connection he was looking for, but it had to be investigated, and fast. He sighed with tiredness and frustration.

"It's not much. But I owe you a favor."

"I suppose an exit visa would be too much to ask?"

"Don't joke, Rizov. I'm not in the mood."

He slammed down the phone. He was already moving toward the door when the telephone jangled again. He went back and lifted the receiver. It was Pasha's voice.

"We need to talk, Yuri."

"It'll have to wait. I thought I told you to rest."

"No, it can't wait. It's important." There was a pause, then Pasha said urgently, "It's about the Wolf. It's about Slanski."

"What do you mean? What about him?"

There was another pause. "Meet me in the Sandunov bathhouse in ten minutes. Ask for me at the door."

"Can't you come here?"

Pasha ignored the question.

The line clicked dead.

52

The faded wooden sign above the blackened granite building said "Sandunov Public Baths."

The double oak doors were closed and locked, but Lukin saw a splinter of light showing at the bottom. He knocked hard and waited.

He glanced back down the cobbled lane. It was deserted. He had left the car parked outside the Berlin Hotel around the next corner and walked.

What the hell was Pasha playing at?

And why meet here; at this hour? Sandunov was one of Moscow's oldest public bathhouses. Pasha had been coming here for almost twenty years, and usually in the evening, when the steam rooms were quiet and he could have some privacy.

He heard the rattle of bolts behind the oak doors and turned.

A middle-aged woman wearing a blue smock stood in the doorway. Her hair was tied in a bun and her huge breasts seemed to unbalance her. "We're closed. Come back tomorrow."

"I believe Pasha Kokunko is expecting me."

The woman hesitated. She studied him carefully for several moments, then looked out into the lane before she gestured for Lukin to enter.

He stepped into a warm tiled hallway. The woman closed the door and slid the bolts.

Most of the lights in the entrance hall were switched off, but across the hallway Lukin saw the cracked stone steps that led down to the bathhouse and the sweat rooms.

The woman crossed to the glass booth in the lobby and came back with a thick white cotton towel and a bunch of birch twigs tied with string. "Go down the steps and take the first door on the right. You'll find Pasha in the sweat room."

Lukin took the towel and birch twigs. The woman went to sit behind the glass booth and began counting a small mountain of kopeck coins and stacking them in neat piles.

Lukin went down the stone steps.

He stopped halfway and sucked in a deep breath. He felt the warm steam mixed with a sharp fragrance of mint reach deep into the pit of his lungs, and it instantly soothed him. At the bottom of the steps he noticed that a glass door on the right was half open.

He stepped inside.

He was in a dressing room lined with metal lockers. Wooden benches were set in a square around the center. Off to the left, another glass-fronted door, fogged with steam, led to one of the sweat rooms. Behind the fogged glass he saw a moving blur of flesh and heard a faint swishing sound.

There were three stages to the ritual of cleansing in the bathhouse.

First came the sweat room, where you steamed and flayed your body with birch twigs until it burned red and the pores opened. Afterwards you washed your body with hot sponges to cleanse your skin. Then you plunged into the icy water pools once it became too hot. And finally, you relaxed in the refreshment lounge.

Lukin could feel a wave of heat from the next room, pleasant after the icy air in the freezing streets outside. On one of the wooden benches were Pasha's clothes. On another lay an enamel basin of hot steaming water, obviously left for Lukin.

He undressed and laid his clothes neatly on one of the benches. He left the metal hook strapped to his arm; it looked ugly and awkward. He placed the cotton towel over his head and soaked the birch leaves in the basin of hot water.

Then he opened the glass door and stepped into the scented mist.

Pasha lay naked on a damp stone bench, looking terribly pale, a white cotton towel around his shoulders, a patch of blood on his bandaged wound.

A bearded, elderly Uzbek wearing a towel around his waist stood over him. The Uzbek was vigorously flaying Pasha's sweating legs and buttocks with a bundle of damp birch leaves.

On the floor lay a small enamel tub of hot water, fresh sponges and a small pile of mint leaves laid out on a wooden tray. Next to the tray was a bottle of vodka and two glasses, and beside them Pasha's worn leather briefcase. The Uzbek stopped flaying and looked around at Lukin. Slit eyes squinted out of a cautious yellow face.

Pasha stirred and raised his body painfully from the stone bench. He saw Lukin and turned to the Uzbek.

"Leave us, Itzkhan."

The Uzbek nodded and went out. Pasha waited until he heard the outer door close, then gestured to one of the stone benches.

"Sit down, Yuri."

There was something odd in his tone, but Lukin removed the towel from his head and put it around his waist, then sat on a bench opposite. The steam room was hot. He put down the birch leaves; he was too tired to flay his skin.

He watched as Pasha picked up one of the sponges and soaked it in hot water and began to sponge himself, his face strained with pain, although he seemed in no hurry.

Lukin said impatiently. "You said this was important, Pasha."

Pasha studied his face. "You look like you haven't slept in a week."

Lukin felt on the verge of collapse but managed a weak smile. "I guess a good night's sleep wouldn't hurt. How do you feel?"

"It could be worse. The morphine the doctor gave me to ease the pain is wearing off. But this place helps me to relax."

He stopped sponging his body and stood. He crossed to a hot-water tap in the corner, filled an enamel basin with steaming water and crushed a handful of mint leaves into the basin. He came back and cupped Lukin's chin in his hand. For several moments he studied Lukin's face oddly, like an examining physician, then handed him the basin and a fresh sponge.

"Your adrenaline's flowing like sweat. Here, soak yourself and inhale the steam. You know what we old bathers say. 'The steam bath makes you sweat to get tough and get slim. It cleanses the body and the devils within.' " He smiled faintly at the old Moscow rhyme. The smile faded and his face became more serious. "You look like you have devils in your soul, Yuri."

Lukin lifted the basin and inhaled. The aroma of the hot fragrant water was like a balm. He dipped the sponge in the steaming basin, closed his eyes, and slowly ran it over his face. The scent of mint filled his nostrils, the fragrant liquid soothing on his skin. He stopped sponging, opened his wet eyes, and saw Pasha staring at him.

"The mint helps?"

"A little. Tell me what this is about. Tell me what's so important?"

Pasha stood and picked up his leather briefcase. He nodded toward the door that led to the dressing room. "Come, let's go inside. There's something I have to show you."

When they stepped into the dressing room Pasha closed the door. He crossed to the wooden bench and undid the straps on the briefcase, removed a red-covered file, and looked back.

"Did anything about the Wolf strike you as strange?"

Lukin frowned. "What do you mean, strange?"

"For one, we know there were several pages missing from the copy of his file. Like I said before, it's usual that an investigator be given access to *all* information for the case he's working on."

"Look, what's this about, Pasha?"

Pasha paused. "I've known you a long time, Yuri. I've always liked and admired you. We've seen good and bad times together."

Lukin said almost irritably, "Will you tell me what all this is about?"

For several long moments Pasha's eyes seemed to search Lukin's face, then he said, "You were right when you said you didn't trust Beria. You were right to doubt why he picked you. And tonight I found out why."

"I don't understand."

"You're a good man, Yuri Lukin. And a good investigator. However, they've fooled you."

"Who has?"

"Stalin and Beria."

Lukin frowned in confusion.

Pasha sat down next to him on the bench. He looked away for a moment, at nothing in particular, then looked back.

Lukin searched the Mongolian's face. He saw fear there. Pasha wasn't hesitating in order to prolong telling him. He seemed genuinely afraid. As he handed the file over, his hands shook.

"I want you to see this."

"What is it?"

"It came from Alex Slanski's original file."

"Pasha, you fool."

"Don't lecture me, Yuri. We're desperate. We're down a dead end so I went to the Archives office and stole a key and had a look for the original file. I was seen by one of the clerks who came in, but not before I managed to get the file."

"Pasha . . ."

"Listen to me. It couldn't get any worse for me if I was caught. It couldn't get any worse for both of us. We're in deep enough trouble. Me, I may as well be hung for a sheep as a lamb."

"Pasha, you've put yourself in real danger."

"No more than I'm in already." Pasha hesitated. "Yuri, there's something in the file you were deliberately not allowed to see. And there's more, but first you should examine what I've given you."

Pasha stood and crossed to the door, opened it softly. He looked back at Lukin, a wistful look on his face.

"I'm going to leave you alone now. Look and read carefully, Yuri. Afterwards, we'll talk."

The door closed and Pasha was gone.

Lukin opened the file.

There was a single photograph and a single, faded flimsy page inside.

Lukin looked at the photograph first. It was old and yellowed and its edges were frayed. It showed a man and a woman, laughing out at the camera. The man was handsome and clean-shaven, with a fine chiseled face and dark soft eyes. The woman was blond and quite beautiful, with high cheekbones and a strong, determined face. She sat on the man's knee with her arms around his neck. They looked happy and very much in love.

From the style and cut of the couple's clothes, Lukin guessed the photograph had been taken some time in the late twenties or early thirties.

He flipped it over and saw a blue ink stamp in the lower right-hand corner which gave the name of a photographer's studio on Marx Prospect. There was something familiar about the couple's features and he guessed they were Slanski's parents. He had the odd feeling he had seen their faces somewhere before. He guessed they could have been well-known Party members.

He put the photograph aside.

The single page gave brief details of Slanski's family background. His real family name was Stefanovitch and his father was a rural doctor living in Smolensk. The report stated that the OGPU, the precursor to the KGB secret police, had called to arrest him and his family. But no reason was given.

According to the report, the doctor had resisted arrest and had been killed trying to escape. His wife had tried to assist his escape and was shot also. The three children were arrested and the order stated they were to be shot. The death warrant for the doctor and his wife had been authorized personally by Joseph Stalin.

It didn't make sense. How had Slanski survived if he was one of the children?

Again, Lukin read the file carefully. In many ways the information seemed unimportant. The tragedy made him better understand a powerful motive of revenge on Slanski's part, but little else. But there was nothing there that could really help his investigation. Nothing that would point a way for him.

No names of family friends Slanski might try to contact in Moscow. And it did not explain how Slanski had survived while all the other members of his family had perished.

That puzzled Lukin. For a long time he sat there. He lit a cigarette and watched the smoke curl in front of his face.

There had to be something in all this he didn't see. Had to be.

But what?

And why? That was the question.

Why had Pasha given him the file?

A little later the door opened softly.

Pasha stood there. He had the bottle of vodka and the two glasses. He poured a generous measure into each before putting the bottle down on the bench and handing one of the glasses to Lukin.

"Take it."

"Are you trying to get me drunk?"

"No, but I think you're going to need it."

"Why?"

Pasha studied Lukin's face. "Did you find nothing familiar in what you just read and saw?"

"In what way familiar?"

Pasha stared back, unblinking. "I meant the way the information in the file fits together like a puzzle."

Lukin shook his head, confused. "I'm afraid I don't understand."

Pasha sat down opposite. He placed his glass beside him and sighed. "Nothing in the file about Slanski's parents struck you as odd? Who they were? What happened to them?"

"What happened to his father and mother happened to many children during the purges. What I don't understand is how Slanski survived. The file said the entire family were killed."

Pasha slowly shook his head. "That's not what I meant, Yuri. Let me remind you of something about Stalin, something all of us in the KGB know. Some evil streak in him gets delight in inflicting a very personal form of punishment. It was especially so during the purges in the thirties. When Stalin's victims were parents, their children over the age of twelve were killed also.

"Those younger were sent to the orphanages controlled by the KGB. Many of the boys, when they came of age, were inducted into the same KGB. And so they became the one thing their parents would probably never have wanted them to become. Dedicated to Stalin, the sword and shield of the Party, a member of his secret police. Most likely to become the same kind of man as the one who arrested and killed their parents. Stalin finds it cruelly amusing." He paused. "You see, there's another reason you were chosen to find and kill this American, but you still haven't figured it out yet. A reason why the page and photograph were missing from the Wolf's file."

"Why?"

A look of concern crossed Pasha's face. "Stalin probably told Beria not to let you see them. Because once you did you'd see through his sick joke. It was no doubt Stalin's idea to pick you to hunt down and kill Slanski. He had a perverted reason which amused him. Think back, Yuri. Like me you were an orphan. What happened to my parents could have happened to Slanski's. Think back to your own life, before you were sent to the orphanage. Think back to your family."

"I . . . I can't remember."

"You can. But you don't want to. You've tried to blot everything about your past from your mind, and were made to do so at the orphanage, just like me, weren't you?"

Pasha removed another flimsy page and a photograph from his tunic pocket. He handed the photograph over.

"That was also in Slanski's file. It's a photograph of the couple's children." He held up the page. "So was this—the second missing page. It says the order to kill the children was rescinded at the last moment. Instead, they were sent to an orphanage in Moscow. It says two of them, a boy and a girl, were later given different names. One of the names you know well. Study the photograph, Yuri. Study it closely."

Lukin looked down at the photograph. It was of two small boys and a very young girl with blond hair. They stood together in a wheat field laughing out at the camera. The oldest of the three, the one in the middle, was obviously Slanski as a child. He had his arms around the smaller children protectively.

Suddenly the two other faces in the photograph jolted Lukin. The girl was aged no more than four or five, her pale face angelic. And the second boy, his face was suddenly and frighteningly familiar.

Lukin felt a shock go through him and looked up.

Pasha said, "The little girl's name was Katya. She was your sister. The couple in the photograph were your parents. The boy on the right is you, Petya Stefanovitch, before you were given the name Yuri Lukin. You were seven years old."

Lukin turned white. Not a muscle moved on his face as he stared back at Pasha, his body numbed with shock.

Pasha said, "Alex Slanski is your brother."

53

Lukin signed in at the entrance hall of the Officer's Club on Dzerzhinsky Square and climbed the winding marble staircase to the second floor.

The large room he entered looked like a miniature palace, with its marble columns and gilded chandeliers and red-carpeted floors. The air was thick with cigarette smoke and a babble of voices. Lukin pushed his way through the crowd to the bar and ordered a large vodka, but as the white-coated orderly poured he said, "I've changed my mind. Give me the bottle."

He took the bottle and glass to an empty table by the window.

He was hardly conscious of the noise at the bar behind him as he filled the glass to the brim and swallowed. He had swallowed three glasses and poured a fourth before he noticed he was shaking.

He felt icy cold and sweat poured down his temples. He felt anger and a terrible feeling of confusion. He felt . . .

He didn't know what he felt.

As he sat there he stared out through the window. The massive form of the KGB Headquarters stood on the far side of the square, lit up by the soft white glow of the security arc lamps. For a long time he stared out at the building in a daze.

Suddenly he felt tears welling up and a powerful feeling of distress overcame him. He could hardly believe what Pasha had told him.

The man and woman in the photograph were his parents.

The little girl his sister Katya.

Alex Slanski his brother, Mischa.

Lukin's own name was Petya Ivan Stefanovitch.

But now he had read the second missing page from the file he knew it was true. He shuddered and a wave of anger rose and almost smothered him. He swallowed the fourth vodka in one gulp and poured another.

His mind fogged. Then cleared. He racked his brains for memories from his past, a past he had always been forced to block at the Moscow orphanage. Racked his brains until his head hurt. Once he had always tried to forget; now he could do nothing but remember.

That day he had gone to collect Anna Khorev's daughter and saw the urchin faces at the orphanage window he had shuddered. He had shuddered because it was his own past. He remembered always looking out of the window after his brother had escaped; always hoping. Hoping Mischa would come back. Hoping Mischa was still alive. But they told him Mischa was dead.

Not dead.

Alive.

He had been lied to. Katya had been lied to.

Lukin felt so overcome with emotion he thought his brain would burst a blood vessel.

He had a vague recollection of the man who had been his father; but a stronger memory of his mother. Lukin was a small boy. She was walking with him in a wood. It was summer. She was picking flowers. One of her hands held his, another held his brother's. The woman smiled down at him . . .

Think.

Remember.

And then he saw his brother's face clearly, as if a curtain had lifted inside his head. The same face as in the photograph.

Slanski.

He *knew* there was something oddly familiar about the face at the checkpoint in Tallinn.

A fog rolled away. He remembered the day the wolves came and he had run to his father's arms.

"Wolves, Papa!"

"Bah! He's afraid of everything," Mischa laughed.

"Then why did *you* run too?"

"Because *you* ran, little brother. And I couldn't stop you."

His father carried them into the warm, happy house and his mother fussed over them. And afterwards, that same night, lying in his bed, the storm came and he heard the wolves again, howling in the woods, and Mischa's voice saying across the darkened room, "Are you afraid?"

Lightning flashed and thunder rolled beyond the bedroom window. Lukin had started to cry then, fearful of the noise and light, and the wild animals out there in the woods baying in the terrible storm.

"Don't be afraid, little brother. Mischa will protect you. Come, sleep beside me."

He had snuggled in beside his brother, still crying, and Mischa's arms went around him and hugged him close.

"Don't cry, Petya. Mischa will always protect you. And if anyone or anything ever tries to hurt you I will kill them. You understand, little brother? And when Mama has her baby, Mischa will protect baby too."

And all through the night Mischa had held him close, warm and safe and comforted.

Mischa—

"I'm surprised you find time to relax. Enjoy it while it lasts, Lukin."

He started at the voice behind him and turned, not even aware of the tears at the edges of his eyes. Romulka stood there, a mocking grin on his face, a glass of brandy in his hand.

Lukin wiped his face and turned away. "Go to hell."

Romulka smirked. "Now that's no way to speak to a fellow officer. You ought to be more respectful. What's wrong, Lukin? Worried what might happen to you and your wife when Beria learns you've failed him? I just thought you'd like to know the Frenchman still hasn't talked yet, he's holding out remarkably well." He held up his glass and grinned."It's thirsty work, and I needed a little refreshment before I really go to work on him. But if a little more torture fails, then I have something in store for Lebel that's certain to loosen his tongue. That can only mean one thing, Lukin. Once I find the American you'll be finished and the woman will be my responsibility."

"I said go to hell."

"Only something bothers me. I hear you had the woman transferred to Lefortovo this evening. But you know what's odd? The prison has no record of receiving her. Now why is that?"

When Lukin didn't reply, Romulka leaned in closer and said threateningly, "If you're trying to hide her from me I'll make you shorter by a head. Where's the woman, Lukin? Where is she?"

As Lukin stared up at the man's face he felt a terrible overpowering rage.

"You know what your trouble is, Romulka? You and your type are the scum of the KGB. Goddamned cowards all of you. And like all cowards you get pleasure inflicting pain. You bastard, you haven't an ounce of pity in you. You want to know where the woman is? Here's your answer."

He threw his drink in Romulka's face.

Romulka flung away his glass in a rage and reached over and grabbed Lukin by the collar, twisting him around in the chair. A fist smashed into Lukin's face and he was flung back.

As he crashed onto the floor Romulka was already moving in for the kill. For a big man he moved fast, but not fast enough.

Lukin stumbled to his feet and ducked right as Romulka punched the air. He saw his chance and swung his hand up and the metal hook impaled itself in Romulka's forearm.

Romulka's eyes snapped open and he screamed in agony.

Lukin pulled him in like a baited fish and his knee smashed into the man's groin. Romulka yelled in pain as Lukin pulled out the hook and blood spurted on the carpet.

Romulka fell to the floor, still screaming in agony, and a couple of army captains rushed forward to break up the fight.

Lukin roared, "Leave him!"

The men took one look at the rage on Lukin's face and stopped in their tracks.

Romulka stared back up, murder in his eyes, pain twisting his face. "Understand one thing, Lukin—I'm going to find the Wolf. Do you hear me? I'm going to succeed and you'll have failed. And then you're finished, Lukin! *Dead*!"

Lukin took a handkerchief from his pocket and wiped the metal hook. "And you understand this—I see you within two paces and so help me I'll kill you."

He noticed the entire room had gone deathly silent. Faces gaped at him and a few stern-faced elderly officers scowled their disapproval. But no one moved, and from the look on their faces they obviously thought he was deranged.

Lukin turned to the two officers. "I suggest you call a doctor before the colonel here ruins the carpet."

Then he turned and strode out of the door.

When Lebel came around he started to cry.

The pain in his testicle was unbearable and the sickening feeling of nausea still hadn't left him.

Suddenly a bucket of water was splashed in his face and Romulka's voice roared, "Wake up, Jew! Wake up!"

Lebel spluttered behind the wet gag as Romulka leaned over the table. He looked pale and in a savage mood. Lebel noticed a bloodied bandage on his forearm.

"You're being stupid, Lebel, don't you think? A simple question is all you have to answer. Who is helping your friends in Moscow? You tell me how I find them and I release you. Not only release you but do you a favor. I promise your friends won't be hurt. It's the American I'm after. The American and his bitch friend. No one else concerns me."

Sweat and water ran down Lebel's face and he mumbled behind the gag. Romulka tore it off.

"You have something to say?"

"You bastard . . . you're . . . making . . . a mistake . . ."

There was a murderous look in Romulka's face. "Have it your way."

Lebel felt the implement being attached to his scrotum again, tightened, and the pain again shot through his spine, only this time more intensely. His screams rang around the walls and tears flooded his eyes.

It was too much . . .

Too much to bear. His tortured cry rang around the cell.

"NO . . . !"

Romulka shouted to one of the men, "Get the scopolamine."

The man came back from the table with a syringe filled with a yellowish liquid and Romulka said to Lebel, "The truth drug. Either way you're going to talk, Lebel, but let's just see how much more pain you can stand, shall we?"

Romulka turned the screw more tightly and the pain increased until it flooded Lebel's body from head to toe.

He screamed again.

Too much.

He couldn't bear it. It felt as if his testicle was about to burst. He tried to tell Romulka he would talk, tell him everything, anything to stop the pain, and then he passed out again.

It was 11:30 when they reached the street.

There was no street lighting and Massey had to strain his eyes to see the van parked at the end of the road. The glass was iced but he saw that patches had been scraped away so that the driver could see out. The Ukrainian tapped on the side window.

"Open up, Sergei, it's me."

The driver's door opened and a young man peered out, his icy breath fogging the air. He looked almost frozen to death, despite the fact that he was wearing a heavy coat and hat and a scarf covering the lower half of his face.

"About fucking time, *Kapitän*."

Massey and the Ukrainian slid into the freezing cab. When the driver recognized Massey he said, "What the devil . . . !"

When he had got over the shock, he said to Massey, "You going to tell me what's happening?"

"Later. What's the situation?"

"They're still in there. They haven't moved so far as I can tell. The dacha's the third on the left."

Massey rubbed a patch in the icy window. He saw the dark outline of houses across the street and counted off the third one, a bank of trees in front. He turned to the driver and explained everything he had told his companion. Massey would go in alone first. If he wasn't out in half an hour or the men heard shooting they were to enter the house back and front and finish the job.

As the driver checked the action of his weapon and screwed on the silencer, Massey said, "I want you to cover the rear."

The young man grinned. "No problem. Anything to get out of Moscow."

Massey looked at the red-haired man. "You stay out front and keep under cover in the front garden. If anyone other than me comes out you both know what to do."

"You're sure you don't need help inside?"

Massey shook his head. "Just understand one thing. The man will be armed and he's dangerous, very dangerous. So be careful."

The red-haired man grinned. "Whatever you say, *Americanski*. But we were SS, remember? We know how to handle ourselves. Right, Sergei?"

"As the *Kapitän* says."

"For your sakes I hope you're right," said Massey.

He looked back toward the dacha. There was no way out for Slanski if he tried to leave. And if Massey himself failed, then the two men would finish the job.

He checked the silenced Tokarev. His hands were shaking and a sudden nausea in the pit of his stomach made him want to vomit.

The driver said, "Hey, are you OK, *Americanski*?"

Massey nodded and took a deep breath.

They synchronized their watches and Massey said, "OK, let's go."

The three of them stepped from the car.

Lukin sat in the operations room leafing through the lists of car registrations. He had been *stupid* to do what he did to Romulka. But his rage had been so overpowering he couldn't help himself. He tried to concentrate on the papers in front of him.

By law and for internal security, all public and private transport vehicles in the Soviet Union were registered with the militia and the KGB 2nd Directorate. Vehicle licenses and ownership were strictly controlled and both were automatically refused to those convicted of serious criminal and political crimes, so Lukin had disregarded the lists of dissidents.

He had gone to the registrations office and showed the officer in charge his letter from Beria, and ten minutes later the man had come back with a ten-page list of Skoda owner registrations for Moscow.

It had taken Lukin another fifteen minutes to find a couple of likely suspects. There were a dozen gray Skodas registered to women owners. Lukin considered that it was also likely the car could be registered in the woman's husband's name if she was married, but two female owners stood out on the lists.

One was named Olga Prinatin. Lukin knew she was a famous ballerina with the Bolshoi and her description was nothing like the one Rizov had given him.

Another woman, named Irena Dezov, also had a gray Skoda registered in her name. Her address was in the Ramenki district, southwest of Moscow. He knew the area. It was a place where many senior army officers had weekend dachas. The kind of place Nadia could have been held. As Lukin noted all the other brief details in the file, he felt his pulse quicken. A widow, Irena Dezov was aged thirty-eight, and there was a photograph that showed a handsome dark-haired woman. He could check further on her background in the 2nd Directorate records office and see if he could come up with anything that suggested her motive. But some instinct told him he was on the right track.

As he scrambled to his feet, the door opened.

Pasha came in. His face still looked gaunt and pale.

Lukin said, "Why aren't you at home? I want you to keep out of this. You're in enough trouble as it is."

"I wanted to see if you were OK." He hesitated. "And I need to talk. Something's come up." He saw the notebook in Lukin's hand. "What have you got there?"

When Lukin explained about the woman, Pasha smiled. "Maybe you've struck gold. You think Alex Slanski could be using her place as a safe house?"

"It's all I've got, Pasha."

"There's something you ought to know. I just saw Romulka getting into a Zis out in the courtyard. He seemed in a hurry and there was another car following behind with some nasty-looking heavies, armed to the teeth. I phoned the cellars. Apparently, the Frenchman's in a bad state and the prison doctor had to give him a shot of morphine."

Lukin whitened.

Pasha said, "Looks like maybe Romulka was right and Lebel's cracked or been drugged up to the eyeballs with scopolamine to make him talk. What are you going to do?"

Lukin reached for his belt and holster and hurriedly buckled it on. "Follow them and see what direction they're going in. If it's toward Ramenki, as I suspect, I'll try and get to the woman's address before Romulka does. If it's not, I'm in trouble. There's no time to check her background further. Give me those car keys, man, quick!"

"You're going alone?"

"I'm going to take a couple of men along," Lukin lied.

"And what happens if Anna Khorev's there? How do you explain that?"

"That's my problem. But you're out of it, Pasha. That's an order."

"You forget, I'm on sick leave. I don't have to take orders."

"Pasha, for once do as you're told."

"I wouldn't miss this for anything." Pasha hesitated, his face suddenly bleak. "What do we do if we find Slanski?"

"God knows."

"If Romulka gets his hands on him and the woman, they're finished. So are we."

Lukin was suddenly gripped by a terrible feeling of confusion and panic. The whole business was a mess and he didn't know exactly what he was going to do once he reached the woman's address, *if* she was the right one. He didn't want Pasha to come with him, but he knew it was pointless arguing and he didn't have the time. The man was disobeying him more out of loyalty than any disrespect.

Lukin said, "I've got a better idea. Where's Lebel now?"

"In the prison surgery. The doctor's still patching him up."

"Get Lebel and bring him up to the courtyard. We're taking him with us. I could be wrong about Irena Dezov. Let's see if he can tell us what he told Romulka."

"According to one of the guards he's barely able to walk."

"Then get him some more morphine from the doctor. Do whatever you have to, but just get the Frenchman." He handed Pasha Beria's letter. "And if anyone questions you show them that."

He picked up his car keys from the desk and was already moving toward the door. "Let's get going. Romulka's got a head start."

54

It took Massey five minutes to thread his way through the woods to the rear of the dacha, and when he came out of the trees he found himself at the end of a large garden with withered fruit trees covered in snow.

The shutters on the dacha's windows were open, but all the windows were closed, and no light showed behind the curtains. He could make out what looked like an open woodshed off to the left with a car parked in it.

He moved forward, staying in the shadows, and made his way to a small stone-flagged patio at the rear. He tried the back door, turning the handle gently. It was unlocked. He pushed. The door creaked a little, then opened quietly on its hinges.

The room inside was in pitch darkness. Massey stood there for several moments, tensed for a reaction, aware of the sweat on his face as he listened for any sound within the house or for something to happen.

Nothing.

The silence rang like thunder in his ears.

He stepped inside. There was a strong smell of rancid food. From the location of the room and the smell he guessed he was in the kitchen.

He flicked on his flashlight. The room was large and basic; a table and some chairs and some pots and kitchen utensils. He saw a hallway ahead, a door halfway down. A yellow crack of light spilled out from under the door. He moved carefully toward the light, his heart beating in his ribs.

When he reached the door, he hesitated and listened again. Silence. He cocked the Tokarev.

Click.

In the stillness the faint noise sounded like an explosion.

Jesus.

Again, he waited for a reaction.

Nothing.

He took a deep breath, then pushed in the door and stepped quickly into the room.

As he sought a target, he felt the cold tip of a gun against his neck.

He froze, then tried to look around as someone stepped from behind the door.

Slanski's voice said, "I wouldn't, Jake. Now how about you drop the gun. I think we need to talk."

As the BMW drove over Lutznikovski Bridge toward October Square, Lukin wiped the perspiration from his face and checked his watch.

Eleven-thirty.

There was a groan in the back seat from Lebel. The Frenchman was out of it, his eyes closed. Lukin had put handcuffs on him but the man was going nowhere, still drowsy after the drugs. The doctor had given them some extra morphine, but by the look of it Lebel was already drugged up to the eyeballs. According to the doctor, the combination of the scopolamine and morphine acted as a strong painkiller but caused drowsiness, and Lukin wondered if taking the Frenchman along had been a waste of time.

Now Pasha looked out beyond the windshield. "At this rate we'll be lucky to make Ramenki before sunrise."

For some reason the late-night traffic was slow and thick over the bridge. Suddenly it had ground to a halt in both directions.

"Something's wrong up ahead."

October Square lay at the far end of the bridge. There seemed to be a pileup of traffic, and drivers were climbing out of their cars. Lukin had no siren and Romulka already had a five-minute head start.

He hit the brakes and Pasha went to step out of the car but Lukin beat him to it.

"Stay here. I'll find out what's going on."

Lukin ran toward the pileup. Up ahead he saw that a delivery truck had skidded across the bridge and the traffic toward October Square was blocked. Tire tracks slashed across the slushy surface and the scene was chaotic. He swore.

He saw a pedestrian walking past on the footpath, head down against the freezing cold, and he roared at the man, "What the hell's wrong up there?"

The man looked back at the tangle of traffic and shrugged. "A truck's blocking the way. A couple of cars came too fast over the bridge and the truck had to swerve to avoid them."

Lukin saw no sign of Romulka's Zis. The bastards must have caused the pileup and driven on. He raced back to the car. When he climbed in he slammed his fist on the steering wheel in frustration.

Pasha said, "What's up?"

Lukin told him. Pasha said, "That's all we need. We'll never catch up with Romulka now."

Lukin ran his hand over his face and tried to think. Below the sweep of the bridge lay the entrance to Gorky Park, its expanse stretching along the bank of the frozen Moscow River. Farther on, in the hollow below the bridge, he saw the towering shape of the Warsaw Hotel. There was a narrow road off to the right of the hotel which Lukin knew finally came out onto Lenin Prospect. It was throwing him off course by minutes but it was the only way he could escape the pileup.

He said to Pasha, "Hold on to your hat. This is where it starts to get interesting."

He shifted into gear, pulled out of the line of traffic and bumped onto the footpath, lights on and horn blaring as he headed down toward the park.

Massey sat in a chair, the Tokarev pointed at him.

He looked over at Slanski steadily. "It's over, Alex, whichever way you look at it. Lebel's been taken by the KGB and it can't be long before he talks. And that can only mean one thing—the boys in black are going to pay this place a visit."

"If you think I'm giving up now, Jake, you're crazy."

"I told you, it's over. Why be a damned fool?"

There was a slight smile on Slanski's face but no trace of humor in his voice. "Instinct, if you like. A lifetime of bad habits. Besides, it would be one hell of a waste of an opportunity."

Massey shook his head. "You're throwing away your life and the lives of Anna and Irena."

"Washington didn't send you all this way just to have a talk. You came here to put a bullet in me, didn't you, Jake?"

Massey was silent but Slanski saw the reaction on his face. "Could you do that, Jake? Kill Anna and me?"

"If I have to," Massey said flatly.

"The look in your eyes says different. You don't want to do it, Jake."

"There's a bigger picture at stake. It's not just your lives. Moscow will want you both alive. And once they have their evidence they'll have enough reason to start a war."

"What you mean is, heads will roll in Washington if this goes wrong." Slanski stood. "You didn't come here alone, did you?"

Massey said quietly, "The dacha is covered, front and back. There's no way out."

Slanski thought for a moment, then said, "What proof has Moscow got that I'm here to kill Stalin?"

"They've got proof, I told you. And they'll use it once they find you."

"I wouldn't be so sure about that. Besides, I'd never let them take me alive. You think Moscow would tell the world that someone got close enough to kill Stalin? That's where you're wrong. It'd be the biggest loss of face the Kremlin's ever had. They'd keep their mouths shut and pretend nothing had happened. And if I succeeded some of them might even be grateful."

Massey started to stand.

Slanski said, "Stay right where you are."

"Then you mind if I smoke?"

"Go right ahead. But move nice and slowly. And light one for me while you're at it."

As Massey handed him a cigarette, Slanski sat down again. "I never thought it would come to this, Jake. You and me. Like *High Noon*."

"It doesn't have to be that way. You give me your word you'll stop this now and I'll take you and the women back with me. It's against my orders but I'm prepared to take that risk. Like you guessed, I don't want to see any of you wind up dead."

"Considerate of you, Jake. But how do you plan on getting us out now that Lebel's out of the picture?"

"There's a military transport flight to Vienna tomorrow morning. I can arrange papers for all of us."

"And if I don't agree?"

"You won't get out of here alive. You, Anna or Irena."

"You'd really kill Anna too?"

When Massey didn't reply, Slanski said, "How about you just take her and Irena and leave me to finish this?"

Massey shook his head. "No deal, Alex. It's all of you or nothing. So I guess her life's in your hands. What's it to be?"

Slanski smiled faintly. "What a terrible world we live in, Jake. We were friends, and now you're ready to kill me. Anna too. It makes my heart bleed, but there you have it."

He held up two fingers, tips close. "I'm that much away from putting a bullet in the head of the biggest madman the world's ever known and you want me to forget it. You're crazier than me."

"I told you the reasons. Washington can't take the risk."

"And you always do what Washington says?"

Massey said impatiently, "Something tells me I'm wasting my time here."

As he reached over to crush out his cigarette suddenly his hand came up to grab the silenced pistol.

But Slanski was too quick. He fired once, the pistol spat and the bullet nicked Massey's wrist.

Massey fell back in pain, gripping the wound.

"You're getting slow, Jake. I could have taken your eye out. Maybe I should just kill you and be done with it."

He took a handkerchief from his pocket and tossed it over. Blood oozed through Massey's fingers and he put the cloth on the wound.

"Alex, you're making a big mistake . . . listen to me . . . for Anna's sake."

There was a sudden hard edge to Slanski's voice. "What the hell do you care about Anna? Sorry, Massey, I'm past listening. Get up."

As Massey struggled to move, there was noise on the stairs and then Anna appeared in the doorway.

When she saw Massey she opened her mouth to speak but no words came, a look of utter shock on her face.

Slanski turned to her. "I'll explain later. Get some water and look after Massey. Then wake Irena. We're getting out of here."

Five minutes later Lukin had cut onto Lenin Prospect and was headed toward the Ramenki district.

Pasha had tried to rouse Lebel, slapping him hard and shouting in his face, but the Frenchman was still unconscious.

The Mongolian said in frustration, "Damn, it's no good, we've wasted our time bringing him with us."

"Try again!"

He tried again but the Frenchman only groaned in his sleep.

Lukin swore with frustration. "Leave him."

The traffic out to the country was thin and the roads covered in hard-packed snow. When they reached the intersection with Lomonossow Prospect and turned right, Lukin saw the taillights of another vehicle a hundred meters in front.

When he narrowed the gap he saw that it was a black Zis and that there was another large car ahead of it.

Pasha said, "I think we're in luck."

The two cars up ahead were moving fast over the snow, but Lukin had snowchains and the BMW had a powerful engine. He put his foot down and pulled out to get a better look. The car in the lead was definitely also a Zis.

Pasha said, "If it's Romulka and you overtake him he'll smell a rat."

"What else can I do?"

Pasha grinned. "Nothing, but I'd like to see the bastard's face when he sees us. Let's do it."

Lukin hit the accelerator. For a split second there was a dragging sensation as the BMW's tires threaded the packed snow, then the chains on the tires gripped and the powerful engine roared as Lukin swung the steering wheel to the left.

He overtook the rear car. There were four burly plain-clothes men inside and they glanced at the BMW as it roared past.

And then suddenly Lukin was alongside the lead Zis.

He glanced right just as Pasha did, and caught a glimpse of the driver, then Romulka sitting in the passenger seat. He gave another burst of power and the BMW shot forward.

The driver and Romulka glanced over, just as Lukin overtook them.

For a moment Romulka's face was illuminated in a wash of street light. There was a look of astonishment when he saw Lukin's car.

Pasha rolled down his window and raised his middle finger at Romulka. "Sit on that, you asshole."

Romulka reacted at the gesture and then his twisted, angry face was gone from view as the BMW raced ahead.

Moments later, Lukin pulled back into the lane, but kept the speed up.

Pasha laughed.

Lukin said, "Do you always have to be the diplomat?"

"Fuck him. I'll worry about the consequences afterwards."

"You Mongolians, you're beyond redemption."

"It's in the blood. With Genghis Khan for an ancestor, what do you expect?"

Lebel groaned in the back, seemed to come around, then fell silent. Lukin glanced in the rearview mirror.

Already the cars behind were picking up speed, challenging him. He felt the sweat drip from his brow as he said to Pasha, "How much farther?"

"I reckon another four kilometers. Keep up the speed and, with luck, we'll just have time to do our business at the dacha before that bastard's up our ass."

Slanski blew out the oil lamp and the room was plunged into darkness.

He flicked on the flashlight and held the Tokarev in his other hand. He shone the beam into a corner of the room.

Massey was sitting on the floor, his hands tied behind his back. Anna and Irena sat huddled beside him. They had dressed and Irena's face was white with fear. Slanski said to Massey, "How about you let the women go free and I take my chances?"

Massey avoided looking at Anna as he said, "I told you, I can't do that, Alex."

"You're a bastard, Massey. They're out of this already. What harm can it do?"

"I was given orders . . ."

Massey saw that Anna was staring at him, hurt on her face. Slanski had told her why Massey had come and he had seen the disbelief in her reaction.

Massey said suddenly, "Anna, I'm sorry. This isn't my doing. If Alex goes ahead with this we're all dead. He has to stop this madness."

There was a look of hopelessness on her face as she turned away. "I don't think it matters now, does it, Jake? Nothing matters."

"Tell him to stop because it's the only way we all walk away from this alive . . . You've nowhere left to run to."

Before Anna could reply, Slanski said, "Shut up, Massey. Make another sound and it'll be your last."

He flicked off the flashlight and moved to the window. He waited until his eyes became accustomed to the dark, then pulled back the curtain a crack and peered out. The front garden looked eerily quiet in the moonlight. He thought he saw a figure move near the gate, and then it was gone. He let the curtain fall back into place, switched on the torch again and shone the light on Massey.

"How many people have you got outside?"

Massey didn't reply. Slanski cocked the Tokarev and aimed at Massey's head. "You hesitate again and I take your head off. How many?"

"Two men."

"Who are they?"

"Agents we dropped months back."

"Tell me more."

"They're former Ukrainian SS."

"Nice company you're keeping, Jake. I'm surprised."

"It was either a war crimes trial or work for us." There was an edge of panic in Massey's voice. "For God's sake let me talk to them, Alex . . ."

Slanski shook his head. "You're sure about the number? You don't want to reconsider?"

"I told you, two."

"You'd better not be lying to me." He tossed Massey's weapon to Anna. "He moves, you shoot him. If you don't he'll kill you."

He handed the flashlight to Irena.

"Switch it off. And keep it off until I get back. Give me the keys to the car."

Irena looked at him wildly. "We'll never get out of this alive. We're all dead . . . Oh my God . . . !"

The woman was trembling with fear and Slanski slapped her face and said firmly, "Shut up and just do as I tell you. That way we may get out of here in one piece. The keys. Then turn off the damned flashlight."

Irena fumbled for the keys, handed them to Slanski, then flicked off the flashlight. Suddenly the room was plunged into darkness again.

They heard the door creak faintly and Slanski was gone.

The kitchen was in darkness and freezing cold.

As Slanski stepped inside he saw that the door that led outside was ajar. He crossed the room silently and peered out into the courtyard, the Tokarev at the ready.

The snowed-under garden was pale gray in the watery moonlight. He trained his eyes for a long time on the woodshed and the car, trying to discern movement, but saw only shadows and darkness.

He didn't know whether Massey was telling the truth. There could be more than two men out there and they could be anywhere, but there was only one way to find out.

He cocked the Tokarev, lay flat on his stomach and crawled out of the door. Moments later he was slithering across the freezing stone-flagged courtyard until he reached the woodshed.

He waited for any movement or sound and when none came he stood and unlocked the driver's door and inserted the key in the ignition, then left the door ajar.

He was about to move forward when he heard a faint click from behind him and a voice said in Russian, "Drop the weapon and keep your hands in the air. Then turn around slowly."

He dropped the Tokarev and it clattered to the ground. He turned and saw a young man standing in the shadows ten feet away.

The man stepped out. He was heavily built and held a pistol in his hand. He grinned. "I'll say this for you, you move pretty silently, but not silently enough. Where's my American friend?"

"Back in the house."

"Dead?"

"Very much alive, I'm afraid." Slanski nodded back toward the garden. "There were supposed to be two of you. Where's your comrade?"

"You'll soon find out. Turn around and move toward the house. I warn you not to try anything, I'm an excellent shot."

"Whatever you say. Except there's something you forgot."

"Oh? And what's that?"

"This."

The silenced Nagant came up and spat once. The man had no chance. The single shot hit him square in the bridge of the nose and he fell back against the car and slid to the ground.

Slanski crouched and waited at the ready for a reaction to the silenced gunshot, and when none came he retrieved the Tokarev, then dragged the body to the back of the woodshed.

The second Ukrainian crouched in the bushes in the front garden and cocked his ears. He had definitely heard something.

What, he wasn't sure.

Voices? Or the wind in the trees? He shifted his bulk and raised himself slightly. He laid the Kalashnikov beside him on the ground and rubbed his legs to get the circulation going. What the fuck was going on? The American should have come out by now.

He checked his watch.

The luminous hands read a quarter to midnight. He'd give it another couple of minutes, then he'd move toward the house. In the meantime, anyone who came out of the door was dead, no question.

Odd, but the situation gave him a strange sense of exhilaration. It was just like the old days, stalking Red partisans in the Caucasus. All that was missing was his SS uniform and a decent German MP40 machine-pistol.

He smiled, picked up his weapon, squatted again, and waited.

* * *

"Turn on the flashlight."

Irena flicked it on and Slanski stood there looking down at Massey. "Looks like maybe you were right about the numbers, Jake. But now you're one down. Tell me about the man out front."

When Massey didn't reply, Slanski put the Tokarev to his head. "Tell me, or I might be tempted."

"His name's Boris Koval. A former Ukrainian SS captain."

"Is he good?"

Massey nodded.

"How good?"

"One of the best we trained. Not that he needed much training. He was good before we started."

"Weapons?"

Massey fell silent. Slanski said, "Either you can tell me, or I shove you out the front door and we learn the hard way."

"A Kalashnikov."

Slanski gave a low whistle. "Then I guess we're in trouble." He turned to Irena and Anna. "We're going out the back way. Massey too. When I give the word you pile into the back of the car and keep your heads down. Leave the rest to me."

As Anna stood, Massey looked up at her. Their eyes met for a moment and he saw the look on her face, all trust between them destroyed.

He went to speak, to explain, but already she was gone, moving toward the door, Irena walking shakily behind her. Then Slanski dragged Massey to his feet and pushed him after them.

Pasha checked the street map as Lukin drove.

Lukin said, "How much farther?"

"Take the next left and we're there."

"You said that a minute ago."

"These streets all look the fucking same in the snow."

Lukin swung right and they entered a long, wide, tree-lined road with dachas on either side. He halted at the junction where the two roads met. The homes looked dark and deserted.

Pasha grabbed a machine-pistol from the back seat and laid it ready on his lap.

"So what's the drill?"

Lukin doused the lights. Only the moon on the snow ahead provided light, and the road looked eerily quiet.

"I wish I knew."

"Damn it, Yuri . . . Romulka will be here in no time!"

"I need to talk to Slanski."

"Then I hope he listens, because if not you're dead."

"I'm going in alone. I want you to wait outside."

"What are you going to do? Knock on the door and say you've come by for a visit? Slanski's going to blow your head off as quick as look at you. There has to be another way."

"There isn't time to think of one."

Suddenly in the rearview mirror Lukin saw a blaze of headlights sweep into view behind them at the far end of the road.

Pasha looked back and said, "The bastards are here already. Looks like we've got the right place."

Lukin watched the headlights moving toward them and said, "You think you could hold them off a little longer?"

"You mean fire on Romulka?"

"In the darkness they're not going to know what the hell's going on or who's shooting. Just blow the tires, that'll slow them, then meet me at the dacha."

"Presuming you're still alive. OK, let's do it."

"Be careful," Lukin said.

Pasha slipped from the car and disappeared around the corner clutching the machine-pistol.

The Frenchman, Lebel, still lay slumped on the back seat.

Lukin slipped into gear and swung the BMW into the street. He counted off the numbers as he drove, and then he saw the dacha.

The lights were out. He drove on another fifty meters to the next dacha on the same side of the street. The place looked deserted, the driveway empty, all the lights out and the windows shuttered for the winter. He slowed, then backed up quickly into the driveway. As he went to step out of the car Lebel moaned and seemed to come to drowsily, then his head listed to one side and he was gone again.

Lukin unlocked the Frenchman's handcuffs and shackled one to the grip on the back door and stepped out of the car.

What exactly he was going to do he still didn't know. But whatever it was he had to do it fast. Any second now Romulka would come tearing around the corner and Pasha would start firing. If Slanski was inside he'd hear the shooting and that wasn't going to help.

The file Pasha had stolen was tucked into Lukin's tunic.

He lifted the flap on his holster, released the safety on his pistol, but left the weapon in the holster. He didn't intend to use it but he wasn't taking a chance.

He went around quickly to the back of the car and unlocked the trunk. He fumbled among the tools and the spare wheel until he found an oily rag. The remnant of a white shirt, it was covered in grease and oil stains. He found the jack and tied the white rag on the end.

It was a crude flag of peace but it would have to do for what he had in mind. It was ridiculous when he thought of it. He was going to knock on the front door, call out to Slanski and hope he got a cooperative response. It was risky, inviting almost certain death, but he could think of nothing else to do.

He moved quickly, closing the trunk again.

Suddenly he heard a blaze of gunfire followed by a screech of tires from the far end of the street.

The noise seemed to fill the air and a split second later came another volley of shots, and then the night seemed to explode with chattering weapons.

Pasha had opened up on Romulka's convoy and by the sound of it Romulka and his men were firing back.

Sweat pumping from every pore, Lukin swore and ran toward the dacha.

The Ukrainian smelled trouble.

He didn't like it. Didn't like it one little bit.

It had been half an hour since the American had left and there was still no sign of him.

What was going on? Was he dead? Or still stalking his quarry inside the house?

The Ukrainian was a man of infinite patience and could have waited in the freezing garden all night, but this time he was reacting to instinct.

And instinct told him there was trouble.

Moments ago a car had driven up on the street outside. He had tensed, every muscle in his body suddenly alert and ready for action. He peered into the street through the bushes and saw a German BMW drive slowly past, snow-chains crunching over the packed surface.

Odd that, a BMW. Its dark paintwork gleamed in the watery moonlight. A beautiful car. He couldn't make out the driver's face but the figure was definitely looking toward the dacha, and there looked to be another figure in the back.

What the fuck was going on?

He had readied himself to fire but the car had driven on past. He heard the vehicle turn into a driveway farther on and the engine die. He waited, heard a car door opening, then another, the sounds loud in the darkness, but heard nothing more.

The dachas were all deserted and he guessed only used on weekends. Perhaps one of the owners had decided to drive out of Moscow and spend the night? Maybe the man had a woman with him in the back of the car? He had barely glimpsed the figure in the back and he wasn't sure if it was a woman.

Fuck.

He listened further for any sound, heard nothing, then got to his feet silently.

Perhaps he ought to check it out? But whatever way you looked at it, he shouldn't stick around waiting. He cocked the Kalashnikov and started to move out of the shadows.

As he did so he heard a crackle of gunfire explode down the street. He froze.

At the kitchen door, Slanski peered out into the moonlit back garden.

Behind him Anna and Irena waited expectantly. Massey was out in front, his hands still tied, and Slanski had the gun pressed into the base of his skull.

"You first, Massey," he whispered, and turned to the others. "We're going to move to the car. Keep it quiet and remember what I told you."

He pushed Massey out into the flagstoned courtyard. He crouched, half expecting gunfire, but when none came they moved hurriedly across to the woodshed and the Skoda.

He opened the rear door and pushed Massey quickly inside, then Anna slid in beside him.

Irena was already in the passenger seat, and as Slanski jumped into the driver's seat beside her he said, "So far so good."

He rolled down the driver's window quietly and then his fingers found the ignition key and he tensed. He shifted into first gear, but kept his foot firmly down on the clutch. He hesitated, and stared out toward the driveway and the snowed-under street beyond it.

It looked empty, no traffic in sight.

The distance was about thirty meters and he could clear it in seconds if he could get quickly up to speed.

He turned the ignition key.

The engine spluttered and died and Slanski's heart sank.

But at that exact moment all hell seemed to break loose.

A crackle of gunfire erupted like fireworks from somewhere off in the darkness, followed by the screech of tires and brakes. Everyone in the Skoda tensed and Slanski went deathly still.

"What the hell . . . ?"

There was another burst of gunfire from far away. Slanski turned the ignition key again and this time the engine exploded into life.

He flicked a switch and the headlights flooded the driveway. At the same time he eased off the clutch, hit the accelerator, and the Skoda shot forward and tore down the path.

As Lukin approached the dacha he tensed.

Blood pumped furiously through his veins as the sound of gunfire still raged in the distance. He had the white rag in his hand, and as he jogged toward the driveway he caught sight of a figure moving out of the bushes at the front of the garden.

A big man, ruggedly built. He had a Kalashnikov in his hands and was moving toward the front of the dacha.

Lukin froze.

The man was partly in shadow and he couldn't make out if it was Slanski.

Before he could react an engine suddenly burst into life and two powerful beams of light illuminated the driveway. Lukin stood there totally confused. The man with the Kalashnikov seemed to freeze too, but then a car roared out of the darkness and down the driveway, headlights blazing.

Lukin stood stunned as the man in the garden spun around and fired off a rapid burst as the Skoda shot past.

Lukin flung himself down as the weapon chattered, and he heard the sound of lead rip into metal as a volley of fire answered from the driver's window.

The Skoda shot onto the street and the man with the Kalashnikov ran after it, firing wildly.

Windows shattered as the car skewed and slid on the snow, then it suddenly righted itself and swung left out into the middle of the street.

As it swung, a rear door burst open with the sudden force of the turn and a figure came hurtling out onto the snow and rolled across the street.

Lukin watched in disbelief as the man with the Kalashnikov kept firing at the Skoda, and then suddenly he caught a glimpse of Slanski at the steering wheel.

The man with the Kalashnikov had emptied his magazine and he tore another from his pocket and hastily reloaded and cocked the weapon.

Lukin wrenched out his pistol just as the man turned, horror on his face when he saw Lukin.

As he went to raise the Kalashnikov, Lukin got off two shots, hitting him in the chest and neck and punching him back into the snow.

He ran out into the street and saw the Skoda's taillights disappear, racing over the snow.

"NO . . . !" he roared.

There was a groan of pain from behind, and when he turned back Lukin saw the figure from the car writhing in the snow. He was wounded in the chest and his face was twisted in agony. Then he saw that his hands were tied behind his back.

"Jesus . . . help me . . ."

The man spoke in English.

For several moments Lukin stood there in total confusion, then suddenly he heard shouts and saw a knot of men come down the street, flashlights in their hands as they moved toward him at a trot.

Romulka led the way, his pistol out. "Halt! Stay where you are!"

Where the hell was Pasha?

Lukin turned back frantically and saw that the taillights of the Skoda had vanished. He knelt and gripped the wounded man by the collar and dragged him back to the BMW.

After ten seconds Lukin was almost out of breath. A volley of shots rang out, kicking up puffs of snow in front of him.

He glanced back. Romulka and his men were less than fifty meters away.

"Halt! Do you hear me? Halt!"

Lukin kept going, the man's weight like lead. When he reached the driveway, he flung open the passenger door of the BMW and lifted the man inside, then climbed into the driver's seat, turned the ignition key and the engine roared.

As he reversed out onto the street two men ran up, firing pistols at the car.

Lukin heard shots puncture metal and glass and the rear window shattered.

As Lukin glanced back, Lebel suddenly became conscious and Lukin heard a moan and a voice saying drowsily, "Where am I . . . ?"

"Keep down!"

He didn't wait to see if Lebel had obeyed. He shifted frantically into gear as he ducked his head, hit the accelerator and the car roared forward.

Bullets cracked into the chassis as he raced down the street.

The last thing Lukin glimpsed in the rearview mirror was Romulka running after him in the middle of the street, firing wildly, his face twisted in rage.

Lukin sweated as he drove.

He had kept the headlights off in case he caught up with the Skoda, but the road was unlit and he found it difficult to keep the BMW straight.

Every now and then he got too close to the curb and the front wheel hit the right side of the road and he had to wrench the steering wheel over.

What he had done was crazy, but he knew he had to follow Slanski. All he saw up ahead now though was night and empty white streets.

The Skoda had a head start of maybe only a minute, but the BMW was faster, so it couldn't get far ahead. Besides, Lukin could just make out the single set of tire marks in the virgin snow and knew it had to be the Skoda.

He came to a fork in the road. He saw tire marks leading left and followed them, picking up as much speed in the darkness as he dared.

What had happened to Pasha? Lukin guessed that once the firing became too intense he had tried to double back to the dacha.

Unless Romulka had killed him? At that thought Lukin sank into despair. But then he knew Pasha. He was headstrong but he had the native cunning of his Mongol blood. Lukin guessed—hoped—the man would somehow find his way out of it.

The Frenchman was conscious now in the back, the drug wearing off. The shooting had obviously startled him awake. When Lebel finally saw the wounded man in the front seat he suddenly seemed to come alive, a bewildered look on his face as he spoke.

"Jake . . ."

Lukin didn't know what the word meant or if it was French or English. The man beside him was barely conscious. His head was slumped on his chest and he was gurgling and coughing up blood.

The Frenchman leaned over shakily and felt the passenger's pulse and said in confusion, "What's going on? For God's sake, can't you see he's dying!"

There was something in his tone and action that suggested Lebel knew the man. The car bumped as it hit the curb, then Lukin righted it again and kept following the tracks in the snow. The man in the passenger seat groaned and his head rolled to the right.

Lukin said urgently, "You know him?"

"Yes."

"Who is he?" Lukin demanded.

Lebel looked at him, perplexed. "Who are you? How did I get here?"

"Major Lukin, KGB. I released you from the Lubyanka."

Confusion filled the Frenchman's face and he fell silent. Lukin guessed that he was still too disoriented from the morphine to recognize him from the hotel. And the Frenchman looked to be in considerable pain. Before Lukin could speak again he suddenly noticed the red taillights of a car a hundred meters ahead and his heart skipped. He had almost reached the Moscow River and a bridge ahead led across to Novodevichy. When the car in front trundled over the bridge and the taillights kept straight on, Lukin realized the vehicle was headed toward the old convent.

It had to be Slanski.

The marks in the snow were the only ones Lukin had seen all the way from the dacha. Slanski was obviously desperate and had nowhere else to run. The deserted convent would offer brief cover.

Lukin slowed and peered beyond the windshield. Just then he saw the beginning of the convent walls on the left-hand side of the road. He felt his heart thumping against his ribs as he saw the car slow and then turn left toward the convent entrance. He had kept a safe distance behind and still had the headlights off, and he guessed the occupants of the car hadn't noticed him. But even from a distance he thought the car was a light-colored Skoda.

As he came toward the left turn, Lukin increased his speed, flicked on the lights, and drove straight on past. He turned to look and saw the Skoda halted outside the convent entrance, fifty meters away. He glimpsed the shattered rear window and sighed with relief. A hundred meters farther on, he doused the headlights, swung the BMW back around facing the convent, then eased on the brakes and switched off the engine. As he sat there he could just make out a figure moving into the arched entrance. Moments later the figure returned, climbed back into the driver's side, and the Skoda drove in through the archway and disappeared.

Lukin waited, then started the car again and drove closer to the convent. Fifty meters from the entrance he switched off the engine and let the BMW coast silently to a halt just outside the archway. He saw the gate inside was open.

The man in the passenger seat groaned again.

The Frenchman said, "He's dying. For God's sake do something, quick!"

"Listen to me, Lebel, and listen well. I mean you no harm. If you do as I say, you go free. Do you want to go free?"

Lebel stared back in disbelief. "Would someone kindly tell me what the hell's going on? I've been abducted and spent two days in a stinking cell, had one of my balls half crushed by a deranged maniac who said I'd never see sunlight again. And now you're asking me if I want to go free, like it's all been some terrible mistake?"

Lukin handed over the key to the handcuffs. "Here, release yourself."

The gesture seemed to amaze the Frenchman and he quickly unlocked the cuffs. Lukin asked, "Who's your friend?"

Lebel hesitated, then said, "An American. His name's Jake Massey. And if you want to know any more ask your comrade Colonel Romulka."

"Time for explanations later. And Romulka's no friend. If I hadn't taken you from the cellars he would have had worse in store for you, I can assure you. But right now I want you to deliver a message to the convent."

There was a puzzled look on Lebel's pained face. "I don't understand."

"Your friends from the dacha just drove in there. There's a man named Slanski with them. Tell him I want to talk. Tell him that it's important and I mean him no harm."

Lukin saw the confusion on the Frenchman's face.

"He'll doubt you, Lebel, but assure him this is no trick. Here, I want you to give him this." He removed the file from his tunic and handed it over. "Tell him to read what's inside carefully. Tell him Major Yuri Lukin has discovered the reason why he was chosen to find the Wolf. When he's read it I need to talk."

Lebel frowned uncertainly.

Lukin said, "*Please*, trust me and do as I ask. I haven't been followed and I mean none of you any harm. Assure Slanski of that. Take my gun if you don't believe me."

He removed the Tokarev from his holster and handed it to Lebel. When the Frenchman didn't take the weapon, he grabbed his hand and forced the gun into his palm and closed his fingers around it.

"*Take it.* Can you drive?"

Lebel looked bewildered. He nodded.

Lukin said, "Take my car and drive into the convent. Tell Slanski I'll be waiting by the river. Take your friend with you. The others may be able to help him."

He climbed out of the car and helped Lebel out of the back and into the driver's seat, the Frenchman wincing in pain.

"Take it easy," he groaned.

Lukin stuffed the Tokarev and the file into Lebel's pockets. "Do you think you can manage it?"

"*Mon ami*, so long as I don't have to return to the Lubyanka, I'll manage anything."

"How do you feel?"

Lebel grunted. "Like someone's set fire to my right testicle."

Lukin found the white rag in the car and rolled down the driver's window. "Take this. Keep waving it as you go inside."

The Frenchman looked alarmed. "You think there'll be shooting?"

"For your sake I hope not."

"I think it's time to get out of the Moscow fur business. Move somewhere safer and more peaceful, like Hell's Kitchen, New York. Wish me luck."

"Go, please. Quickly. And remember what I told you."

Lebel drove unsteadily toward the convent gate. As Lukin watched him disappear into the dark courtyard beyond he heard the distant sound of a clock strike half past midnight.

He walked on down to the river. The place was deserted, the frozen water silver in the pale moonlight. He found a bench and sat. He removed the cigarette case from his pocket, lit one with a shaking hand, and waited.

Massey became conscious again as he sat in the car.

A draft of icy cold rushed in through the open window and stung his face. Then shock waves of pain flooded his entire body. He moaned in agony and tasted blood on his lips. His lungs and chest felt as if they were in flames, but his brow felt cold as ice. He coughed up blood and it spewed onto his coat.

He thought: *God, I'm dying.*

A voice said, "Take it easy, Jake. We're almost there, you goddamned son-of-a-bitch. Don't die on me now."

Massey was faintly aware of a silver light at the end of an alcove, an open trellis gate and a courtyard with gardens beyond. The car drove through very slowly and finally came to a halt and the engine died. And then the man beside him was waving something and shouting. "I've got a wounded man here, for Christ's sake! Give me some help!"

The voice rang around the courtyard walls.

In the freezing silence that followed the moments seemed like hours. Then Massey heard another voice, distant, too distant to hear clearly.

Then the voice beside him called out, "Don't shoot! I've got Massey with me. He's badly wounded."

Slanski appeared out of nowhere holding a gun.

Massey tried to move, but all his senses seemed to go out of focus, a strange fog started to envelope him, and he slumped forward in his seat.

57

The buildings set around the convent courtyard had long been allowed to go to ruin, and the vestry at the back of the old church was no different. It had no electricity and stank of urine and excrement, and the plaster walls were peeling.

Anna held a flashlight while Irena supported Lebel and Slanski carried Massey inside. The Frenchman had difficulty walking, but when she shone the light on Massey she put a hand over her mouth in horror. Blood streamed through his clothes from his wounds and his face was deathly white.

Once they were inside the room, Slanski put Massey down and said to Irena, "Take off his coat, quick as you can."

Irena went to do as he said but when she had opened a couple of buttons and saw the wounds she said, "You're wasting your time. He's not going to make it. He's lost too much blood." She turned on Lebel, anger blazing in her eyes now she had got over the shock of seeing him again. "What a mess you've got me into."

"I could say the same for myself."

"Lebel, I could cheerfully kill you, you bastard."

"Not my doing, my love. Sometimes things have a way of going wrong. Just be grateful we're both still alive."

Something seemed to snap in Irena then, and she raised a hand to slap Lebel's face, but he deflected it in midair and said, "Don't, *chérie*, can't you see I'm in enough pain?"

Slanski was feeling Massey's pulse and he shouted over at them, "You too can slug it out later. Irena, go outside and see if you can find some water. We need to clean these wounds."

Irena went to protest but when she saw the look on Slanski's face she hurriedly left the room.

Lebel said to Slanski, "I was told to give you these." He held out the file and the Tokarev. "Compliments of a Major Lukin. I presume you two know each other?"

Slanski went very still and his face tightened.

Lebel said, "Lukin drove us here. He was alone and told me to tell you he means you no harm. He said to assure you that it's no trick, and that he hasn't been followed." He saw the look of total confusion on Slanski's face and said, "Take it from me, whoever's side the major is on, it's not the KGB's. He just rescued me. And by the way, that's Lukin's gun you're holding—he's unarmed."

"Do you mind telling me what's going on?"

"My sentiments exactly. This whole thing gets more confusing by the minute. One moment I'm in Paris, the next I'm being tortured in a stinking cell in Moscow, having one of my testicles reshaped. Then, to cap it all, I'm set free by a one-armed renegade KGB major playing the rescuing angel. Life certainly has its surprises."

"Where's Lukin now?"

"Outside by the river waiting for you to join him. He says he wants to talk and it's important." Lebel pointed to the file. "But you're to read that first. Something else he said to tell you. That Major Yuri Lukin has discovered the reason why he was chosen to find the Wolf. Whatever that means."

Slanski switched on his flashlight, confusion on his face, and opened the folder.

Lebel turned to Anna. "You must be one of my intended passengers? I'm afraid after tonight we'll be lucky to get out of Moscow, let alone make it to Finland. It looks hopeless."

Before Anna could speak, Massey groaned and she turned to him. He was losing blood fast. She put a hand on his fevered brow, leaned closer and whispered, "Don't die on me, Jake."

Suddenly Massey's eyelids flickered and his voice gurgled. "Anna . . ."

"Don't move or talk, Jake. Take it easy."

"Anna . . . forgive me . . ."

"No talk, Jake. Please."

Massey coughed up blood and it dribbled down his chin. His eyes closed and his head slumped to one side. There were tears in Anna's eyes as she turned to Slanski. "For God's sake, can't you do something?"

But he wasn't listening. As he stood there holding the file there was an odd look on his face, which was dazed and suddenly very pale, paler than she had ever seen it before, and he was very still. He held a photograph in his hand and he stared at it silently.

Anna screamed at Lebel, "Do something!"

Lebel moved closer and felt Massey's pulse, just as Irena came in carrying a battered zinc bucket slopping with liquid.

"It's all I could find, some ice water from an overflow barrel."

Lebel looked up and let Massey's limp wrist fall.

"I'm afraid we're wasting our time. He's dead."

* * *

Snow started to drift down and the icy river looked ghostly white in the darkness.

Beyond the silver birch trees on the far bank, Lukin could see the lights of Moscow. In the distance the red star on top of the Kremlin winked on and off like a beacon through the mist of lightly falling snow.

Slanski sat beside him. There was a timelessness to it all both men were conscious of. The look of shock hadn't left Slanski and he still held the file in his hand. He had made his way down to the riverbank, warily at first, until he had seen the trauma on Lukin's face when their eyes met, a look that told him he had nothing to fear. For a long time the two men sat there, neither speaking, and then, as if to break the tension and silence, Lukin said, "Your friend. Will he make it?"

"He's dead."

"I'm sorry."

"It comes to us all. Nothing could be done."

Lukin looked at Slanski intently. "You read all of the file?"

"Yes."

"And you believed everything you read?"

"I had my doubts, but now . . . now I see you up close, yes, I believe it. And from what Lebel tells me you saved his life and ours. You wouldn't have gone to that trouble if you weren't serious."

Lukin looked out at the darkness. "Who would have imagined it? Now you know why I was picked to track you down and kill you. A sick joke of Stalin's. Pit brother against brother. Blood against blood." He sucked in a deep breath and blew a cloud of steam into the air and shook his head. "I still can't believe it."

Slanski's voice softened. "Tell me what happened the night I left the orphanage. Tell me what happened afterwards."

Lukin looked at him. There were tears at the edges of his eyes and his voice was thick with emotion.

"Do I have to?"

"I need to know, Petya."

"It's a long time since anyone called me by that name. It seems strange, from another life. So much of what happened in my past I've locked away. It seemed such a terrible nightmare. Until I read the file, I thought I'd managed to bury it all."

"You have to tell me."

Lukin shook his head. "It won't help. For over twenty years I've tried to forget. And maybe it's better you don't know."

For some reason, Slanski reached over and touched Lukin's hand.

And then Lukin was overcome with emotion. Slanski put his hand gently on his brother's shoulder and said, "Take it easy, Petya."

They sat there for several moments, not speaking, then Slanski said, "Being with you and Katya seemed like the only reality I knew. When I left you both behind that night at the orphanage it felt like I'd lost everything. I never knew what had happened to you both. And afterwards that pain seemed worse than knowing you were dead. It was like someone cut my heart out and there was a hollow where both of you used to be. I need to know."

Lukin looked away. Towards the city he saw the lights of traffic moving beyond the mist of snow. The scene seemed so normal, and yet the turmoil in his own soul was so extraordinary. He felt a stab of anguish in his chest and turned back.

"The night you escaped Katya and I watched you from the window. It was like losing Mama and Papa all over again. The same grief, the same pain. Katya was inconsolable. She loved you, Mischa. You were father and mother to her.

"It must have been about four in the morning when you escaped. Katya was broken-hearted, she was shaking with convulsions. I couldn't stop her. One of the wardens came to the dormitory and found us. When she discovered you were gone she raised the alarm and put us both in one of the basement cells. Two men came from the secret police. They demanded we tell them where you had gone. They threatened to kill us if we didn't." His voice shook with anger. "Katya was five years old but they beat her, tormented her, just as they did me.

"After three or four days went by they told us you were never coming back. Your body had been found on a railway track near the Kiev Station, crushed by a train. Something happened to Katya after that. It was like a light went out inside her. When I looked in her face her eyes were empty. She wouldn't eat or drink. A doctor was sent for, but the doctors who came to the orphanage couldn't have cared less if you lived or died. There were so many orphans, one less didn't matter."

He hesitated. "The next day they sent me to a correction school. From that institution the secret police often picked their recruits. Katya they sent to an orphanage in Minsk and I never saw her again." He looked up. "Only it wasn't an orphanage. It was a special hospital. For special children."

"What do you mean?"

"It was a home for the retarded. The really bad ones were kept in locked cells, chained to their beds like animals. Katya had become so withdrawn they locked her in a cell on her own. But there was nothing really wrong with her except her heart was broken and no one could reach her." Lukin paused. "When the war came and the Germans advanced, Stalin ordered that the inmates of all special hospitals were to be liquidated to conserve food supplies. They took the patients out in batches to the woods and shot them. Katya was one of them."

After a long silence Slanski said palely, "So Katya died because of me."

"No, not because of you. Don't blame yourself. You did what you had to."

"If I'd stayed she would have survived."

"No matter what you think, you were right to escape. To have stayed would have destroyed you too. Just like it destroyed me. Not physically, but in spirit. Me, I became the one thing our parents would never have wanted me to become."

Slanski stood. He took a deep breath and closed his eyes tightly, as if the pain of what he had heard was too much to bear. After a long time he looked down.

"Tell me what happened to you. Tell me how you learned the truth. How your people knew about my mission?"

Lukin told him. Slanski just stood there listening, not speaking.

Finally, Lukin said, "You must know now it's impossible to kill Stalin."

"Maybe the impossible appeals to me. Besides, it can still be done."

"How?"

Slanski said warily, "First, I need your word you won't betray me. I need to know I can really trust you."

"I'd never betray you, Mischa. Not ever. You have my word. And you trusted me by coming out here. So trust me now."

Slanski thought for a moment. "One of the Tsar's old escape tunnels leads from the Bolshoi Theater to the third floor of the Kremlin and comes out near Stalin's quarters. That's my way in."

Lukin shook his head. "You'd be wasting your time. Stalin has moved to his dacha at Kuntsevo because of the threat to his life. And because of this threat it's even more tightly guarded than the Kremlin. Besides, all the secret Kremlin tunnels are also under extra guard. You'd be dead before you got near the place."

Slanski half smiled. "When the cards are stacked against you, reshuffle the deck. There's an alternative plan. A secret underground train line runs from the Kremlin to the Kuntsevo villa. The line is only ever used when Stalin needs to travel in haste or in an emergency. It can be breached near the Kremlin and leads right under the villa."

"I know about the underground train but you can be sure the line is also heavily guarded, especially now. You'd be dead before you got anywhere near Stalin's villa. Besides, there are armed guards everywhere and the woods around it are mined. You'd be committing suicide."

"I knew that from the start. But it's a chance I'm going to have to take."

"And even if you got close enough, how would you kill him?"

"I'm afraid even you can't know that, brother. But if I do get close enough, I'll make certain Stalin's punishment fits his crimes."

Lukin thought for a moment, his brow creased in concentration. "Maybe there's another way into the dacha that stands some chance. Only there's a price to pay."

"What price?"

"Both our lives."

Slanski hesitated, then shook his head. "Me, I figured on dying anyway. But this isn't your battle."

"You're wrong. It's as much mine as yours. You and I, we're two sides of the same coin. We can both repay everything that happened to us. Stalin has an appointment with death. It's an appointment long overdue. I'm going to make sure he keeps it."

"What about your wife? The child she's carrying? You can't do that."

"I must. And you can't do what I have in mind without me. Your friends might still make it to the border with Lebel. The colonel I told you about, Romulka, may suspect that Lebel's train will be used, and try to stop it. But if things go the way I plan, the entire Moscow KGB will be in chaos and your friends just may get away in the confusion. It's the only chance they have, however small. I'll see to it they get on board safely. Nadia can go with them. After tonight, I'm dead anyway. Staying in Russia, Nadia stands no chance. Going with Lebel, she may make it over the border."

Slanski looked at him intently. "You're sure about this?"

"I've never been more certain about anything in my life." Lukin paused. His voice became firm. "But one condition. It's best Nadia doesn't know what we're going to do. Or why we're doing it. She'll be confused enough as it is. As far as she's concerned, I caught you, but we've come to a mutual understanding. I've allowed Anna and your friends to escape and you've agreed in return for her to go with them because of the risk to her life. You make sure your friends tell her I'll be joining her later in Finland. Make sure they tell her that. She'll worry less. But you don't tell any of them about our past. They'd never believe it, and things are confusing enough for them as it is."

"So what *do* I tell them?"

"That I've failed Beria and my life is at risk. And now we've reached an accommodation in return for letting your friends escape."

"You think they'll believe it?"

"I don't see why not. Anna and Lebel know I'm finished after releasing them. They know what Beria's capable of and that Nadia's life would be in danger because of what I've done." He hesitated. "There's something else I want to do before the train leaves. Something important."

"What?"

Lukin told him. Slanski's forehead creased in thought as he sat there in the cold night, as if trying to take it all in.

Lukin said finally, "So, brother, do you agree?"

"You know, I never thought I'd be glad I didn't kill you when I had the chance."

Lukin smiled, a sad smile. "Maybe it was fate."

Suddenly Slanski seemed to crumple and his shoulders sagged, a lifetime of hardened anguish peeled away, as if his soul was exposed. He said, "God, Petya . . . it's good to see you again."

Lukin put a hand on his shoulder, then embraced him.

As they sat together the snow started to fall more heavily, drifting against the silver birch trees. Beyond the far bank of the frozen river the lights of Moscow were dying slowly. The whole city seemed to be growing still in the cottony silence.

After a long time Slanski seemed to compose himself, wiped his face, looked across at Lukin and asked, "So tell me, how do we kill Stalin?"

58

Henri Lebel sat uncomfortably at the window of the deserted station house outside Moscow, smoking a cigarette and staring out worriedly beyond the thickly falling snow.

The man who stood beside Lebel was painfully thin and had a cigarette dangling from the corner of his mouth. He wore a greasy cap and a train driver's overalls under a filthy overcoat, and there was a troubled expression on his face as he wiped his hands with an oily rag.

A train stood waiting on the tracks outside, its black paintwork muddied, a limp plume of smoke rising from its funnel.

The man said, "For a while there you had me worried, Henri. When I didn't get your call yesterday as we arranged I phoned your hotel. They said you hadn't arrived in Moscow. Then you call me at the last minute and tell me everything's still on as we agreed. And now I find you hobbling about like you need crutches. Mind telling me what's going on?"

Lebel was barely enjoying his first smoke in three days. Lukin had given him another shot of morphine, and the pain in his crotch had subsided, replaced by a feeling of numbness. But he was barely able to walk, and really he needed rest and a decent doctor. But both would have to wait for now. He brushed a fleck of ash from his sable coat and turned to the man.

"Forget it, Nicolai. Let's just say I had a rather unpleasant experience, but I'm here now." He looked at the cheap makkorka cigarette with distaste. "You could have found me something better than this Bolshevik firecracker."

"They're good enough for me."

"With the money you earn from me you ought to be smoking Havanas. What time is it?"

The man consulted his watch. "Almost one. Your friends are cutting it a bit fine. You're sure they'll come? If they don't they'll save us both a lot of bother."

Lebel fixed him with a stare. "They'll come. Just don't forget our agreement."

"Hey, have I ever let you down? But whether they appear or not, I still get my money, that was what we agreed."

"You'll get your reward, Nicolai. Just as soon as the goods are delivered."

At that moment the headlights of a car swept up to the right of the station house and Lebel's heart skipped. Slanski stepped out of the BMW, followed by Lukin, still wearing his KGB uniform.

When Nicolai saw the uniform the cigarette dropped from his mouth and he said with horror, "On Lenin's life . . . what the fuck's going on?"

"Nothing for you to worry about. Relax, Nicolai, your passengers have arrived."

"Relax? In case you hadn't noticed, that's a KGB uniform your friend's wearing."

Lebel said wearily, "Help me up." Nicolai eased him to his feet and the Frenchman said, "Wait here."

He opened the station house door and hobbled out. He hadn't gone very far when Slanski crossed the platform to meet him and said, "Everything's in order?"

"I haven't told the driver about our new arrangement yet. I thought it best to wait until you came. Something tells me Nicolai isn't going to like it. How has Major Lukin's wife taken the news?"

Slanski glanced back toward the car where Lukin was helping the other passengers out. His wife took his arm shakily as she stepped from the car clutching a single small suitcase, looking totally lost.

"She's bewildered to say the least, and upset. But that's to be expected."

At that moment they heard a door bang and the train driver came marching across the platform toward Lebel.

"Henri, what the fuck's going on here . . . ?"

Slanski said briskly, "A change of plan. You have two extra passengers."

The driver's face turned red with anger and he glared at Lebel. "This wasn't our agreement. Two was the limit. You want to get me put up against a wall?"

"Nicolai, I'm afraid the situation's changed."

"You can say that again. The deal's off. No way do I go along with this."

Lebel said, "Listen to me, Nicolai. The only way you're going to get your money is to take the extra people along. Besides, I'll see there's a bonus in it for you."

"It wasn't what we agreed. And our lives are on the line quite enough as it is. I may never get to spend the money. Don't fuck with me, Henri. I haven't got the time or the patience. The train's already behind schedule. I take two people, no more, take it or leave it. What do you think I'm running here, a fucking wooden horse of Troy?"

"Ten thousand rubles more as soon as everyone's safely over the border. I guarantee it. That's a lot of champagne and underwear for your girlfriend in Karelia."

Nicolai seemed to hesitate, then he looked over at the green BMW as the uniformed KGB major ushered more passengers out of the back, but in the slanting snow the driver couldn't see their faces.

"Who are *they*?"

"Your passengers, that's all you need to know. Three women and a child."

"This is starting to sound like a widows and orphans outing. Children are trouble. What happens if the border guards decide to take a look at the carriage and the kid starts crying?"

"If you've done your job and bribed them as usual, they shouldn't. Besides, the child will be given a sedative. She'll sleep all the way through."

Nicolai looked doubtful and shook his head. "It's still too big a risk." He jerked his chin at Slanski. "And who might this be?"

Slanski produced a KGB identity card from his pocket and flashed it at the driver.

"Someone who's about to save your life, comrade." He looked over toward the BMW, as Lukin led the others toward the platform. "The man you see over there is a colleague of mine, Major Lukin." Slanski paused for effect. "He knows all about your little smuggling operation. In fact, until Monsieur Lebel and I intervened, he wanted to arrest you."

Nicolai turned even paler and looked at Lebel in alarm. "You bastard. You said I had nothing to worry about."

"You don't so long as you do as you're told," Slanski interrupted. "One of the passengers is an agent of ours we want transported to the west. You leave her behind and I personally guarantee to have you up against a wall and shot before morning."

Nicolai's face drained completely of color as he looked helplessly at Lebel.

Lebel said, "It's true, I'm afraid."

"Then tell me exactly what's going on."

Slanski said, "That's a matter of state security and none of your business. You'll proceed as normal with the transport and give no indication, as usual, of your hidden cargo. Fail us, and you'll suffer the consequences. You think you can do that?"

Nicolai crumpled and sighed. "I don't have much choice, do I?"

Slanski turned and crossed the platform smartly toward the others.

Lebel said, "Relax, Nicolai. Look on the bright side."

"Which is ?"

"Now you're working for the KGB."

Slanski stood on the platform, Lebel beside him as they watched Nicolai slide open the door of one of the goods trucks. He stepped inside carrying a steel crowbar and a bag of tools.

Lebel said, "It shouldn't take him long to loosen the floorboards. He's already vented the wood so they won't suffocate. Your friends will be able to come out once we have a clear run to the border, but they'll have to go back in hiding before we cross the checkpoint. That is, assuming we make it that far."

"Give me a cigarette."

Lebel handed Slanski a cigarette and looked over at the group huddled on the platform beside the open carriage. Lukin was embracing his wife and Lebel saw that the woman was crying. Next to them Anna Khorev was holding her daughter tightly in her arms as Irena fussed over the child.

Lebel said, "Your ladyfriend I know about, but who's the little girl?"

Slanski struck a match against one of the station pillars and lit his cigarette. "Her daughter. The child was in a KGB orphanage. Major Lukin just forged Beria's signature to release her."

Lebel said palely, "My God, this gets worse by the minute."

"After what happened tonight it's hardly going to matter much."

"Let's hope you're right."

"You did the favor I asked?"

Lebel took a set of car keys from his pocket and handed them to Slanski. "All I could manage was a blue Emka van. One of my contacts from the Trade Ministry who owed me a favor left it parked and waiting where you said. He won't report it stolen until tomorrow morning."

"Thanks. What about the train? Can you manage that too?"

"Slightly more risky. We halt at a station named Klin, an hour out from Moscow, to hook on a cargo of coal for Helsinki. That shouldn't take more than an hour. Nicolai ought to be able to stretch it to two taking on water for the engine and attending to some imaginary repairs, but he won't be able to delay much longer than that. Otherwise, the railway authorities may get suspicious. So if you're going to join us, I suggest you don't delay."

"Try to stretch the halt as long as you can."

Lebel said glumly, "I think we've stretched matters quite far enough as it is, don't you?"

Slanski tossed away his cigarette. "Cheer up, Henri. You're still breathing. It could be a lot worse."

"After this, I'll never see Moscow again. Not that I ever want to. I suppose there's some compensation if Irena is free, if we live long enough to enjoy it. Do you really think we'll still make it to Helsinki?"

"It's a chance worth taking when you consider the alternative."

Lebel frowned. "May I be permitted an observation? After four years in the French resistance, a man gets to know when he's being sold a stinker. And something definitely stinks about this whole arrangement. I suppose it's no use asking what's really going on between you and Lukin?"

"No use at all."

Lebel shrugged and nodded toward the train. "It seems you have a farewell in store, my friend. I'd better see what's keeping Nicolai."

As Anna handed her daughter to Irena and came toward them, Lebel shuffled toward the train.

Then Anna's arms were around Slanski's neck and she pulled him to her tightly.

"What Lukin did, I don't know how to thank him."

"Look after his wife, that'll be thanks enough."

She looked into his face. "You and Lukin aren't really going to join us later, are you?"

"Oh, I don't know about that."

She studied him, her eyes wet. "That's a lie, Alex, and you know it. Please . . . it's not too late to change your mind."

"Far too late, I'm afraid."

And then her lips were on his and he heard her sobbing. Finally he broke away. For a long time he looked at her face, then his hand brushed against her cheek. "Take care, Anna Khorev. I wish you a long life and happiness with Sasha."

"Alex . . . please . . . ! Come with us!"

The train suddenly whistled and Lebel appeared and said, "Another minute and I'll be in tears myself. Nicolai's ready to go. Let's move, my friends, this isn't the Gare du Nord."

The steam engine seemed to burst into life, gave another shrieking whistle, and Slanski took Anna's hand and pulled her toward the train.

Lukin helped Lebel up beside the driver, then got the others on board. A final look passed between them all; Slanski and Anna, Lukin and Nadia, and then Irena slid the carriage door and bolted it shut.

Lebel gave a wave from the engine. "So long, comrades. With luck, maybe we'll all live to crack a bottle of champagne in Helsinki."

Slanski saw a terrible look of anguish on Lukin's face as he stared grimly at the carriage, and then the train whistled again and started to move. Lukin touched the carriage door with his hand as it pulled away from the platform, as if reluctant to let it go, and then the engine picked up speed and the carriage slid away.

Slanski said, "You said your goodbye?"

"As best I could under the circumstances."

"How did Nadia take it?"

Lukin said grimly, "I don't think she believed me when I told her I'd see her again. But she knows what she's doing is for the best. And for our child. On my way to pick up Anna's daughter I called at the Leningrad Station. I showed Beria's letter to the duty official in charge of the railway lines to Helsinki and told him to keep the lines clear for Lebel's train. Under no circumstances was it to be deliberately stopped or delayed, otherwise he'd face Beria's wrath and a firing squad. Let's hope he does what I tell him. All we can do is hope by some miracle they all survive." He looked around, agony in his face. "A terrible world we live in, brother, but there you have it. And Anna? Something passed between you and her, didn't it?"

Slanski shrugged. "Another time, another place, and under different circumstances, who knows what might have come of it? But too late now." He paused, then there was a hint of remorse in his voice. "But it's still not too late for you to change your mind."

Lukin shook his head. "This is for Katya. For our parents. For us."

Slanski touched his arm. "We'd better go. There isn't much time."

59

It was still snowing as Lukin pulled up across the street from the side entrance to KGB Headquarters.

As he switched off the engine he turned to Slanski and said, "Give me fifteen minutes. If I haven't showed up by then get away from here as fast as you can. Ditch the car and go to the nearest Metro. After that I'm afraid you'll have to make your own way to Kuntsevo, as you planned."

Slanski nodded toward the KGB building. "You'll be taking a risk going in there. Is it really necessary?"

"I need to know if Pasha's safe. I want him to leave Moscow, otherwise after everything we've done is discovered he'll be guilty by association and doubtless he'll be shot. There's a train leaving for the Urals in under two hours and I want him on it with a false set of papers. They'll never find him among his own people."

Lukin glanced over at the building. The double oak doors were open, and another glass door led to a hallway beyond. The lights were on and the uniformed guard on duty sat behind a desk in the hall.

"Besides, you're going to need a KGB uniform for what we're planning to do. There's also an important phone call to make, remember?"

Slanski nodded. "Good luck."

Lukin climbed out of the car, crossed the street and went in through the side doors. Slanski watched the guard check his papers before Lukin stepped into an elevator in the hall and was gone.

As Slanski sat in the car he reached anxiously for a cigarette and lit one, then glanced over at the dead body lying on the backseat.

Jake Massey's lifeless eyes stared back at him.

The fourth floor was empty and the office was in darkness.

Lukin stepped into the room and closed the door. He flicked on the light switch. The room flooded with light and he heard the voice at once and turned.

"Welcome back, Lukin. So kind of you to join us."

Romulka stood by the window, a Tokarev in his hand. Two brutal-faced plain-clothes KGB men stood in front of Pasha's desk. They held rubber truncheons. Pasha was tied down in a chair with leather straps binding his arms and legs, his face bloated and bloodied almost beyond recognition. One of the men had his hand over his mouth and as he released it Pasha gurgled with pain and his swollen eyes rolled in their sockets.

Lukin's heart sank. "What's the meaning of this?"

Romulka stepped forward. "Don't fuck with me, Lukin, it's far too late for that. Remove your pistol and place it on the desk. Nice and easy. Or I'll be tempted to take your head off before Comrade Beria has the pleasure of dealing with you."

Lukin removed his Tokarev and placed it on the desk.

Romulka crooked a finger. "Come closer, away from the door."

As Lukin stepped forward, Romulka slammed his fist into his jaw. Lukin fell back against the wall but Romulka moved in smartly and jerked his knee savagely into Lukin's groin.

As he slid to the floor, Romulka stood over him, his hands on his hips.

"I can't understand it, Lukin. I credited you with some brains. Did you really expect to get away with what you did tonight? Preventing me from catching the American? Releasing the woman and taking the child from the orphanage? You must think I'm a fool."

A trickle of blood ran down Lukin's chin. "No, just a callous, brutal bastard."

Romulka lashed out with his boot and it smashed into Lukin's thigh.

"Get up, traitor!"

When Lukin didn't move, Romulka yanked him savagely by the hair and hauled him into a chair. He stared into his face. "You know what I don't understand, Lukin? Motive. But there must be an explanation. There always is. And you're going to give it to me."

He replaced the pistol in his holster and the riding crop appeared. Without warning it swished through the air and struck Lukin a stinging blow across the face.

As he jerked back in pain, Romulka grabbed him by the hair again.

"A small debt repaid. But nothing to the debt you're about to be repaid by Beria. Interesting to know that your wife isn't at home, Lukin. I had my men stop at your apartment half an hour ago. No doubt you thought she'd be safer elsewhere. But don't you worry, we'll find her. And you know what I'll do to that bitch wife of yours when we throw her in a cell? Screw her until she can't walk." He leered. "Of course, cooperate and you may find me a little more lenient. What have you been playing at, Lukin?"

"Go to hell," Lukin spluttered.

The muscles tightened in Romulka's face. "You had your little yellow friend here tie us up nicely until you got away, didn't you? Unfortunately, he hasn't been much help either. But then perhaps we haven't tried hard enough to loosen his tongue." He nodded to the two men standing over Pasha. "Show Lukin what he and his bitch wife can expect in the cellars."

One of the men grinned and slapped the rubber truncheon in his hand. It swished through the air and struck Pasha savagely across the face. The Mongolian screamed in agony as again and again the rubber struck, his head tossing from side to side with the force, until his face was a bloodied pulp.

Lukin screamed, "No!"

The beating went on until finally Romulka said, "Enough."

He put the barrel of Lukin's pistol hard against Pasha's temple.

"Something else I discovered. This yellow bastard was seen sniffing around the records office. That's off limits without a permit." He grinned. "A man could get himself killed for sticking his nose where he shouldn't. I wonder what he was up to? One last chance, Lukin. Either you talk, or I blow this yellow bastard's brains out here and now."

Pasha seemed barely conscious, his eyes unable to focus, a froth of blood on his mouth. Then suddenly a gurgling sound came from his throat and with a burst of rage he came to life.

"Tell him nothing, Yuri . . ." His bloodied face stared up at Romulka, his voice a hoarse whisper. "You . . . go . . . fuck yourself . . ."

Romulka's face erupted in rage and the Tokarev came up so fast Lukin could barely react. The weapon pressed into Pasha's temple, the hammer clicked, and the gun exploded.

Pasha's head snapped sideways with the force, his body suddenly limp like a rag doll's, blood spattering the walls as the bullet tore into his skull.

Lukin roared, "NO!"

As he tried to struggle from the chair the two men held him down.

Romulka turned to him and the gun came up hard and struck him below the jaw, sent him reeling back, then Romulka pressed the barrel painfully hard into his forehead. "Now it's your turn, Lukin. You're going to talk if it's the last thing you do." He put the pistol down and picked up the riding crop and said to the men, "On the desk with him. Pull down his trousers."

He produced what looked like a pair of pliers from his pocket and said to Lukin, "A little implement even the Frenchman couldn't resist. Only in your case, I assure you you'll never walk again. And I can't tell you how much I'm going to enjoy this."

As the two men dragged Lukin onto the desk, a voice said, "I really wouldn't do that."

Romulka and the men turned at once. Slanski stood in the open doorway, the silenced Nagant in his hand.

It happened quickly. One of Romulka's men went to reach for his pistol and Slanski shot him in the eye. As the man reeled back a second shot hit him in the neck, shattering his windpipe, cutting off the scream in his throat.

As the man spun, the second man lunged forward and Slanski fired twice, hitting him in the throat and chest.

Slanski was already reacting as Romulka started to reach for his weapon, but Lukin shouted, "NO! He's mine."

He lunged just as Romulka grabbed for the gun, pushed him back against the wall. His arm came up and the metal claw dug hard into Romulka's chest. The man's eyes opened wide in horror as Lukin's hand went over his mouth to stifle the scream.

Lukin stared into his face. "Have a nice time in hell, you bastard."

He withdrew the claw and stepped back as Romulka slid down, a fountain of blood gushing from the gaping wound in his chest.

Lukin stared at Slanski in disbelief. "How the hell did you get in here?"

"As soon as you stepped into the elevator the guard on the desk couldn't wait to reach for the phone. So I decided to keep you company."

"You took a risk."

"Lucky for you the building's almost empty at this time of night."

"Thanks, Mischa."

Slanski nodded over at Pasha's body. "But too late to help your friend."

Lukin stared at the corpse. For several moments he didn't speak, then he turned back, grief etched on his face.

"He was a good man. A good man wearing a bad uniform." It took several moments for him to compose himself. "What happened to the guard?"

"Dead in one of the offices across the hall. Did you make the call?"

"There wasn't time."

"Then make it now."

Lukin crossed to the desk as Slanski went to stand by the door, leaving it open a crack, the Nagant raised and ready.

It took Lukin less than a minute to make the call, and when he replaced the receiver there was sweat on his face. He looked at Slanski and said, "It's done."

"Then let's get out of here before someone raises the alarm. Don't forget the uniform."

Lukin crossed to his locker in the corner and removed his spare uniform, gloves, boots and cap.

Slanski went out, pausing only to check the hallway, but it was deserted.

Lukin took a long, painful look at Pasha's bloodied face, then followed him out.

They reached the Kuntsevo road ten minutes later.

There was hardly any traffic. Once they had left the suburbs behind, Slanski said, "Pull over. I want to go over the plan one more time. There can't be any mistakes, Petya."

Lukin shook his head. "There's no time. It won't take long before someone discovers the guard on the door is missing. After that, all hell's going to break loose."

"How much time have we got?"

"The shift changes in half an hour. But someone's going to notice the missing guard before then."

"How much longer to Stalin's dacha?"

"Ten minutes, a straight road all the way. Another ten to get in, if we're lucky. We're cutting it fine."

Slanski looked ahead through the falling snow. There was a blaze of lights off to the right side of the Kuntsevo road, some sort of red-brick factory compound with massive gates, and then he saw an ambulance inch slowly out through the gates and realized the place was a hospital. On the left side of the road a narrow track led off into darkness. A squat, flat-roofed derelict building in the same red brick as the hospital stood to the right of the track.

Slanski pointed through the windshield. "What's that?"

"A bomb shelter from the war."

"Pull in beside it."

"But . . ."

"We only get one chance to get this right. Let's go over the plan again. I want no mistakes. Pull in."

Lukin swung the wheel and pulled over in front of the shelter. The flat roof was covered in snow and steps led down beyond the dark mouth of the entrance, the door hanging off its hinges.

As Lukin switched off the engine, he saw the silenced Nagant appear in Slanski's hand. Before he could speak, Slanski had pointed the weapon at him.

Alarmed, Lukin said, "What's going on?"

"Listen to me, Petya. I can do this alone. You have a wife and child to think of. There's no need for you to throw away your life. I want you to live. At least one of us should live. Do it for me. Do it for Katya and our parents."

Lukin saw it then. Saw everything. His face drained of color as he stared at Slanski. "You never intended for us to do this together, did you?"

"I guess not."

"Mischa . . . please . . . you'll never get inside the villa alone."

"That's where you're wrong. You made the call and you're expected. I can get in with your identity card."

"But you don't even look like me!"

"Apart from hair color we're pretty much the same build. As for the rest, let me worry about that."

Lukin shook his head fiercely. "Mischa, this is crazy. Together we stand some chance. Alone you have none."

"It's a better chance than having you explain I'm one of your fellow officers. With security so tight they may not even let me inside." He shook his head. "Like I said, I don't want you to die. If you come with me he'll have killed all of us in the end. I won't let him kill you. I won't let him destroy us all. If there was time, I'd tell you about all the times I missed you. How much I loved you and Katya. How much I longed to be with you both again. But there isn't."

Suddenly there was a hint of tears in Slanski's eyes. He quickly removed a set of keys from his pocket. Then he nodded to the bomb shelter. "I'm going to leave you here. Lebel's waiting with the train at a station called Klin, northwest of Moscow. There's a blue Emka van we passed half a kilometer back down the road, parked and waiting with a full tank of fuel. Here are the keys. You can make it if you hurry." He stuffed the keys into Lukin's breast pocket. "Live your life, brother. Live it for all our family."

"Mischa, no . . . !"

"Goodbye, brother."

Slanski's fingers came up quickly and closed around Lukin's neck like a vice, the thumb pressing hard into the point below his ear. Lukin struggled and fought back, his arms flailing and his body bucking wildly, but Slanski was stronger.

It was only a matter of seconds before Lukin slumped in the seat and blacked out. Slanski stepped out of the car into the freezing night and went down the steps into the shelter.

The building was in darkness and smelled foul. He had to go back to the car and get the flashlight; then he flicked it around the walls and saw that the place was strewn with garbage. He cleared a corner and then quickly carried Lukin down from the car and propped him against a wall.

It took him another five minutes to do everything he had to do, moving quickly, then prying the interior mirror from the car and using it to apply the engine oil to his hair. Only when he had finished did he pull on the single leather uniform glove. He found the identity card with the photograph in Lukin's breast pocket. Everything else he needed was already in the car.

When he had checked himself in the mirror he shone the flashlight at the unconscious figure propped against the shelter wall. In the cold, he wouldn't be out for more than another five minutes.

For a long time Slanski stared at Lukin's face, until he was almost overcome with emotion, then he knelt down and kissed him hard on the cheek, suddenly aware of his struggle to keep back the tears, before he tore himself away and went out and up the steps.

As he climbed back into the BMW, he glanced over his shoulder at Massey's corpse lying across the backseat.

"Well, I guess you got to see it through to the end after all, Jake. If there's a heaven, and you're already there, wish us both luck. We're going to need it."

He checked his watch. It was 1:15 A.M.

He started the car.

60

The guards heard the car long before they saw it.

One of them pulled back a shutter in the green-painted metal gate and peered out into the falling snow. Headlights blazed through the veil of white, and when the BMW drew up in front and its lights were extinguished, searchlights in the watchtower above the gate suddenly sprang on, flooding the area with intense white light.

The man carefully checked the license-plate number against his list before he stepped out through a gate and approached the car. He didn't fail to notice the bullet holes in the bodywork, and that part of the rear window was shattered.

"Papers."

The uniformed KGB major with the gloved hand rolled down the window and smiled as he handed them over.

"Major Lukin. I'm expected."

"This vehicle looks like it's been through the wars."

"I think you could say that."

The guard examined the identity card, then studied the major's face closely.

"Your car keys, comrade."

When the major handed them over the guard flicked on a flashlight and went around the back and unlocked the trunk. Moments later he slammed it shut and shone the flashlight inside the car. When he saw the body lying across the backseat he recoiled in horror and said, "What the fucking hell . . . !"

The major grinned. "I think if you check with the duty watch officer you'll find everything is in order." He glanced back at the corpse with obvious disgust. "An enemy American agent apprehended by the Second Directorate. Comrade Stalin wishes to see the body personally, so don't hang about."

When the shaken guard had regained his composure he said sternly, "Wait here."

He stepped back inside the gate and Slanski heard the jangle of a field telephone. Moments later he reappeared, flicking a distasteful look at the body in the back as he handed Slanski his papers.

"Looks like you're in business, Comrade Major. Follow the road for half a kilometer until you reach the dacha. No stopping until you get to the main entrance."

As the guard stepped back inside the gate, Slanski switched on the ignition and the BMW's headlights sprang to life.

The green metal gates yawned open. Half a dozen elite Kremlin Guards with blue bands on their caps stood inside the entrance, fingering their weapons. The woods beyond the gate were illuminated by the car's headlights, the shafts of light probing the snowy darkness. A narrow road wound around through the trees, the snow cleared away and raised in high banks on either side, and here and there the shadowy figures of more armed Kremlin Guards patrolled the forest with leashed Alsatians.

Slanski shifted into gear and released the clutch, sweat rising on his forehead. He saw the Kremlin Guards stare curiously at the corpse in the back as the car rolled forward.

As he drew up outside the dacha entrance he saw a massive two-story building of pale granite stone that looked like a Boston manor house.

The walls were covered in creeping vines, their leafless tendrils clinging to the granite like dead bones. Lights were on in the downstairs rooms and the white lawns were lit up in front. A miniature wooden pavilion stood off to the left, its onion dome encrusted with huge hanging icicles.

Slanski wiped the sweat from his brow before he switched off the engine and climbed out of the BMW. As he did so, two Kremlin Guards stepped out from behind the double-fronted oak doors of the dacha entrance.

Behind them in the lighted doorway appeared a massive Guards colonel. He stood well over six feet and was ruggedly built, his uniform immaculate, his boots brightly polished. He stood with his hands on his hips and stared at Slanski suspiciously before he strode down the pathway to the car.

"Major Lukin, I believe."

Slanski saluted and the colonel returned the salute smartly. He looked at the damaged BMW, then stared into Slanski's face. "Colonel Zinyatin, Head of Security. Your papers, Major."

"They've already been checked at the gate, sir."

The colonel smiled coldly. "And now they're being checked again. We can't be too careful, can we? I'm the duty officer responsible for Comrade Stalin's personal safety. No one goes inside without my permission." He held out his hand stiffly and Slanski handed over his papers.

The colonel examined them thoroughly, looking from the photograph to Slanski's face, checking the stamp on the identity card and rubbing his thumb vigorously on the print. Then he glanced at the black leather glove on Slanski's hand. He seemed to hesitate, as if uncertain of something, before he slowly handed the papers back and peered into the back of the car.

Slanski said, "Not a pleasant sight, Comrade Colonel. An American agent." He gestured to the bullet holes in the BMW. "He proved to be quite an adversary. Unfortunately, I was unable to capture him alive."

"So I heard."

"Then no doubt you know Comrade Stalin wishes to see the body personally."

The colonel glanced back at Slanski with no expression, then he opened the rear door and examined the body, gripping Massey's stiff jaw and looking into the lifeless white face.

"Definitely dead, I think you'll find, sir," Slanski offered.

"Don't be smart, Lukin. I'm not blind."

The colonel stared down at the corpse before turning back. "I'm certain it won't be necessary to take the body inside. Comrade Stalin will take my word for it the American's dead." The colonel smiled without humor. "If he's in doubt, I'll have the corpse delivered to him personally. I believe congratulations are in order, Lukin."

"Thank you, sir."

The colonel's smile was replaced by a cold stare. "One more thing."

"Comrade?"

"Your sidearm. Procedure forbids visitors to Kuntsevo to carry weapons." The colonel thrust out his hand.

Slanski hesitated, then unholstered the Tokarev and handed it over.

"Now, if you'll follow me, Comrade Stalin is expecting you."

The polished double oak doors opened silently on their hinges and the colonel went in first.

Slanski followed him into a dazzling room. A log fire blazed in one corner, and a long walnut table stood in the center, a dozen or more chairs set around it. An ornate crystal chandelier hung overhead, its light flooding the entire room. Bokhara rugs were set around the floor and rich tapestries draped the gilded walls.

Josef Vissarionovich Djugashvili—Joseph Stalin—General Secretary of the Communist Party, Generalissimo of the Soviet Union, stood at the end of the table. He smoked a pipe and held a glass in his hand, a half-full bottle of vodka on the table beside him. He was dressed in a simple gray smock tunic and his thick graying hair was swept back off a pockmarked face, his mouth half hidden under a bushy gray mustache. Hooded, watery gray eyes stared cautiously at his visitors.

The colonel crossed the room and whispered something into his ear. After a few moments the colonel stepped back.

Stalin put down his pipe and glass and crooked a finger. "Comrade Major Lukin, come here."

As Slanski stepped forward, Stalin turned to the colonel. "Leave us, Zinyatin."

The colonel seemed to hesitate, his cautious eyes flicking to Slanski, then he saluted and left, closing the double doors softly after him.

A thin smile played across Stalin's lips, but the gray eyes regarded Lukin coldly. "Step closer, Major. Let me see you."

His voice sounded slurred. He motioned with the fingers of his right hand and Slanski noticed the stiff and withered left arm. He stepped closer, enough to smell the man's body odor. A strong mixture of alcohol and stale tobacco. He had been drinking heavily, that much was obvious.

Suddenly Stalin leaned forward and kissed Slanski on both cheeks. As he stepped back, he studied Slanski's face. His eyes clouded for a moment in doubtful recognition, then he said, "So, you brought me the American's body."

"Yes, Comrade Stalin."

"And what about the woman?"

"Under lock and key in Lefortovo prison."

The gray eyes smiled coldly. "You have surpassed my expectations, Major Lukin. My congratulations. You will have a drink."

"No thank you, comrade."

Stalin frowned. "I insist. No one refuses a drink with Stalin."

The old man shuffled to the drinks trolley and poured vodka into a tumbler. He came back, handed it to Slanski, and raised his own glass.

"I drink to your success, Comrade Lukin. And to your promotion. You have my thanks and my promised reward. As of now, you are a full colonel."

"I don't know what to say, Comrade Stalin."

"Perhaps, but I do. If only all my officers were as capable. Drink, Lukin. It's good Armenian vodka."

Slanski raised his glass and sipped.

Stalin swallowed his drink in one gulp, put the glass down and moved around the table.

He looked over at Lukin suspiciously.

"But you know, something bothers me."

"Comrade Stalin?"

"A small matter, but an important one. You didn't see fit to follow protocol and inform Comrade Beria of your visit here, nor of the American's capture. I've just been on the phone to him. He's as surprised as I am by your success. According to him, you've been avoiding answering his calls and deliberately obstructing one of his officers, Colonel Romulka, in his duty. Your behavior has been somewhat unusual and unorthodox, Comrade Beria thinks. And I agree. In fact, before I informed him of your call, he wanted you arrested. He's on his way here now, to confront you. He claims you have kept the woman from him." Cold eyes stared into Slanski's face. "Why is that, Lukin? Did you want all the glory for yourself? Or are you keeping a secret? Comrade Stalin doesn't like secrets kept from him."

Slanski put his glass down carefully on the table. "There is a matter I needed to discuss in private. It concerns the American plot. I have information of vital importance for your ears only."

The bushy eyebrows rose slightly. "And what information is that?"

Slanski slipped off the black leather glove and the small Nagant appeared in his hand. There was the softest of clicks as he cocked the hammer and aimed the weapon at Stalin's head.

Horror shone like torchlight in the old man's eyes as Slanski leaned in closer and whispered.

"Not something you're going to enjoy. But you'll listen or I'll take your head off. Sit down. The chair to your right. Make a sound and I kill you."

Stalin's face turned an angry red. "What's the meaning of this . . . ?"

"*Sit.* Or I put a bullet in you here and now."

Stalin lowered himself shakily into the chair. Slanski removed his officer's cap. Stalin stared in shock at the face, then at the ungloved hand.

"You . . . you're not Lukin. Who are you? What do you want?"

"I'm sure the answer to the first two questions should be obvious by now. As for the last, I want you."

There was a terrible look of icy fear on Stalin's face, as if the alcoholic haze had suddenly lifted, everything becoming perfectly clear.

Slanski smiled chillingly. "But first, comrade, I'm going to tell you a story."

Lukin opened his eyes in the freezing blackness of the air-raid shelter and shivered violently.

Icy cold seeped into his bones and his brain throbbed. He shook his head and a million stars exploded inside his skull.

He sat there groggily for several moments, rubbing his neck, before he found the strength to stagger to his feet.

He found a damp, cold wall to support him, and as he stood shakily he smelled the garbage and saw the snow falling beyond an open door. It took several moments before the throbbing in his skull ebbed away, and then he staggered out of the door and up the steps of the shelter, blinking in pain and taking deep breaths, the air steaming in front of his face.

He realized where he was and what had happened.

Then all hell broke loose inside his head and his heart raced wildly. How long had he been unconscious? He looked at his watch and tried to focus in the poor light.

One-twenty A.M.

He must have been out cold for over five minutes.

He suddenly remembered the van. Half a kilometer away. Five minutes if he ran. Nadia's face flashed before his eyes. His grief returned, but he forced the image and the emotion away, letting only anger in, a powerful anger and a terrible lust for revenge, knowing what he had to do, that he wasn't going to be cheated of this moment.

He could still make it to Stalin's villa.

He fumbled madly for the keys, found them, then staggered through the trees toward the road.

"My father's name was Illia Ivan Stefanovitch. Do you remember him?"

Stalin shook his head.

"No."

"Think again."

A clock ticked softly somewhere and beyond the oak doors came faint sounds, distant voices; the click of heels on wood approached and faded. Stalin's nervous eyes flicked to the door, then back.

"I don't remember him."

Slanski pressed the Nagant hard into his temple.

"Think."

"I . . . I don't know who you're talking about."

"Yuri Lukin is my brother. Illia Ivan Stefanovitch was our father. You killed him. You killed his wife. And his daughter. Our sister. You killed them all. Our family."

Slanski stared hard into Stalin's frightened eyes. "And you haven't stopped trying to kill us. You pitted my brother against me."

"No . . . you're mistaken. Who told you this? Who told you I was responsible? Lies!"

The old man ran a trembling hand around his tunic collar. Slanski wrenched it away.

"Move again and I'll tear your heart out."

A wind gusted flurries of snow outside, rattling the windows. Beads of sweat glistened on Stalin's face. His breathing came in short gasps.

"Please, some water . . ."

A crystal water decanter stood on the drinks cart opposite but Slanski ignored it.

"Then let me remind you of the lies you speak of. My father was a village doctor. We lived near Smolensk. One day the secret police came to our village. They demanded the summer harvest. It was the time of the *kulak* wars and there was a famine raging. A famine deliberately caused by you. The villagers barely had enough to feed their children. Already they were starving. Men, women and children thin as corpses and dying by the dozens. So the people refused. Half the men of the village were shot in reprisal and their grain stolen. There was nothing to eat. Women and children starved. My father was spared but he couldn't believe Comrade Stalin would allow such a thing to happen to his village. So he decided to do something." Slanski removed the file from his tunic and placed it on the table. "Open it. Look and read."

When Stalin hesitated, Slanski said again, "*Open it*!"

Stalin opened the file with shaking hands. He glanced at the pages, the photographs, then looked up.

"I don't remember this man."

"What you see was in my file. You read all this before you sent my brother to find me."

Stalin swallowed, ashen-faced.

Slanski said, "I want you to remember what happened to my family. Let me remind you. Illia Ivan Stefanovitch, my father, called on the local commissar and told him he wanted to speak to Stalin, to condemn what had happened in his village in Stalin's name. It was his right as a citizen. He was given a pen and paper and told to write his grievance and it would be passed to Moscow. He wrote about what had happened in his village. He expressed his revulsion and resigned from the Party. You read the letter, but the reply wasn't what my father expected.

"You sentenced him to death as a traitor. The secret police came to his surgery. They thought they'd make this troublesome doctor's death a little more interesting than merely shooting him. So they made his wife watch while they held him down and injected him with a lethal dose of one of his drugs, Adrenalin. Do you know the effect such an amount of Adrenalin has on a body? It's not a pleasant way to die. The heart races, the body weakens and trembles, the lungs swell, the stomach vomits. A fatal dosage can cause the blood vessels in the brain to burst, but death may still come slowly. My father's did.

"They made my mother watch every moment. And then they raped her. All of them raped her. Until one of them had the pity to put a bullet in her head. Only it didn't kill her. They left her lying there, bleeding to death, slowly, for hours. I heard it happen because one of the men held me in the next room. I heard her screams and later I saw her die. Everything that happened after that is in the file. But then you know that, don't you? You knew when you selected Yuri Lukin. You chose him because having him kill me would be another of your sick jokes. One more laugh at your victims' expense."

Slanski leaned in close, his eyes wet, his voice almost a whisper. "You say you don't remember my father, but you will. Illia Ivan Stefanovitch. Remember that name. It's the last name you're going to hear before you go screaming to hell."

Slanski placed the Nagant on the table and removed a hypodermic from his pocket. With one finger he flipped off the metal sheath and exposed the needle. The glass was full of clear liquid.

"Pure Adrenalin. And now I'm going to kill you the way you killed my father."

As Slanski moved in, the old man rose and lunged at him like a bull.

"NO!"

Stalin grabbed at the Nagant and the weapon exploded. As the shot rang around the room Slanski struck him a hard blow to the neck and he slumped back in the chair.

Then everything seemed to happen at once.

The dacha went mad, screams and voices everywhere.

The doors burst open and the big colonel was the first in, crashing into the room like an enraged animal, staring at the scene in horror.

Slanski stabbed the needle into Stalin's neck and the plunger sank.

"For my father."

Then the Nagant came up smartly and pressed against Stalin's temple.

"And this for my mother . . . and sister . . ."

The Nagant exploded and Stalin's head was flung back.

As the colonel frantically wrenched out his weapon, he watched in disbelief as the major smiled in certain death, turning the Nagant toward himself, slipping the barrel into his mouth.

The weapon exploded again.

The Emka's wipers brushed away the snow but it was ceaseless.

A hundred meters from the dacha entrance Lukin heard the sirens going off and his heart jolted. The shrill noise erupted through the woodland air like the shrieks of a thousand wild animals in pain.

Klieg lamps sprang to life, illuminating the woods, beams of powerful light sweeping through the darkness, casting a silver wash over the snowy birch trees. Dogs barked; voices screamed orders. The forest seemed to come alive with light and noise.

Through the windshield, in the distance, Lukin could make out the dacha's green-painted gates, searchlights sweeping wildly through the trees as the sirens wailed ceaselessly.

He slowed the Emka. There was a rutted lane off to the right and he pulled in and switched off the engine. His body was shaking violently, and his heart was racing.

He was too late.

He felt a lump rise in his throat and it almost choked him. He stumbled out of the car and filled his lungs with air, then he fell to his knees and vomited.

For a long time he knelt in the frozen woods, no longer hearing the wailing sirens and the noises in the forest, only his own sobbing and the wild thumping of his heart in his ears as a painful anguish flooded him, almost physical in its intensity.

There was a timelessness to everything, and then it seemed as if a dam burst inside his head, and when the scream finally came, it came from deep inside him.

"Mischa!"

The scream seemed to go on forever in the white darkness.

THE PRESENT

61

It had started to rain again.

The sky over Moscow darkened like twilight, then a flash of forked lightning lit up the clouds and thunder cracked and the heavens opened. Anna Khorev stood at the window and stared out through the sheeting rain toward the distant red walls of the Kremlin. When she finally turned back she smiled, a brief sad smile.

"And there you have your story, Mr. Massey. Not entirely a happy ending, but then life rarely surprises us with happy endings."

"It's a remarkable story."

She lit a cigarette. "Not only remarkable, but true. You're one of the few people to know what happened that night at Kuntsevo. It took almost four days for Stalin to die, but die he did. The drug caused him to have a hemorrhage, the bullet made sure he'd die. And there was nothing his doctors could do to save him. Of course, the irony was they were too afraid to lift a finger after what happened to their Kremlin colleagues."

"So the official version of how Stalin died was a lie."

"The Kremlin claimed he died naturally, of a cerebral hemorrhage. But you'll also read in some history books that the bodies of two men were taken from the dacha grounds the night Stalin fell fatally ill. It's not a widely known fact, but it's the one small grain of truth that hints at something unusual happening that night. The bodies were those of Alex and your father. But of course, there was never any mention of that. Some secrets are best kept just that—secret."

I didn't answer for a moment, then I said, "Why did you tell me your story? Was it because you had to?"

Anna Khorev smiled back. "Partly that, I suppose. But perhaps I needed to tell someone and I'm glad we finally met. What happened all those years ago has been such a secret part of my life. Perhaps too big a secret to keep all to myself until the day I die. And to be honest, now that I've told you I feel quite relieved."

She smiled again, and then a distant, sad look appeared on her face.

"What about afterwards?" I said.

She sat down. "You mean what happened to everyone? Oh, Beria I'm sure you know about. After Stalin's death he made his play for power and failed. He was accused, ironically, of having been an agent for the West. But really he had made too many enemies who wanted him dead. He was arrested in the Kremlin and shot soon afterwards. So he got his just reward in the end. Some even said he was killed because he knew what had really happened to Stalin, and his comrades in the Kremlin wanted to cover it up."

"So what happened after you escaped from Moscow?"

"Russia was in chaos for days afterwards. With Romulka dead, our escape wasn't that difficult. We made it to Finland but there were problems, of course. The CIA, naturally, thought I and the others might be an embarrassment if the mission was ever leaked or discovered. And Henri Lebel was fearful for his life when he realized he had been in a small way party to Stalin's death. But Henri had been rather clever. After your father had first struck a deal with him in Paris he had transcribed all the details and sent them in a sealed envelope to his lawyer, with instructions that the contents be made public if Henri ordered it, or if he or Irena were ever harmed. That way, he was insuring himself against the CIA ever trying to blackmail him into working for them again, or double-crossing him. So the CIA kept your father's promise. They arranged secretly through Mossad for myself and Sasha, along with Henri and Irena, to live in Israel under new identities. They thought we'd all be safer there and out of harm's way, if ever the KGB wanted to exact revenge on us, but thankfully that never happened."

She looked away, toward the window. "Mossad was quite happy with things as they turned out. With Stalin dead, the purge of the Jews stopped, the camps were never completed, and the surviving doctors were released. The Americans arranged a nice apartment for Sasha and me in Tel Aviv and looked after us financially. I was warned never to disclose my real identity or divulge anything about the mission because it might put our lives in danger. But the new rulers in the Kremlin never made public the fact that the mission succeeded, or even that it had ever existed. That would have been an embarrassment for them and would perhaps have caused a war nobody really wanted, least of all the Soviets, who were without a leader, and that suited Washington completely. Khrushchev eventually succeeded Stalin, and later denounced him for his crimes. No one went entirely unpunished for his death, however. Not long after, the KGB systematically and brutally assassinated a number of extremist Russian and Ukrainian émigré leaders in Europe, probably in the mistaken belief that they were in some way partly responsible. But whether the CIA pointed a finger at them or not, I've no way of knowing."

"Why did the CIA claim my father committed suicide?"

"At the time your father's death was a problem for Washington. They had to cover it up somehow and without any of his colleagues becoming suspicious. The official explanation given was that he had committed suicide while traveling in Europe. They said that after he had been recalled to Washington from Munich he had been put on leave, for health reasons. They claimed that he was depressed and unstable. The date they gave for his death was before our mission began, so that no one might ever connect him to what subsequently happened. It wasn't fair to the character of your father, of course, but it had to be done for the sake of security. And, of course, no body was buried, just a coffin full of stones."

"What happened to Lebel and Irena?"

Anna Khorev smiled. "Henri opened a clothing business in Tel Aviv and they married and lived happily together until Henri died ten years ago. Irena followed him soon after."

"And Yuri Lukin?"

For a long time Anna Khorev stared out silently at the sheeting rain. There was a look of sadness on her face. Then she looked back.

"He made it to the train that night, much to the relief of his wife, but he was distraught, as you can imagine. He had found his brother after all those years, and then lost him again. When we arrived in Helsinki we were all debriefed for several days by Branigan. I never saw Yuri Lukin again after that. I would have liked to very much. He was a remarkable man, Mr. Massey."

"Do you know what became of him?"

She crushed out her cigarette and said, "Do you really want to know?"

"He's the final part of the puzzle," I offered.

"I can only tell you what I heard from the CIA. After Helsinki, he and his wife were flown to America. They were given new identities and settled in California, where his wife gave birth to a son. Then three months later they told me Yuri was killed in an automobile accident."

"You think the KGB had him killed?"

"No, I don't believe they did. It was definitely a freak accident, Mr. Massey. And I'm certain the CIA didn't kill him for that matter. In many ways, had it not been for him, the mission wouldn't have been so successful. But I suppose his death was probably convenient for both the Kremlin and Washington. There was one less person alive who knew the real truth."

"What happened to his wife and son?"

"I have no idea, I'm afraid."

I sat there for several moments, taking it all in. Beyond the glass the rain had stopped. The sun appeared from behind the sullen Moscow clouds, glinting off the Kremlin's golden domes and the bright, candy-colored whorls of St. Basil's.

I looked back. "May I ask you a personal question?"

She smiled. "That depends on how personal."

"Did you ever remarry?"

She laughed gently. "Good lord, what an odd question. But the answer is no. Sasha eventually married a nice Russian émigré in Israel. They have a son they named Ivan Alexei Yuri. And a daughter, Rachel, whom you met when you arrived." She smiled. "I loved two remarkable men in my life, Mr. Massey. My husband and Alex. And that's really been quite enough."

"So you really did love Alex Slanski?"

"Yes, I loved him. Not in the way I loved Ivan, but I loved him. It was never destined to have a happy ending, I think we both knew that. What is it they say? A lost soul. That summed up Alex perfectly. I think he knew he'd die on the mission, perhaps even wanted to. I think he always knew his destiny was to die in Moscow. To kill Stalin was worth the sacrifice of his life and the ultimate revenge for what had happened to his family. And in paying that price Alex did the world a great service, Mr. Massey. There were as many sighs of relief in Moscow as in Washington when Stalin died."

The door opened softly. The dark-haired girl stood there. She had changed into a blouse and skirt and she looked remarkably beautiful, her long legs tanned and her hair down about her shoulders.

"Nana, the embassy car is here for the airport."

The girl smiled at me and I smiled back. She had the same features as her grandmother. The same brown eyes and presence. I guessed she must have looked much like Anna Khorev had over forty years before. I could understand Alex Slanski, and even my father, falling in love with her.

"Thank you, Rachel. We're almost finished. Tell the driver we'll be with him in a minute."

The girl smiled at me again. "Promise me you won't keep my grandmother much longer?"

"I promise."

She left, closing the door after her.

Anna Khorev stood. "So there you have it, Mr. Massey. I've told you everything I can. I'm afraid you must excuse me now. Rachel and I have a flight to Israel to catch. I hope you understand? It's been a brief visit, but one I've wanted to make for a long time."

"May I ask one more question?"

"And what's that?"

"Do you really think my father would have killed you and Alex?"

She thought for several moments, then she said, "No, I don't believe he would have. Though God knows what the outcome would have been if Yuri Lukin hadn't done what he did. Your father came to Moscow because he was ordered. But I think if it had come down to it, he wouldn't have killed us. He would have stopped us, certainly, but figured some way of getting us out of Moscow. He was a fine man, Mr. Massey. He was a father you would have been proud of. And to be honest, maybe I was a little in love with him, too."

Finally, she glanced at her watch before picking up the bunch of white orchids I had brought. "We have some time, so why don't you ride with us in the car, Mr. Massey? We can drop you at your hotel on the way to the airport. And if you don't mind I'd like to pay a visit to Novodevichy on the way."

* * *

The sun came out as we walked together to the graves.

Rachel had waited in the car and as the sunlight washed down through the chestnut trees the graveyard hardly seemed like the same place. The sky was clear and blue and the dry heat of the afternoon lingered under the trees. Old women walked among the shaded pathways with bunches of flowers and bottles of vodka, come to sit and talk and drink with their departed.

When we came to the two gravestones Anna Khorev placed a spray of orchids on each of them.

I stood back then, to let her say her final prayer. She wasn't crying, but I saw the pain in her eyes when she finally turned back.

"I decided a long time ago that this will be my final resting place when my day comes, Mr. Massey. I know Ivan, my husband, would have understood."

"I'm certain he would have." I looked at her, stuck for something to say, seeing the faraway look in her brown eyes. "Everything that happened that night must seem like a dream." It was all I could offer.

"Sometimes I wonder did it really happen. And wonder who would believe it."

"I do."

She half smiled and went to say something, glancing at the two graves as if there was something else I should know, but then she seemed to change her mind and shivered.

"Are you ready, Mr. Massey? I'm afraid graveyards are not one of my favorite places. Even on a warm, sunny Moscow day."

I nodded and took her arm and we walked back to the car.

I heard that Anna Khorev died six months later.

There was nothing in the newspapers but Bob Vitali called from Langley and said he thought I'd want to know she had passed away in the Sharet Hospital in Jerusalem. She had suffered from lung cancer. The funeral was to be in Moscow four days later.

I ordered plane tickets, for some reason wanting to be part of the end of things.

It was snowing when I landed at Sheremetyevo, the fields and steppes of Russia frozen like some vast ghostly tapestry, flurries of snow sweeping the Moscow streets, the country in the harsh grip of another bitter winter, and I thought it must have been like this all those years ago when Alex Slanski and Anna made their way across Russia.

The funeral at Novodevichy was a small affair and it had already started when I arrived. A half-dozen or more Israeli embassy staff were huddled around the open grave as an Orthodox priest chanted his prayers for the dead and the snow gusted around us.

I saw Anna Khorev's granddaughter holding on to the arm of a handsome woman in her forties whom I guessed was Sasha, both their faces pale with grief. The coffin was open and I took my turn to kiss Anna Khorev's cold marble face and say my final goodbye. For a brief moment I looked down at her, thinking how beautiful she looked even in death, then I walked back and stood at the edge of the mourners as the gravediggers went to work.

Something remarkable happened then.

As I stood watching the coffin being lowered into the frozen ground, I noticed an old couple standing arm in arm among the mourners. The woman's face was deeply wrinkled, but under the headscarf she wore I could see a fading tint of red in her graying hair. The man was very old, his body almost bent double with age.

He wore a black leather glove on his stiff left hand.

I felt a shiver go through me.

The couple waited until the coffin had been lowered into the ground before the old man came forward and placed a bunch of winter roses in the open grave. When he stepped back he stood there for several moments, then I saw his eyes look over at Alex Slanski's headstone. For a long time the old man stood there, as if lost in thought, until the woman took his arm and kissed his cheek and led him away.

As they shuffled past me, my mind was on fire with excitement.

My heart pounded in my chest as I touched his shoulder and asked the question in Russian. "Major Lukin? Major Yuri Lukin?"

The old man started and his watery eyes looked up to study my face.

For a time he seemed undecided about something, then he glanced over at his wife, before replying to my question in a frail voice.

"I'm sorry, sir. You're mistaken. My name is Stefanovitch."

The couple walked on. I started to say something then, remembering the name, Slanski's family name, but I was struck dumb. I saw the couple step into one of the black cars parked nearby and drive off down the narrow cemetery track before the red taillights disappeared in a mist of snow.

Was it Yuri Lukin?

Perhaps.

I like to think he hadn't really died as Anna Khorev had said.

But it was all such a long time ago. I had found my own truth. I had resurrected my ghosts and now it was time to bury them.

I took one last look at the three graves, then turned and walked back toward the cemetery gates.

AUTHOR'S NOTE

Although the exact date and time cannot be confirmed, history relates that Joseph Stalin was taken fatally ill on the night of 1–2 March 1953. He died almost four days later.

To this day the exact circumstances of his death remain a mystery.

Some sources claim he was poisoned by Lavrenty Beria, whose gloating at Stalin's deathbed is well recorded, but the claim has never been proven.

Stalin's immediate family claimed that he had almost certainly been killed, and had not died of a cerebral hemorrhage as was widely reported, and that the true circumstances of his death were covered up for reasons of state security.

There are historically recorded facts that point to an answer that supports this view.

Some months before Stalin's death, the CIA had been receiving reports of the Soviet leader's worsening mental health.

Stalin was displaying alarming signs of a deep psychological disturbance, and the CIA was also aware of Stalin's almost manic wish to perfect the hydrogen bomb ahead of the USA; and acutely aware of the fact that the Soviets were ahead in their research, and that Stalin intended a "final solution to the Jewish problem," on a par with Hitler's.

All these were serious and troubling signs, especially at the time of a dangerous Cold War. And the likelihood of war, as those who lived during the period will recall, both in America and the Soviet Union, was both very real and very threatening.

Was Stalin assassinated to prevent the situation from worsening?

There were numerous intended plots to kill him. So far as history records, all failed, or never materialized. But history rarely records or reveals its true secrets. What *is* true is that the CIA had already sent a number of agents with military training to Moscow at the time of Stalin's death. It also seems likely that the CIA would at least have considered such a plot. And almost immediately after his demise, the KGB unleashed an unexplained and savage program of assassination against top anti-Soviet émigré leaders who were working with the CIA.

Former senior CIA officers, responsible for such missions during the period, remain curiously tight-lipped, even for very elderly men long since retired. Nor to this day will they reveal the identities of those they dispatched, invoking the fact that certain details of the period remain top secret, and claiming that some of the agents are still alive and living in Russia to this day.

So what exactly happened on the night of 1–2 March at Stalin's dacha seems destined to remain a mystery.

It is known that his last days prior to that eventful night were spent in seclusion, heavily guarded, apparently fearful for his life, and with strict instructions to his guards that all the big wooden log fires in the dacha be kept lit, just as the Russian hunters and shepherds of old kept fires burning to keep away wolves. And on pieces of paper Stalin drew, obsessively, pictures of a wolf with sharp fangs.

But one very remarkable incident, never fully explained, is confirmed fact.

In the early hours of 2 March, after Stalin was reported to have been taken seriously ill, several members of his guard at the Kuntsevo villa witnessed the bodies of two men being removed from the grounds. Both had apparently died from bullet wounds.

Rumors spread within the KGB itself about the mysterious incident, but not until many months later was an official internal explanation offered.

The two men, the KGB report claimed, were bodyguards of Stalin's, so overcome with grief at their leader's certain demise that they had shot themselves.

Stalin certainly incited awe in many of his unsuspecting countrymen, but those closest to him who witnessed his rages and his incredible malice, who knew too well his evil crimes, lived in fear of him and breathed a deep collective sigh of relief when he died.

The names of the two alleged bodyguards were not divulged, nor was any further explanation offered. The matter was firmly closed and the file on the incident destroyed.

The two men who died were buried in a Moscow cemetery.

To this day their graves remain.

Curiously, they each bear a nameless headstone.